Bloom

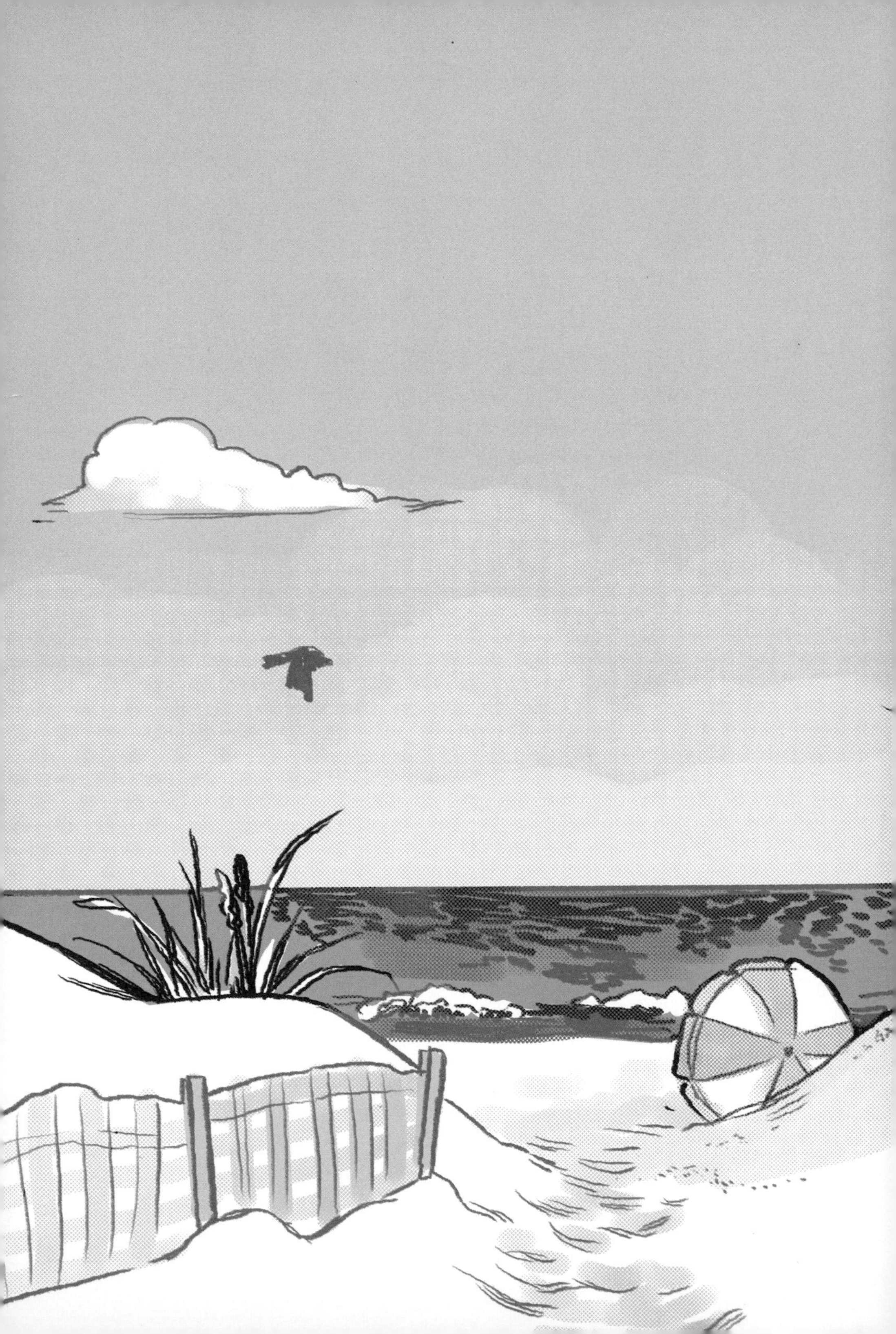

Bloom

Written by
Kevin Panetta

Artwork by
Savanna Ganucheau

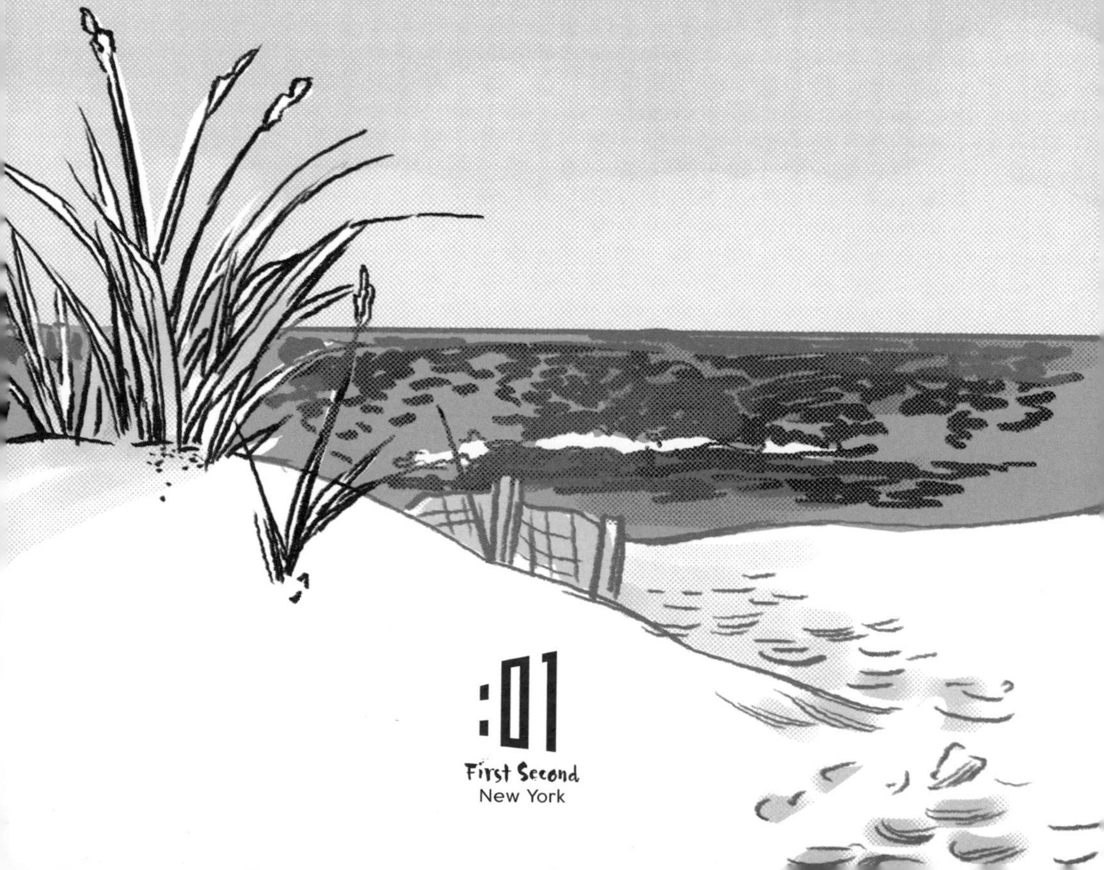

:01
First Second
New York

First Second

Text copyright © 2019 by Kevin Panetta
Illustrations copyright © 2019 by Savanna Ganucheau

Published by First Second
First Second is an imprint of Roaring Brook Press, a division of Holtzbrinck
Publishing Holdings Limited Partnership
175 Fifth Avenue, New York, NY 10010

Don't miss your next favorite book from First Second!
Sign up for our enewsletter to get updates at firstsecondnewsletter.com.

Library of Congress Control Number: 2018937127

Paperback ISBN: 978-1-62672-641-3
Hardcover ISBN: 978-1-250-19691-0

Our books may be purchased in bulk for promotional, educational, or business use.
Please contact your local bookseller or the Macmillan Corporate and Premium Sales Department
at (800) 221-7945 ext. 5442 or by email at MacmillanSpecialMarkets@macmillan.com.

First edition, 2019

Edited by Calista Brill and Sarah Gaydos
Book design by Molly Johanson

Bloom was completely rendered in Photoshop. Inked using GrutBrushes's "papaya grind"
and toned with Kyle T. Webster's halftone brushes.

Printed in China

Paperback: 10 9 8 7 6 5 4 3 2 1
Hardcover: 10 9 8 7 6 5 4 3 2 1

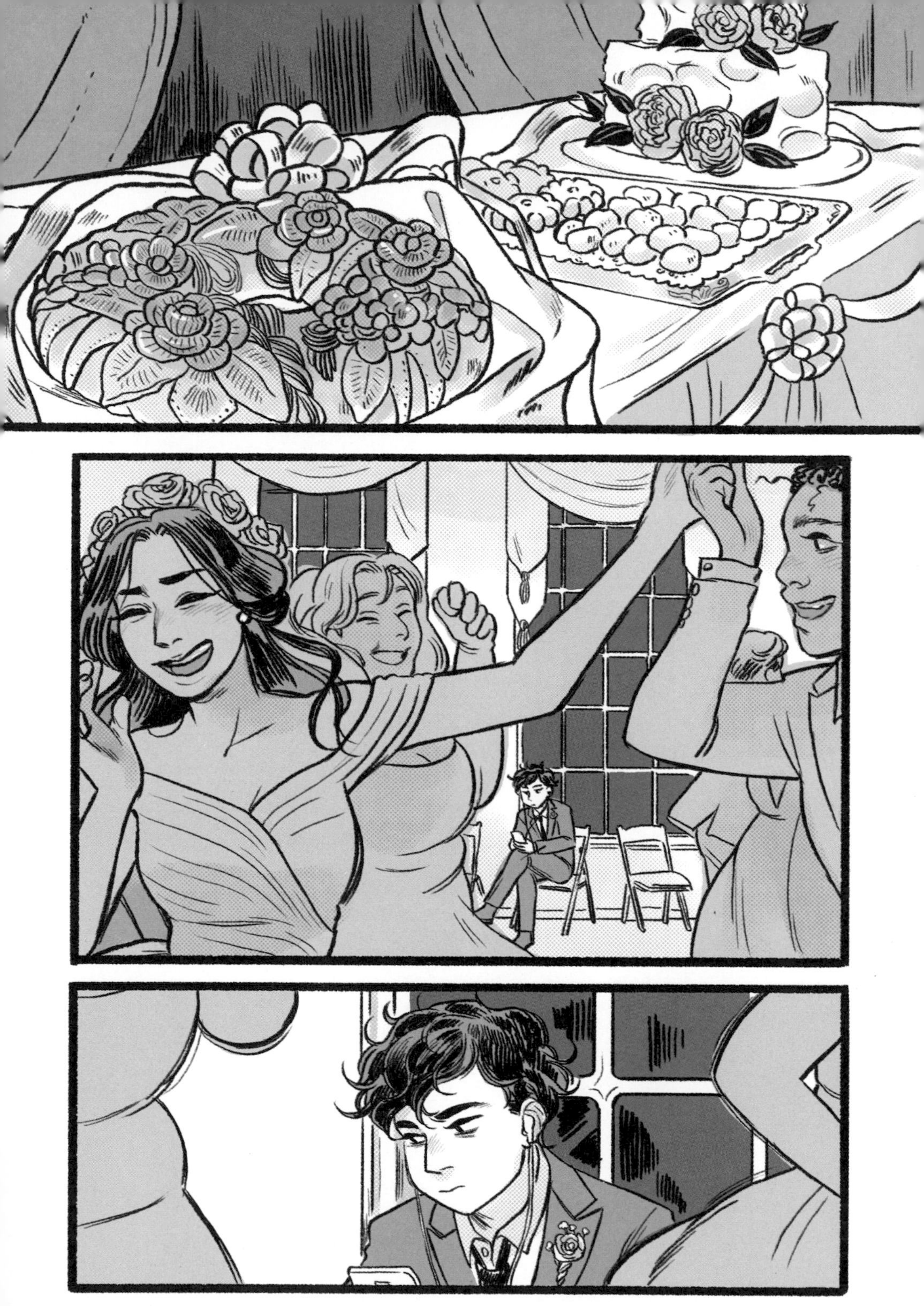

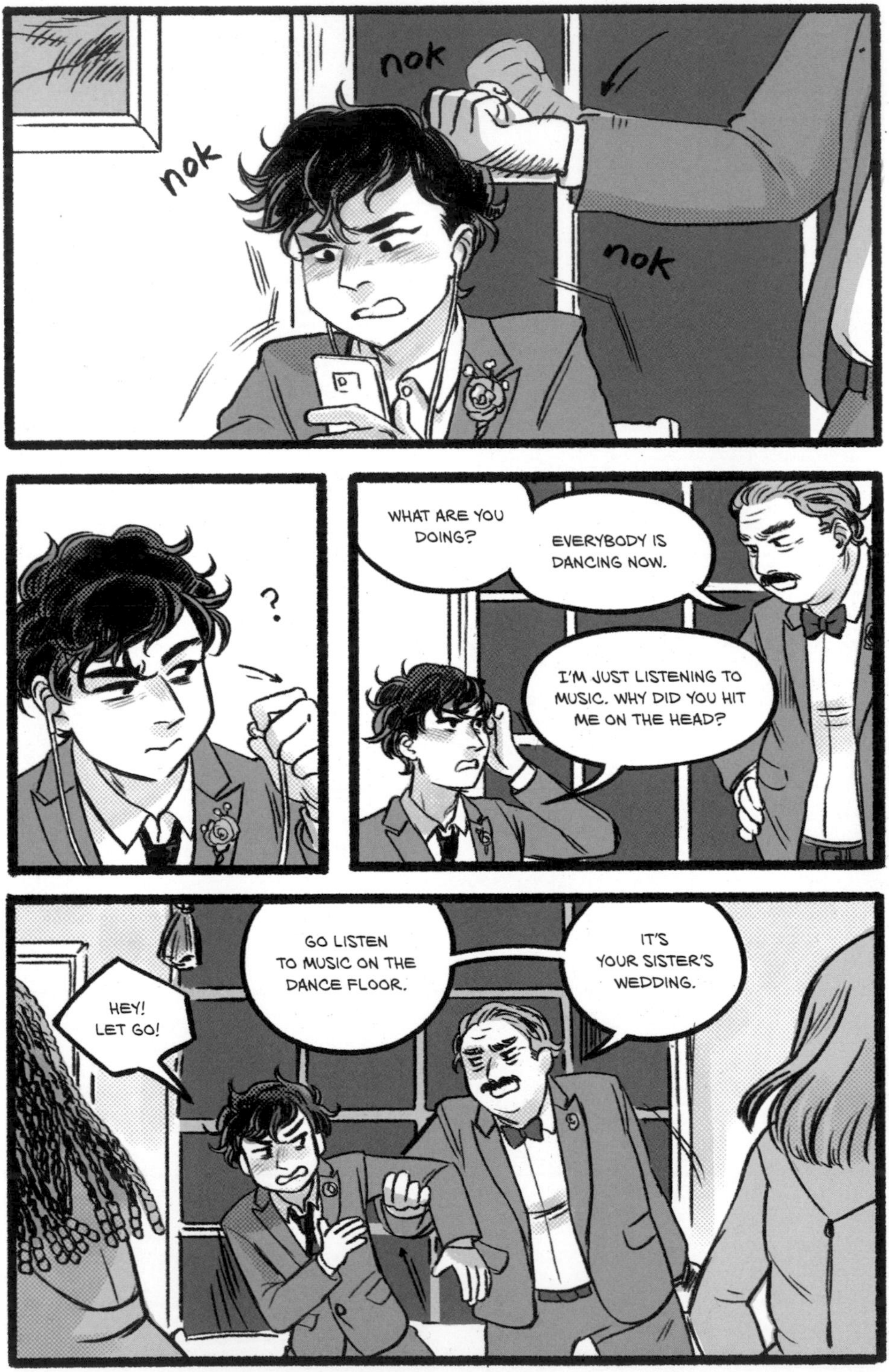
nok
nok
nok
?
WHAT ARE YOU DOING?
EVERYBODY IS DANCING NOW.
I'M JUST LISTENING TO MUSIC. WHY DID YOU HIT ME ON THE HEAD?
HEY! LET GO!
GO LISTEN TO MUSIC ON THE DANCE FLOOR.
IT'S YOUR SISTER'S WEDDING.

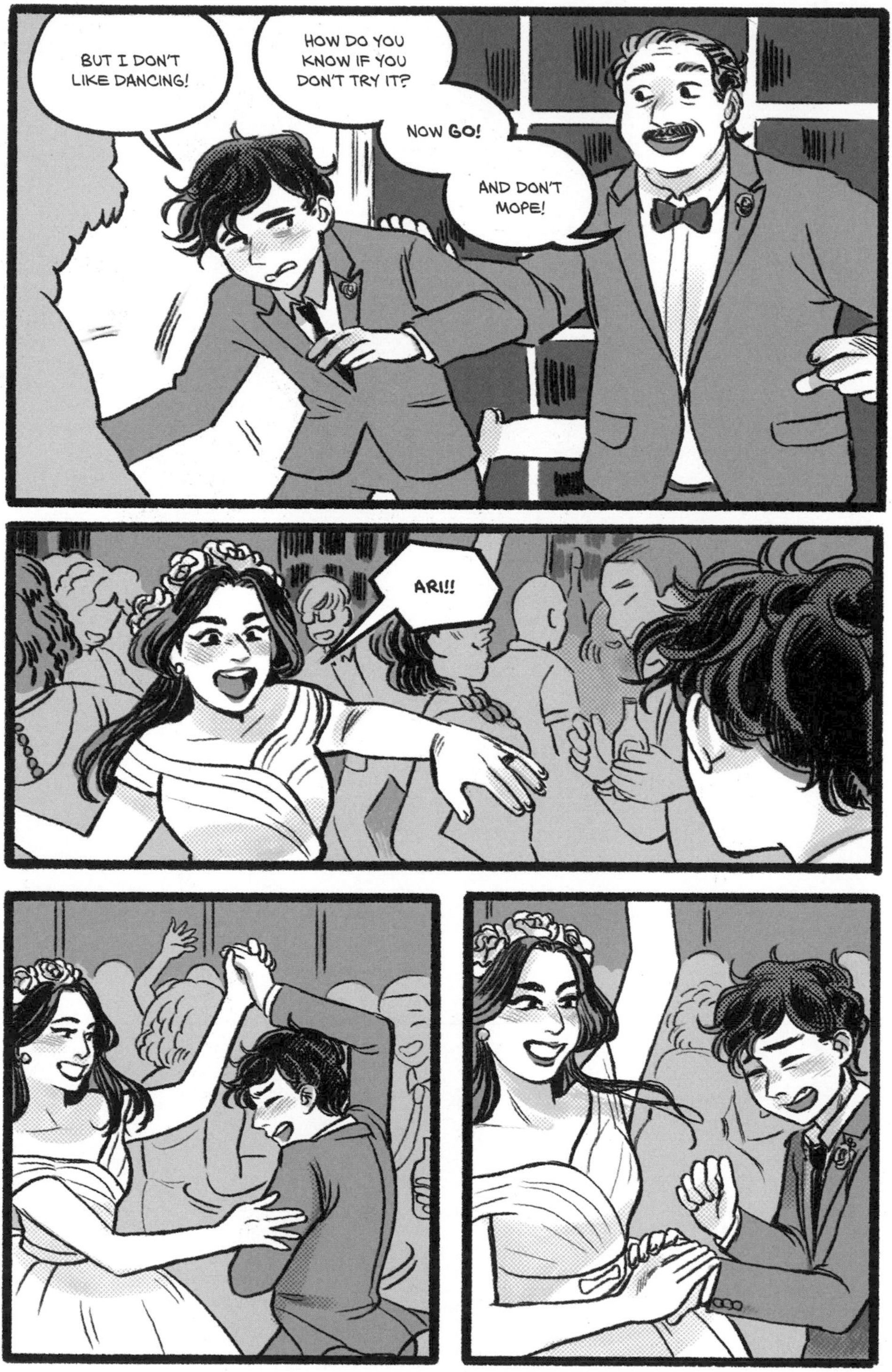
BUT I DON'T LIKE DANCING!
HOW DO YOU KNOW IF YOU DON'T TRY IT?
NOW **GO**!
AND DON'T MOPE!
ARI!!

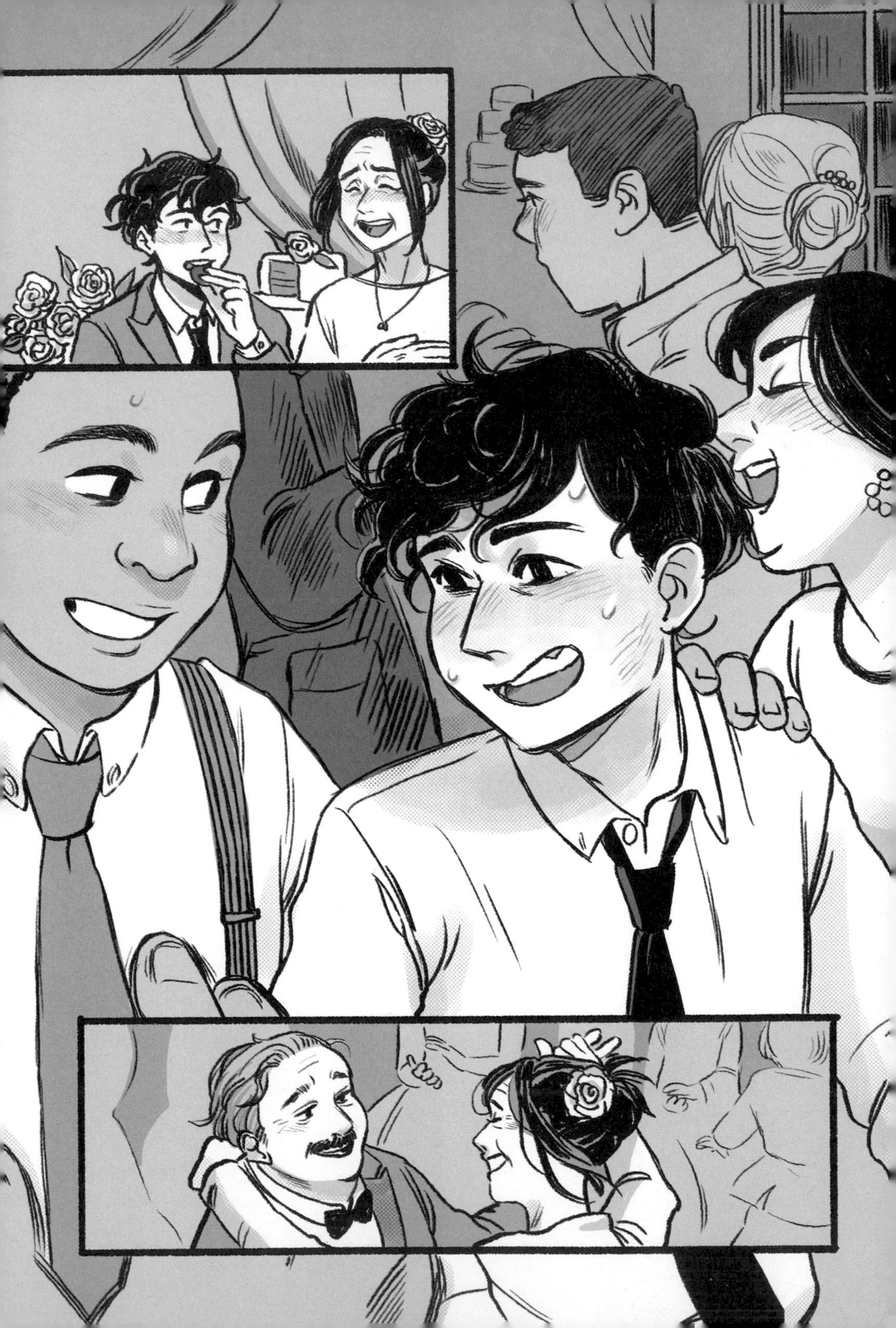

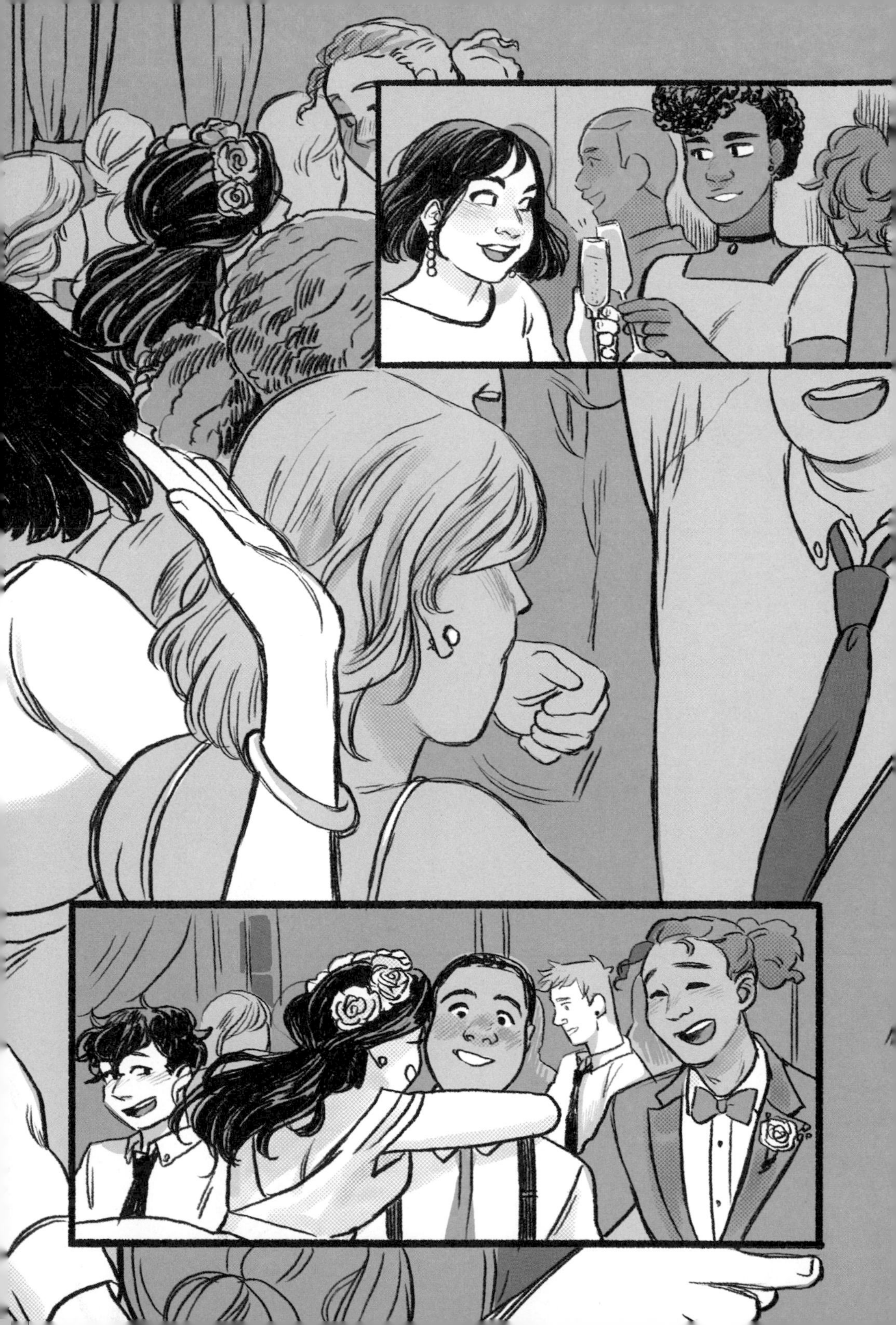

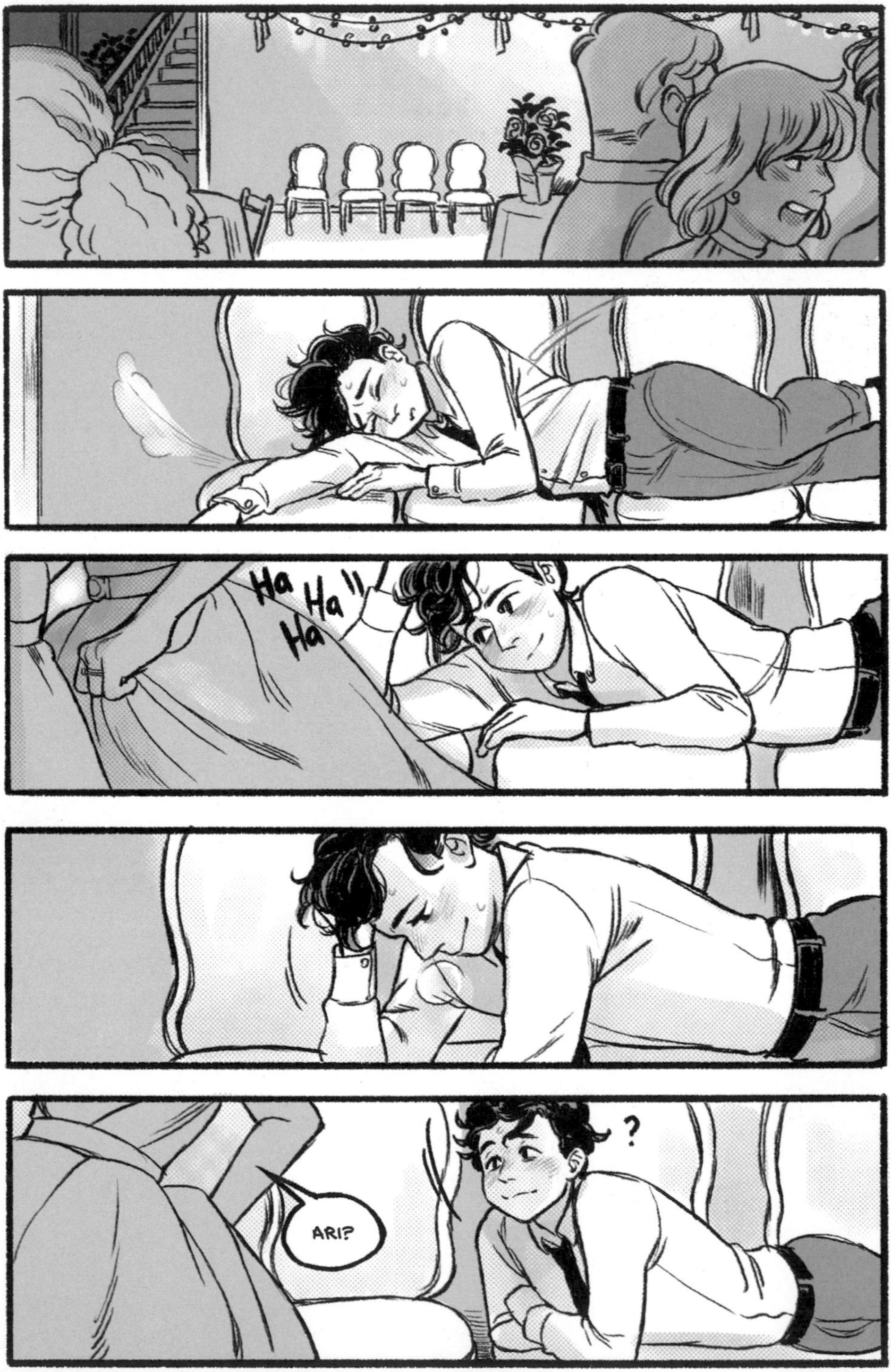
Ha Ha Ha
?
ARI?

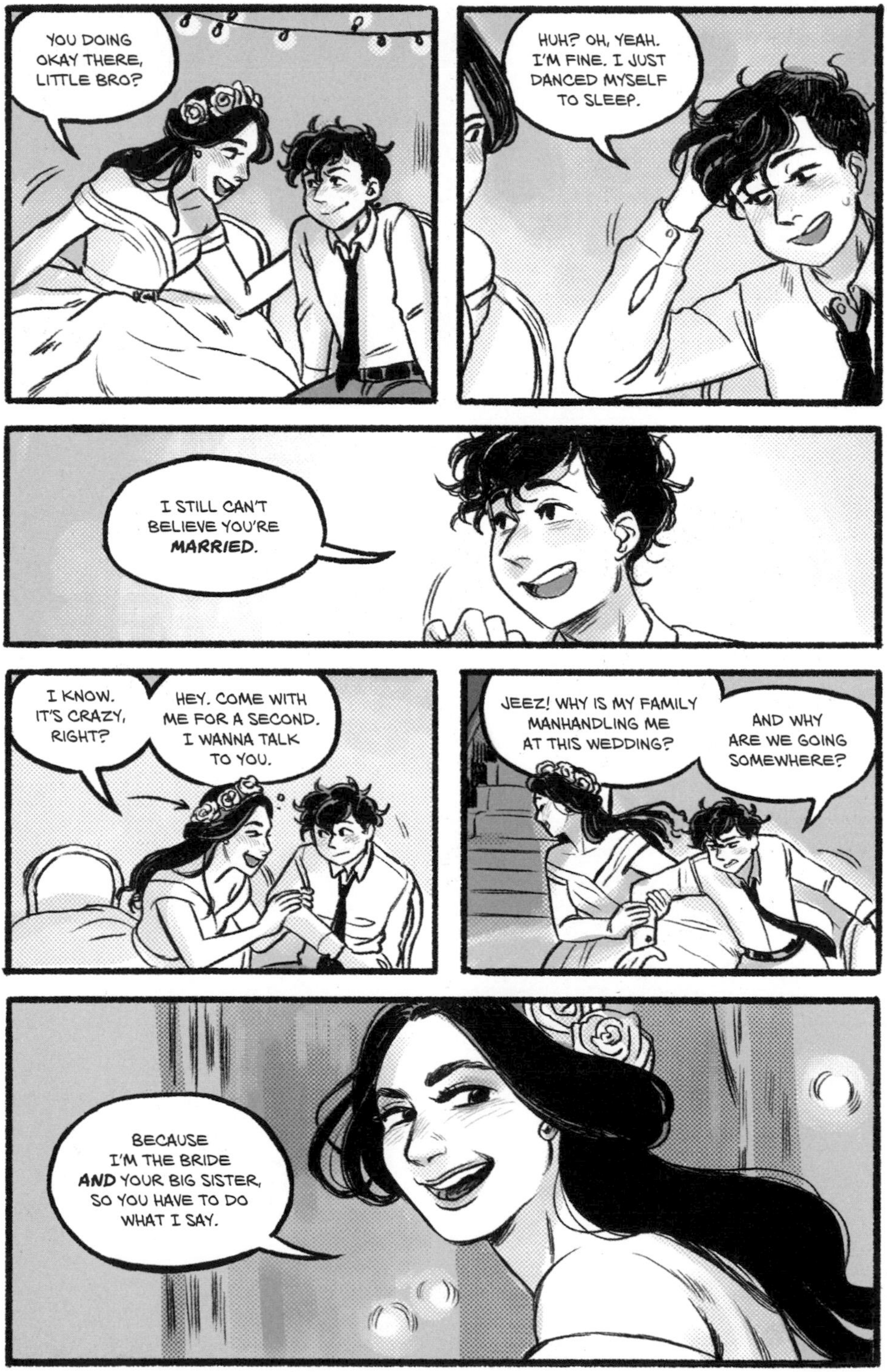
YOU DOING OKAY THERE, LITTLE BRO?
HUH? OH, YEAH. I'M FINE. I JUST DANCED MYSELF TO SLEEP.
I STILL CAN'T BELIEVE YOU'RE **MARRIED**.
I KNOW. IT'S CRAZY, RIGHT?
HEY. COME WITH ME FOR A SECOND. I WANNA TALK TO YOU.
JEEZ! WHY IS MY FAMILY MANHANDLING ME AT THIS WEDDING?
AND WHY ARE WE GOING SOMEWHERE?
BECAUSE I'M THE BRIDE **AND** YOUR BIG SISTER, SO YOU HAVE TO DO WHAT I SAY.

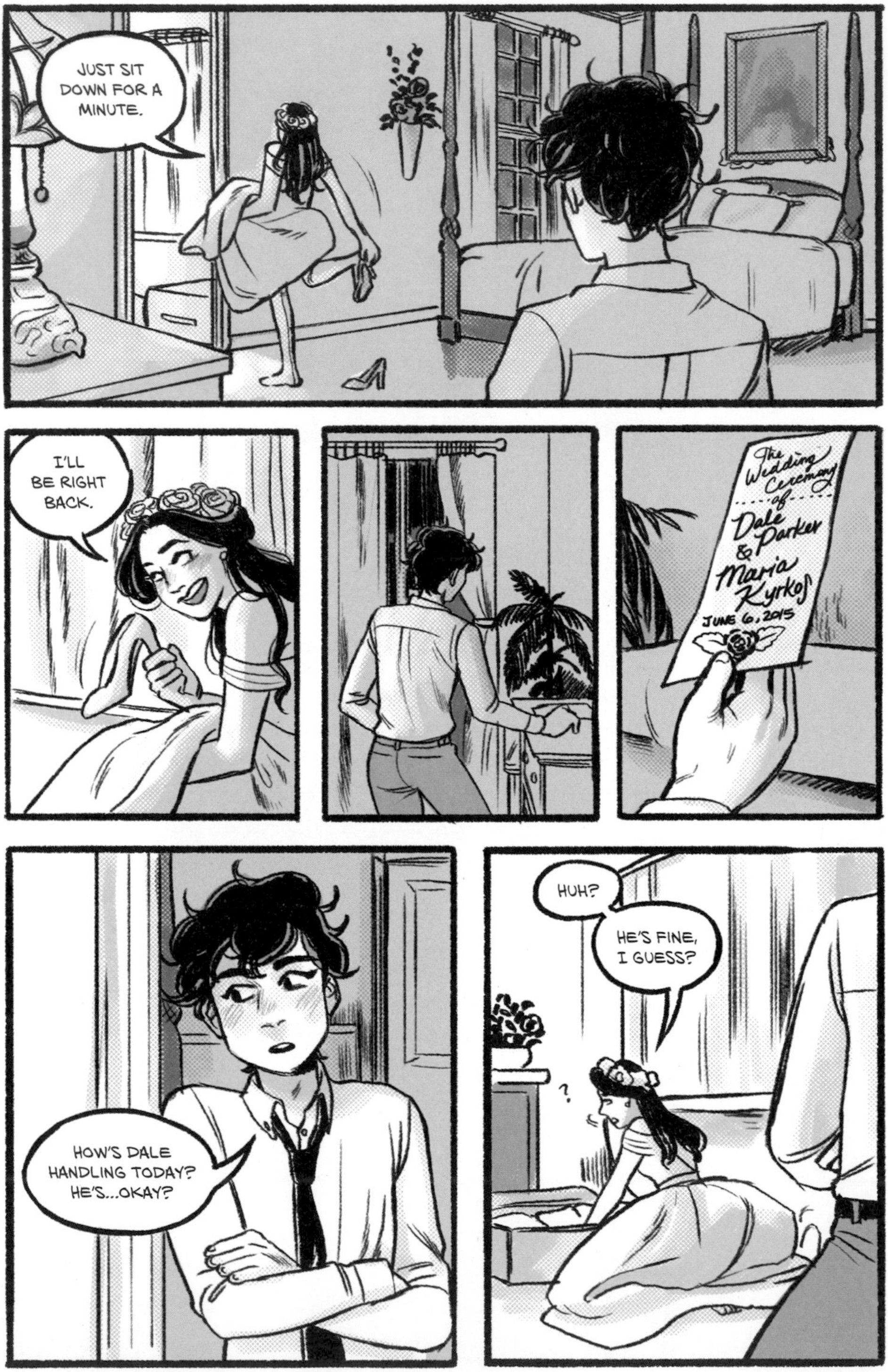
JUST SIT DOWN FOR A MINUTE.
I'LL BE RIGHT BACK.
The Wedding Ceremony of Dale Parker & Maria Kyrkos
JUNE 6, 2015
HOW'S DALE HANDLING TODAY? HE'S...OKAY?
HUH?
HE'S FINE, I GUESS?
?

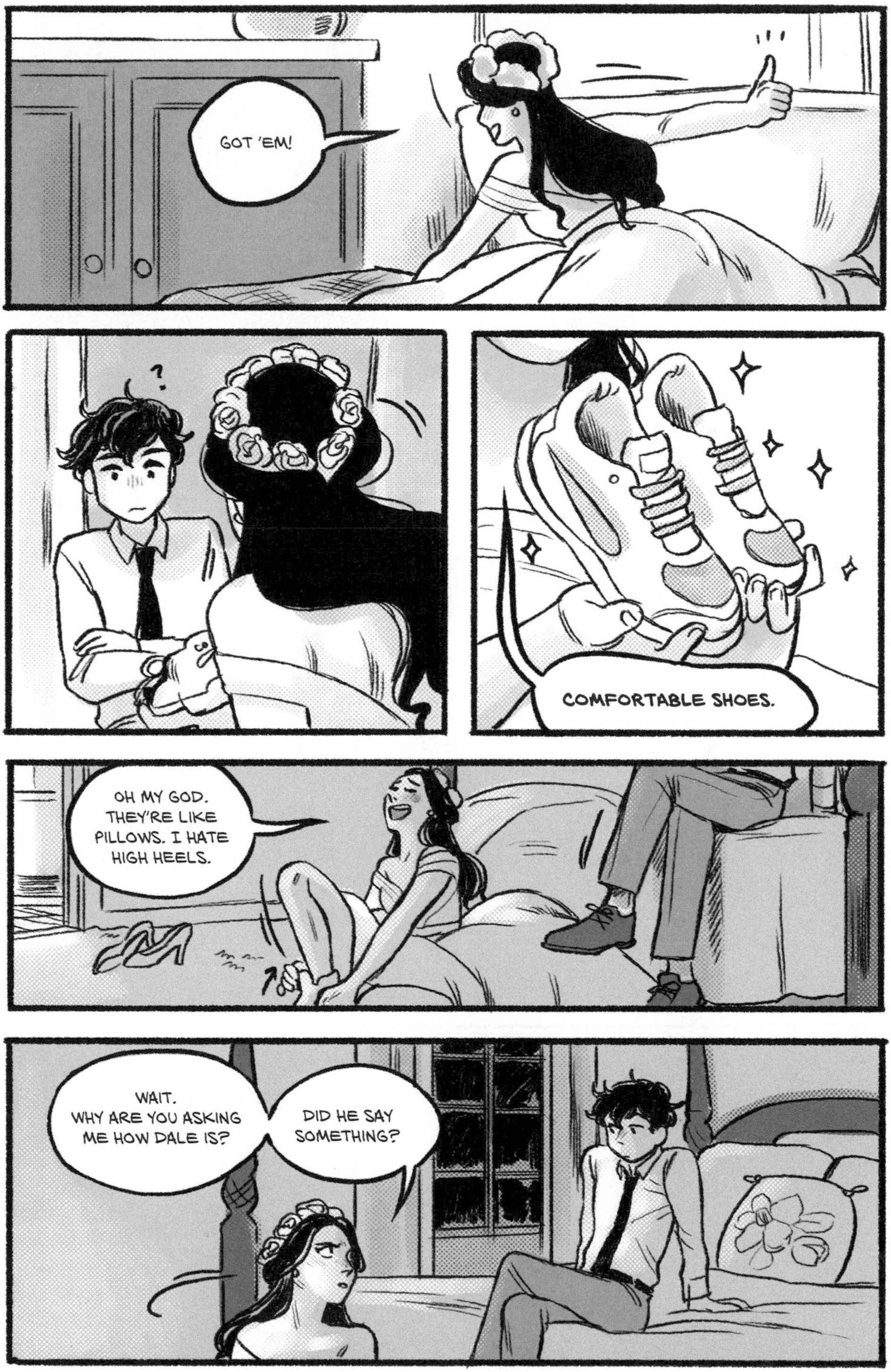
GOT 'EM!
COMFORTABLE SHOES.
OH MY GOD. THEY'RE LIKE PILLOWS. I HATE HIGH HEELS.
WAIT. WHY ARE YOU ASKING ME HOW DALE IS?
DID HE SAY SOMETHING?

WHAT? NONONONO. I JUST KNOW YOU GUYS HAVE BEEN UP AND DOWN RECENTLY. I WAS JUST ASKING, THAT'S ALL.

MHM.

THAT'S JUST HOW RELATIONSHIPS GO, ARI. THEY AREN'T ALWAYS EASY. YOU HAVE TO PUT WORK INTO THEM.

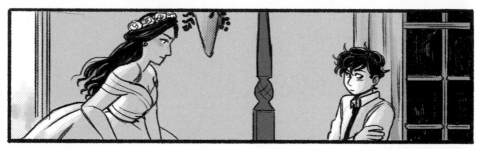

ANYWAY, I DIDN'T BRING YOU UP HERE TO TALK ABOUT DALE.

IT'S ABOUT YOU.

MOM SAID YOU'RE PLANNING ON MOVING AWAY.

DO YOU REALLY THINK THAT'S THE BEST THING RIGHT NOW?

OH, GOD.

YOU SOUND LIKE DAD.

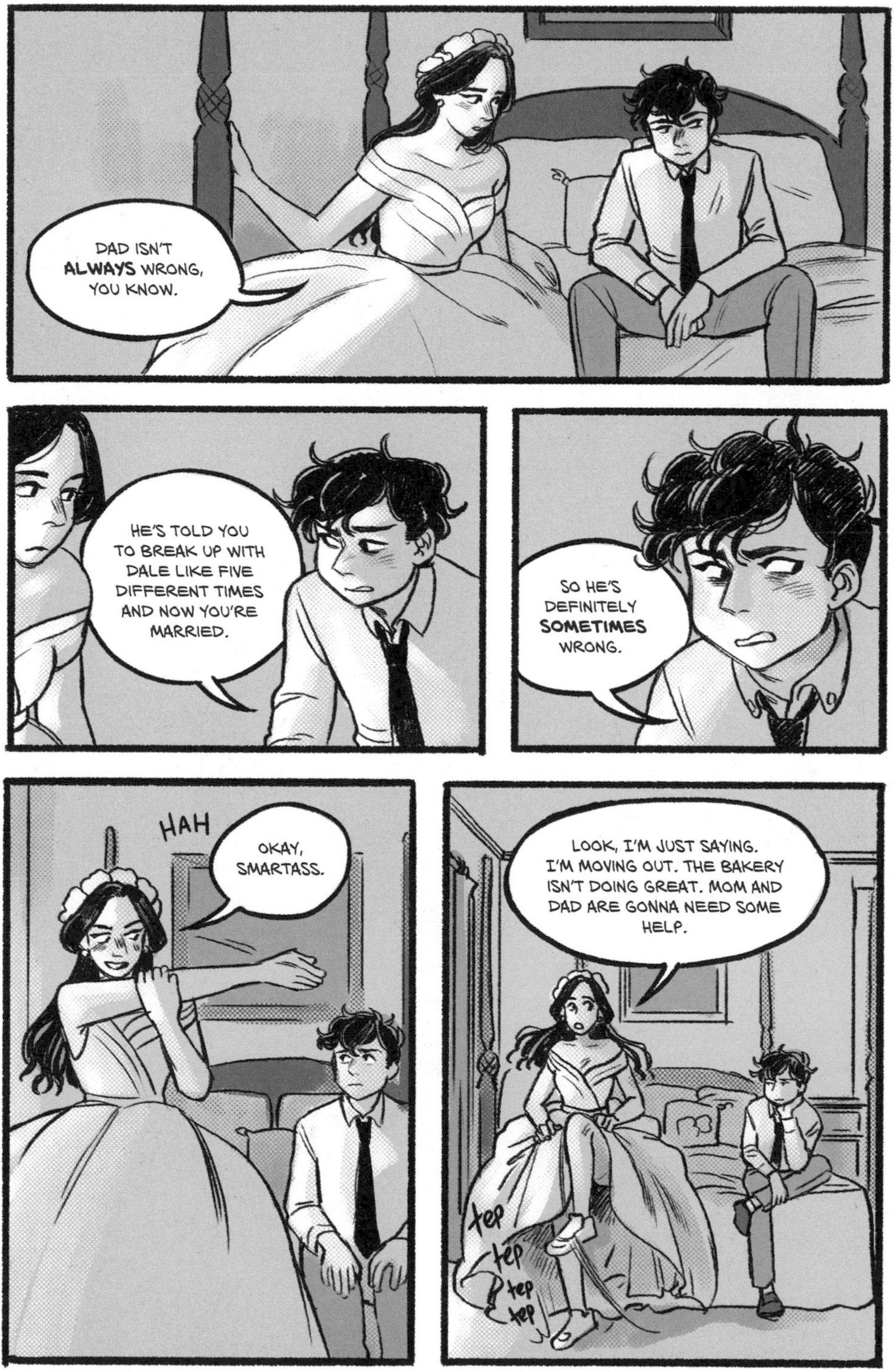
DAD ISN'T **ALWAYS** WRONG, YOU KNOW.
HE'S TOLD YOU TO BREAK UP WITH DALE LIKE FIVE DIFFERENT TIMES AND NOW YOU'RE MARRIED.
SO HE'S DEFINITELY **SOMETIMES** WRONG.
HAH
OKAY, SMARTASS.
LOOK, I'M JUST SAYING. I'M MOVING OUT. THE BAKERY ISN'T DOING GREAT. MOM AND DAD ARE GONNA NEED SOME HELP.
tep
tep
tep
tep

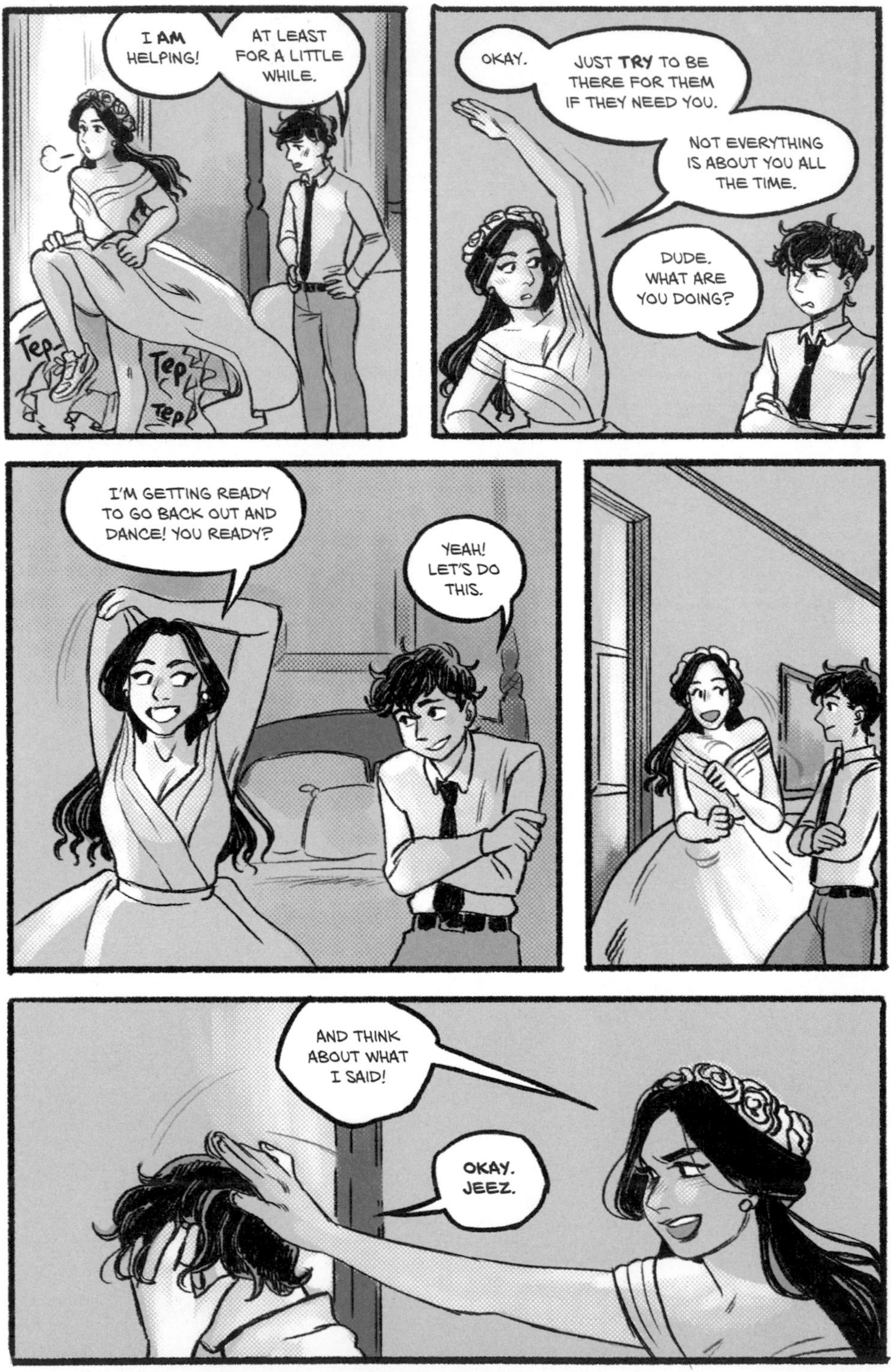
I **AM** HELPING!
AT LEAST FOR A LITTLE WHILE.
Tep
Tep
Tep
OKAY.
JUST **TRY** TO BE THERE FOR THEM IF THEY NEED YOU.
NOT EVERYTHING IS ABOUT YOU ALL THE TIME.
DUDE. WHAT ARE YOU DOING?
I'M GETTING READY TO GO BACK OUT AND DANCE! YOU READY?
YEAH! LET'S DO THIS.
AND THINK ABOUT WHAT I SAID!
OKAY. JEEZ.

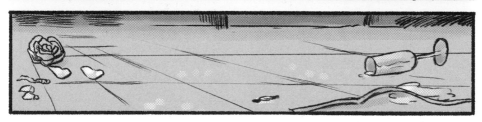

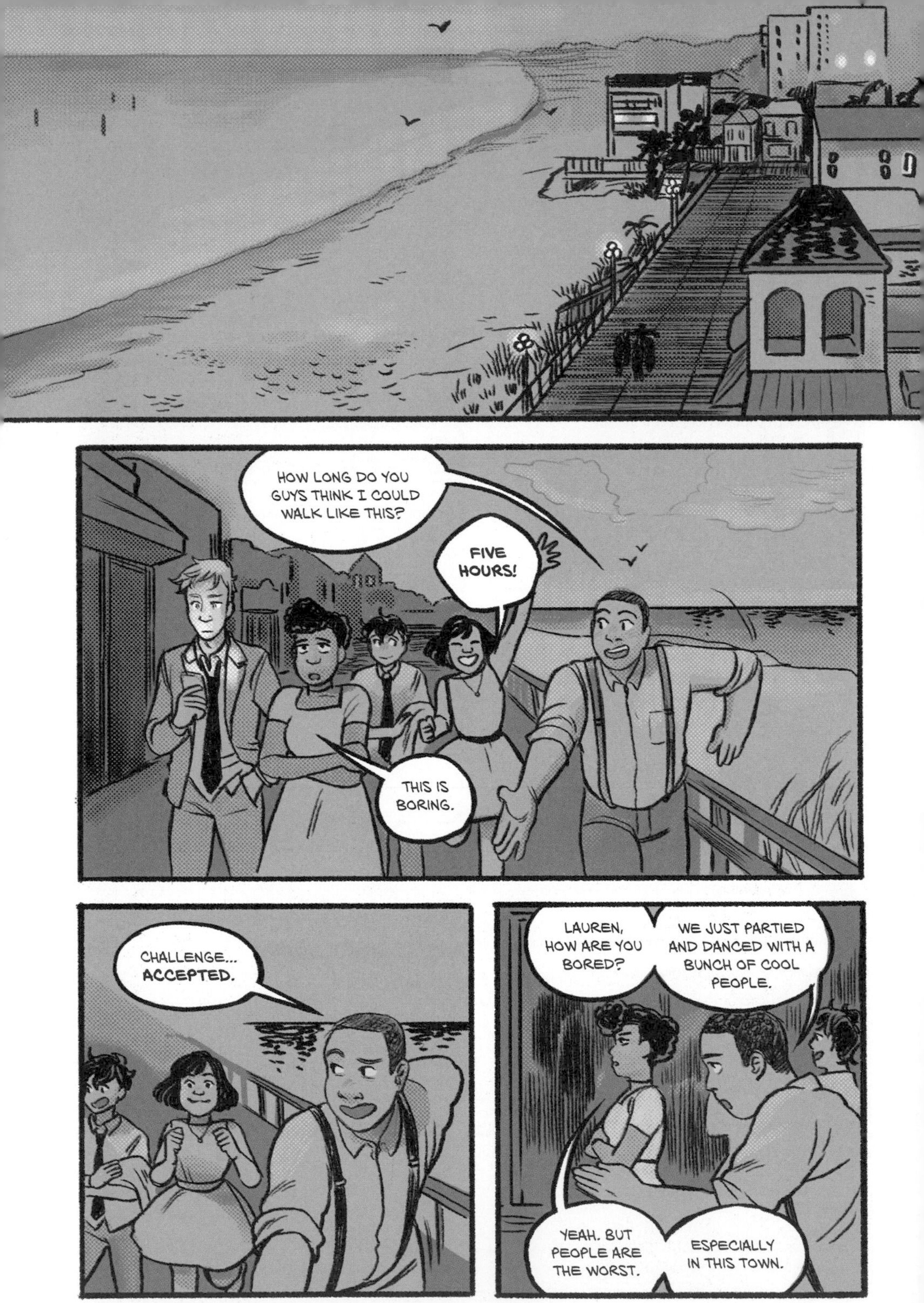
HOW LONG DO YOU GUYS THINK I COULD WALK LIKE THIS?
FIVE HOURS!
THIS IS BORING.
CHALLENGE... ACCEPTED.
LAUREN, HOW ARE YOU BORED?
WE JUST PARTIED AND DANCED WITH A BUNCH OF COOL PEOPLE.
YEAH. BUT PEOPLE ARE THE WORST.
ESPECIALLY IN THIS TOWN.

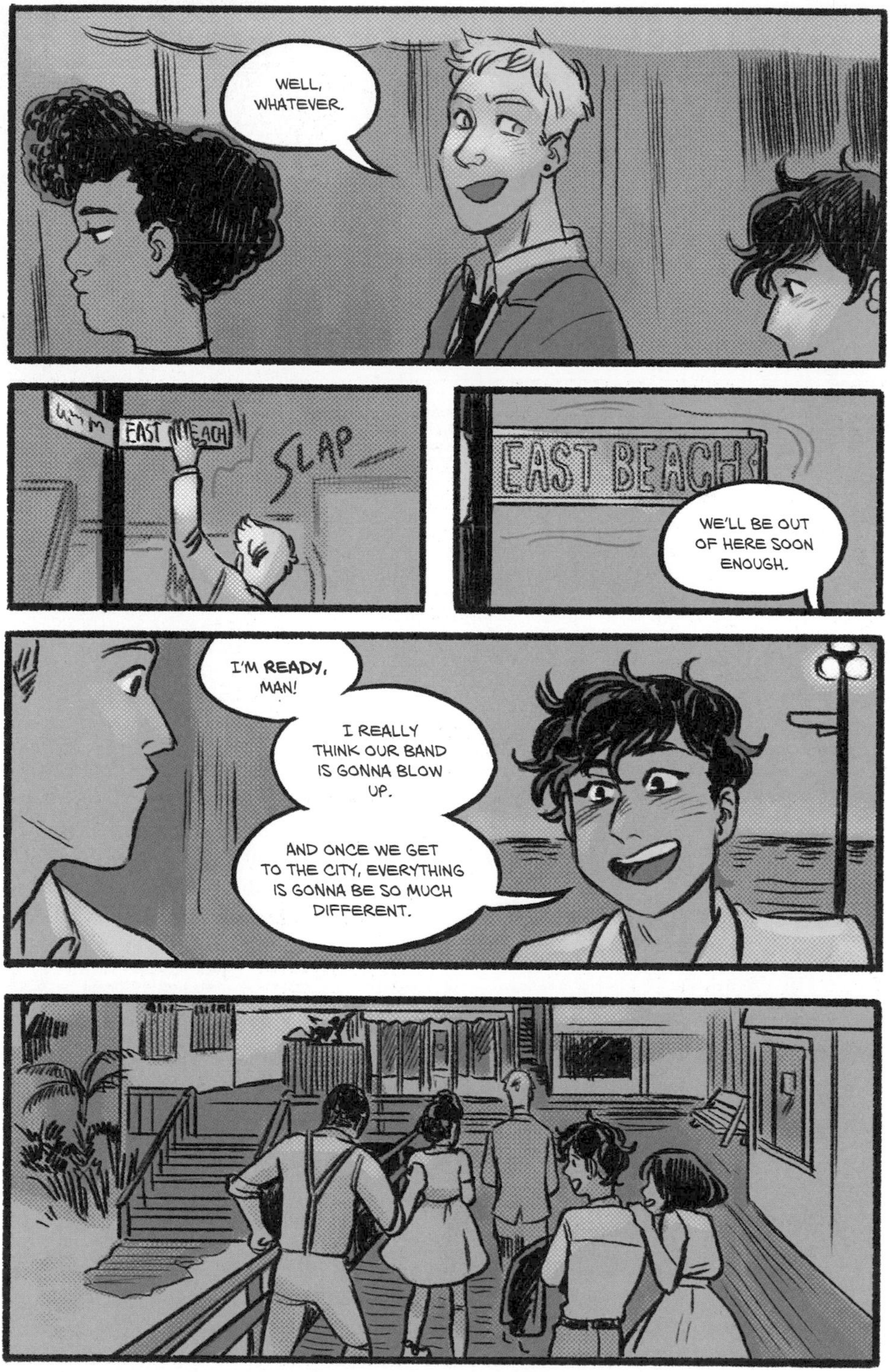
WELL, WHATEVER.
SLAP
EAST BEACH
WE'LL BE OUT OF HERE SOON ENOUGH.
I'M **READY,** MAN!
I REALLY THINK OUR BAND IS GONNA BLOW UP.
AND ONCE WE GET TO THE CITY, EVERYTHING IS GONNA BE SO MUCH DIFFERENT.

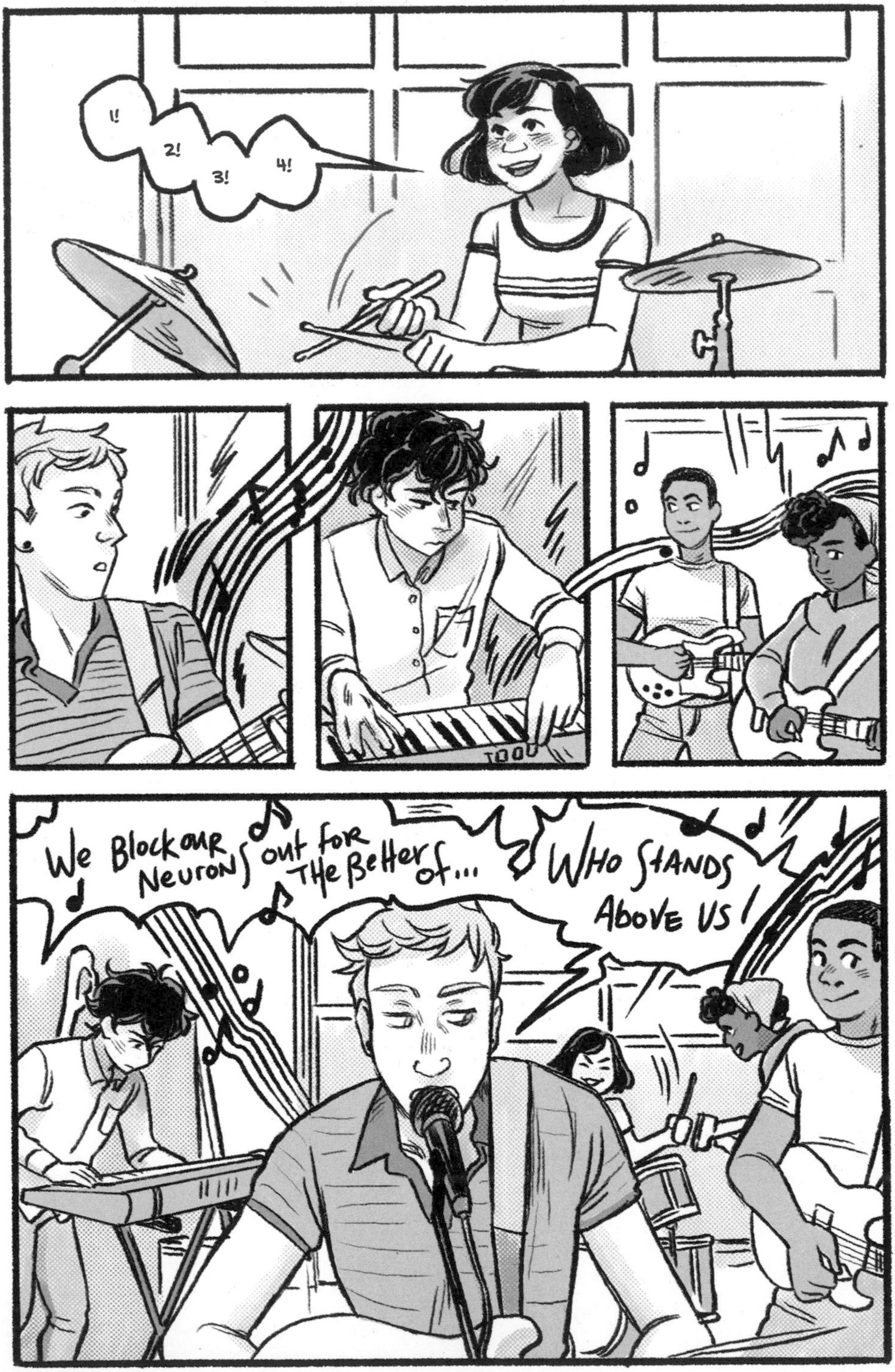

1!
2!
3!
4!
We Block our Neurons out for The Better of...
Who Stands Above Us!

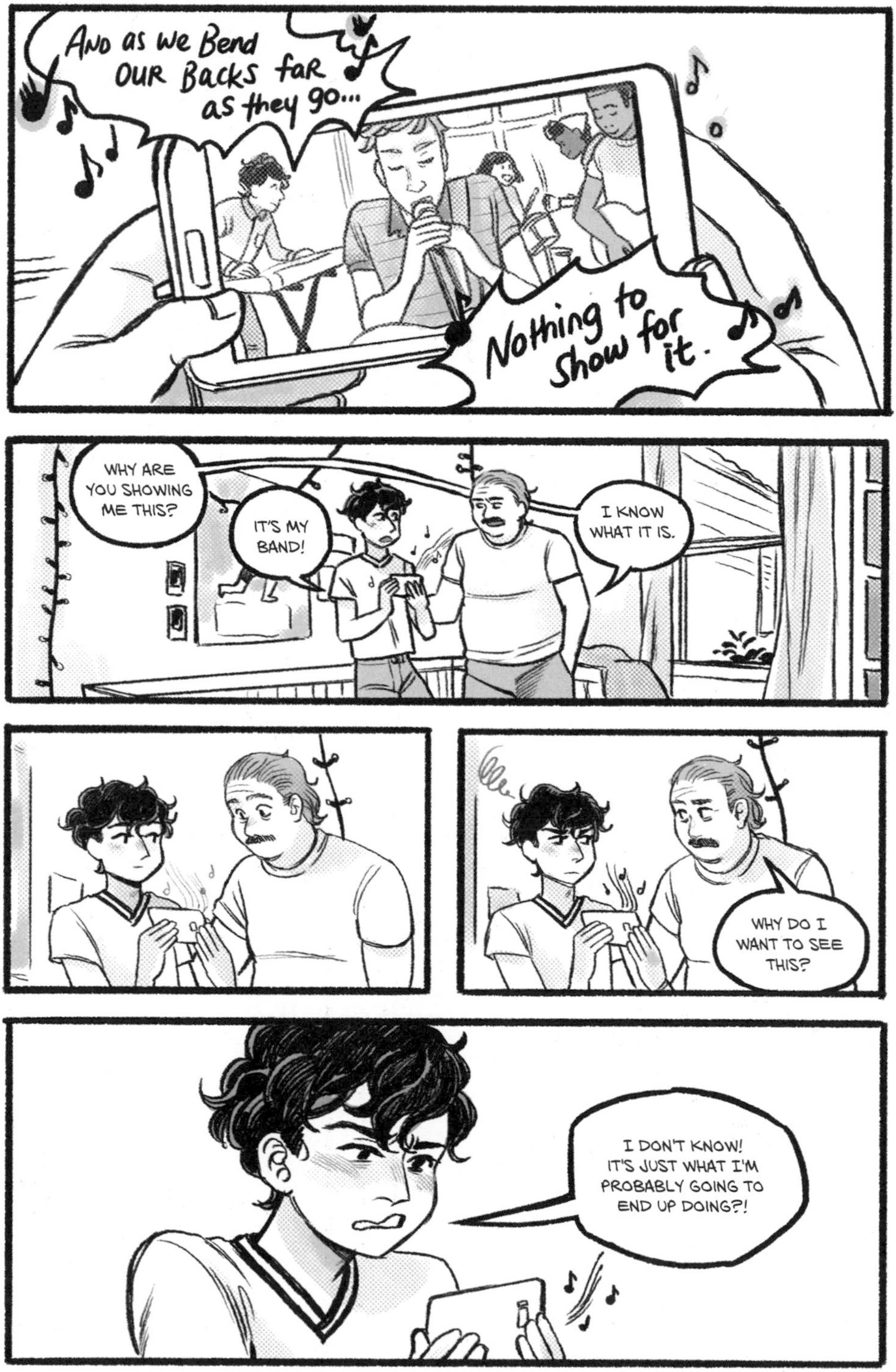
And as we Bend our Backs far as they go...
Nothing to Show for it.
WHY ARE YOU SHOWING ME THIS?
IT'S MY BAND!
I KNOW WHAT IT IS.
WHY DO I WANT TO SEE THIS?
I DON'T KNOW! IT'S JUST WHAT I'M PROBABLY GOING TO END UP DOING?!

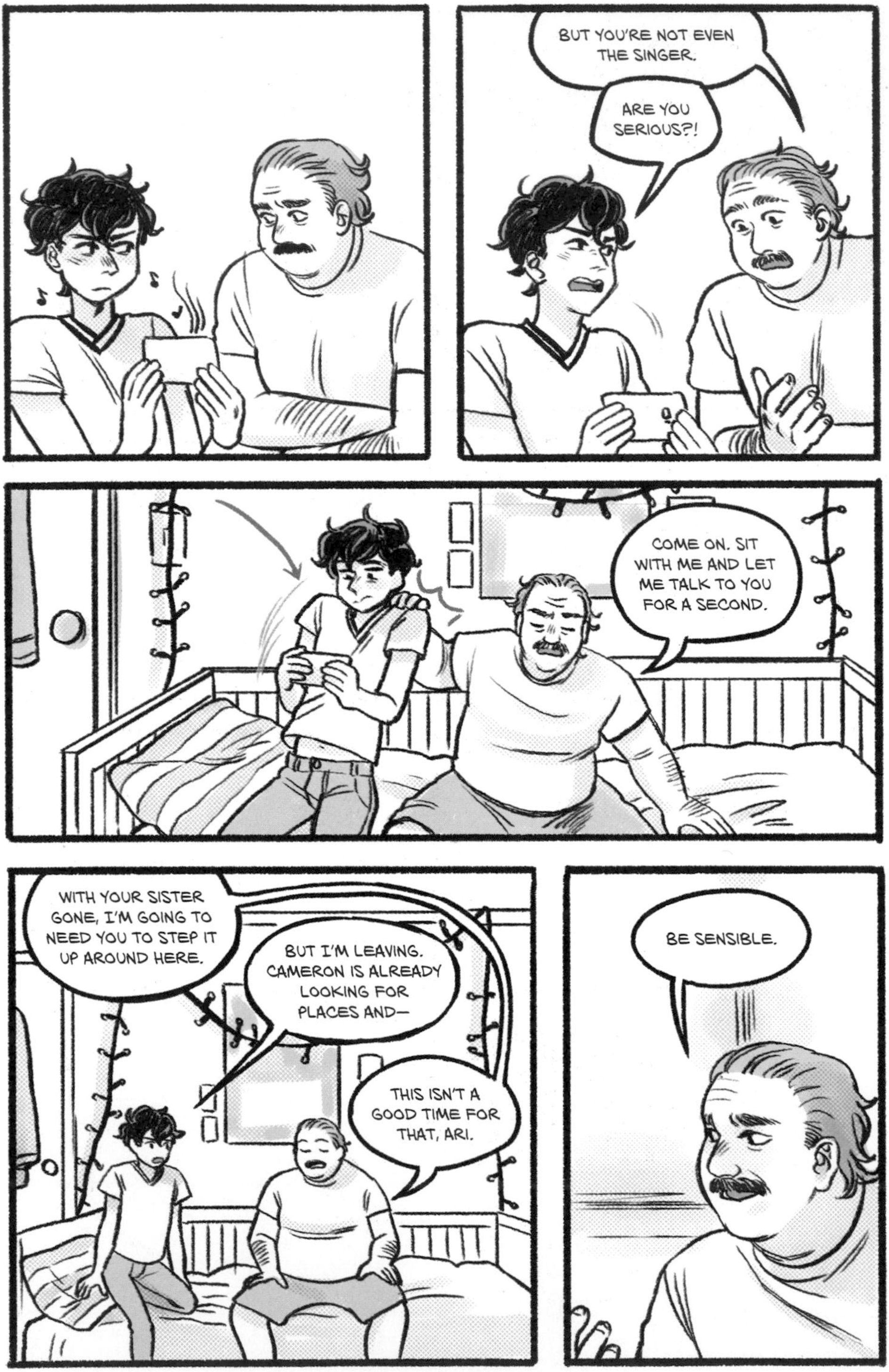
BUT YOU'RE NOT EVEN THE SINGER.
ARE YOU SERIOUS?!
COME ON. SIT WITH ME AND LET ME TALK TO YOU FOR A SECOND.
WITH YOUR SISTER GONE, I'M GOING TO NEED YOU TO STEP IT UP AROUND HERE.
BUT I'M LEAVING. CAMERON IS ALREADY LOOKING FOR PLACES AND—
THIS ISN'T A GOOD TIME FOR THAT, ARI.
BE SENSIBLE.

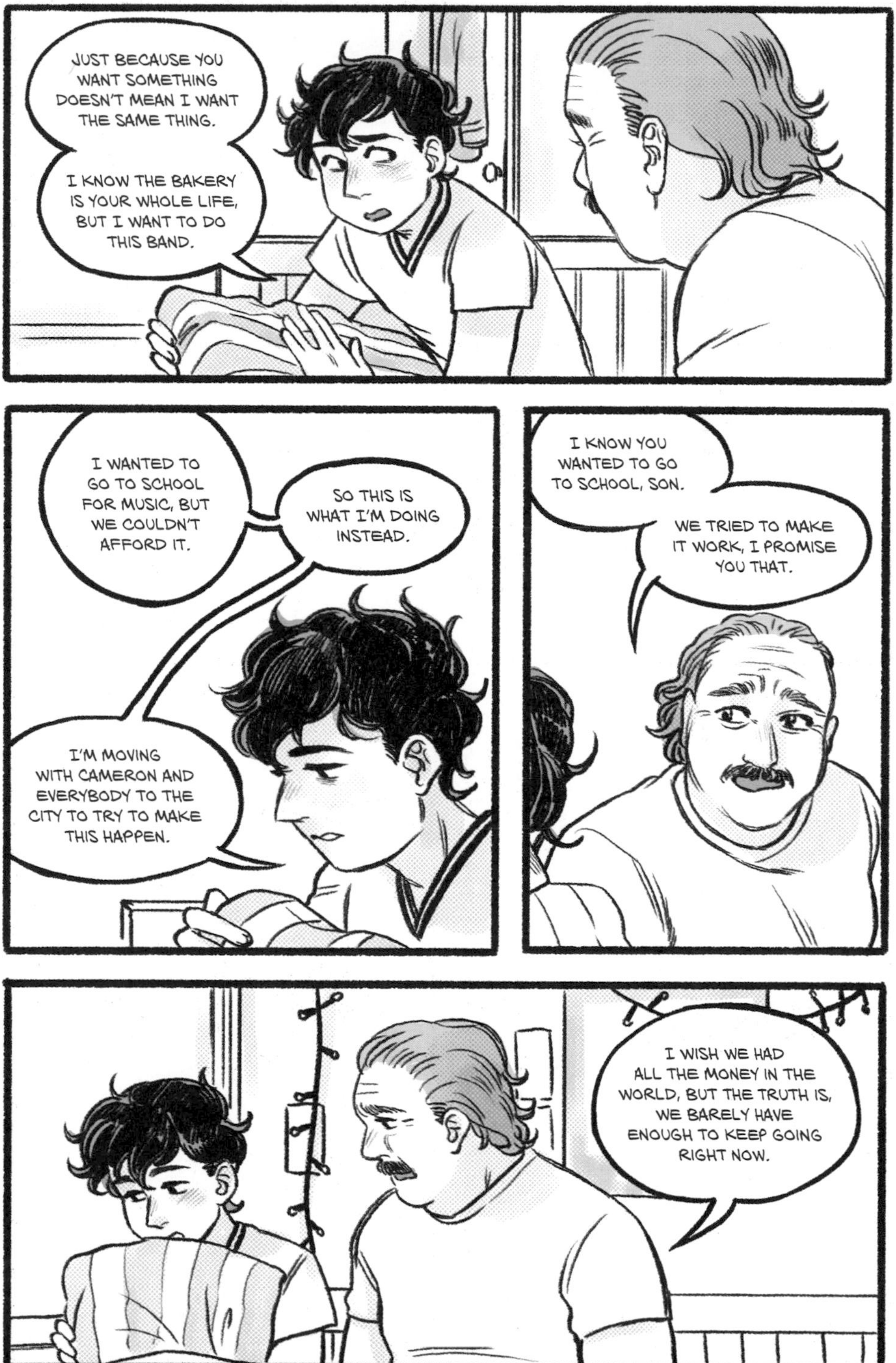
JUST BECAUSE YOU WANT SOMETHING DOESN'T MEAN I WANT THE SAME THING.
I KNOW THE BAKERY IS YOUR WHOLE LIFE, BUT I WANT TO DO THIS BAND.
I WANTED TO GO TO SCHOOL FOR MUSIC, BUT WE COULDN'T AFFORD IT.
SO THIS IS WHAT I'M DOING INSTEAD.
I'M MOVING WITH CAMERON AND EVERYBODY TO THE CITY TO TRY TO MAKE THIS HAPPEN.
I KNOW YOU WANTED TO GO TO SCHOOL, SON.
WE TRIED TO MAKE IT WORK, I PROMISE YOU THAT.
I WISH WE HAD ALL THE MONEY IN THE WORLD, BUT THE TRUTH IS, WE BARELY HAVE ENOUGH TO KEEP GOING RIGHT NOW.

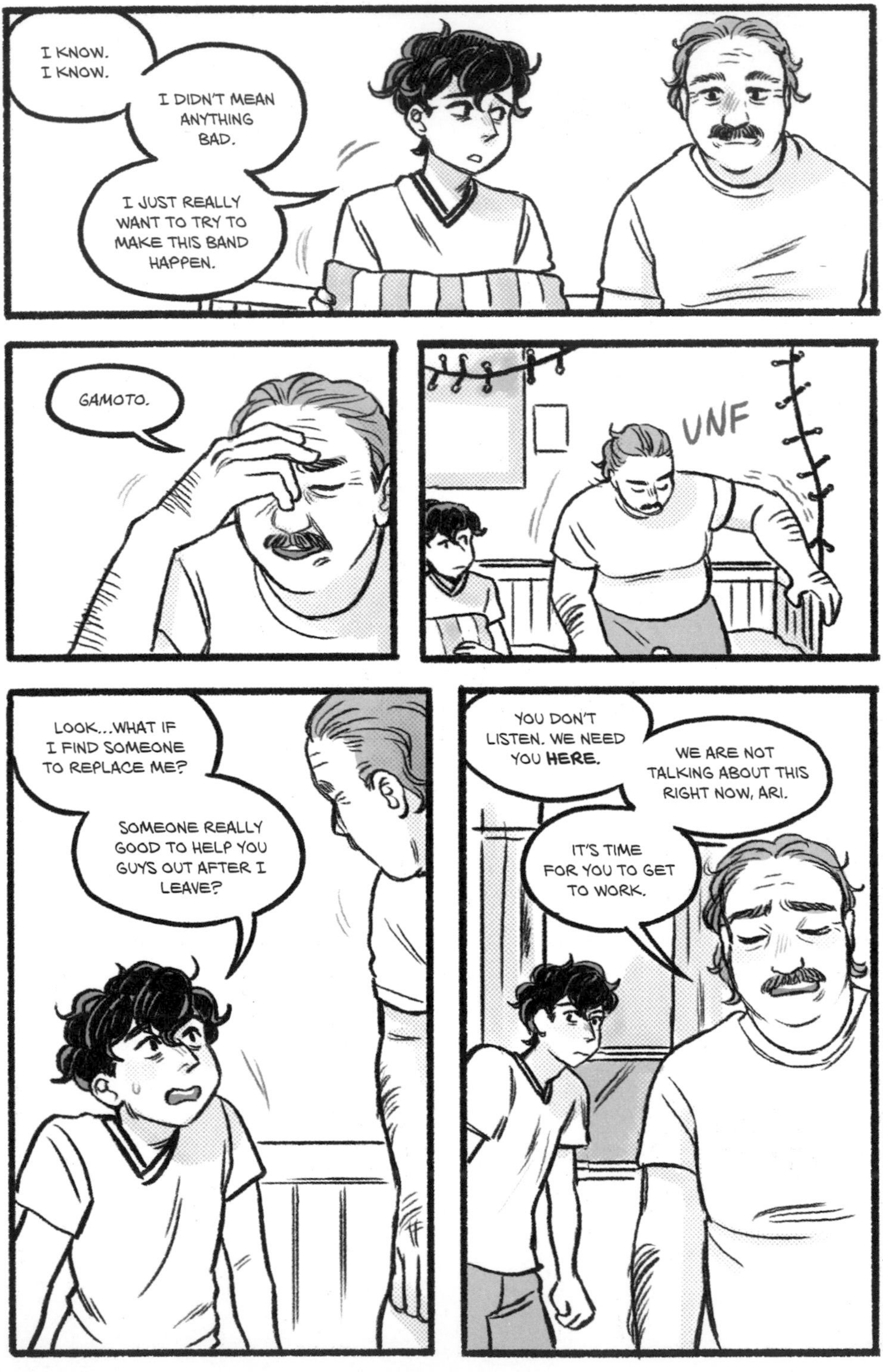
I KNOW.
I KNOW.
I DIDN'T MEAN ANYTHING BAD.
I JUST REALLY WANT TO TRY TO MAKE THIS BAND HAPPEN.
GAMOTO.
UNF
LOOK...WHAT IF I FIND SOMEONE TO REPLACE ME?
SOMEONE REALLY GOOD TO HELP YOU GUYS OUT AFTER I LEAVE?
YOU DON'T LISTEN. WE NEED YOU **HERE**.
WE ARE NOT TALKING ABOUT THIS RIGHT NOW, ARI.
IT'S TIME FOR YOU TO GET TO WORK.

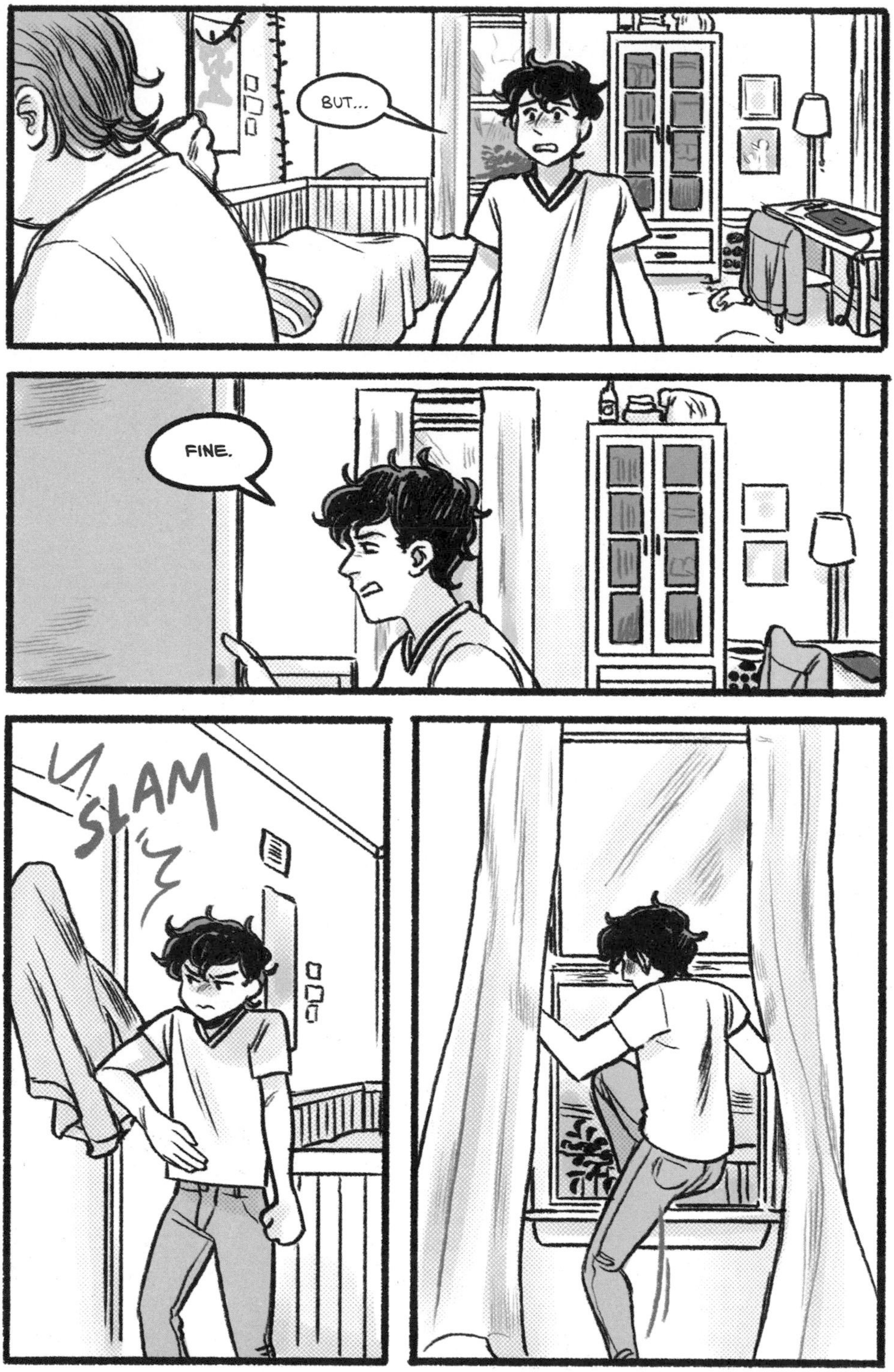
BUT...
FINE.
SLAM

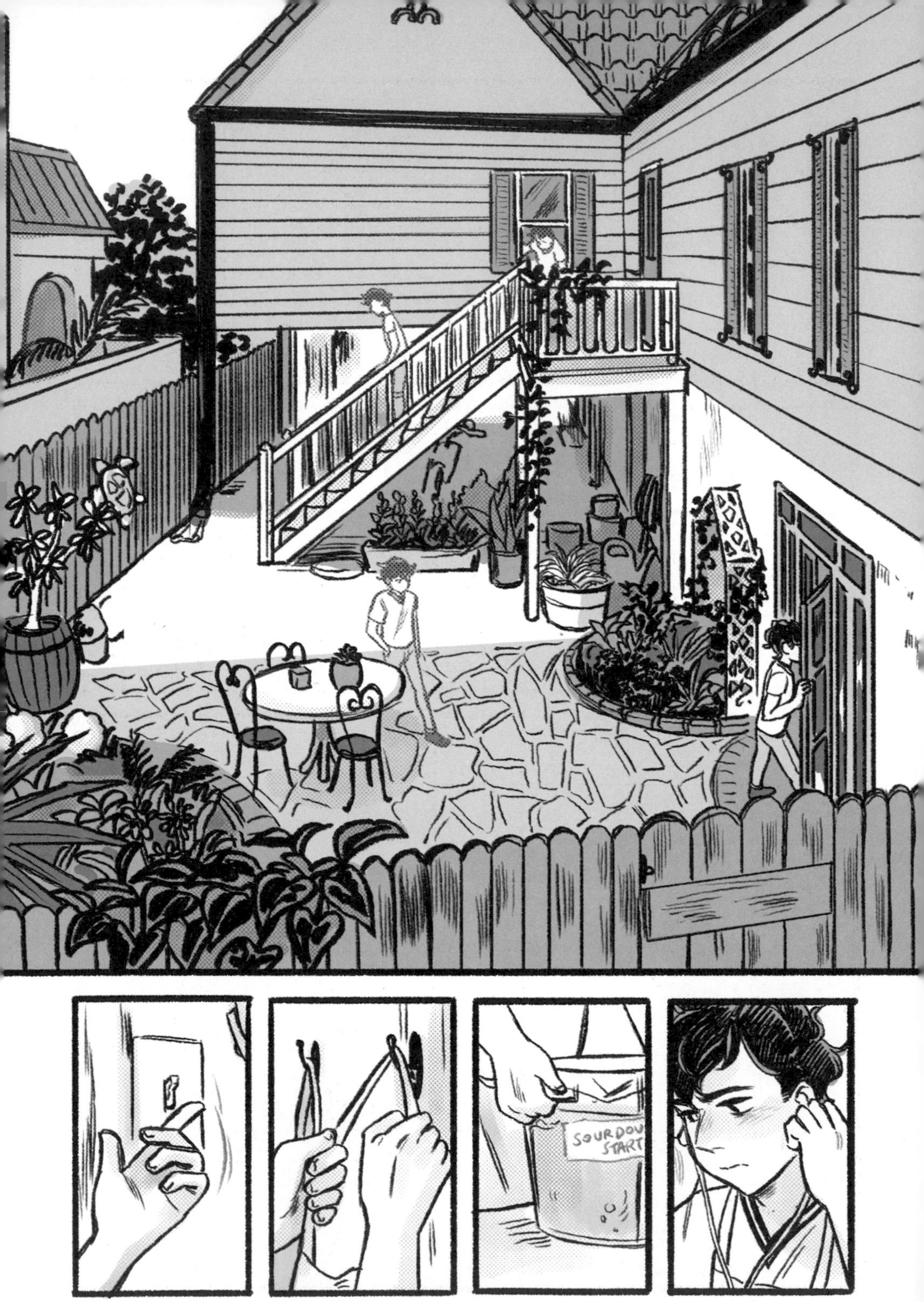
SOURDOU
START

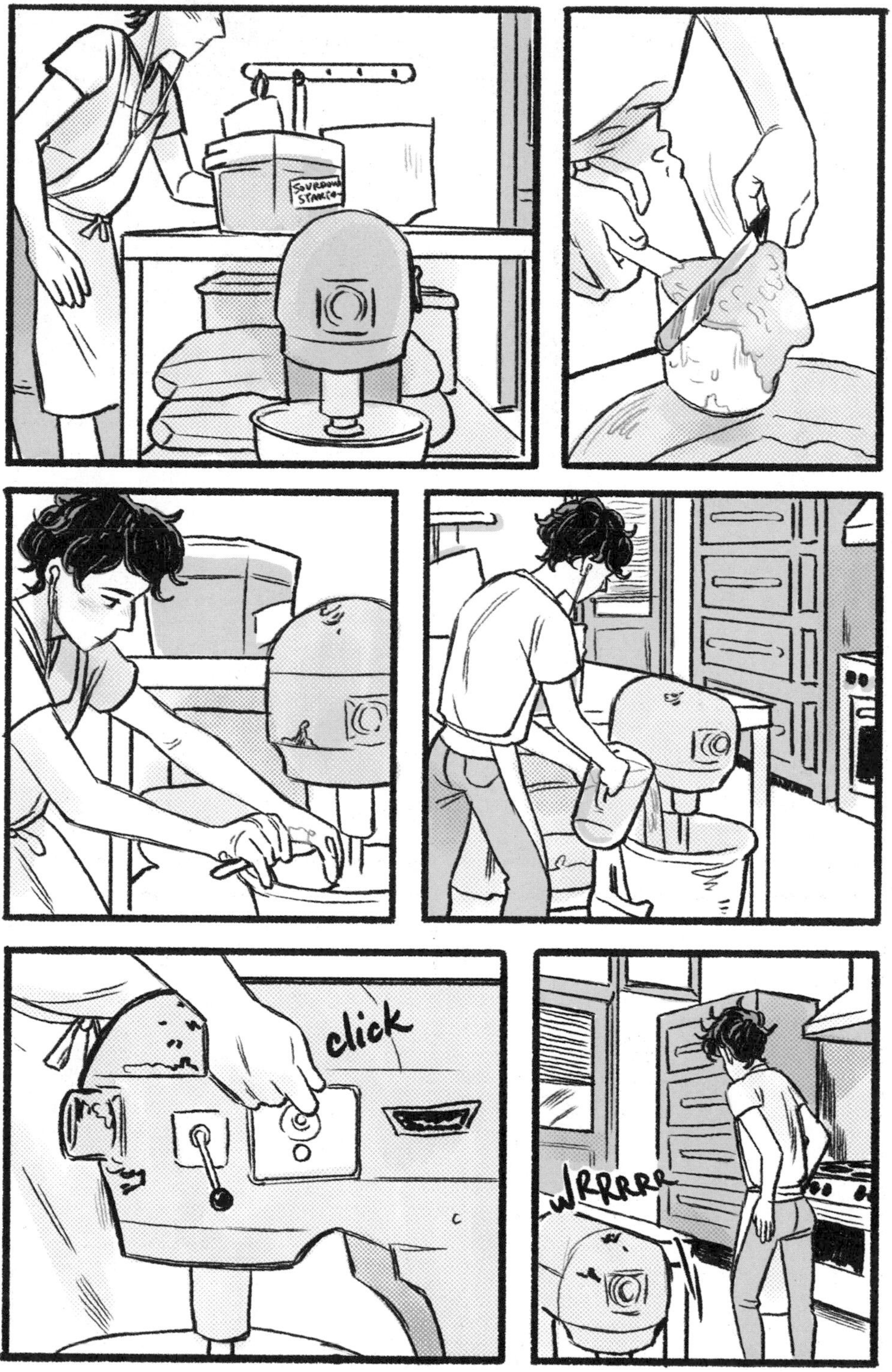
click
WRRRRR

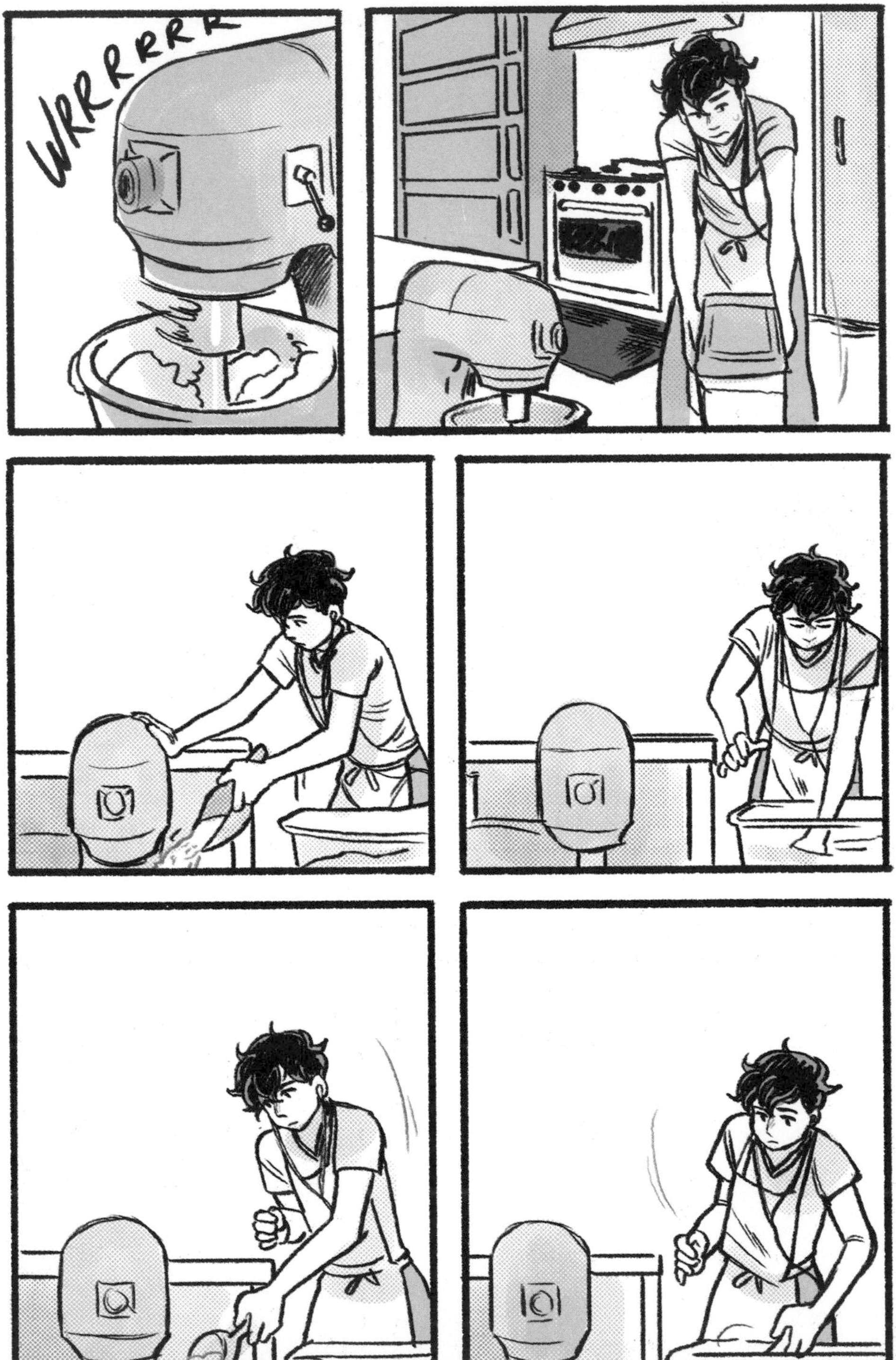
WRRRRRR

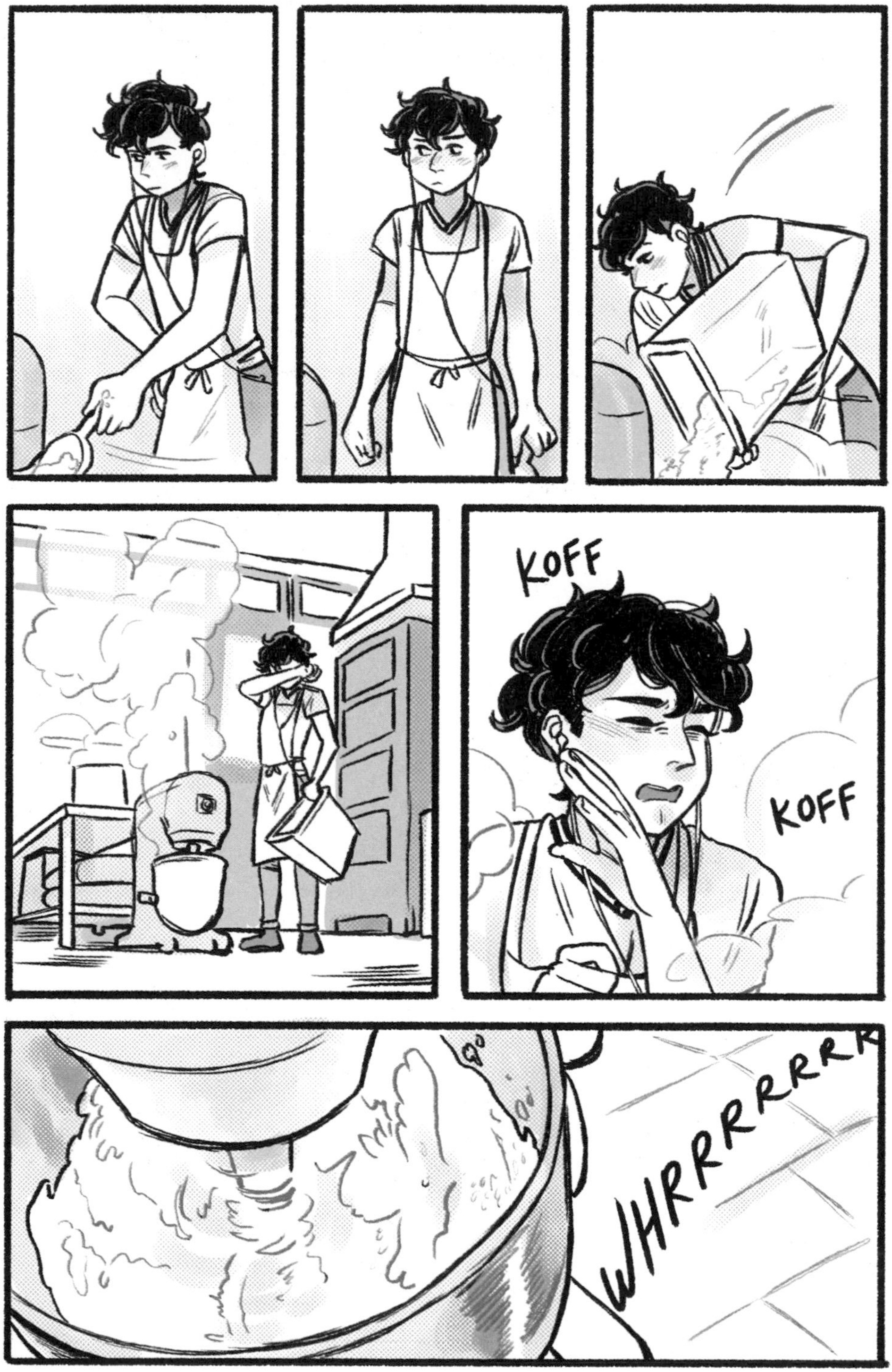
KOFF
KOFF
WHRRRRRRR

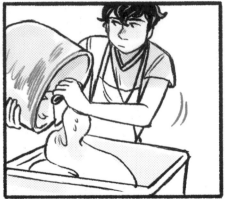

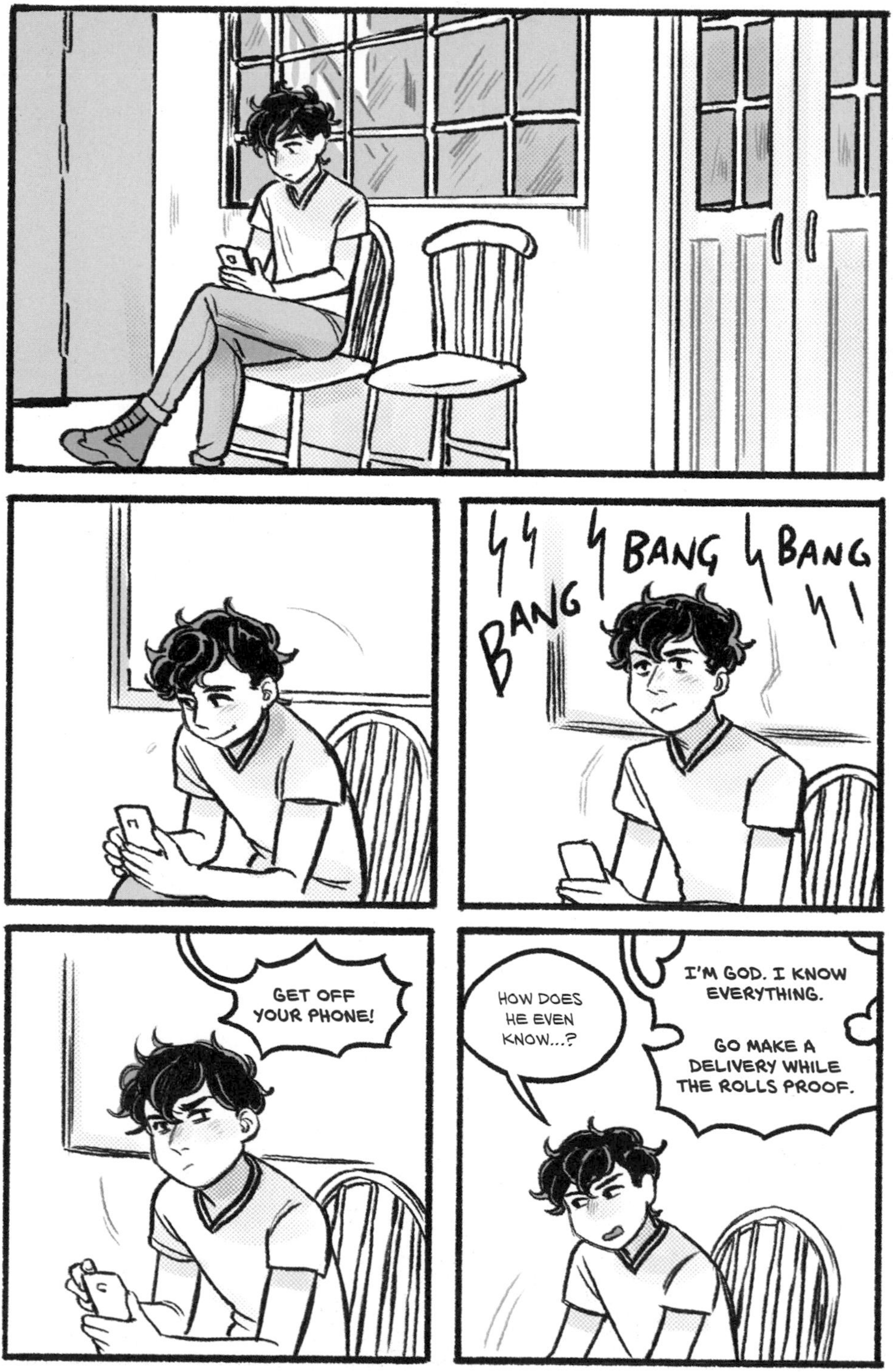
BANG
BANG
BANG
GET OFF YOUR PHONE!
HOW DOES HE EVEN KNOW...?
I'M GOD. I KNOW EVERYTHING.
GO MAKE A DELIVERY WHILE THE ROLLS PROOF.

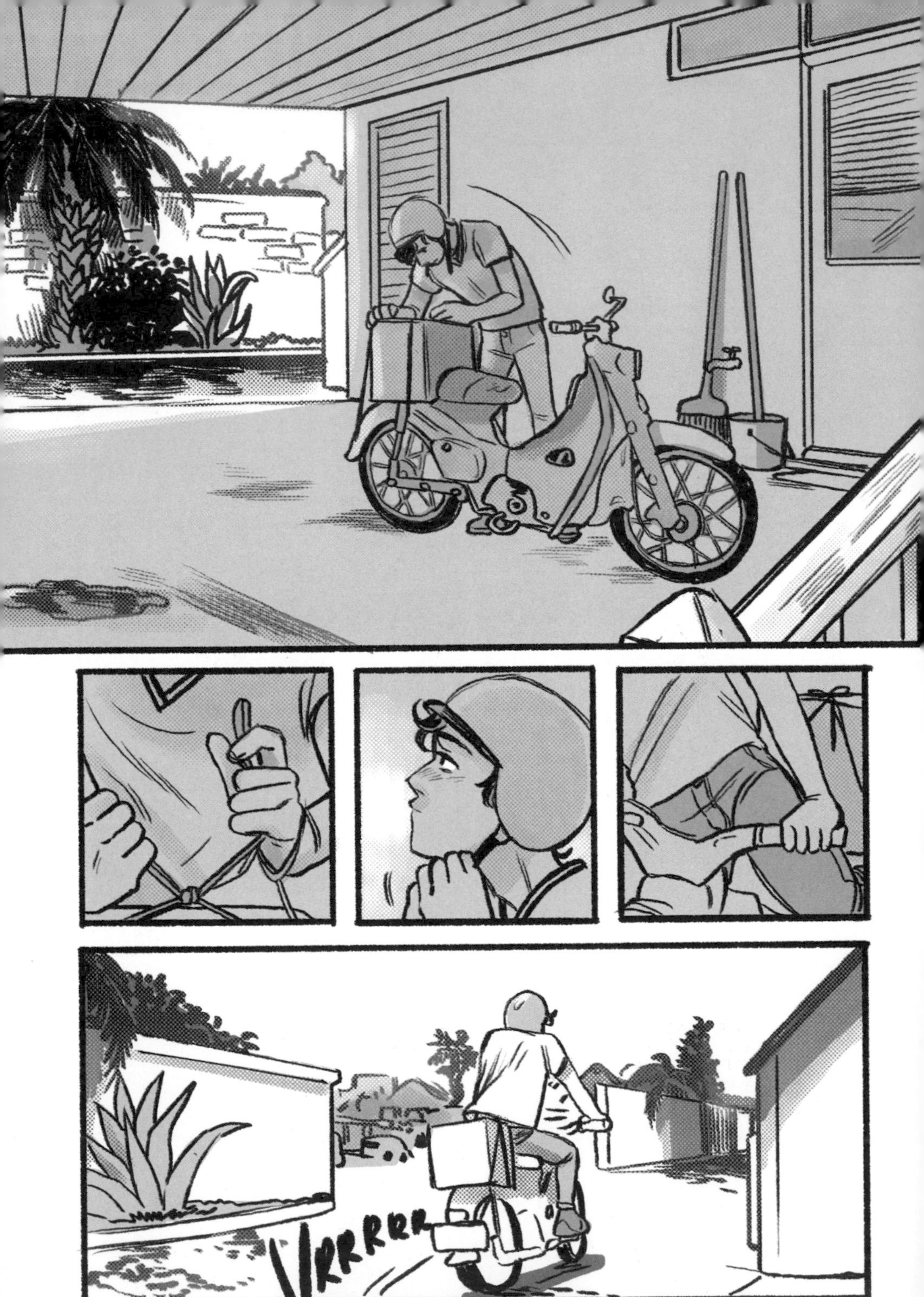
VRRRRR

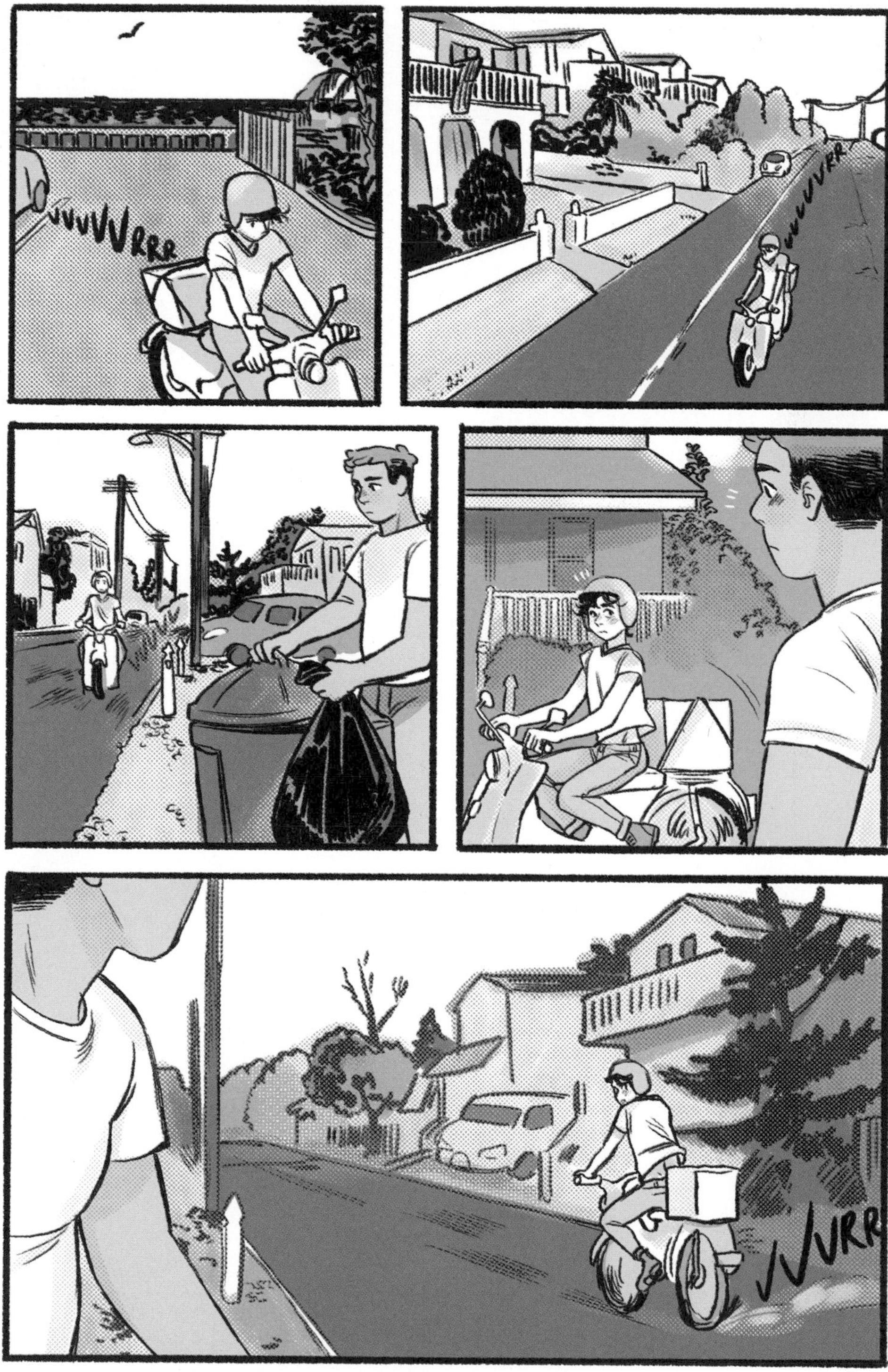
VVVVVRRR
VVVVVRR
VVRR

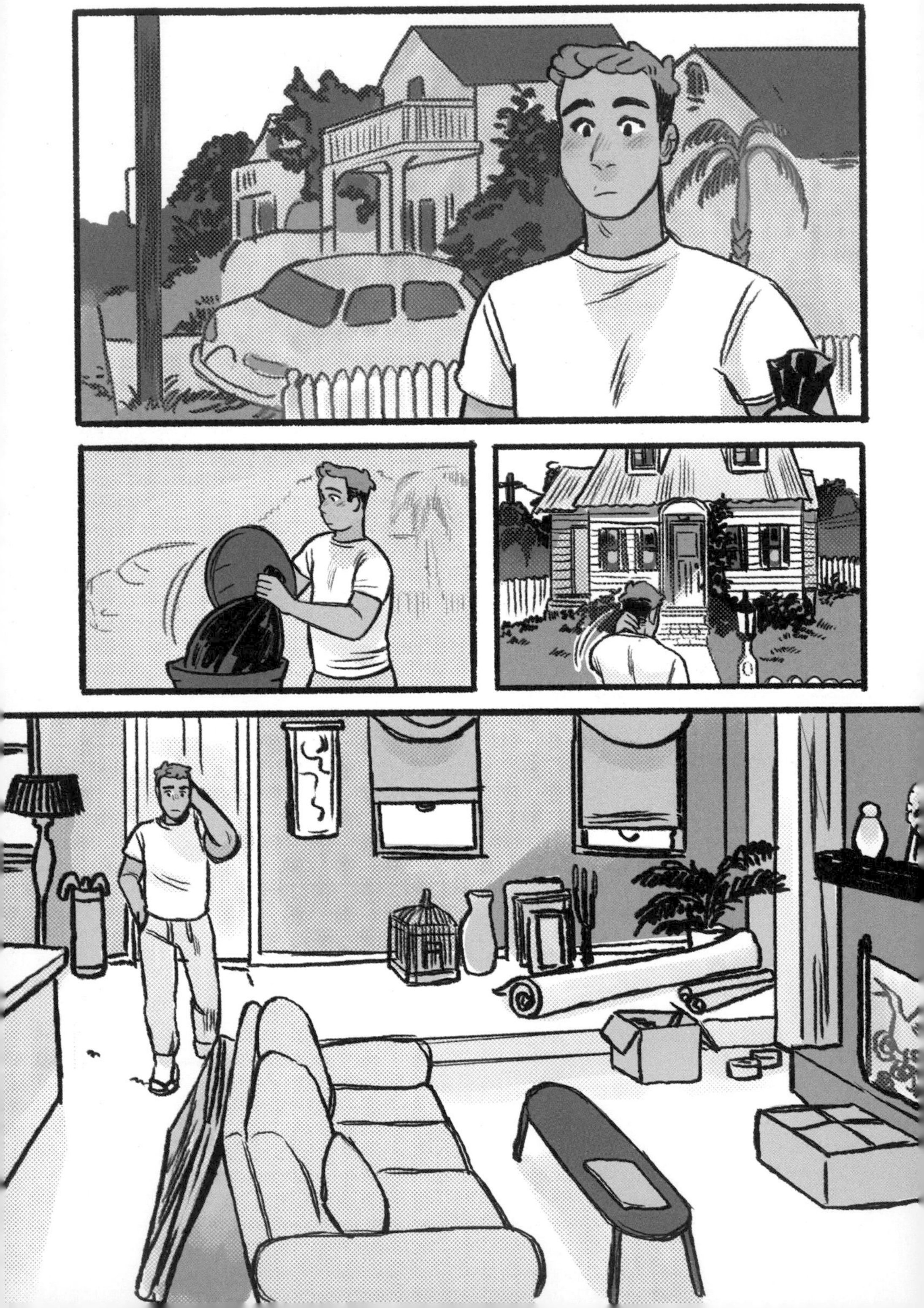

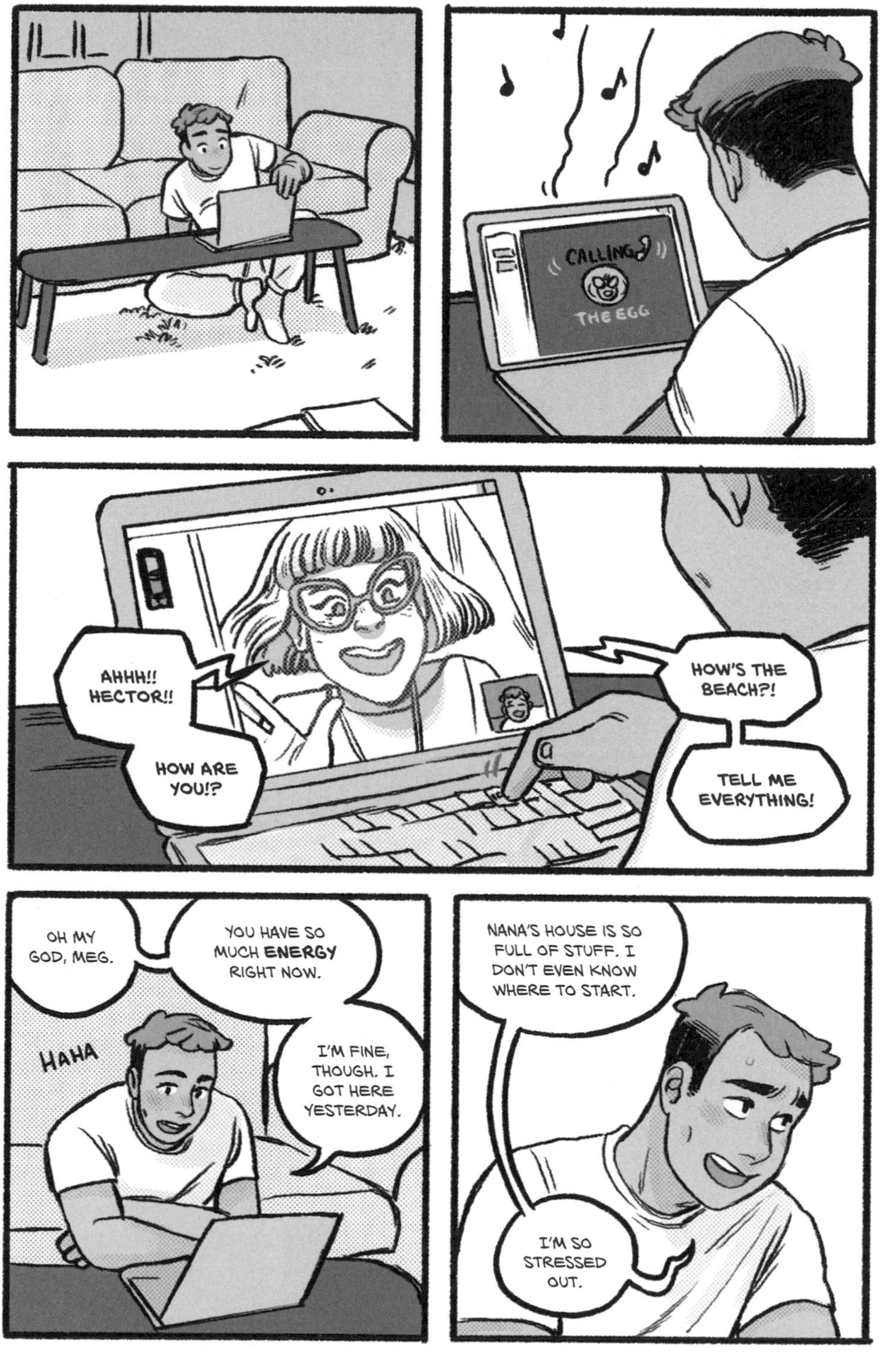
CALLING
THE EGG
AHHH!! HECTOR!!
HOW ARE YOU!?
HOW'S THE BEACH?!
TELL ME EVERYTHING!
OH MY GOD, MEG.
YOU HAVE SO MUCH **ENERGY** RIGHT NOW.
HAHA
I'M FINE, THOUGH. I GOT HERE YESTERDAY.
NANA'S HOUSE IS SO FULL OF STUFF. I DON'T EVEN KNOW WHERE TO START.
I'M SO STRESSED OUT.

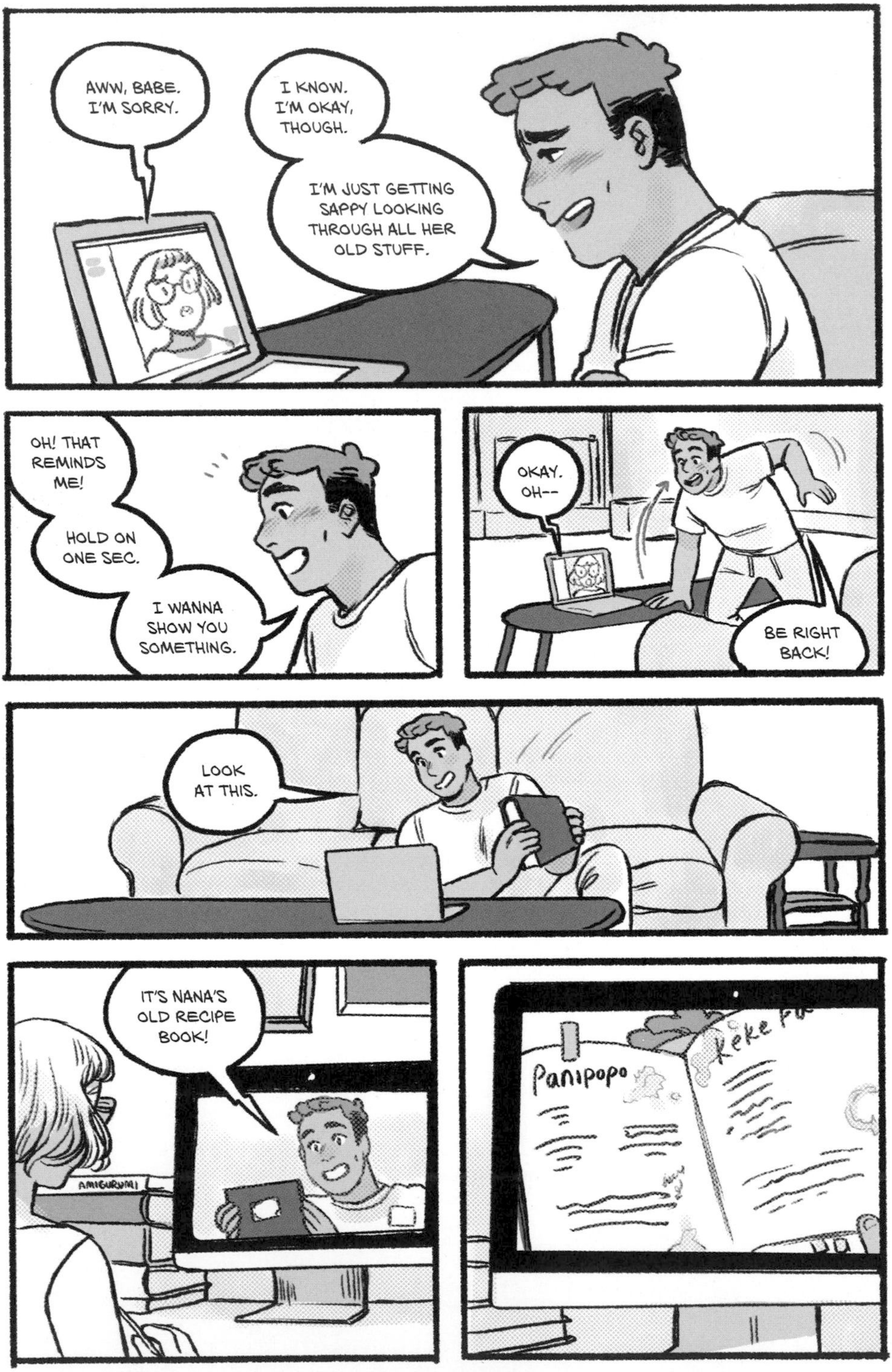
AWW, BABE. I'M SORRY.
I KNOW. I'M OKAY, THOUGH.
I'M JUST GETTING SAPPY LOOKING THROUGH ALL HER OLD STUFF.
OH! THAT REMINDS ME!
HOLD ON ONE SEC.
I WANNA SHOW YOU SOMETHING.
OKAY. OH--
BE RIGHT BACK!
LOOK AT THIS.
IT'S NANA'S OLD RECIPE BOOK!
AMIGURUMI
Panipopo

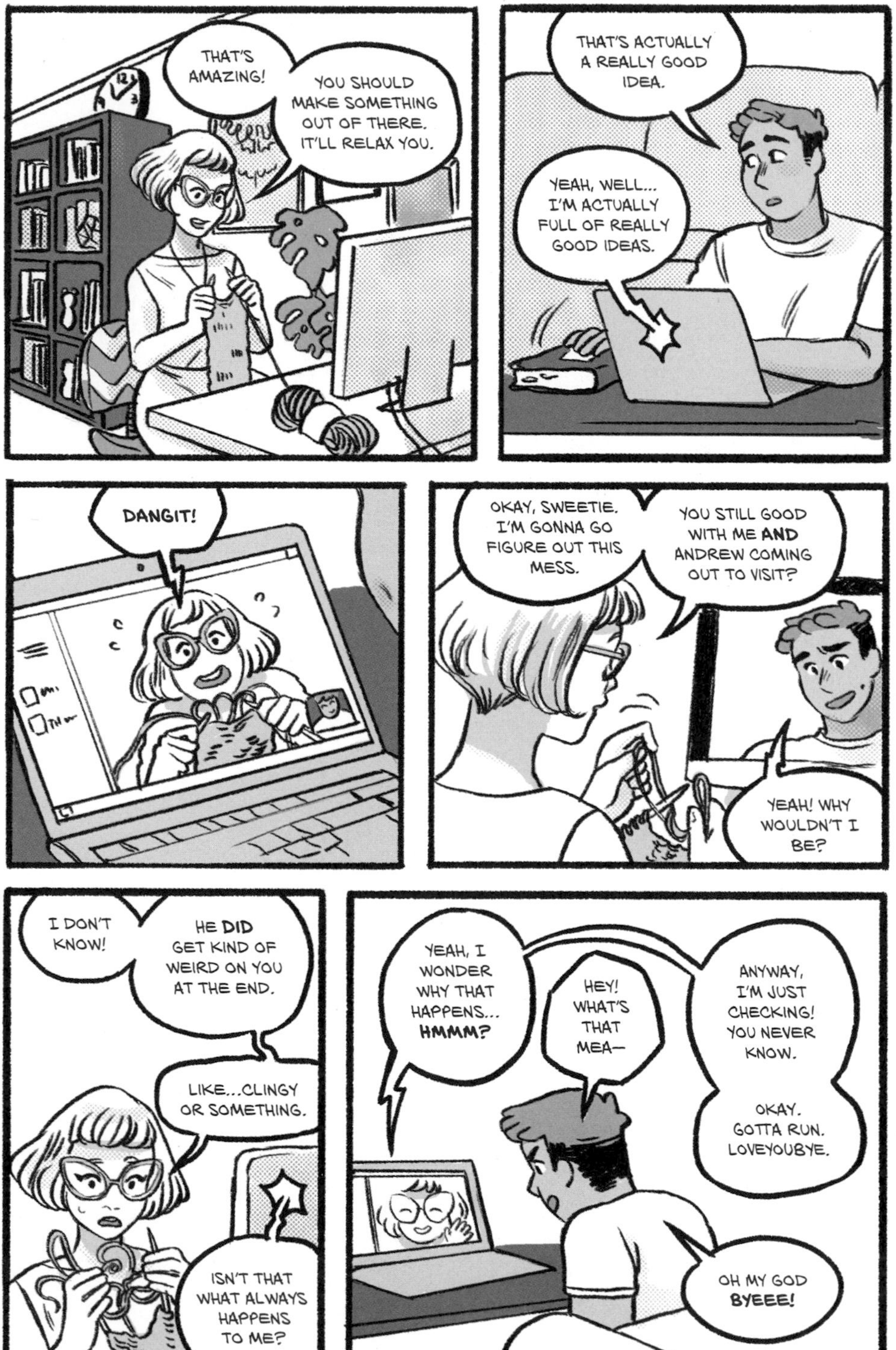
THAT'S AMAZING!
YOU SHOULD MAKE SOMETHING OUT OF THERE. IT'LL RELAX YOU.
THAT'S ACTUALLY A REALLY GOOD IDEA.
YEAH, WELL... I'M ACTUALLY FULL OF REALLY GOOD IDEAS.
DANGIT!
OKAY, SWEETIE. I'M GONNA GO FIGURE OUT THIS MESS.
YOU STILL GOOD WITH ME **AND** ANDREW COMING OUT TO VISIT?
YEAH! WHY WOULDN'T I BE?
I DON'T KNOW!
HE **DID** GET KIND OF WEIRD ON YOU AT THE END.
LIKE...CLINGY OR SOMETHING.
ISN'T THAT WHAT ALWAYS HAPPENS TO ME?
YEAH, I WONDER WHY THAT HAPPENS... **HMMM?**
HEY! WHAT'S THAT MEA—
ANYWAY, I'M JUST CHECKING! YOU NEVER KNOW.
OKAY. GOTTA RUN. LOVEYOUBYE.
OH MY GOD **BYEEE!**

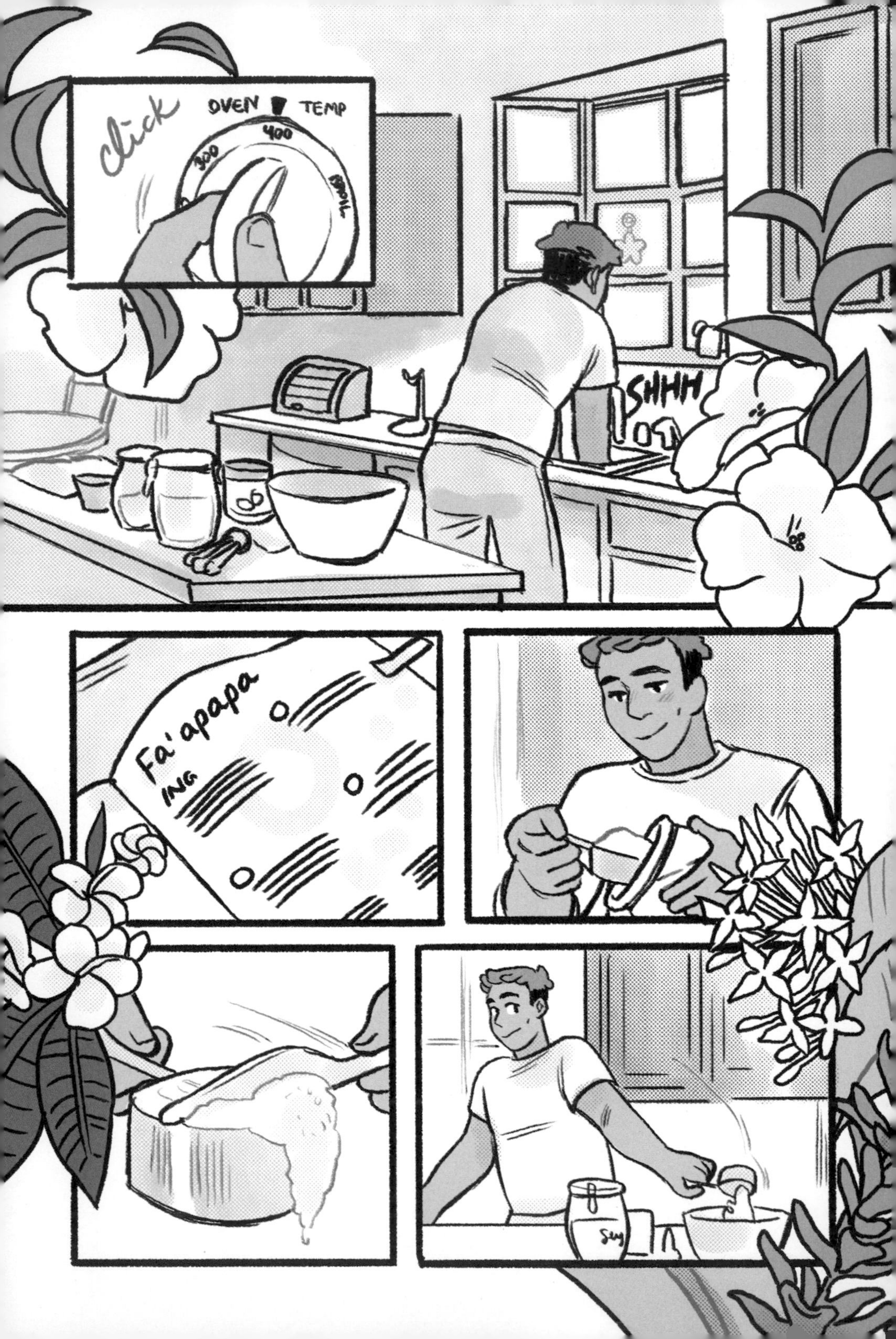
click
OVEN TEMP
300
400
BROIL
SHHH
Fa'apapa
ING

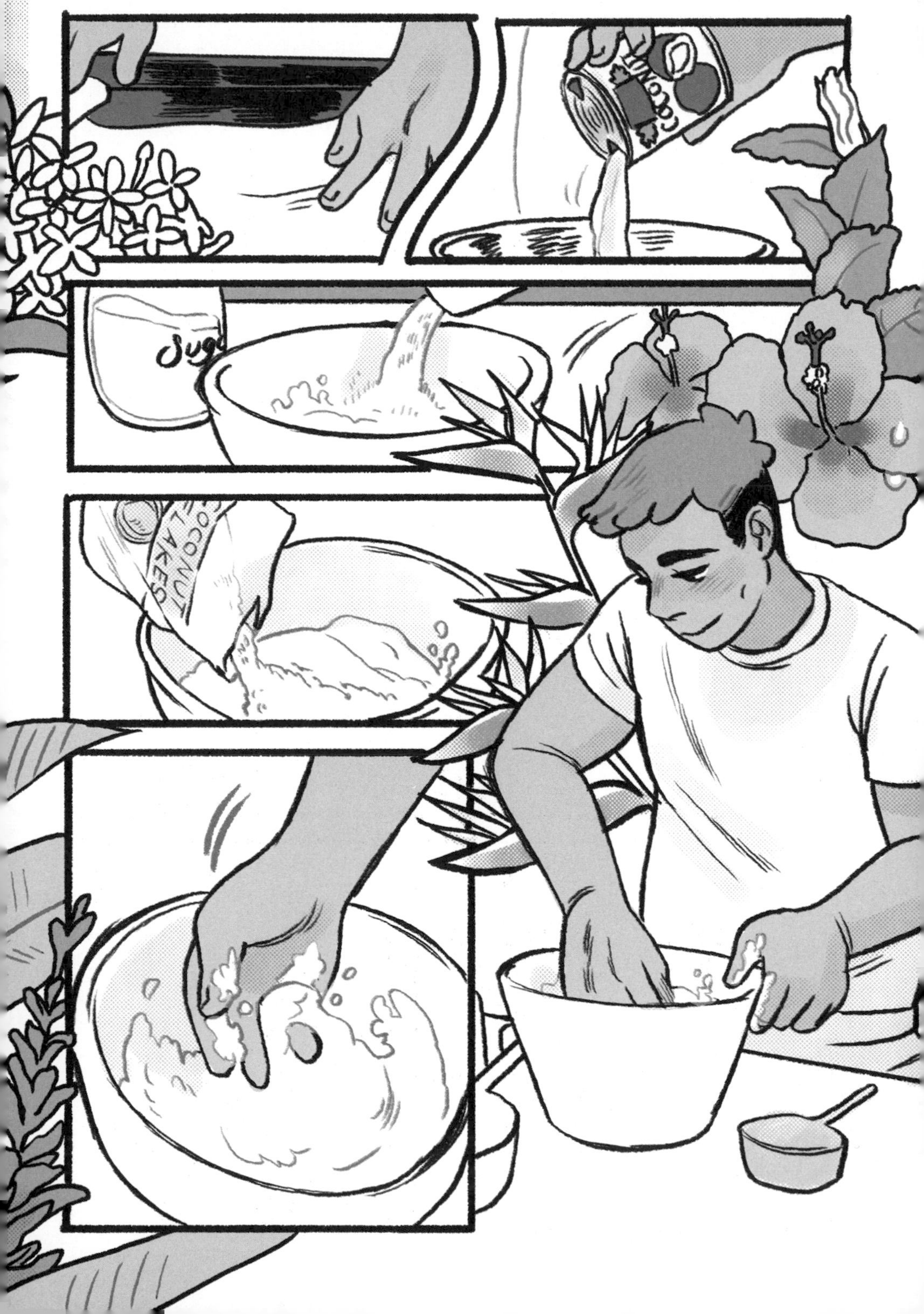
COCONUT

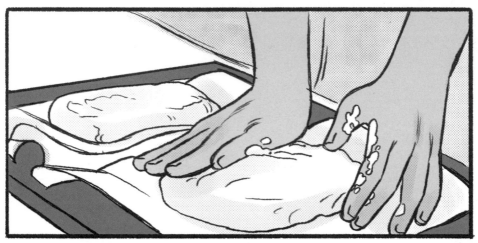

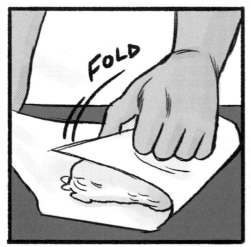

FOLD

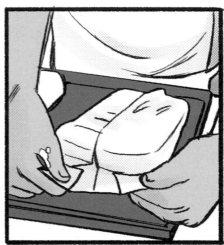

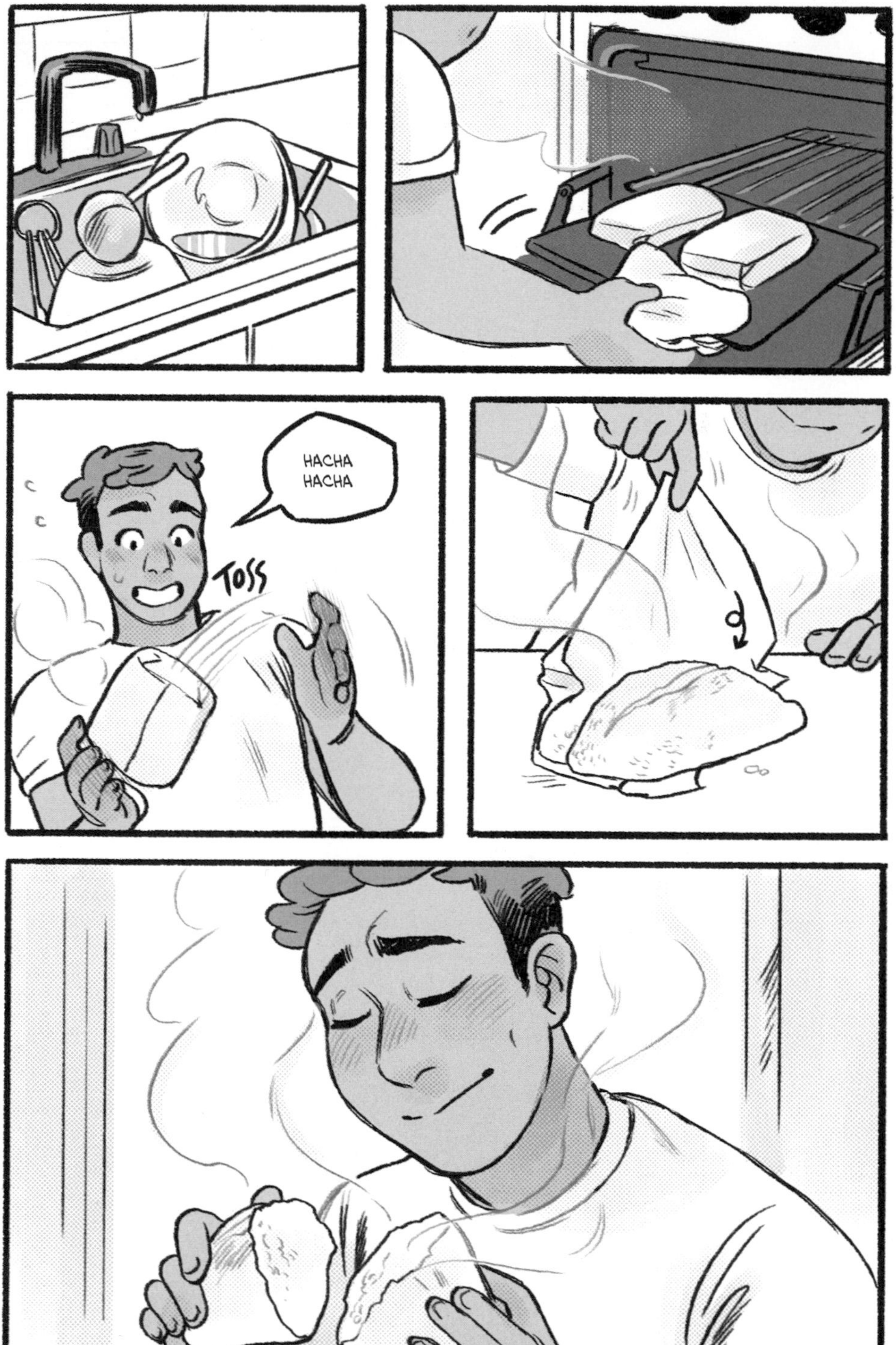
HACHA
HACHA
TOSS

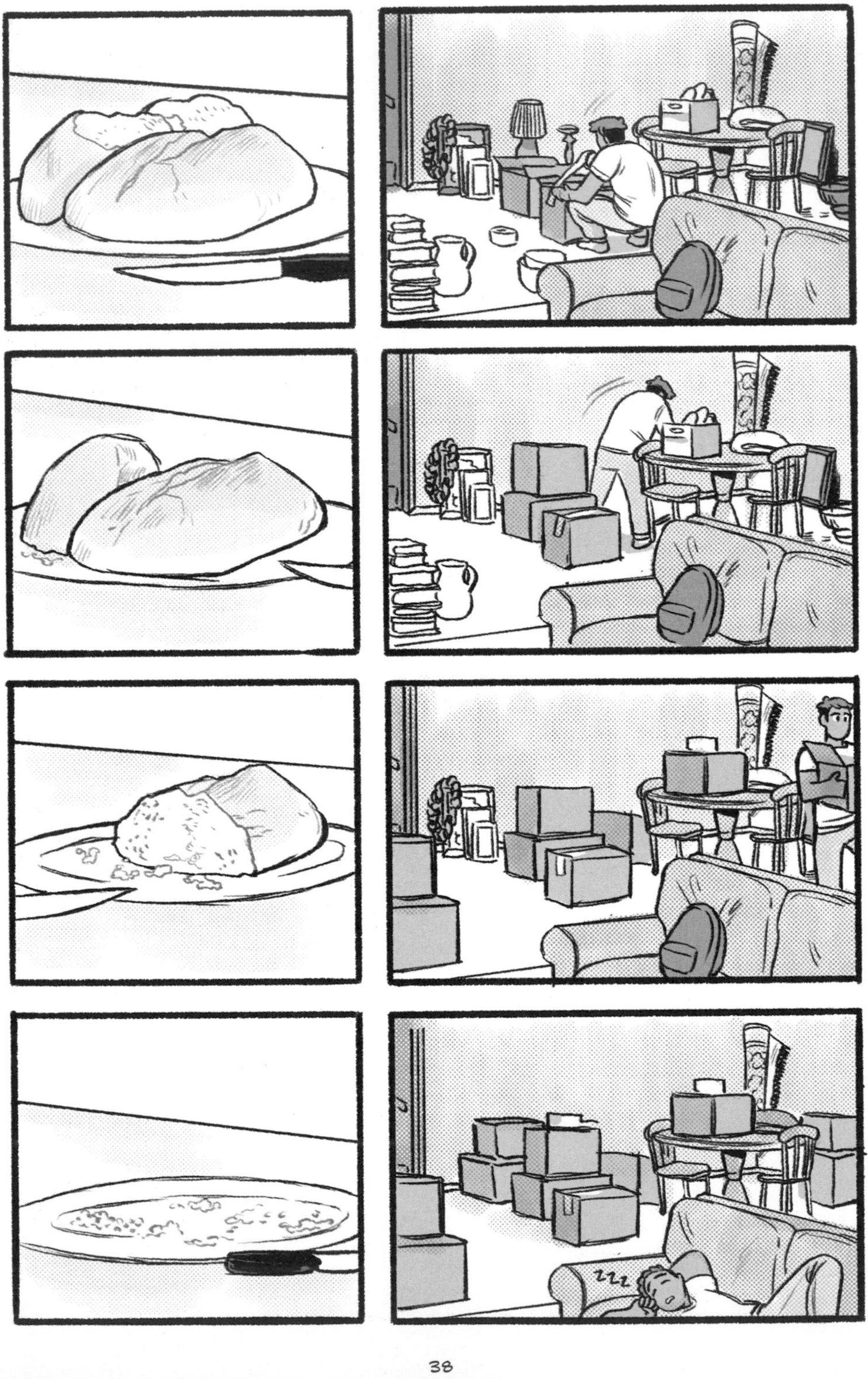
zzz

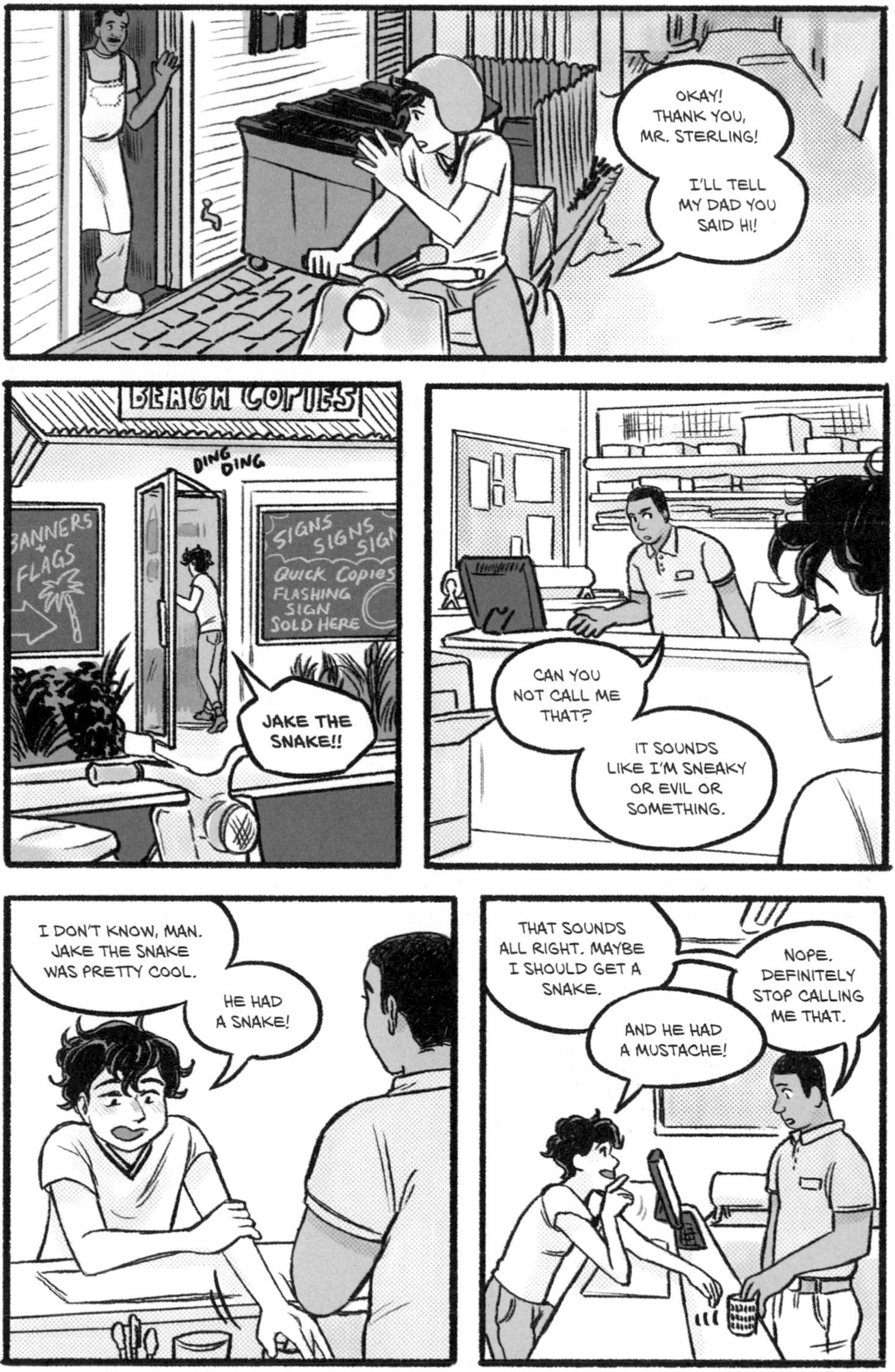
OKAY! THANK YOU, MR. STERLING!
I'LL TELL MY DAD YOU SAID HI!
BEACH COPIES
DING DING
BANNERS + FLAGS
SIGNS SIGNS SIGN
Quick Copies
FLASHING SIGN SOLD HERE
JAKE THE SNAKE!!
CAN YOU NOT CALL ME THAT?
IT SOUNDS LIKE I'M SNEAKY OR EVIL OR SOMETHING.
I DON'T KNOW, MAN. JAKE THE SNAKE WAS PRETTY COOL.
HE HAD A SNAKE!
THAT SOUNDS ALL RIGHT. MAYBE I SHOULD GET A SNAKE.
AND HE HAD A MUSTACHE!
NOPE. DEFINITELY STOP CALLING ME THAT.

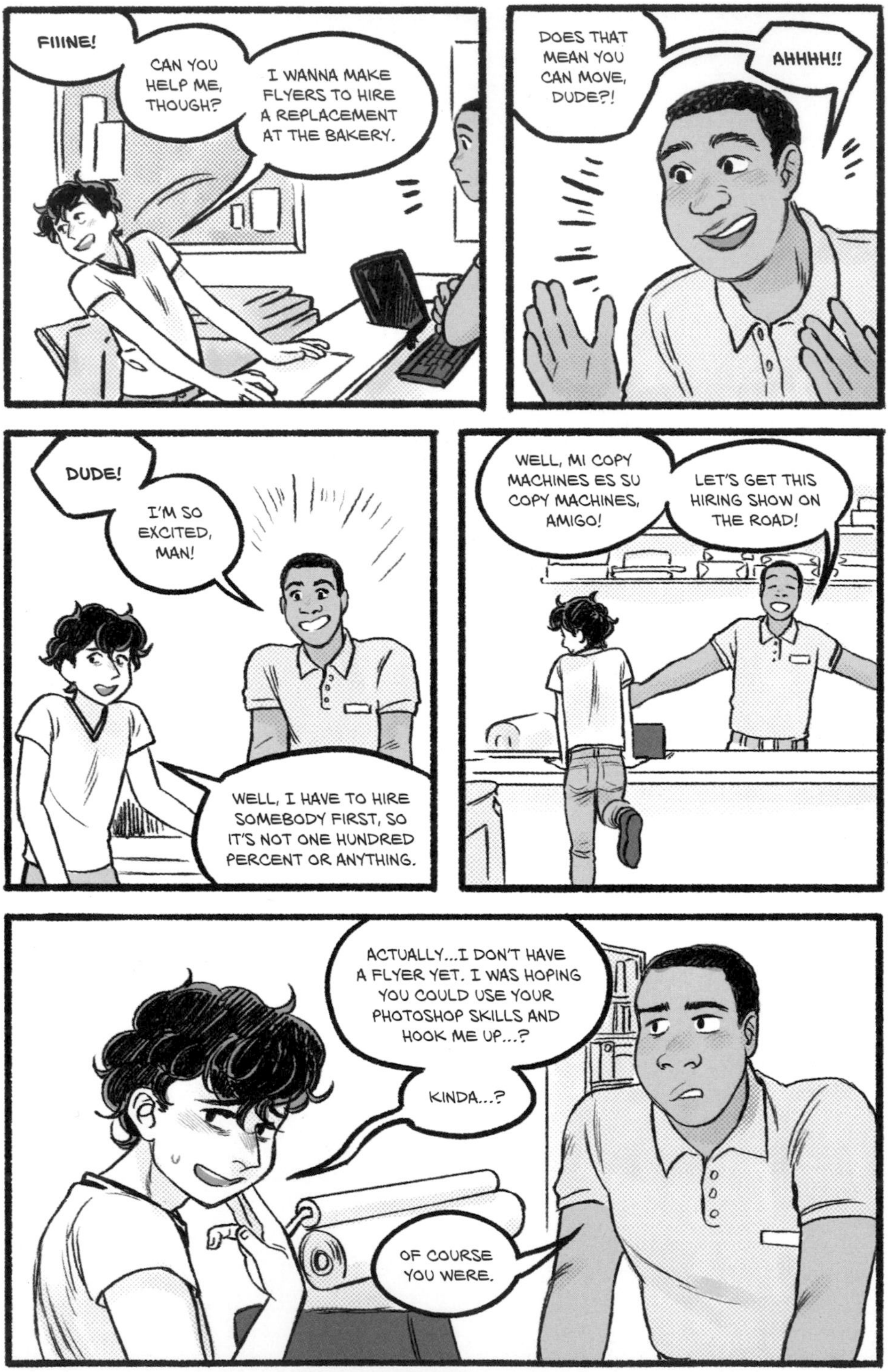
FIIINE!
CAN YOU HELP ME, THOUGH?
I WANNA MAKE FLYERS TO HIRE A REPLACEMENT AT THE BAKERY.
DOES THAT MEAN YOU CAN MOVE, DUDE?!
AHHHH!!
DUDE!
I'M SO EXCITED, MAN!
WELL, I HAVE TO HIRE SOMEBODY FIRST, SO IT'S NOT ONE HUNDRED PERCENT OR ANYTHING.
WELL, MI COPY MACHINES ES SU COPY MACHINES, AMIGO!
LET'S GET THIS HIRING SHOW ON THE ROAD!
ACTUALLY...I DON'T HAVE A FLYER YET. I WAS HOPING YOU COULD USE YOUR PHOTOSHOP SKILLS AND HOOK ME UP...?
KINDA...?
OF COURSE YOU WERE.

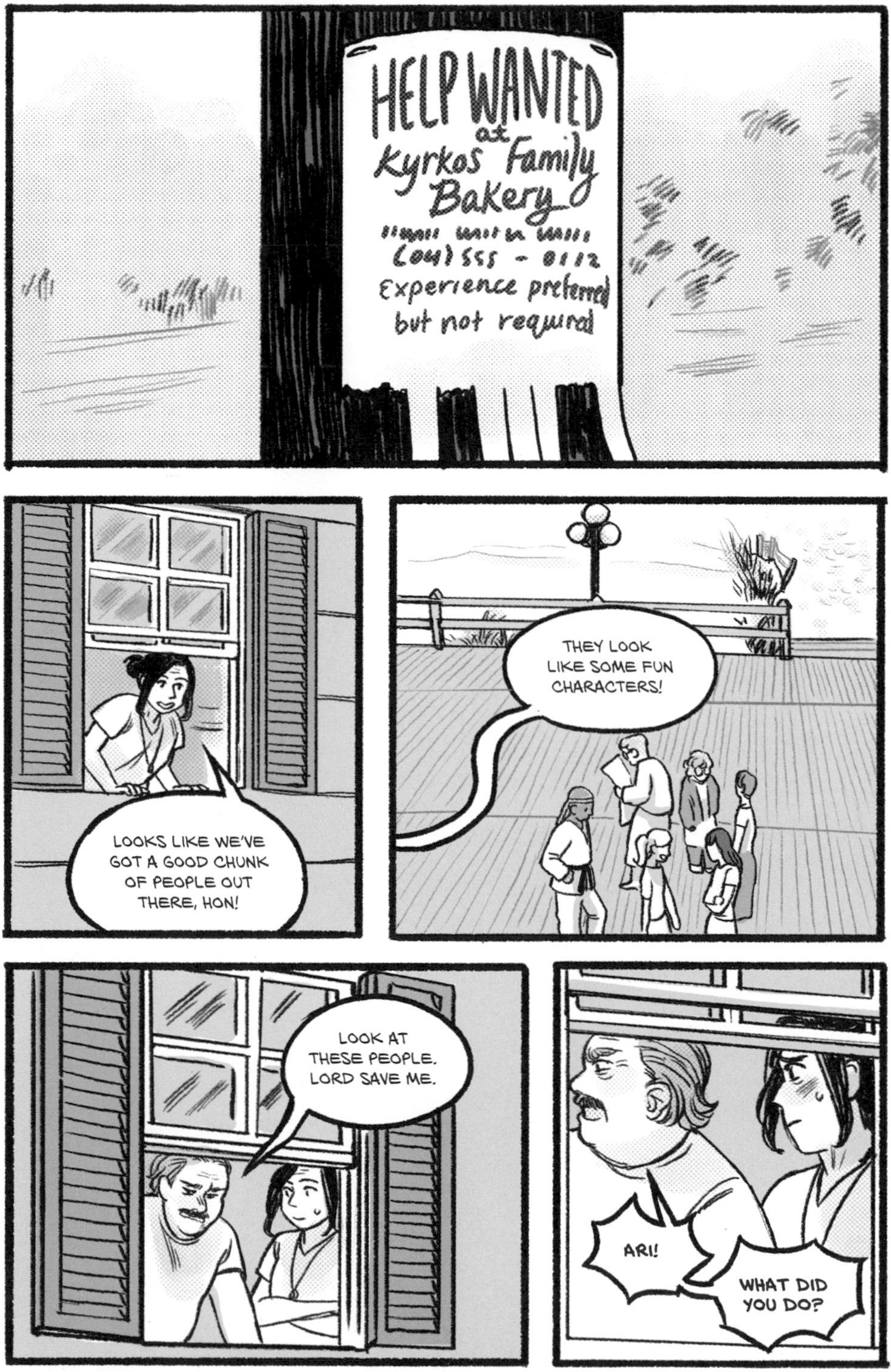
HELP WANTED
at
Kyrkos Family
Bakery
(041) 555 - 0112
Experience preferred
but not required
LOOKS LIKE WE'VE GOT A GOOD CHUNK OF PEOPLE OUT THERE, HON!
THEY LOOK LIKE SOME FUN CHARACTERS!
LOOK AT THESE PEOPLE. LORD SAVE ME.
ARI!
WHAT DID YOU DO?

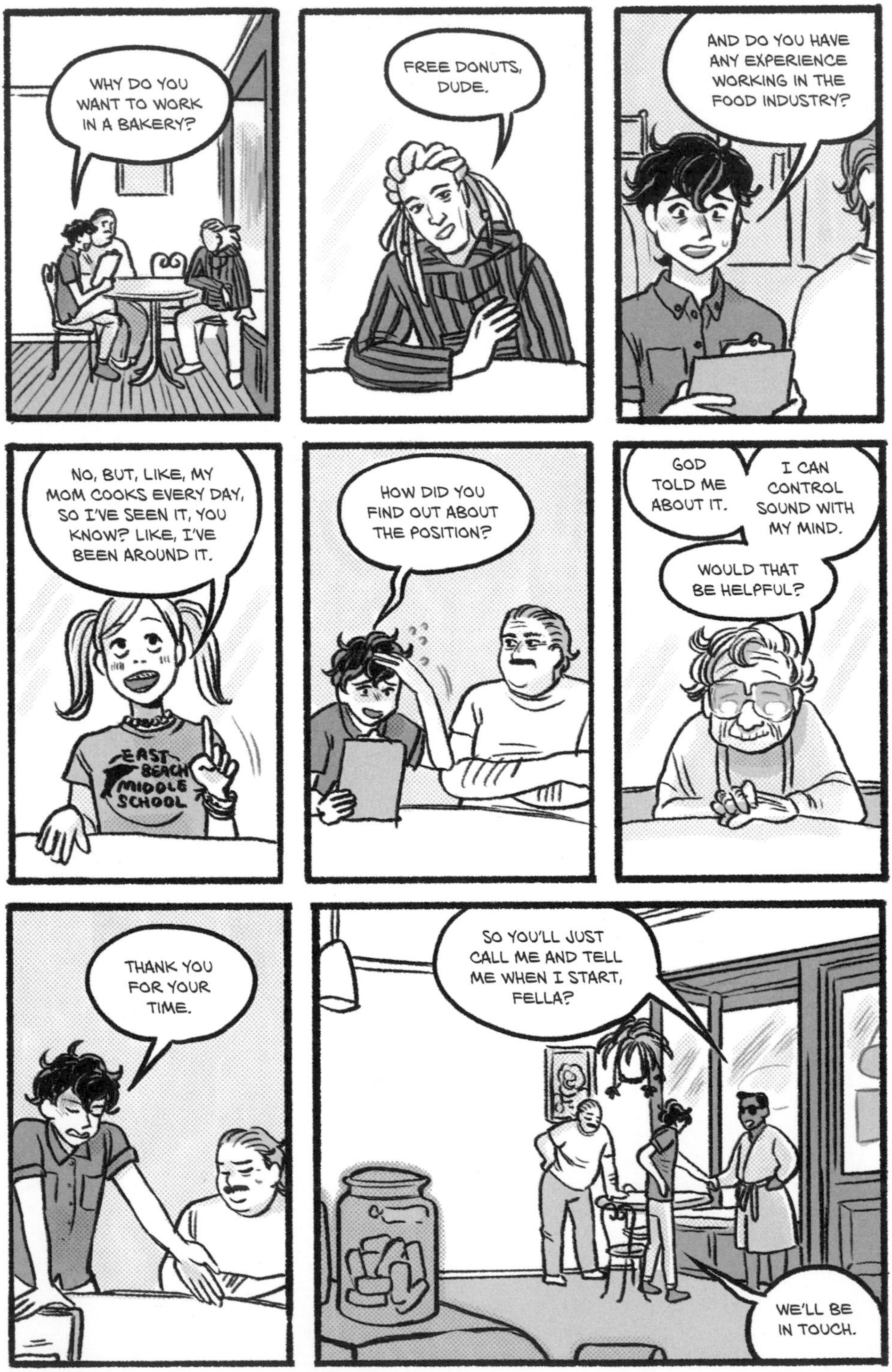
WHY DO YOU WANT TO WORK IN A BAKERY?
FREE DONUTS, DUDE.
AND DO YOU HAVE ANY EXPERIENCE WORKING IN THE FOOD INDUSTRY?
NO, BUT, LIKE, MY MOM COOKS EVERY DAY, SO I'VE SEEN IT, YOU KNOW? LIKE, I'VE BEEN AROUND IT.
EAST BEACH MIDDLE SCHOOL
HOW DID YOU FIND OUT ABOUT THE POSITION?
GOD TOLD ME ABOUT IT.
I CAN CONTROL SOUND WITH MY MIND.
WOULD THAT BE HELPFUL?
THANK YOU FOR YOUR TIME.
SO YOU'LL JUST CALL ME AND TELL ME WHEN I START, FELLA?
WE'LL BE IN TOUCH.

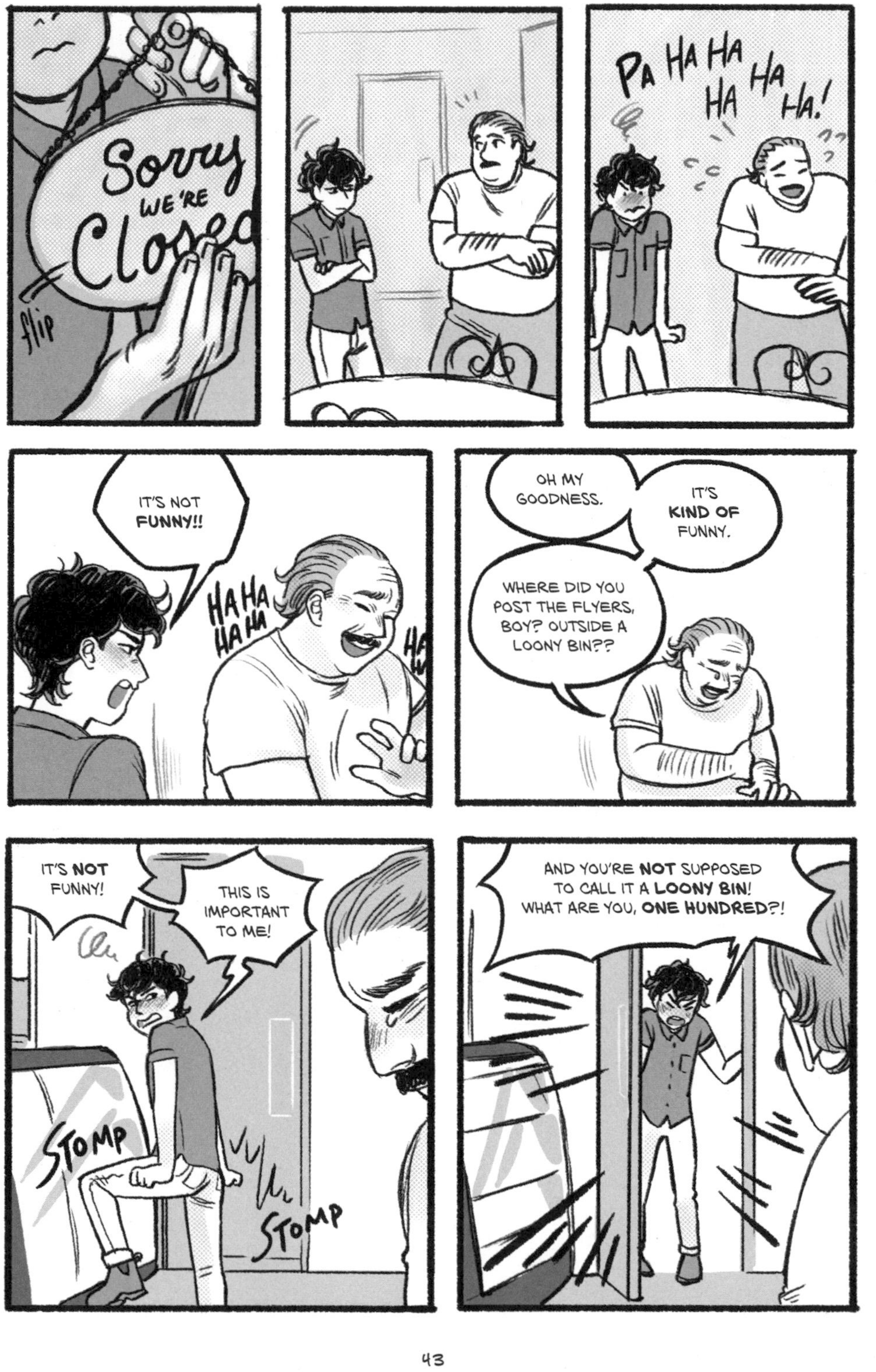
Sorry WE'RE Closed
flip
PA HA HA HA HA HA!
IT'S NOT **FUNNY!!**
HA HA HA HA
OH MY GOODNESS.
IT'S **KIND OF** FUNNY.
WHERE DID YOU POST THE FLYERS, BOY? OUTSIDE A LOONY BIN??
IT'S **NOT** FUNNY!
THIS IS IMPORTANT TO ME!
STOMP
STOMP
AND YOU'RE **NOT** SUPPOSED TO CALL IT A **LOONY BIN**! WHAT ARE YOU, **ONE HUNDRED**?!

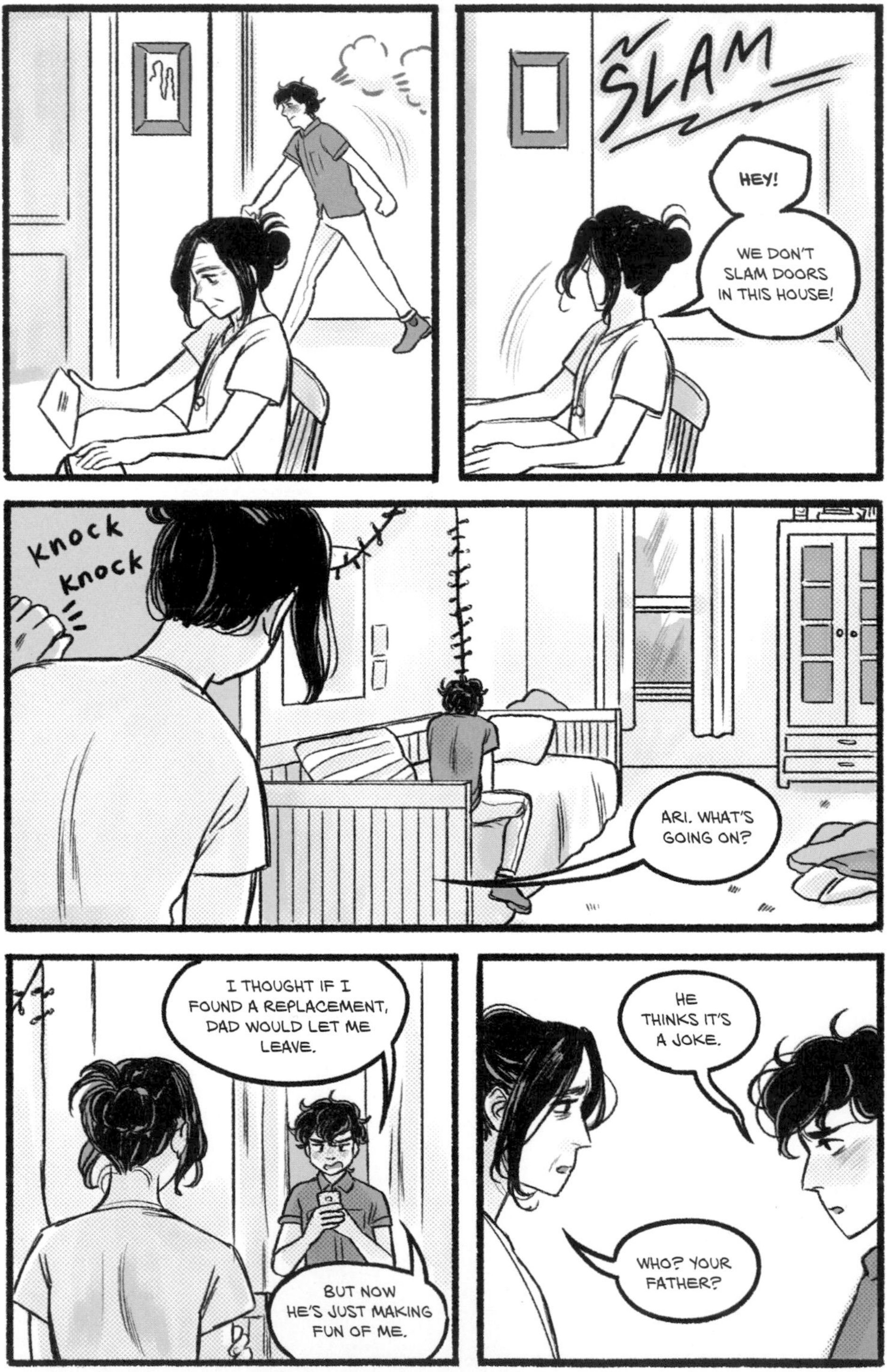
SLAM
HEY!
WE DON'T SLAM DOORS IN THIS HOUSE!
knock knock
ARI. WHAT'S GOING ON?
I THOUGHT IF I FOUND A REPLACEMENT, DAD WOULD LET ME LEAVE.
BUT NOW HE'S JUST MAKING FUN OF ME.
HE THINKS IT'S A JOKE.
WHO? YOUR FATHER?

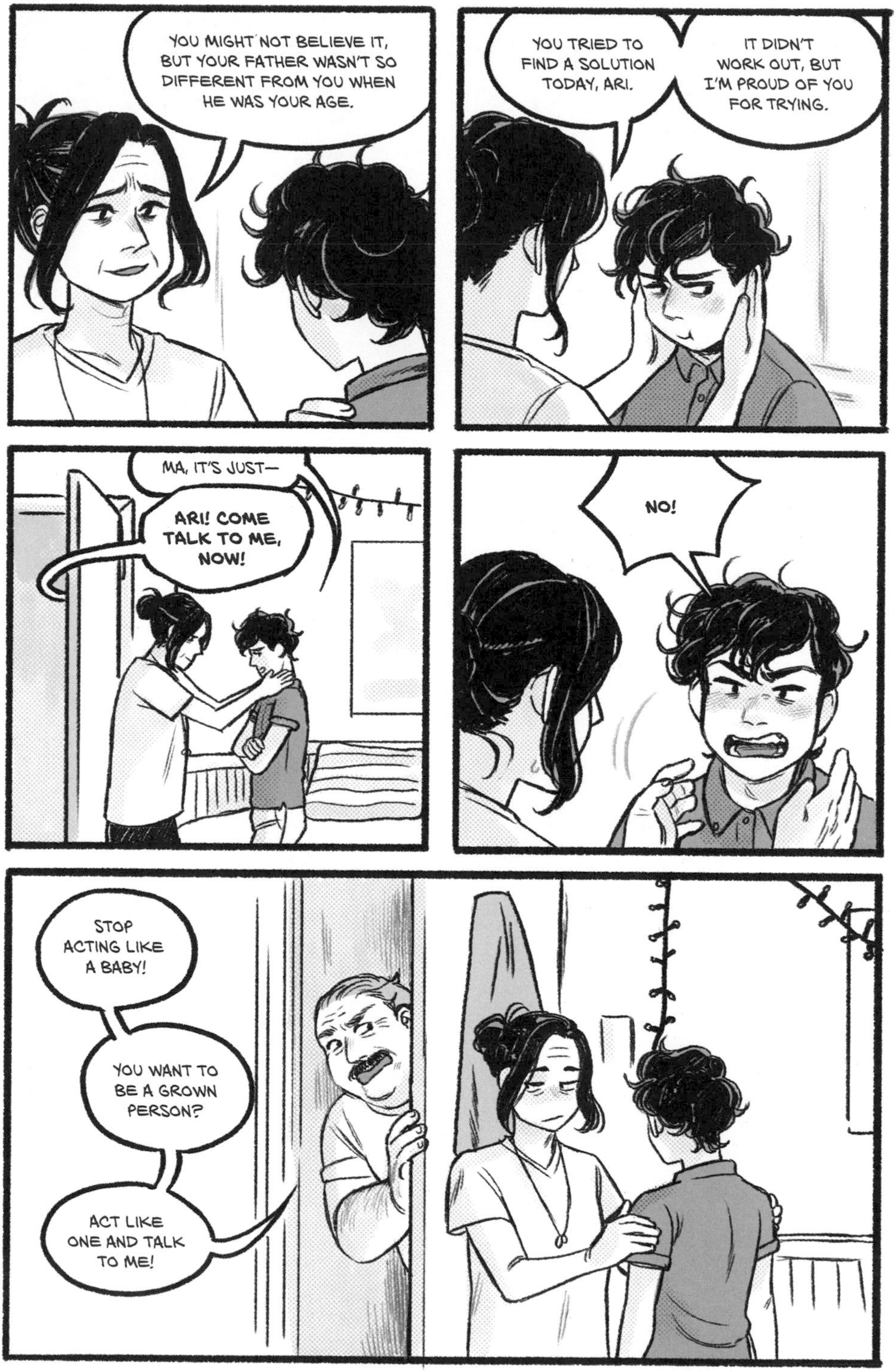
YOU MIGHT NOT BELIEVE IT, BUT YOUR FATHER WASN'T SO DIFFERENT FROM YOU WHEN HE WAS YOUR AGE.
YOU TRIED TO FIND A SOLUTION TODAY, ARI.
IT DIDN'T WORK OUT, BUT I'M PROUD OF YOU FOR TRYING.
MA, IT'S JUST—
ARI! COME TALK TO ME, NOW!
NO!
STOP ACTING LIKE A BABY!
YOU WANT TO BE A GROWN PERSON?
ACT LIKE ONE AND TALK TO ME!

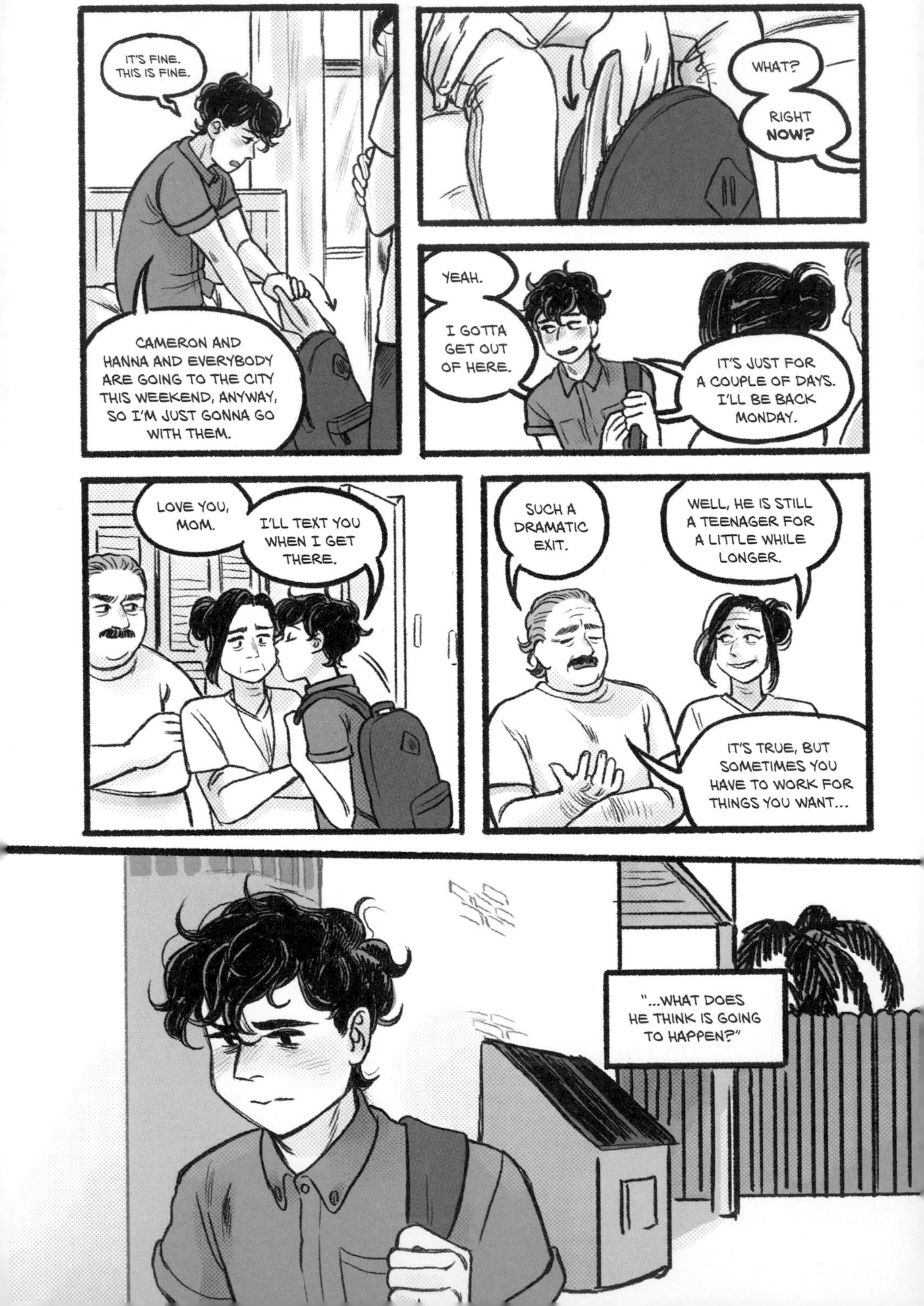
IT'S FINE. THIS IS FINE.
CAMERON AND HANNA AND EVERYBODY ARE GOING TO THE CITY THIS WEEKEND, ANYWAY, SO I'M JUST GONNA GO WITH THEM.
WHAT?
RIGHT NOW?
YEAH.
I GOTTA GET OUT OF HERE.
IT'S JUST FOR A COUPLE OF DAYS. I'LL BE BACK MONDAY.
LOVE YOU, MOM.
I'LL TEXT YOU WHEN I GET THERE.
SUCH A DRAMATIC EXIT.
WELL, HE IS STILL A TEENAGER FOR A LITTLE WHILE LONGER.
IT'S TRUE, BUT SOMETIMES YOU HAVE TO WORK FOR THINGS YOU WANT...
"...WHAT DOES HE THINK IS GOING TO HAPPEN?"

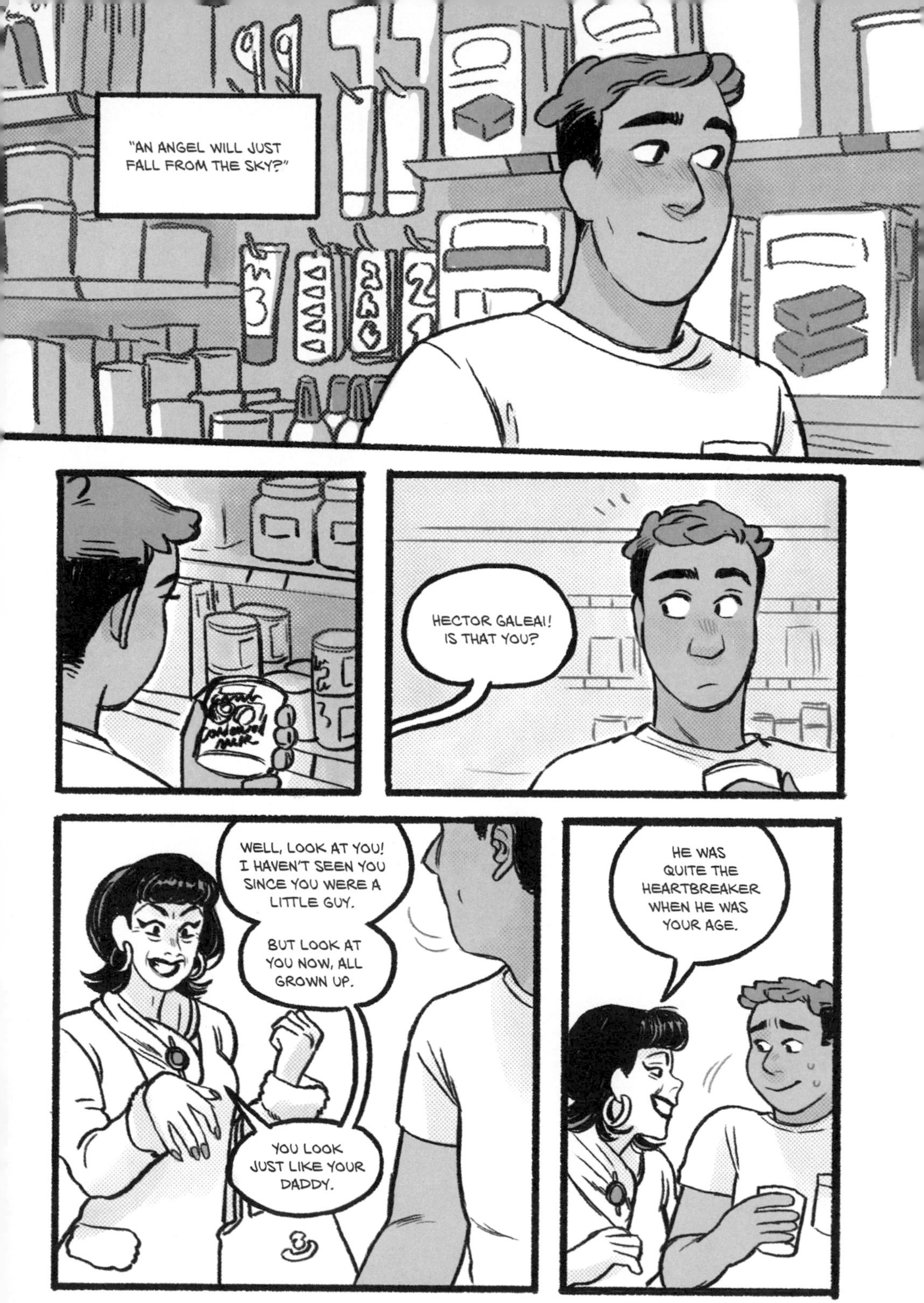
"AN ANGEL WILL JUST FALL FROM THE SKY?"
HECTOR GALEA!! IS THAT YOU?
WELL, LOOK AT YOU! I HAVEN'T SEEN YOU SINCE YOU WERE A LITTLE GUY.
BUT LOOK AT YOU NOW, ALL GROWN UP.
YOU LOOK JUST LIKE YOUR DADDY.
HE WAS QUITE THE HEARTBREAKER WHEN HE WAS YOUR AGE.

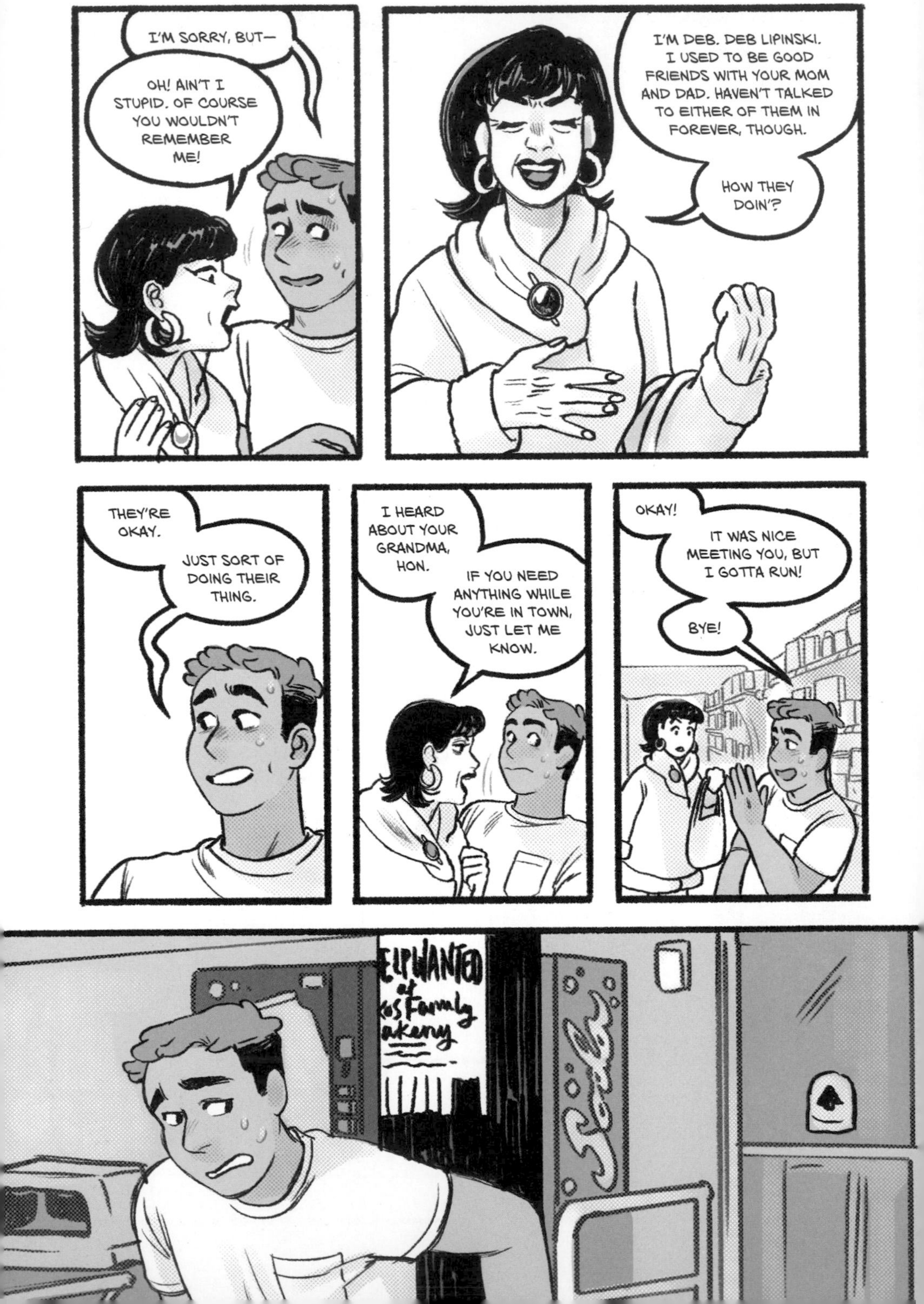
I'M SORRY, BUT—
OH! AIN'T I STUPID. OF COURSE YOU WOULDN'T REMEMBER ME!
I'M DEB. DEB LIPINSKI. I USED TO BE GOOD FRIENDS WITH YOUR MOM AND DAD. HAVEN'T TALKED TO EITHER OF THEM IN FOREVER, THOUGH.
HOW THEY DOIN'?
THEY'RE OKAY.
JUST SORT OF DOING THEIR THING.
I HEARD ABOUT YOUR GRANDMA, HON.
IF YOU NEED ANYTHING WHILE YOU'RE IN TOWN, JUST LET ME KNOW.
OKAY!
IT WAS NICE MEETING YOU, BUT I GOTTA RUN!
BYE!
ELP WANTED

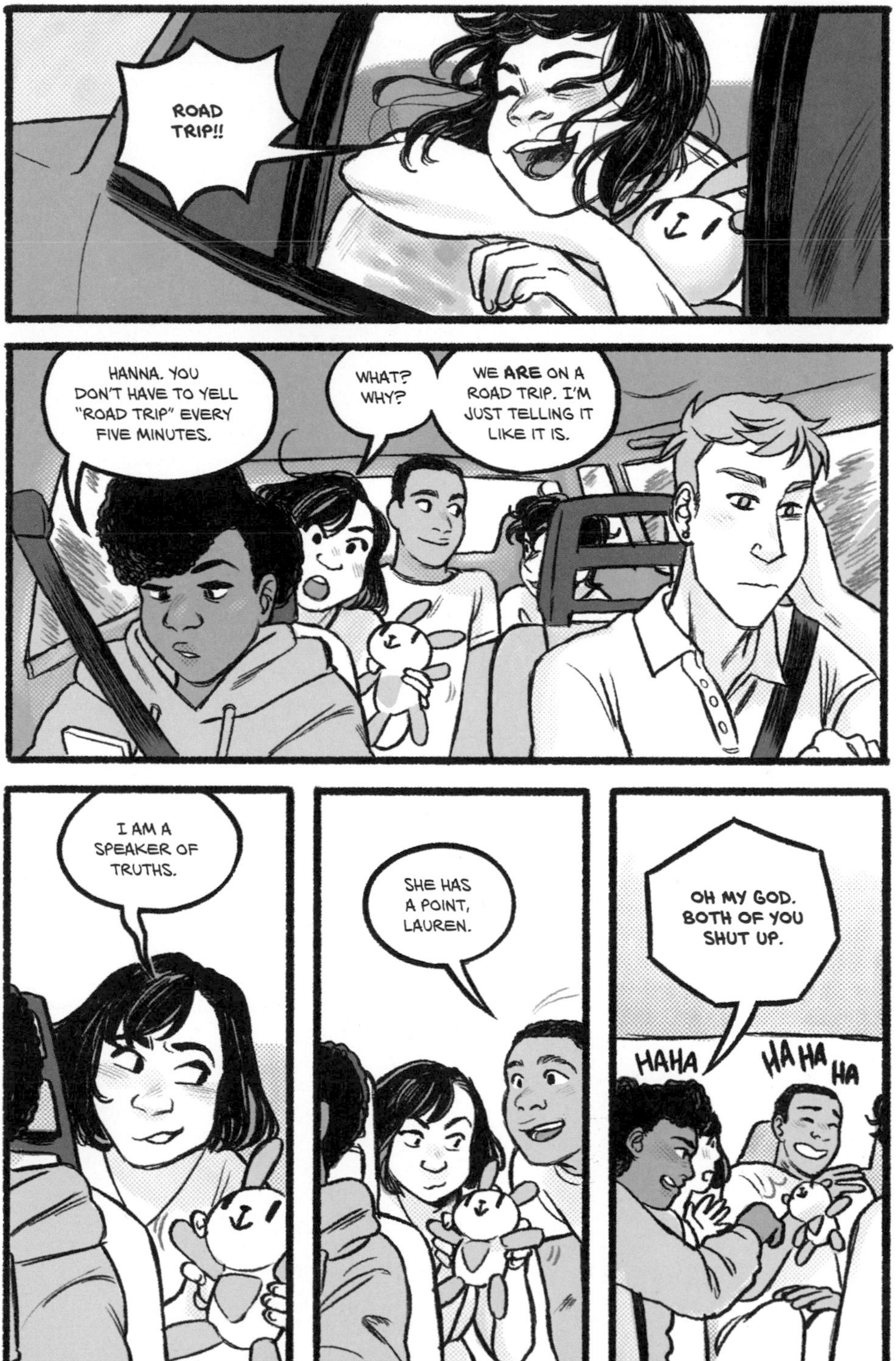

ROAD TRIP!!
HANNA. YOU DON'T HAVE TO YELL "ROAD TRIP" EVERY FIVE MINUTES.
WHAT? WHY?
WE ARE ON A ROAD TRIP. I'M JUST TELLING IT LIKE IT IS.
I AM A SPEAKER OF TRUTHS.
SHE HAS A POINT, LAUREN.
OH MY GOD. BOTH OF YOU SHUT UP.
HAHA
HA HA HA

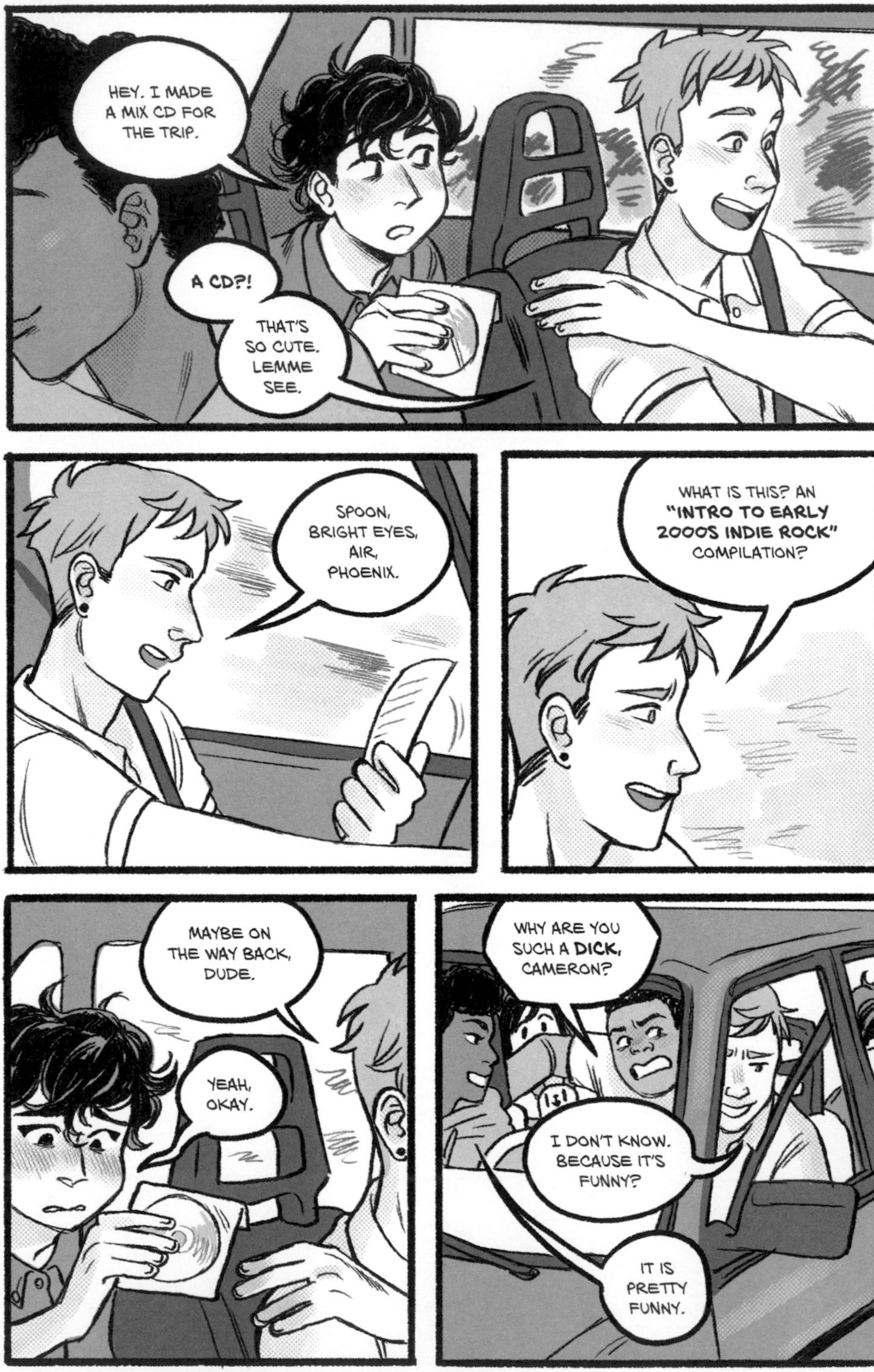
HEY. I MADE A MIX CD FOR THE TRIP.
A CD?!
THAT'S SO CUTE. LEMME SEE.
SPOON, BRIGHT EYES, AIR, PHOENIX.
WHAT IS THIS? AN **"INTRO TO EARLY 2000S INDIE ROCK"** COMPILATION?
MAYBE ON THE WAY BACK, DUDE.
YEAH, OKAY.
WHY ARE YOU SUCH A **DICK,** CAMERON?
I DON'T KNOW. BECAUSE IT'S FUNNY?
IT IS PRETTY FUNNY.

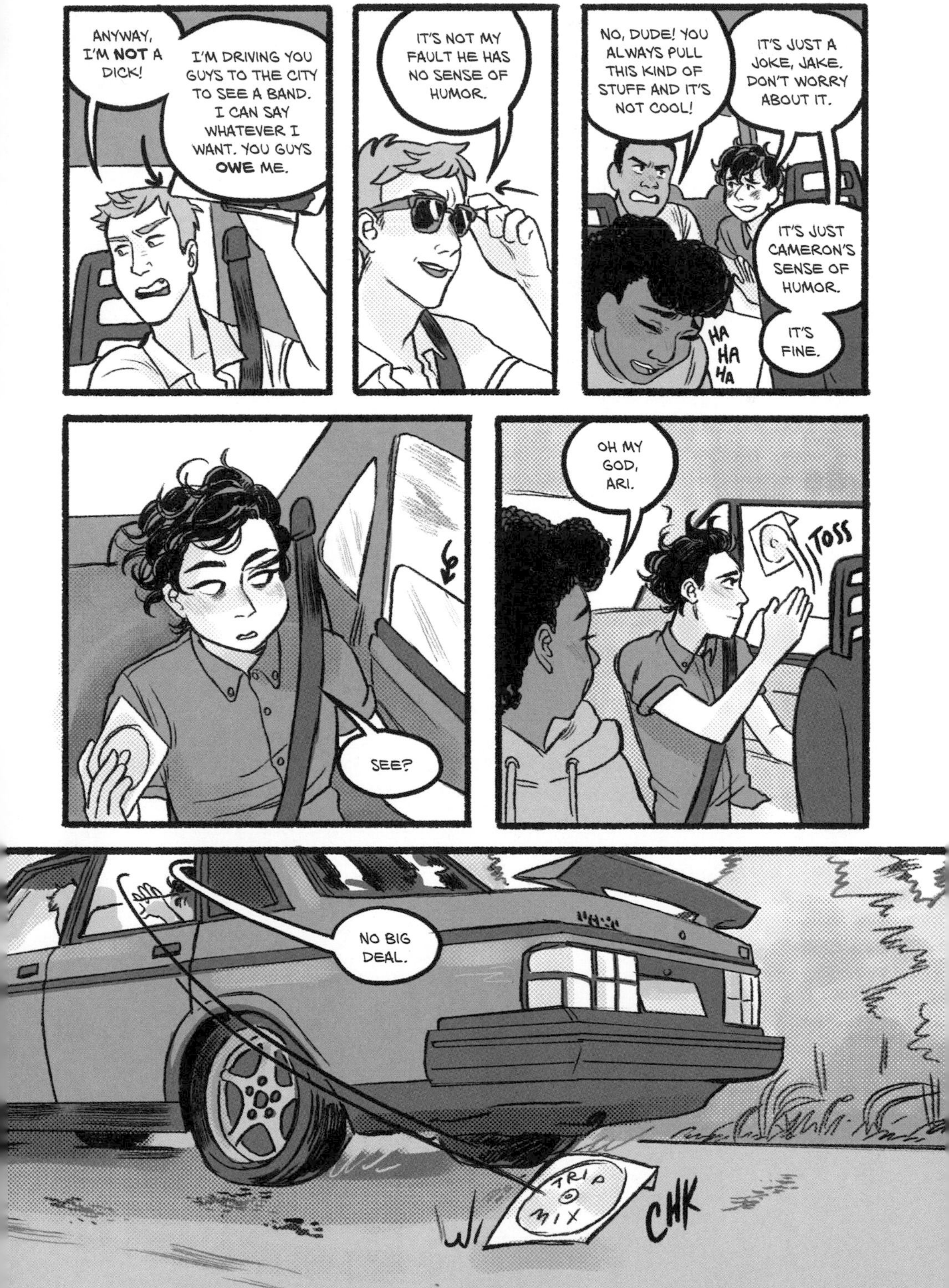
ANYWAY, I'M **NOT** A DICK!
I'M DRIVING YOU GUYS TO THE CITY TO SEE A BAND. I CAN SAY WHATEVER I WANT. YOU GUYS **OWE** ME.
IT'S NOT MY FAULT HE HAS NO SENSE OF HUMOR.
NO, DUDE! YOU ALWAYS PULL THIS KIND OF STUFF AND IT'S NOT COOL!
IT'S JUST A JOKE, JAKE. DON'T WORRY ABOUT IT.
IT'S JUST CAMERON'S SENSE OF HUMOR.
HA HA HA
IT'S FINE.
SEE?
OH MY GOD, ARI.
TOSS
NO BIG DEAL.
TRIP MIX
CHK

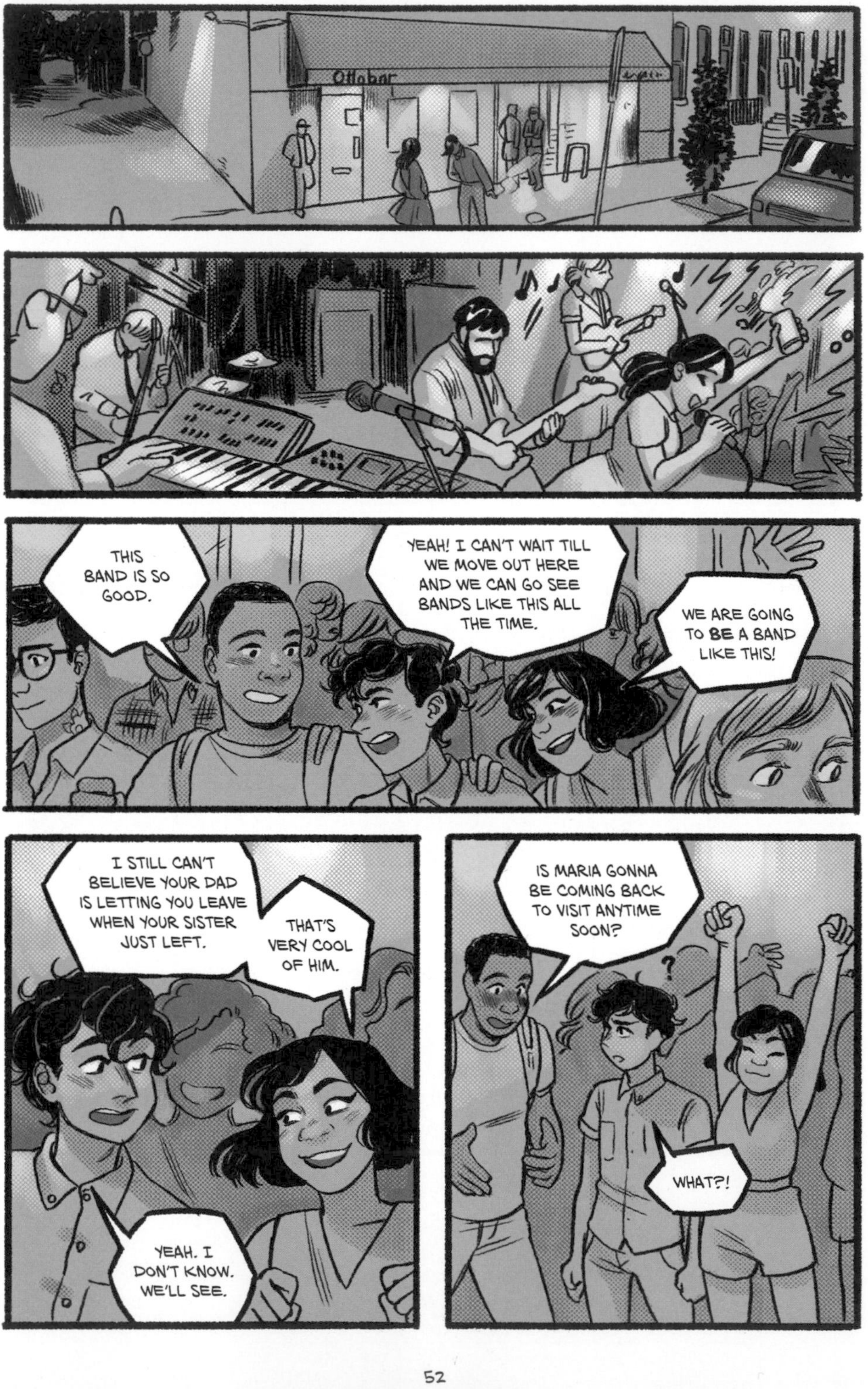

Ottobar
THIS BAND IS SO GOOD.
YEAH! I CAN'T WAIT TILL WE MOVE OUT HERE AND WE CAN GO SEE BANDS LIKE THIS ALL THE TIME.
WE ARE GOING TO BE A BAND LIKE THIS!
I STILL CAN'T BELIEVE YOUR DAD IS LETTING YOU LEAVE WHEN YOUR SISTER JUST LEFT.
THAT'S VERY COOL OF HIM.
YEAH. I DON'T KNOW. WE'LL SEE.
IS MARIA GONNA BE COMING BACK TO VISIT ANYTIME SOON?
?
WHAT?!

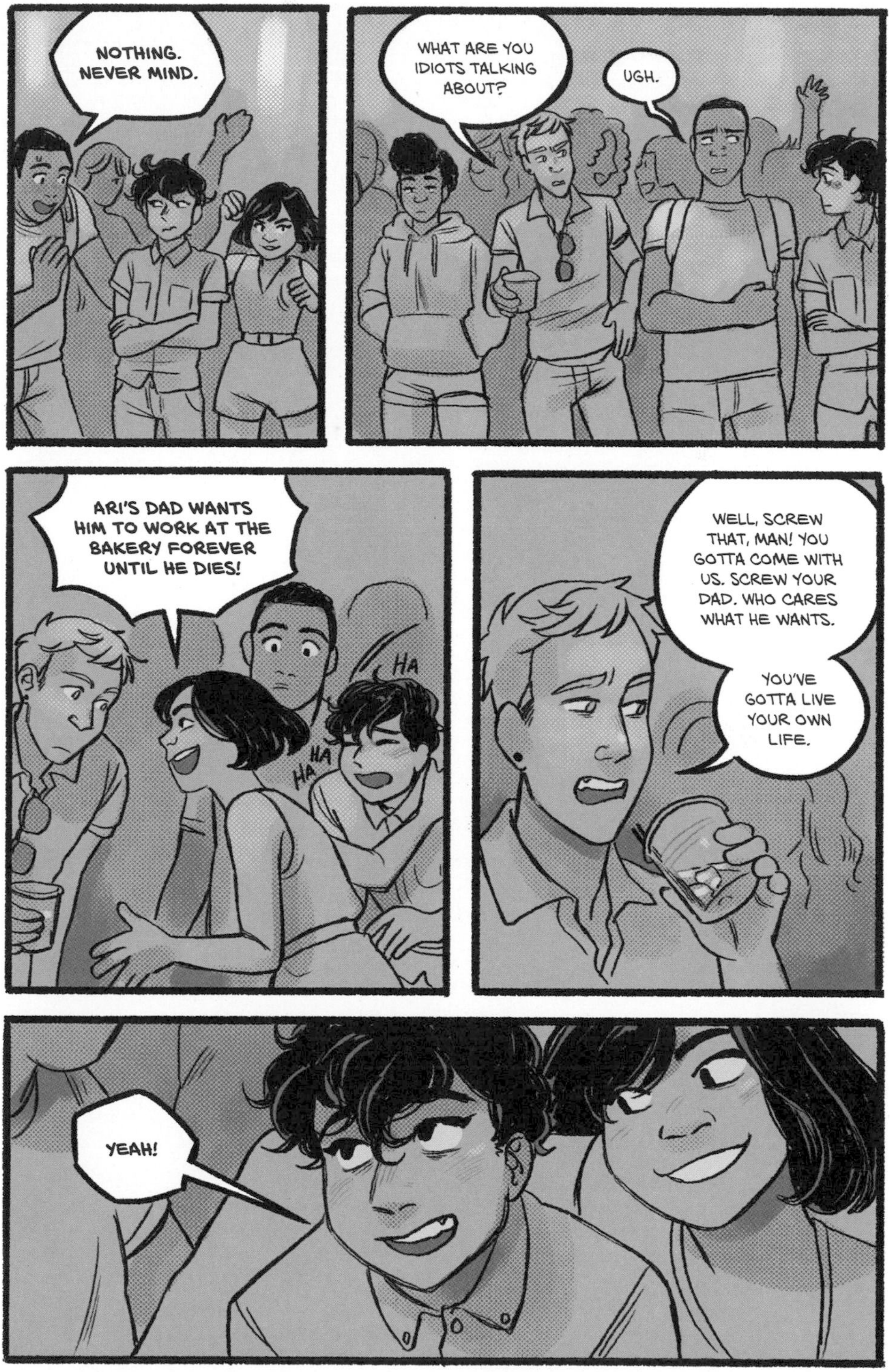
NOTHING. NEVER MIND.
WHAT ARE YOU IDIOTS TALKING ABOUT?
UGH.
ARI'S DAD WANTS HIM TO WORK AT THE BAKERY FOREVER UNTIL HE DIES!
HA
HA
HA
WELL, SCREW THAT, MAN! YOU GOTTA COME WITH US. SCREW YOUR DAD. WHO CARES WHAT HE WANTS.
YOU'VE GOTTA LIVE YOUR OWN LIFE.
YEAH!

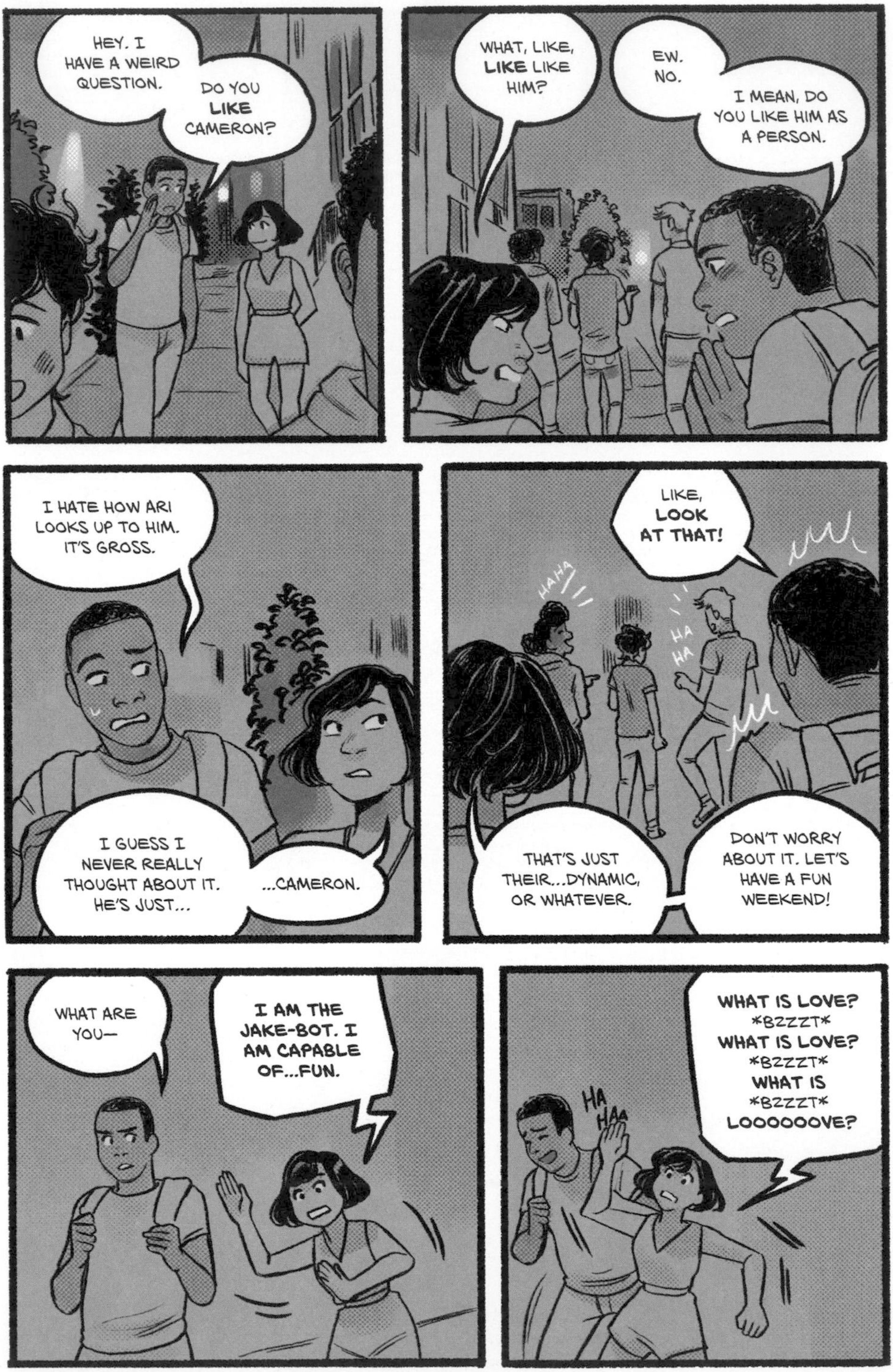
HEY. I HAVE A WEIRD QUESTION.
DO YOU **LIKE** CAMERON?
WHAT, LIKE, **LIKE** LIKE HIM?
EW. NO.
I MEAN, DO YOU LIKE HIM AS A PERSON.
I HATE HOW ARI LOOKS UP TO HIM. IT'S GROSS.
I GUESS I NEVER REALLY THOUGHT ABOUT IT. HE'S JUST...
...CAMERON.
LIKE, **LOOK AT THAT!**
HAHA
HA HA
THAT'S JUST THEIR...DYNAMIC, OR WHATEVER.
DON'T WORRY ABOUT IT. LET'S HAVE A FUN WEEKEND!
WHAT ARE YOU—
I AM THE JAKE-BOT. I AM CAPABLE OF...FUN.
HA HAA
WHAT IS LOVE? *BZZZT* WHAT IS LOVE? *BZZZT* WHAT IS *BZZZT* LOOOOOOVE?

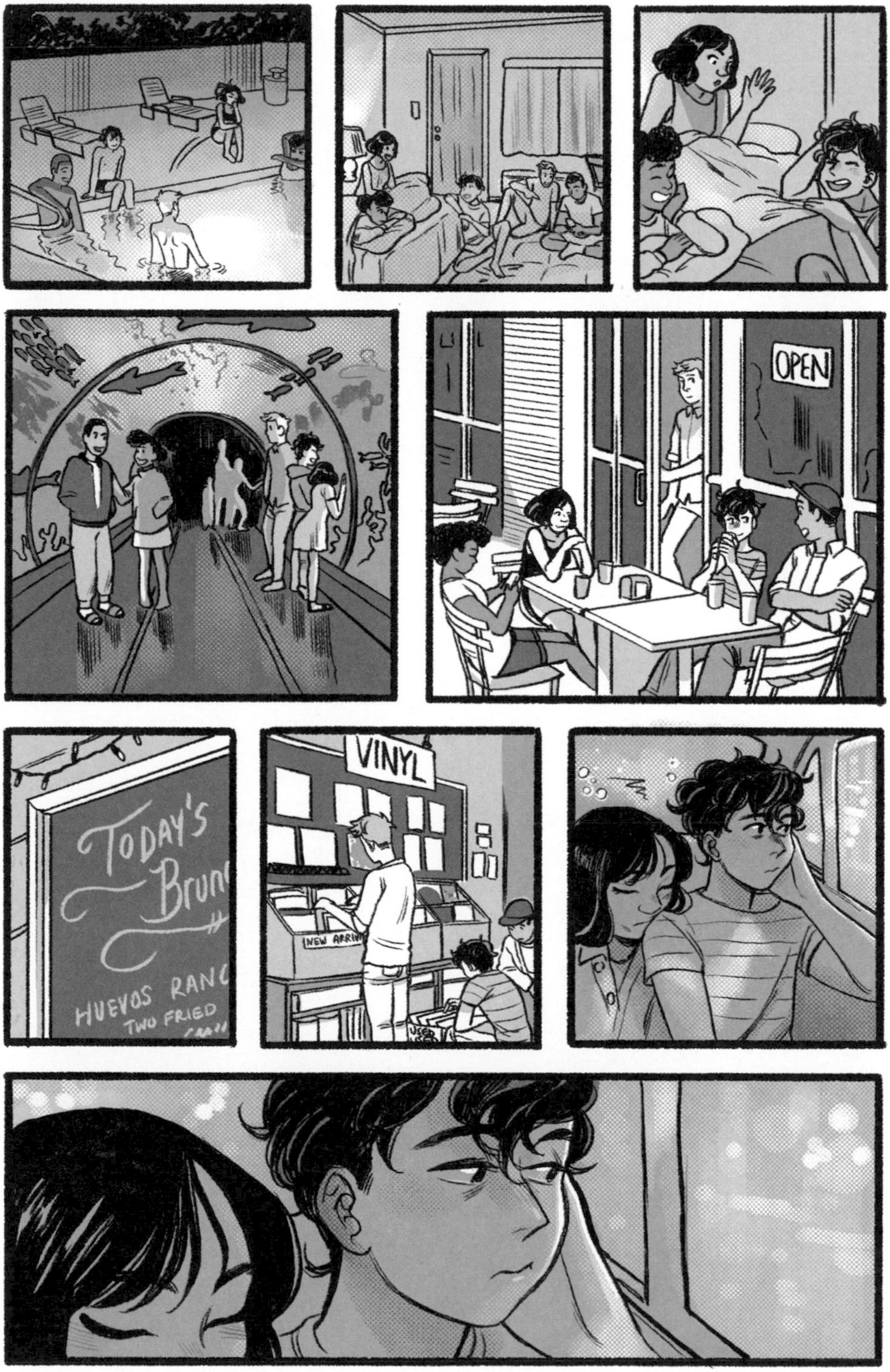
OPEN
TODAY'S
Brunc
HUEVOS RANC
TWO FRIED
VINYL

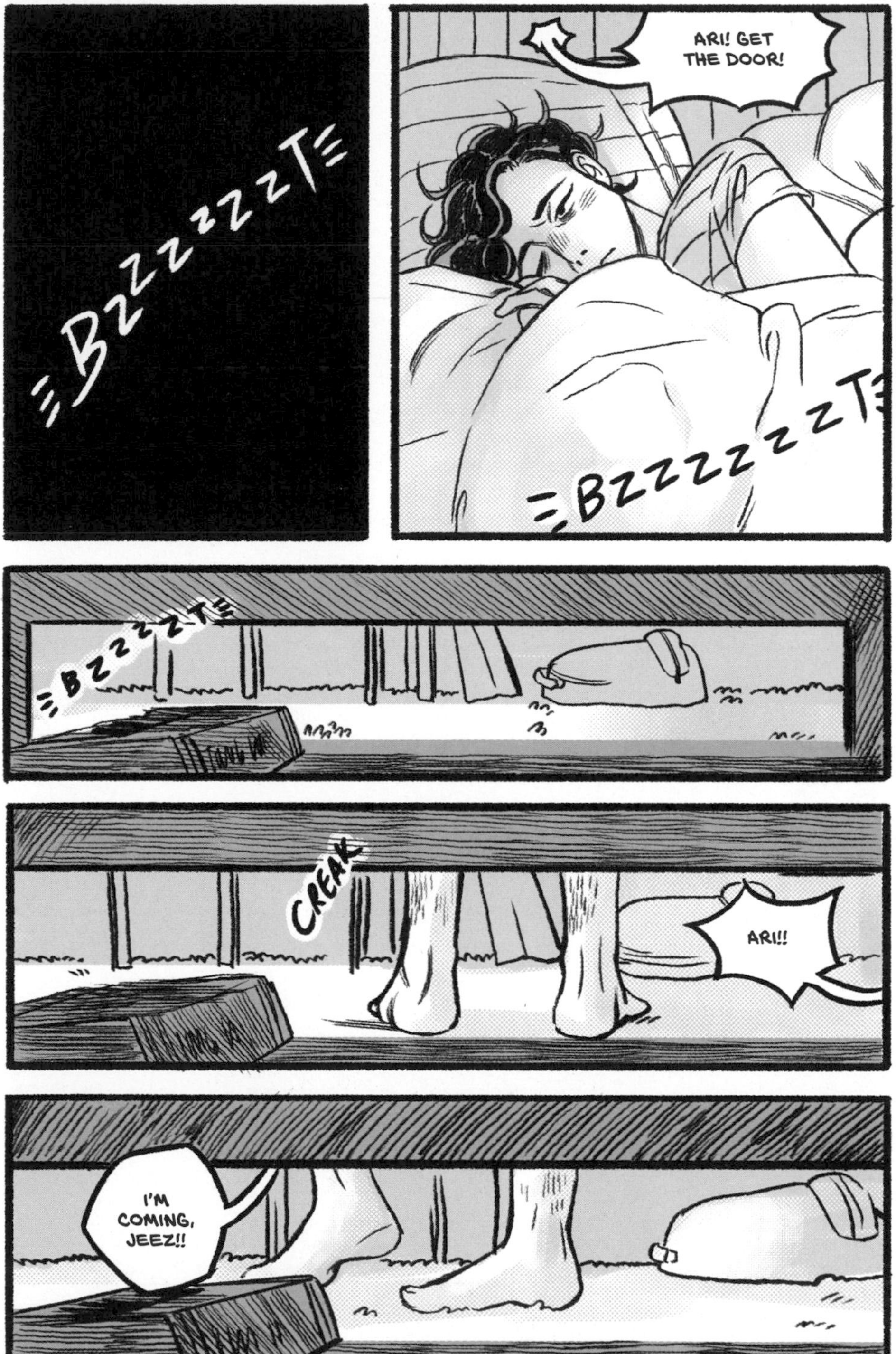
BZZZZZZZT
ARI! GET THE DOOR!
BZZZZZZZZT
BZZZZZT
CREAK
ARI!!
I'M COMING, JEEZ!!

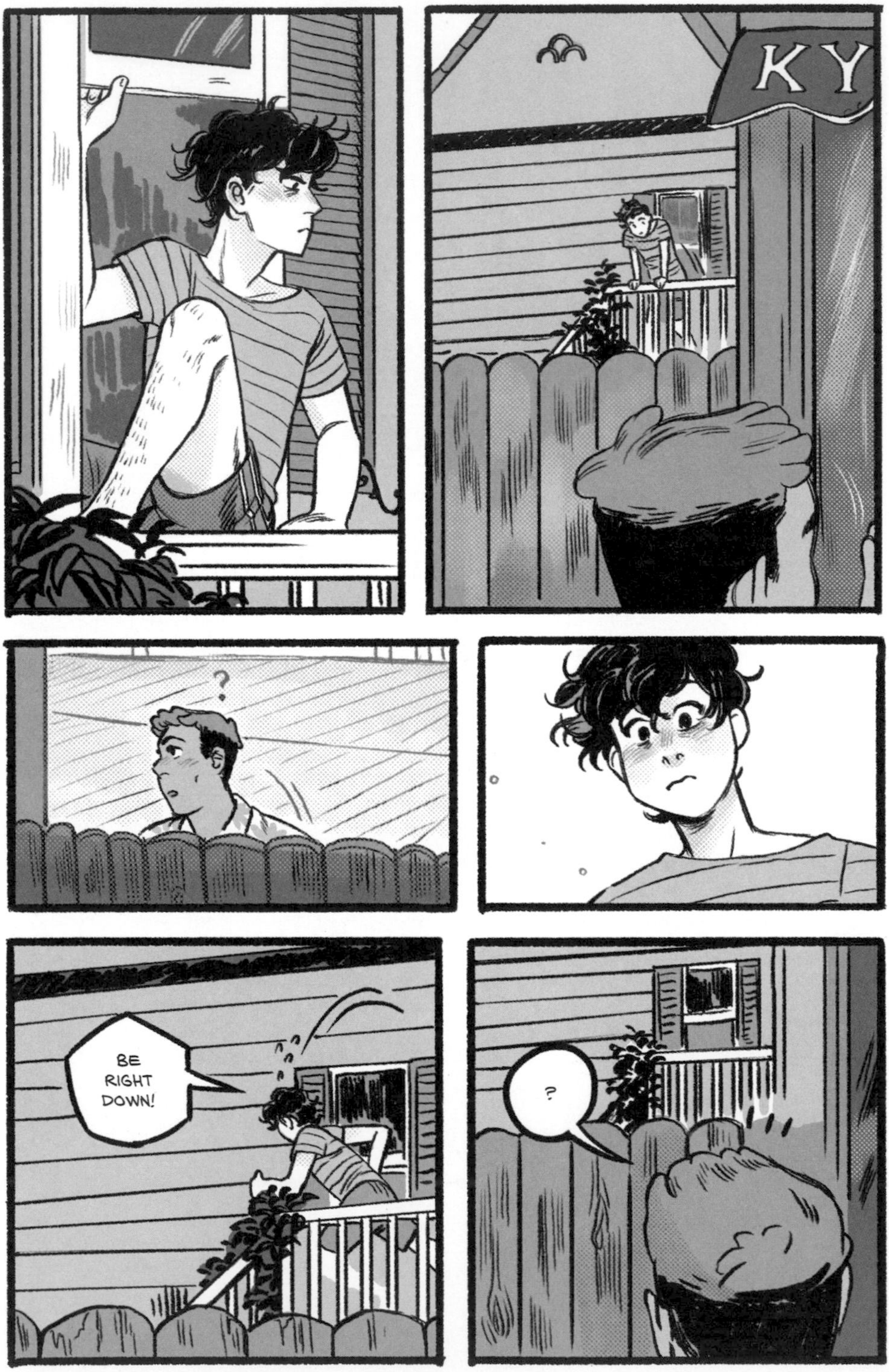
KY
?
BE RIGHT DOWN!
?

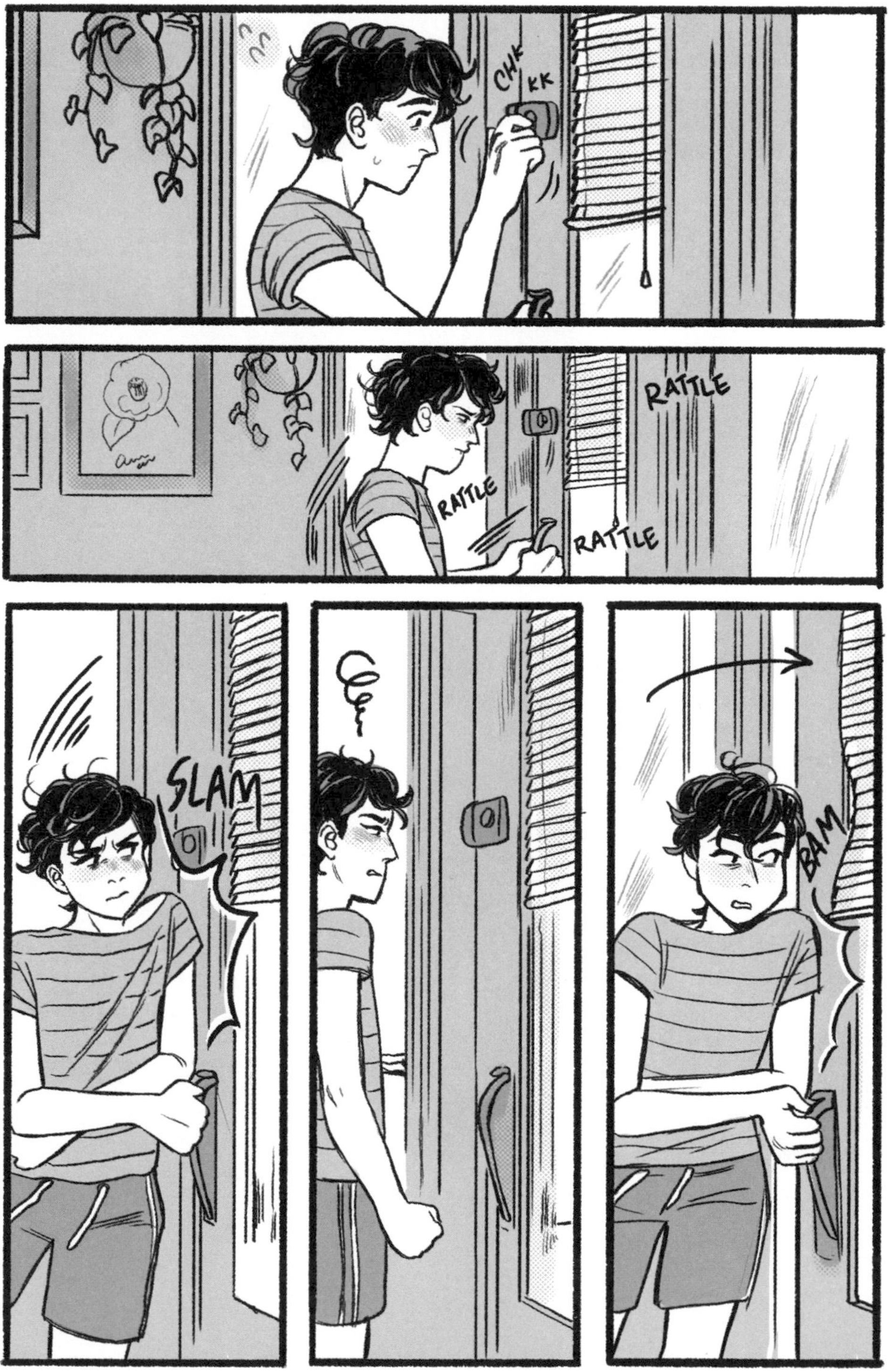
CHK
KK
RATTLE
RATTLE
RATTLE
SLAM
BAM

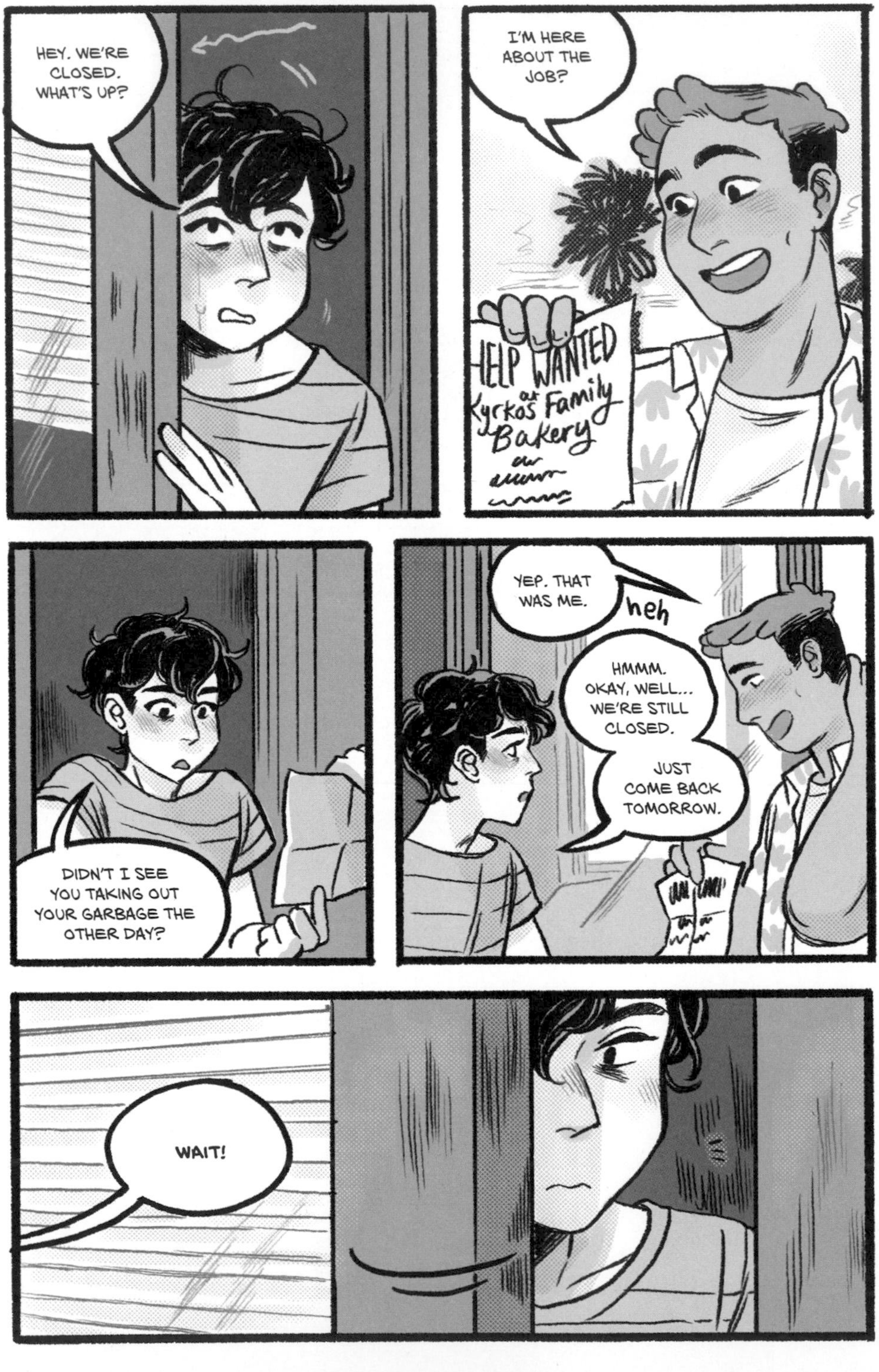

HEY. WE'RE CLOSED. WHAT'S UP?
I'M HERE ABOUT THE JOB?
HELP WANTED at Kyrkos Family Bakery
DIDN'T I SEE YOU TAKING OUT YOUR GARBAGE THE OTHER DAY?
YEP. THAT WAS ME.
heh
HMMM. OKAY, WELL... WE'RE STILL CLOSED.
JUST COME BACK TOMORROW.
WAIT!

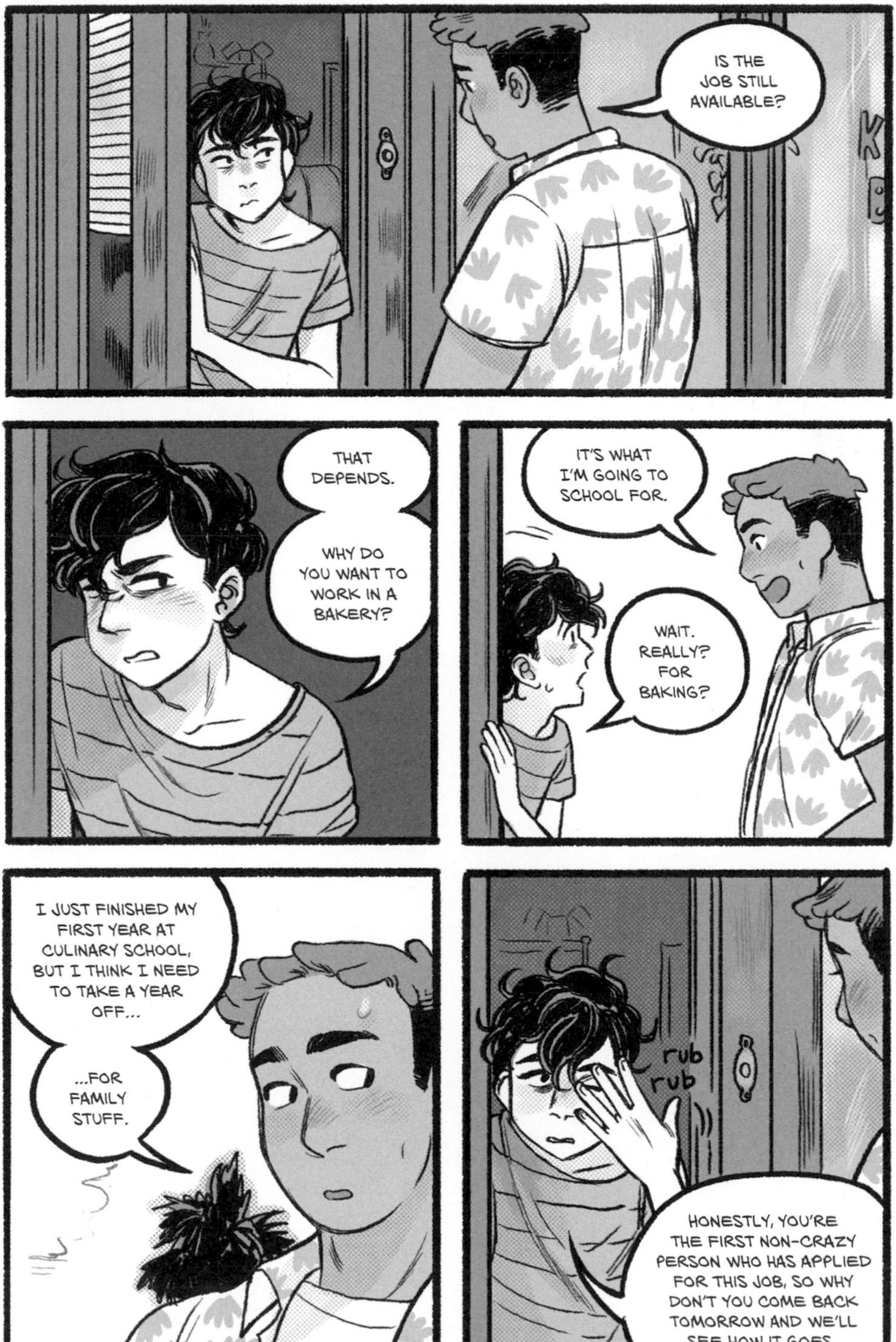
IS THE JOB STILL AVAILABLE?
THAT DEPENDS.
WHY DO YOU WANT TO WORK IN A BAKERY?
IT'S WHAT I'M GOING TO SCHOOL FOR.
WAIT. REALLY? FOR BAKING?
I JUST FINISHED MY FIRST YEAR AT CULINARY SCHOOL, BUT I THINK I NEED TO TAKE A YEAR OFF...
...FOR FAMILY STUFF.
rub rub
HONESTLY, YOU'RE THE FIRST NON-CRAZY PERSON WHO HAS APPLIED FOR THIS JOB, SO WHY DON'T YOU COME BACK TOMORROW AND WE'LL SEE HOW IT GOES.

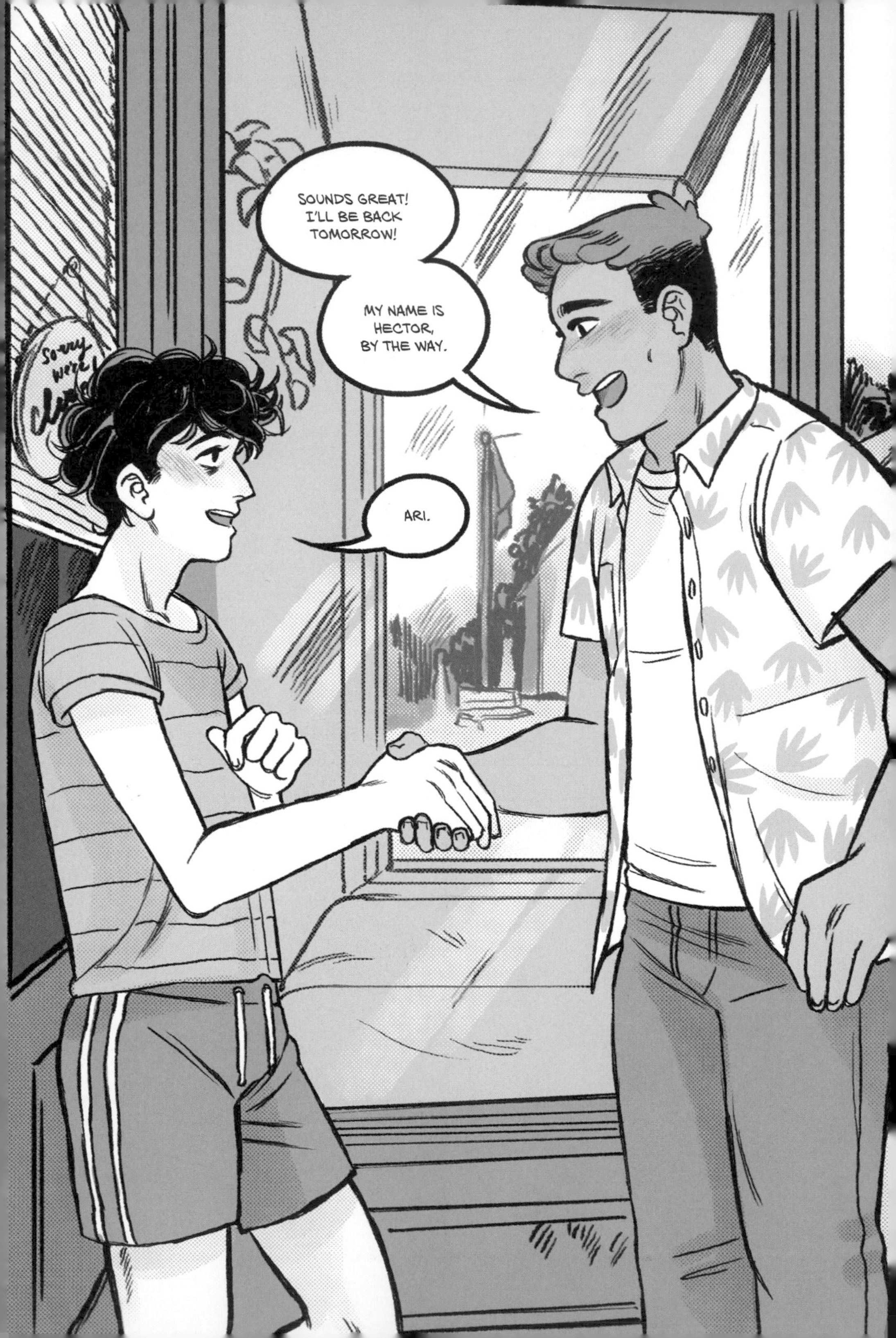
Sorry we're
SOUNDS GREAT! I'LL BE BACK TOMORROW!
MY NAME IS HECTOR, BY THE WAY.
ARI.

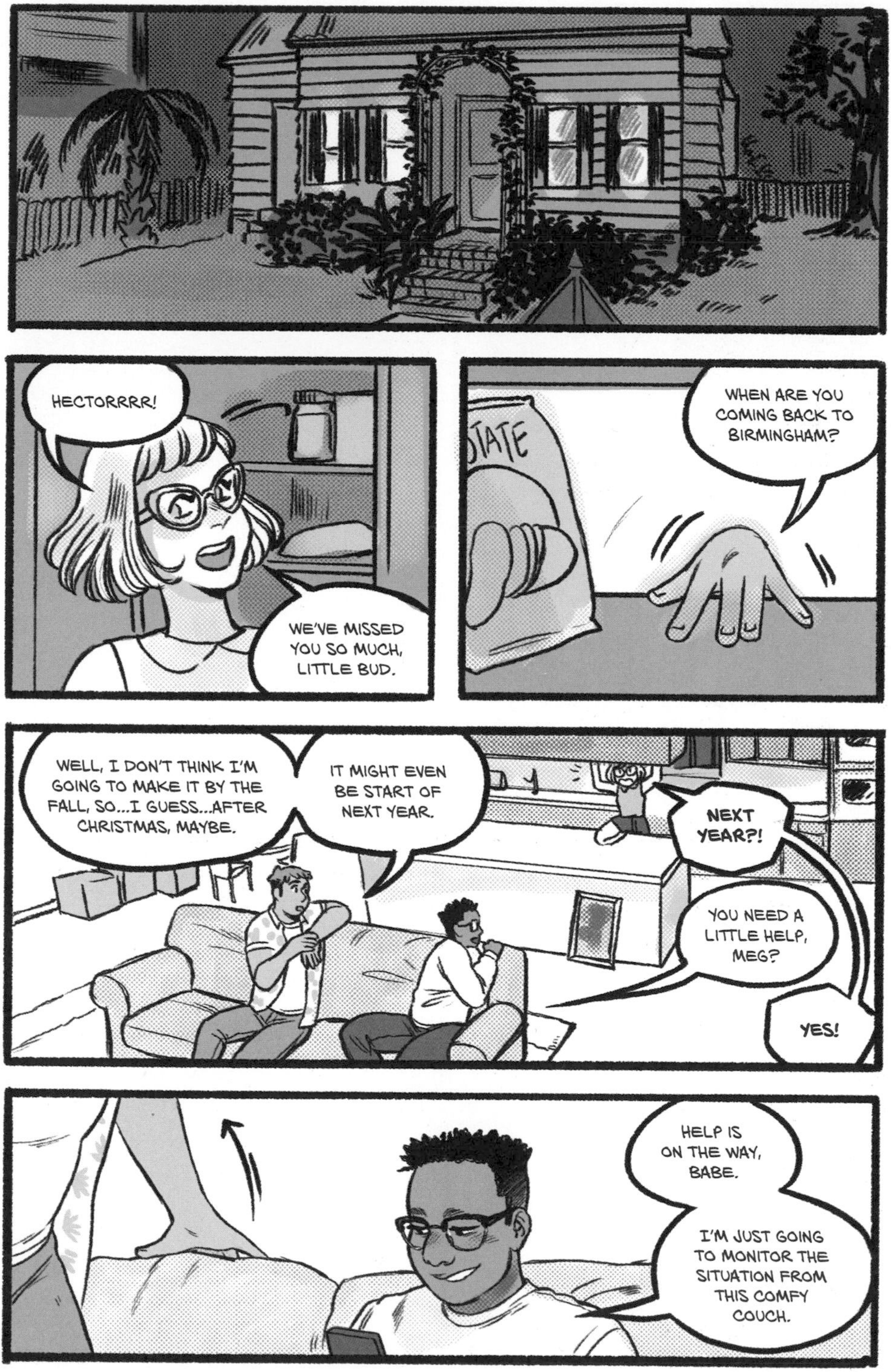
HECTORRRR!
WE'VE MISSED YOU SO MUCH, LITTLE BUD.
STATE
WHEN ARE YOU COMING BACK TO BIRMINGHAM?
WELL, I DON'T THINK I'M GOING TO MAKE IT BY THE FALL, SO...I GUESS...AFTER CHRISTMAS, MAYBE.
IT MIGHT EVEN BE START OF NEXT YEAR.
NEXT YEAR?!
YOU NEED A LITTLE HELP, MEG?
YES!
HELP IS ON THE WAY, BABE.
I'M JUST GOING TO MONITOR THE SITUATION FROM THIS COMFY COUCH.

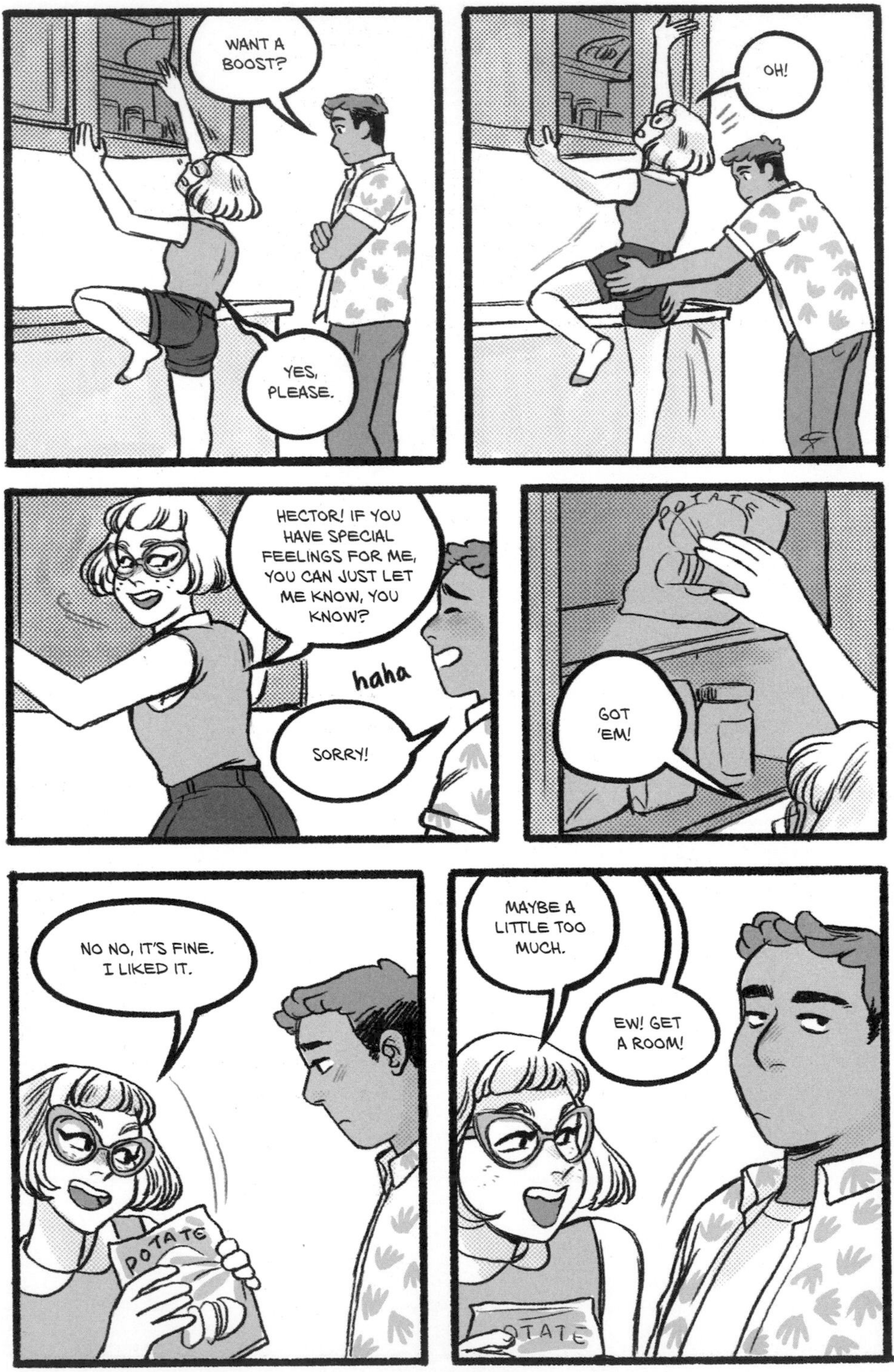
WANT A BOOST?
YES, PLEASE.
OH!
HECTOR! IF YOU HAVE SPECIAL FEELINGS FOR ME, YOU CAN JUST LET ME KNOW, YOU KNOW?
haha
SORRY!
POTATE
GOT 'EM!
NO NO, IT'S FINE. I LIKED IT.
POTATE
MAYBE A LITTLE TOO MUCH.
EW! GET A ROOM!

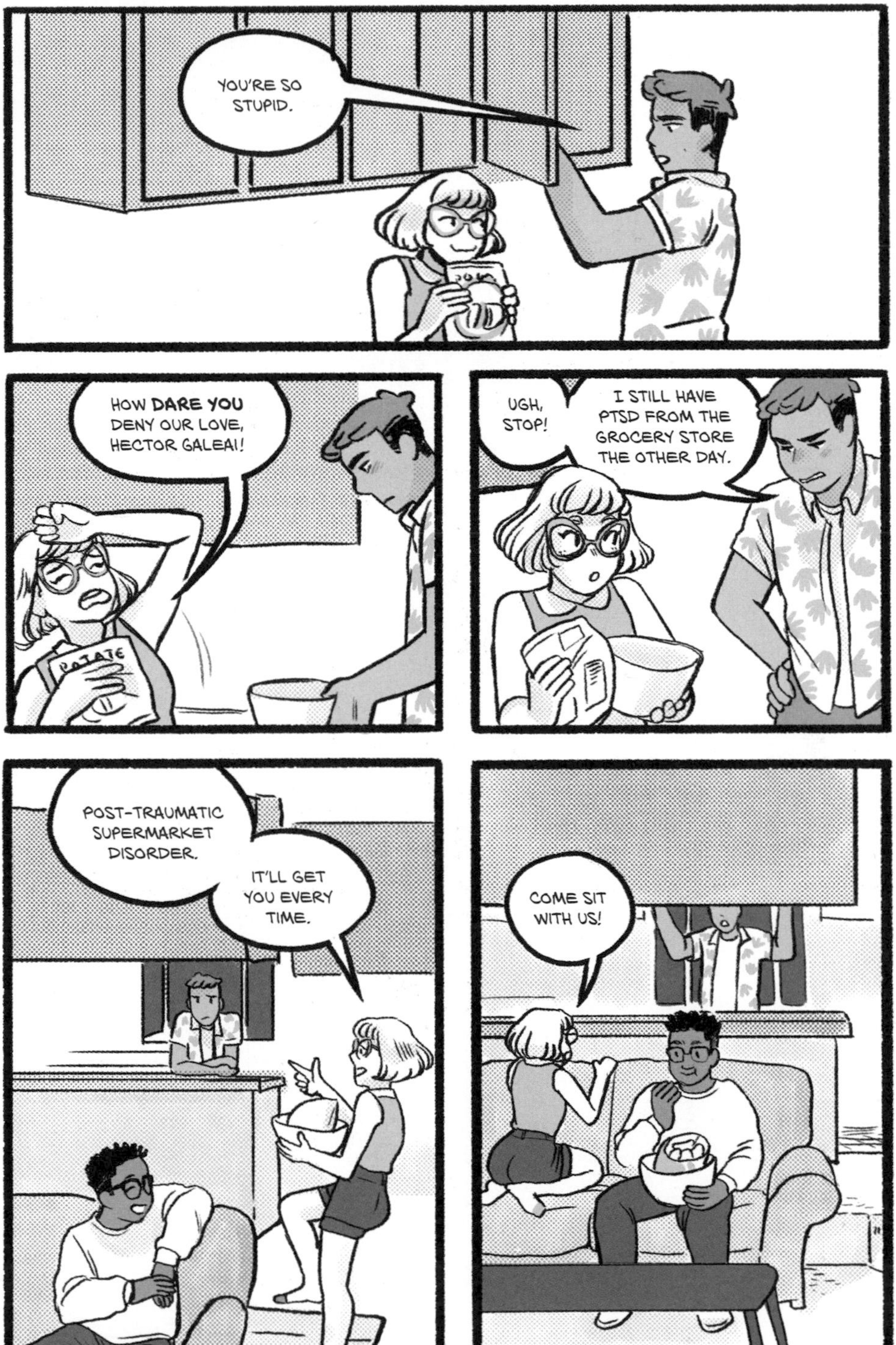
YOU'RE SO STUPID.
HOW **DARE YOU** DENY OUR LOVE, HECTOR GALEAI!
UGH, STOP!
I STILL HAVE PTSD FROM THE GROCERY STORE THE OTHER DAY.
POST-TRAUMATIC SUPERMARKET DISORDER.
IT'LL GET YOU EVERY TIME.
COME SIT WITH US!

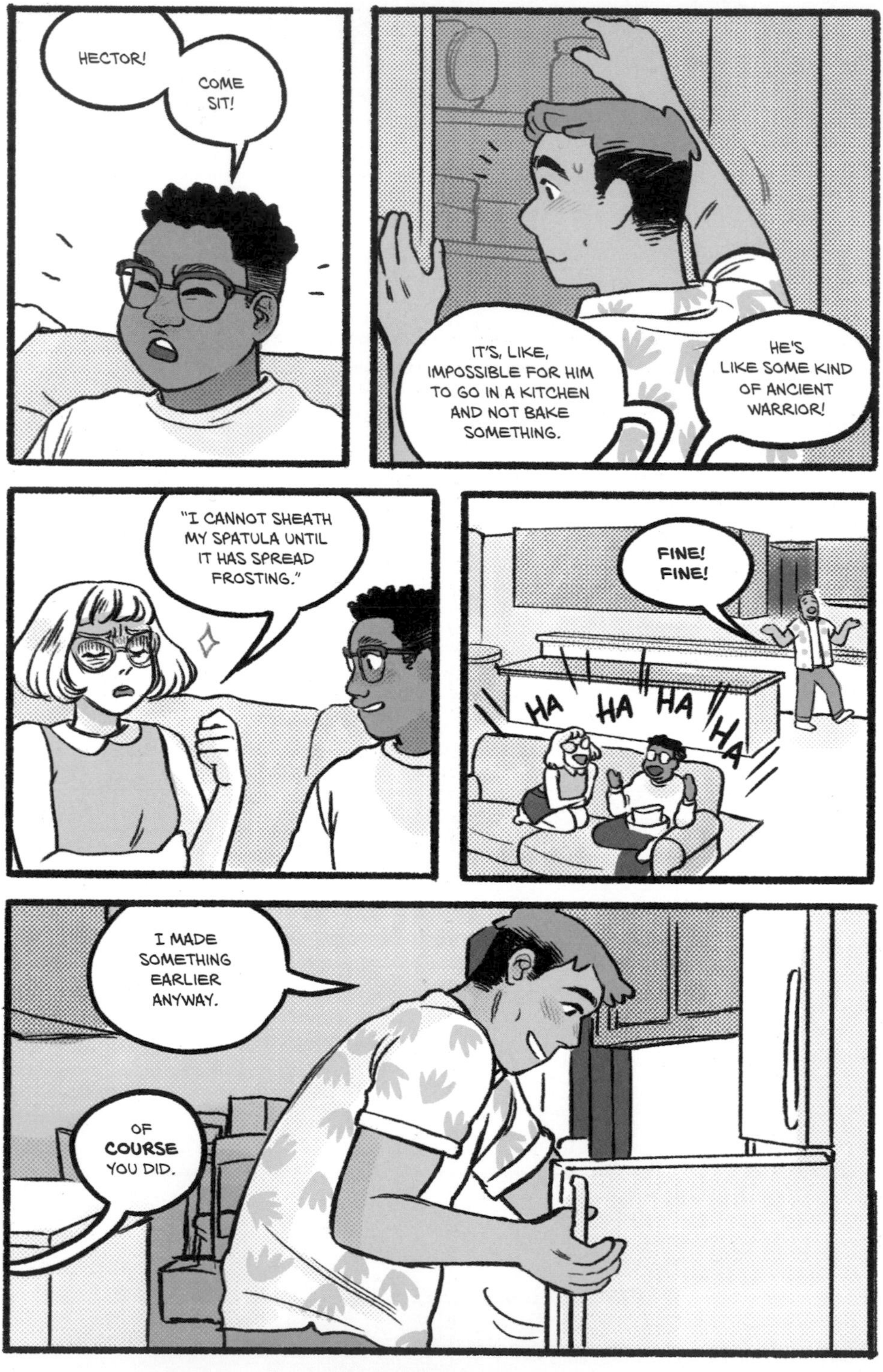
HECTOR!
COME SIT!
IT'S, LIKE, IMPOSSIBLE FOR HIM TO GO IN A KITCHEN AND NOT BAKE SOMETHING.
HE'S LIKE SOME KIND OF ANCIENT WARRIOR!
"I CANNOT SHEATH MY SPATULA UNTIL IT HAS SPREAD FROSTING."
FINE! FINE!
HA HA HA HA
I MADE SOMETHING EARLIER ANYWAY.
OF COURSE YOU DID.

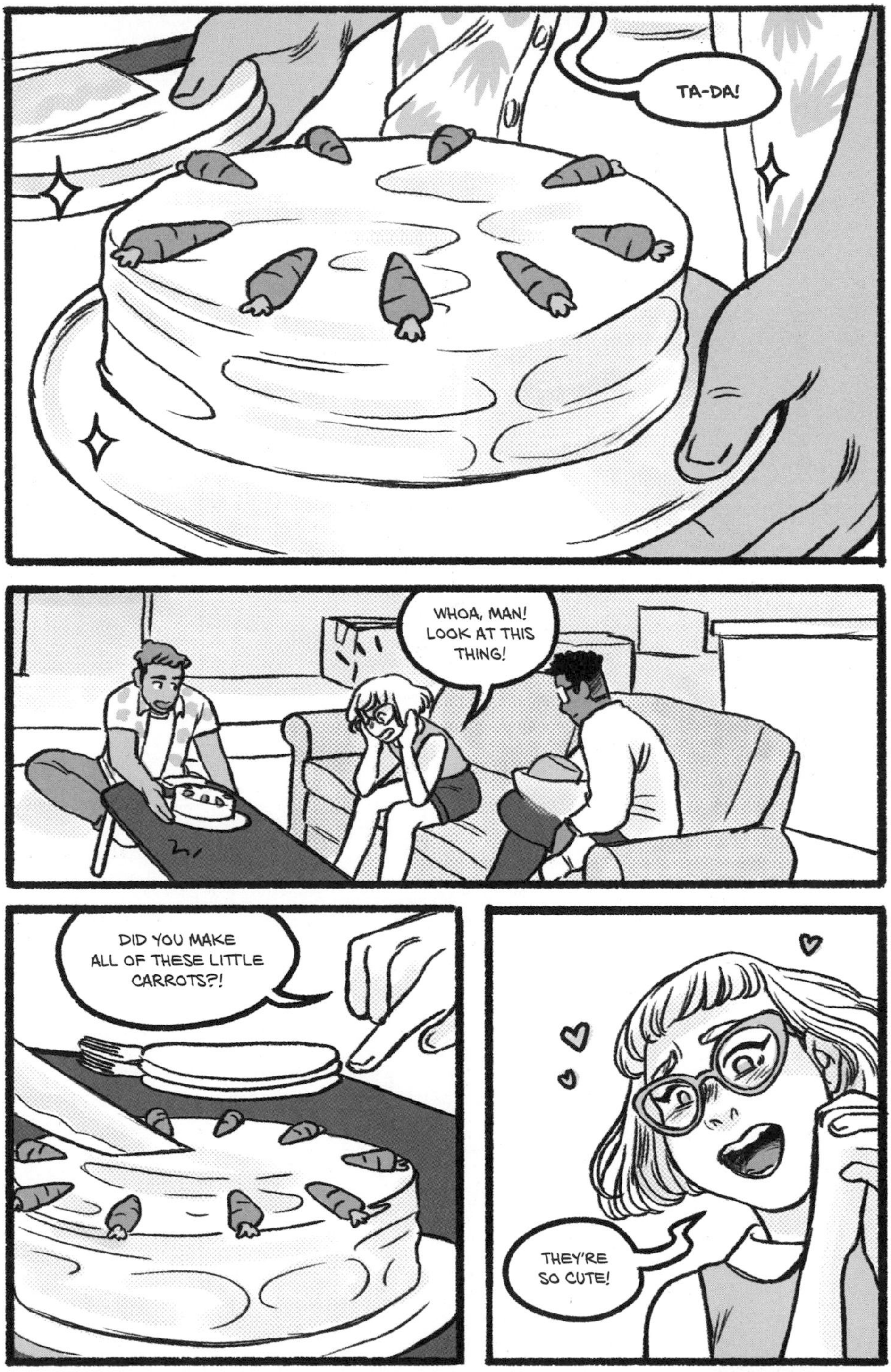
TA-DA!
WHOA, MAN! LOOK AT THIS THING!
DID YOU MAKE ALL OF THESE LITTLE CARROTS?!
THEY'RE SO CUTE!

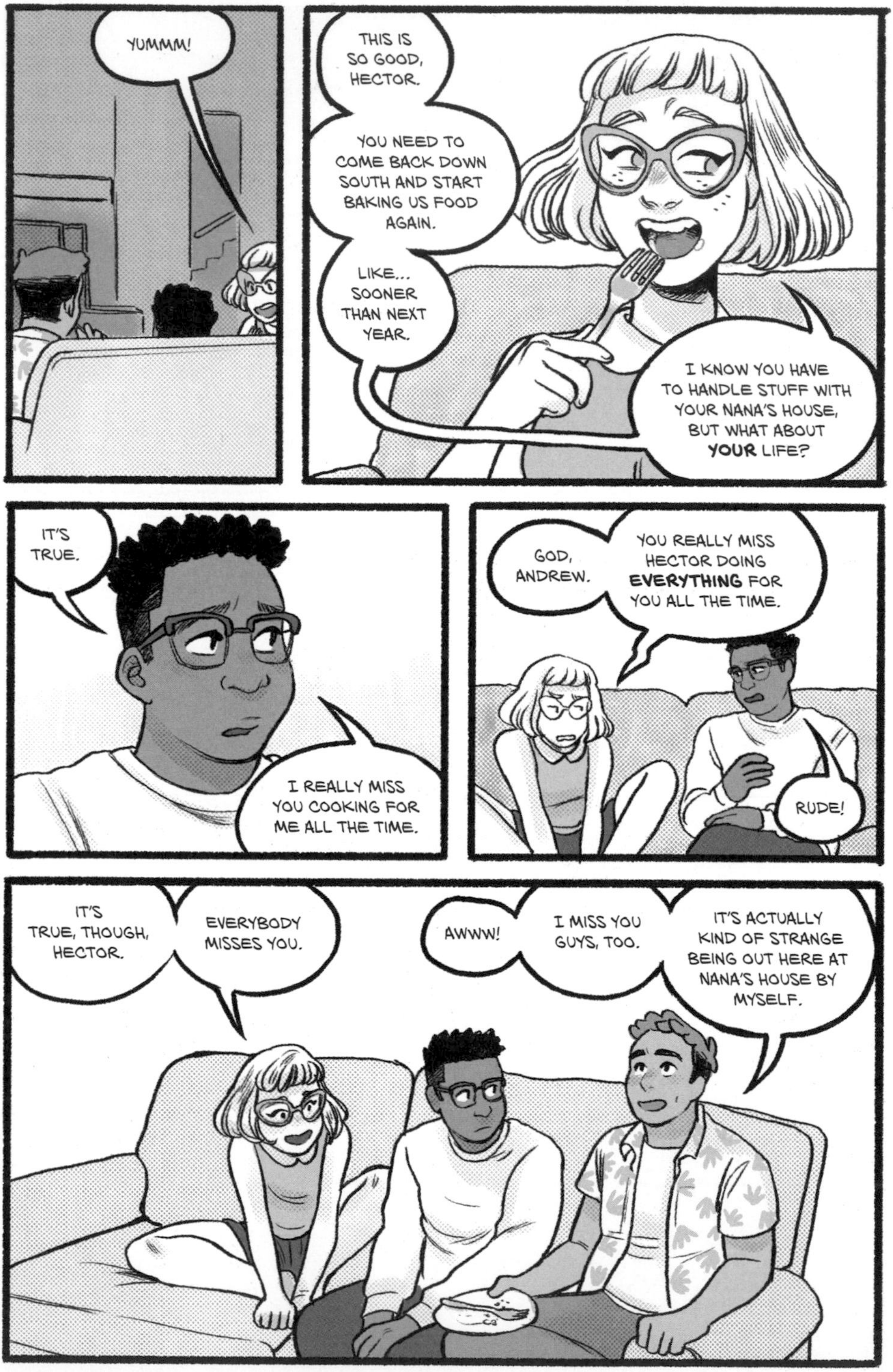
YUMMM!
THIS IS SO GOOD, HECTOR.
YOU NEED TO COME BACK DOWN SOUTH AND START BAKING US FOOD AGAIN.
LIKE... SOONER THAN NEXT YEAR.
I KNOW YOU HAVE TO HANDLE STUFF WITH YOUR NANA'S HOUSE, BUT WHAT ABOUT **YOUR** LIFE?
IT'S TRUE.
I REALLY MISS YOU COOKING FOR ME ALL THE TIME.
GOD, ANDREW.
YOU REALLY MISS HECTOR DOING **EVERYTHING** FOR YOU ALL THE TIME.
RUDE!
IT'S TRUE, THOUGH, HECTOR.
EVERYBODY MISSES YOU.
AWWW!
I MISS YOU GUYS, TOO.
IT'S ACTUALLY KIND OF STRANGE BEING OUT HERE AT NANA'S HOUSE BY MYSELF.

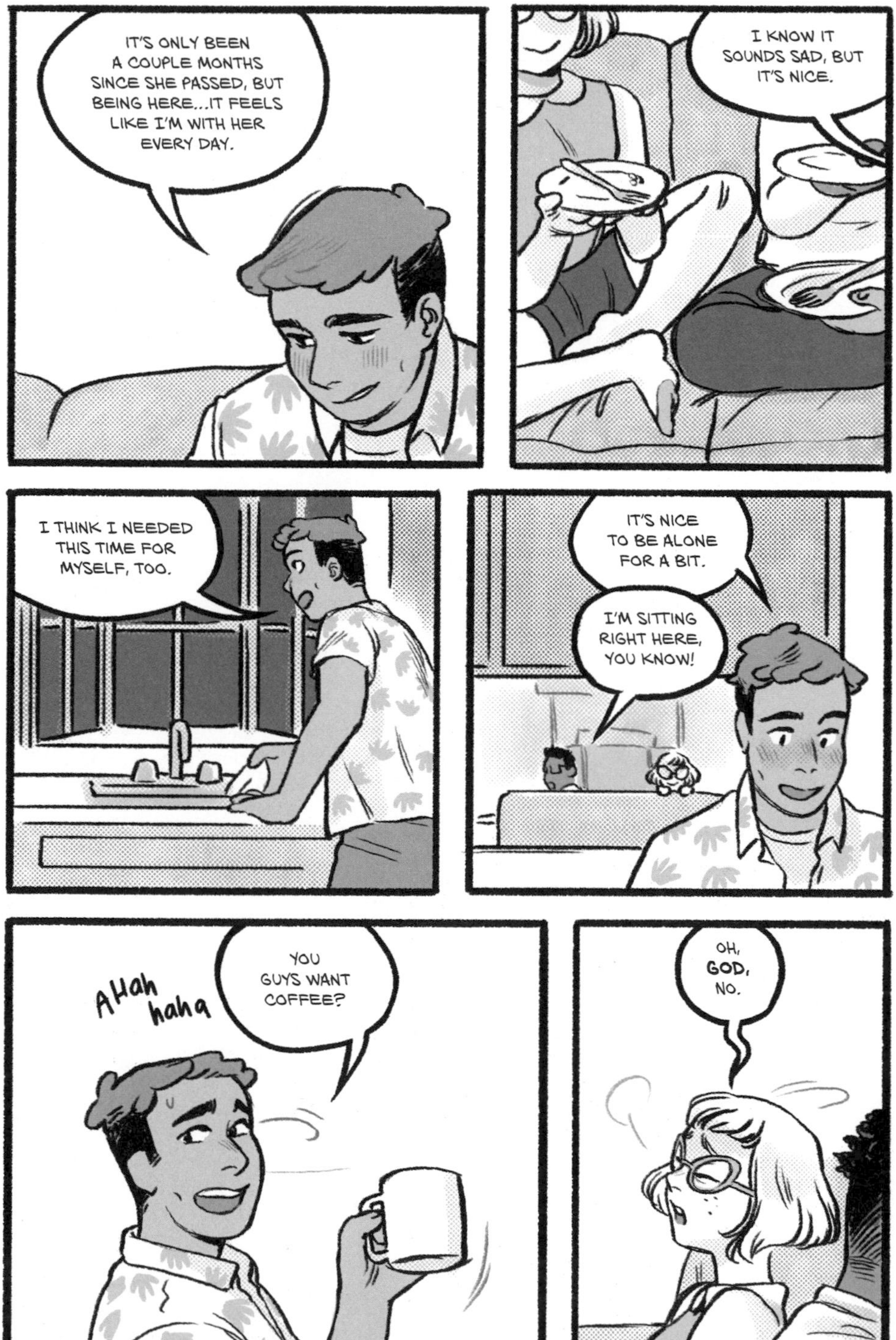
IT'S ONLY BEEN A COUPLE MONTHS SINCE SHE PASSED, BUT BEING HERE...IT FEELS LIKE I'M WITH HER EVERY DAY.
I KNOW IT SOUNDS SAD, BUT IT'S NICE.
I THINK I NEEDED THIS TIME FOR MYSELF, TOO.
IT'S NICE TO BE ALONE FOR A BIT.
I'M SITTING RIGHT HERE, YOU KNOW!
AHah haha
YOU GUYS WANT COFFEE?
OH, GOD, NO.

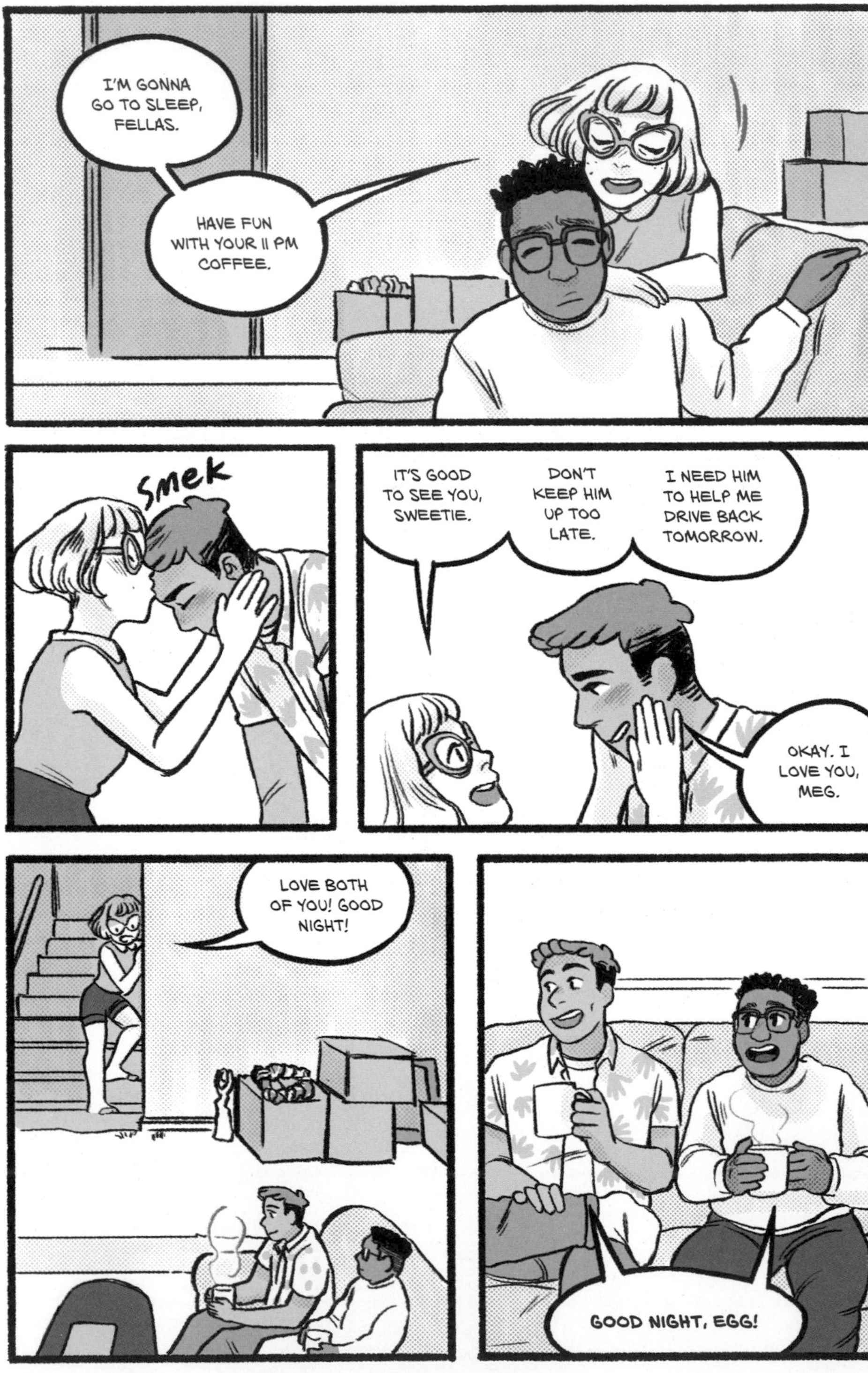
I'M GONNA GO TO SLEEP, FELLAS.
HAVE FUN WITH YOUR 11 PM COFFEE.
SMEK
IT'S GOOD TO SEE YOU, SWEETIE.
DON'T KEEP HIM UP TOO LATE.
I NEED HIM TO HELP ME DRIVE BACK TOMORROW.
OKAY. I LOVE YOU, MEG.
LOVE BOTH OF YOU! GOOD NIGHT!
GOOD NIGHT, EGG!

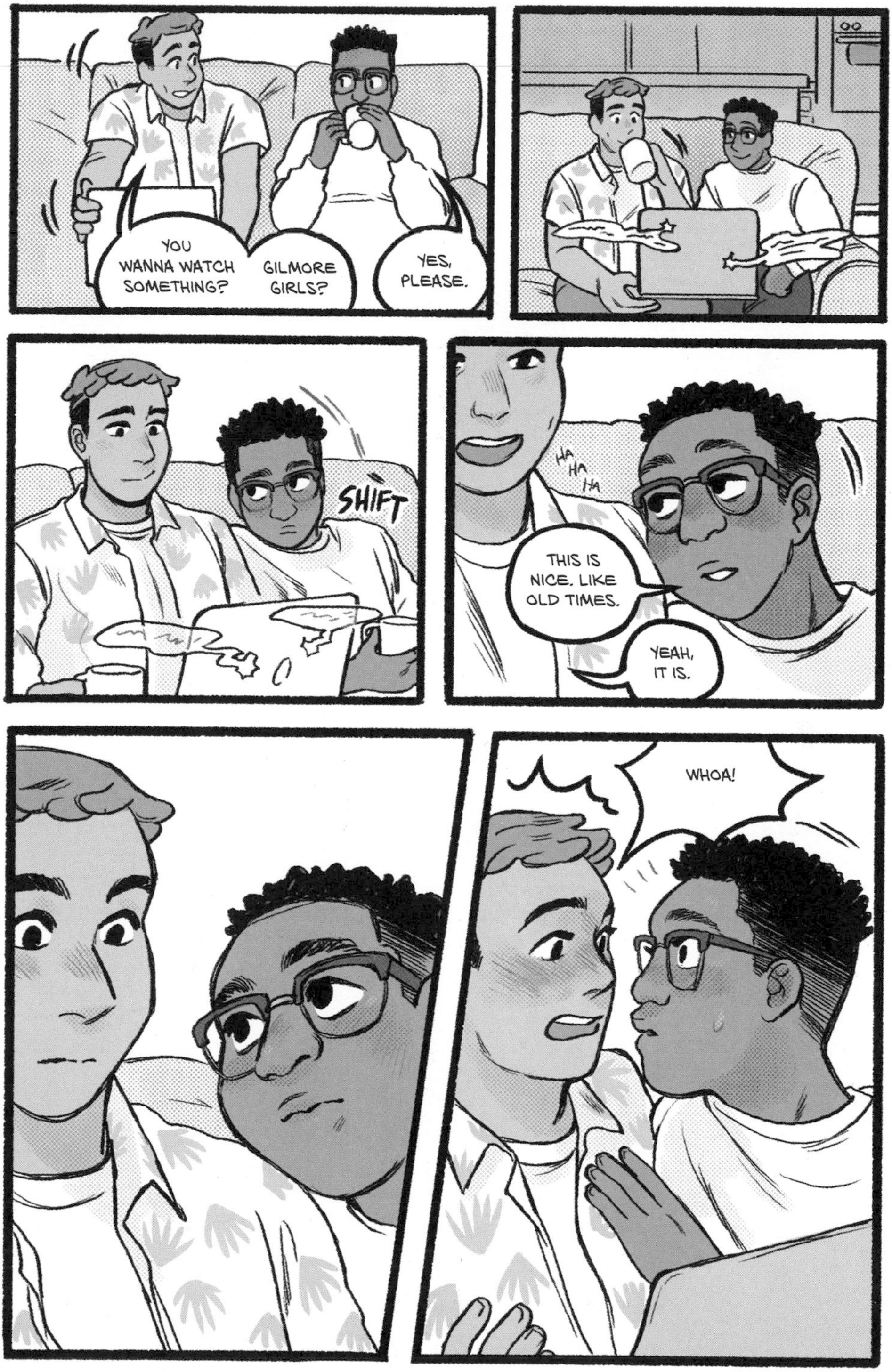
YOU WANNA WATCH SOMETHING?
GILMORE GIRLS?
YES, PLEASE.
SHIFT
HA HA HA
THIS IS NICE. LIKE OLD TIMES.
YEAH, IT IS.
WHOA!

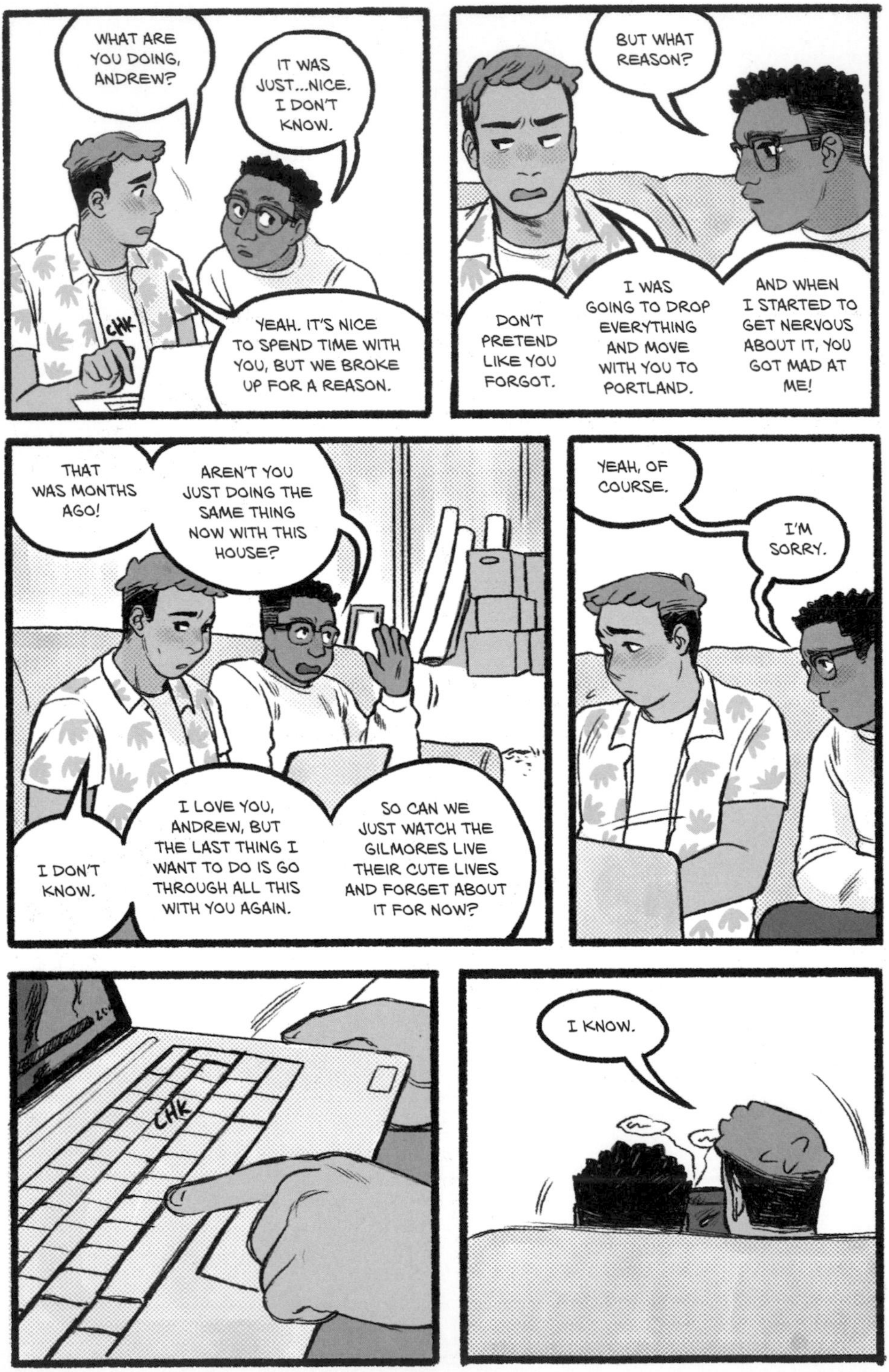
WHAT ARE YOU DOING, ANDREW?
IT WAS JUST...NICE. I DON'T KNOW.
YEAH. IT'S NICE TO SPEND TIME WITH YOU, BUT WE BROKE UP FOR A REASON.
CHK
BUT WHAT REASON?
DON'T PRETEND LIKE YOU FORGOT.
I WAS GOING TO DROP EVERYTHING AND MOVE WITH YOU TO PORTLAND.
AND WHEN I STARTED TO GET NERVOUS ABOUT IT, YOU GOT MAD AT ME!
THAT WAS MONTHS AGO!
AREN'T YOU JUST DOING THE SAME THING NOW WITH THIS HOUSE?
I DON'T KNOW.
I LOVE YOU, ANDREW, BUT THE LAST THING I WANT TO DO IS GO THROUGH ALL THIS WITH YOU AGAIN.
SO CAN WE JUST WATCH THE GILMORES LIVE THEIR CUTE LIVES AND FORGET ABOUT IT FOR NOW?
YEAH, OF COURSE.
I'M SORRY.
CHK
I KNOW.

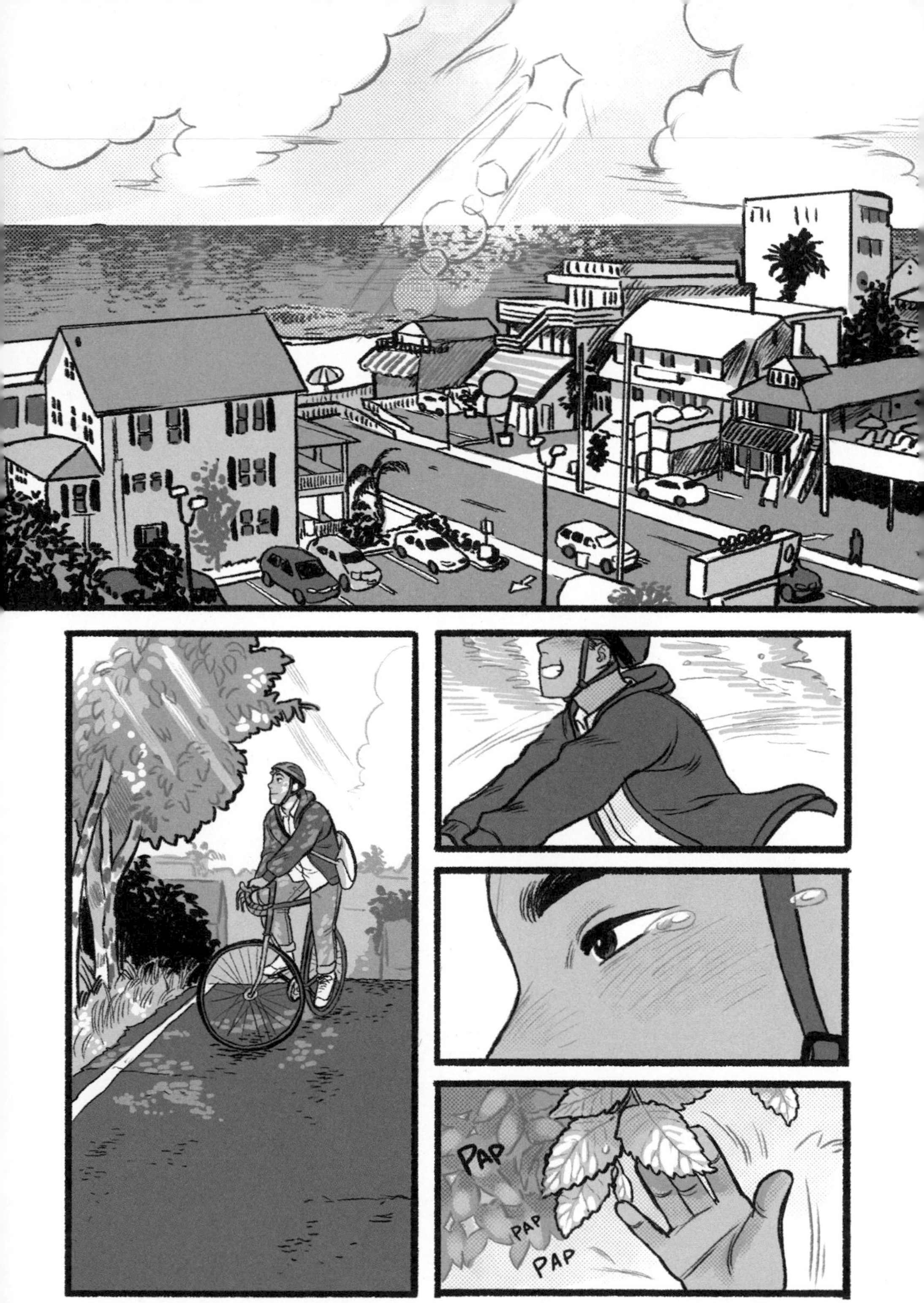
PAP
PAP
PAP

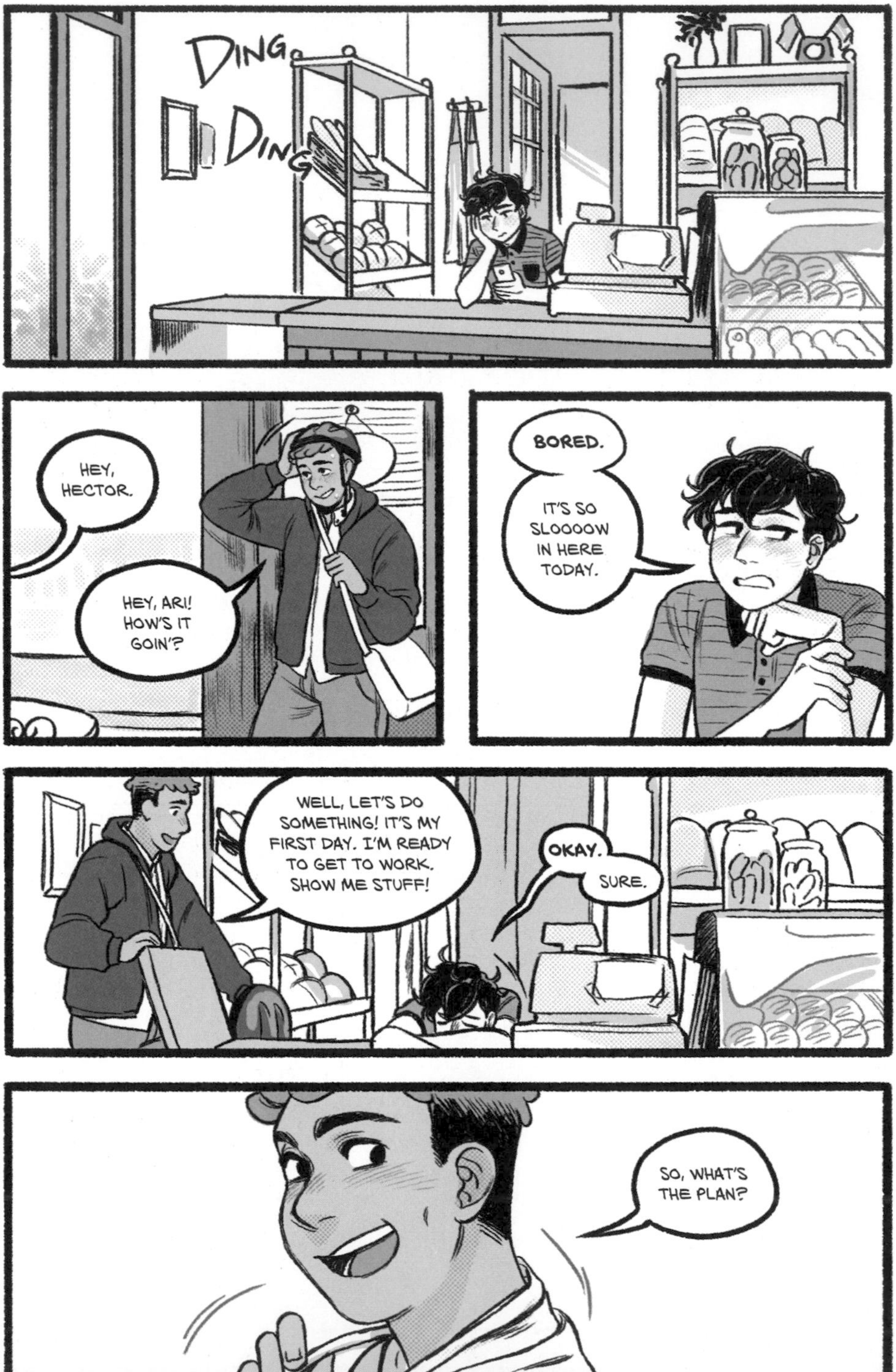
DING
DING
HEY, HECTOR.
HEY, ARI! HOW'S IT GOIN'?
BORED.
IT'S SO SLOOOOW IN HERE TODAY.
WELL, LET'S DO SOMETHING! IT'S MY FIRST DAY. I'M READY TO GET TO WORK. SHOW ME STUFF!
OKAY.
SURE.
SO, WHAT'S THE PLAN?

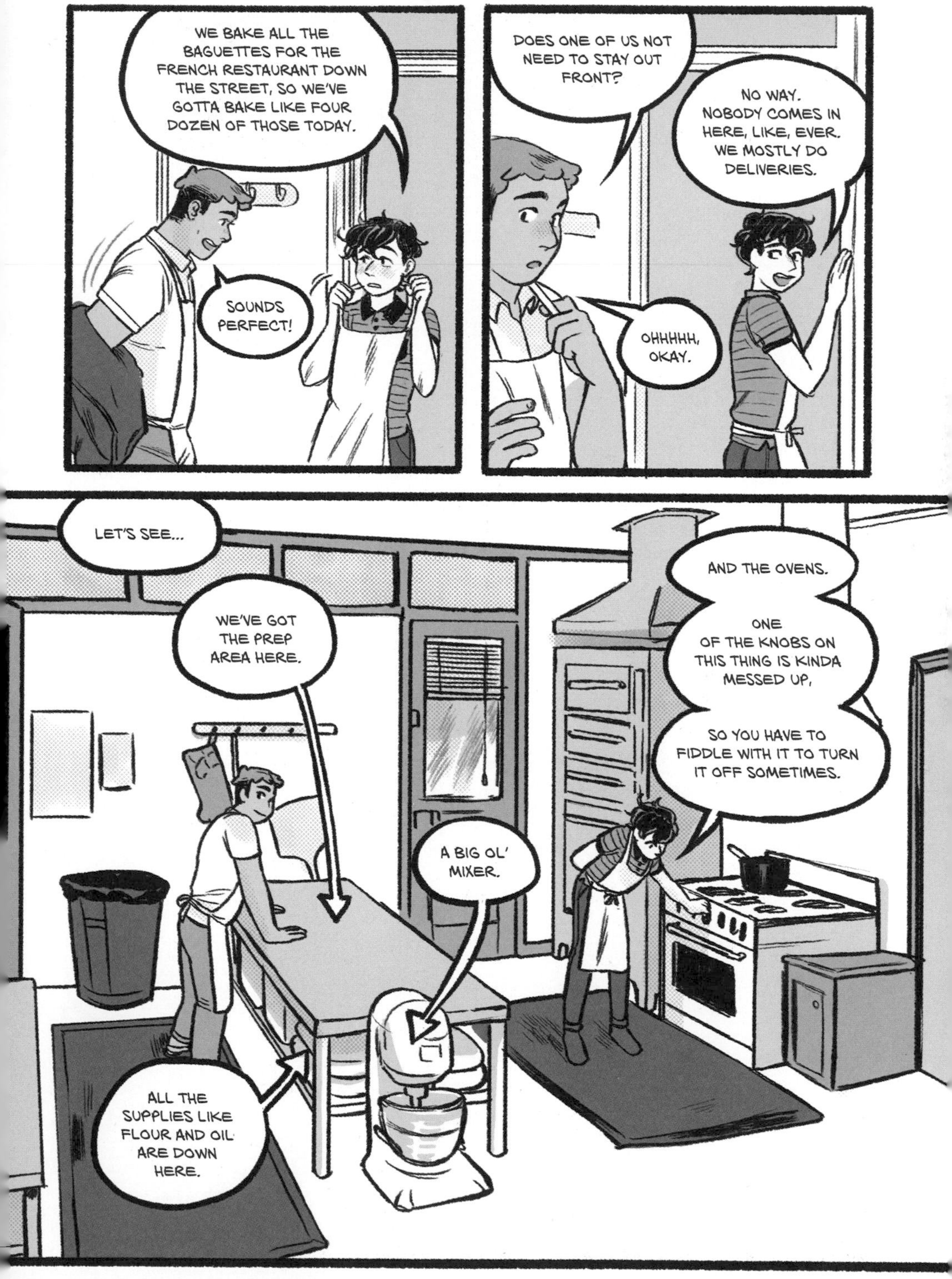
WE BAKE ALL THE BAGUETTES FOR THE FRENCH RESTAURANT DOWN THE STREET, SO WE'VE GOTTA BAKE LIKE FOUR DOZEN OF THOSE TODAY.
SOUNDS PERFECT!
DOES ONE OF US NOT NEED TO STAY OUT FRONT?
NO WAY. NOBODY COMES IN HERE, LIKE, EVER. WE MOSTLY DO DELIVERIES.
OHHHHH, OKAY.
LET'S SEE...
WE'VE GOT THE PREP AREA HERE.
A BIG OL' MIXER.
ALL THE SUPPLIES LIKE FLOUR AND OIL ARE DOWN HERE.
AND THE OVENS.
ONE OF THE KNOBS ON THIS THING IS KINDA MESSED UP,
SO YOU HAVE TO FIDDLE WITH IT TO TURN IT OFF SOMETIMES.

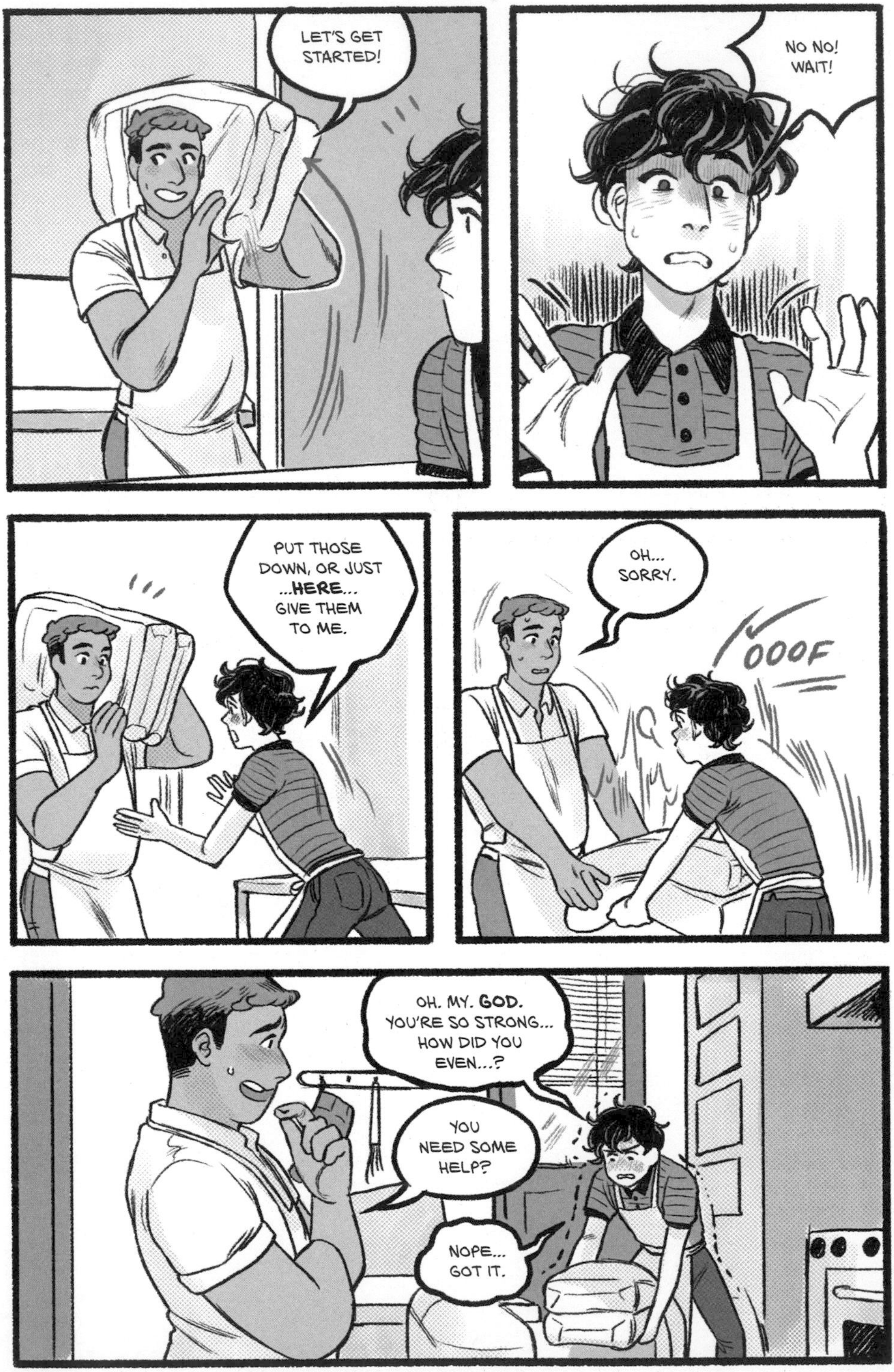
LET'S GET STARTED!
NO NO! WAIT!
PUT THOSE DOWN, OR JUST ...HERE... GIVE THEM TO ME.
OH... SORRY.
OOOF
OH. MY. GOD. YOU'RE SO STRONG... HOW DID YOU EVEN...?
YOU NEED SOME HELP?
NOPE... GOT IT.

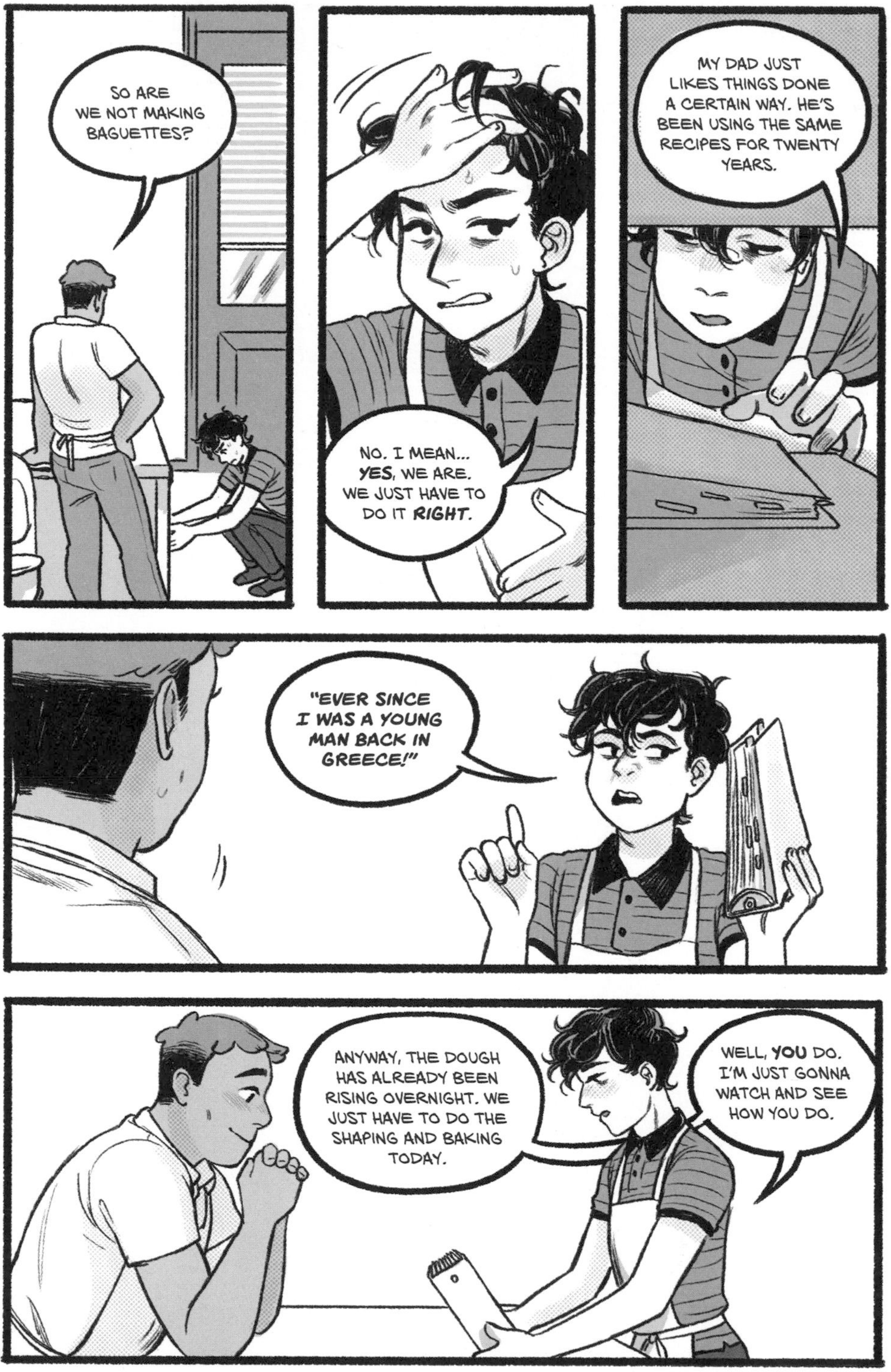
SO ARE WE NOT MAKING BAGUETTES?
NO. I MEAN... YES, WE ARE. WE JUST HAVE TO DO IT RIGHT.
MY DAD JUST LIKES THINGS DONE A CERTAIN WAY. HE'S BEEN USING THE SAME RECIPES FOR TWENTY YEARS.
"EVER SINCE I WAS A YOUNG MAN BACK IN GREECE!"
ANYWAY, THE DOUGH HAS ALREADY BEEN RISING OVERNIGHT. WE JUST HAVE TO DO THE SHAPING AND BAKING TODAY.
WELL, YOU DO. I'M JUST GONNA WATCH AND SEE HOW YOU DO.

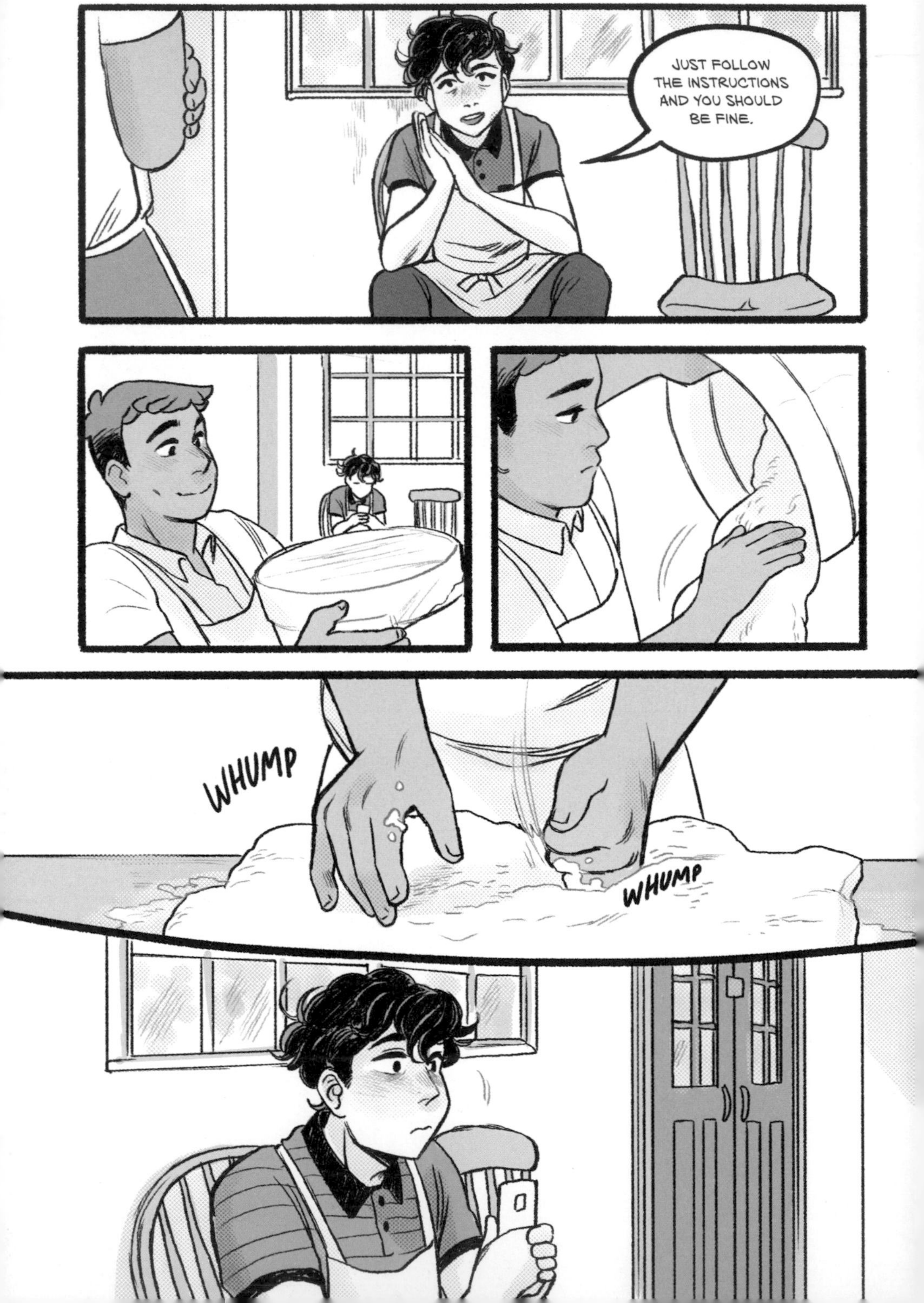
JUST FOLLOW THE INSTRUCTIONS AND YOU SHOULD BE FINE.
WHUMP
WHUMP

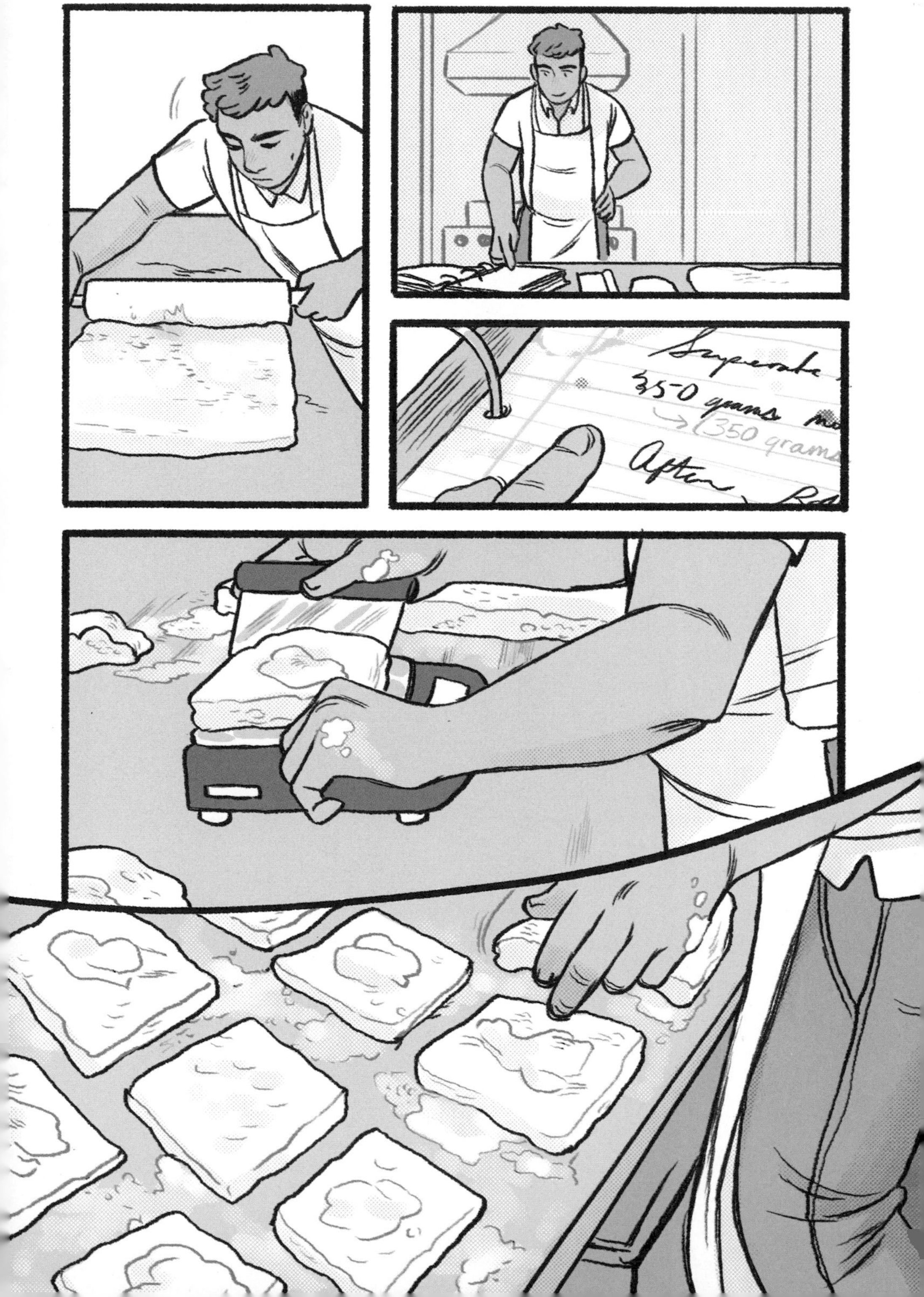

3͟5-0 grams
(350 grams
After

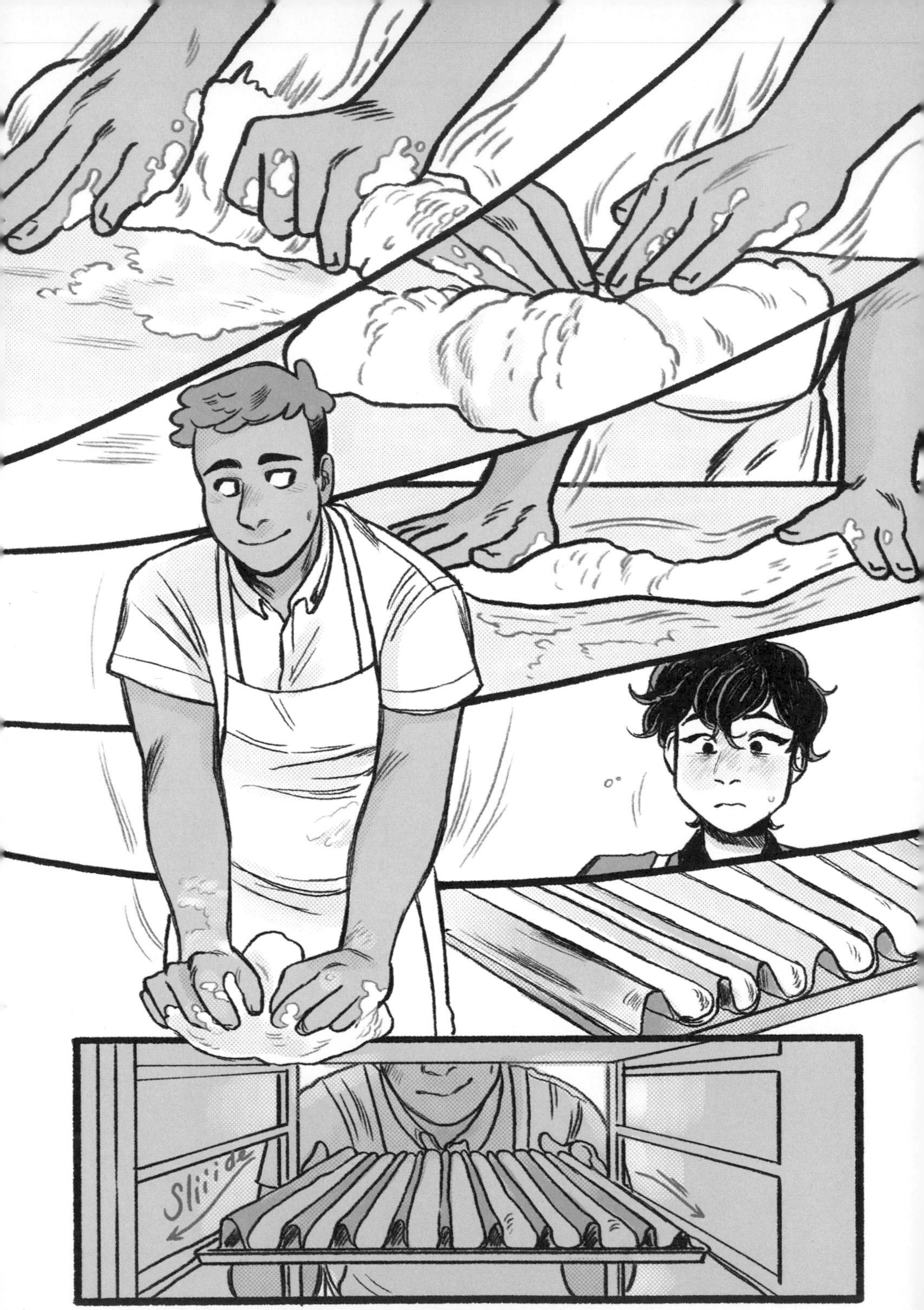
Sliiide

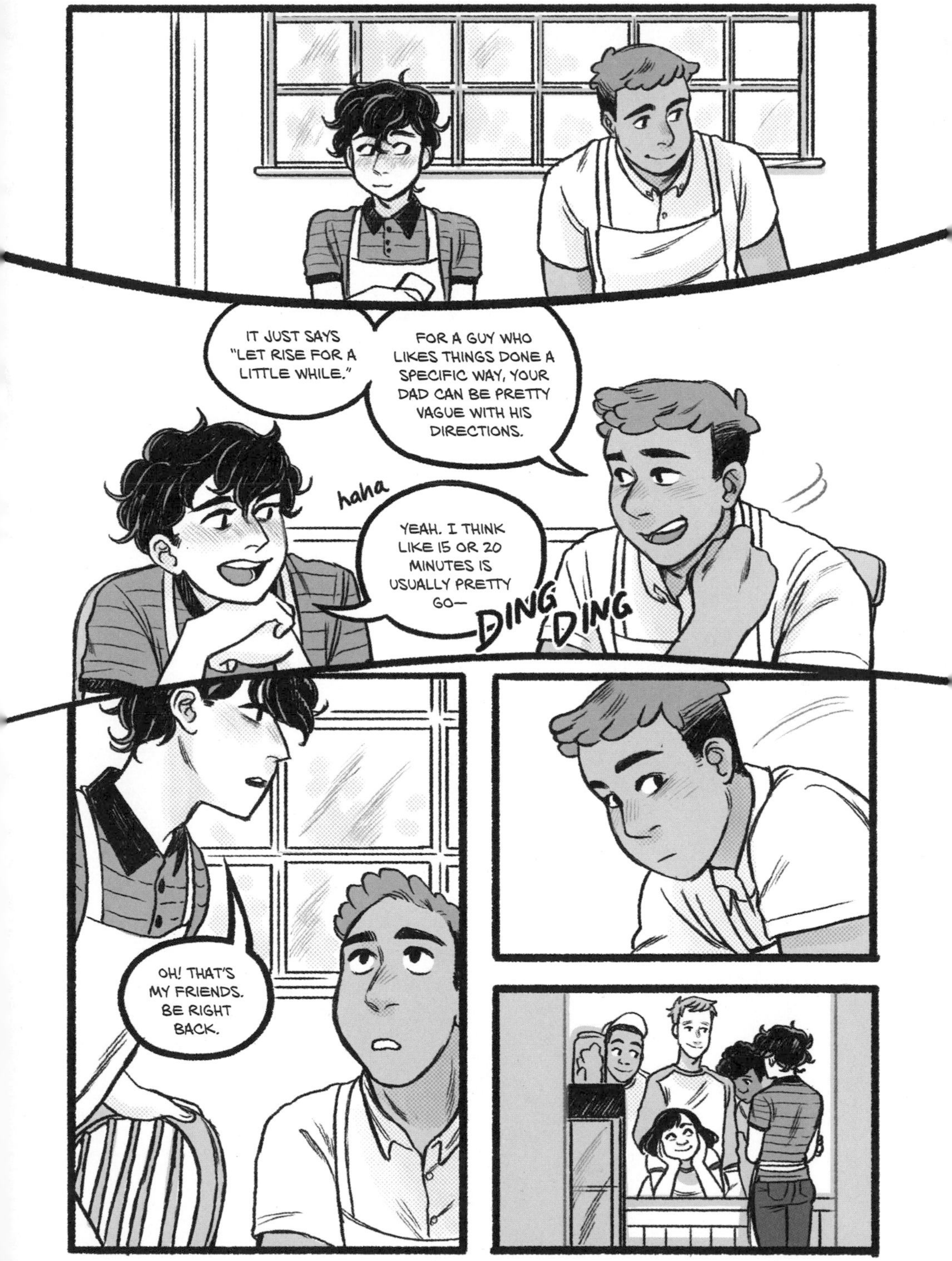
IT JUST SAYS "LET RISE FOR A LITTLE WHILE."
FOR A GUY WHO LIKES THINGS DONE A SPECIFIC WAY, YOUR DAD CAN BE PRETTY VAGUE WITH HIS DIRECTIONS.
haha
YEAH. I THINK LIKE 15 OR 20 MINUTES IS USUALLY PRETTY GO—
DING DING
OH! THAT'S MY FRIENDS. BE RIGHT BACK.

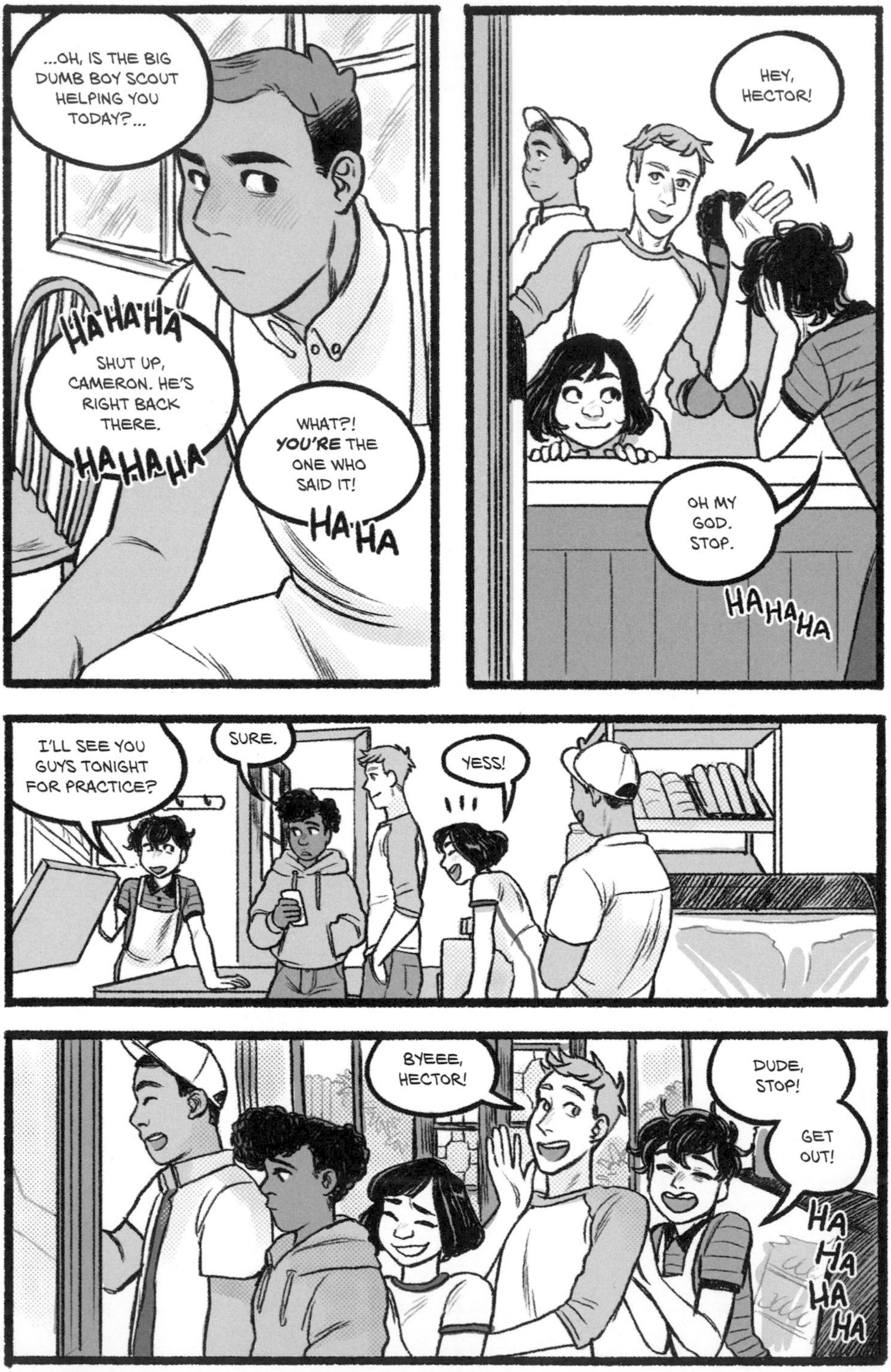
...OH, IS THE BIG DUMB BOY SCOUT HELPING YOU TODAY?...
HA HA HA
SHUT UP, CAMERON. HE'S RIGHT BACK THERE.
HA HA HA
WHAT?! *YOU'RE* THE ONE WHO SAID IT!
HA HA
HEY, HECTOR!
OH MY GOD. STOP.
HA HA HA
I'LL SEE YOU GUYS TONIGHT FOR PRACTICE?
SURE.
YESS!
BYEEE, HECTOR!
DUDE, STOP!
GET OUT!
HA HA HA HA

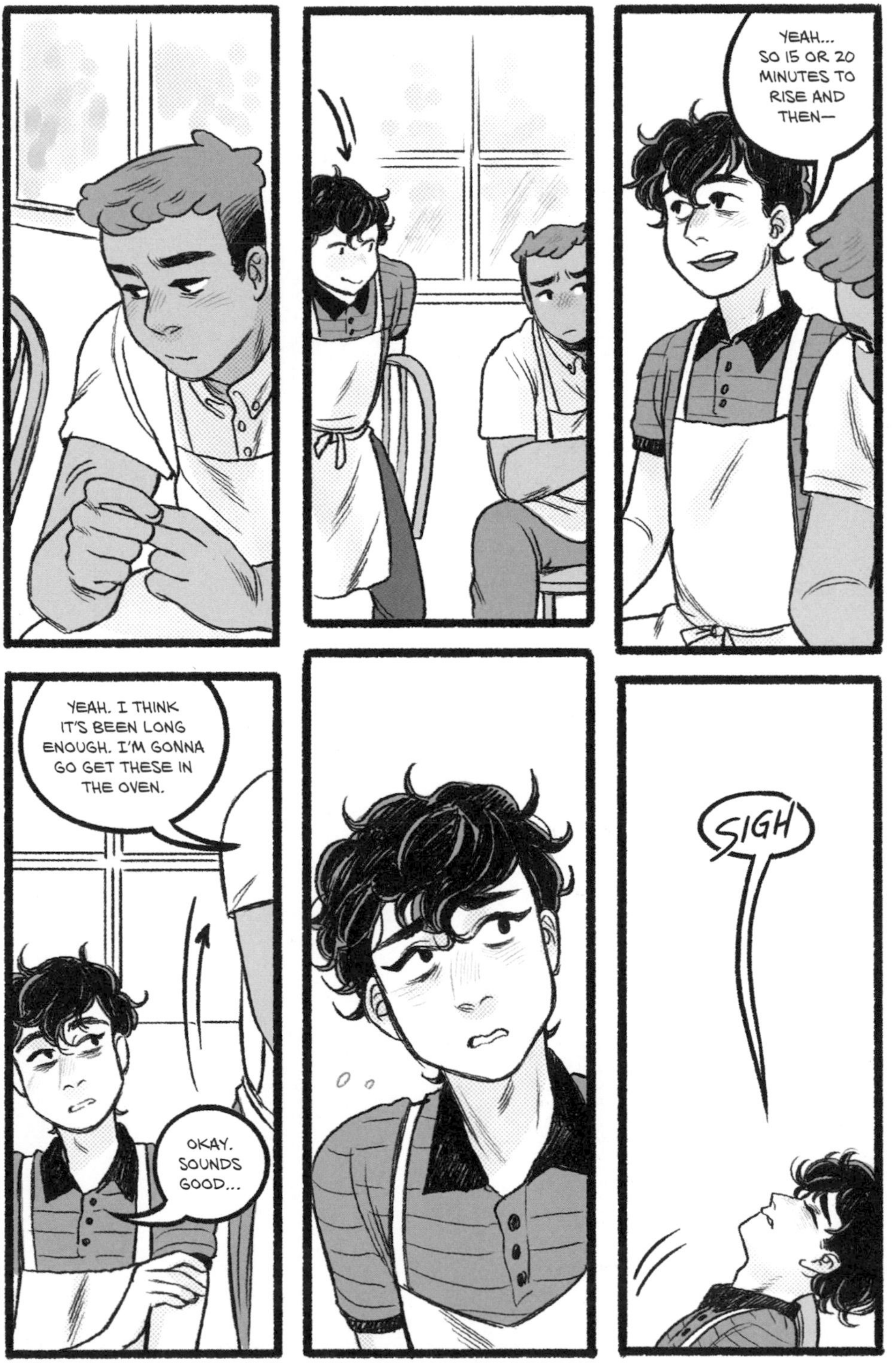
YEAH... SO 15 OR 20 MINUTES TO RISE AND THEN—
YEAH. I THINK IT'S BEEN LONG ENOUGH. I'M GONNA GO GET THESE IN THE OVEN.
OKAY. SOUNDS GOOD...
SIGH

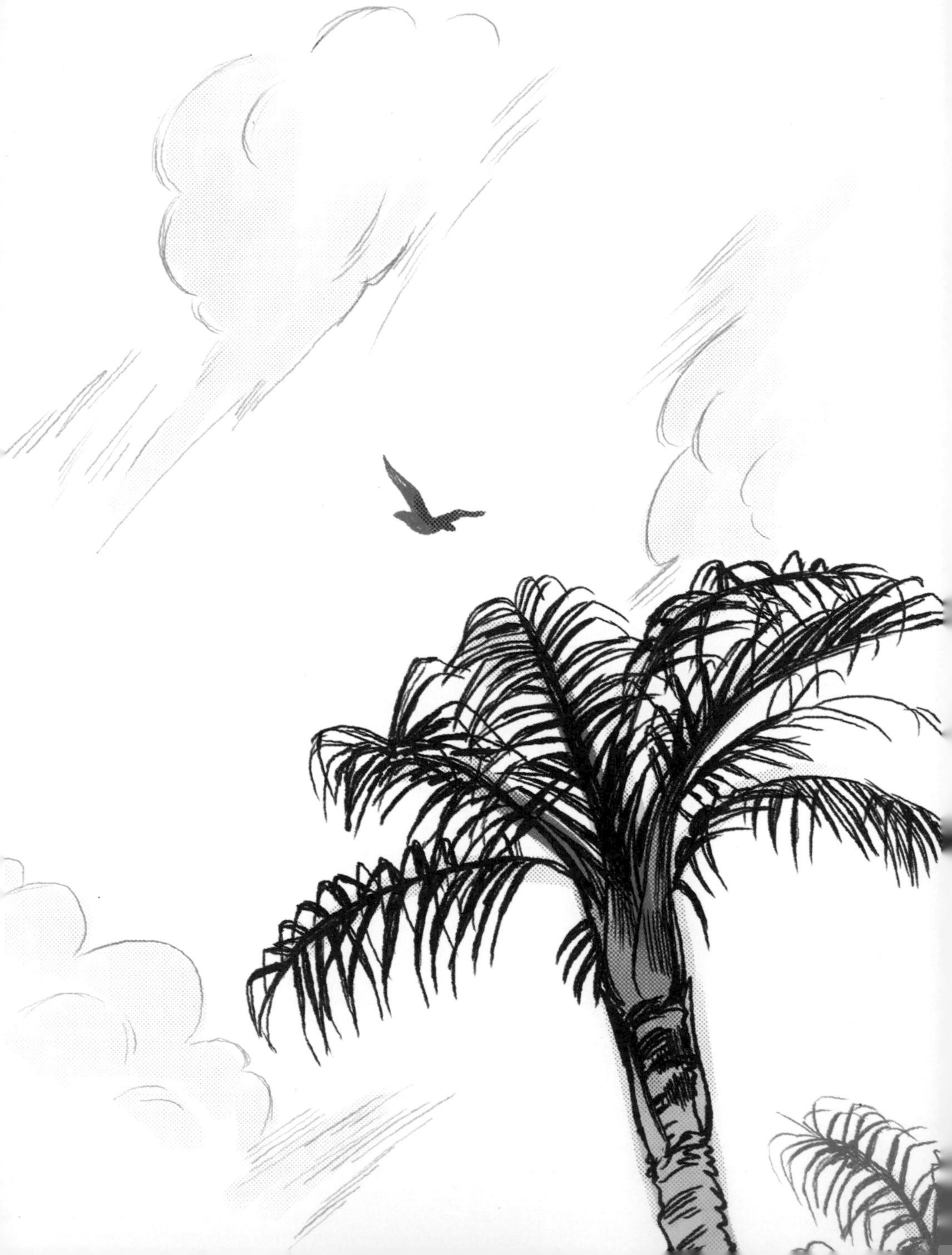

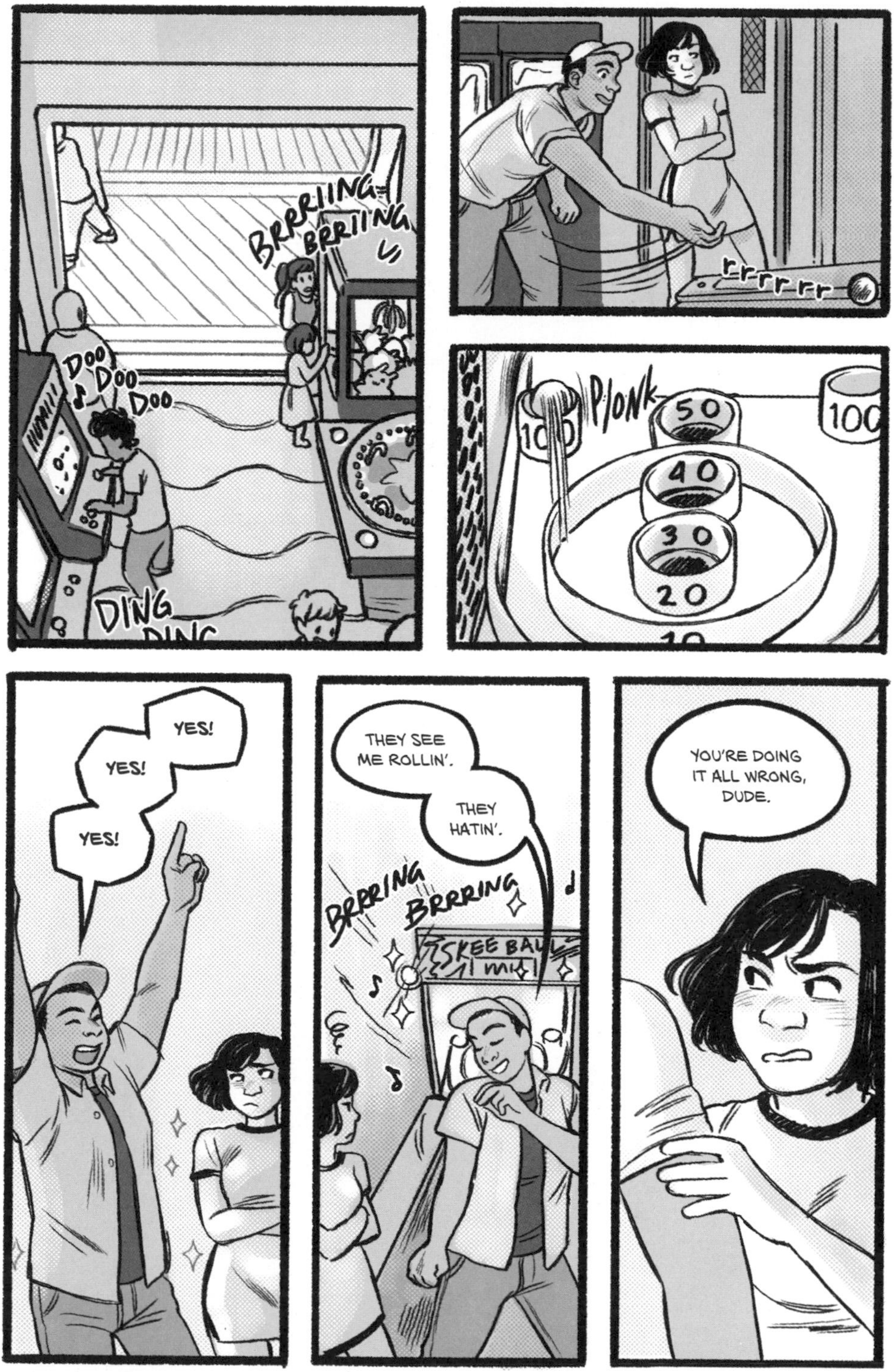
BRRRIING
BRRIING
DOO
DOO
DOO
DING
rrrrrr
PLONK
50
40
30
20
100
100
YES!
YES!
YES!
THEY SEE ME ROLLIN'.
THEY HATIN'.
BRRRING
BRRRING
SKEE BALL
YOU'RE DOING IT ALL WRONG, DUDE.

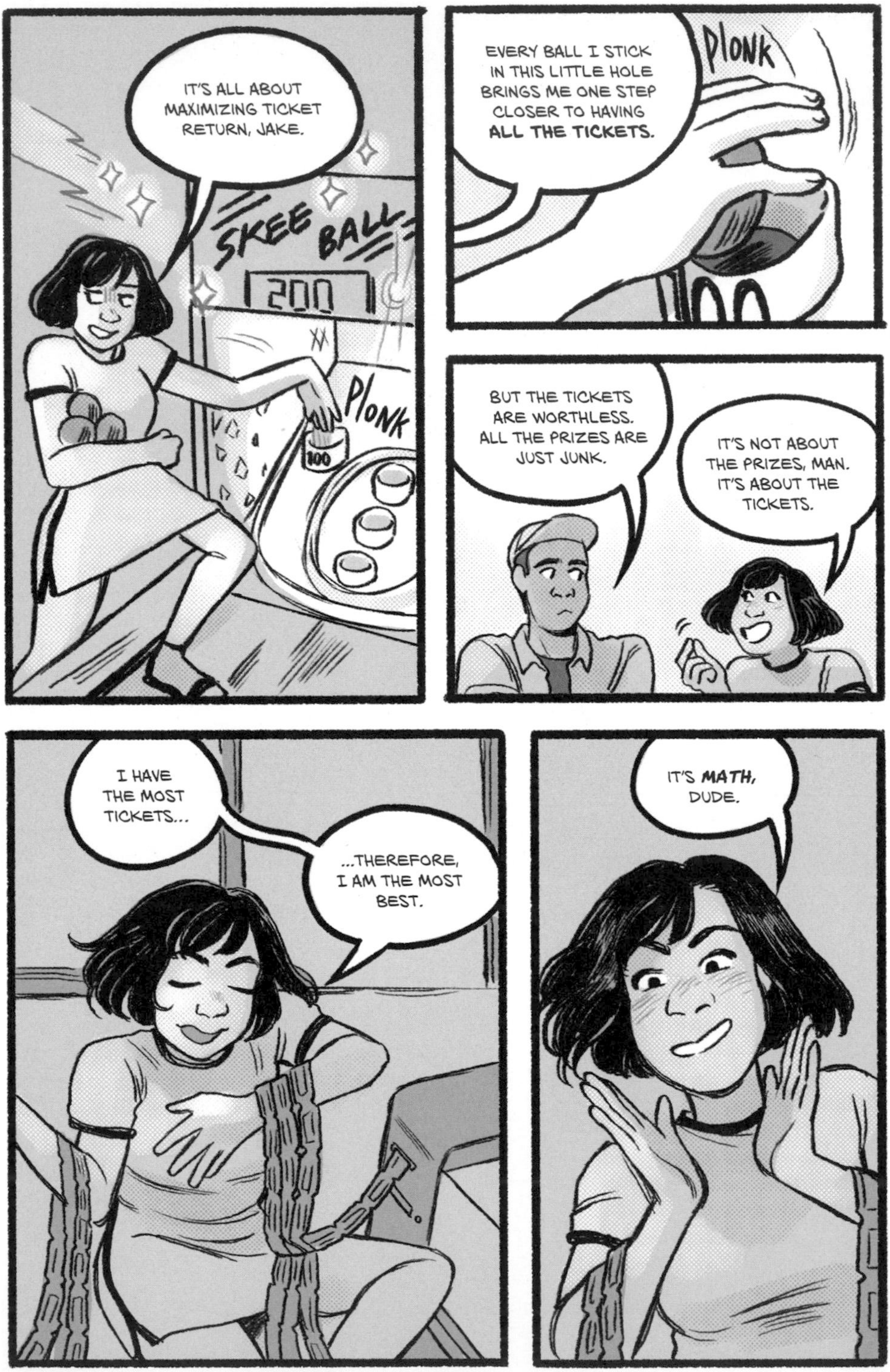
IT'S ALL ABOUT MAXIMIZING TICKET RETURN, JAKE.
SKEE BALL
200
PLONK
EVERY BALL I STICK IN THIS LITTLE HOLE BRINGS ME ONE STEP CLOSER TO HAVING **ALL THE TICKETS.**
PLONK
BUT THE TICKETS ARE WORTHLESS. ALL THE PRIZES ARE JUST JUNK.
IT'S NOT ABOUT THE PRIZES, MAN. IT'S ABOUT THE TICKETS.
I HAVE THE MOST TICKETS...
...THEREFORE, I AM THE MOST BEST.
IT'S ***MATH,*** DUDE.

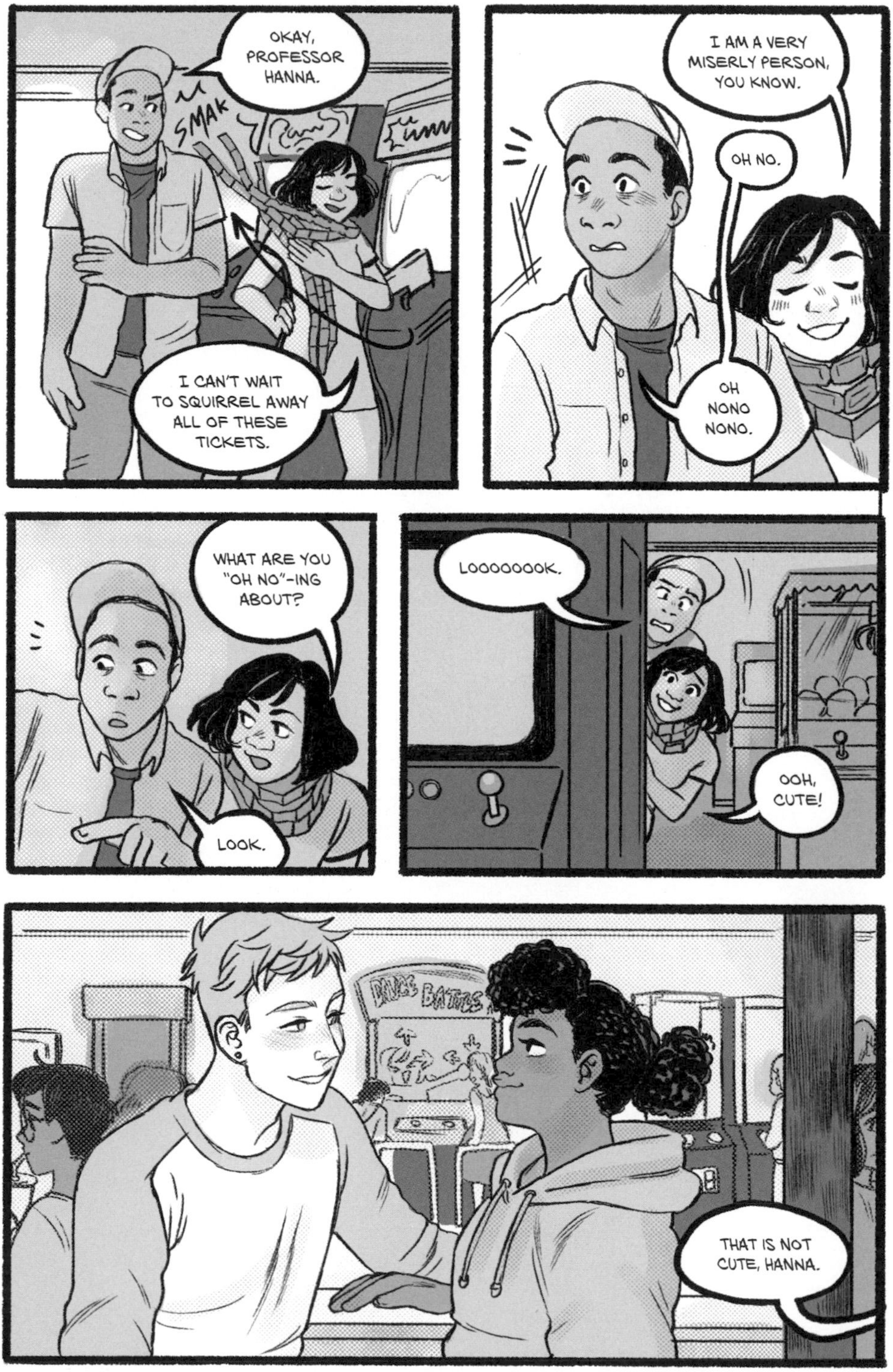
OKAY, PROFESSOR HANNA.
SMAK
I CAN'T WAIT TO SQUIRREL AWAY ALL OF THESE TICKETS.
I AM A VERY MISERLY PERSON, YOU KNOW.
OH NO.
OH NONO NONO.
WHAT ARE YOU "OH NO"-ING ABOUT?
LOOK.
LOOOOOOOK.
OOH, CUTE!
THAT IS NOT CUTE, HANNA.

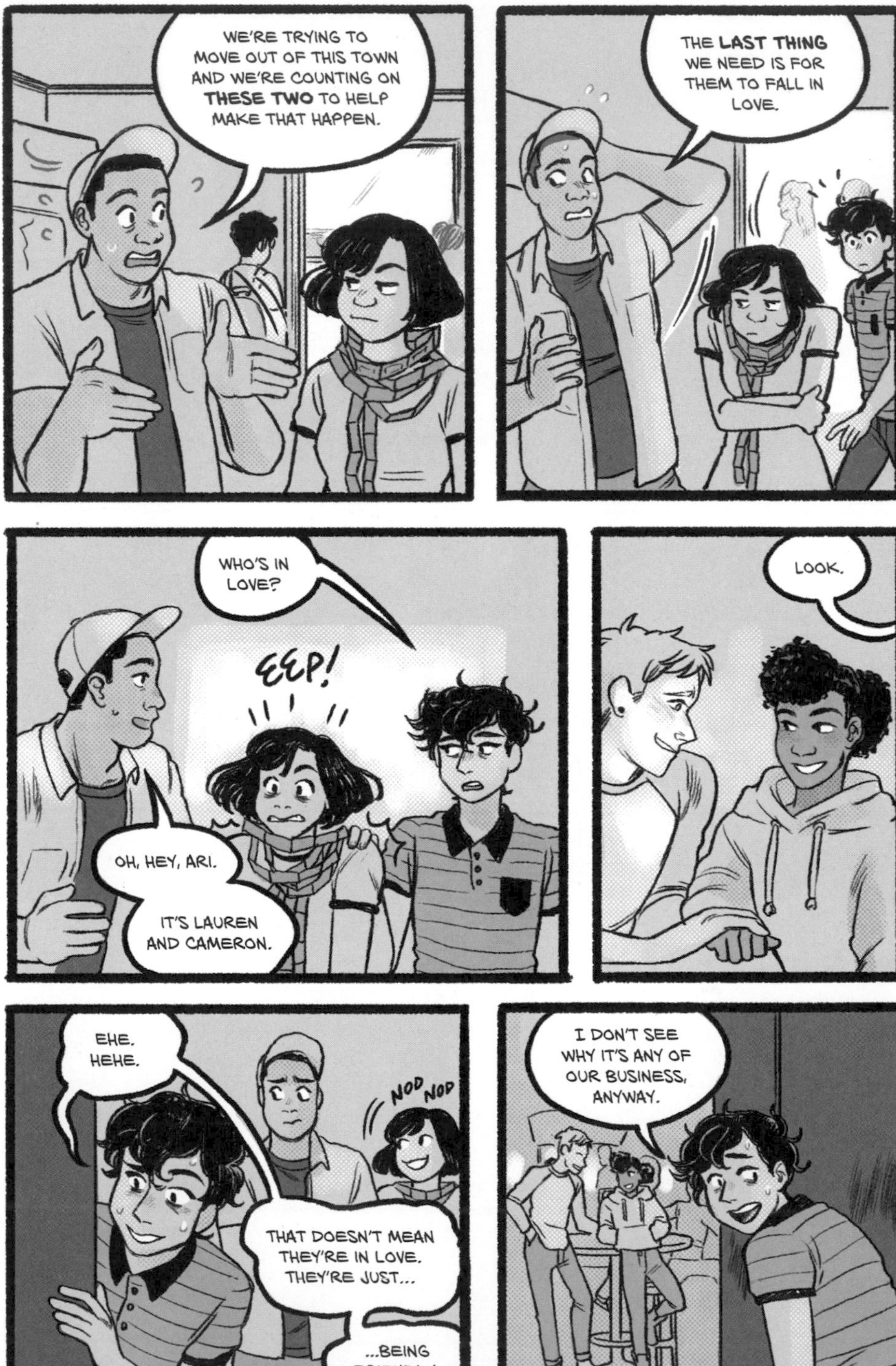
WE'RE TRYING TO MOVE OUT OF THIS TOWN AND WE'RE COUNTING ON **THESE TWO** TO HELP MAKE THAT HAPPEN.
THE **LAST THING** WE NEED IS FOR THEM TO FALL IN LOVE.
WHO'S IN LOVE?
EEP!
OH, HEY, ARI.
IT'S LAUREN AND CAMERON.
LOOK.
EHE. HEHE.
NOD NOD
THAT DOESN'T MEAN THEY'RE IN LOVE. THEY'RE JUST...
...BEING FRIENDLY.
I DON'T SEE WHY IT'S ANY OF OUR BUSINESS, ANYWAY.

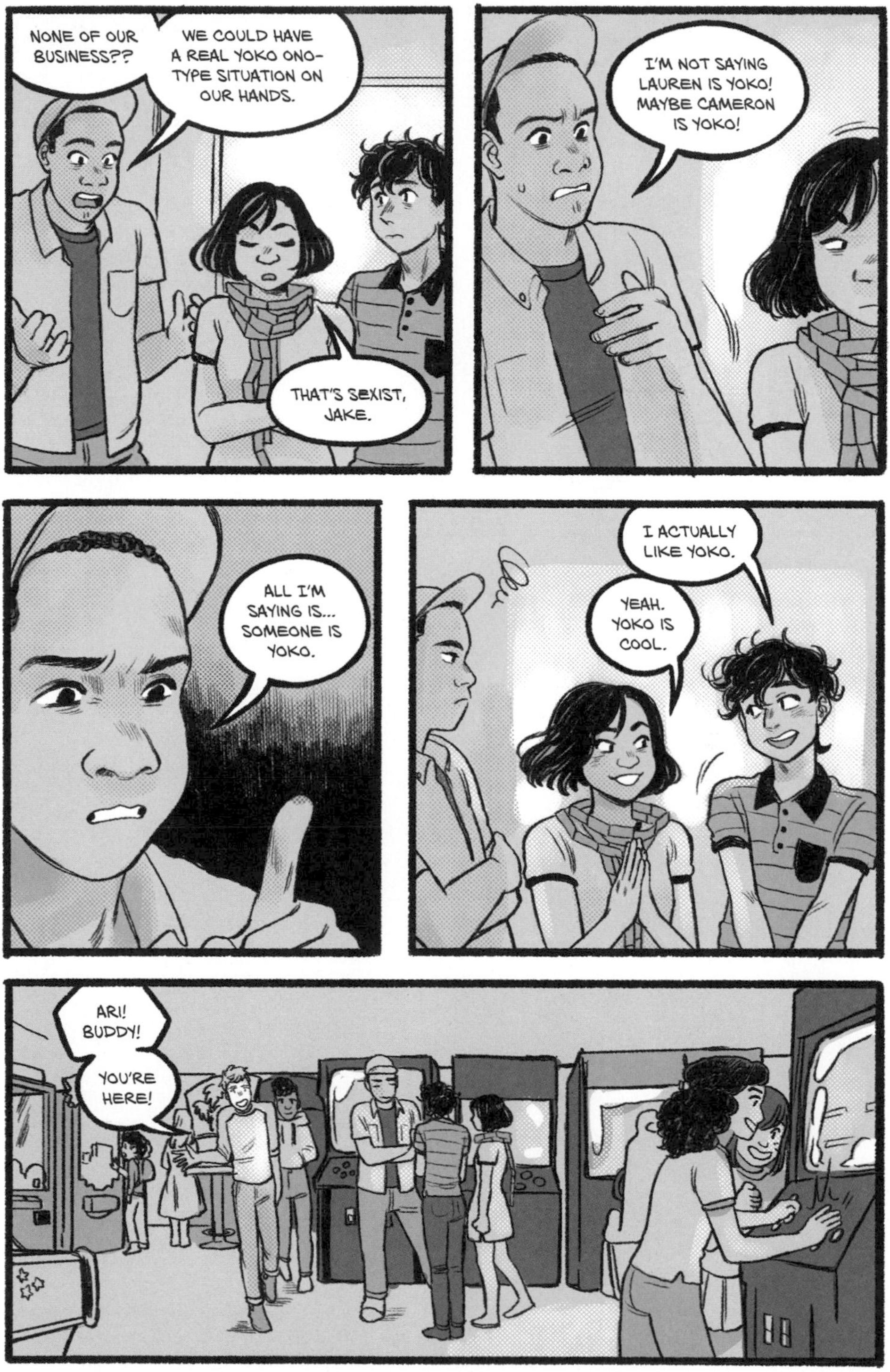
NONE OF OUR BUSINESS??
WE COULD HAVE A REAL YOKO ONO-TYPE SITUATION ON OUR HANDS.
THAT'S SEXIST, JAKE.
I'M NOT SAYING LAUREN IS YOKO! MAYBE CAMERON IS YOKO!
ALL I'M SAYING IS... SOMEONE IS YOKO.
I ACTUALLY LIKE YOKO.
YEAH. YOKO IS COOL.
ARI! BUDDY!
YOU'RE HERE!

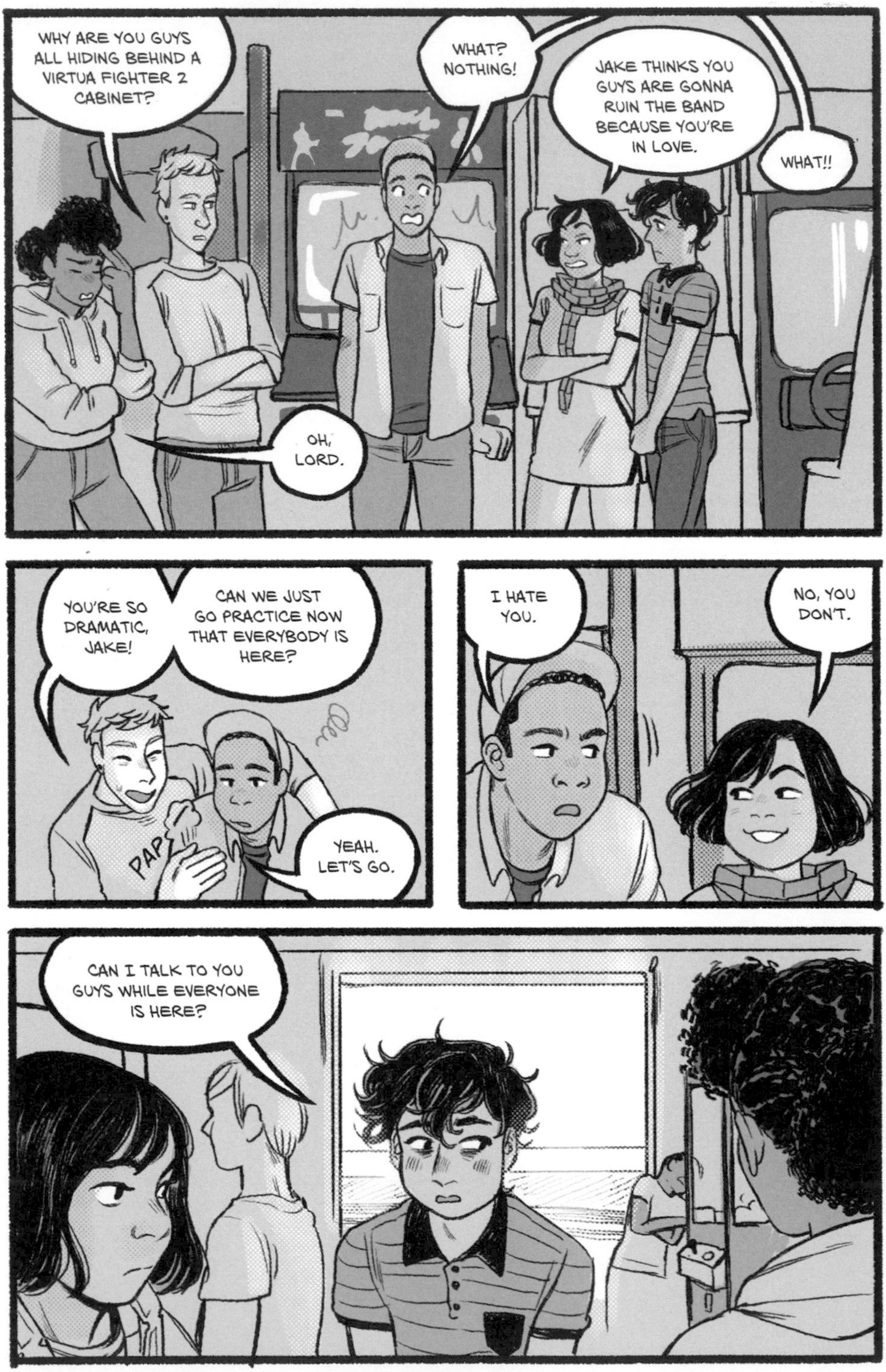
WHY ARE YOU GUYS ALL HIDING BEHIND A VIRTUA FIGHTER 2 CABINET?
WHAT? NOTHING!
JAKE THINKS YOU GUYS ARE GONNA RUIN THE BAND BECAUSE YOU'RE IN LOVE.
WHAT!!
OH, LORD.
YOU'RE SO DRAMATIC, JAKE!
CAN WE JUST GO PRACTICE NOW THAT EVERYBODY IS HERE?
PAP
YEAH. LET'S GO.
I HATE YOU.
NO, YOU DON'T.
CAN I TALK TO YOU GUYS WHILE EVERYONE IS HERE?

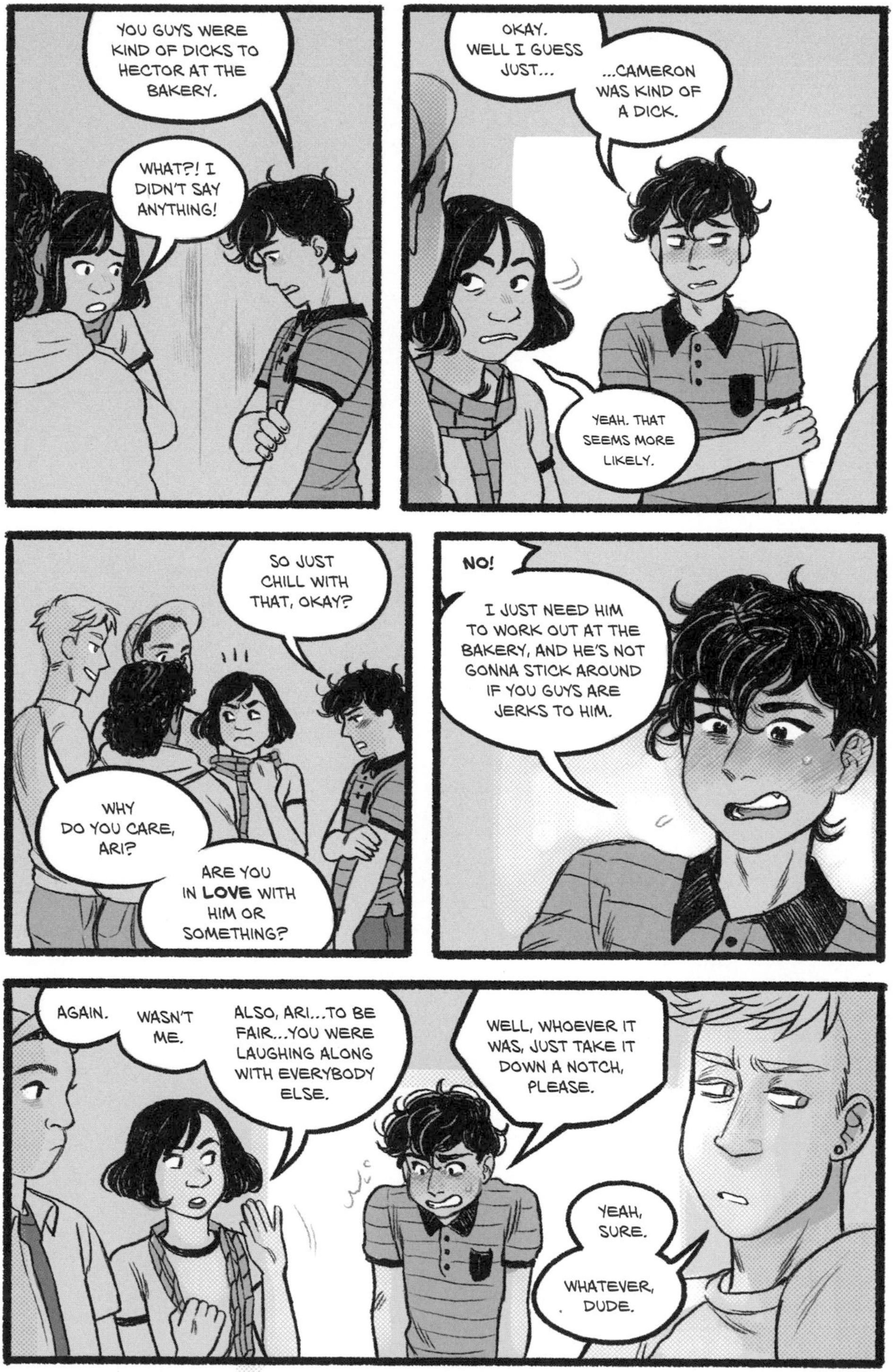
YOU GUYS WERE KIND OF DICKS TO HECTOR AT THE BAKERY.
WHAT?! I DIDN'T SAY ANYTHING!
OKAY. WELL I GUESS JUST...
...CAMERON WAS KIND OF A DICK.
YEAH. THAT SEEMS MORE LIKELY.
SO JUST CHILL WITH THAT, OKAY?
WHY DO YOU CARE, ARI?
ARE YOU IN **LOVE** WITH HIM OR SOMETHING?
NO!
I JUST NEED HIM TO WORK OUT AT THE BAKERY, AND HE'S NOT GONNA STICK AROUND IF YOU GUYS ARE JERKS TO HIM.
AGAIN.
WASN'T ME.
ALSO, ARI...TO BE FAIR...YOU WERE LAUGHING ALONG WITH EVERYBODY ELSE.
WELL, WHOEVER IT WAS, JUST TAKE IT DOWN A NOTCH, PLEASE.
YEAH, SURE.
WHATEVER, DUDE.

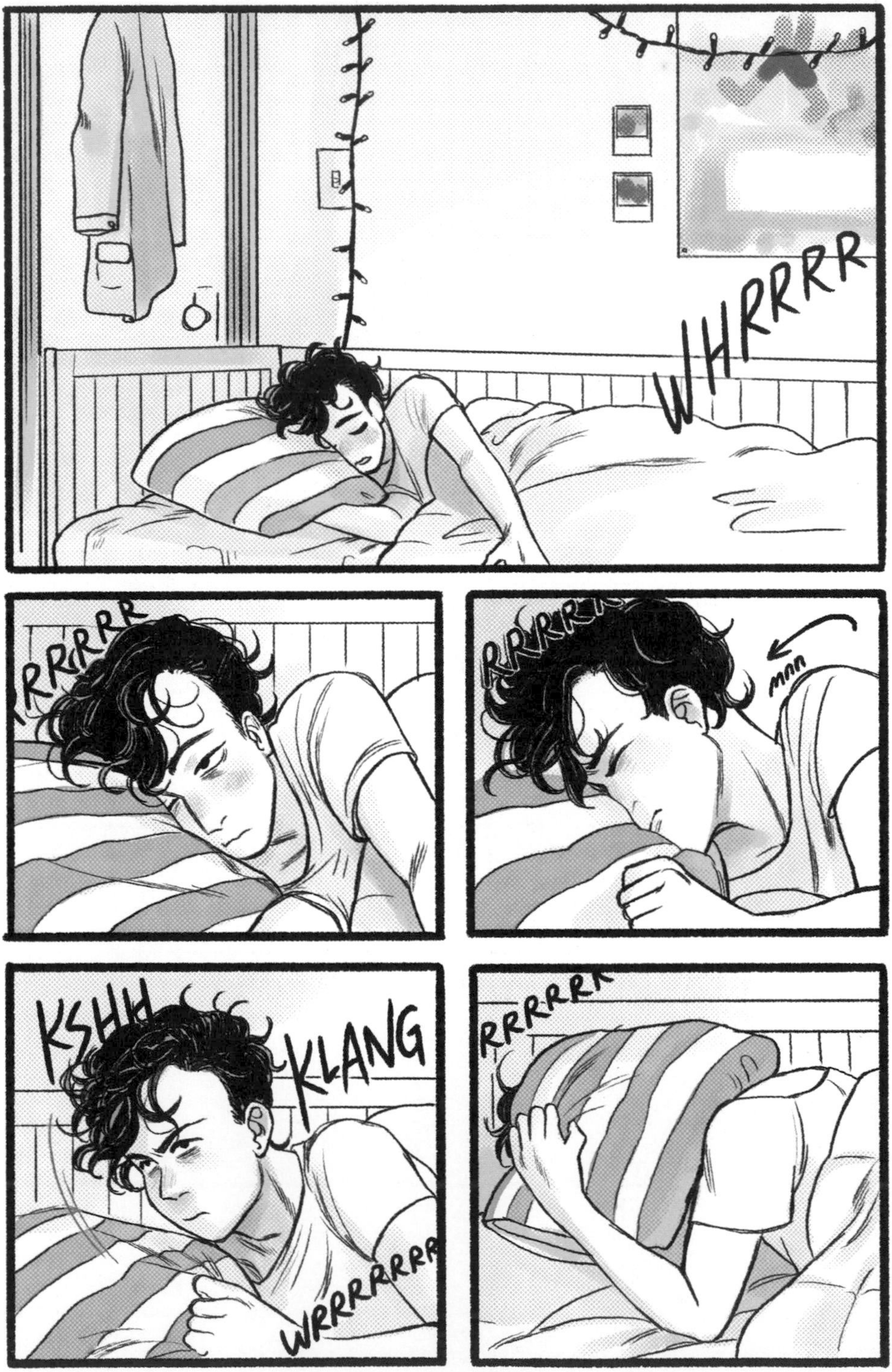
WHRRRR
RRRRRRR
RRRRR
mnn
KSHH
KLANG
WRRRRRR
RRRRRR

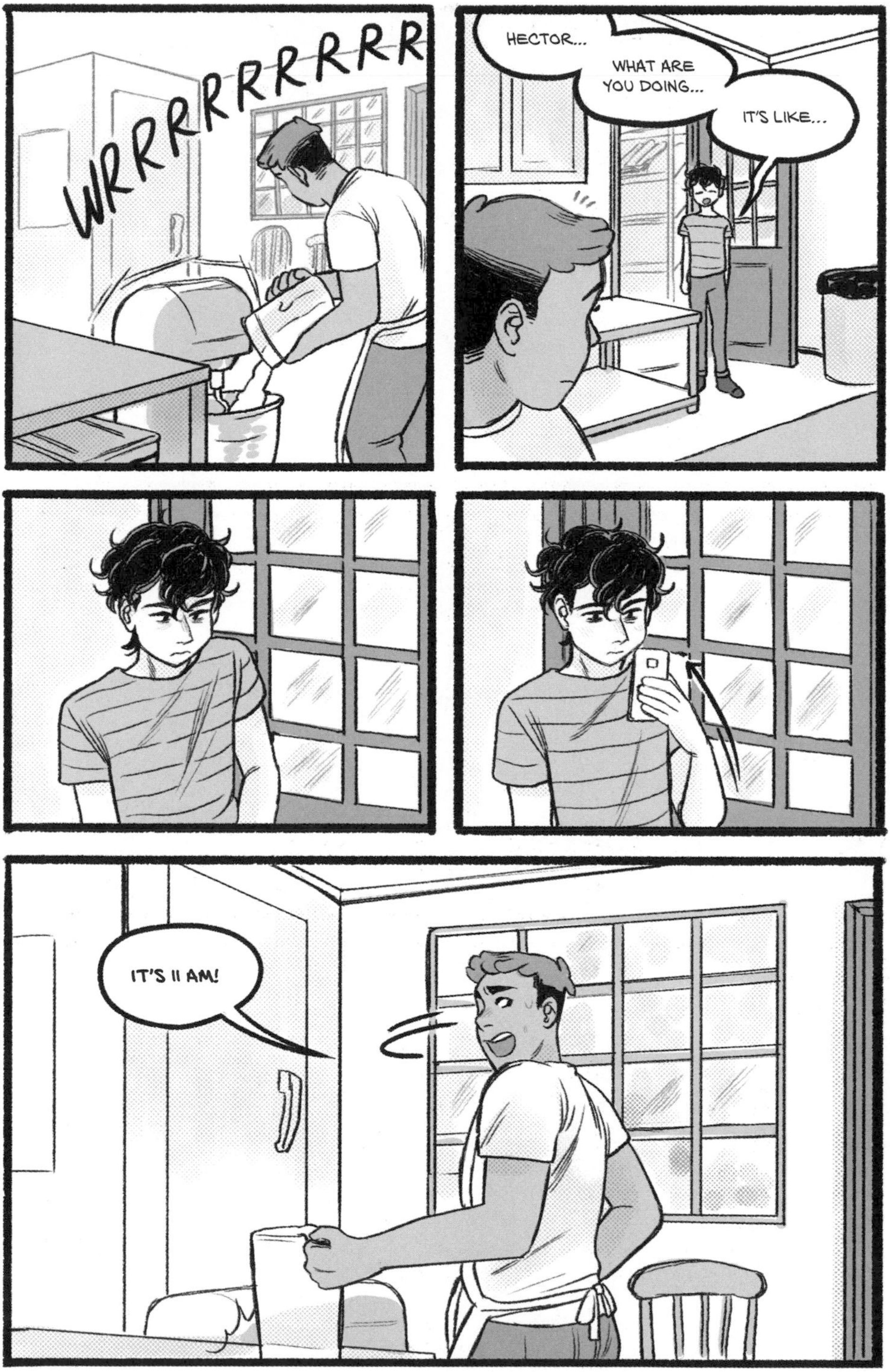
WRRRRRRRRRR
HECTOR...
WHAT ARE YOU DOING...
IT'S LIKE...
IT'S 11 AM!

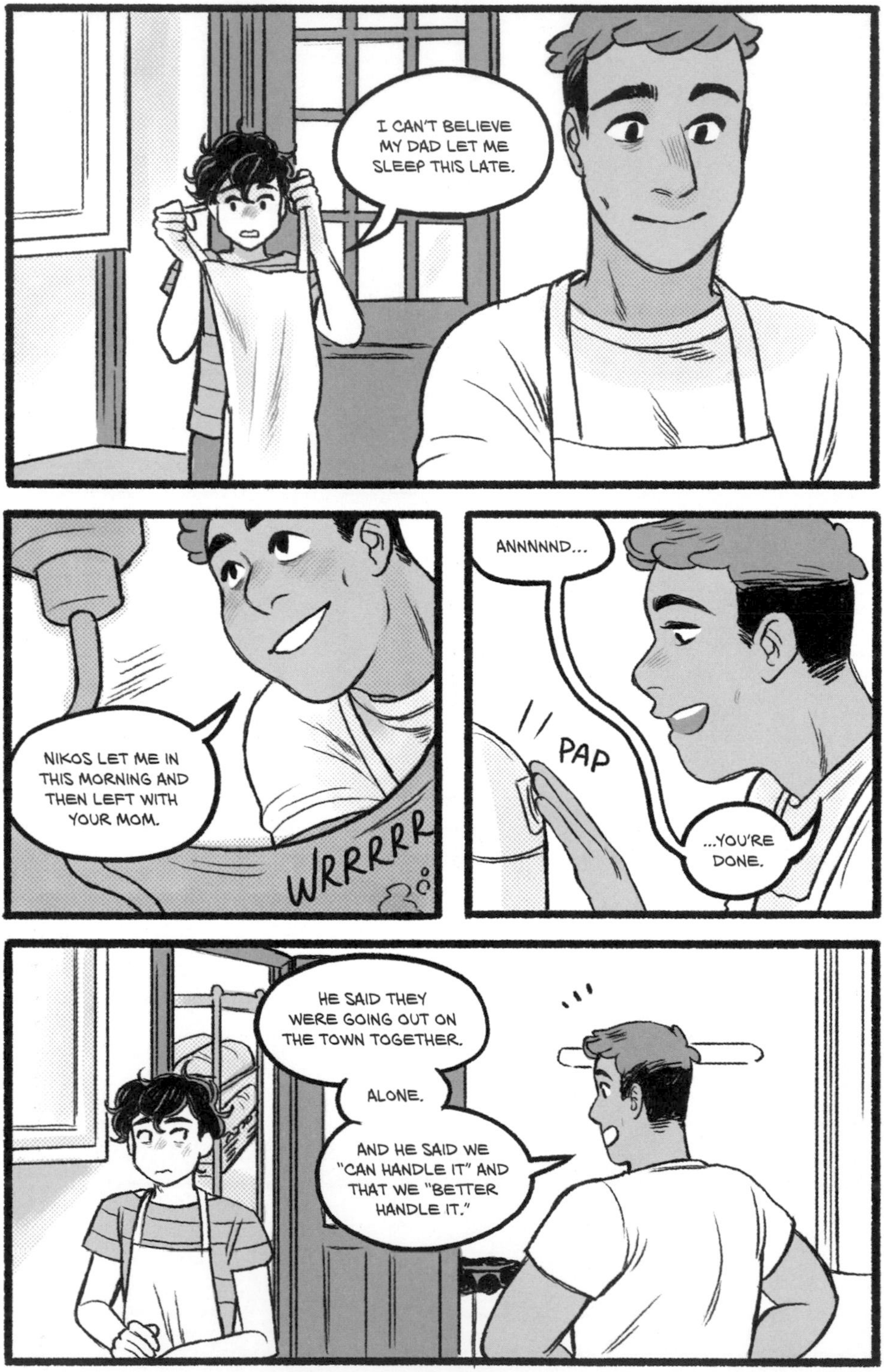
I CAN'T BELIEVE MY DAD LET ME SLEEP THIS LATE.
NIKOS LET ME IN THIS MORNING AND THEN LEFT WITH YOUR MOM.
WRRRRR
ANNNNND...
PAP
...YOU'RE DONE.
HE SAID THEY WERE GOING OUT ON THE TOWN TOGETHER.
ALONE.
AND HE SAID WE "CAN HANDLE IT" AND THAT WE "BETTER HANDLE IT."

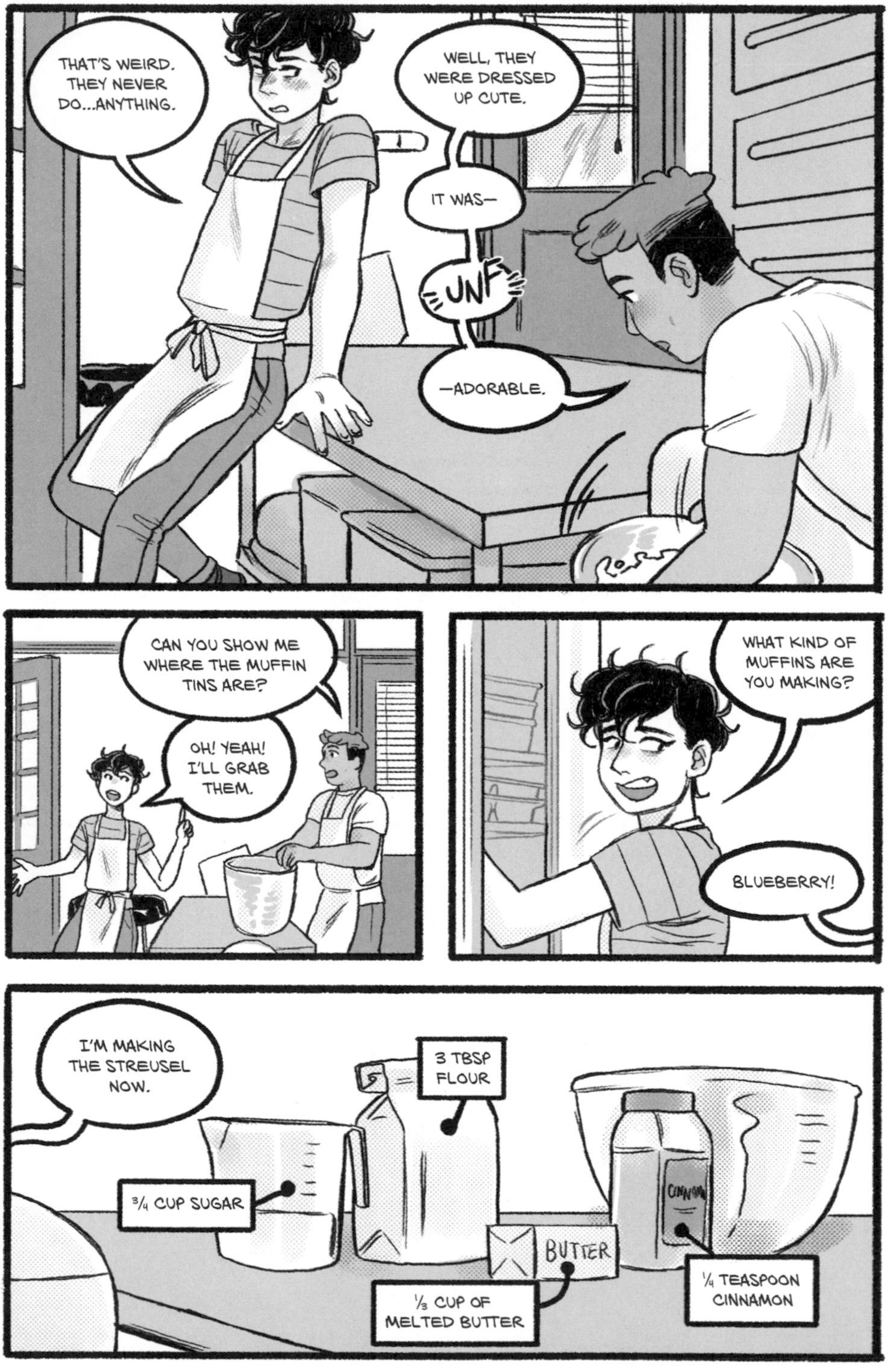
THAT'S WEIRD. THEY NEVER DO...ANYTHING.
WELL, THEY WERE DRESSED UP CUTE.
IT WAS—
UNF
—ADORABLE.
CAN YOU SHOW ME WHERE THE MUFFIN TINS ARE?
OH! YEAH! I'LL GRAB THEM.
WHAT KIND OF MUFFINS ARE YOU MAKING?
BLUEBERRY!
I'M MAKING THE STREUSEL NOW.
3 TBSP FLOUR
3/4 CUP SUGAR
BUTTER
1/3 CUP OF MELTED BUTTER
CINNAMON
1/4 TEASPOON CINNAMON

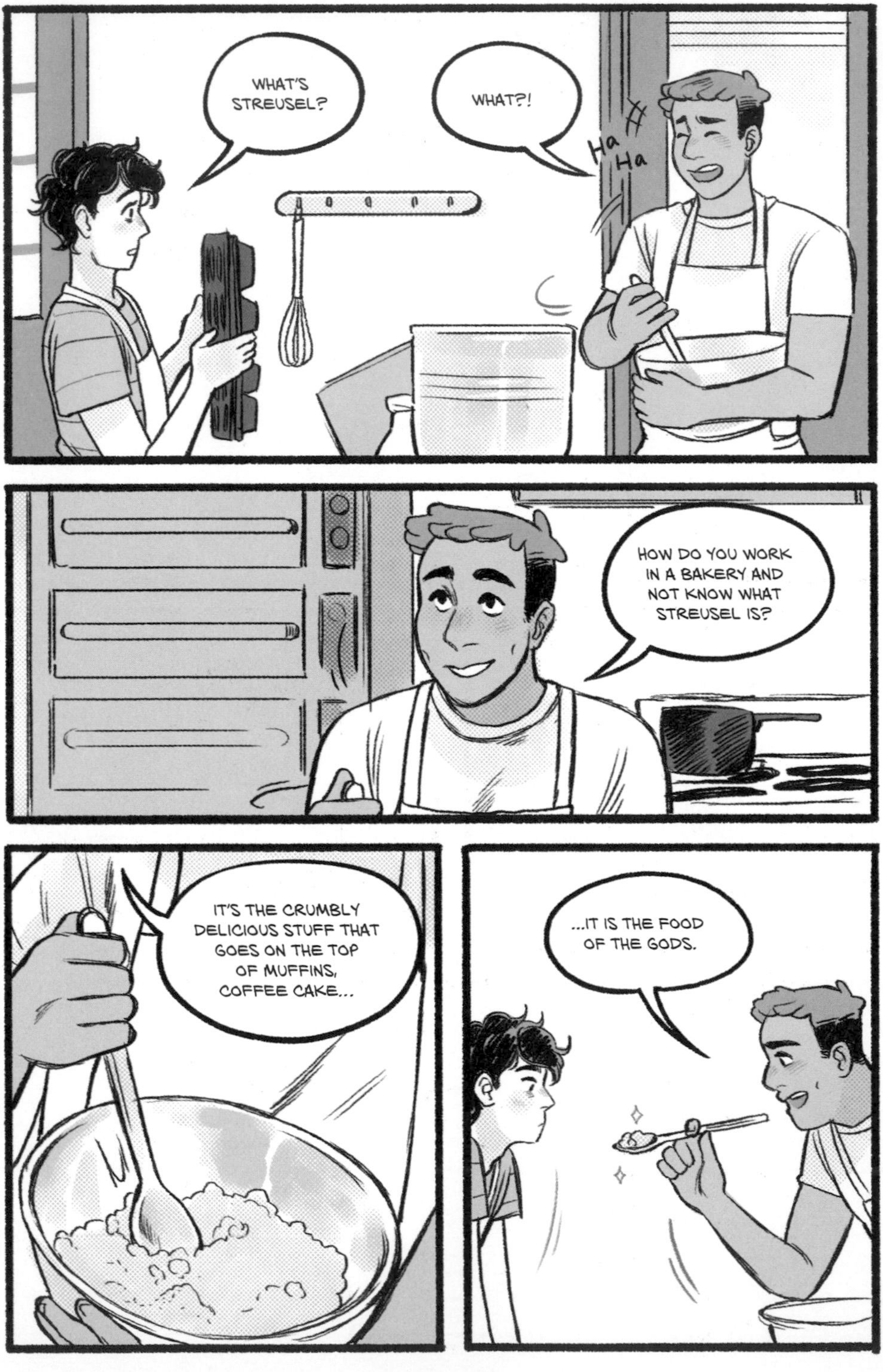
WHAT'S STREUSEL?
WHAT?!
Ha Ha
HOW DO YOU WORK IN A BAKERY AND NOT KNOW WHAT STREUSEL IS?
IT'S THE CRUMBLY DELICIOUS STUFF THAT GOES ON THE TOP OF MUFFINS, COFFEE CAKE...
...IT IS THE FOOD OF THE GODS.

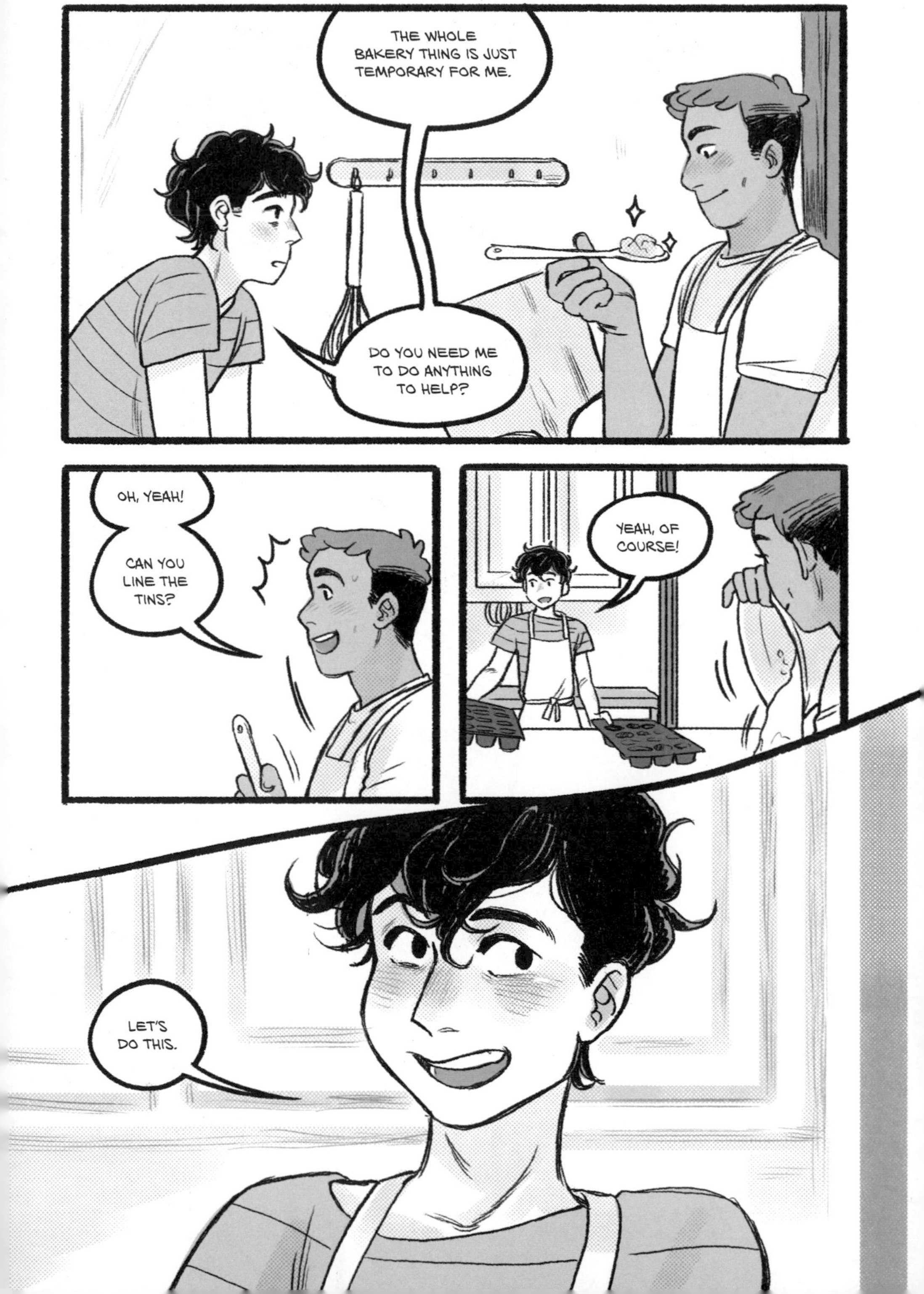
THE WHOLE BAKERY THING IS JUST TEMPORARY FOR ME.
DO YOU NEED ME TO DO ANYTHING TO HELP?
OH, YEAH!
CAN YOU LINE THE TINS?
YEAH, OF COURSE!
LET'S DO THIS.

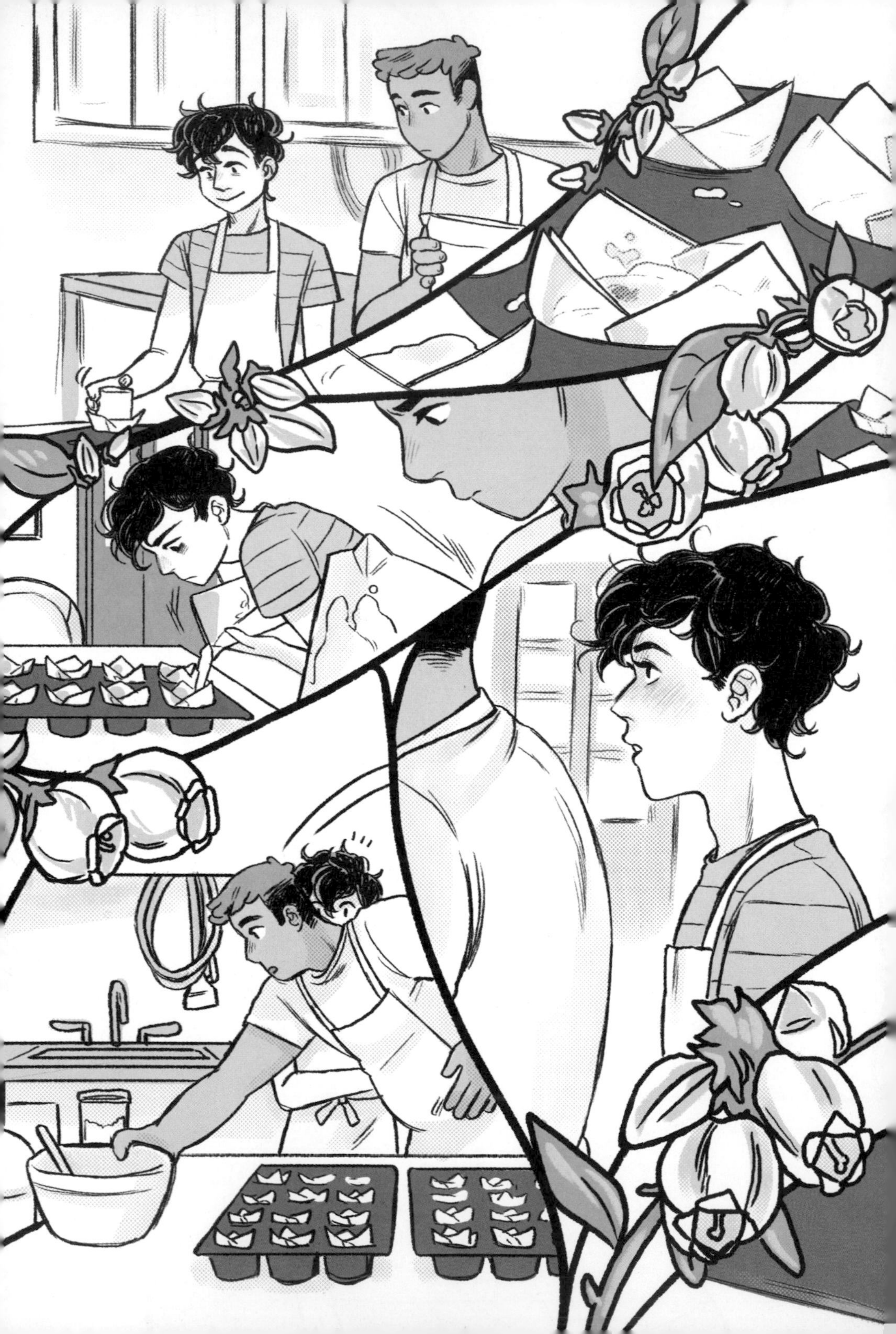

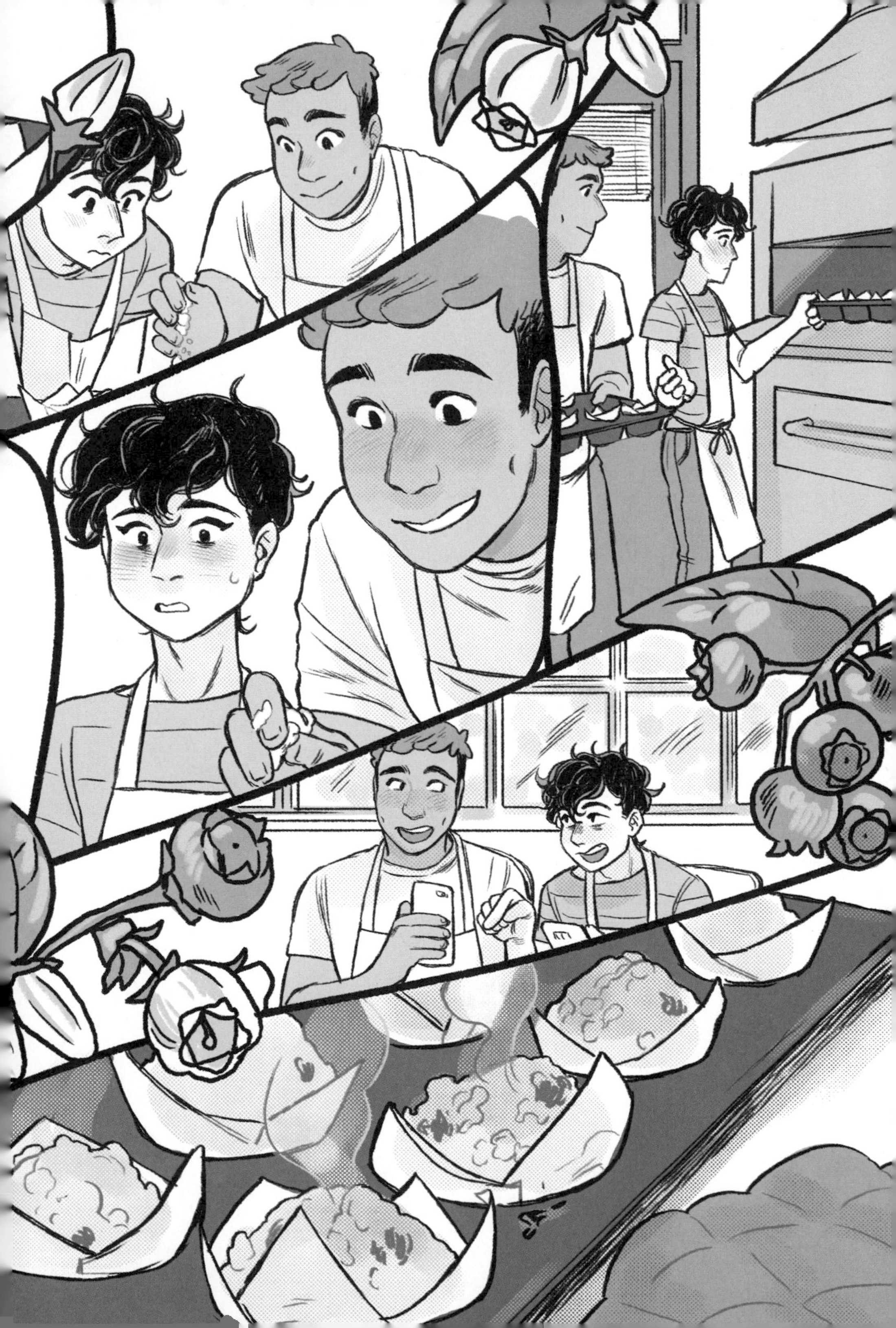

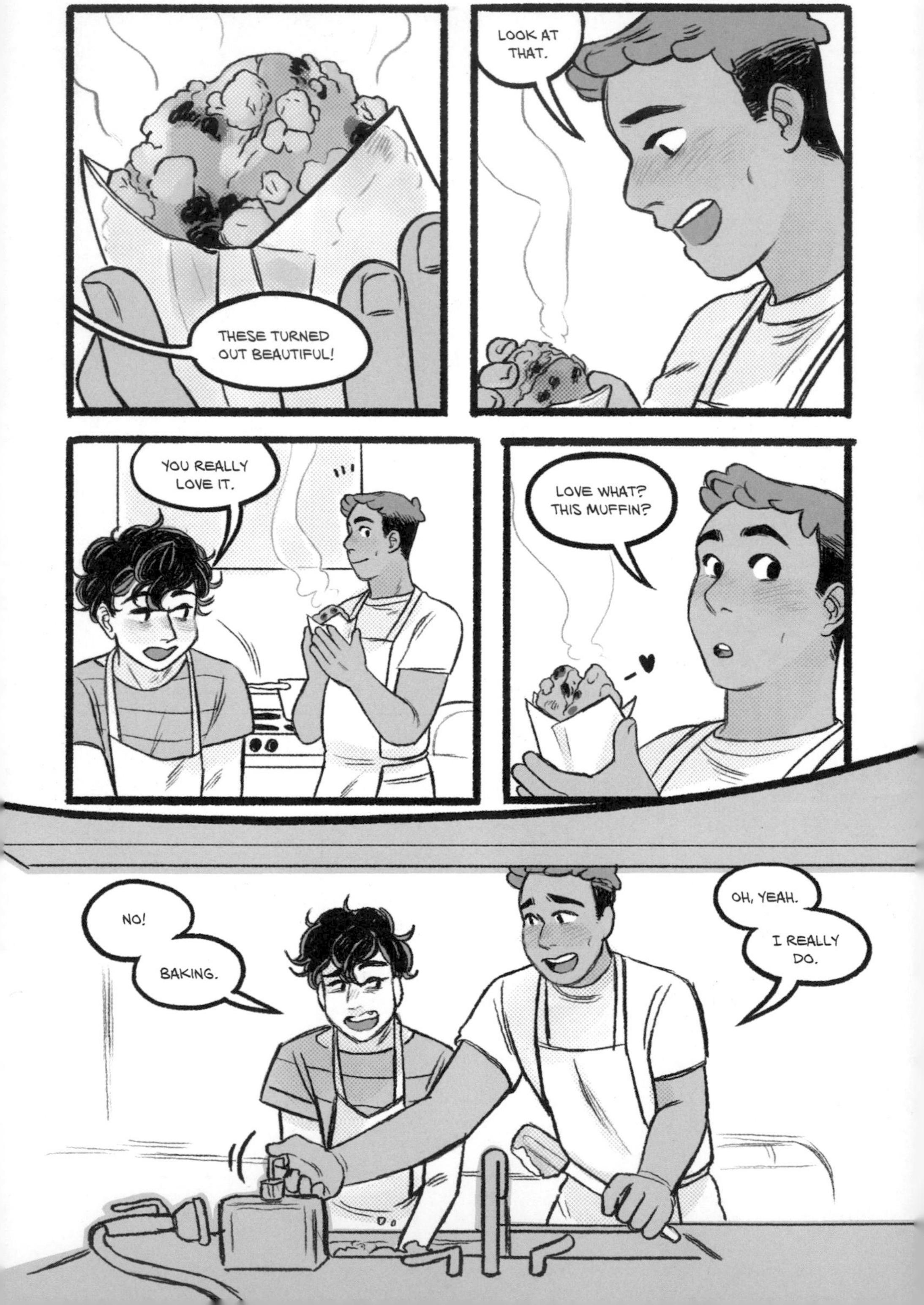
THESE TURNED OUT BEAUTIFUL!
LOOK AT THAT.
YOU REALLY LOVE IT.
LOVE WHAT? THIS MUFFIN?
NO!
BAKING.
OH, YEAH.
I REALLY DO.

KYROS FAMILY BAKERY
KYROS FAMILY BAKERY

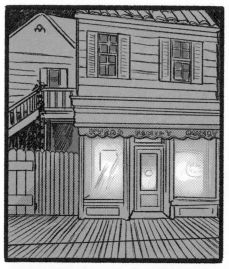

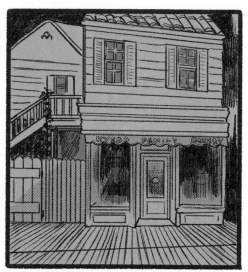

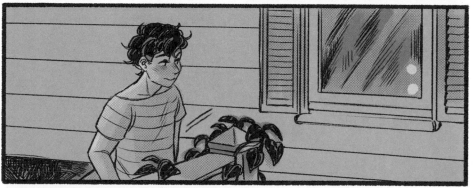

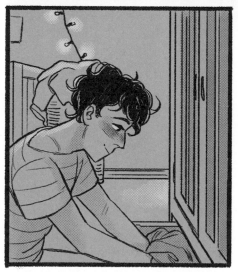

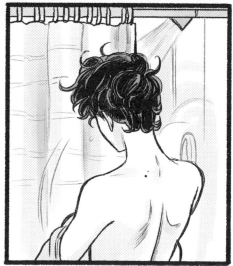

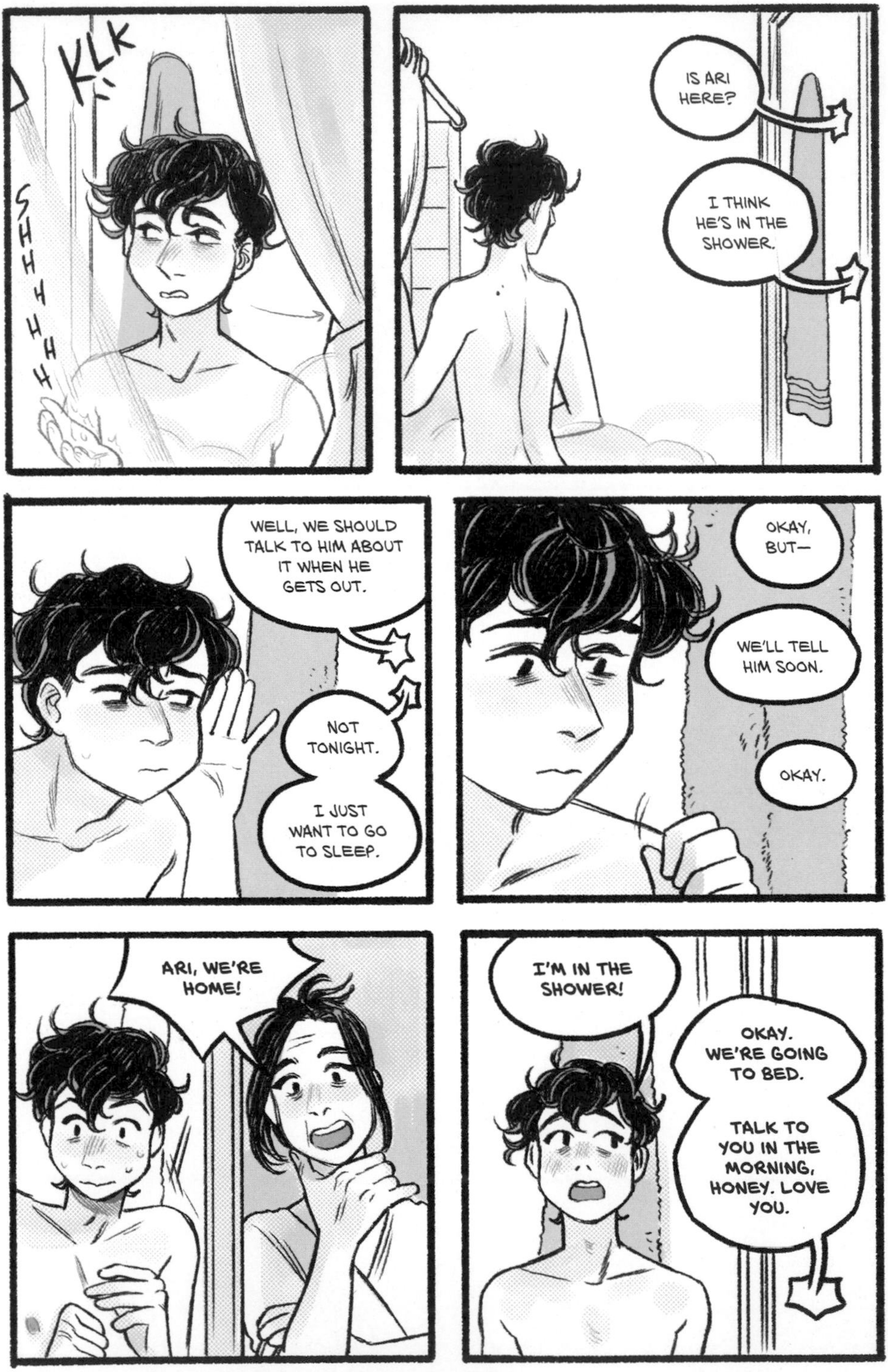
KLK
SHHHHHHH
IS ARI HERE?
I THINK HE'S IN THE SHOWER.
WELL, WE SHOULD TALK TO HIM ABOUT IT WHEN HE GETS OUT.
NOT TONIGHT.
I JUST WANT TO GO TO SLEEP.
OKAY, BUT—
WE'LL TELL HIM SOON.
OKAY.
ARI, WE'RE HOME!
I'M IN THE SHOWER!
OKAY. WE'RE GOING TO BED.
TALK TO YOU IN THE MORNING, HONEY. LOVE YOU.

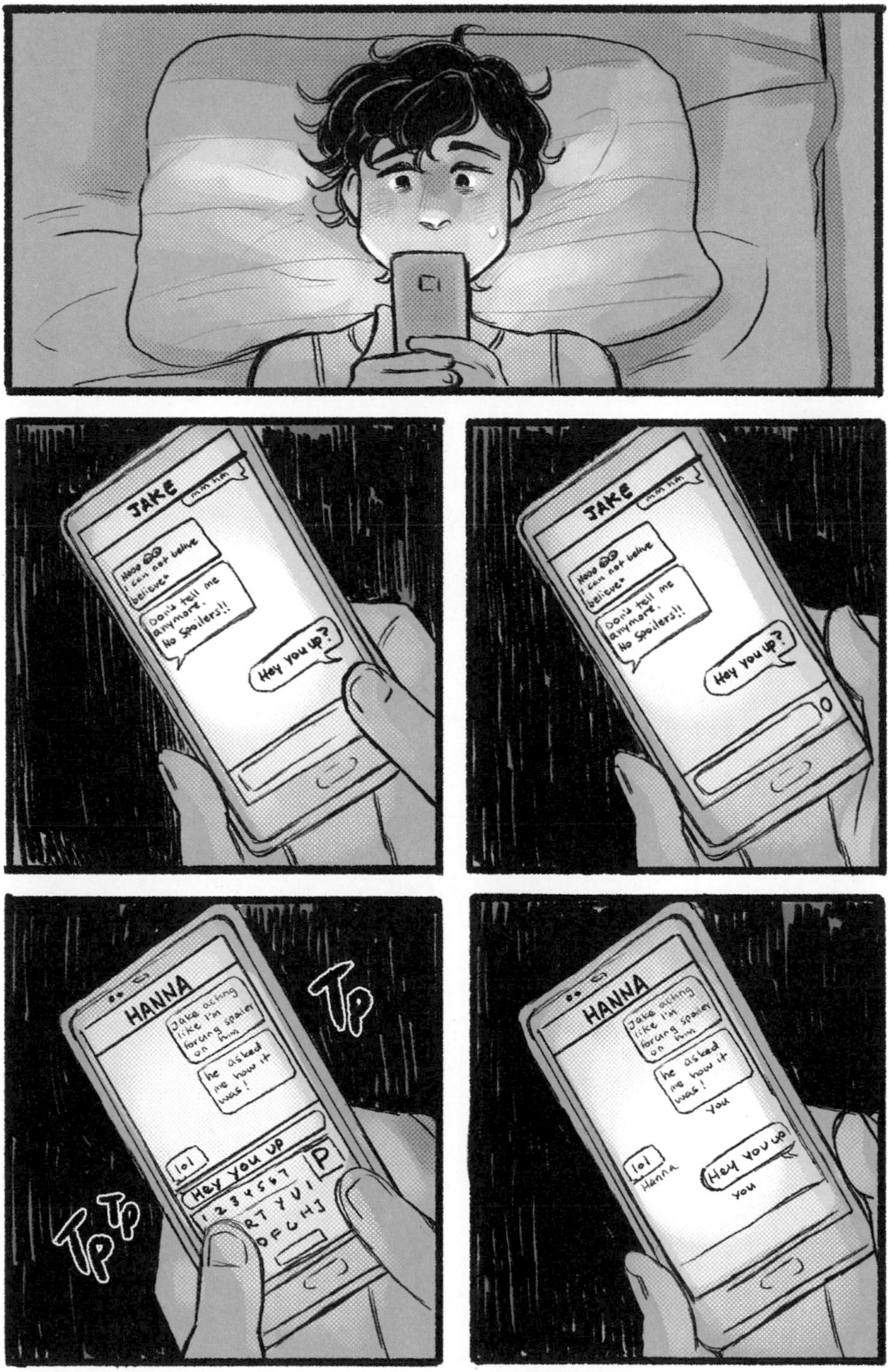
JAKE
mm hm
Nooo I can not belive believe*
Don't tell me anymore. No Spoilers!!
Hey you up?
JAKE
mm hm
Nooo I can not belive believe*
Don't tell me anymore. No Spoilers!!
Hey you up?
HANNA
Jake acting like I'm forcing spoiler on him
he asked me how it was!
lol
Hey you up
Tp
Tp Tp
HANNA
Jake acting like I'm forcing spoiler on him
he asked me how it was!
You
lol
Hanna
Hey you up
you

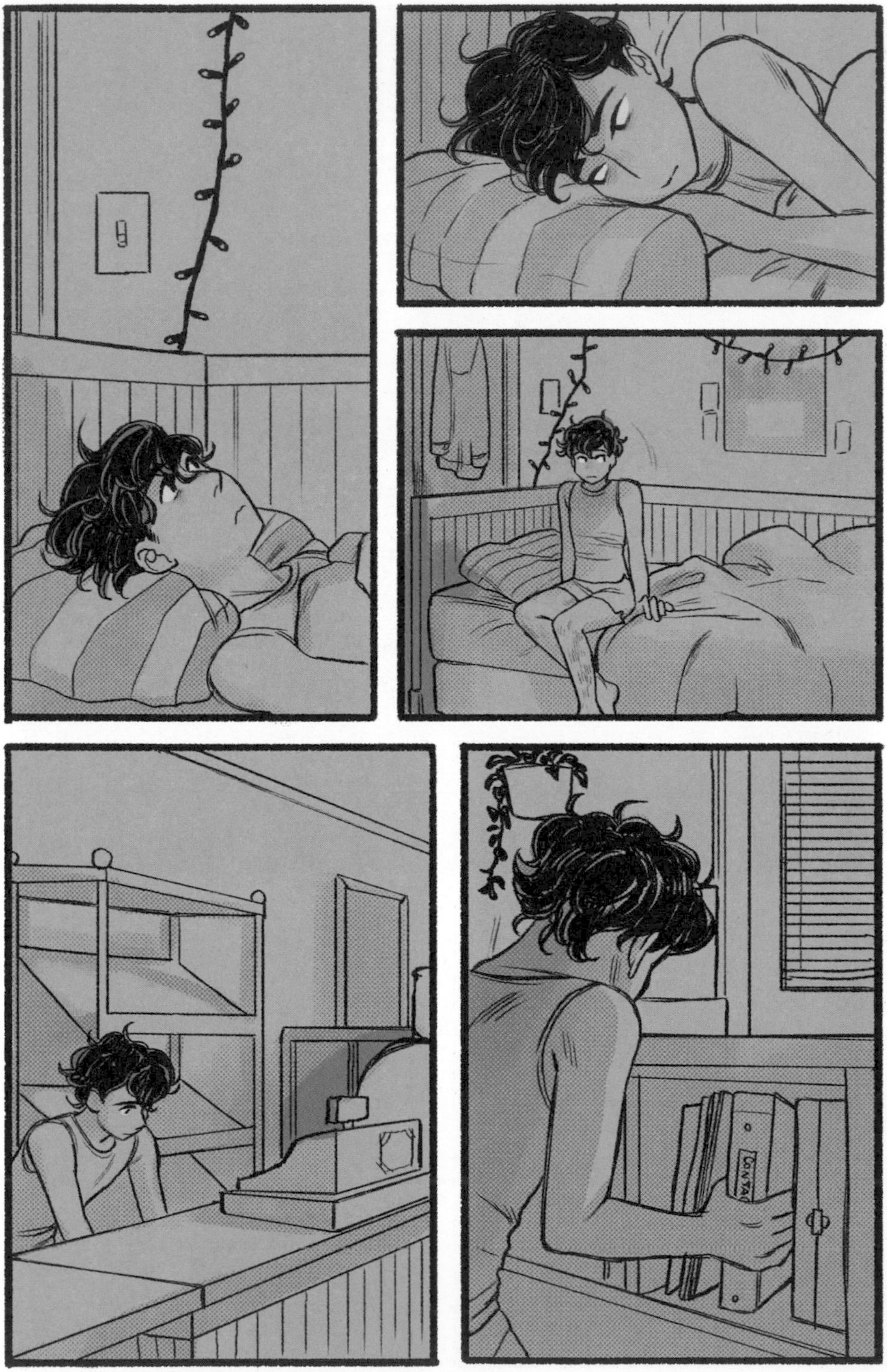

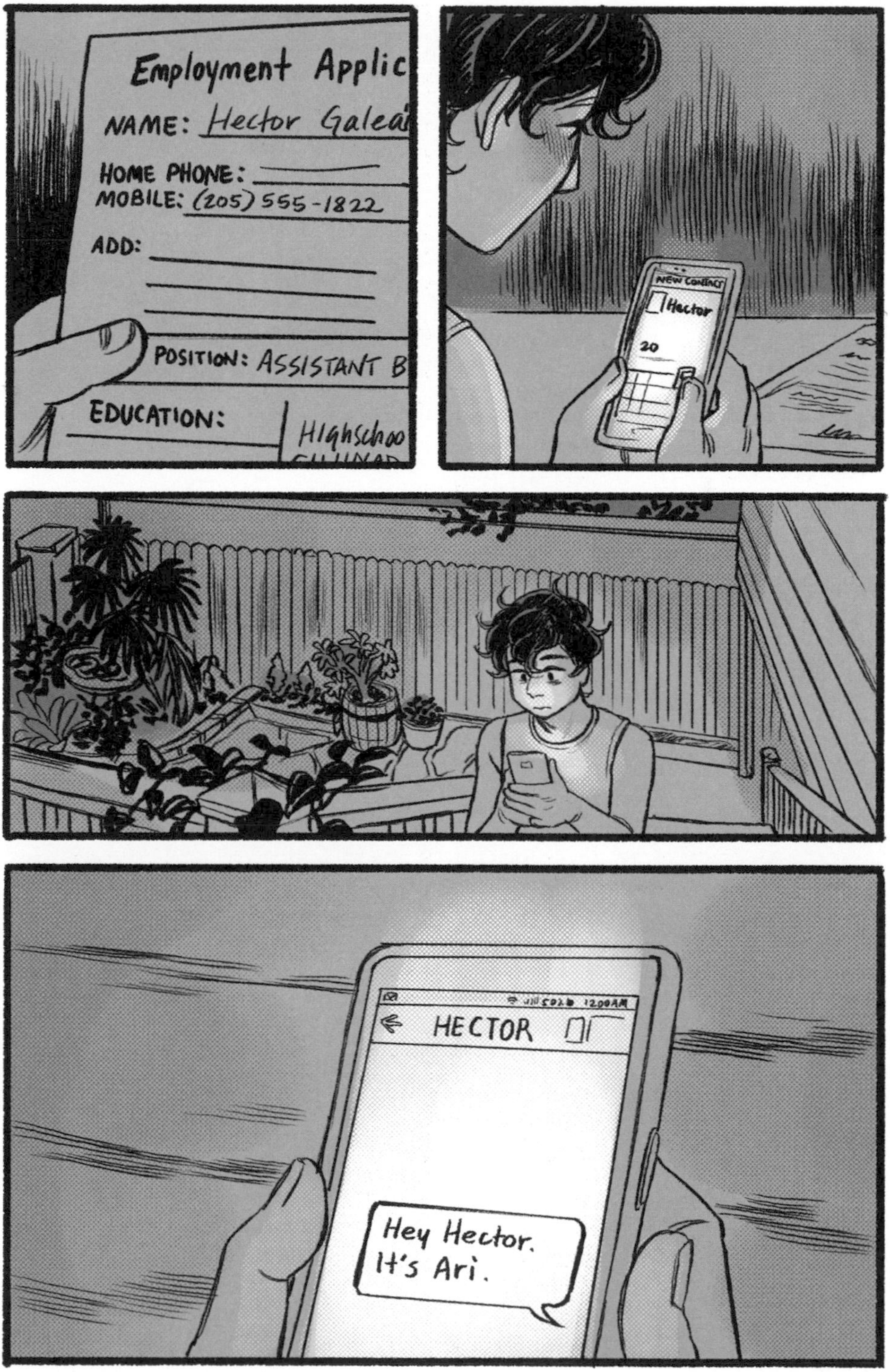
Employment Applic
NAME: Hector Galea
HOME PHONE:
MOBILE: (205) 555-1822
ADD:
POSITION: ASSISTANT B
EDUCATION:
Highschoo
NEW CONTACT
Hector
20
HECTOR
Hey Hector. It's Ari.

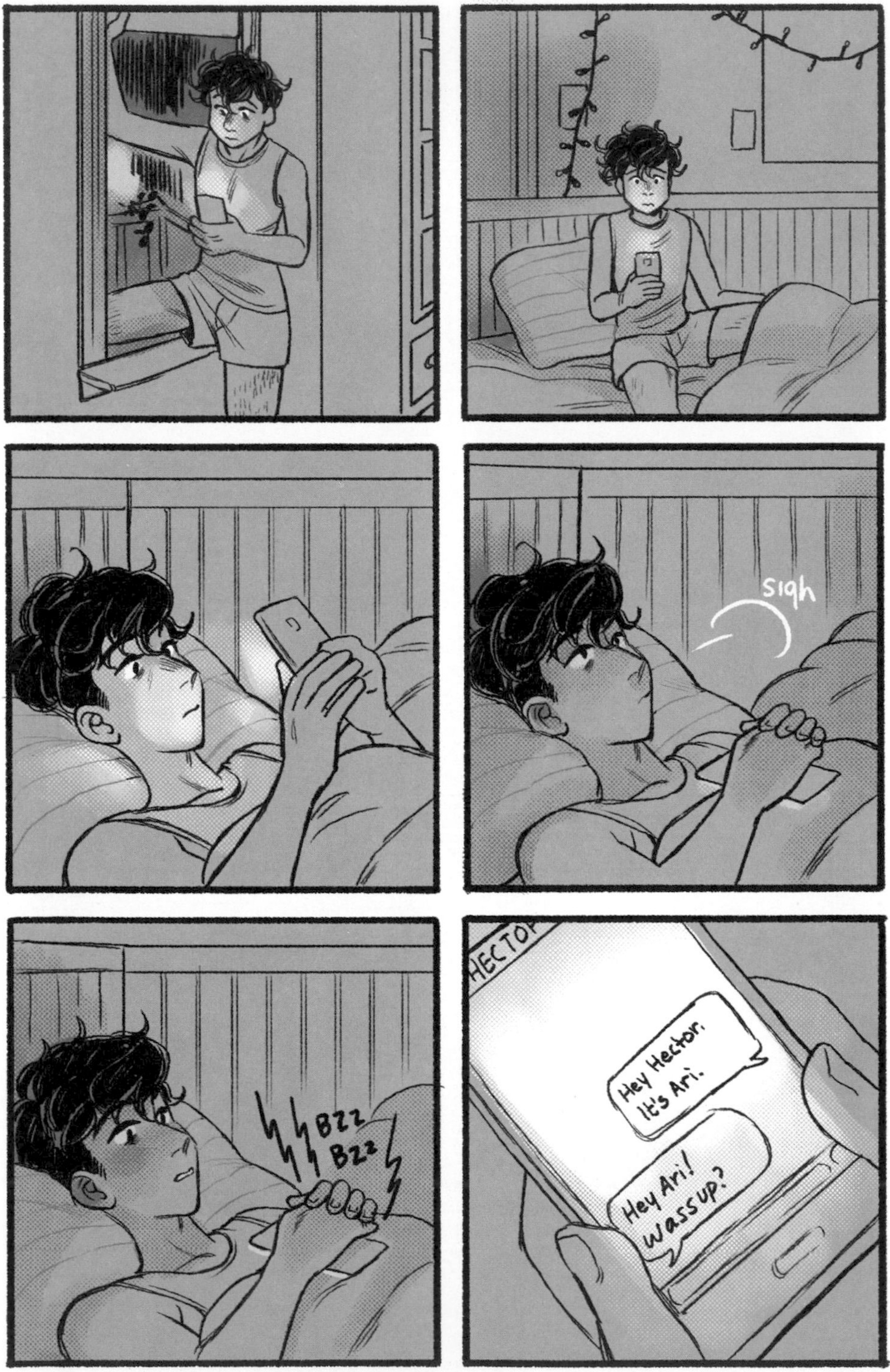

sigh
BZZ
BZZ
HECTOR
Hey Hector.
It's Ari.
Hey Ari!
Wassup?

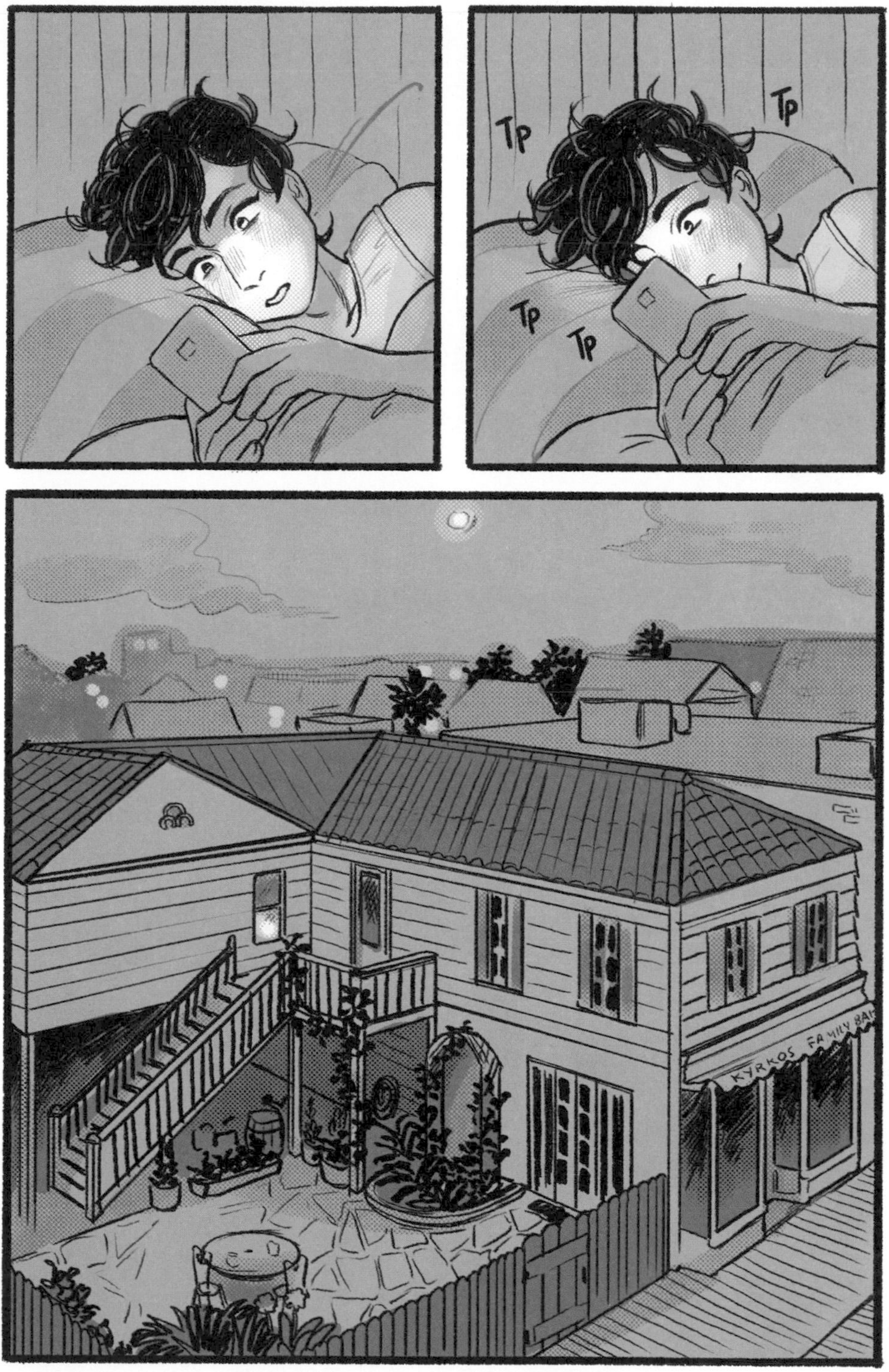
Tp
Tp
Tp
Tp
KYRKOS FAMILY

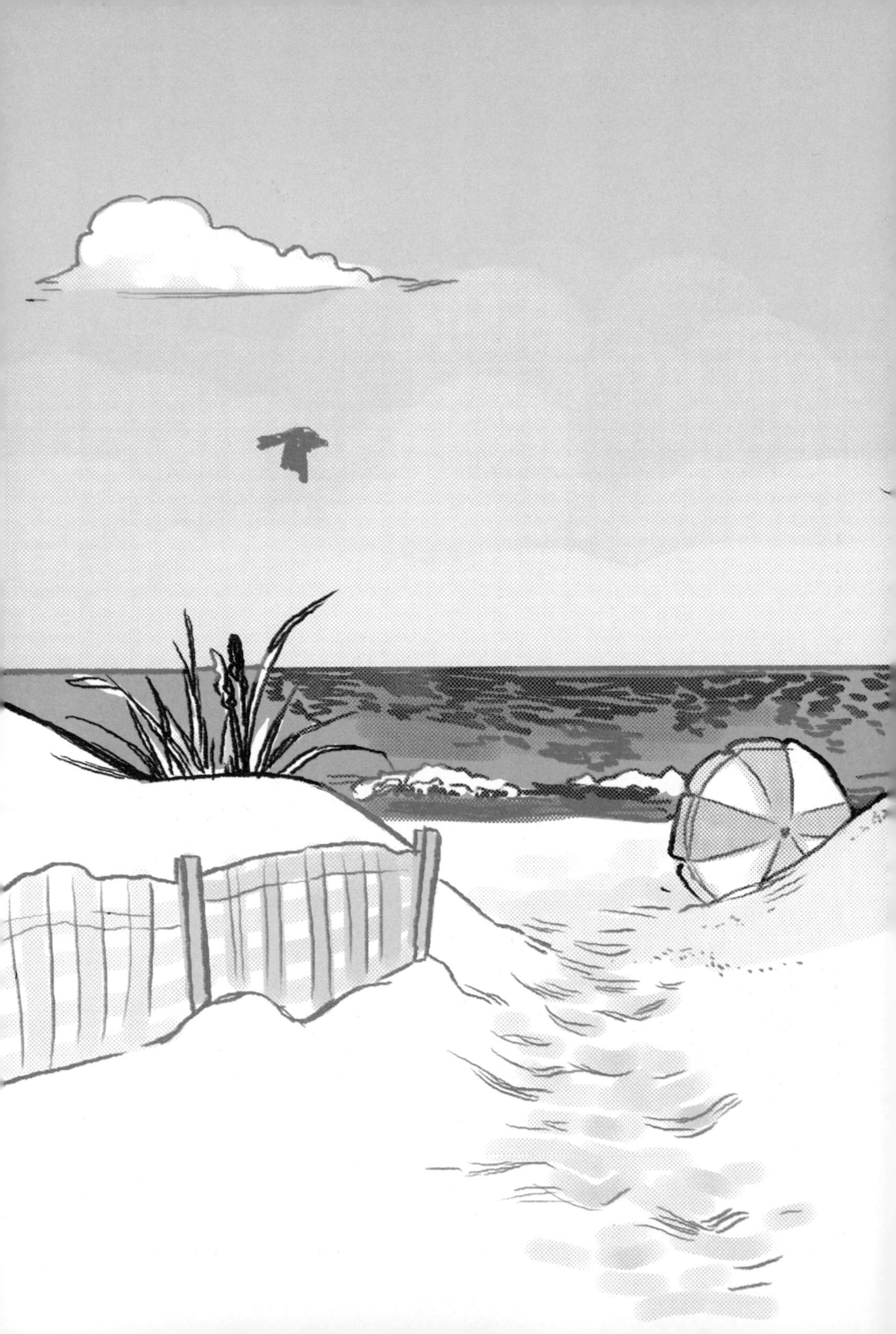

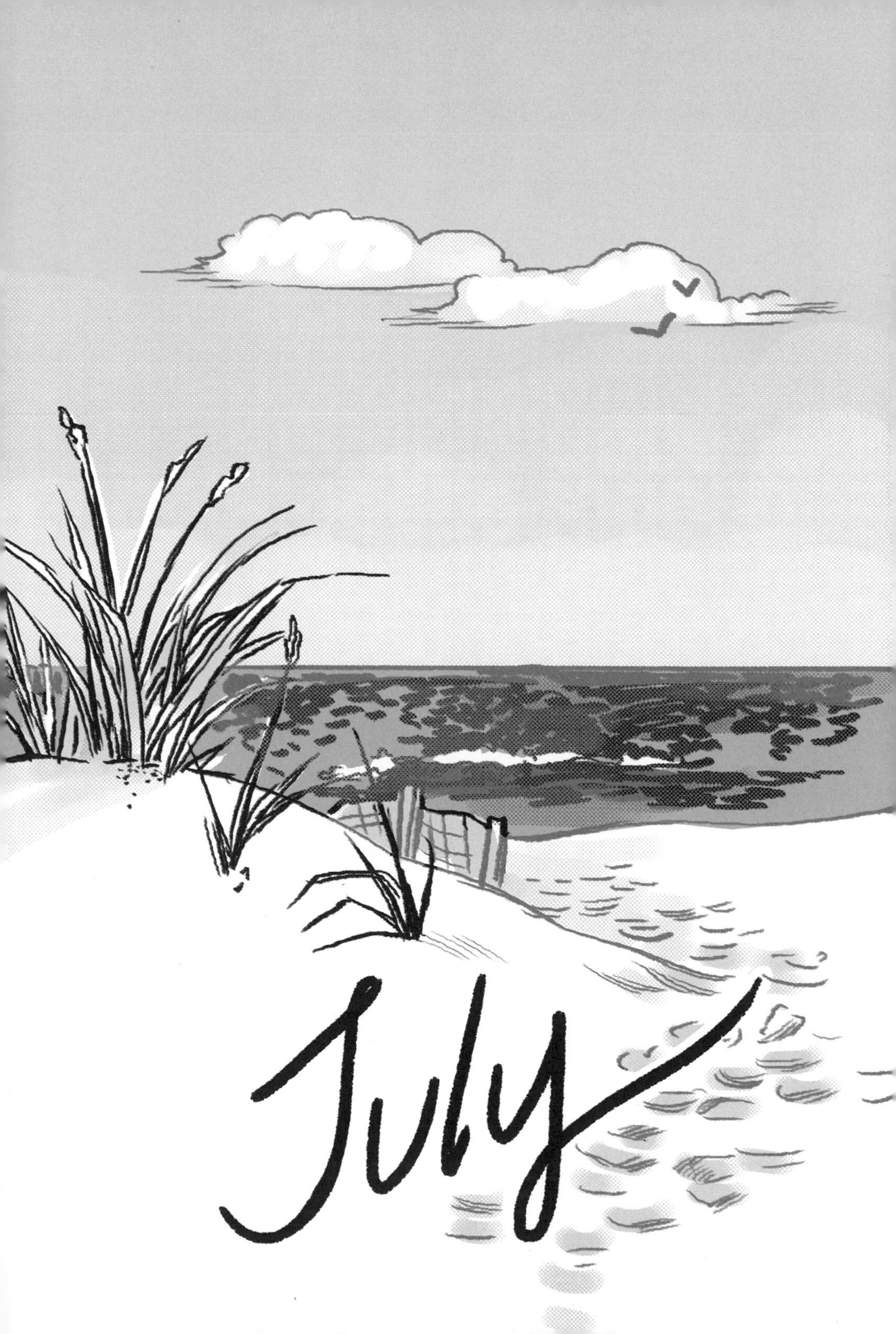
July

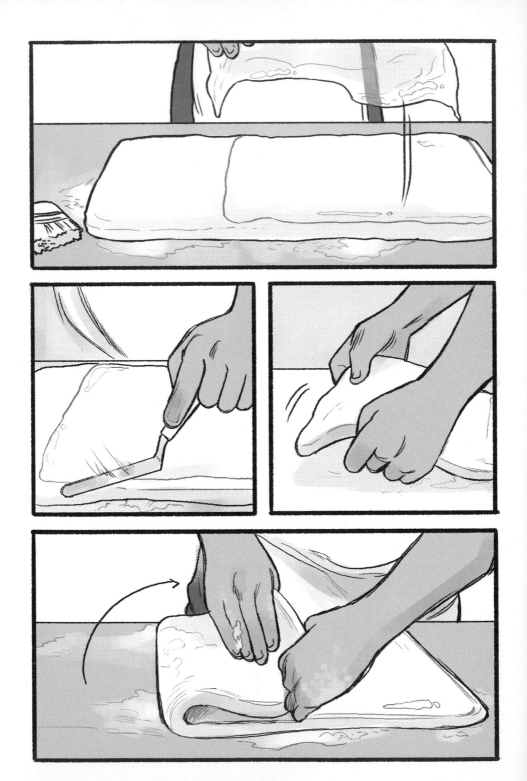

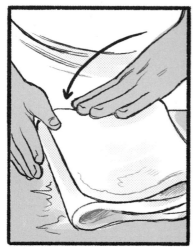

Wipe

HECTOR!

WHAT'S UP, BOSS?

HaHaHa

WE NEED MORE SOURDOUGH ROLLS.

HOW MUCH LONGER?

FIVE MINUTES, PROBABLY?

LEMME FINISH LAMINATING THIS CROISSANT DOUGH AND I'LL BRING THEM OUT.

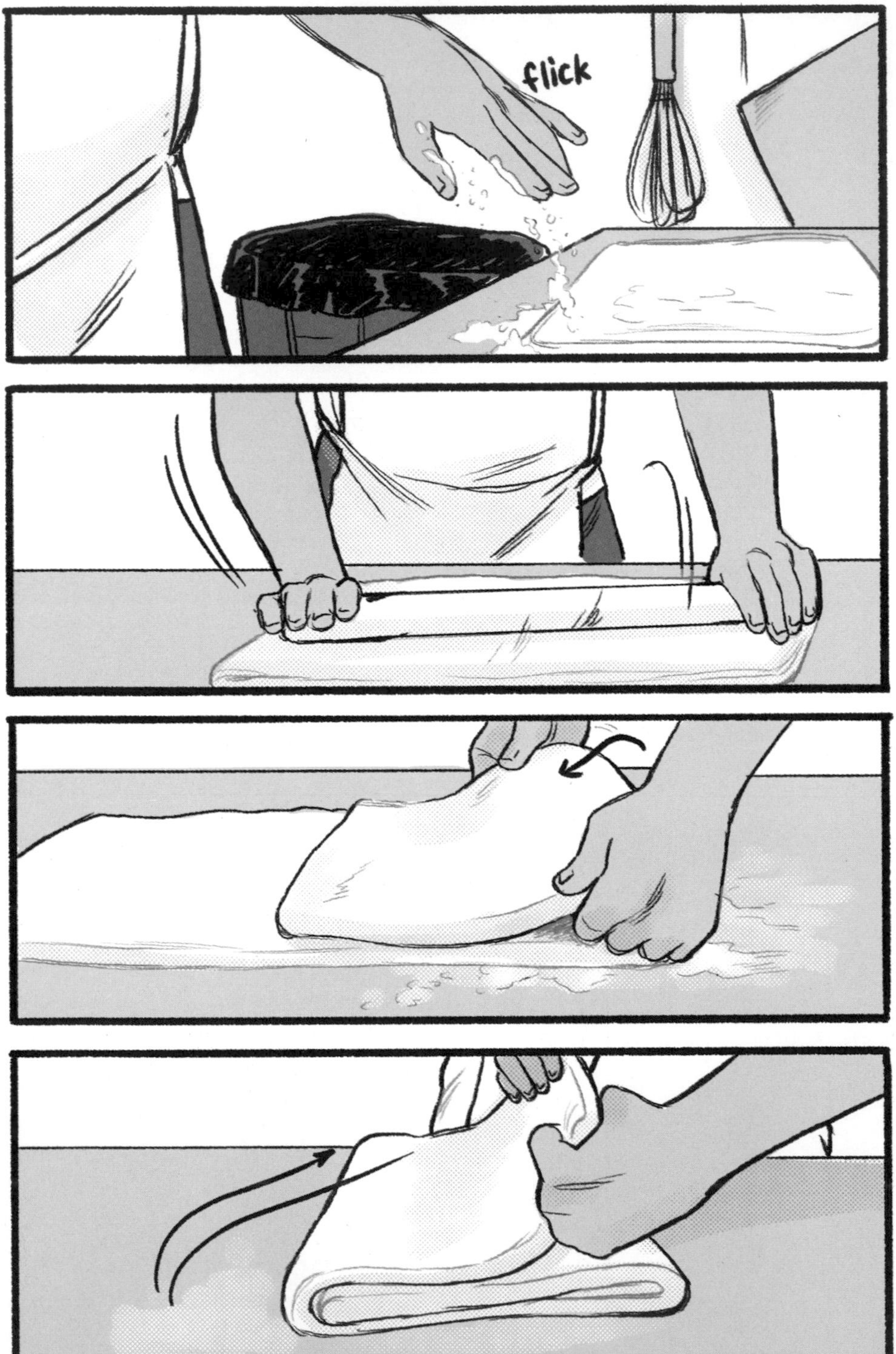
flick

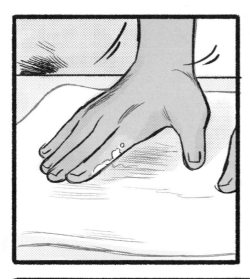

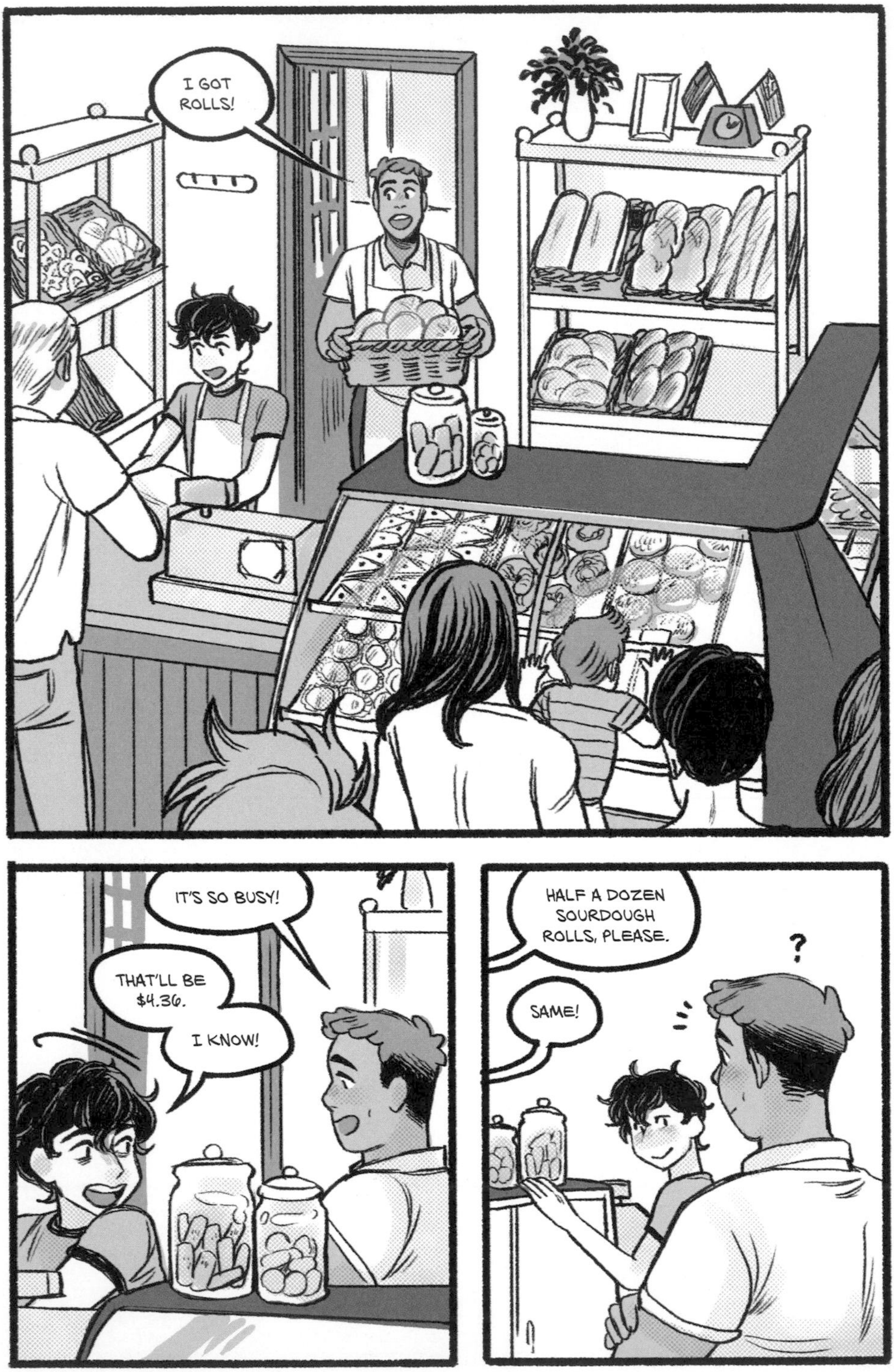
I GOT ROLLS!
IT'S SO BUSY!
THAT'LL BE $4.36.
I KNOW!
HALF A DOZEN SOURDOUGH ROLLS, PLEASE.
SAME!
?

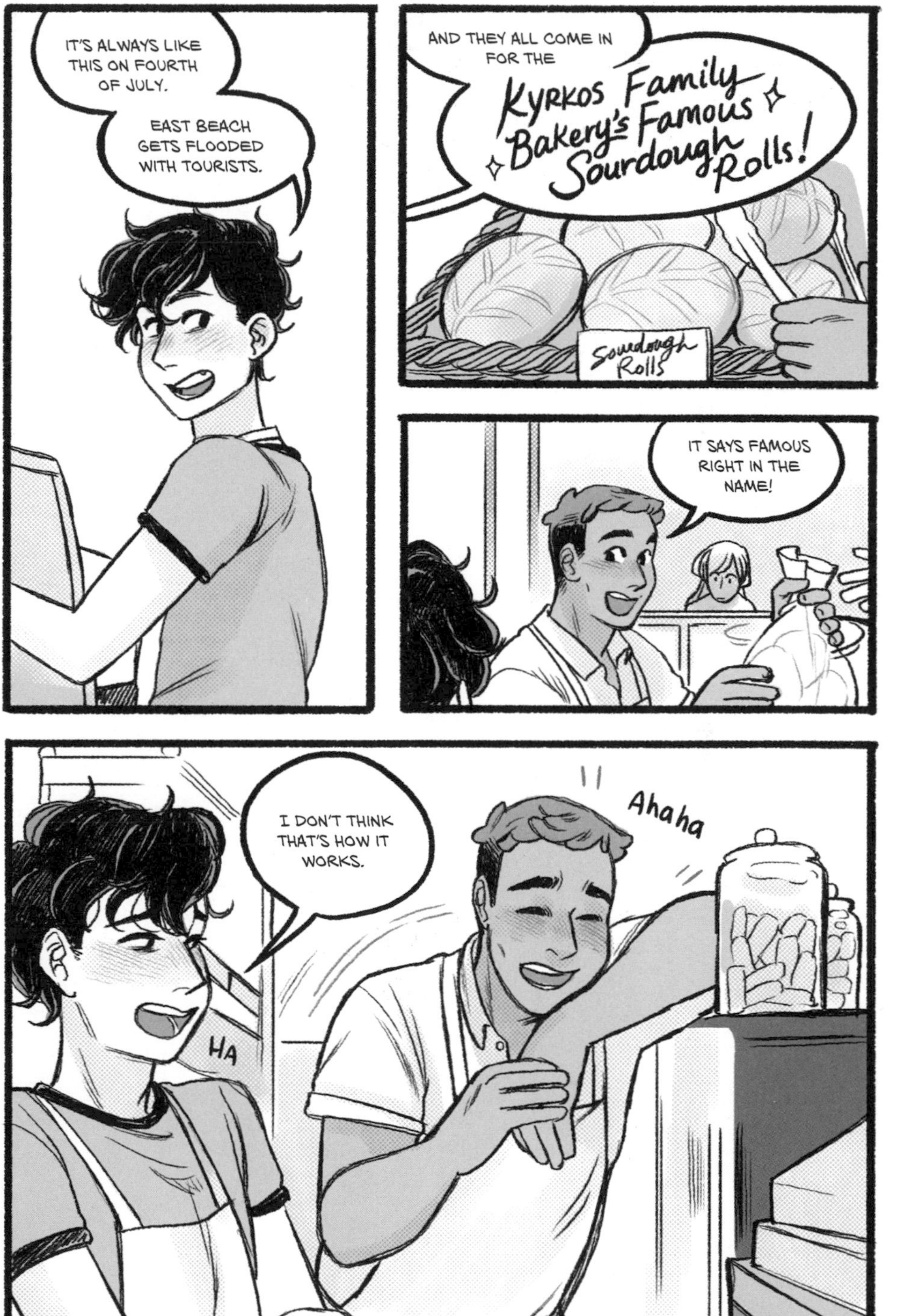
IT'S ALWAYS LIKE THIS ON FOURTH OF JULY.
EAST BEACH GETS FLOODED WITH TOURISTS.
AND THEY ALL COME IN FOR THE
Kyrkos Family Bakery's Famous Sourdough Rolls!
Sourdough Rolls
IT SAYS FAMOUS RIGHT IN THE NAME!
I DON'T THINK THAT'S HOW IT WORKS.
Ahaha
HA

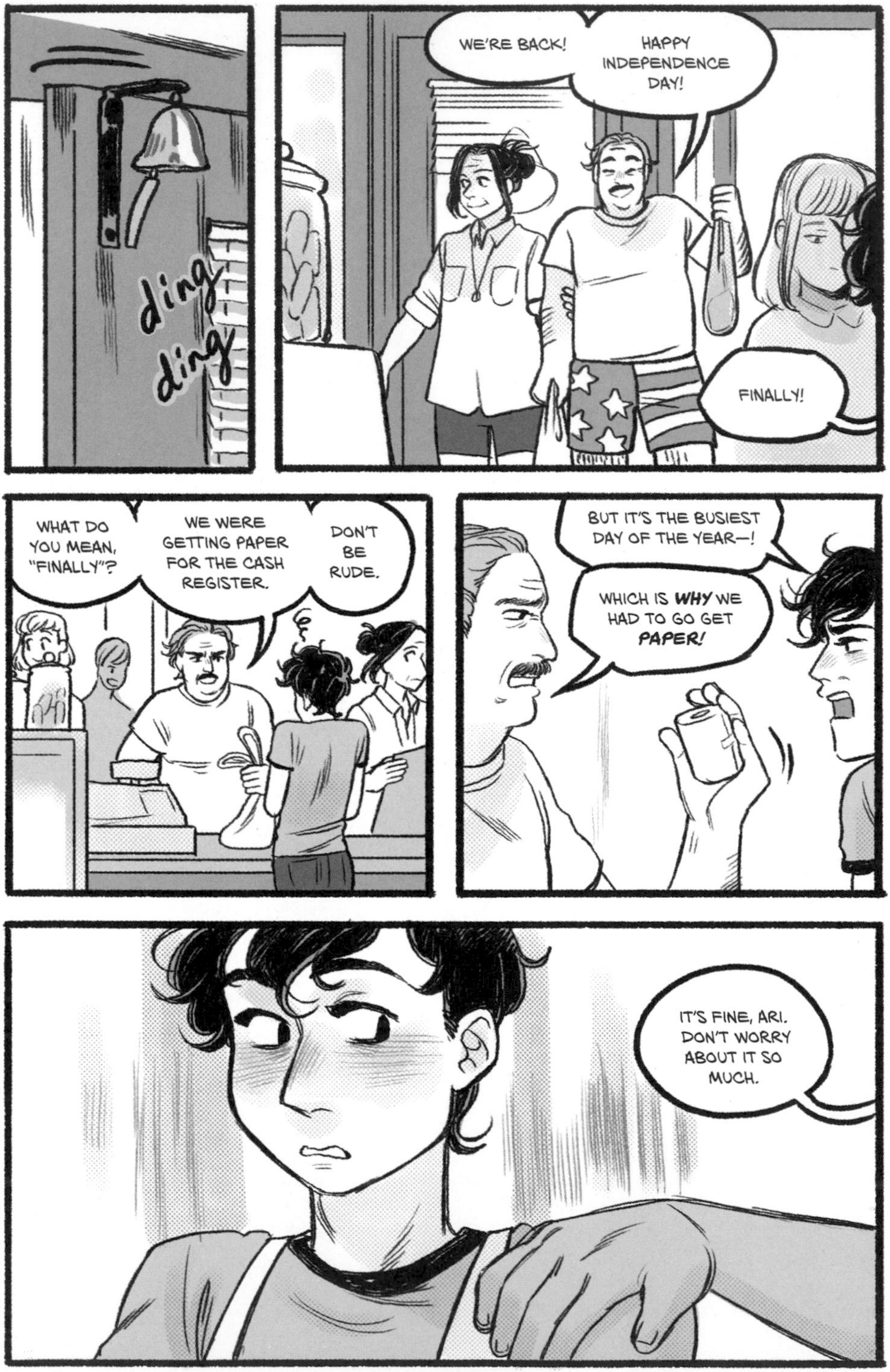
ding ding
WE'RE BACK!
HAPPY INDEPENDENCE DAY!
FINALLY!
WHAT DO YOU MEAN, "FINALLY"?
WE WERE GETTING PAPER FOR THE CASH REGISTER.
DON'T BE RUDE.
BUT IT'S THE BUSIEST DAY OF THE YEAR—!
WHICH IS **WHY** WE HAD TO GO GET **PAPER!**
IT'S FINE, ARI. DON'T WORRY ABOUT IT SO MUCH.

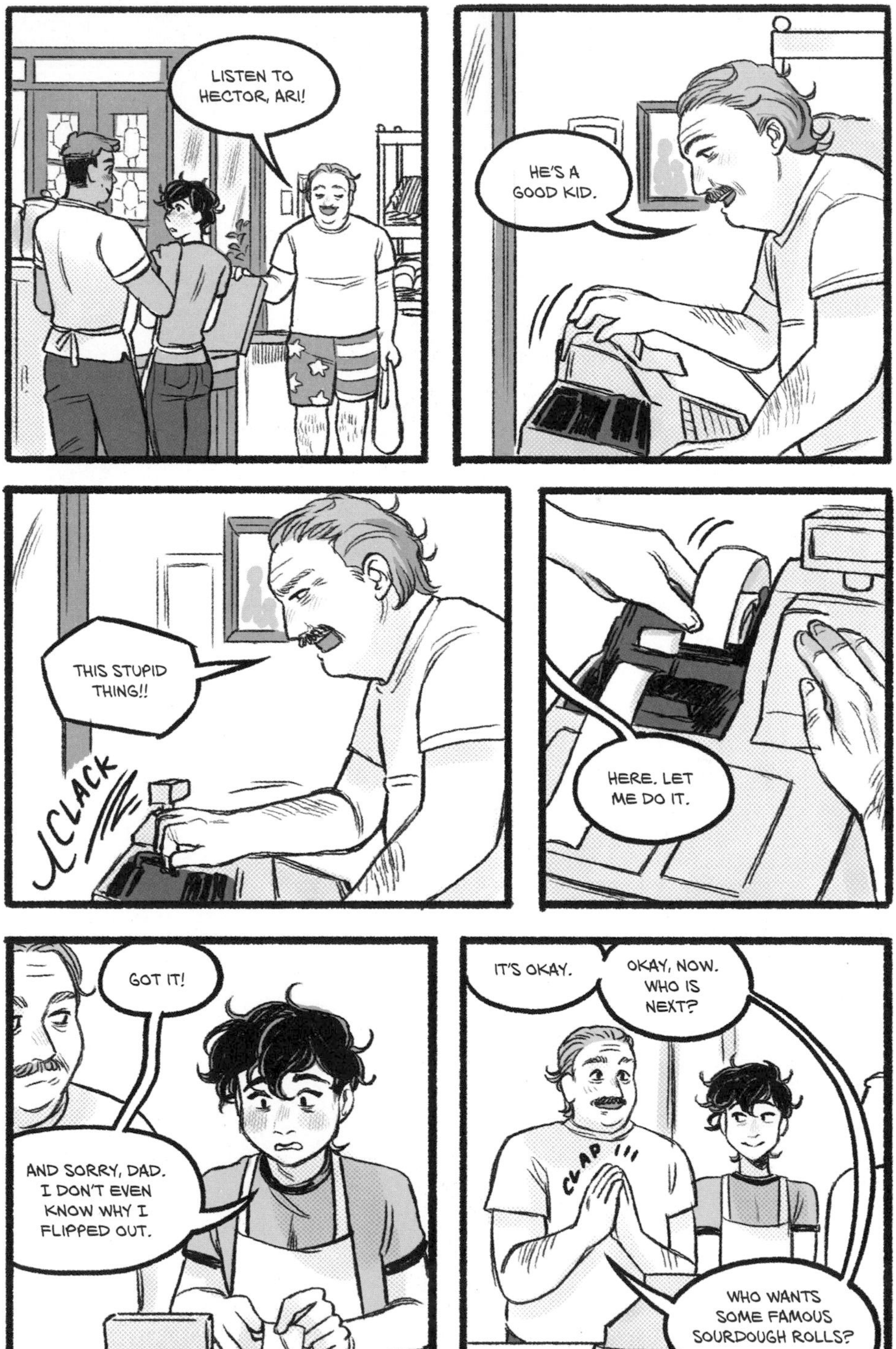
LISTEN TO HECTOR, ARI!
HE'S A GOOD KID.
THIS STUPID THING!!
CLACK
HERE. LET ME DO IT.
GOT IT!
AND SORRY, DAD. I DON'T EVEN KNOW WHY I FLIPPED OUT.
IT'S OKAY.
OKAY, NOW. WHO IS NEXT?
CLAP !!!
WHO WANTS SOME FAMOUS SOURDOUGH ROLLS?

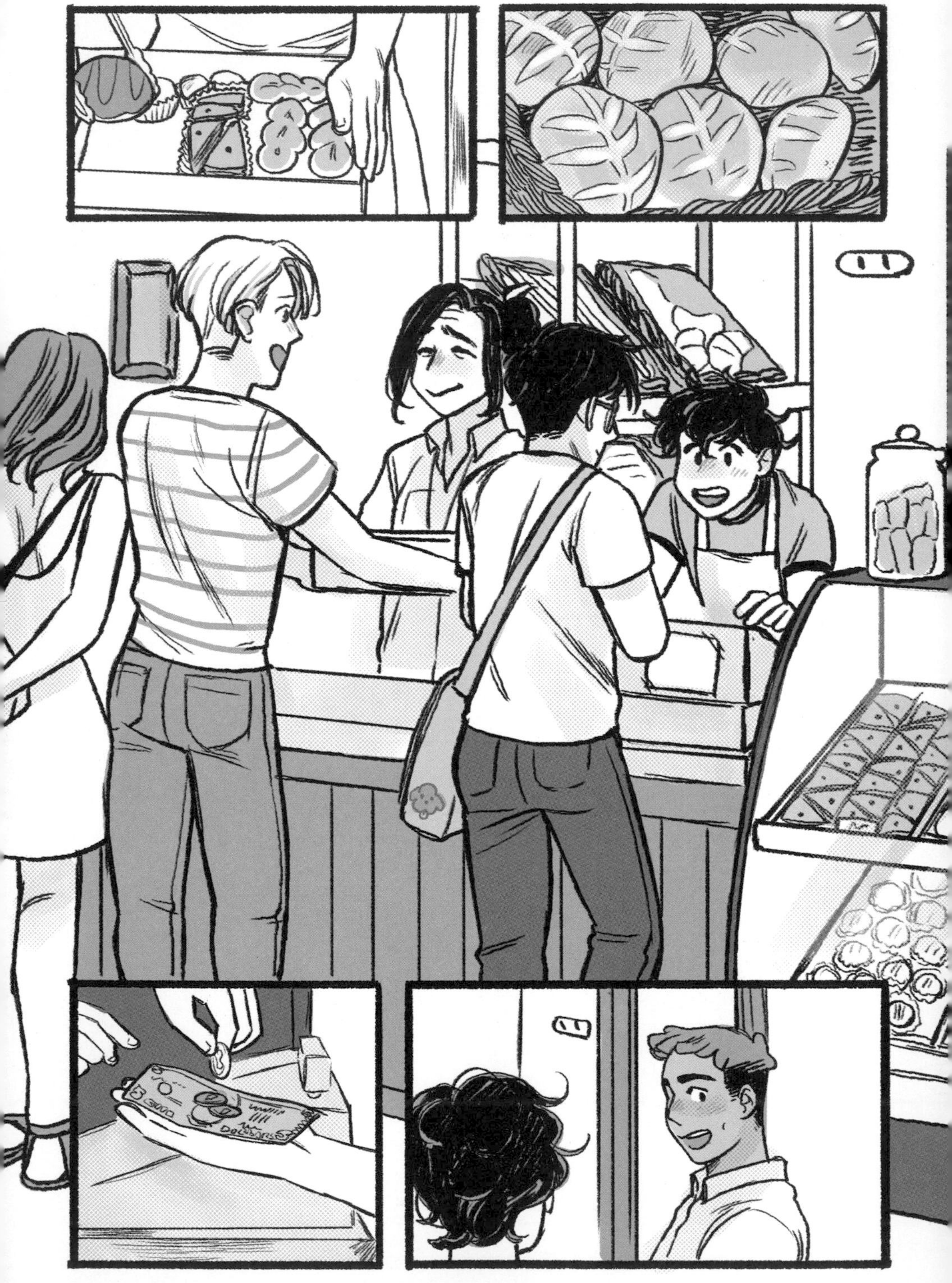

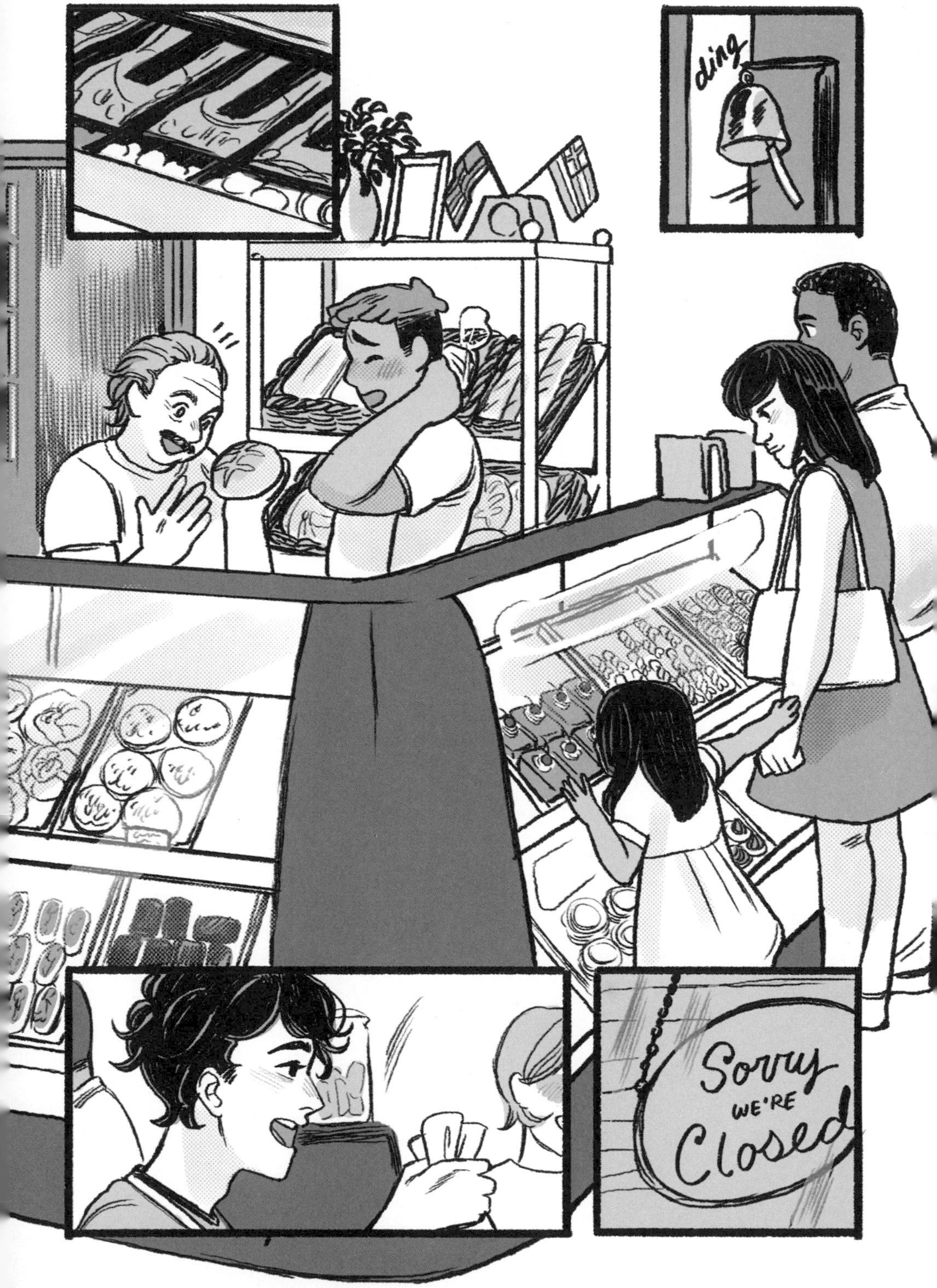
ding
Sorry
WE'RE
Closed

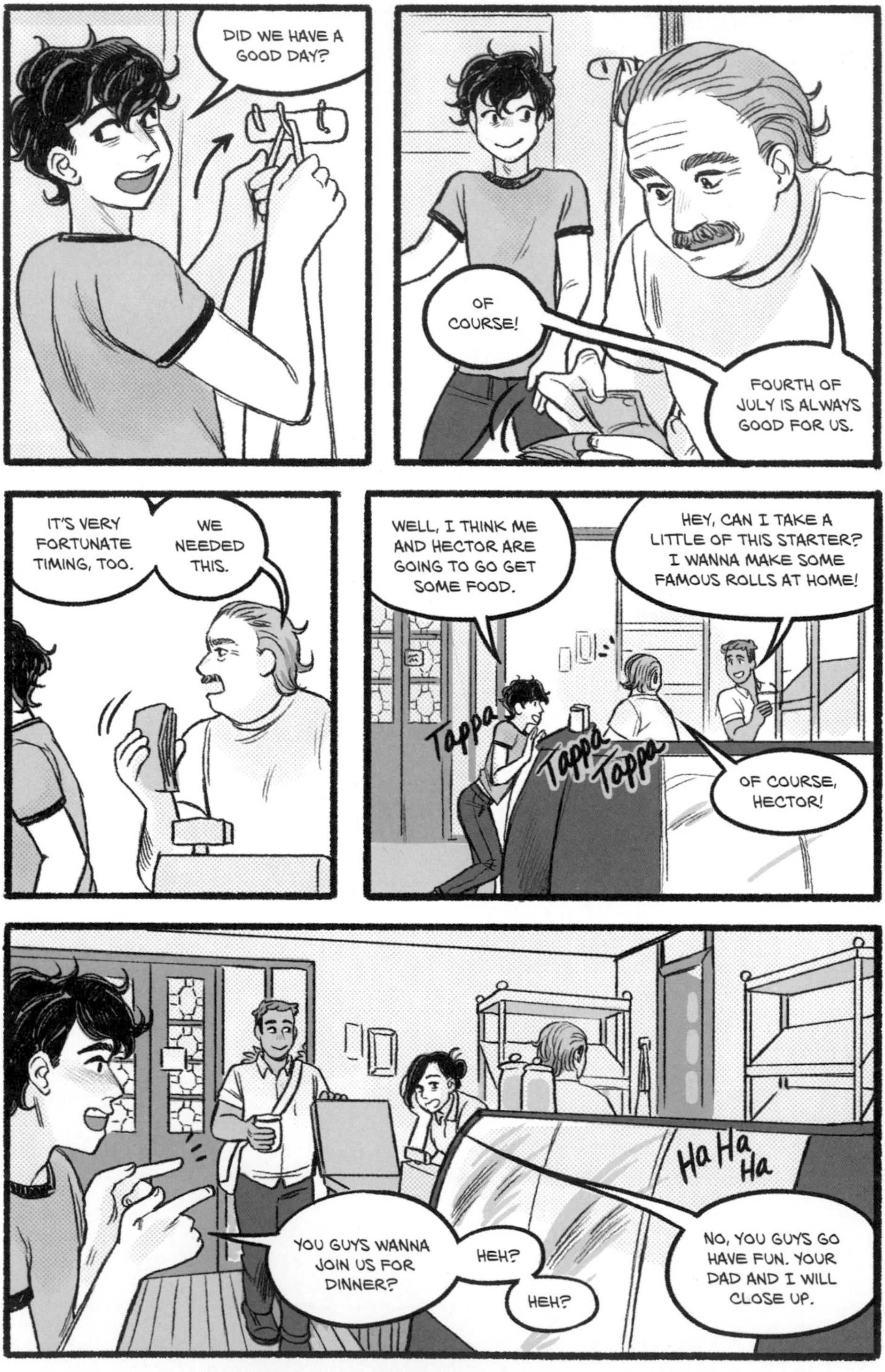
DID WE HAVE A GOOD DAY?
OF COURSE!
FOURTH OF JULY IS ALWAYS GOOD FOR US.
IT'S VERY FORTUNATE TIMING, TOO.
WE NEEDED THIS.
WELL, I THINK ME AND HECTOR ARE GOING TO GO GET SOME FOOD.
Tappa
Tappa
Tappa
HEY, CAN I TAKE A LITTLE OF THIS STARTER? I WANNA MAKE SOME FAMOUS ROLLS AT HOME!
OF COURSE, HECTOR!
Ha Ha Ha
YOU GUYS WANNA JOIN US FOR DINNER?
HEH?
HEH?
NO, YOU GUYS GO HAVE FUN. YOUR DAD AND I WILL CLOSE UP.

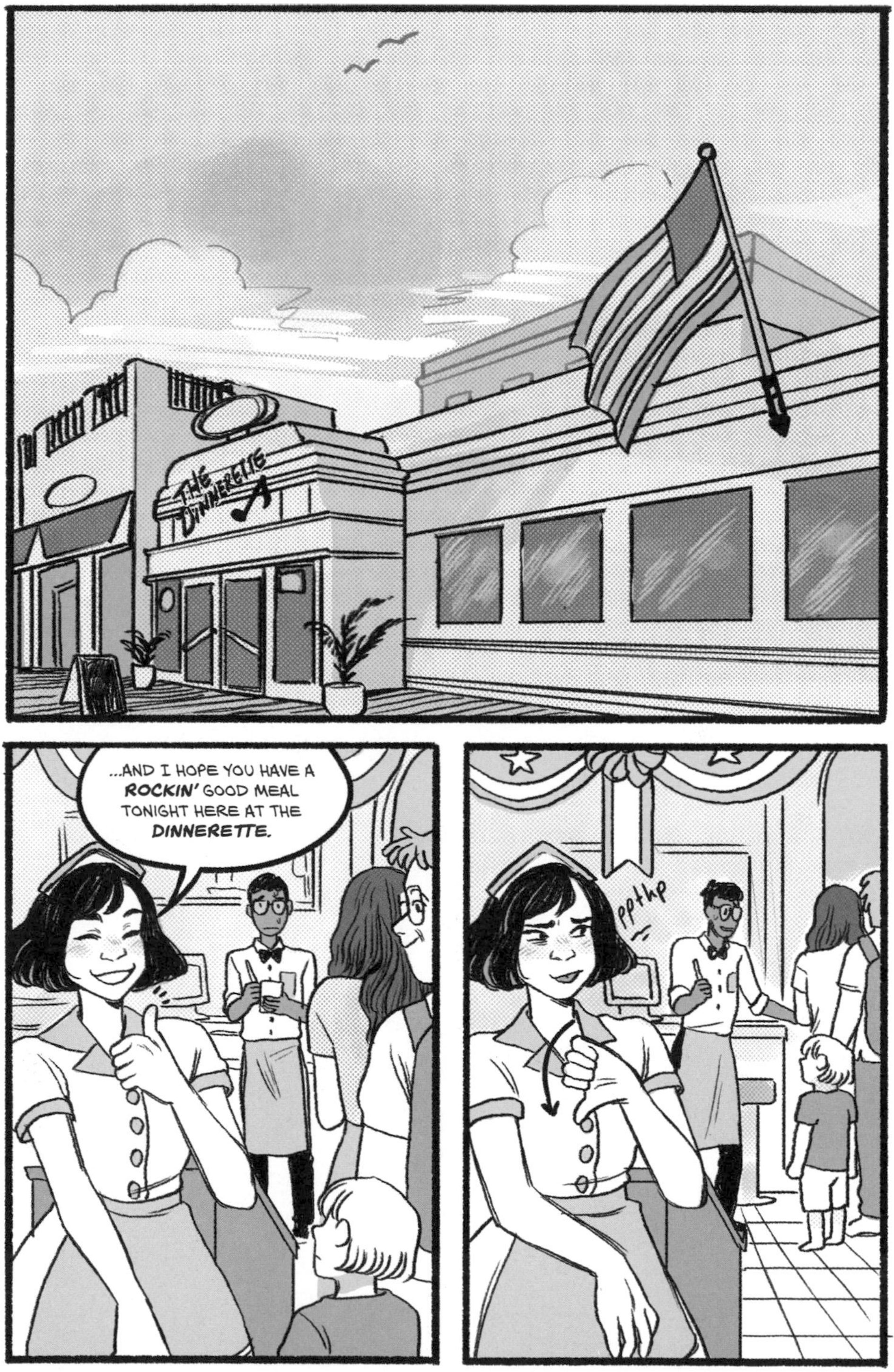
THE DINNERETTE
...AND I HOPE YOU HAVE A ROCKIN' GOOD MEAL TONIGHT HERE AT THE DINNERETTE.
ppthp

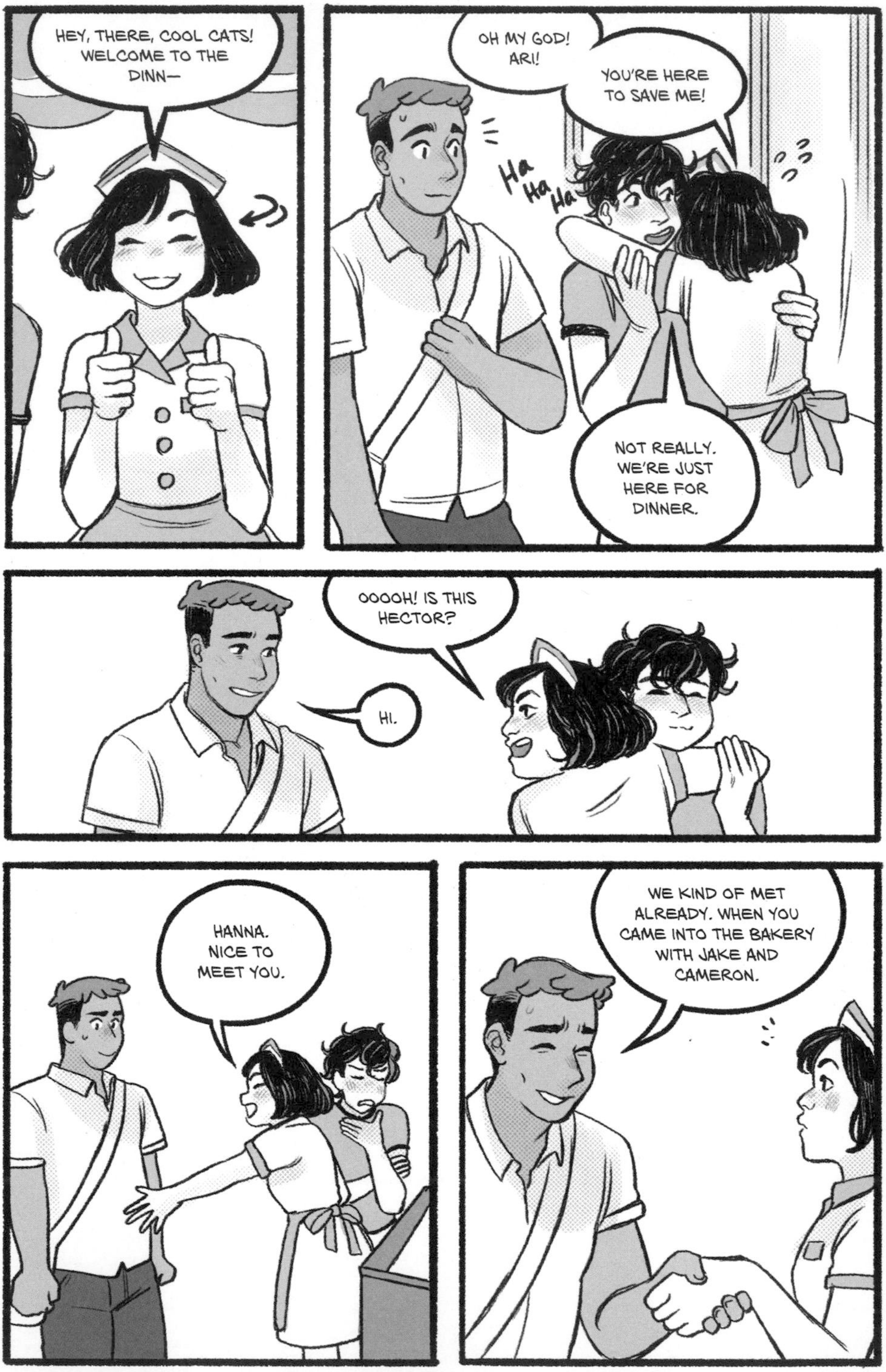
HEY, THERE, COOL CATS! WELCOME TO THE DINN—
OH MY GOD! ARI!
YOU'RE HERE TO SAVE ME!
Ha Ha Ha
NOT REALLY. WE'RE JUST HERE FOR DINNER.
OOOOH! IS THIS HECTOR?
HI.
HANNA. NICE TO MEET YOU.
WE KIND OF MET ALREADY. WHEN YOU CAME INTO THE BAKERY WITH JAKE AND CAMERON.

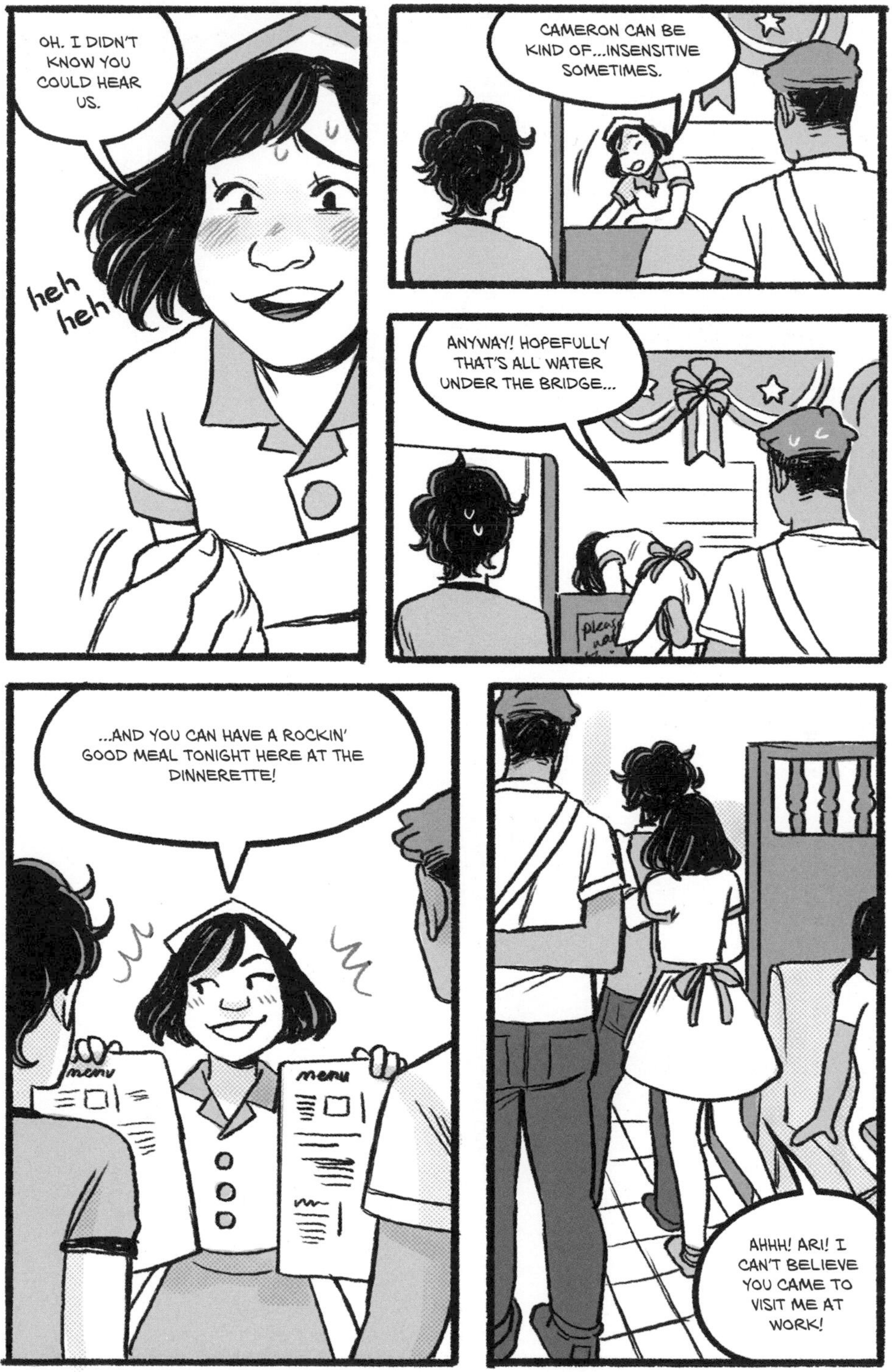
OH. I DIDN'T KNOW YOU COULD HEAR US.
heh heh
CAMERON CAN BE KIND OF...INSENSITIVE SOMETIMES.
ANYWAY! HOPEFULLY THAT'S ALL WATER UNDER THE BRIDGE...
...AND YOU CAN HAVE A ROCKIN' GOOD MEAL TONIGHT HERE AT THE DINNERETTE!
menu
menu
AHHH! ARI! I CAN'T BELIEVE YOU CAME TO VISIT ME AT WORK!

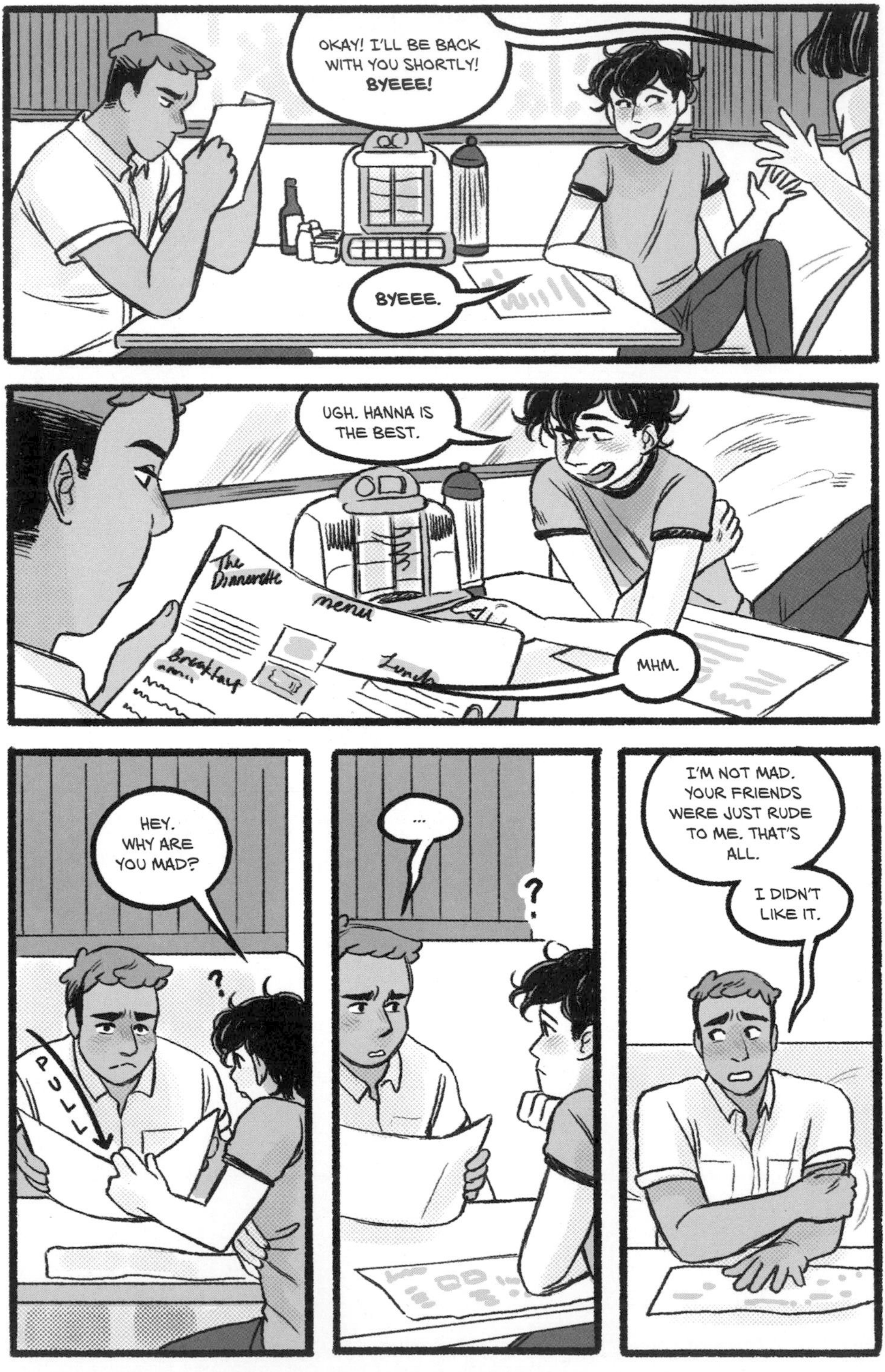
OKAY! I'LL BE BACK WITH YOU SHORTLY! **BYEEE!**
BYEEE.
UGH. HANNA IS THE BEST.
The Dinnerette menu
Breakfast
Lunch
MHM.
HEY. WHY ARE YOU MAD?
?
PULL
...
?
I'M NOT MAD. YOUR FRIENDS WERE JUST RUDE TO ME. THAT'S ALL.
I DIDN'T LIKE IT.

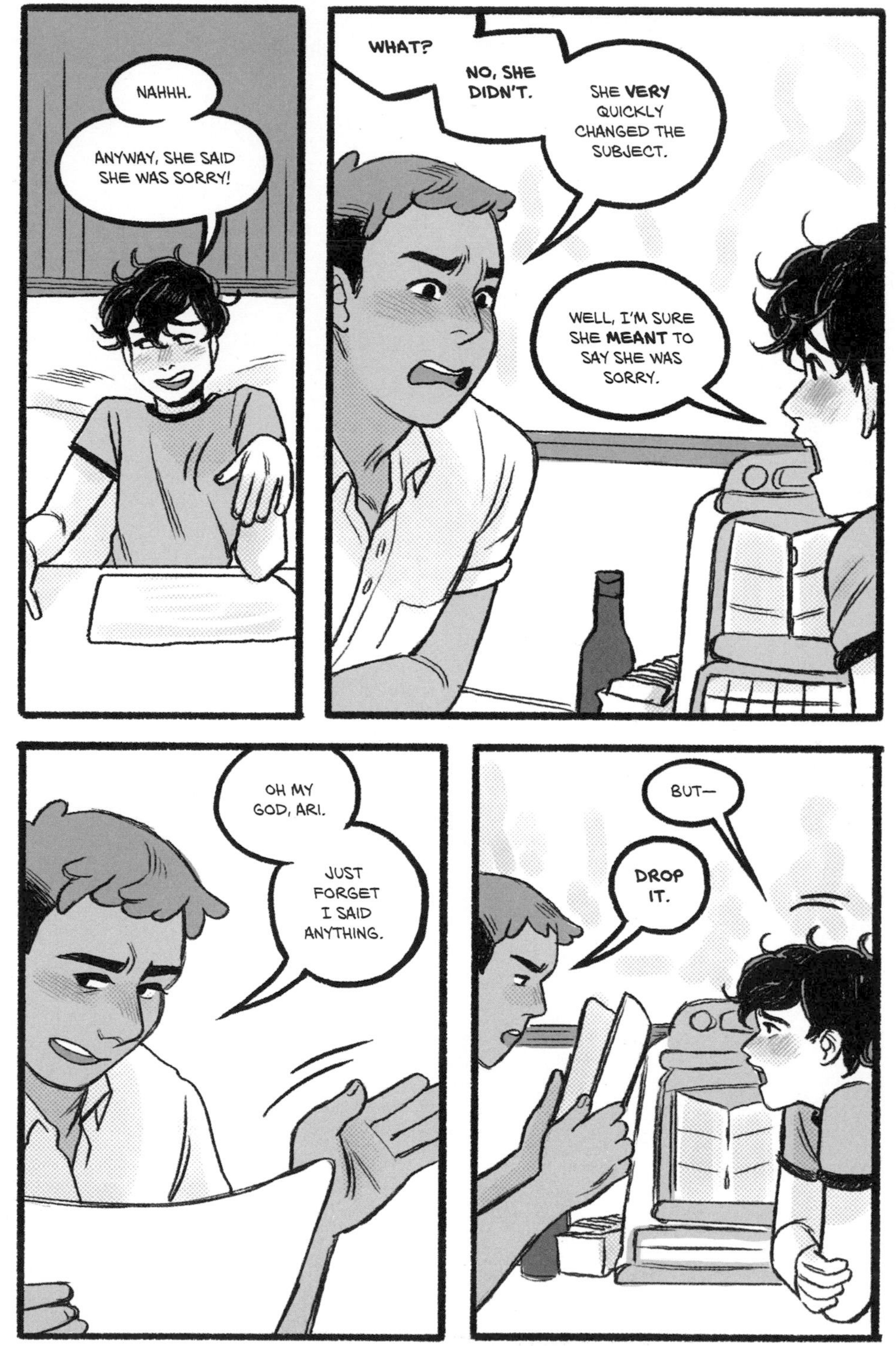
NAHHH.
ANYWAY, SHE SAID SHE WAS SORRY!
WHAT?
NO, SHE DIDN'T.
SHE VERY QUICKLY CHANGED THE SUBJECT.
WELL, I'M SURE SHE MEANT TO SAY SHE WAS SORRY.
OH MY GOD, ARI.
JUST FORGET I SAID ANYTHING.
BUT—
DROP IT.

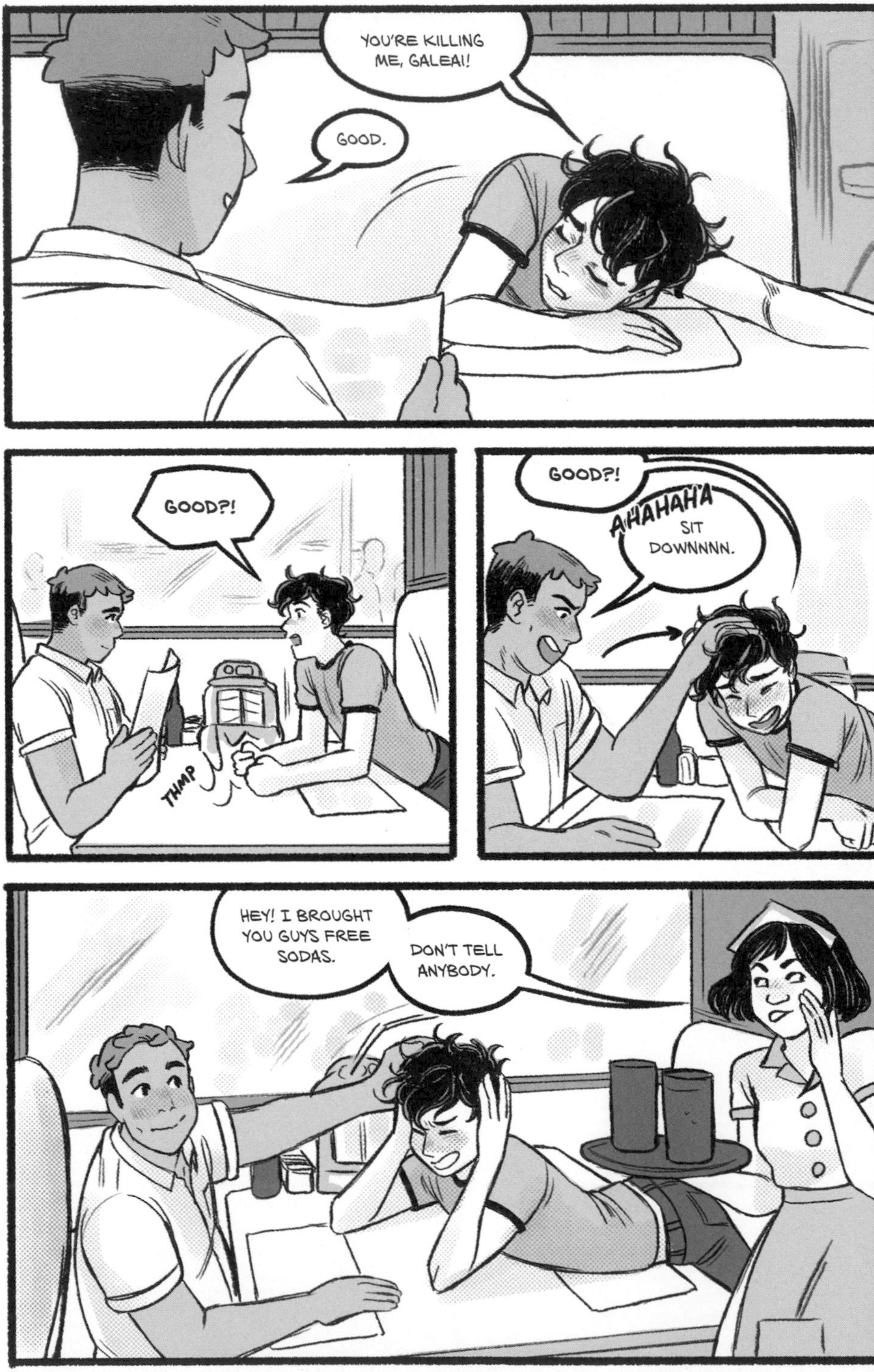
YOU'RE KILLING ME, GALEAI!
GOOD.
GOOD?!
THMP
GOOD?!
AHAHAHA
SIT DOWNNNN.
HEY! I BROUGHT YOU GUYS FREE SODAS.
DON'T TELL ANYBODY.

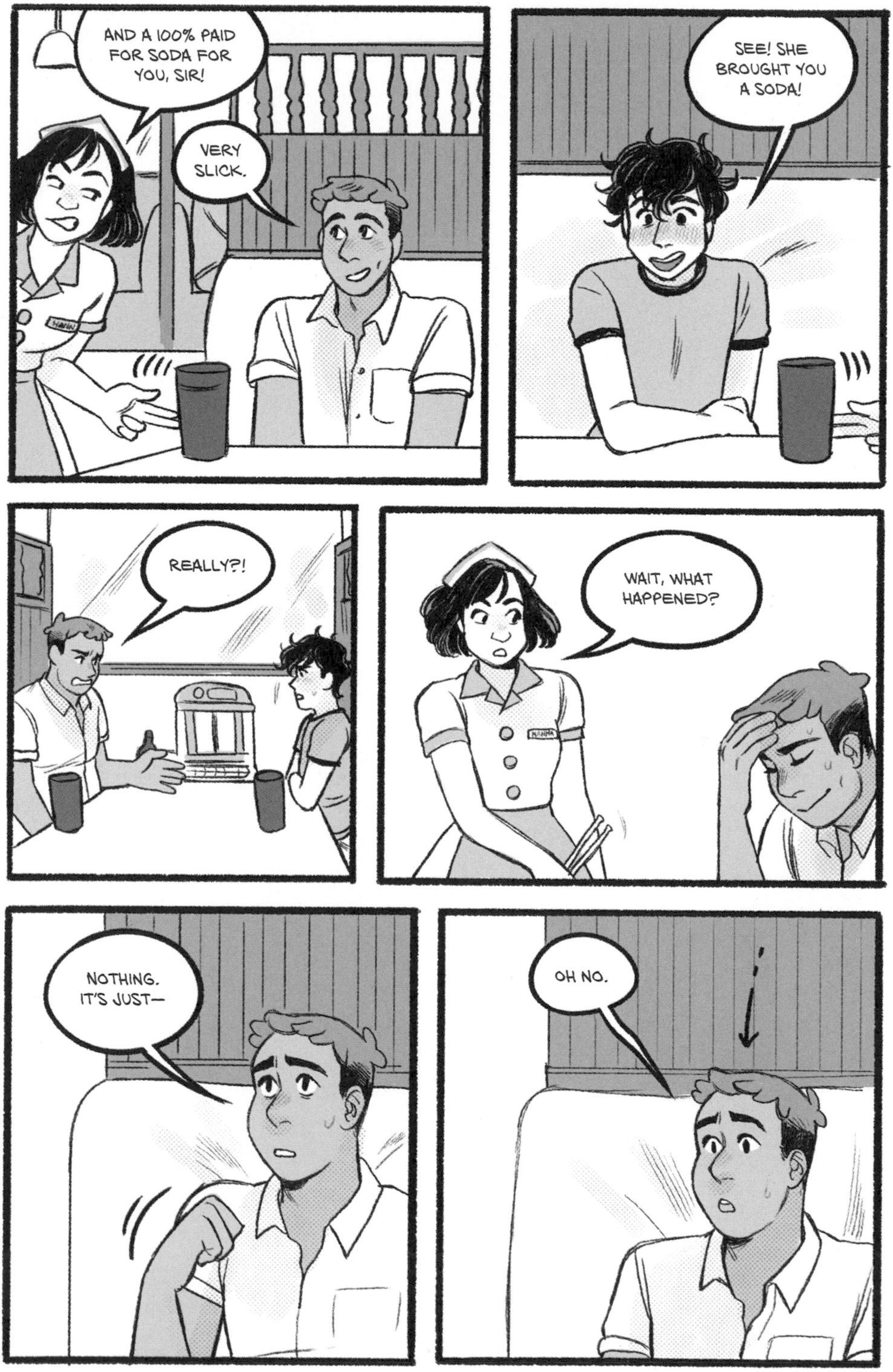
AND A 100% PAID FOR SODA FOR YOU, SIR!
VERY SLICK.
SEE! SHE BROUGHT YOU A SODA!
REALLY?!
WAIT, WHAT HAPPENED?
NOTHING. IT'S JUST—
OH NO.

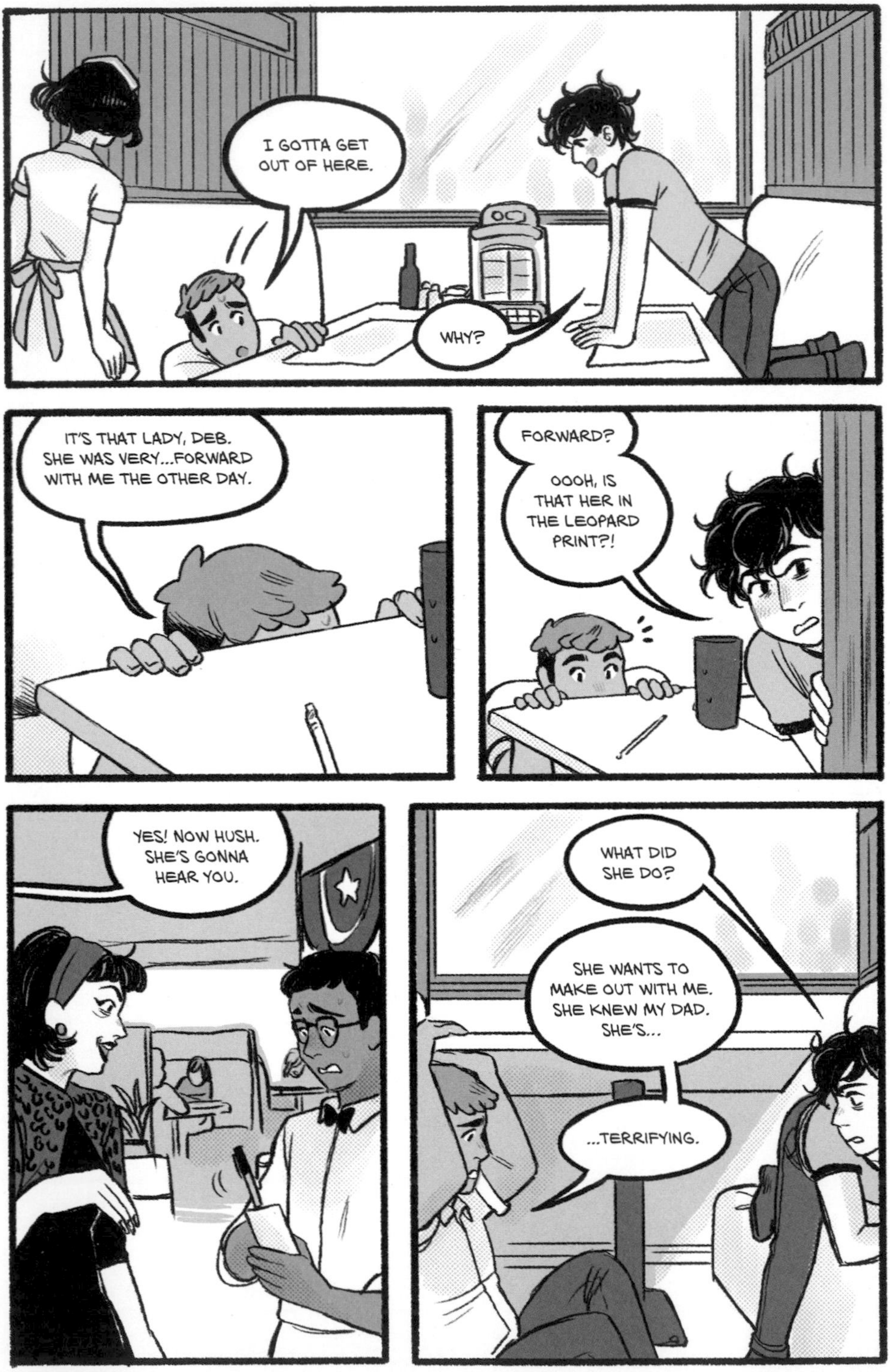
I GOTTA GET OUT OF HERE.
WHY?
IT'S THAT LADY, DEB. SHE WAS VERY...FORWARD WITH ME THE OTHER DAY.
FORWARD?
OOOH, IS THAT HER IN THE LEOPARD PRINT?!
YES! NOW HUSH. SHE'S GONNA HEAR YOU.
WHAT DID SHE DO?
SHE WANTS TO MAKE OUT WITH ME. SHE KNEW MY DAD. SHE'S...
...TERRIFYING.

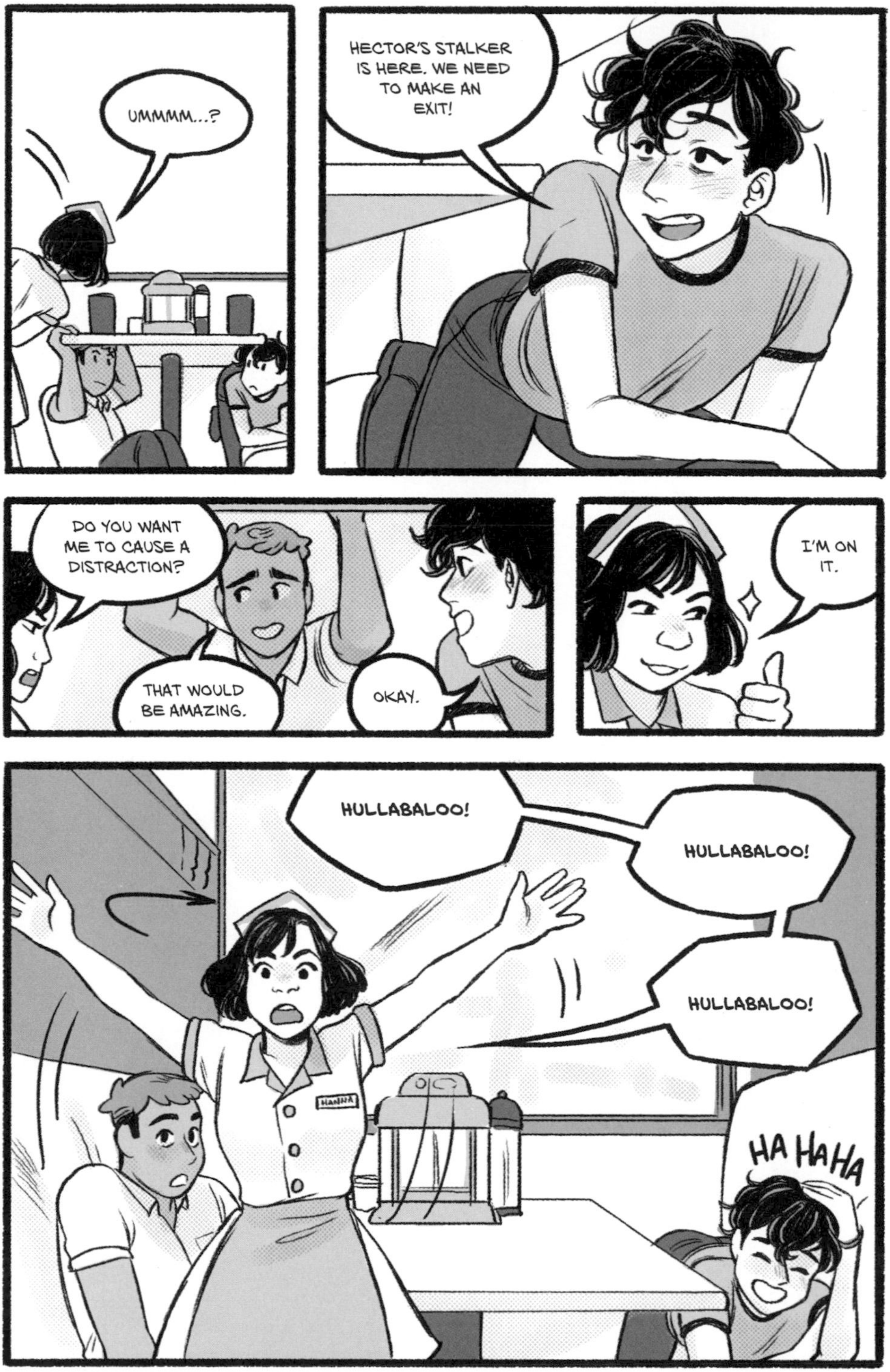
UMMMM...?
HECTOR'S STALKER IS HERE. WE NEED TO MAKE AN EXIT!
DO YOU WANT ME TO CAUSE A DISTRACTION?
THAT WOULD BE AMAZING.
OKAY.
I'M ON IT.
HULLABALOO!
HULLABALOO!
HULLABALOO!
HA HA HA

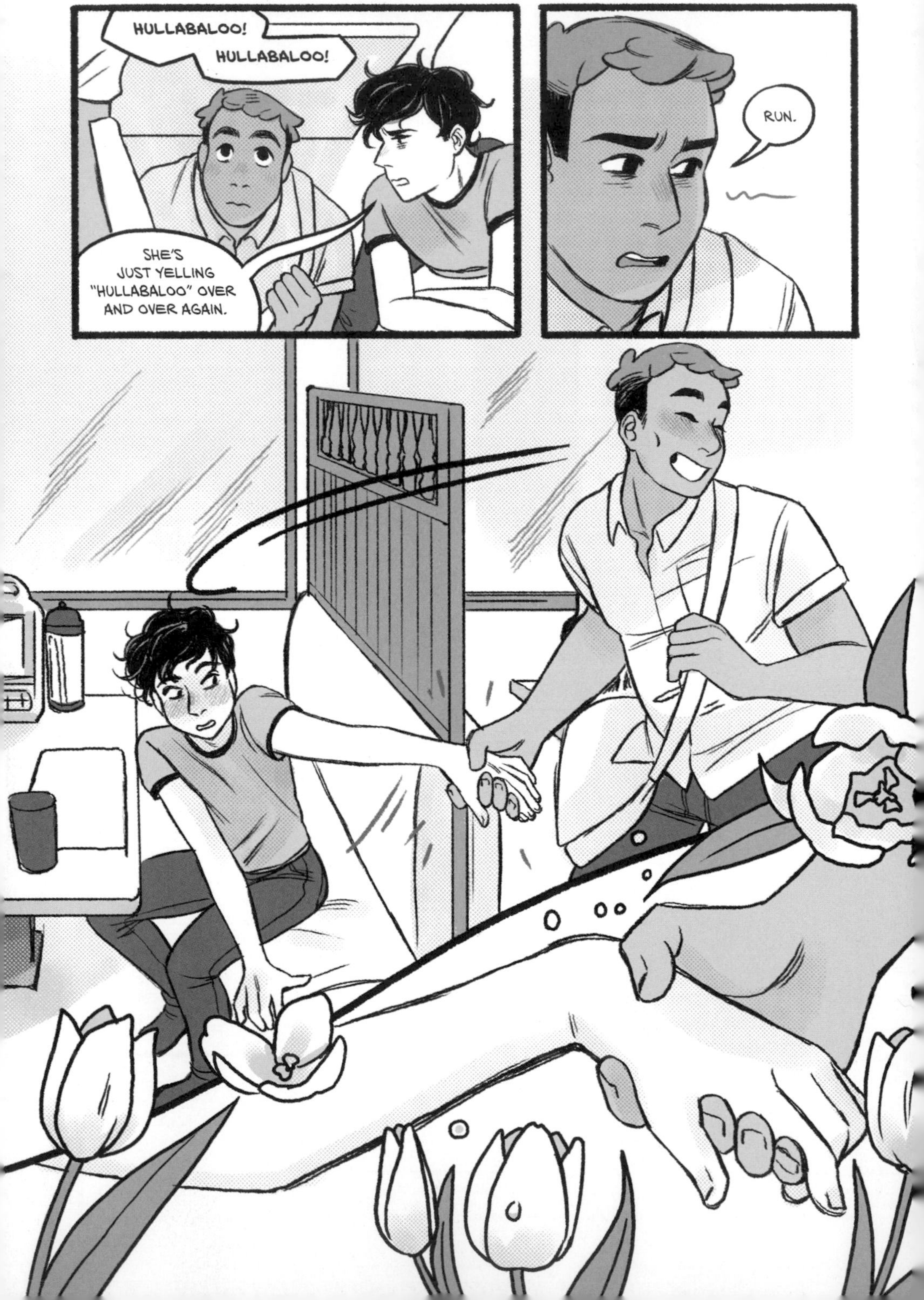
HULLABALOO!
HULLABALOO!
SHE'S JUST YELLING "HULLABALOO" OVER AND OVER AGAIN.
RUN.

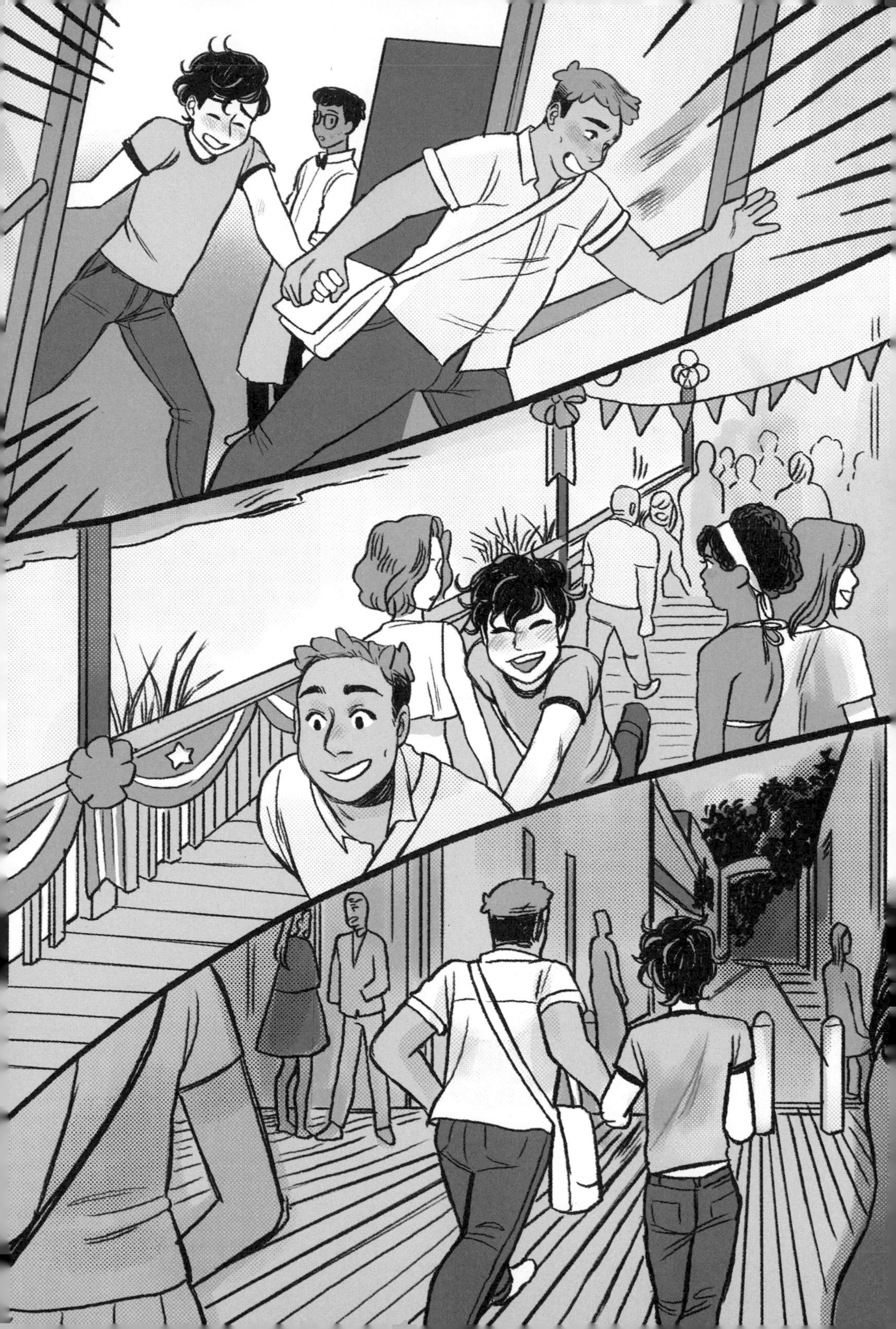

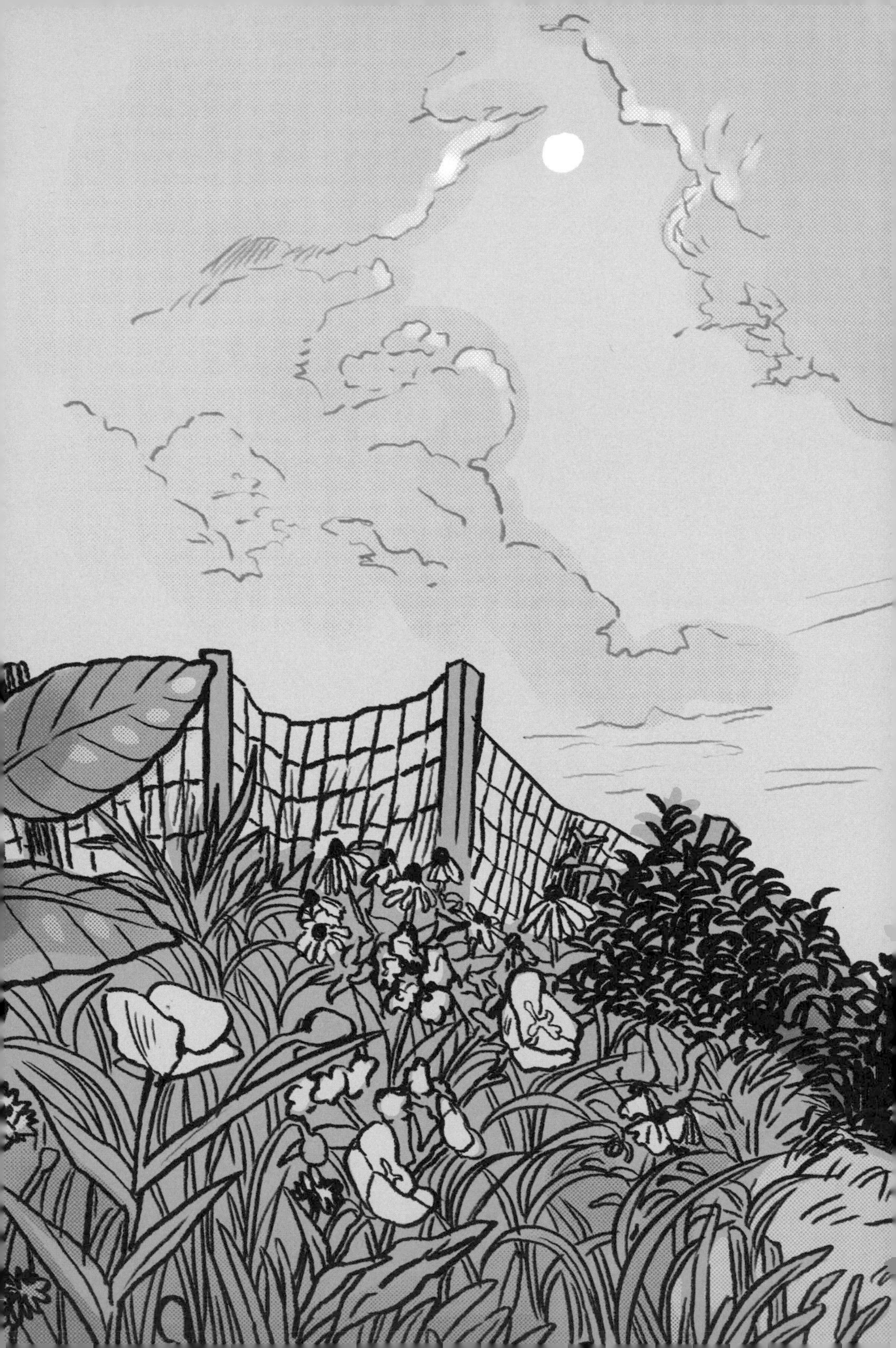

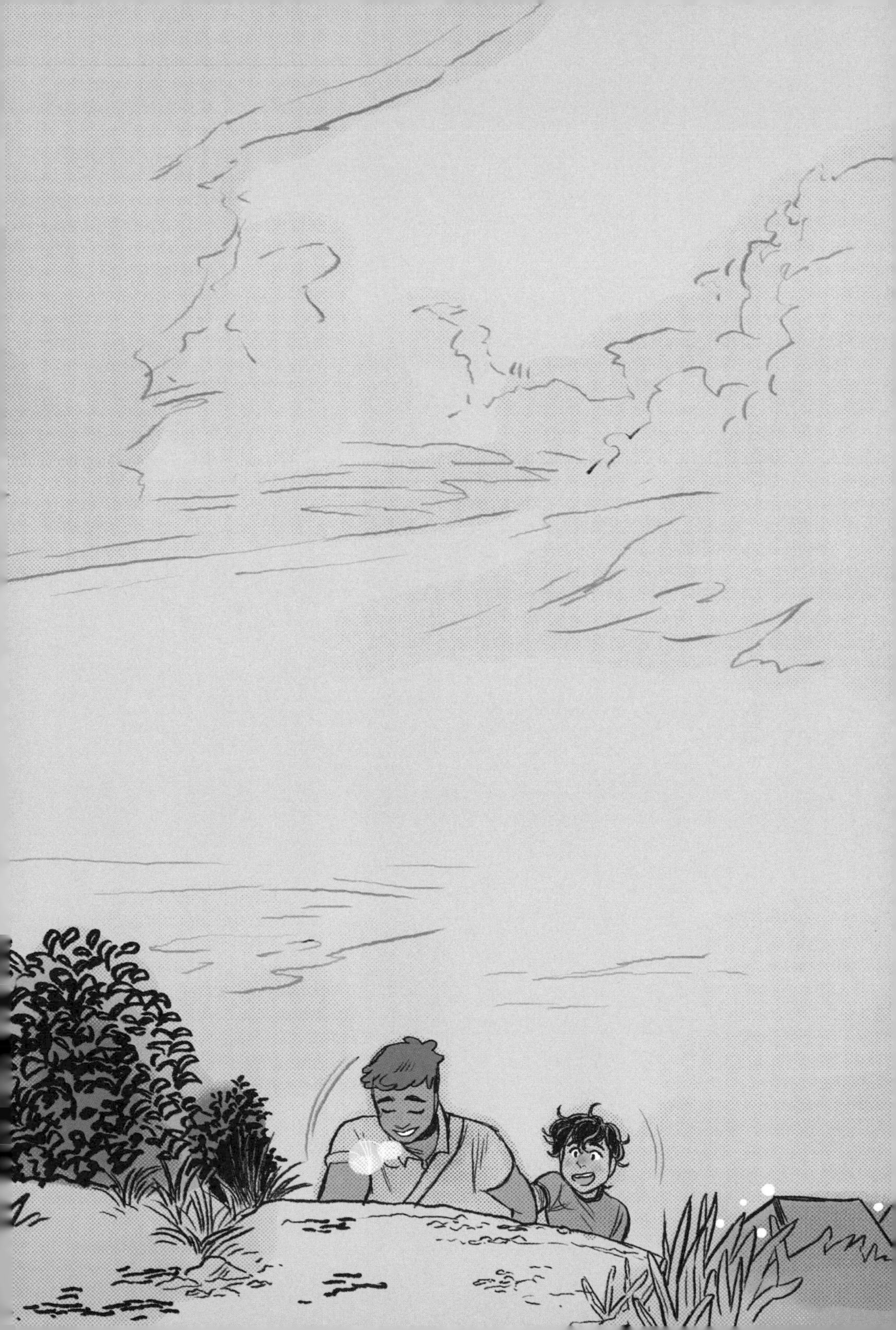

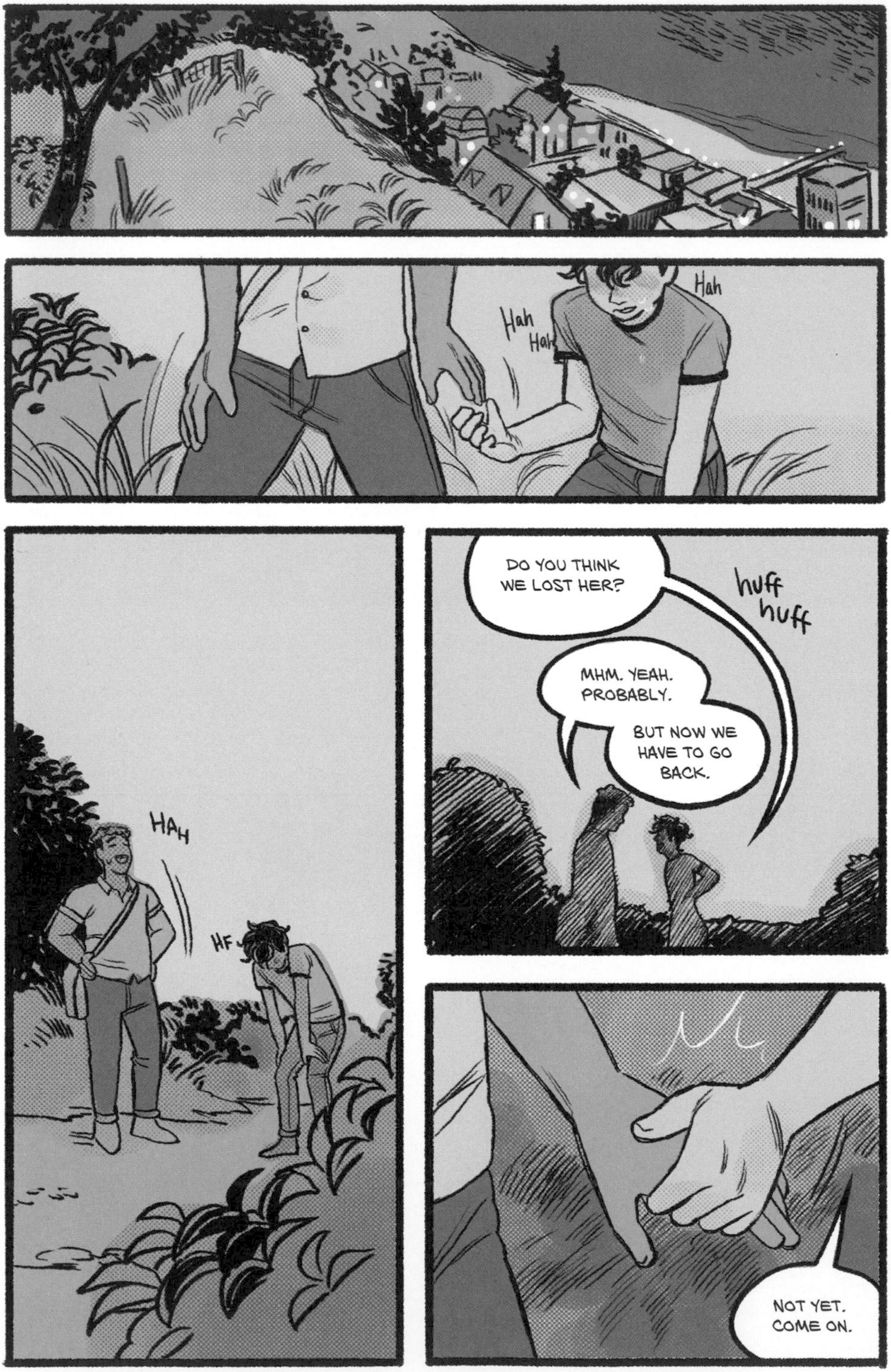
Hah
Hah
Hah
HAH
HF
DO YOU THINK WE LOST HER?
huff huff
MHM. YEAH. PROBABLY.
BUT NOW WE HAVE TO GO BACK.
NOT YET. COME ON.

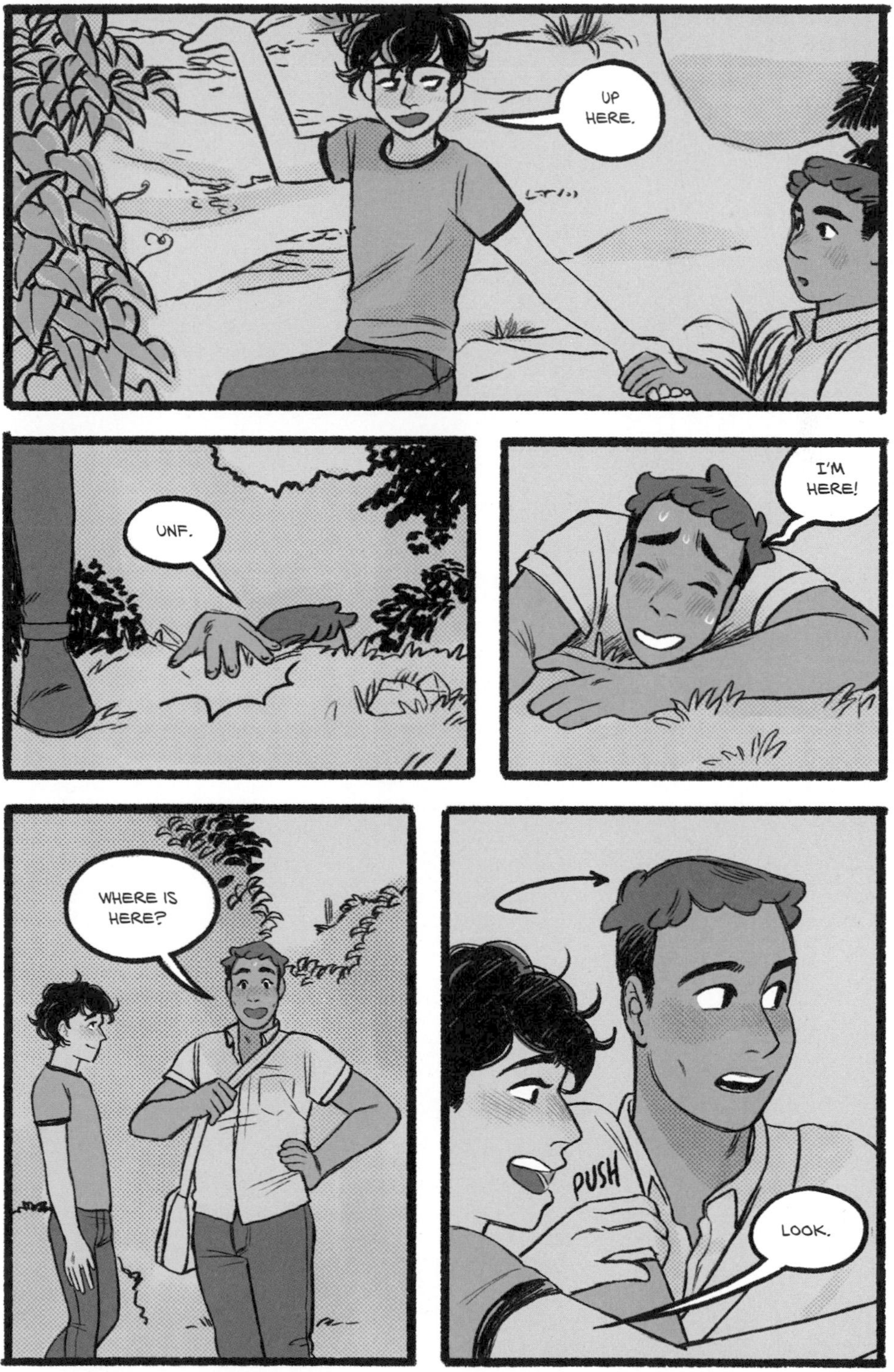
UP HERE.
UNF.
I'M HERE!
WHERE IS HERE?
PUSH
LOOK.

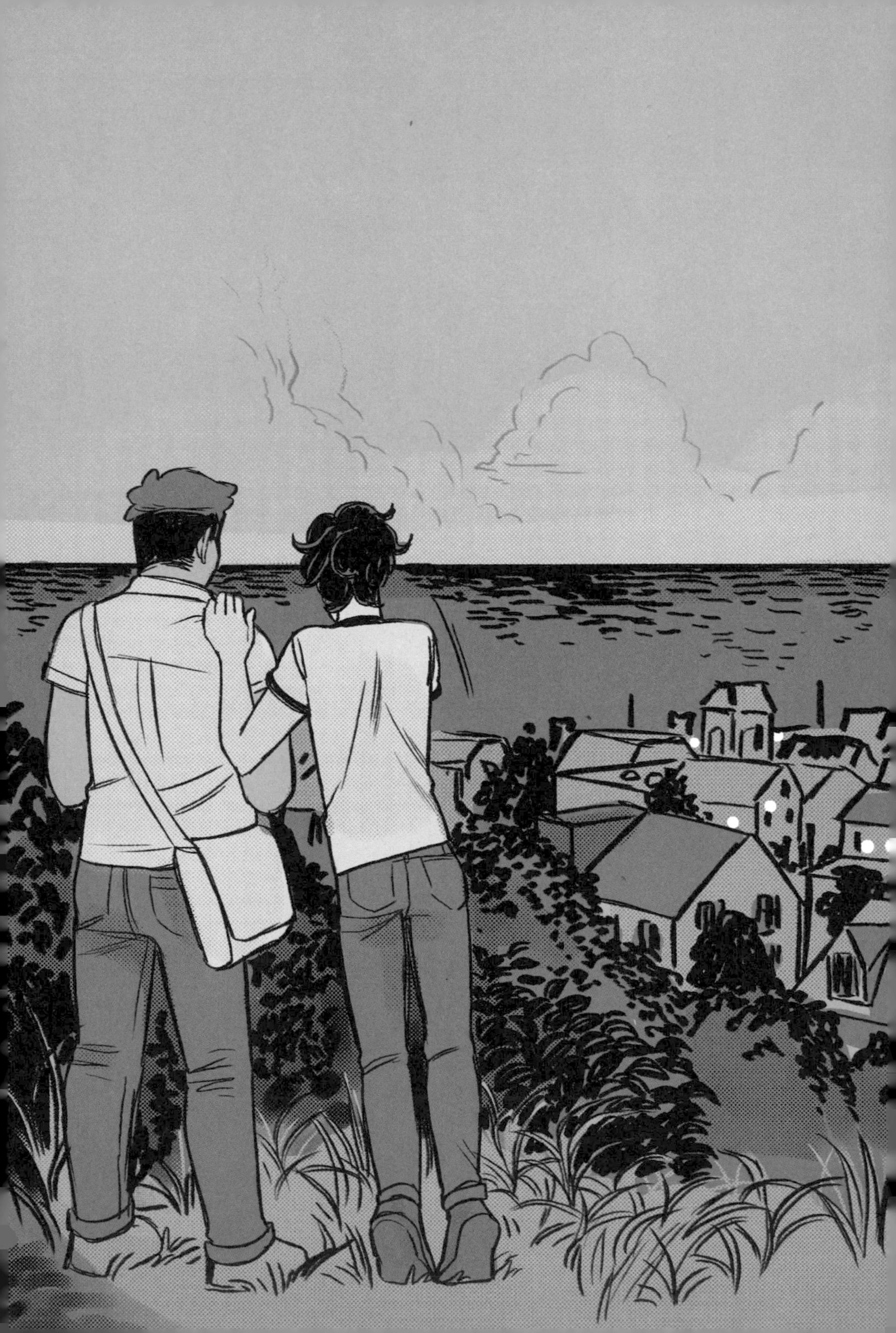

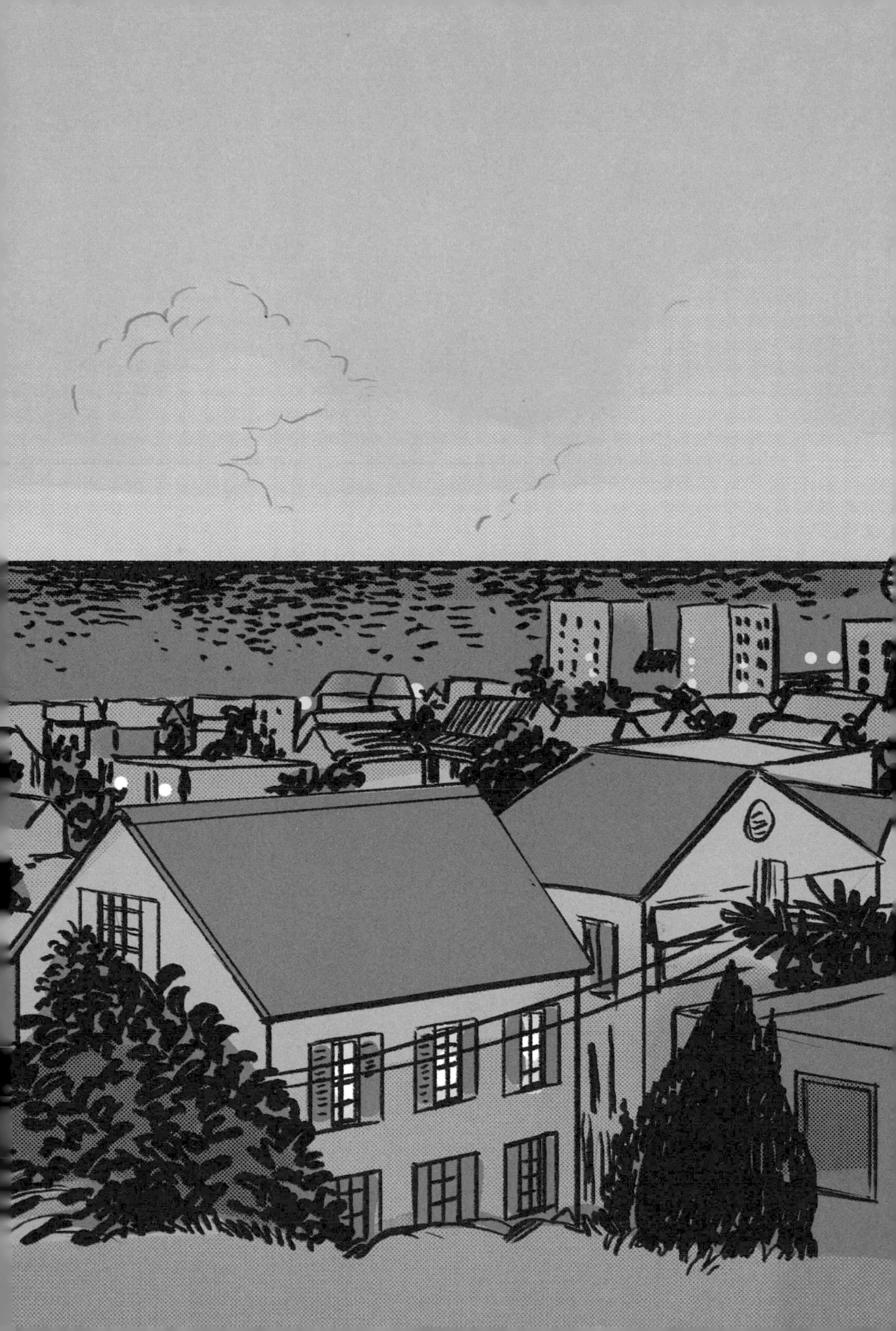

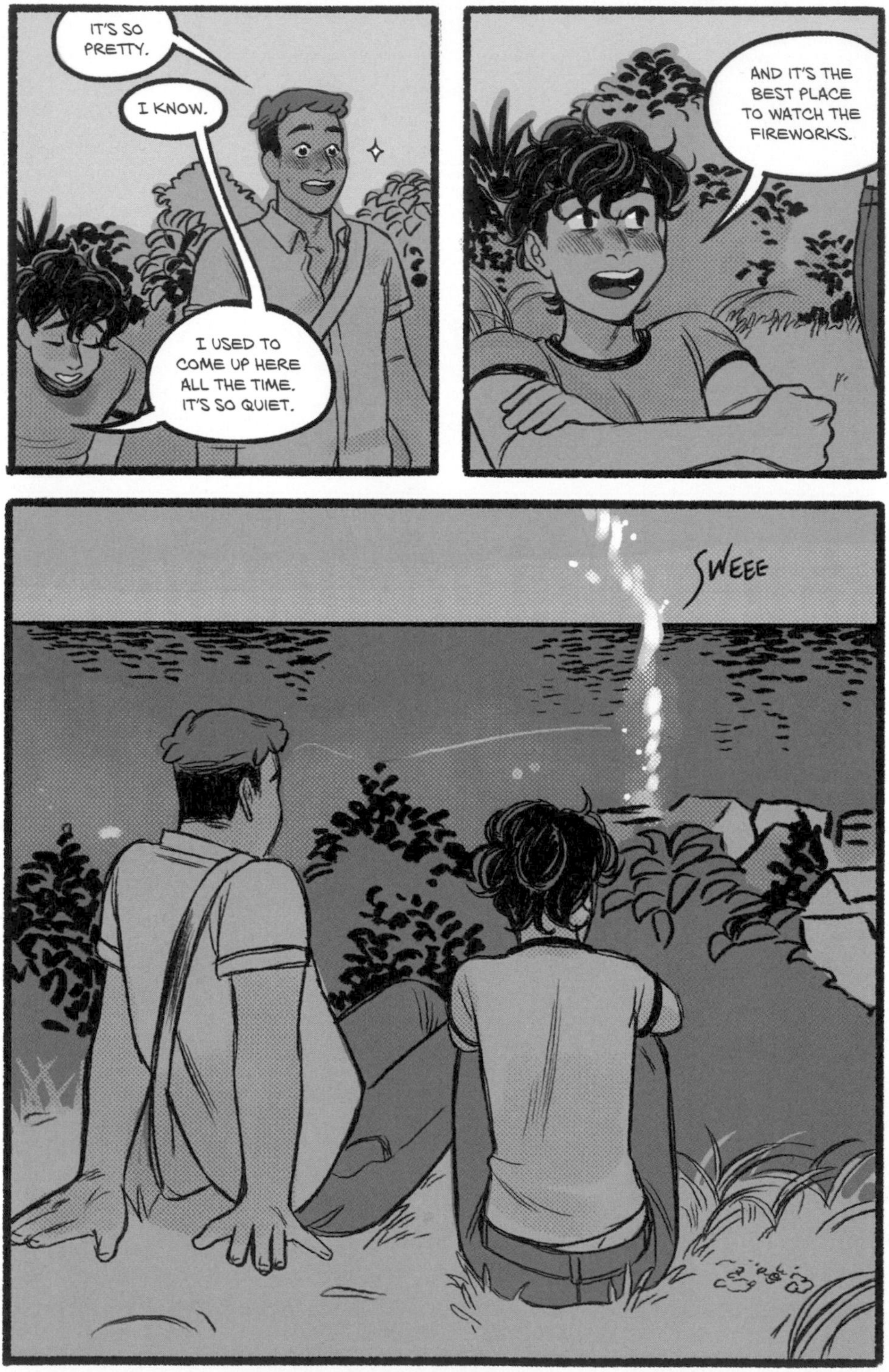
IT'S SO PRETTY.
I KNOW.
I USED TO COME UP HERE ALL THE TIME. IT'S SO QUIET.
AND IT'S THE BEST PLACE TO WATCH THE FIREWORKS.
SWEEE

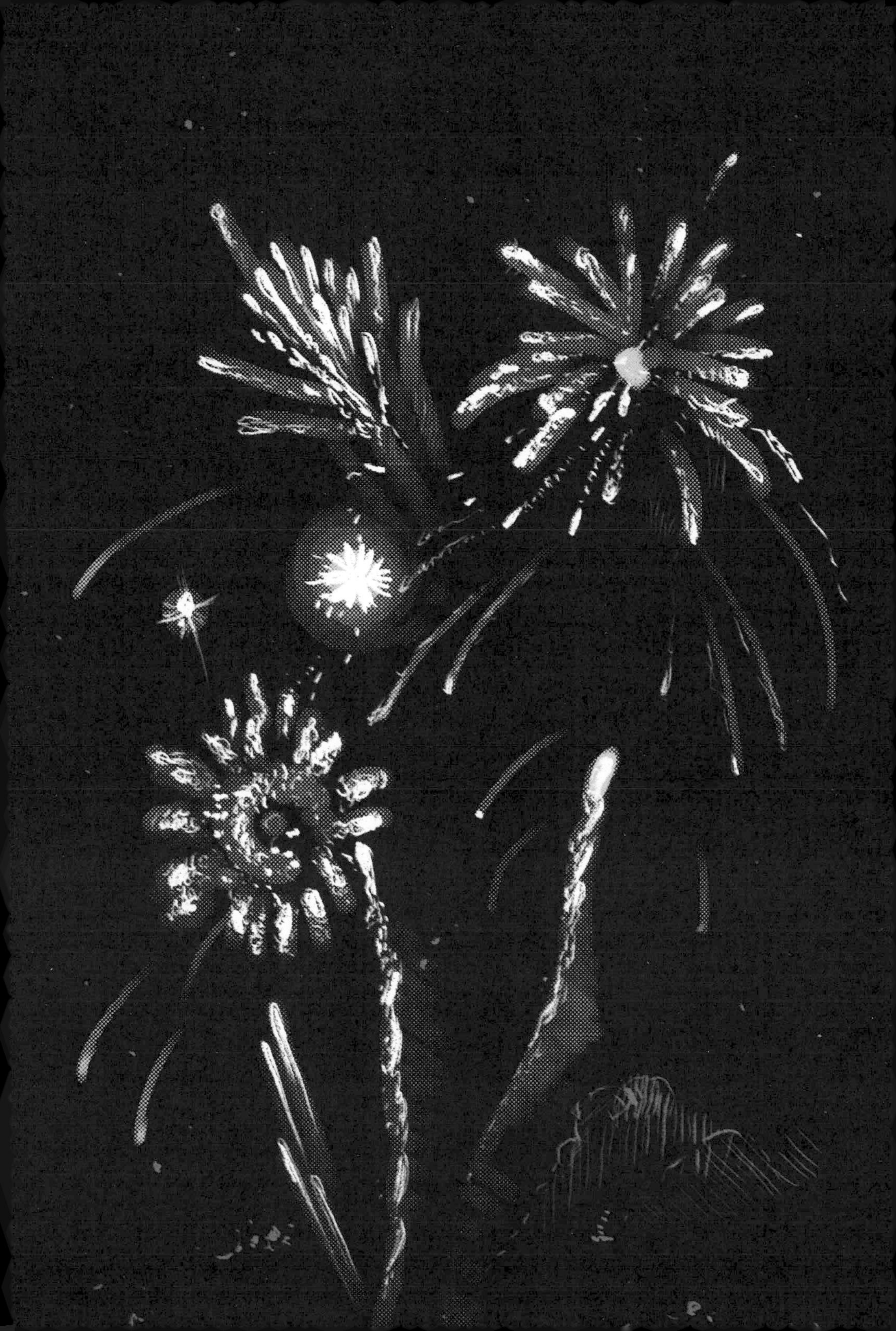

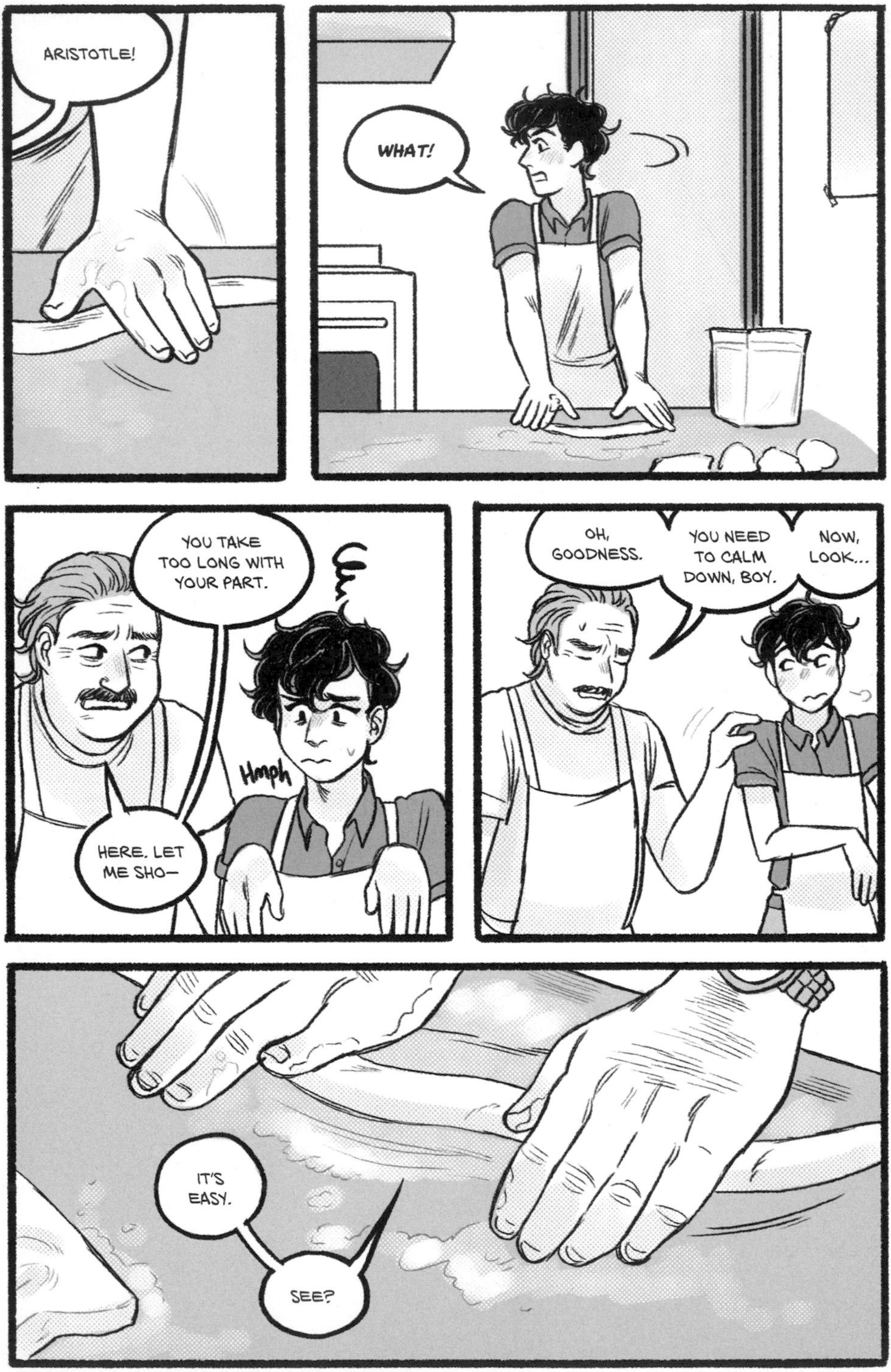
ARISTOTLE!
WHAT!
YOU TAKE TOO LONG WITH YOUR PART.
Hmph
HERE. LET ME SHO—
OH, GOODNESS.
YOU NEED TO CALM DOWN, BOY.
NOW, LOOK...
IT'S EASY.
SEE?

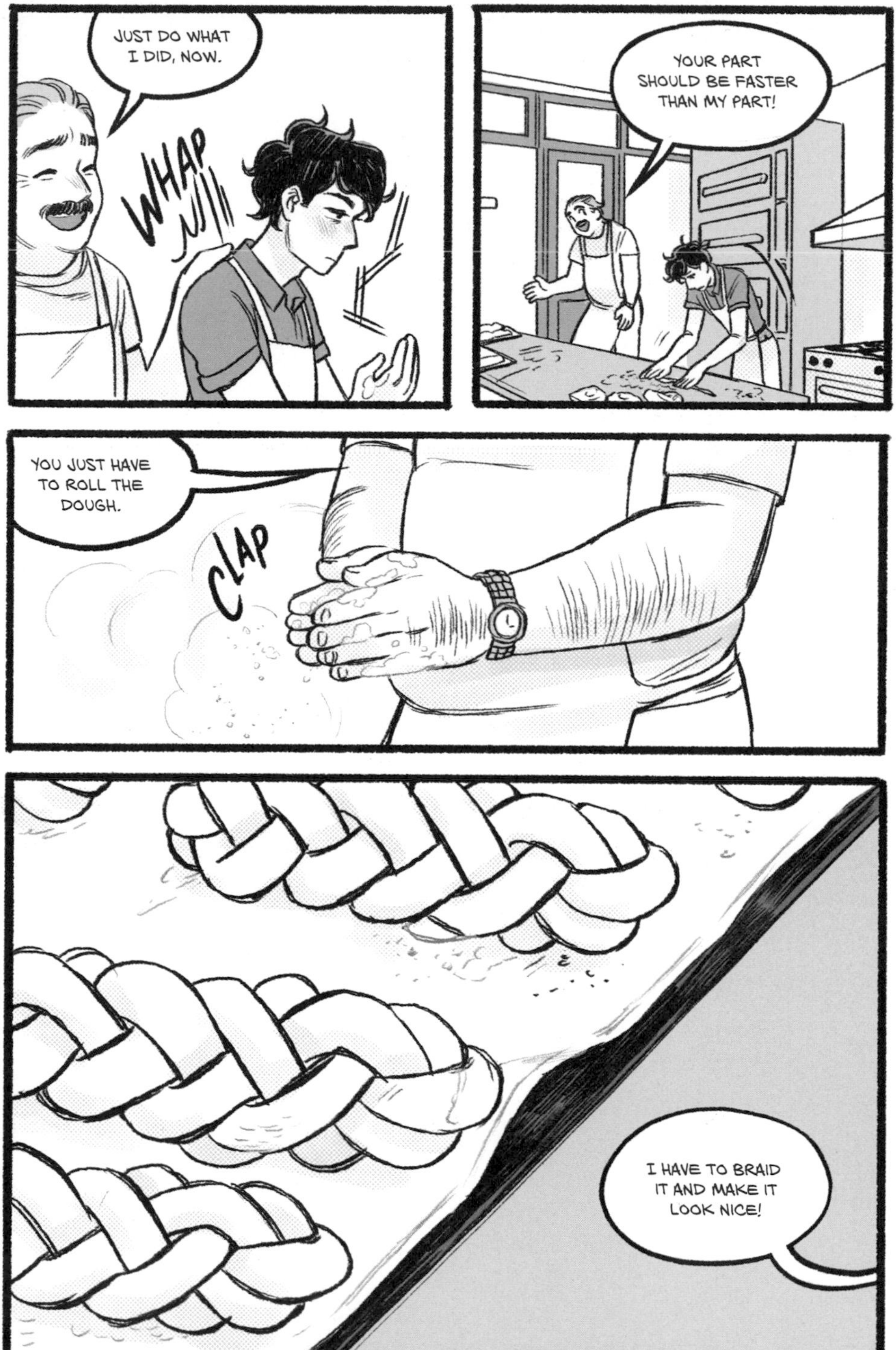

JUST DO WHAT I DID, NOW.
WHAP
YOUR PART SHOULD BE FASTER THAN MY PART!
YOU JUST HAVE TO ROLL THE DOUGH.
CLAP
I HAVE TO BRAID IT AND MAKE IT LOOK NICE!

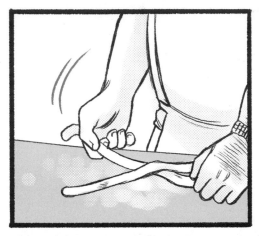
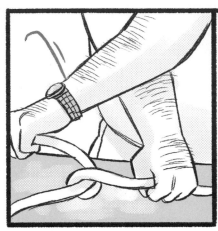
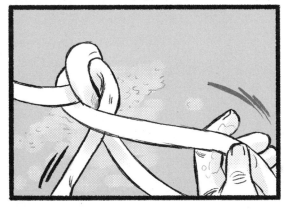
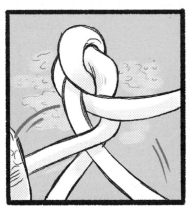

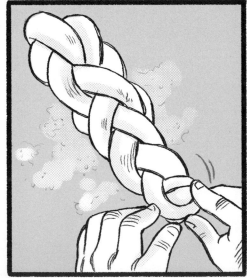

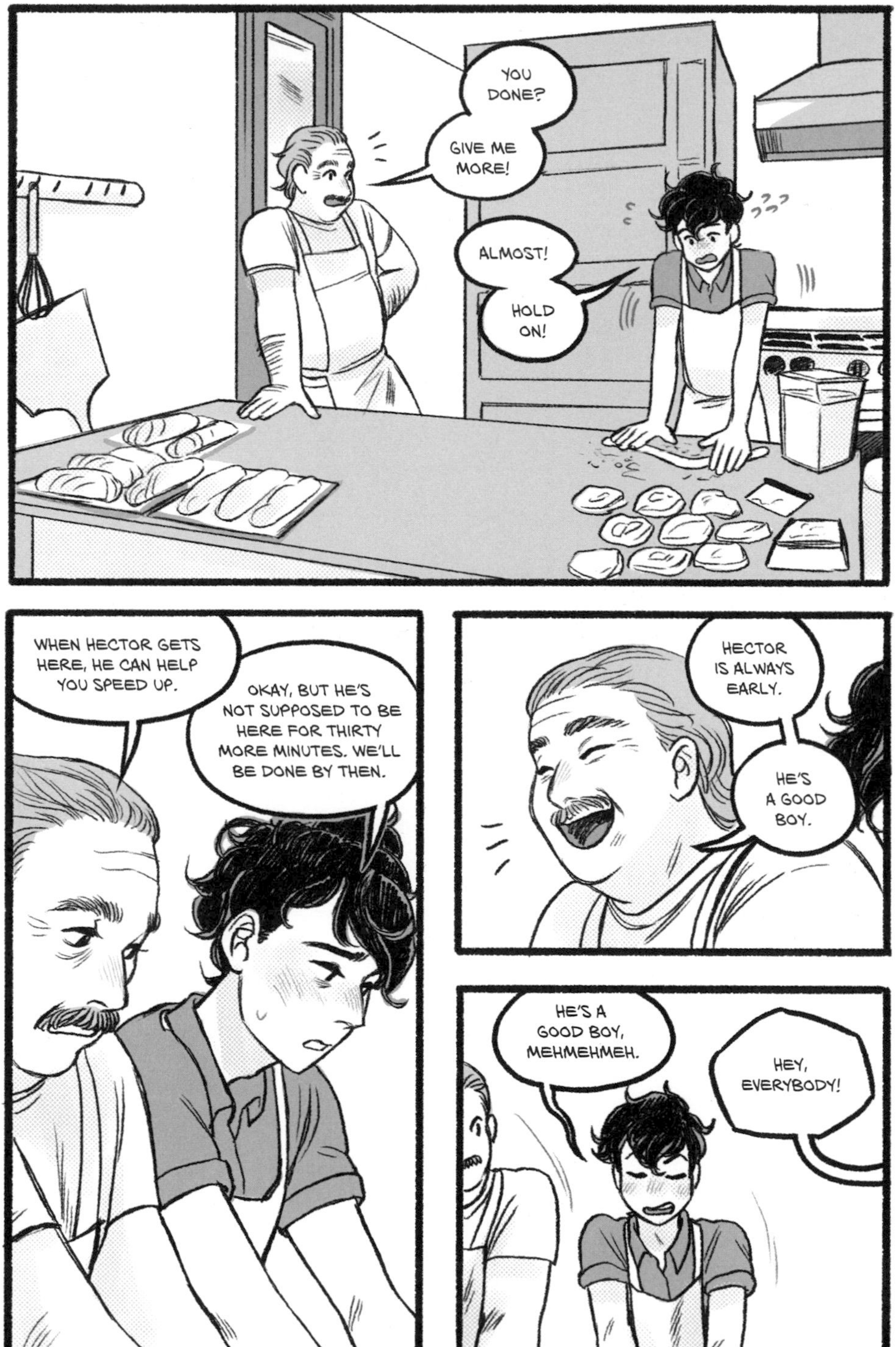
YOU DONE?
GIVE ME MORE!
ALMOST!
HOLD ON!
WHEN HECTOR GETS HERE, HE CAN HELP YOU SPEED UP.
OKAY, BUT HE'S NOT SUPPOSED TO BE HERE FOR THIRTY MORE MINUTES. WE'LL BE DONE BY THEN.
HECTOR IS ALWAYS EARLY.
HE'S A GOOD BOY.
HE'S A GOOD BOY, MEHMEHMEH.
HEY, EVERYBODY!

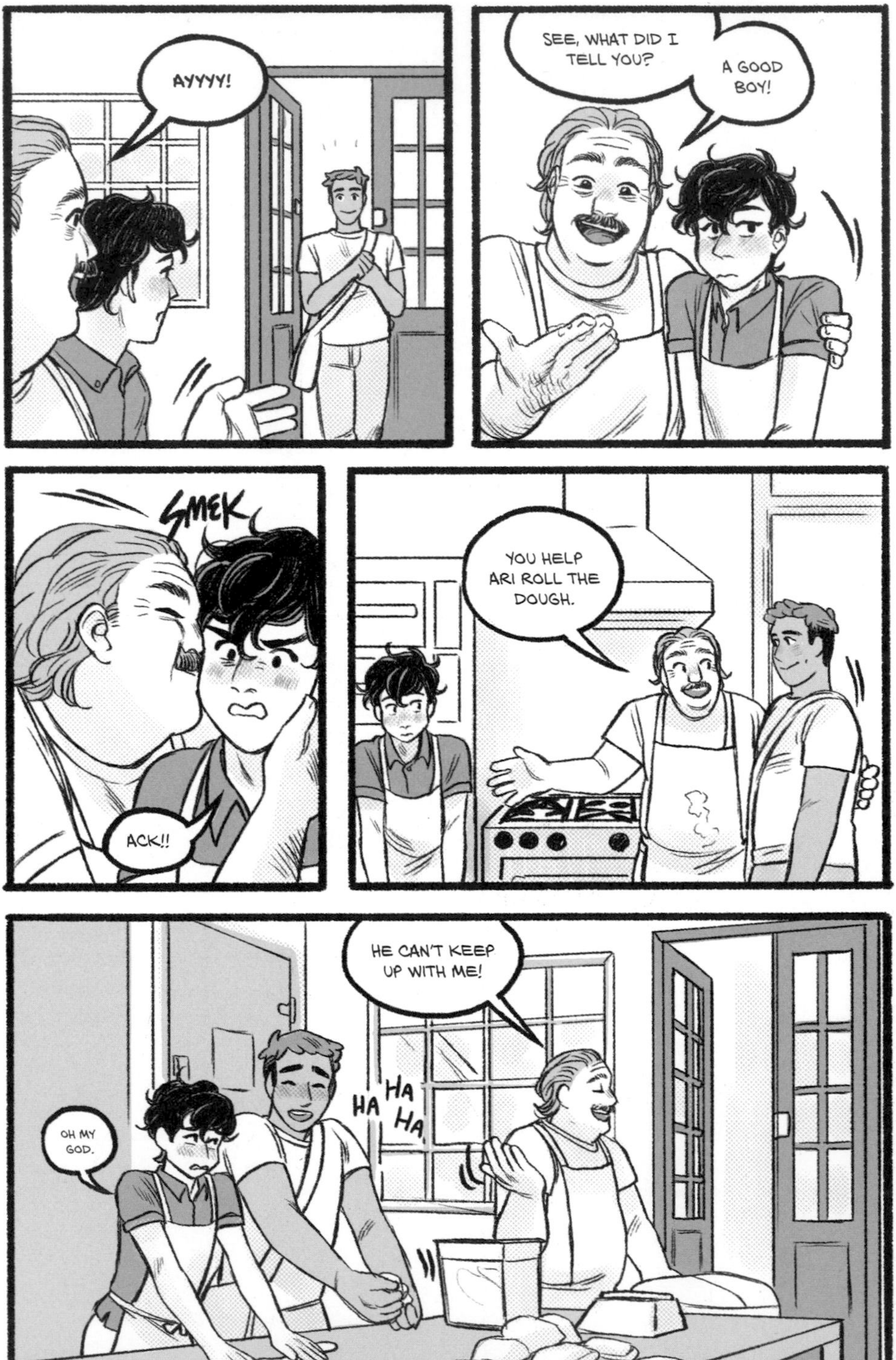
AYYYY!
SEE, WHAT DID I TELL YOU?
A GOOD BOY!
SMEK
ACK!!
YOU HELP ARI ROLL THE DOUGH.
HE CAN'T KEEP UP WITH ME!
HA HA HA
OH MY GOD.

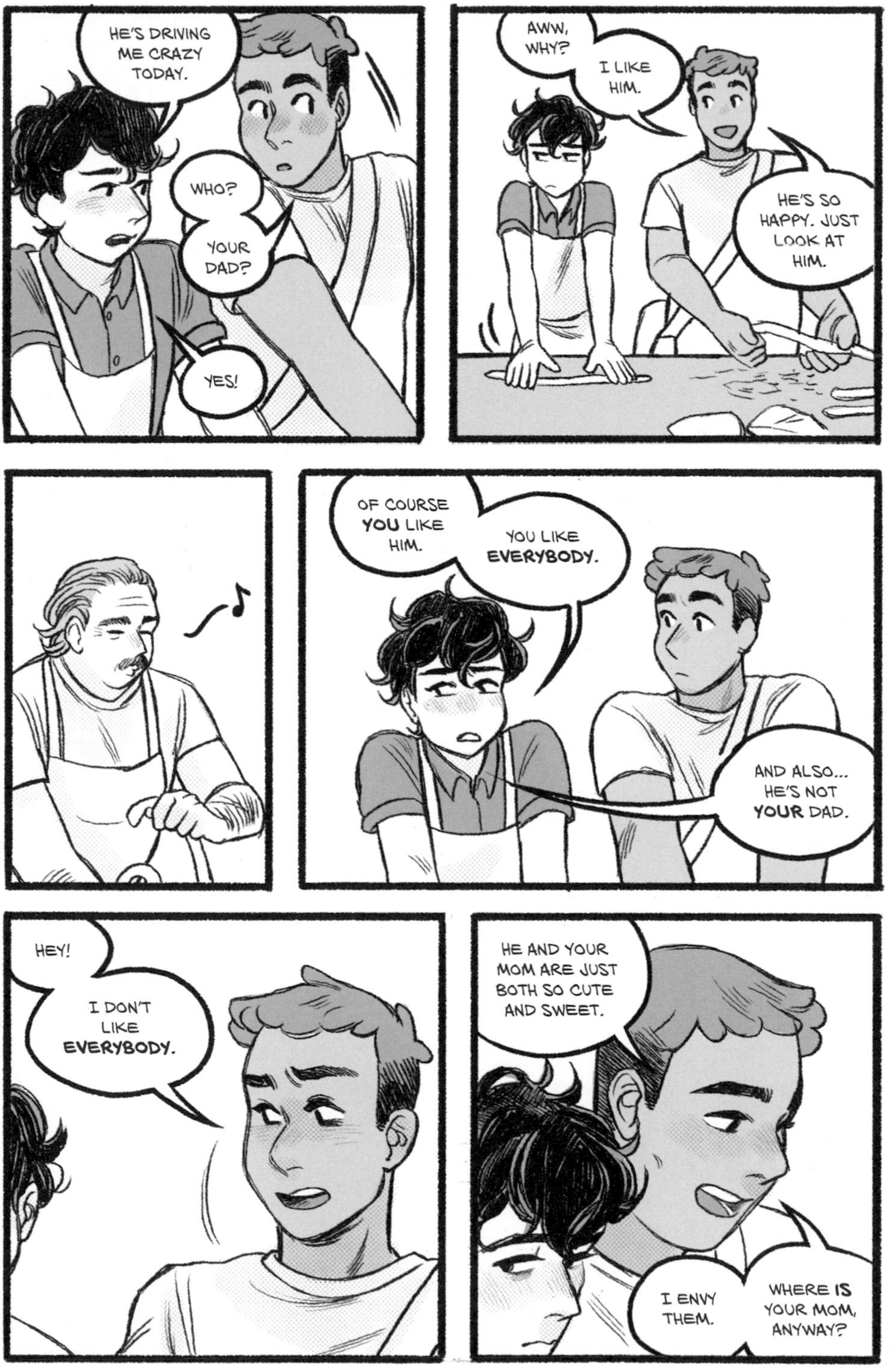
HE'S DRIVING ME CRAZY TODAY.
WHO?
YOUR DAD?
YES!
AWW, WHY?
I LIKE HIM.
HE'S SO HAPPY. JUST LOOK AT HIM.
OF COURSE YOU LIKE HIM.
YOU LIKE EVERYBODY.
AND ALSO... HE'S NOT YOUR DAD.
HEY!
I DON'T LIKE EVERYBODY.
HE AND YOUR MOM ARE JUST BOTH SO CUTE AND SWEET.
I ENVY THEM.
WHERE IS YOUR MOM, ANYWAY?

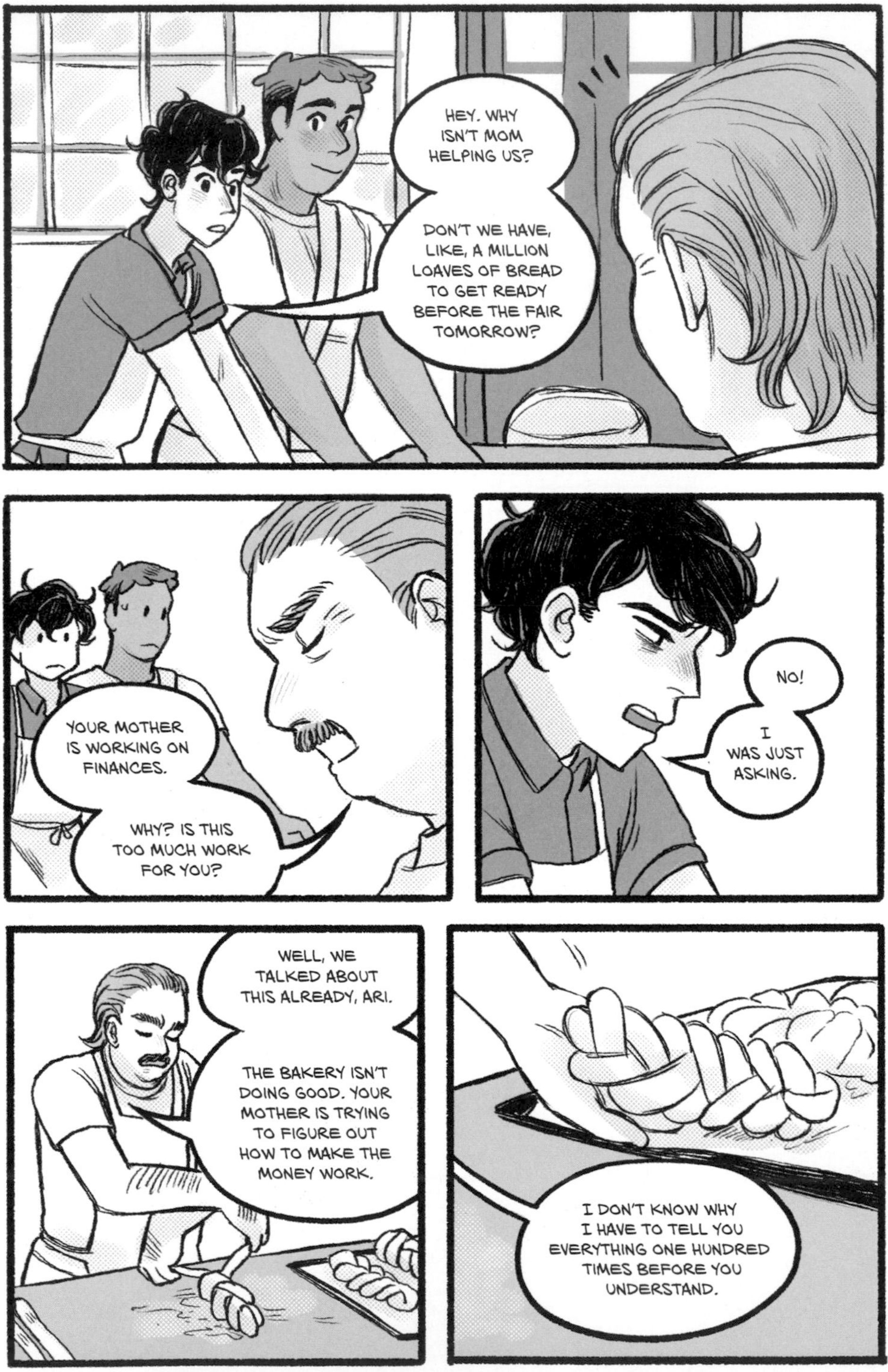
HEY. WHY ISN'T MOM HELPING US?
DON'T WE HAVE, LIKE, A MILLION LOAVES OF BREAD TO GET READY BEFORE THE FAIR TOMORROW?
YOUR MOTHER IS WORKING ON FINANCES.
WHY? IS THIS TOO MUCH WORK FOR YOU?
NO!
I WAS JUST ASKING.
WELL, WE TALKED ABOUT THIS ALREADY, ARI.
THE BAKERY ISN'T DOING GOOD. YOUR MOTHER IS TRYING TO FIGURE OUT HOW TO MAKE THE MONEY WORK.
I DON'T KNOW WHY I HAVE TO TELL YOU EVERYTHING ONE HUNDRED TIMES BEFORE YOU UNDERSTAND.

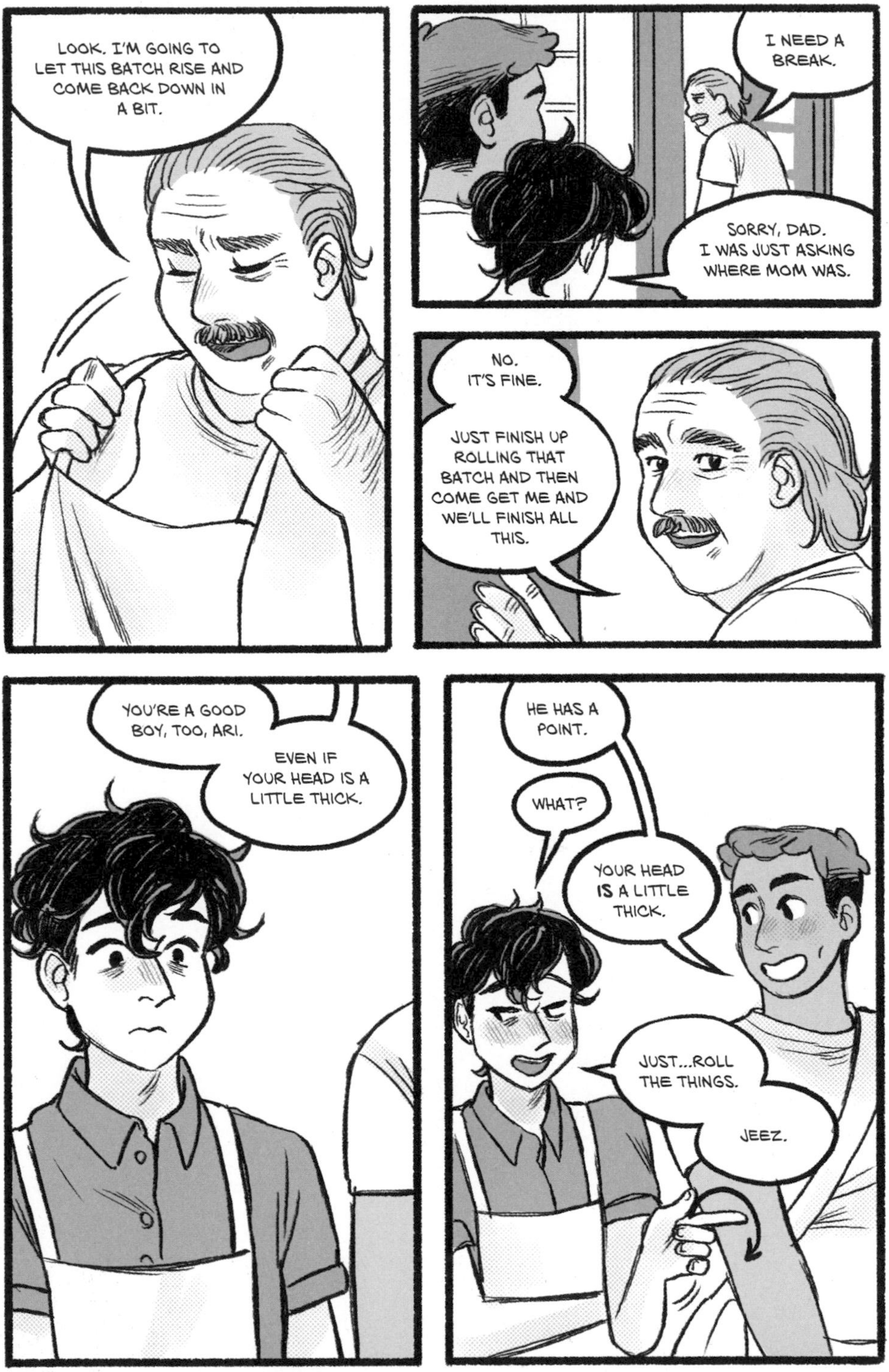
LOOK. I'M GOING TO LET THIS BATCH RISE AND COME BACK DOWN IN A BIT.
I NEED A BREAK.
SORRY, DAD. I WAS JUST ASKING WHERE MOM WAS.
NO. IT'S FINE.
JUST FINISH UP ROLLING THAT BATCH AND THEN COME GET ME AND WE'LL FINISH ALL THIS.
YOU'RE A GOOD BOY, TOO, ARI.
EVEN IF YOUR HEAD IS A LITTLE THICK.
HE HAS A POINT.
WHAT?
YOUR HEAD **IS** A LITTLE THICK.
JUST...ROLL THE THINGS.
JEEZ.

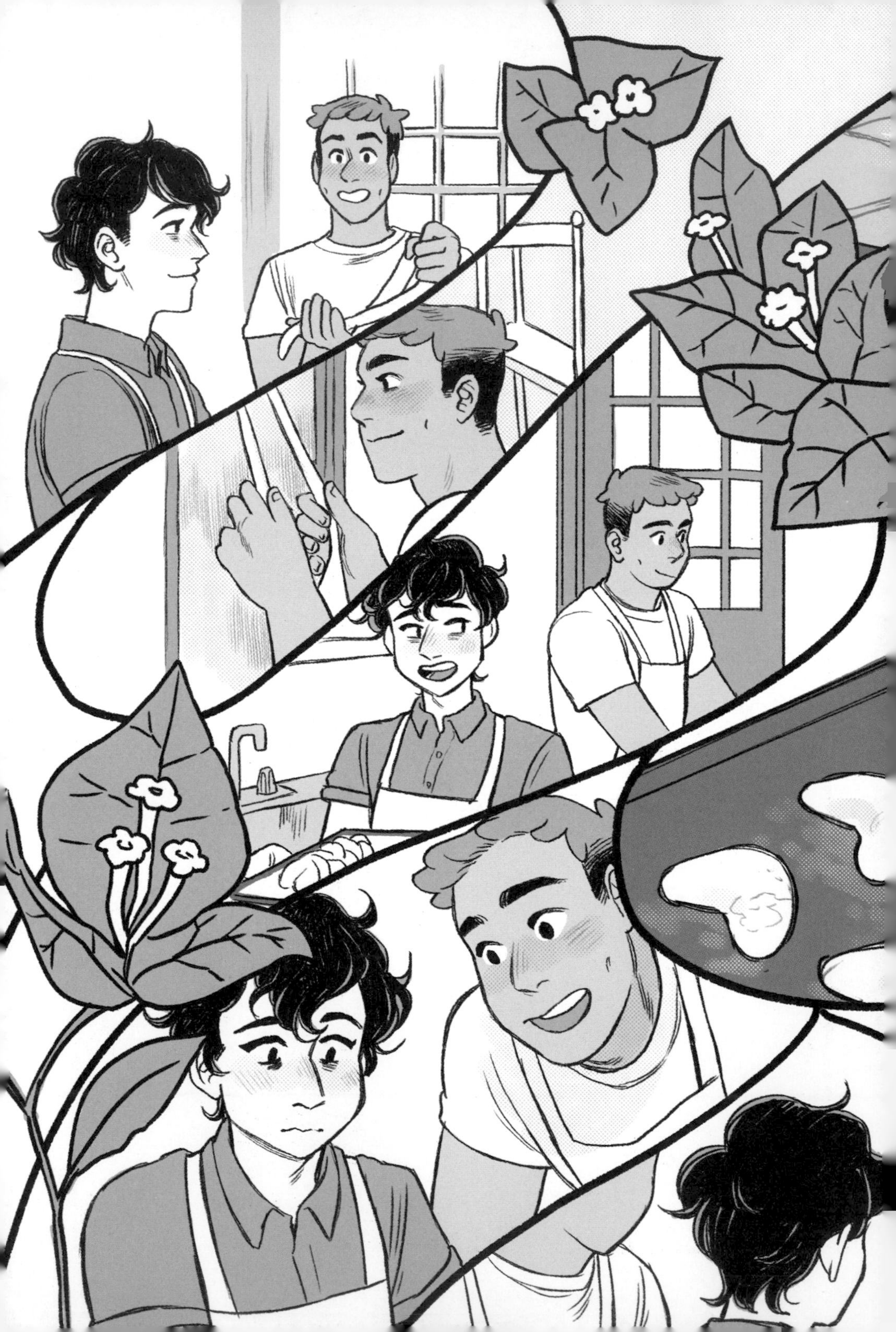

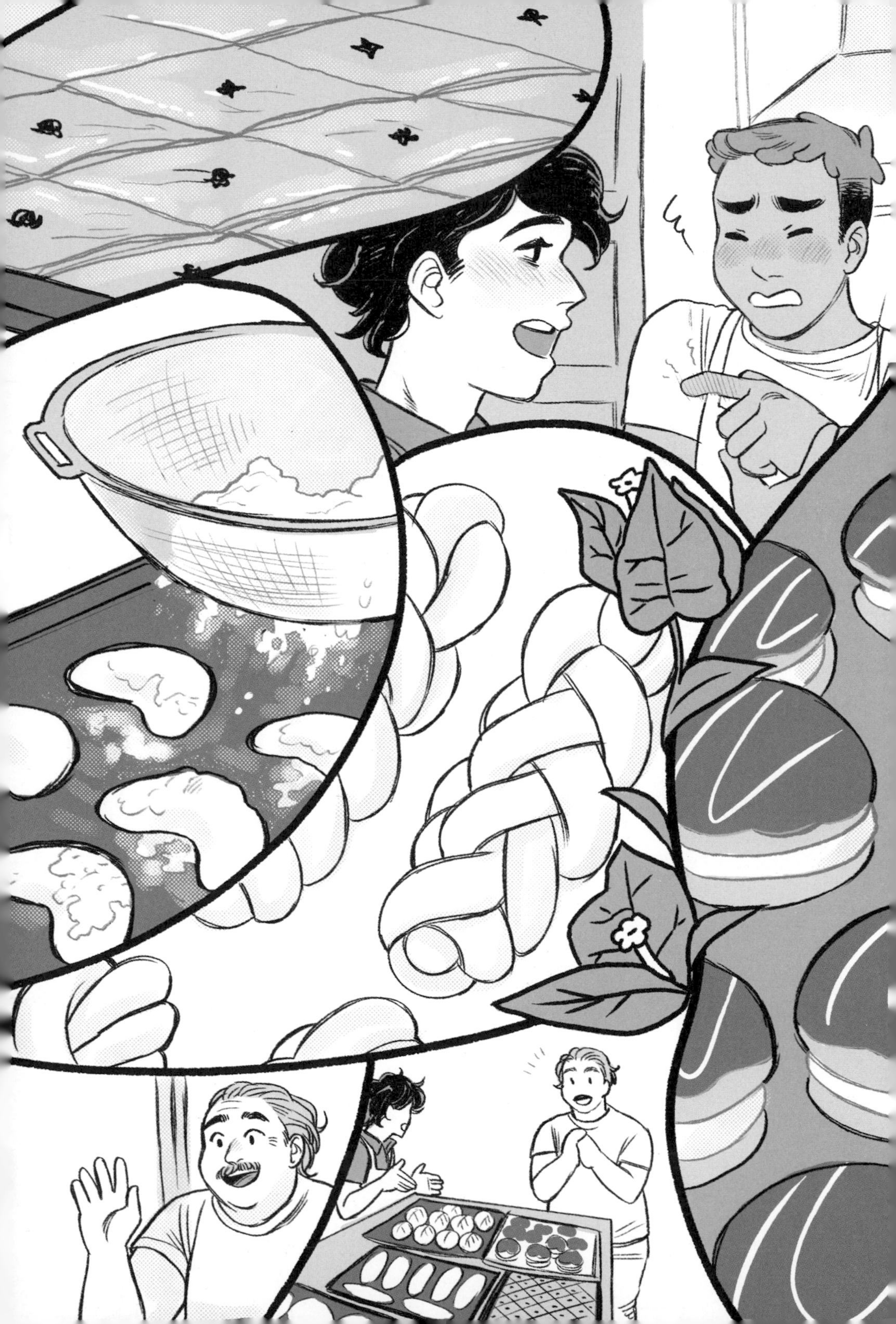

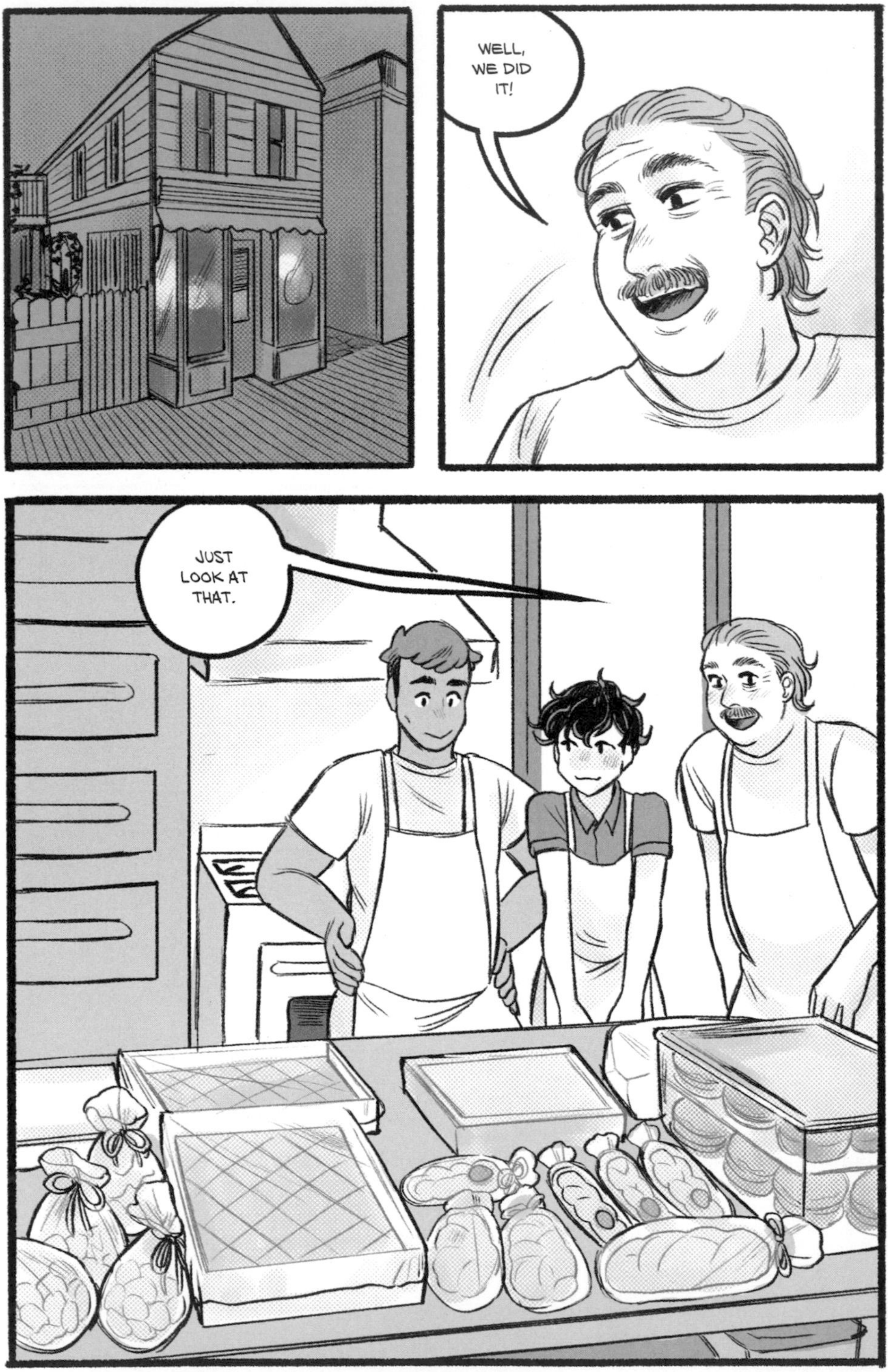
WELL, WE DID IT!
JUST LOOK AT THAT.

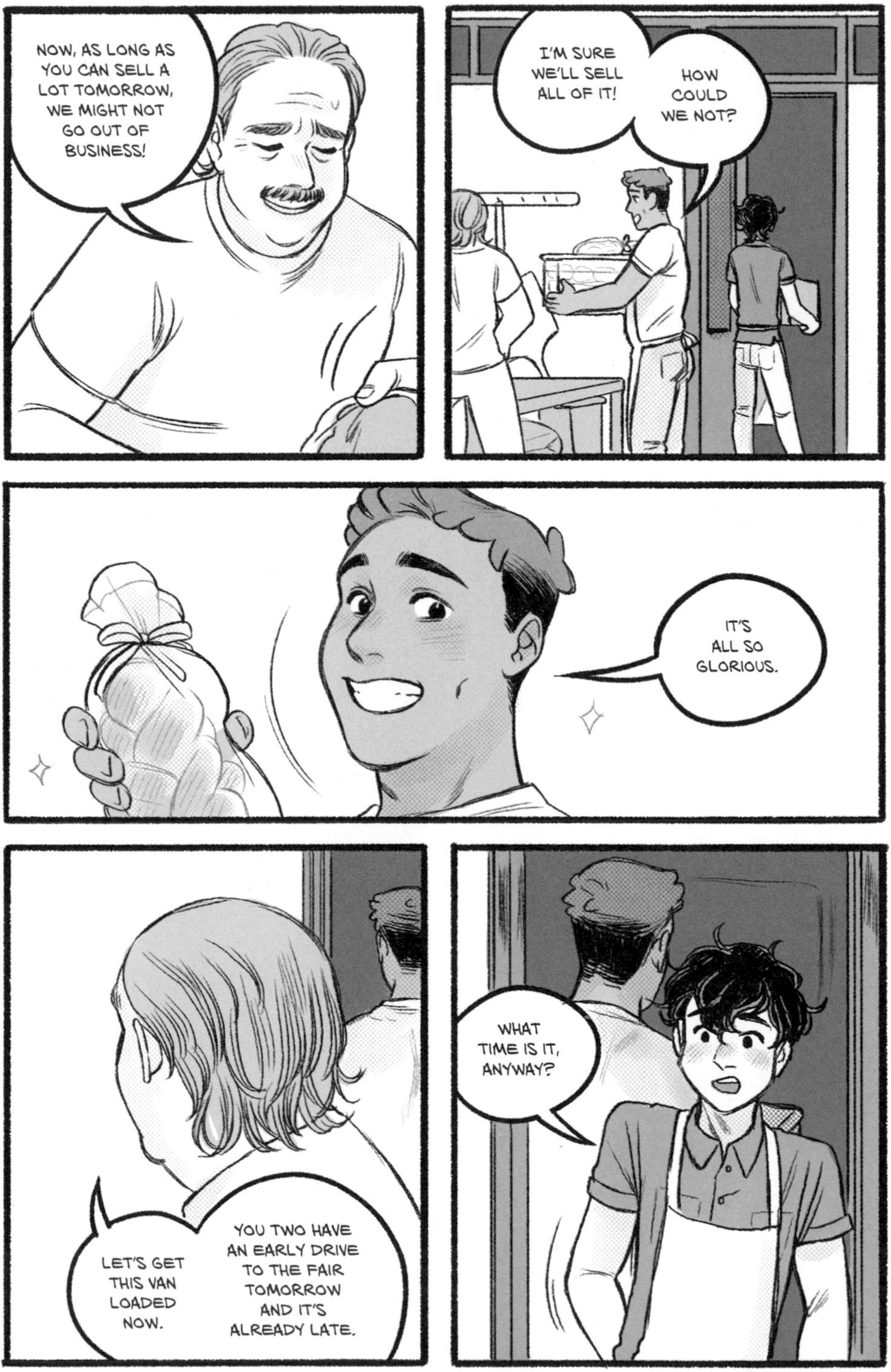
NOW, AS LONG AS YOU CAN SELL A LOT TOMORROW, WE MIGHT NOT GO OUT OF BUSINESS!
I'M SURE WE'LL SELL ALL OF IT!
HOW COULD WE NOT?
IT'S ALL SO GLORIOUS.
LET'S GET THIS VAN LOADED NOW.
YOU TWO HAVE AN EARLY DRIVE TO THE FAIR TOMORROW AND IT'S ALREADY LATE.
WHAT TIME IS IT, ANYWAY?

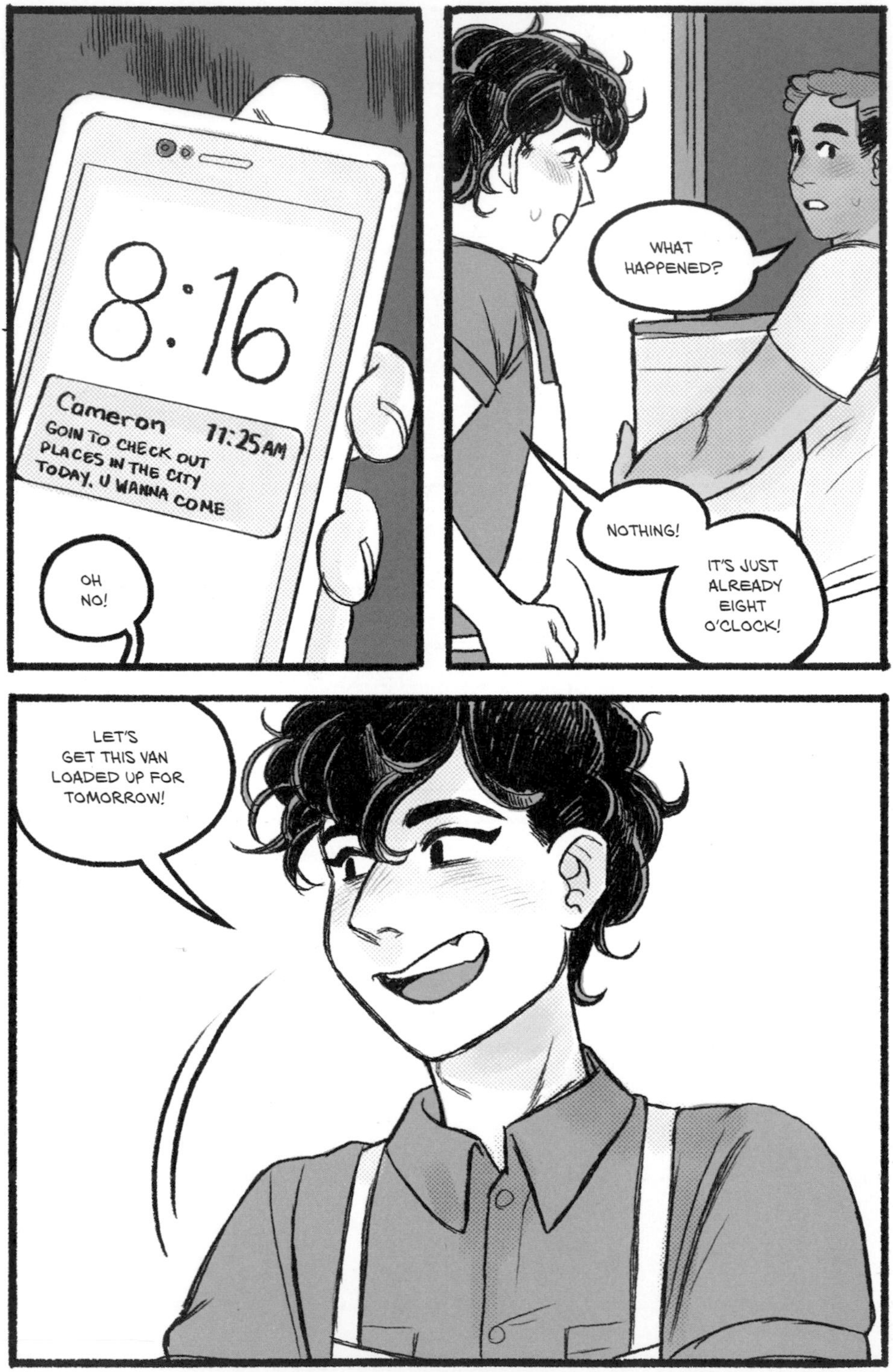
8:16
Cameron 11:25AM
GOIN TO CHECK OUT PLACES IN THE CITY TODAY, U WANNA COME
OH NO!
WHAT HAPPENED?
NOTHING!
IT'S JUST ALREADY EIGHT O'CLOCK!
LET'S GET THIS VAN LOADED UP FOR TOMORROW!

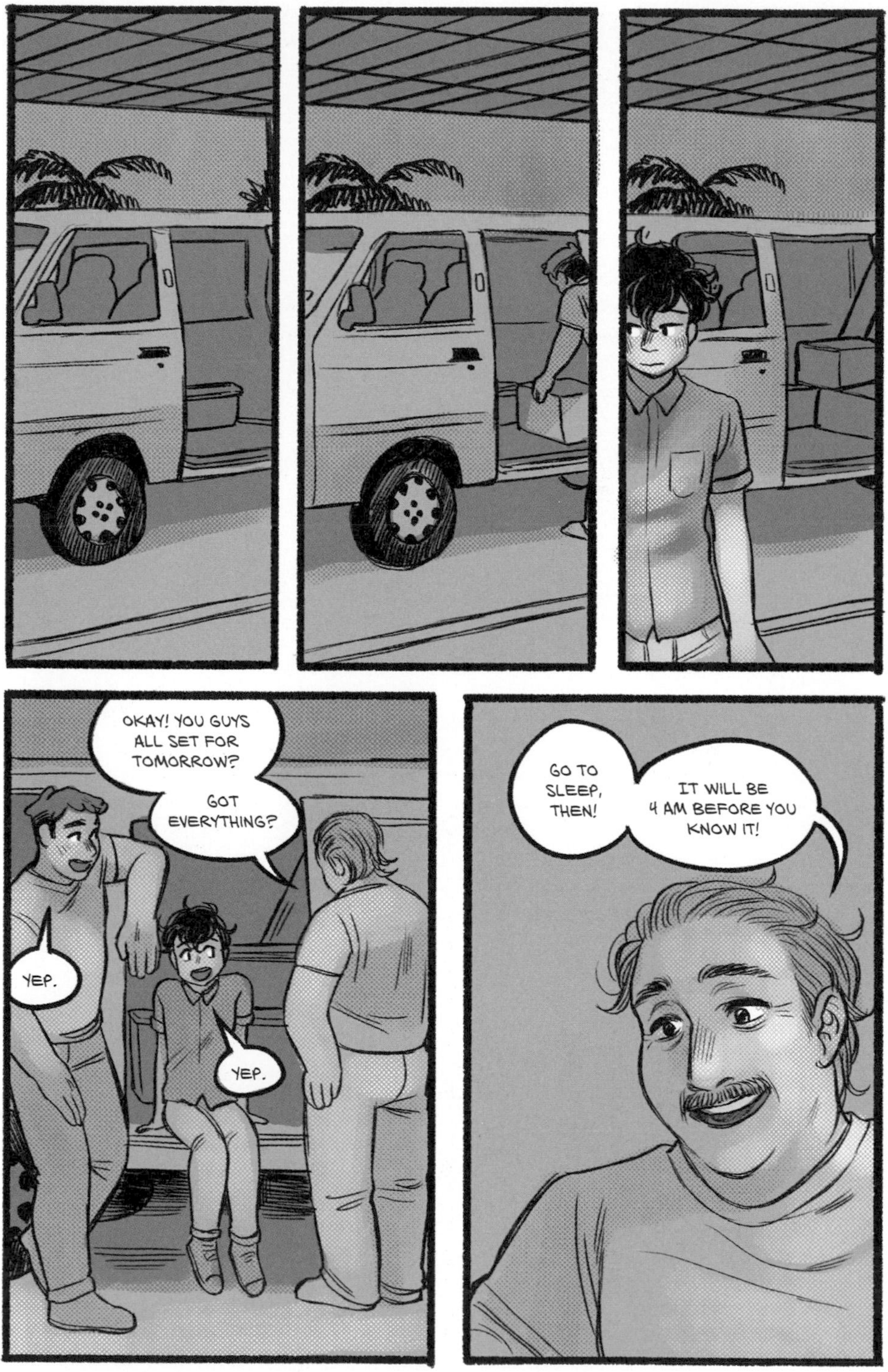
OKAY! YOU GUYS ALL SET FOR TOMORROW?
GOT EVERYTHING?
YEP.
YEP.
GO TO SLEEP, THEN!
IT WILL BE 4 AM BEFORE YOU KNOW IT!

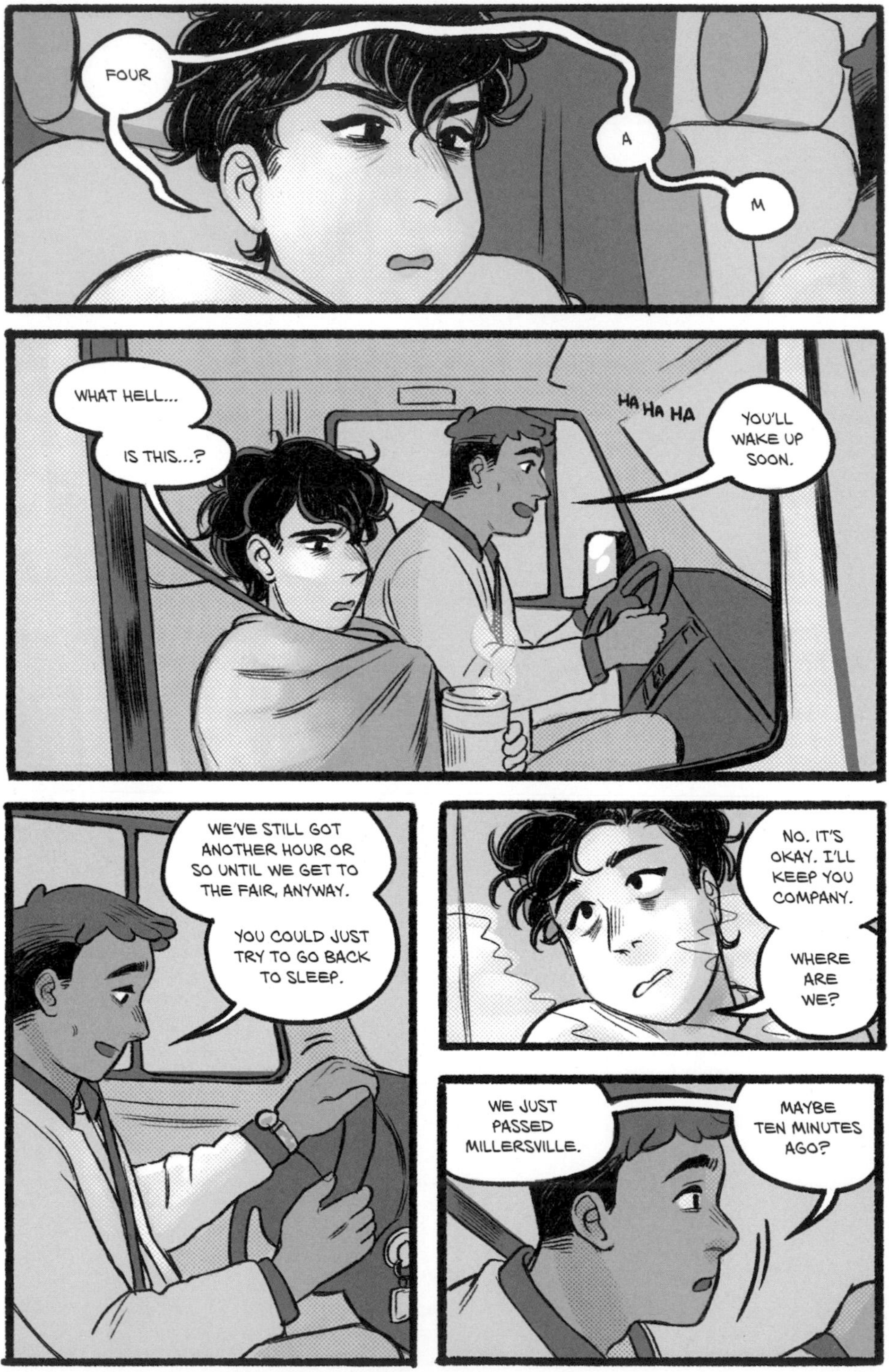
FOUR
A
M
WHAT HELL...
IS THIS...?
HA HA HA
YOU'LL WAKE UP SOON.
WE'VE STILL GOT ANOTHER HOUR OR SO UNTIL WE GET TO THE FAIR, ANYWAY.
YOU COULD JUST TRY TO GO BACK TO SLEEP.
NO. IT'S OKAY. I'LL KEEP YOU COMPANY.
WHERE ARE WE?
WE JUST PASSED MILLERSVILLE.
MAYBE TEN MINUTES AGO?

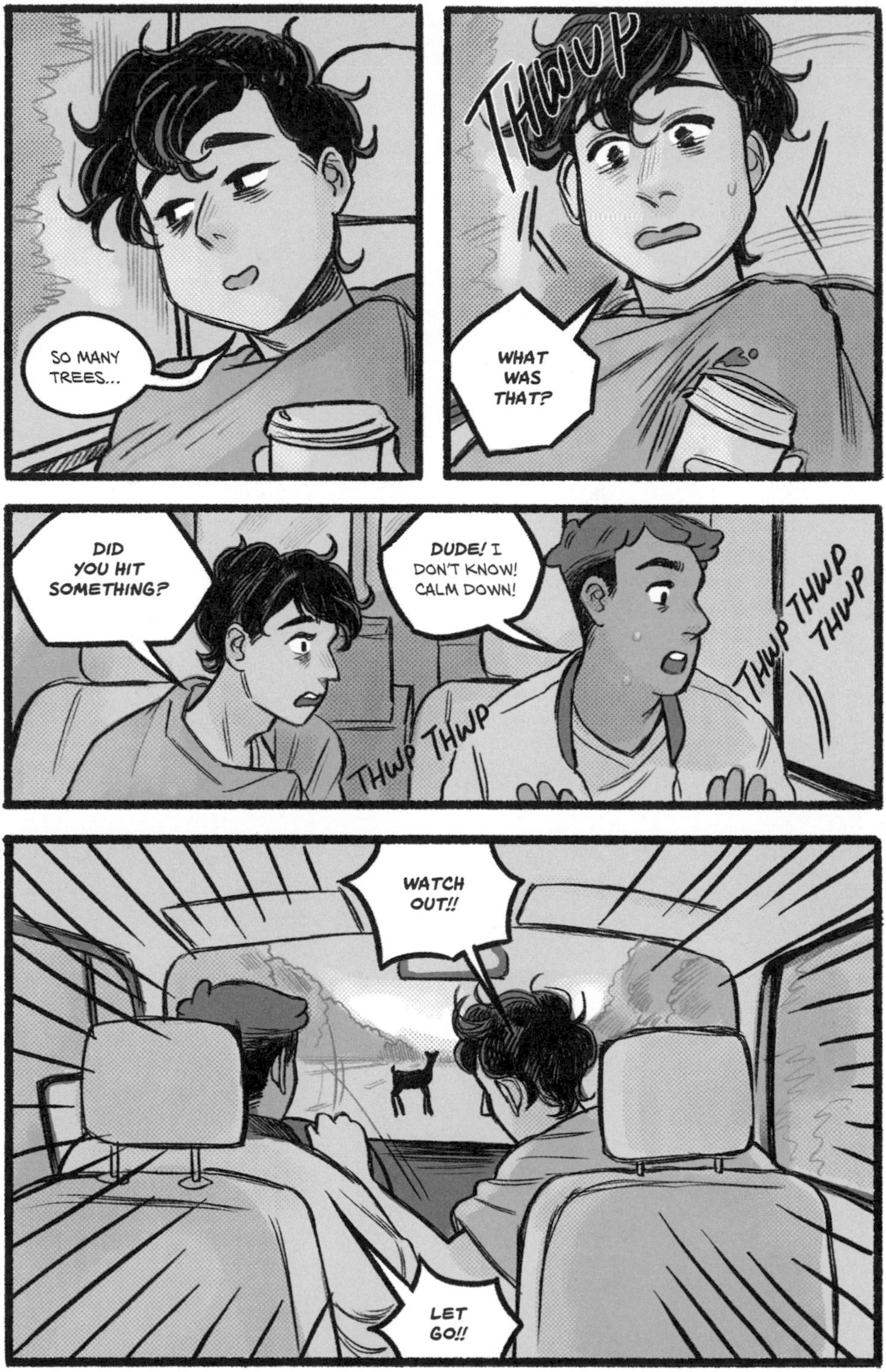

SO MANY TREES...
THWUP
WHAT WAS THAT?
DID YOU HIT SOMETHING?
DUDE! I DON'T KNOW! CALM DOWN!
THWP THWP
THWP THWP THWP
WATCH OUT!!
LET GO!!

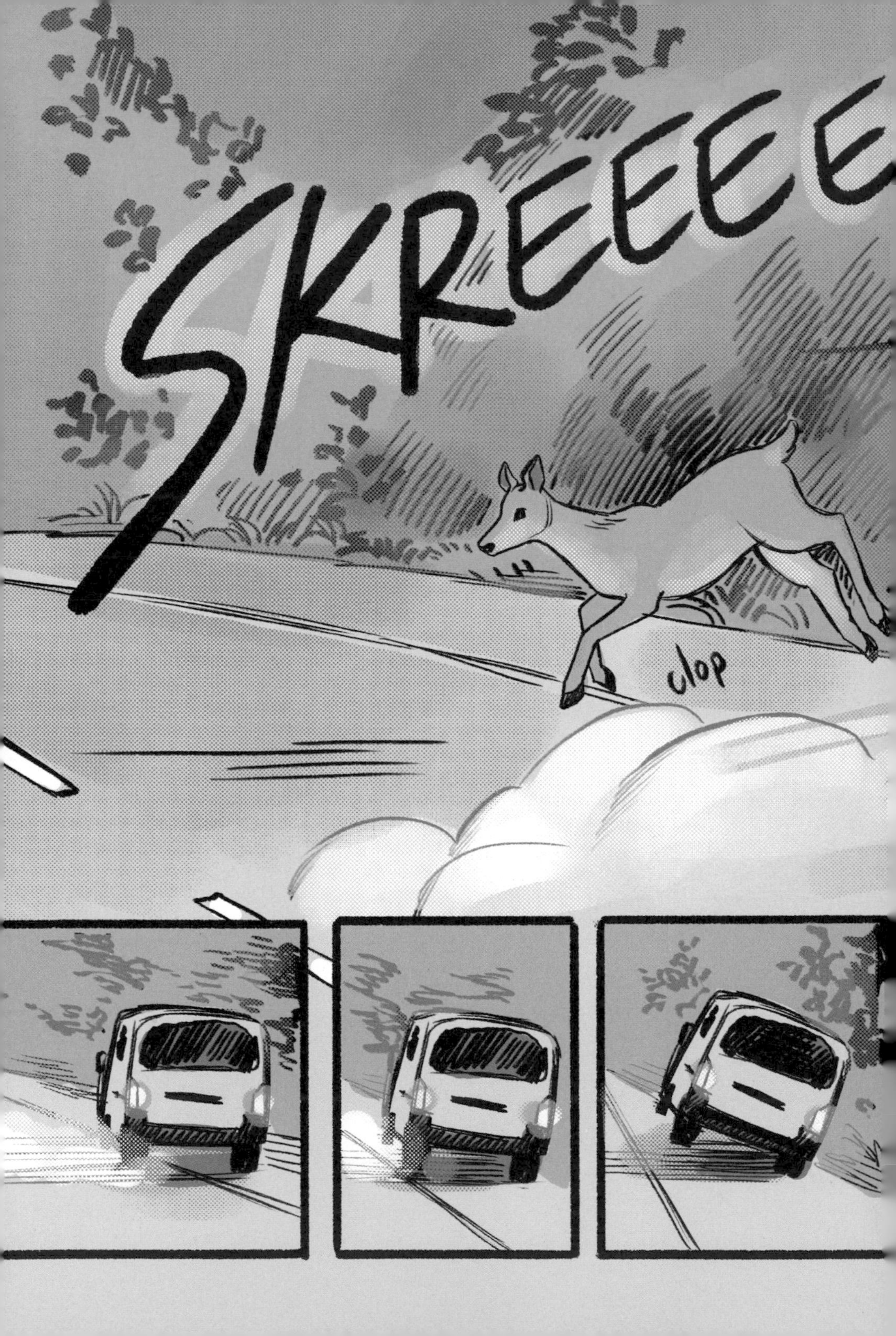
SKREEEEE
clop

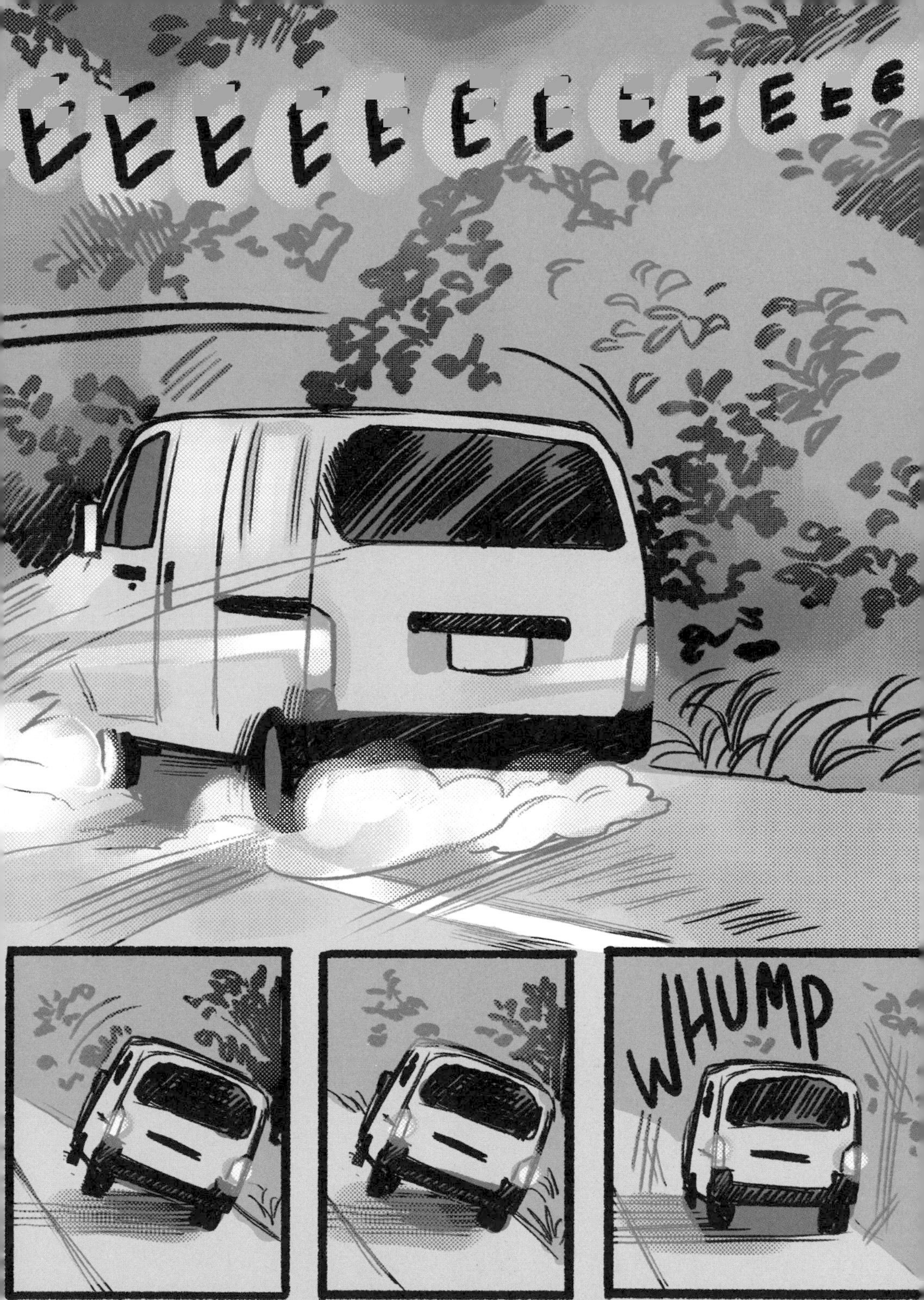
EEEEEEEEEEEE
WHUMP

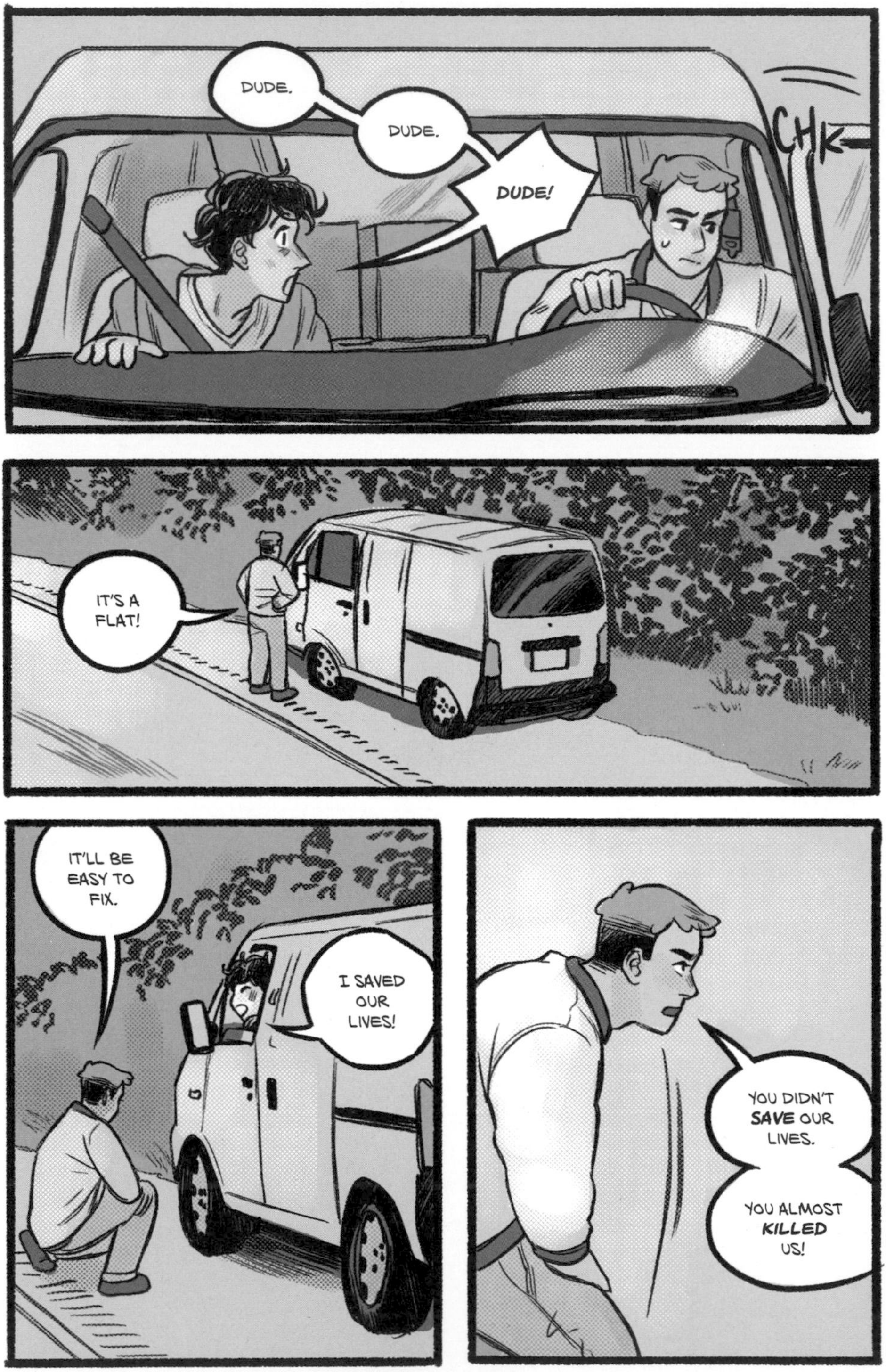
DUDE.
DUDE.
DUDE!
CHK
IT'S A FLAT!
IT'LL BE EASY TO FIX.
I SAVED OUR LIVES!
YOU DIDN'T SAVE OUR LIVES.
YOU ALMOST KILLED US!

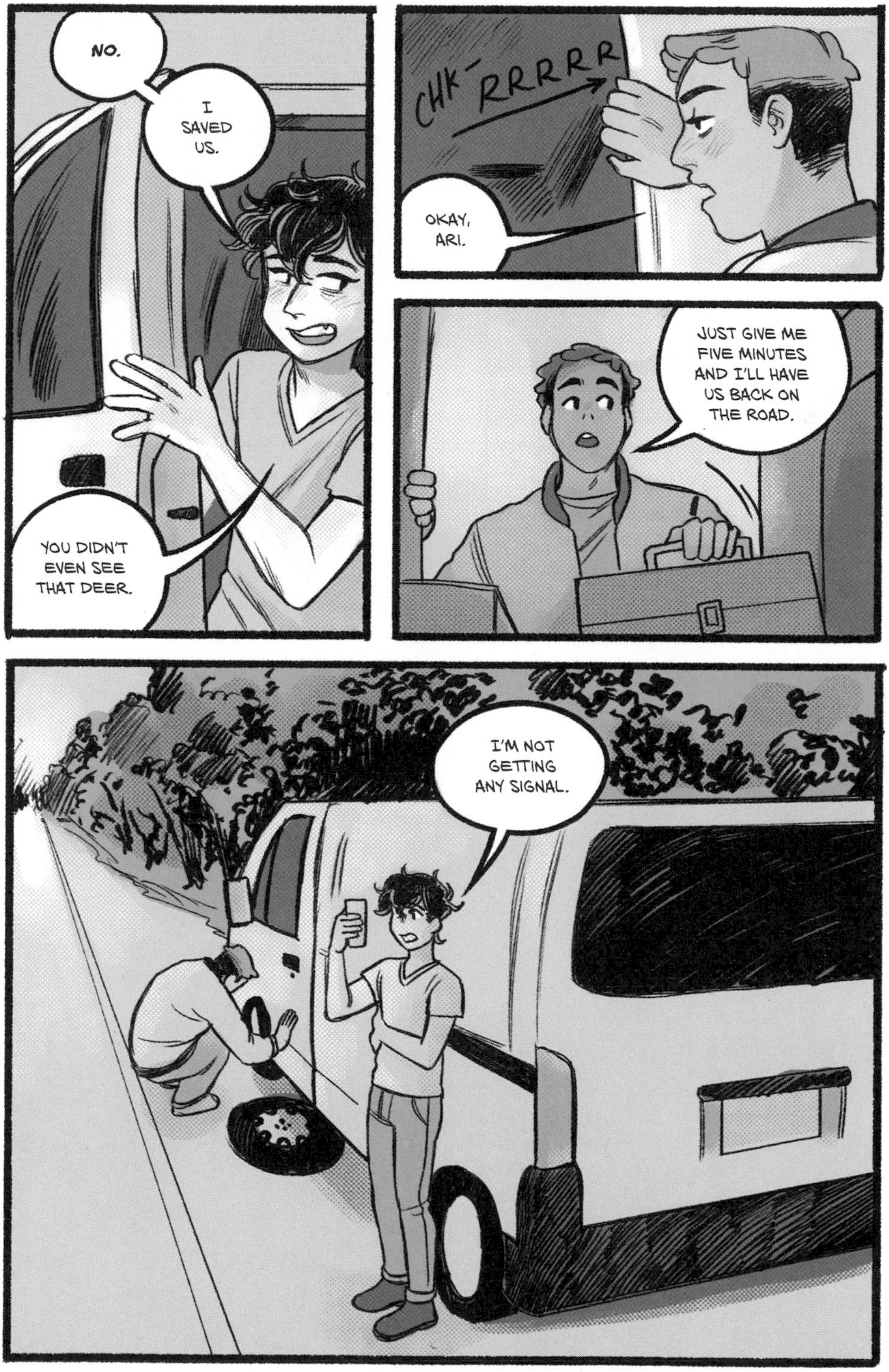
NO.
I SAVED US.
YOU DIDN'T EVEN SEE THAT DEER.
CHK-RRRRR
OKAY, ARI.
JUST GIVE ME FIVE MINUTES AND I'LL HAVE US BACK ON THE ROAD.
I'M NOT GETTING ANY SIGNAL.

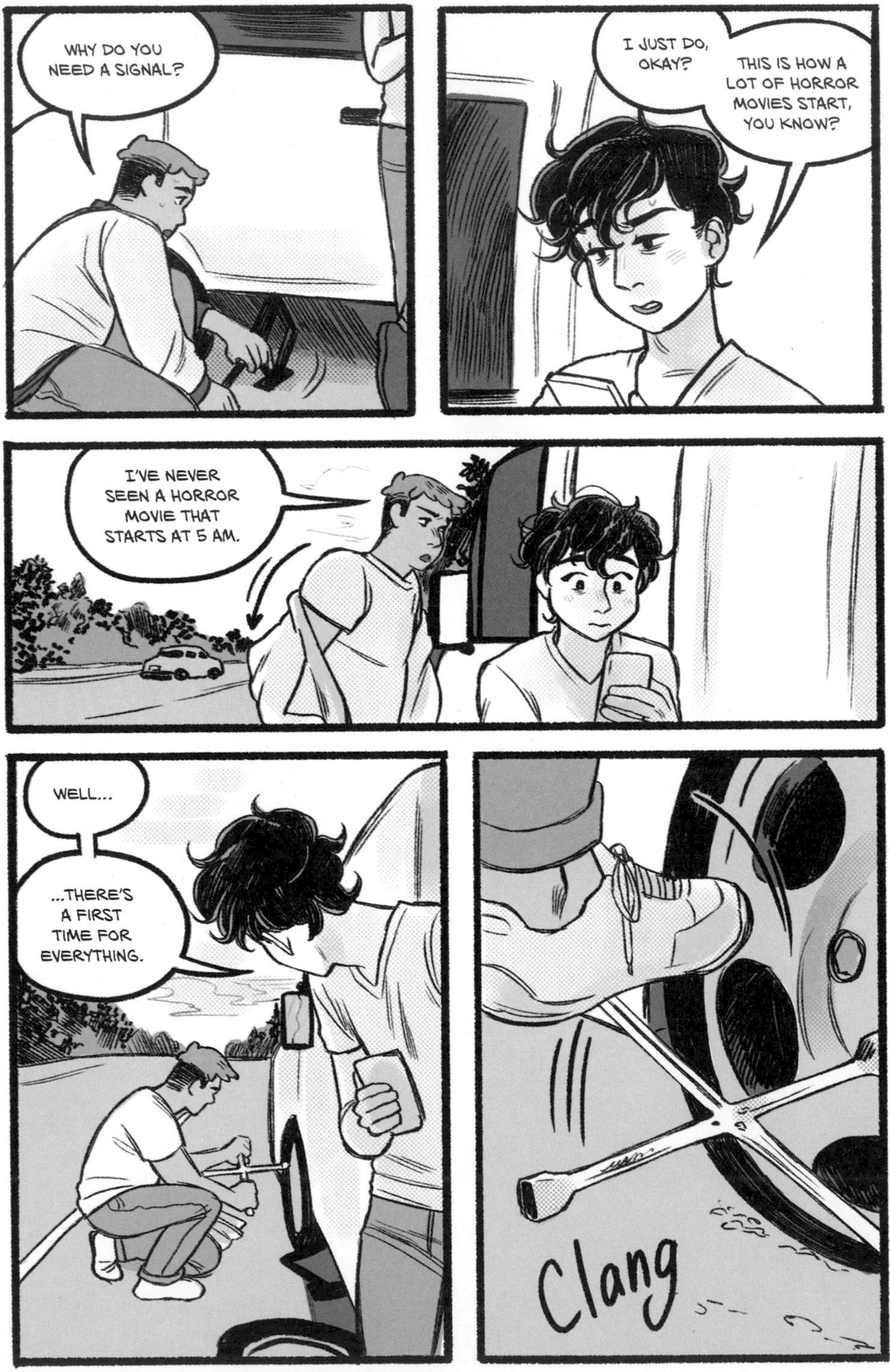
WHY DO YOU NEED A SIGNAL?
I JUST DO, OKAY?
THIS IS HOW A LOT OF HORROR MOVIES START, YOU KNOW?
I'VE NEVER SEEN A HORROR MOVIE THAT STARTS AT 5 AM.
WELL...
...THERE'S A FIRST TIME FOR EVERYTHING.
Clang

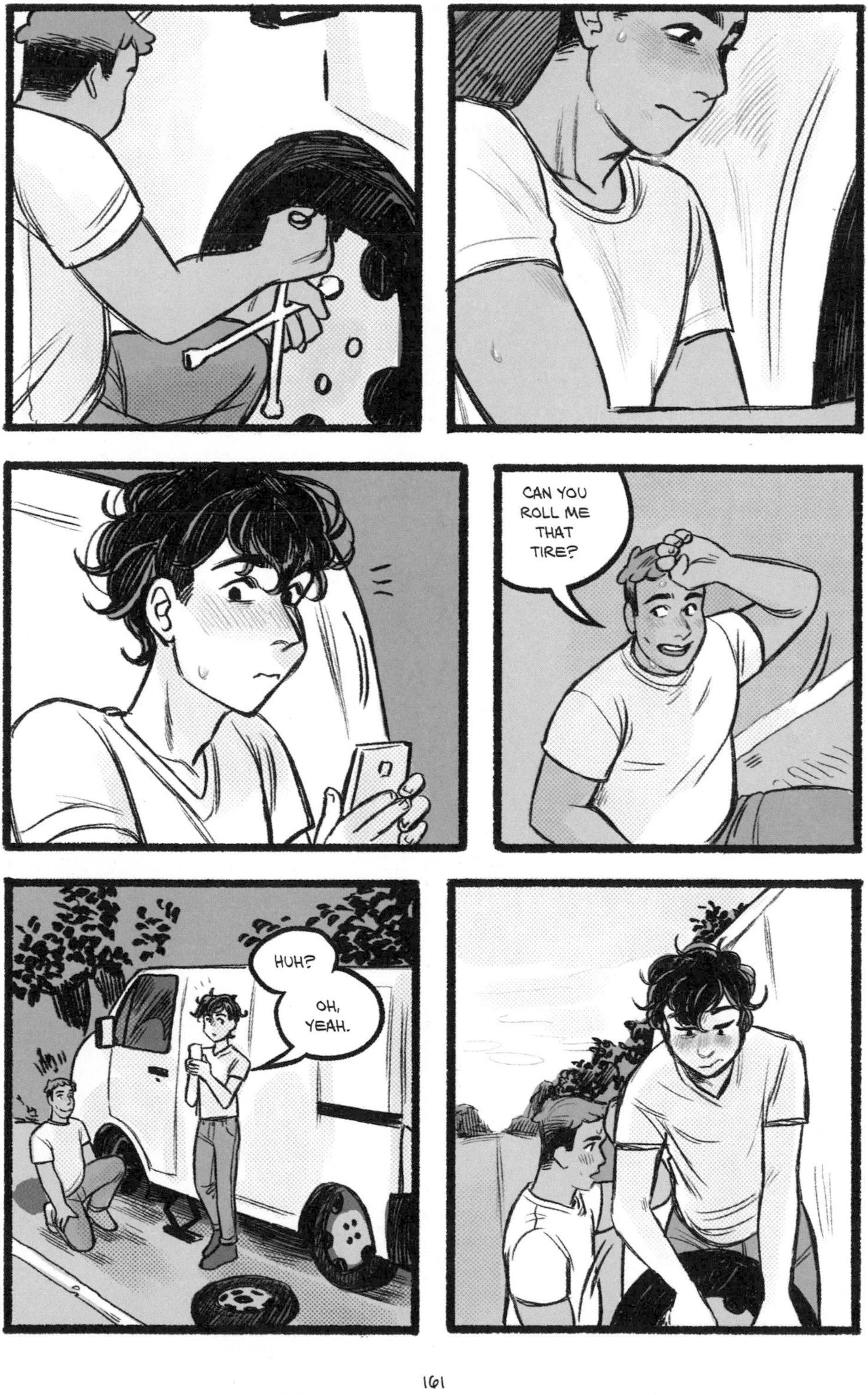
CAN YOU ROLL ME THAT TIRE?
HUH?
OH, YEAH.

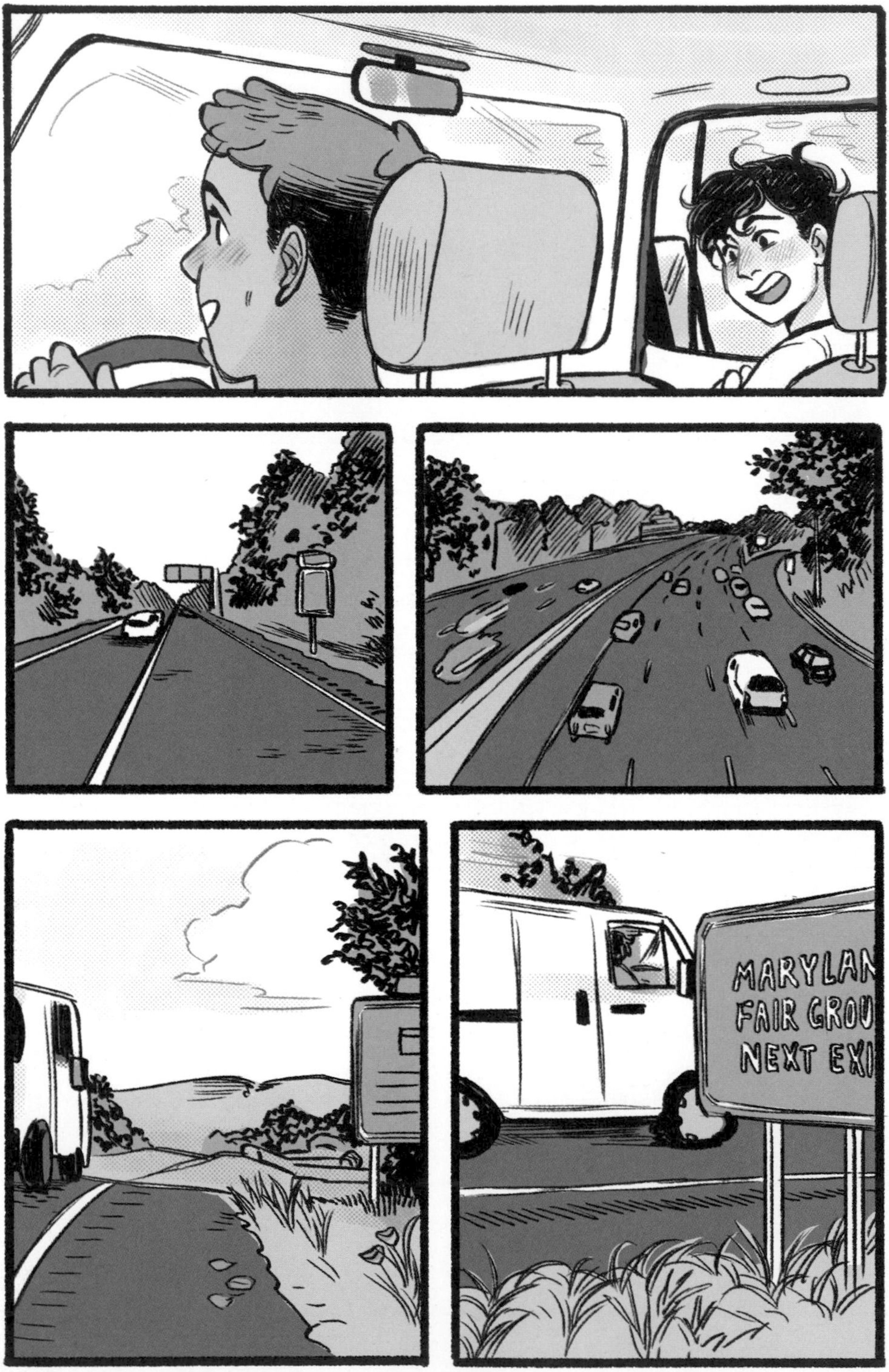
MARYLAN
FAIR GROU
NEXT EXI

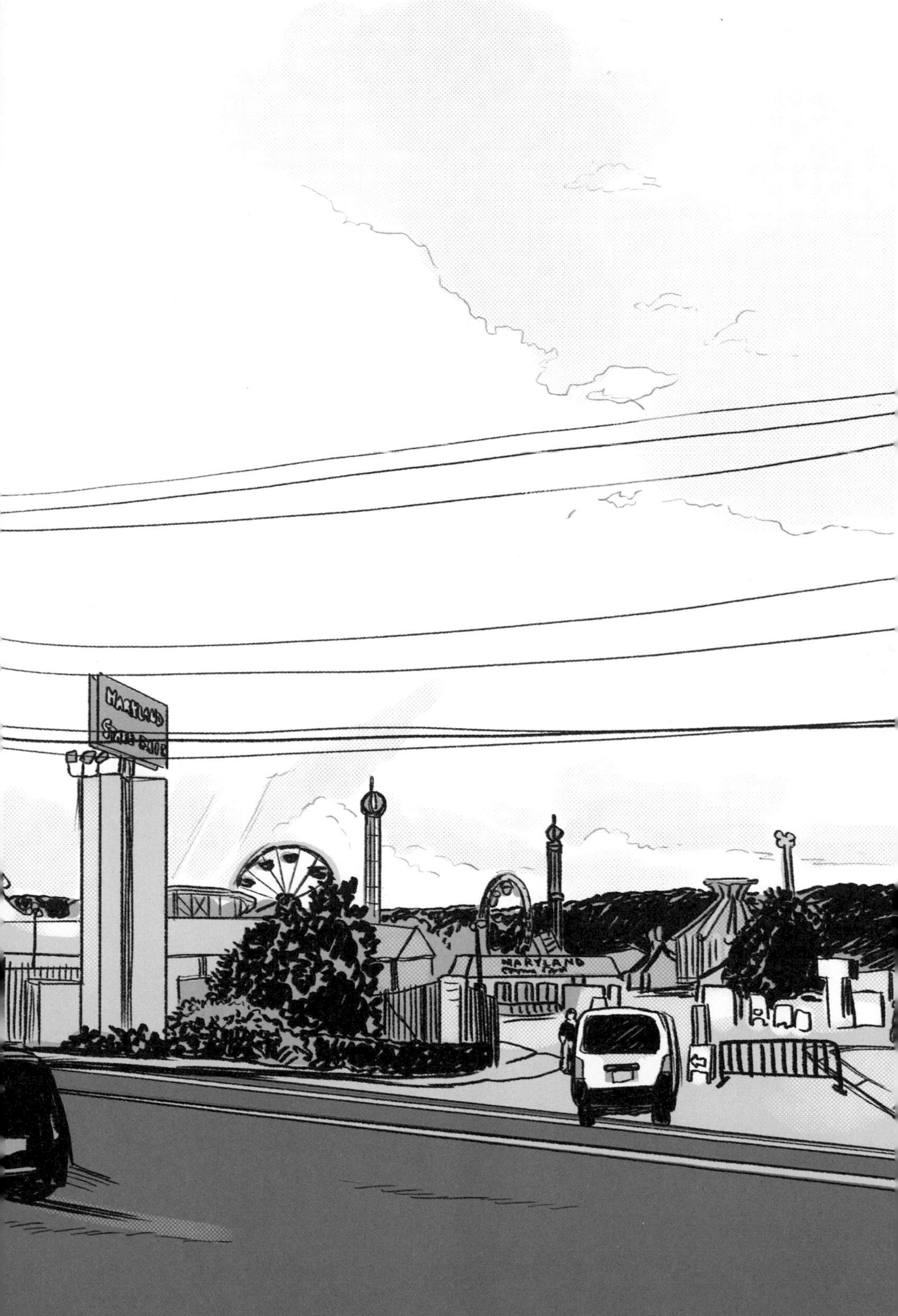
MARYLAND
MARYLAND

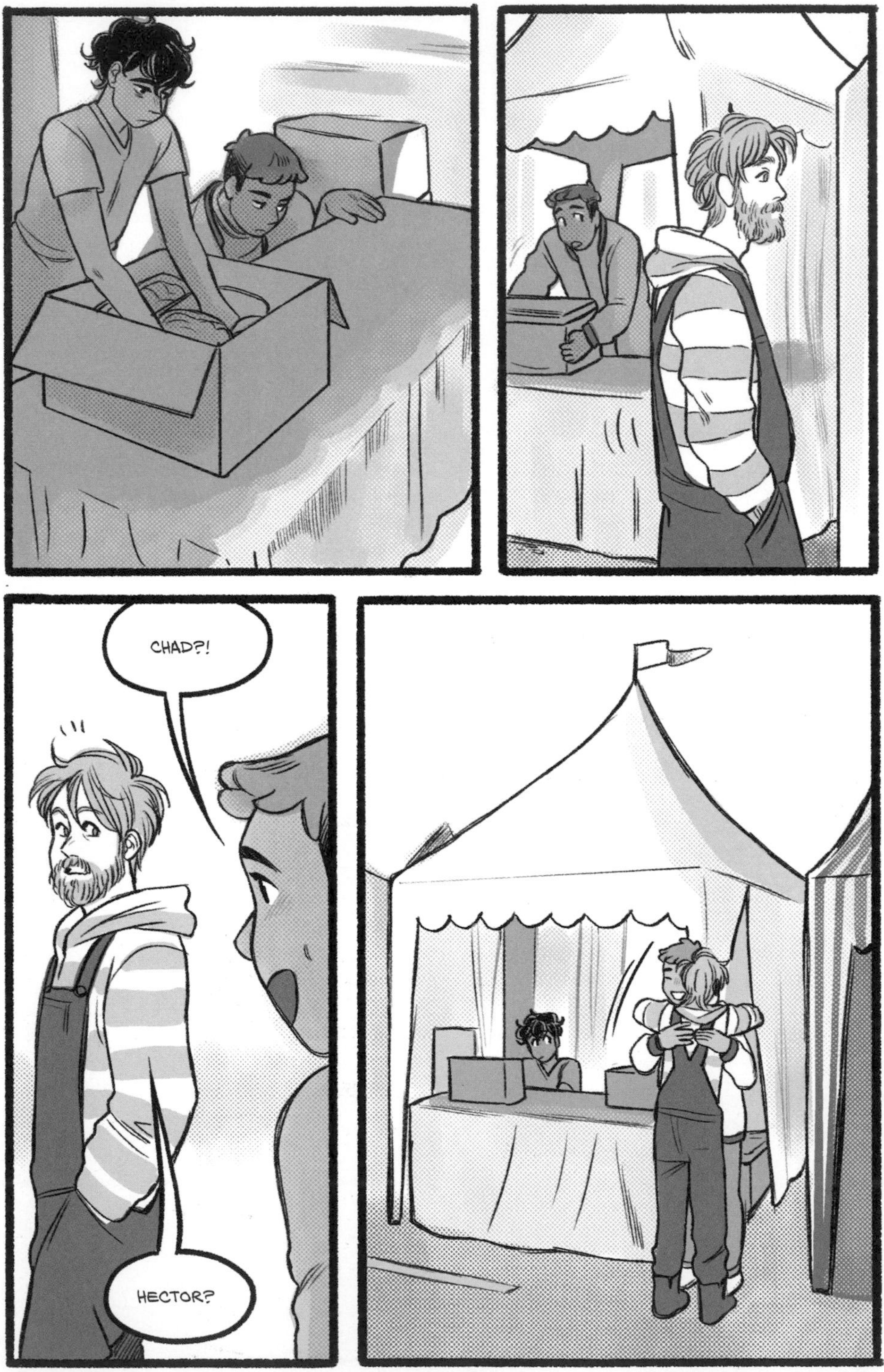
CHAD?!
HECTOR?

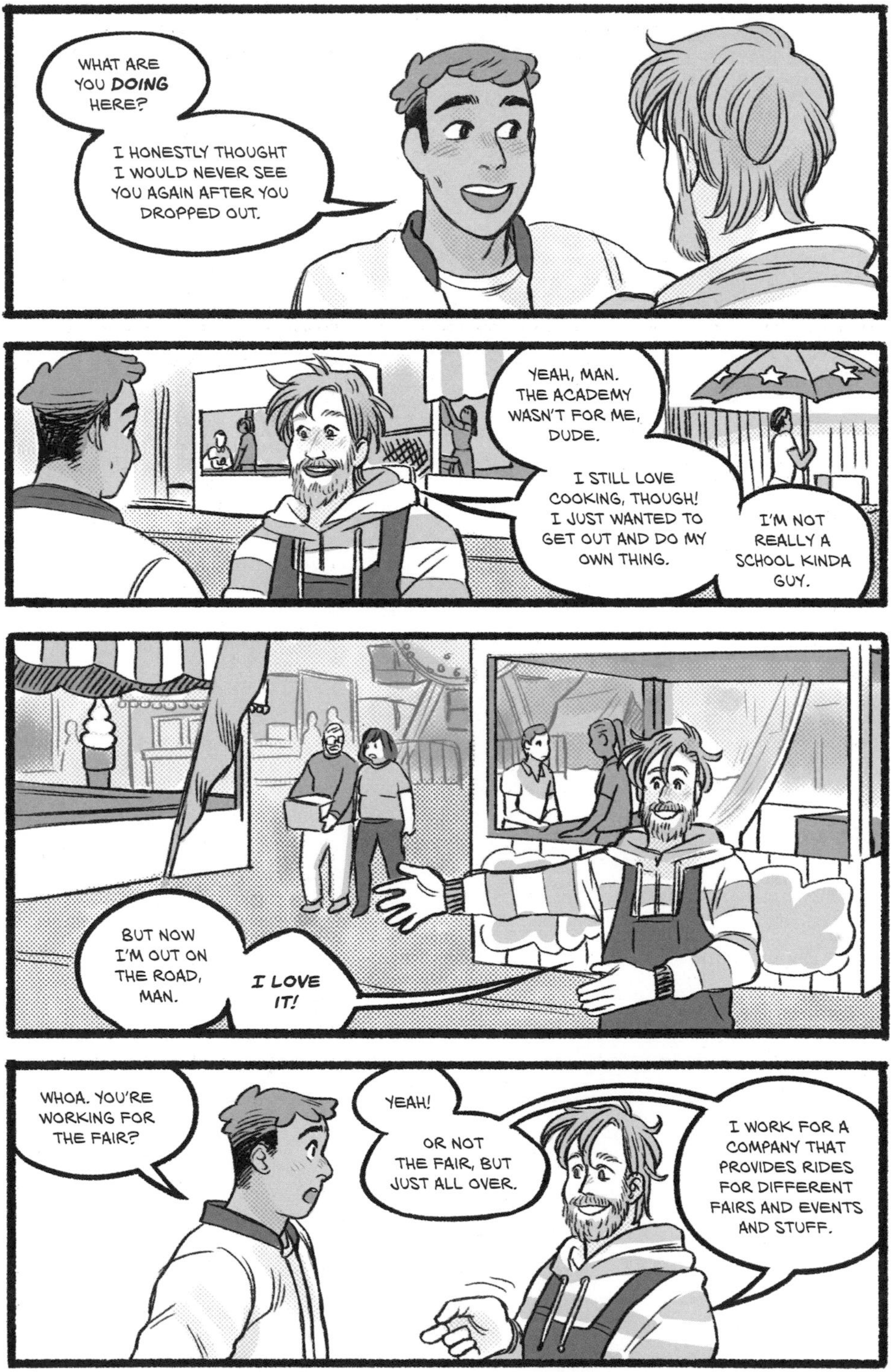
WHAT ARE YOU **DOING** HERE?
I HONESTLY THOUGHT I WOULD NEVER SEE YOU AGAIN AFTER YOU DROPPED OUT.
YEAH, MAN. THE ACADEMY WASN'T FOR ME, DUDE.
I STILL LOVE COOKING, THOUGH! I JUST WANTED TO GET OUT AND DO MY OWN THING.
I'M NOT REALLY A SCHOOL KINDA GUY.
BUT NOW I'M OUT ON THE ROAD, MAN.
I LOVE IT!
WHOA. YOU'RE WORKING FOR THE FAIR?
YEAH!
OR NOT THE FAIR, BUT JUST ALL OVER.
I WORK FOR A COMPANY THAT PROVIDES RIDES FOR DIFFERENT FAIRS AND EVENTS AND STUFF.

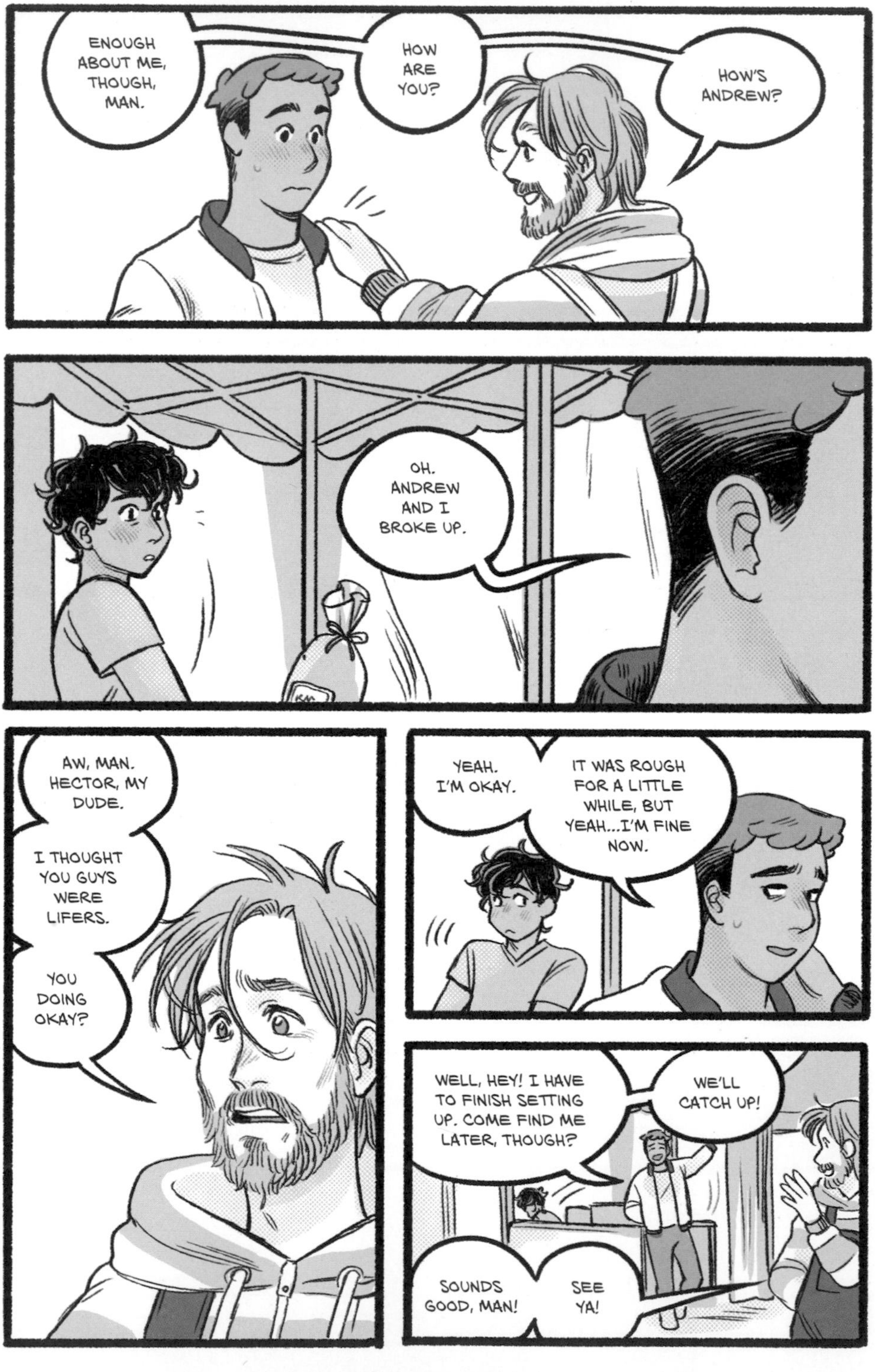
ENOUGH ABOUT ME, THOUGH, MAN.
HOW ARE YOU?
HOW'S ANDREW?
OH. ANDREW AND I BROKE UP.
AW, MAN. HECTOR, MY DUDE.
I THOUGHT YOU GUYS WERE LIFERS.
YOU DOING OKAY?
YEAH. I'M OKAY.
IT WAS ROUGH FOR A LITTLE WHILE, BUT YEAH...I'M FINE NOW.
WELL, HEY! I HAVE TO FINISH SETTING UP. COME FIND ME LATER, THOUGH?
WE'LL CATCH UP!
SOUNDS GOOD, MAN!
SEE YA!

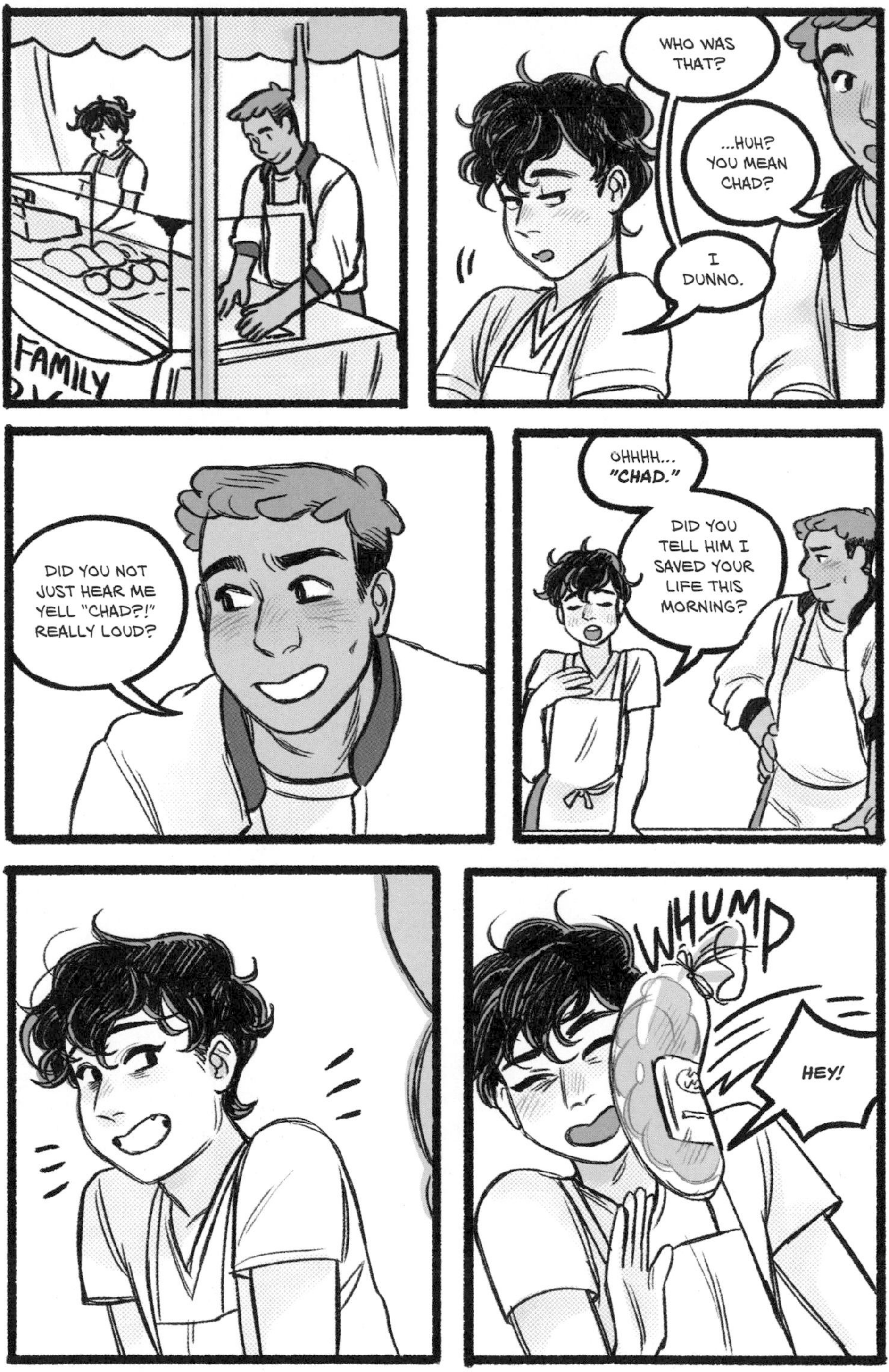
FAMILY
WHO WAS THAT?
...HUH? YOU MEAN CHAD?
I DUNNO.
DID YOU NOT JUST HEAR ME YELL "CHAD?!" REALLY LOUD?
OHHHH... "CHAD."
DID YOU TELL HIM I SAVED YOUR LIFE THIS MORNING?
WHUMP
HEY!

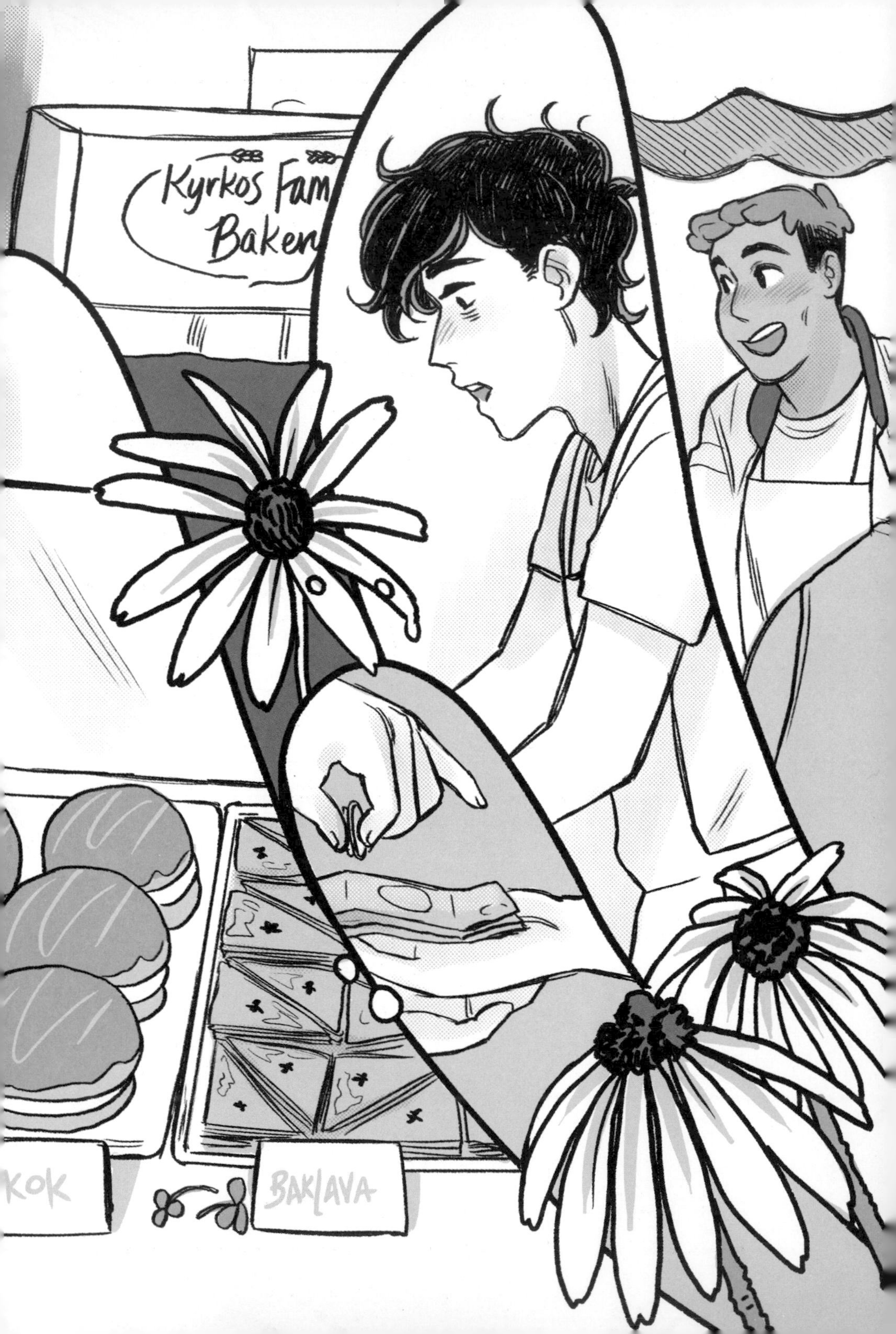
Kyrkos Fam
Baker
KOK
BAKLAVA

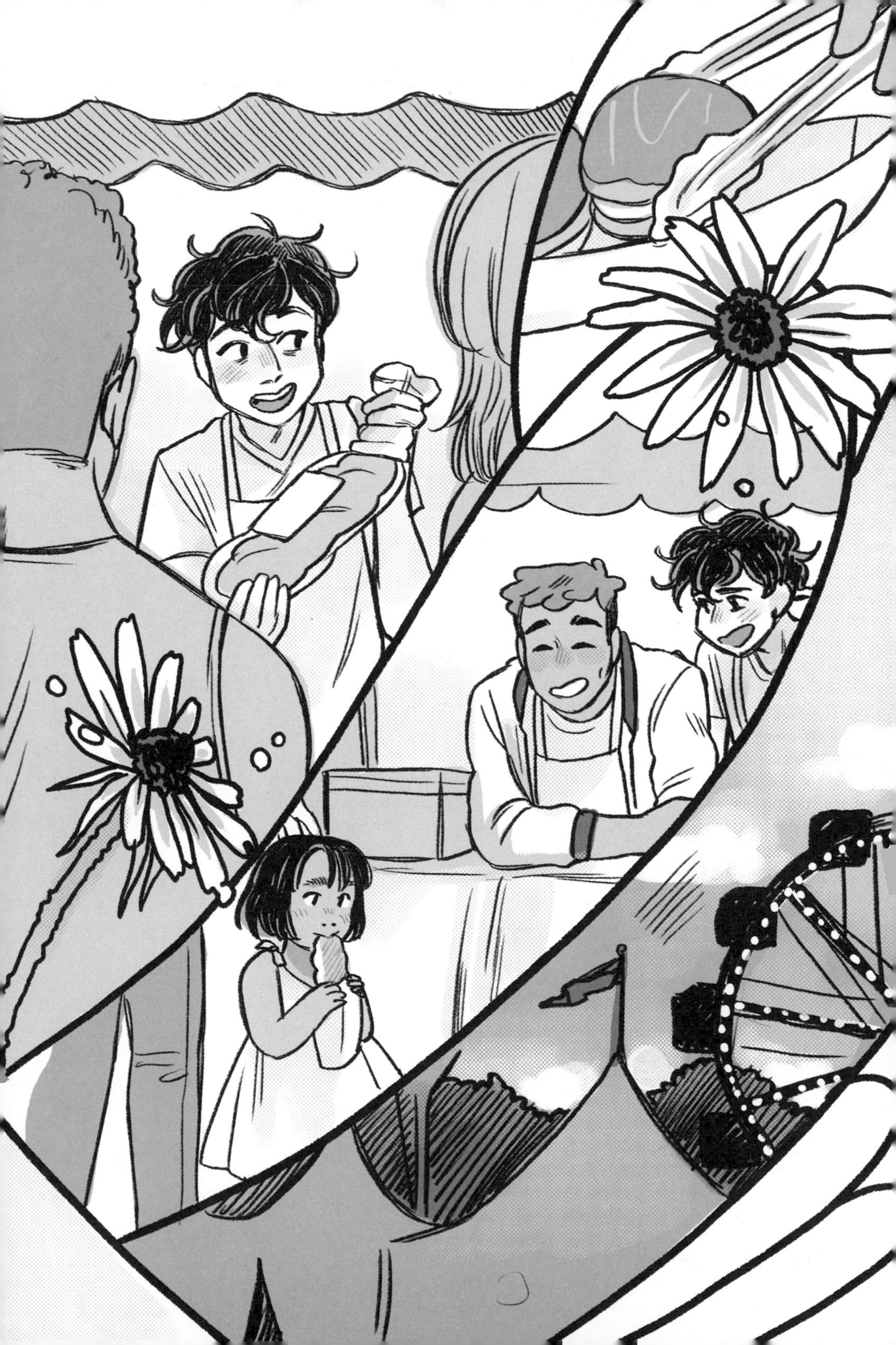

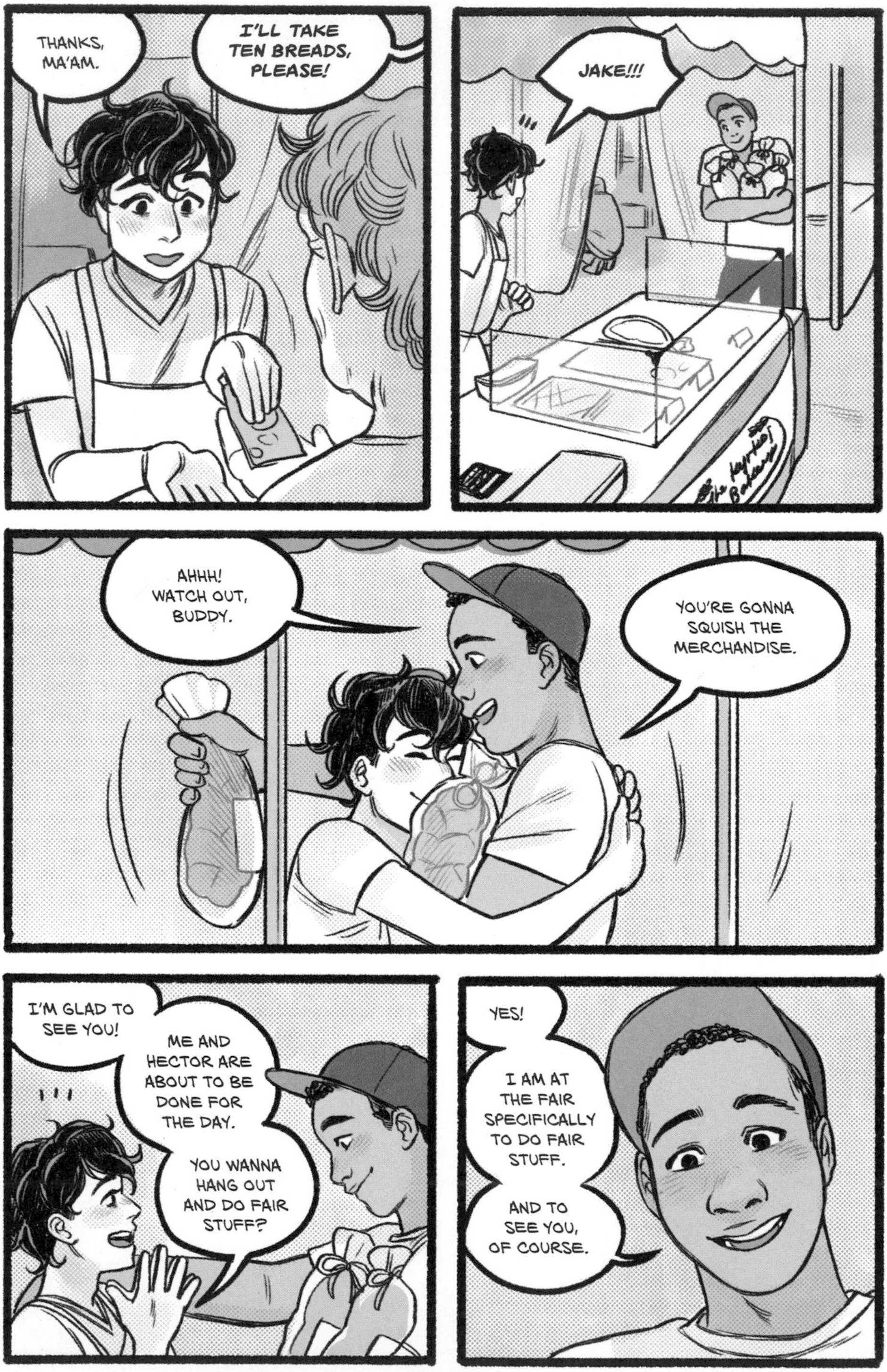
THANKS, MA'AM.
I'LL TAKE TEN BREADS, PLEASE!
JAKE!!!
AHHH! WATCH OUT, BUDDY.
YOU'RE GONNA SQUISH THE MERCHANDISE.
I'M GLAD TO SEE YOU!
ME AND HECTOR ARE ABOUT TO BE DONE FOR THE DAY.
YOU WANNA HANG OUT AND DO FAIR STUFF?
YES!
I AM AT THE FAIR SPECIFICALLY TO DO FAIR STUFF.
AND TO SEE YOU, OF COURSE.

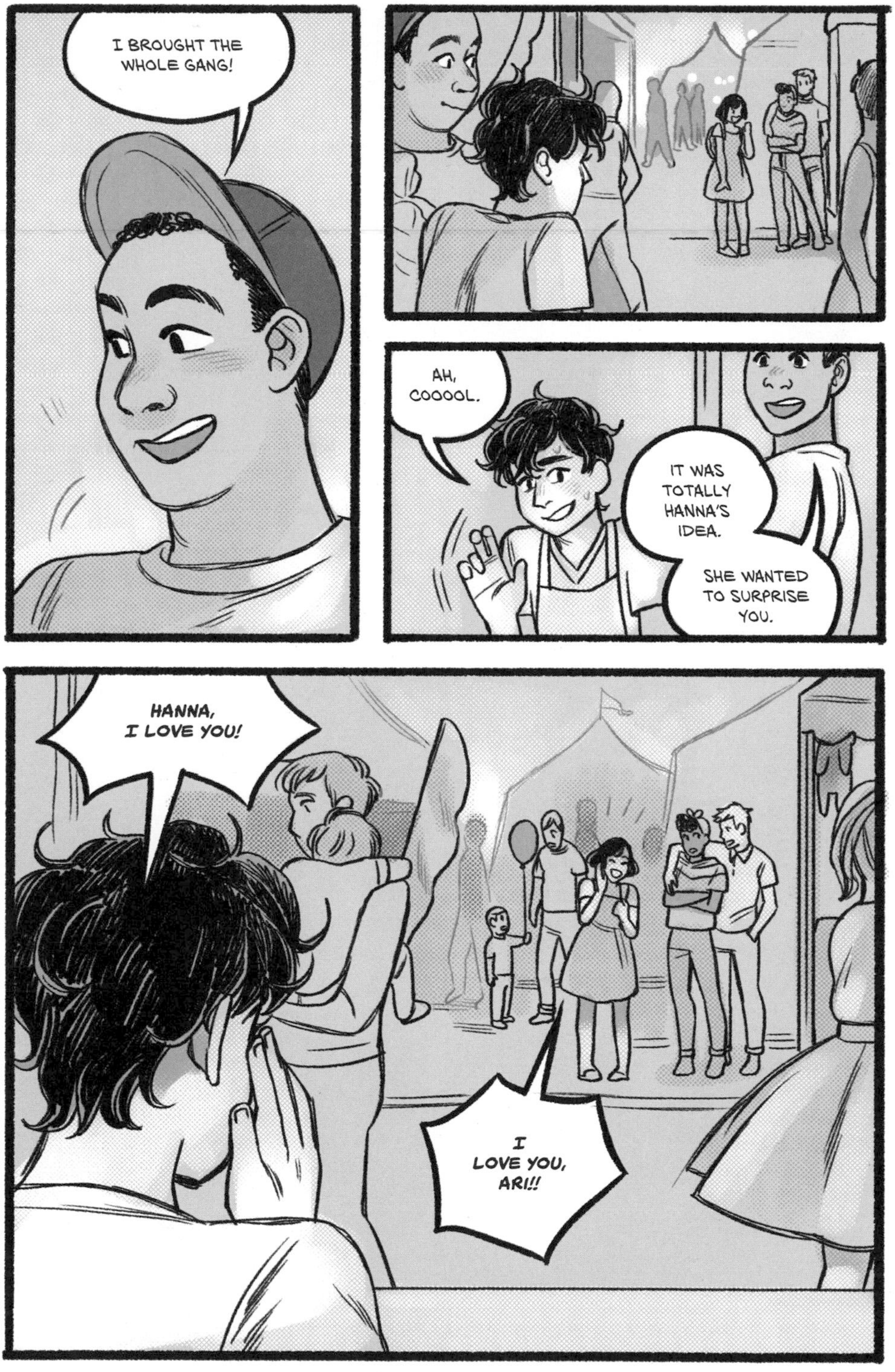
I BROUGHT THE WHOLE GANG!
AH, COOOOL.
IT WAS TOTALLY HANNA'S IDEA.
SHE WANTED TO SURPRISE YOU.
HANNA, I LOVE YOU!
I LOVE YOU, ARI!!

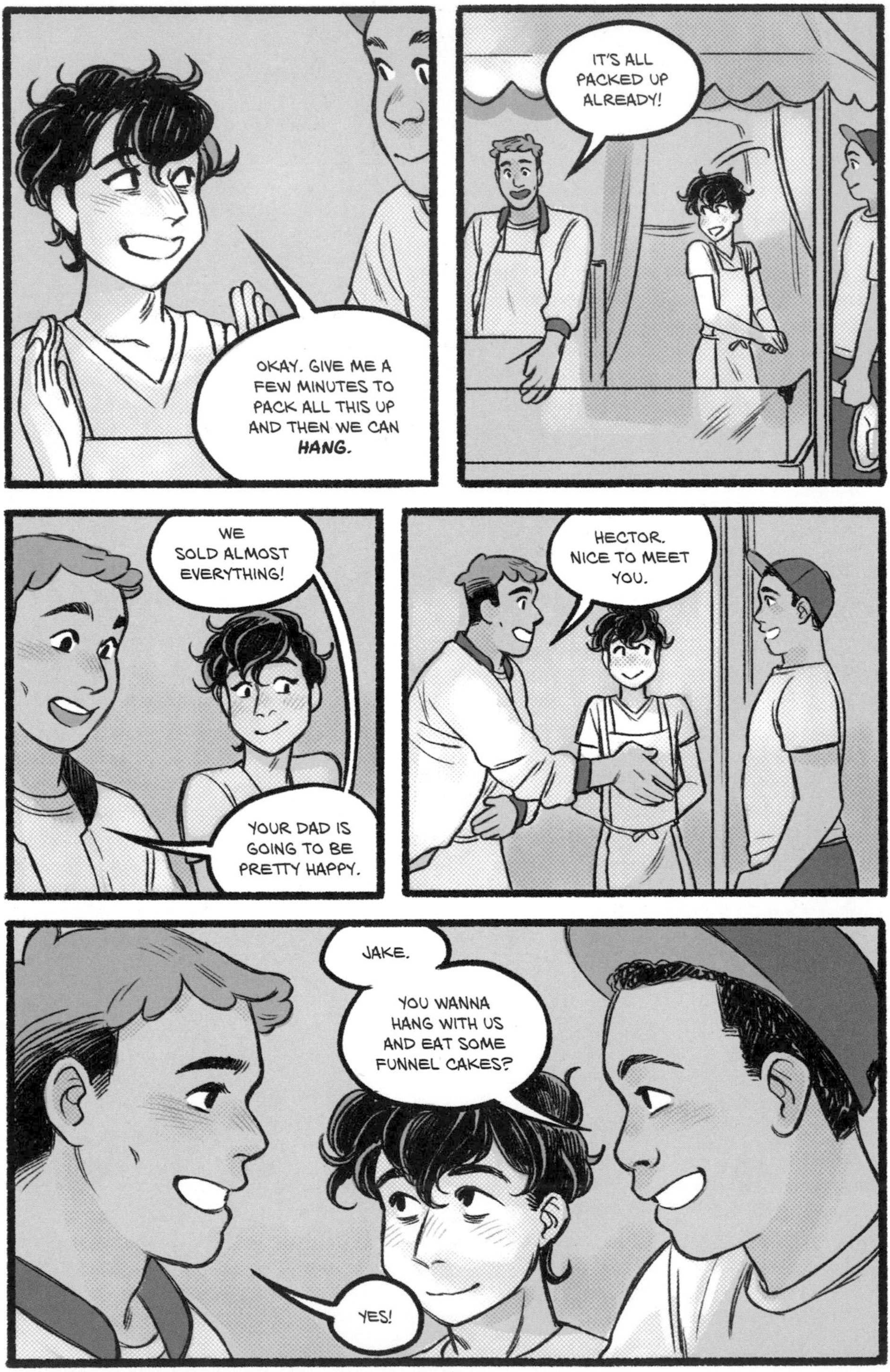
OKAY. GIVE ME A FEW MINUTES TO PACK ALL THIS UP AND THEN WE CAN **HANG.**
IT'S ALL PACKED UP ALREADY!
WE SOLD ALMOST EVERYTHING!
YOUR DAD IS GOING TO BE PRETTY HAPPY.
HECTOR. NICE TO MEET YOU.
JAKE.
YOU WANNA HANG WITH US AND EAT SOME FUNNEL CAKES?
YES!

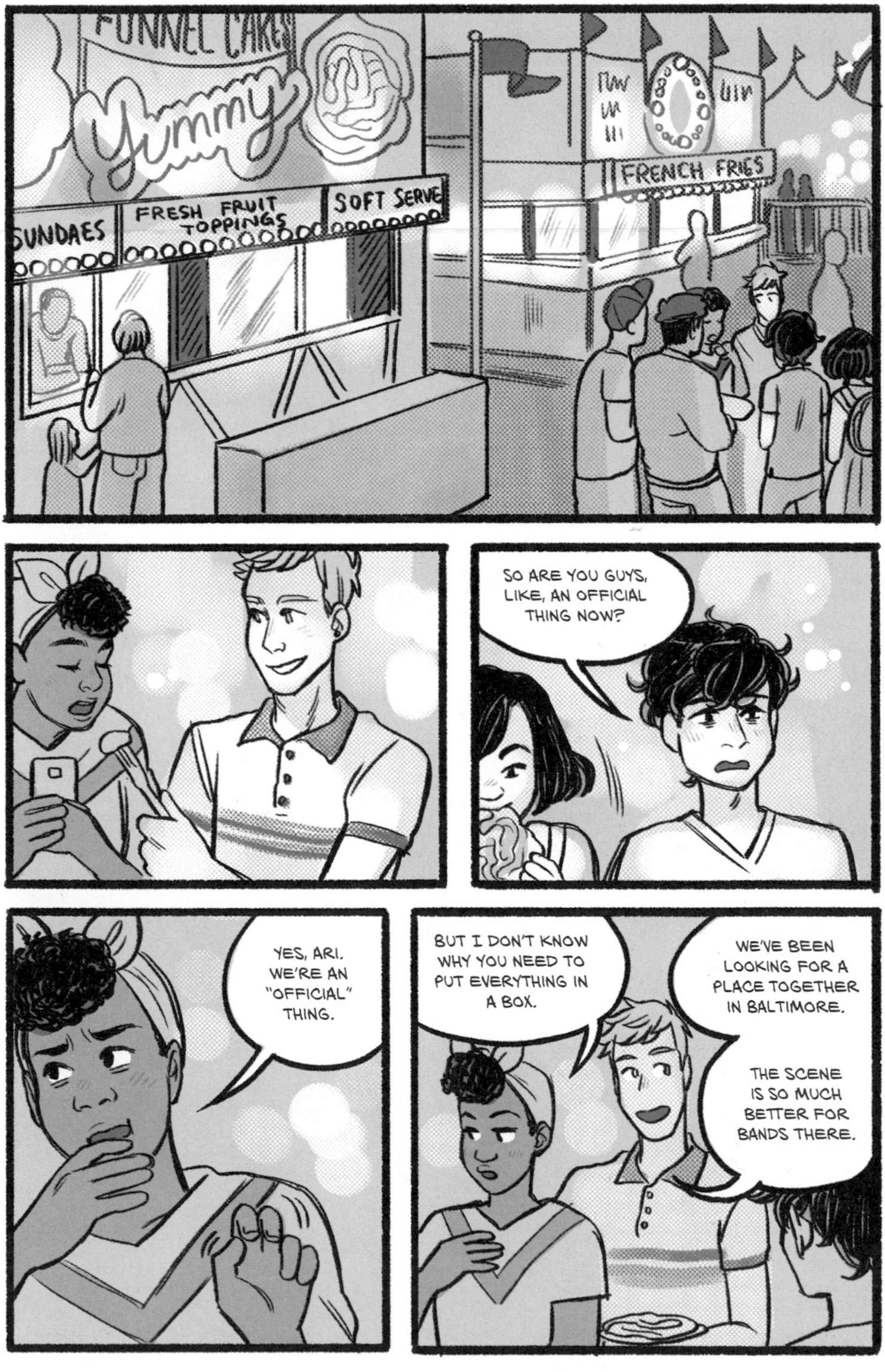
FUNNEL CAKES
Yummy
SUNDAES
FRESH FRUIT TOPPINGS
SOFT SERVE
FRENCH FRIES
SO ARE YOU GUYS, LIKE, AN OFFICIAL THING NOW?
YES, ARI. WE'RE AN "OFFICIAL" THING.
BUT I DON'T KNOW WHY YOU NEED TO PUT EVERYTHING IN A BOX.
WE'VE BEEN LOOKING FOR A PLACE TOGETHER IN BALTIMORE.
THE SCENE IS SO MUCH BETTER FOR BANDS THERE.

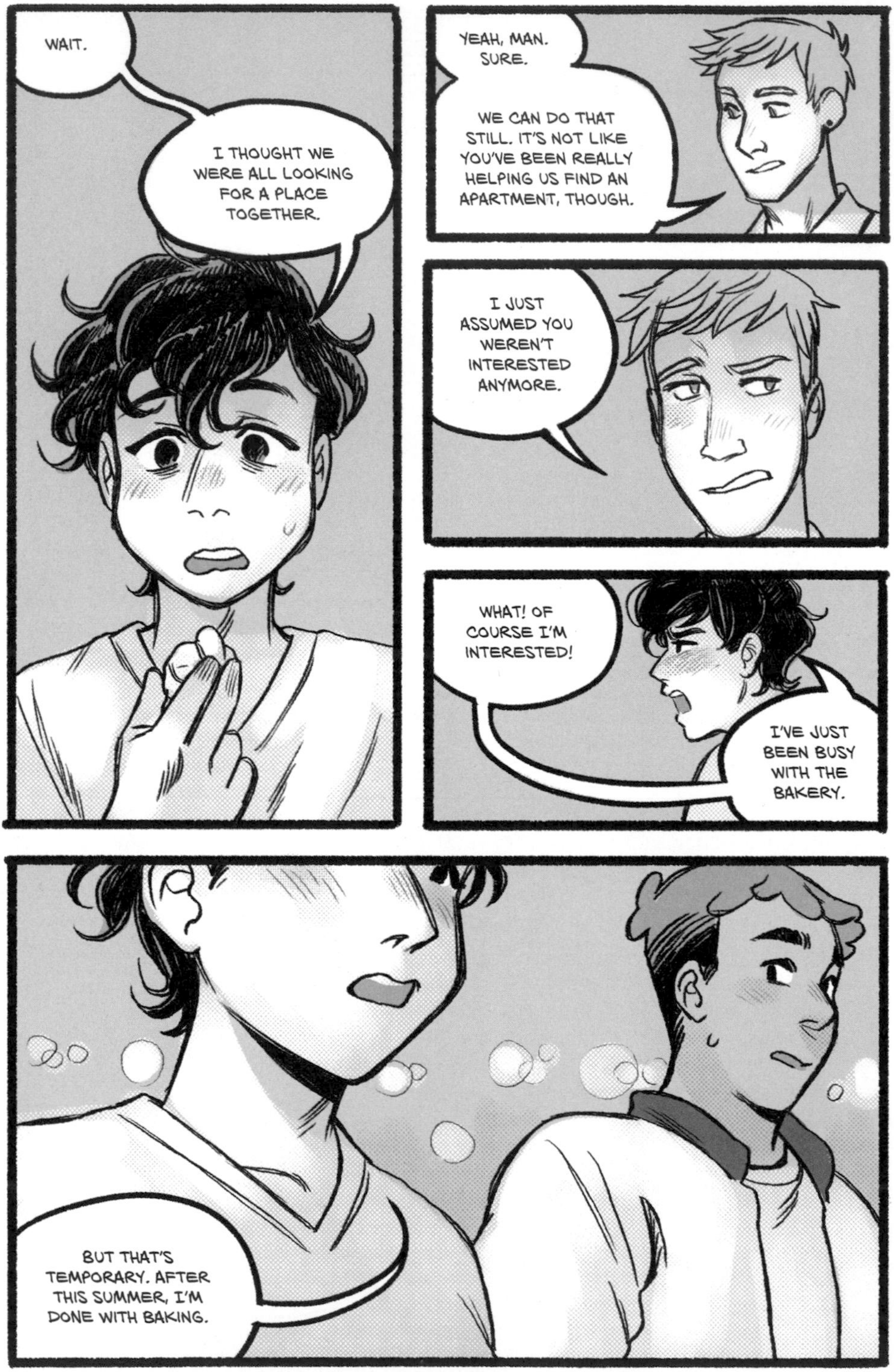
WAIT.
I THOUGHT WE WERE ALL LOOKING FOR A PLACE TOGETHER.
YEAH, MAN. SURE.
WE CAN DO THAT STILL. IT'S NOT LIKE YOU'VE BEEN REALLY HELPING US FIND AN APARTMENT, THOUGH.
I JUST ASSUMED YOU WEREN'T INTERESTED ANYMORE.
WHAT! OF COURSE I'M INTERESTED!
I'VE JUST BEEN BUSY WITH THE BAKERY.
BUT THAT'S TEMPORARY. AFTER THIS SUMMER, I'M DONE WITH BAKING.

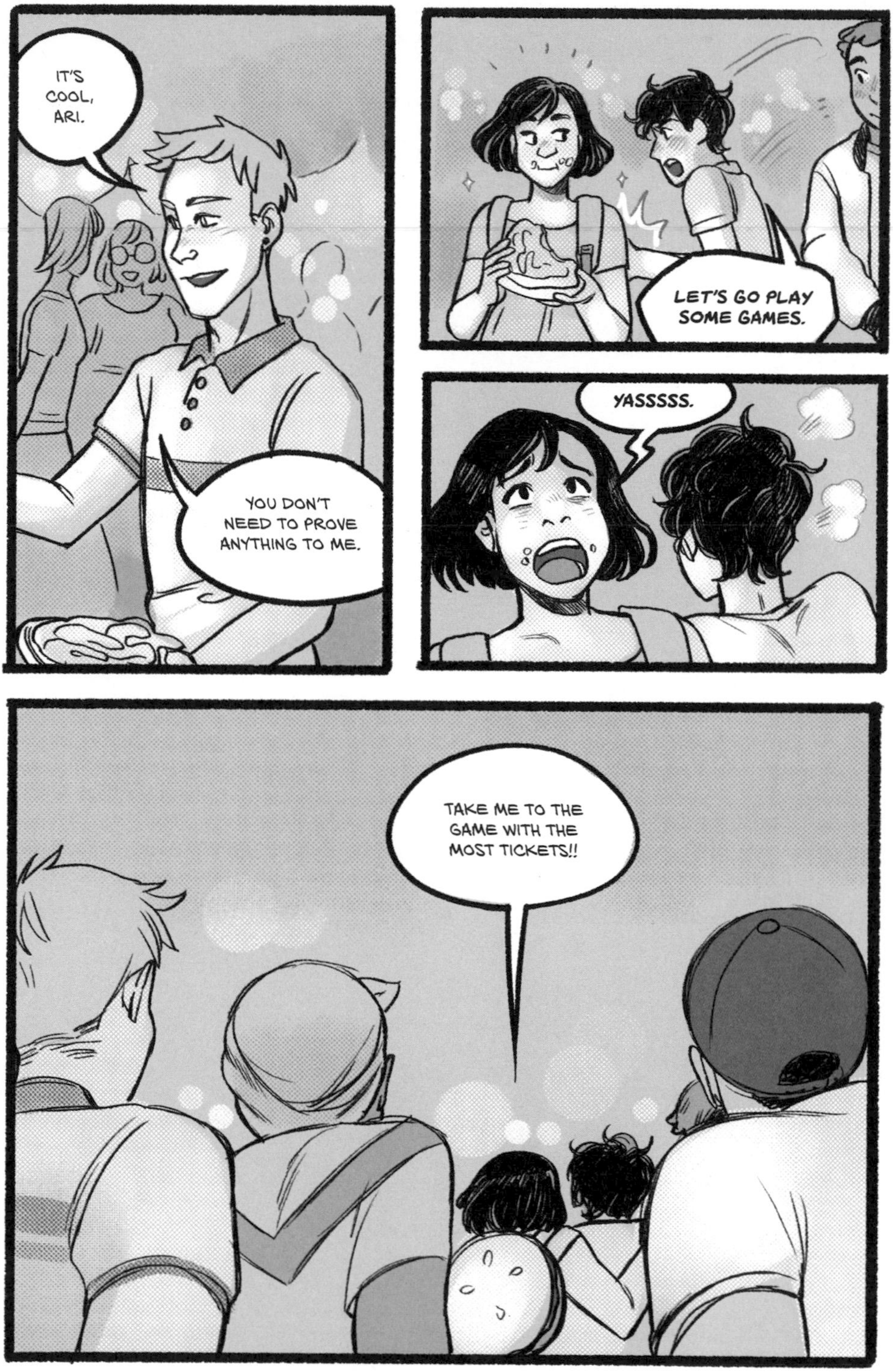
IT'S COOL, ARI.
YOU DON'T NEED TO PROVE ANYTHING TO ME.
LET'S GO PLAY SOME GAMES.
YASSSSS.
TAKE ME TO THE GAME WITH THE MOST TICKETS!!

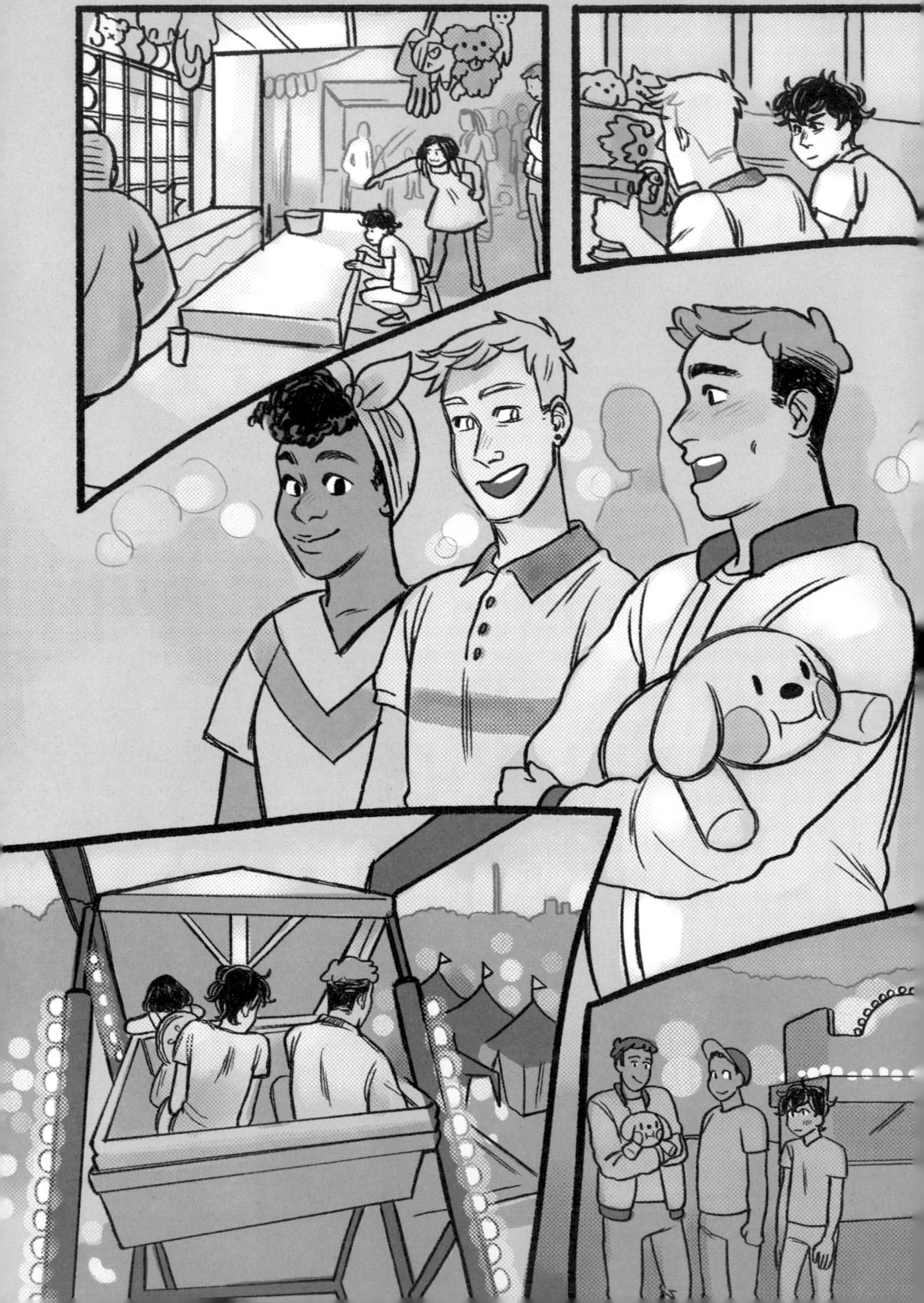

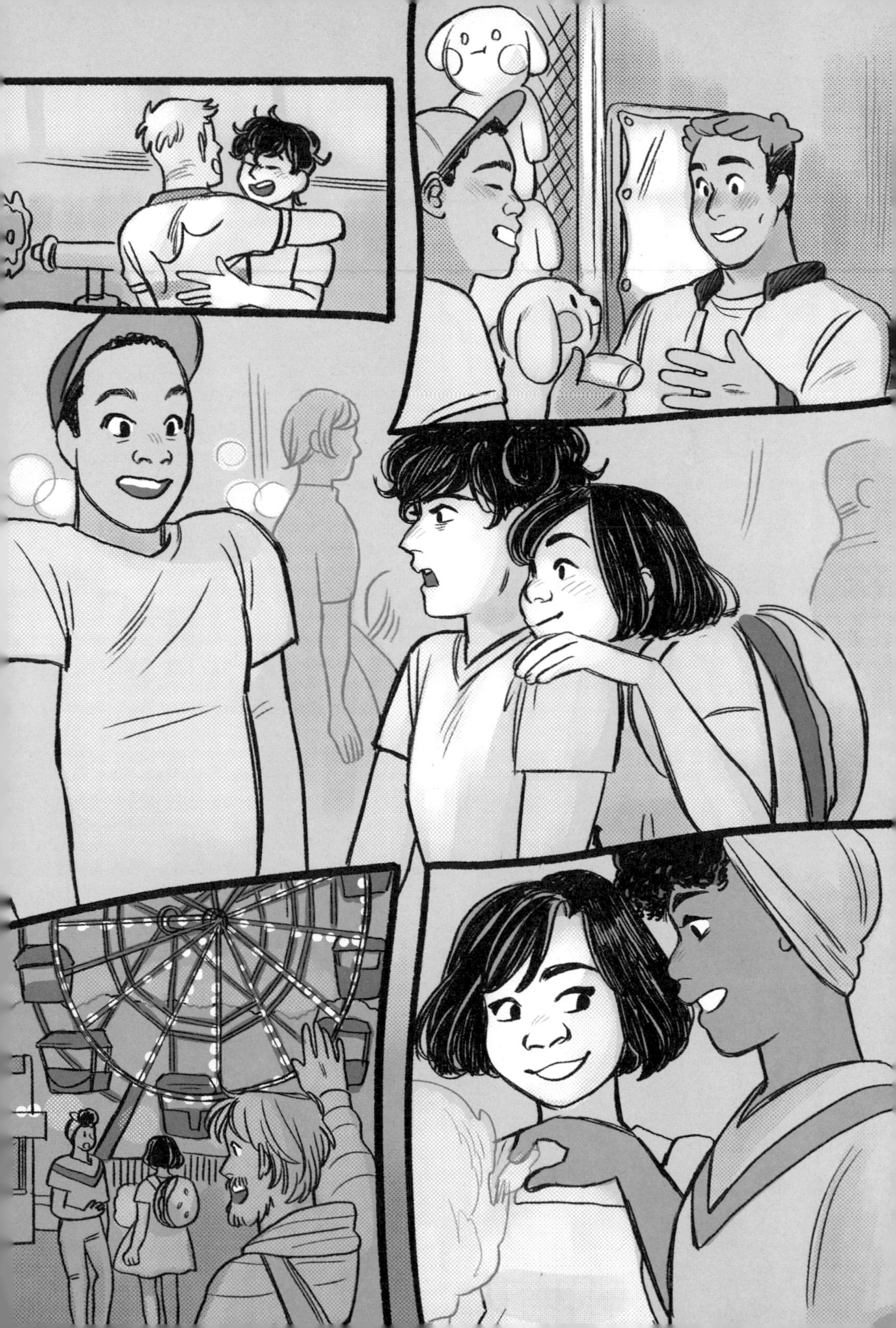

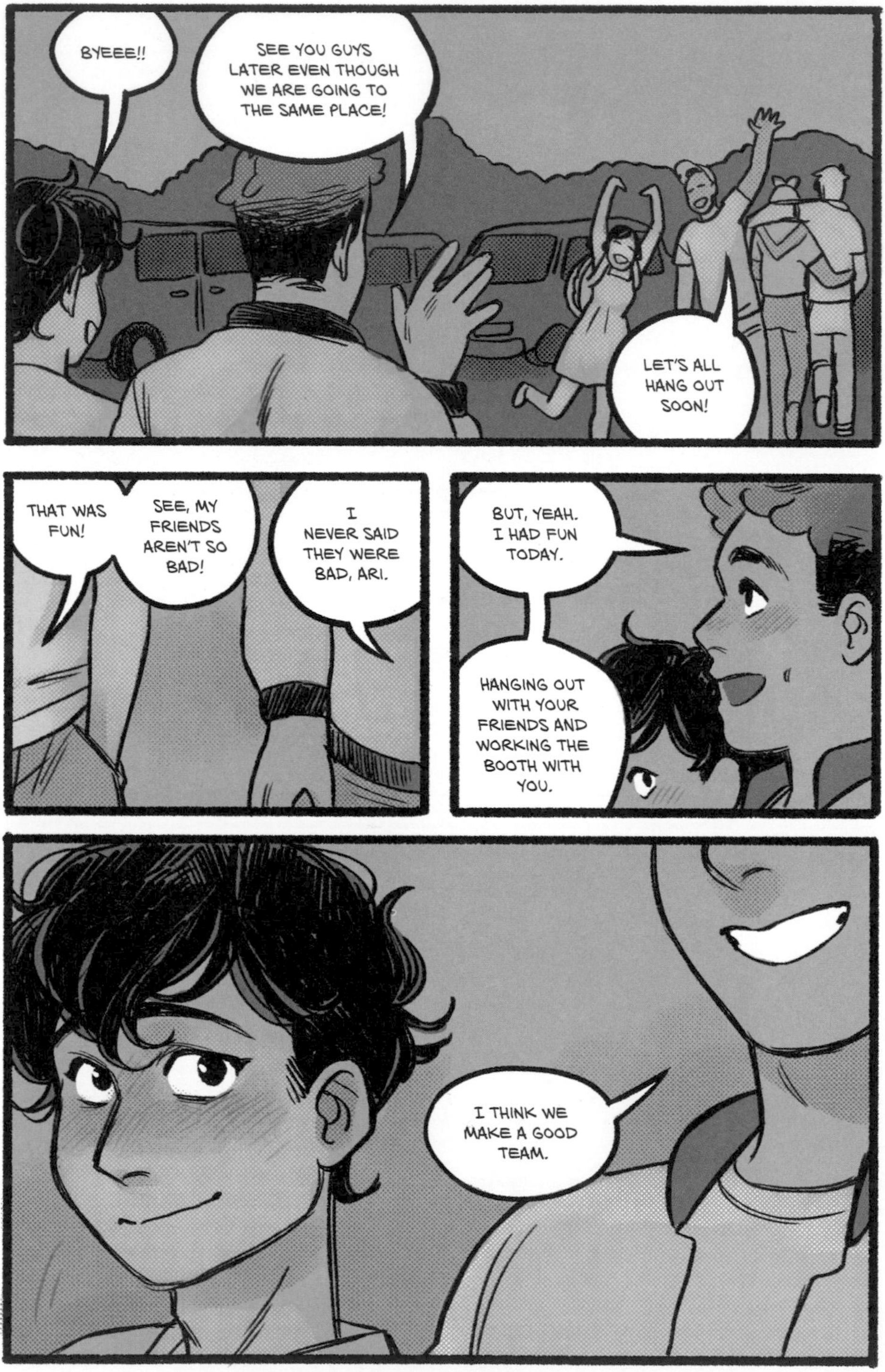
BYEEE!!
SEE YOU GUYS LATER EVEN THOUGH WE ARE GOING TO THE SAME PLACE!
LET'S ALL HANG OUT SOON!
THAT WAS FUN!
SEE, MY FRIENDS AREN'T SO BAD!
I NEVER SAID THEY WERE BAD, ARI.
BUT, YEAH. I HAD FUN TODAY.
HANGING OUT WITH YOUR FRIENDS AND WORKING THE BOOTH WITH YOU.
I THINK WE MAKE A GOOD TEAM.

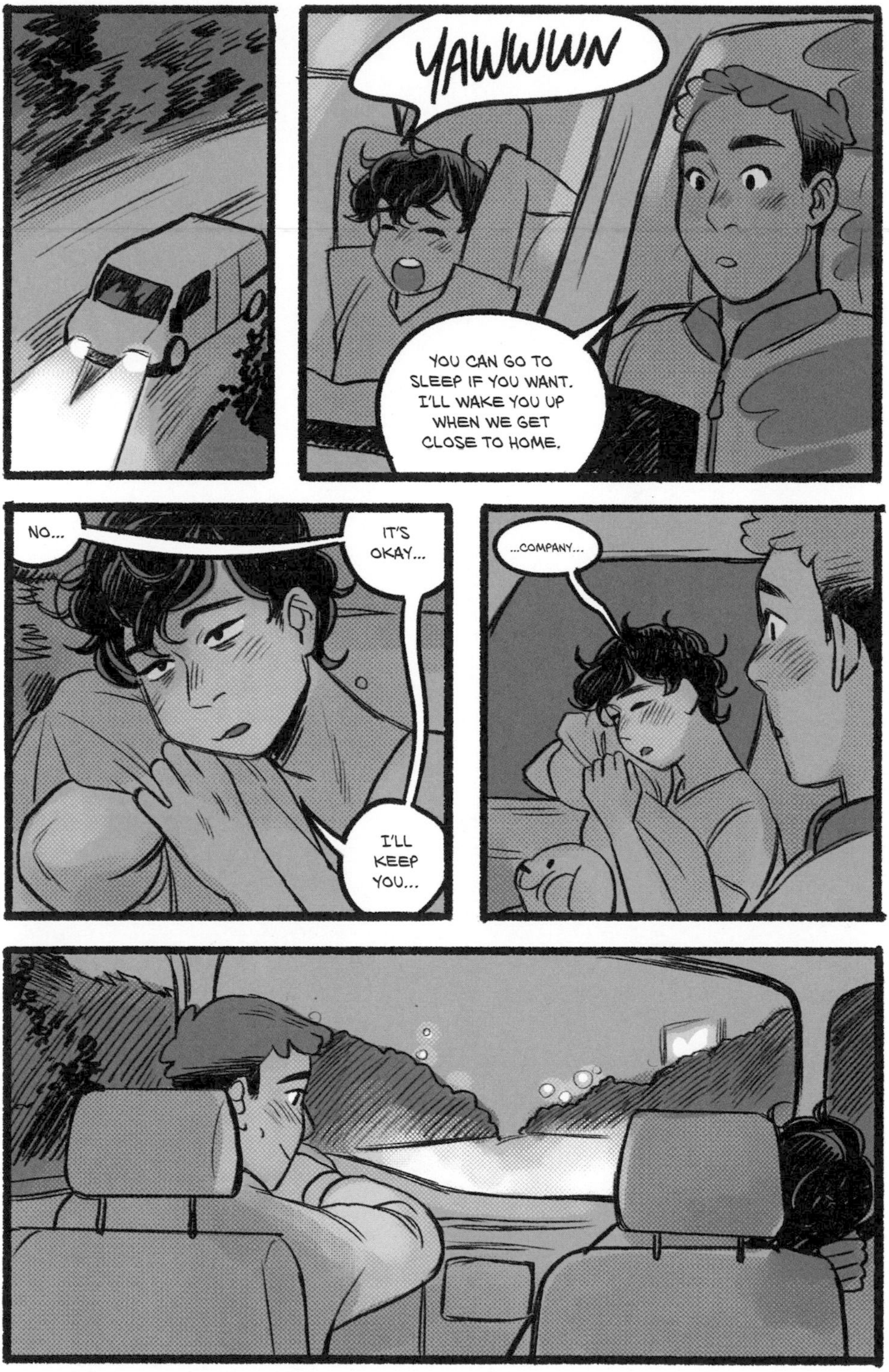
YAWWUN
YOU CAN GO TO SLEEP IF YOU WANT. I'LL WAKE YOU UP WHEN WE GET CLOSE TO HOME.
NO...
IT'S OKAY...
I'LL KEEP YOU...
...COMPANY...

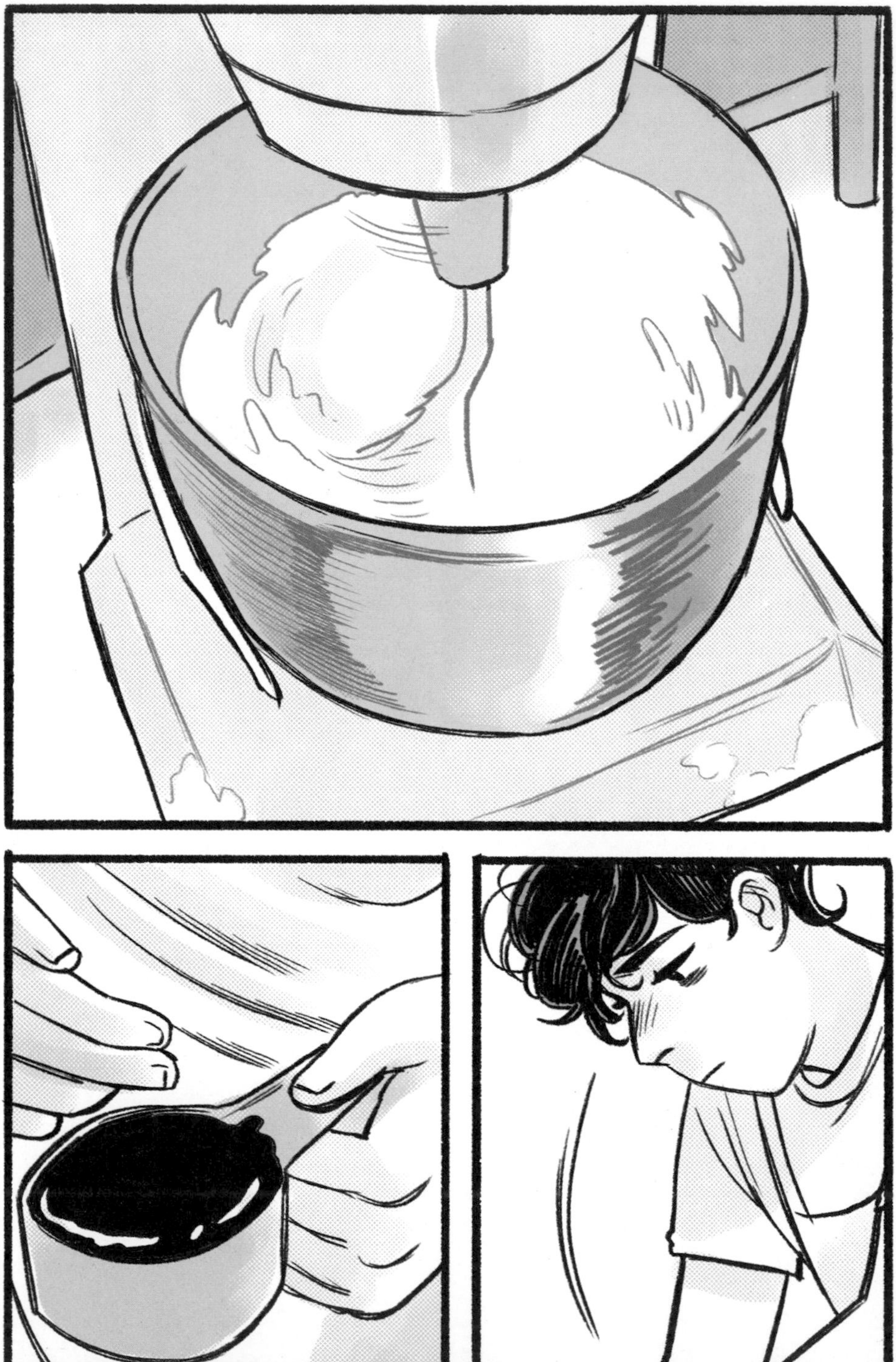

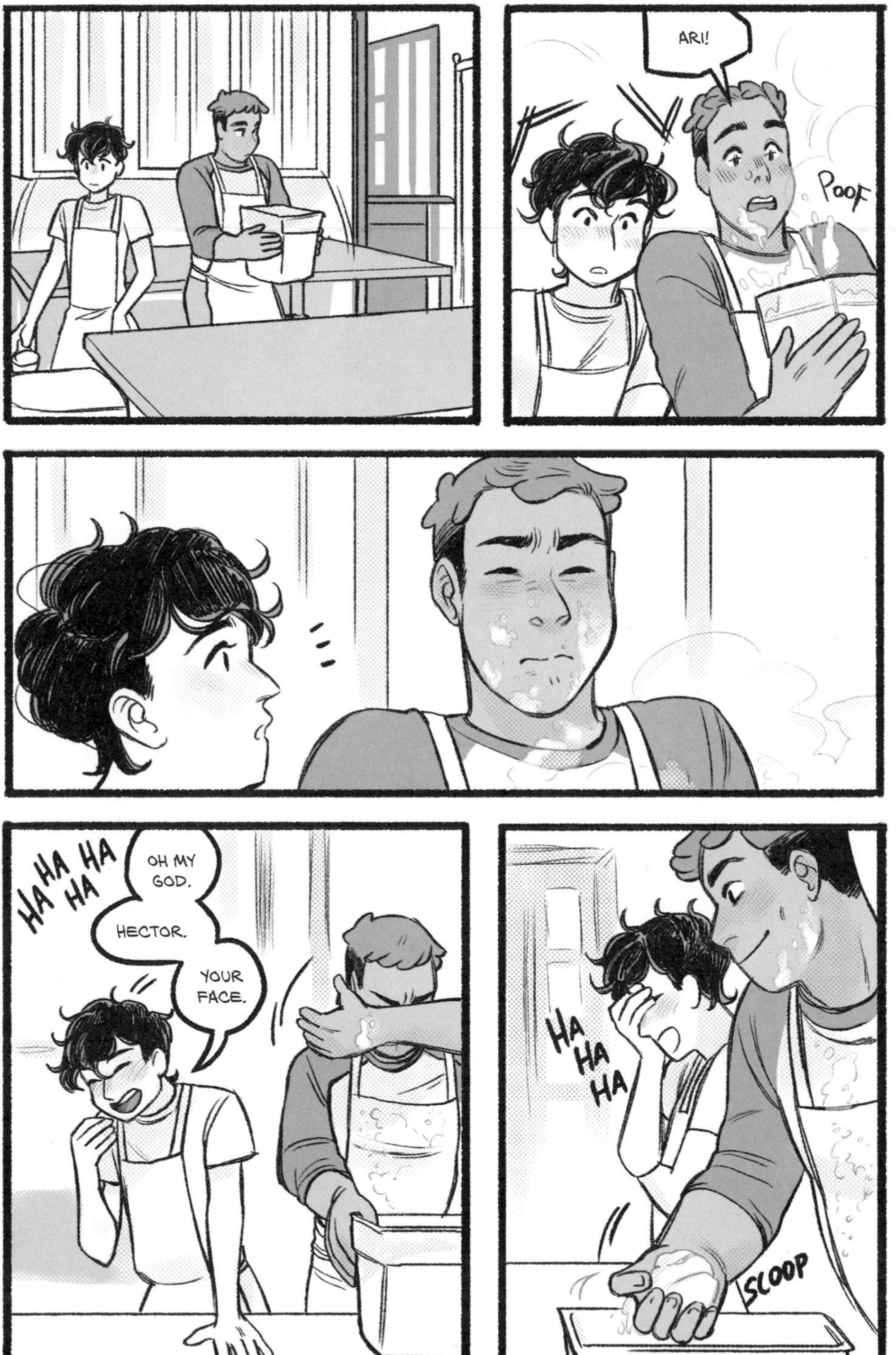
ARI!
POOF
HA HA HA HA HA
OH MY GOD.
HECTOR.
YOUR FACE.
HA HA HA
SCOOP

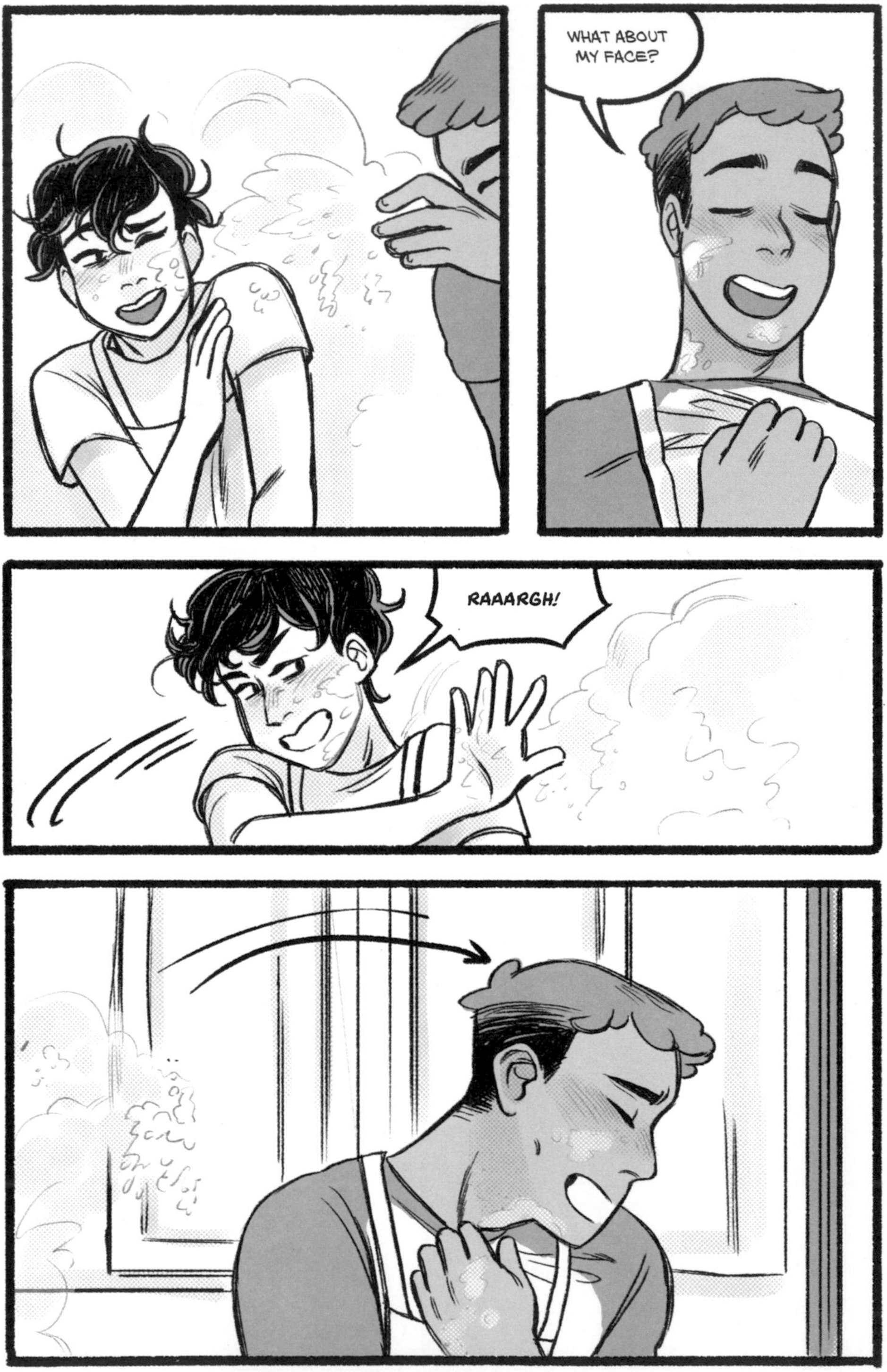
WHAT ABOUT MY FACE?
RAAARGH!

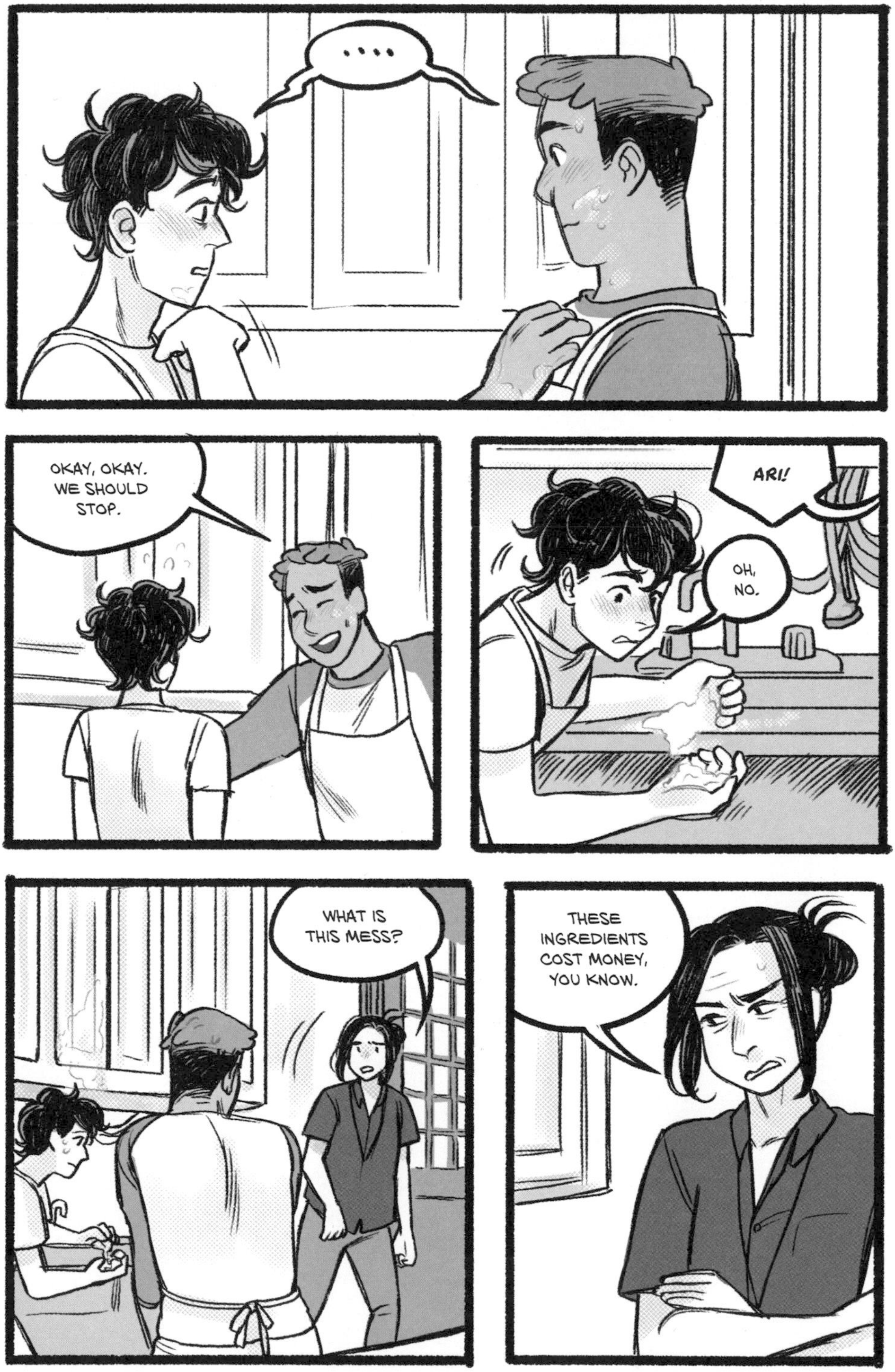
....
OKAY, OKAY. WE SHOULD STOP.
ARI!
OH, NO.
WHAT IS THIS MESS?
THESE INGREDIENTS COST MONEY, YOU KNOW.

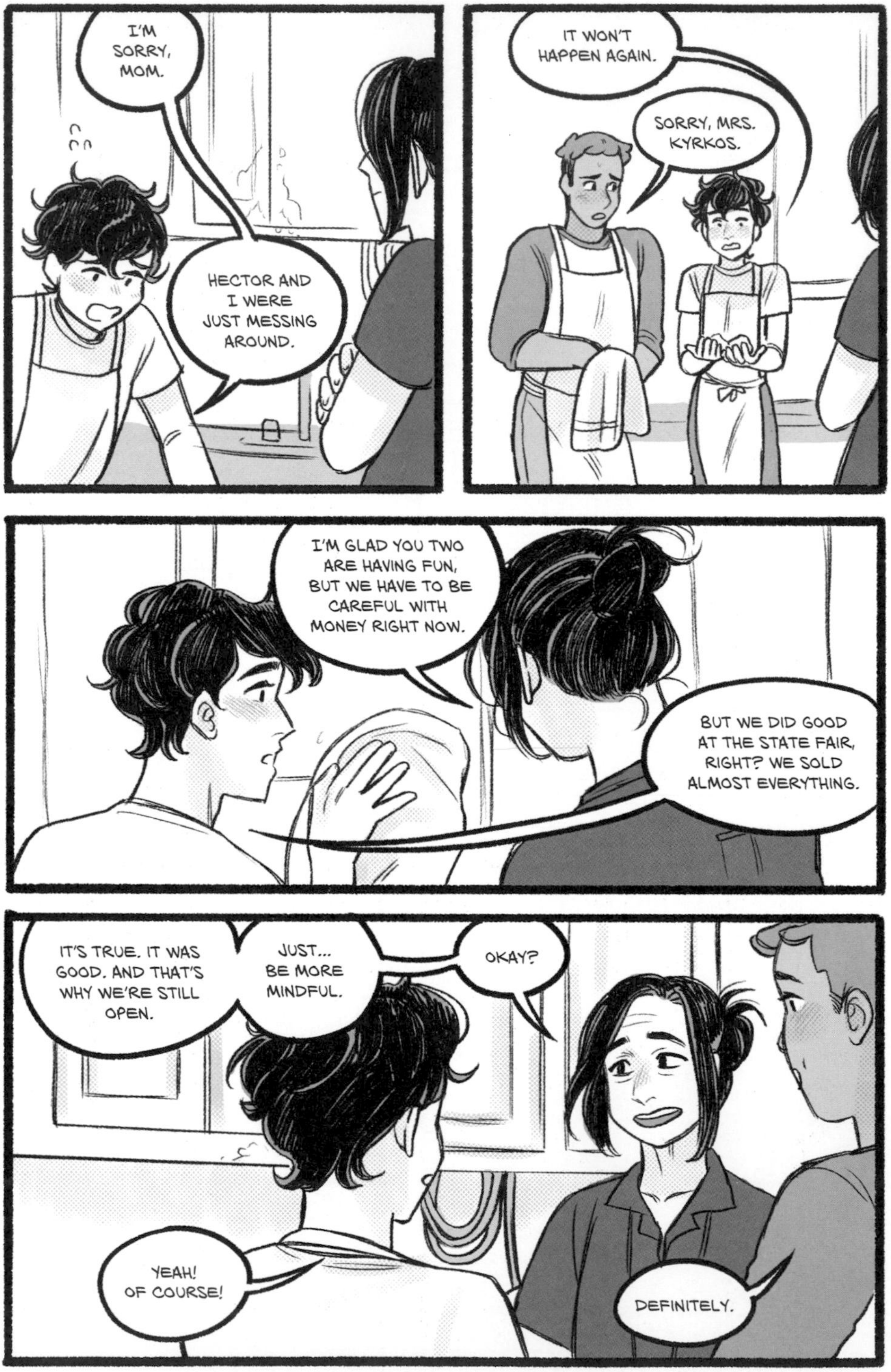
I'M SORRY, MOM.
HECTOR AND I WERE JUST MESSING AROUND.
IT WON'T HAPPEN AGAIN.
SORRY, MRS. KYRKOS.
I'M GLAD YOU TWO ARE HAVING FUN, BUT WE HAVE TO BE CAREFUL WITH MONEY RIGHT NOW.
BUT WE DID GOOD AT THE STATE FAIR, RIGHT? WE SOLD ALMOST EVERYTHING.
IT'S TRUE. IT WAS GOOD. AND THAT'S WHY WE'RE STILL OPEN.
JUST... BE MORE MINDFUL.
OKAY?
YEAH! OF COURSE!
DEFINITELY.

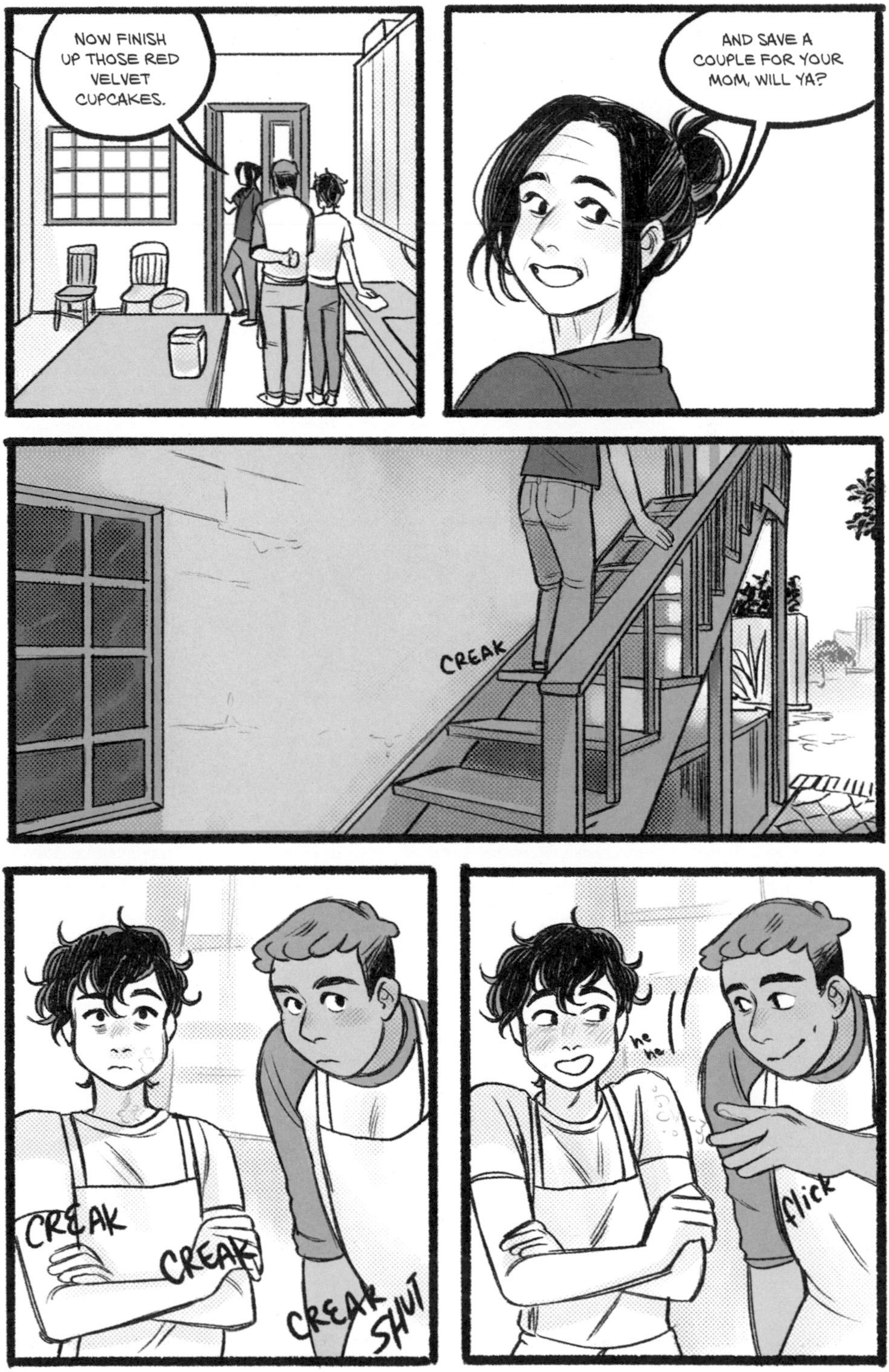
NOW FINISH UP THOSE RED VELVET CUPCAKES.
AND SAVE A COUPLE FOR YOUR MOM, WILL YA?
CREAK
CREAK
CREAK
CREAK
SHUT
he he
flick

OKAY!

I STILL NEEEED...

SEVEN CUPS OF FLOUR.

GOT IT!

OKAY, AND THREE CUPS OF MILK.

SHHHK

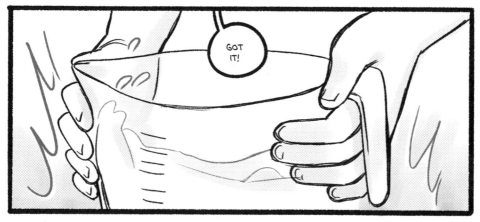

GOT IT!

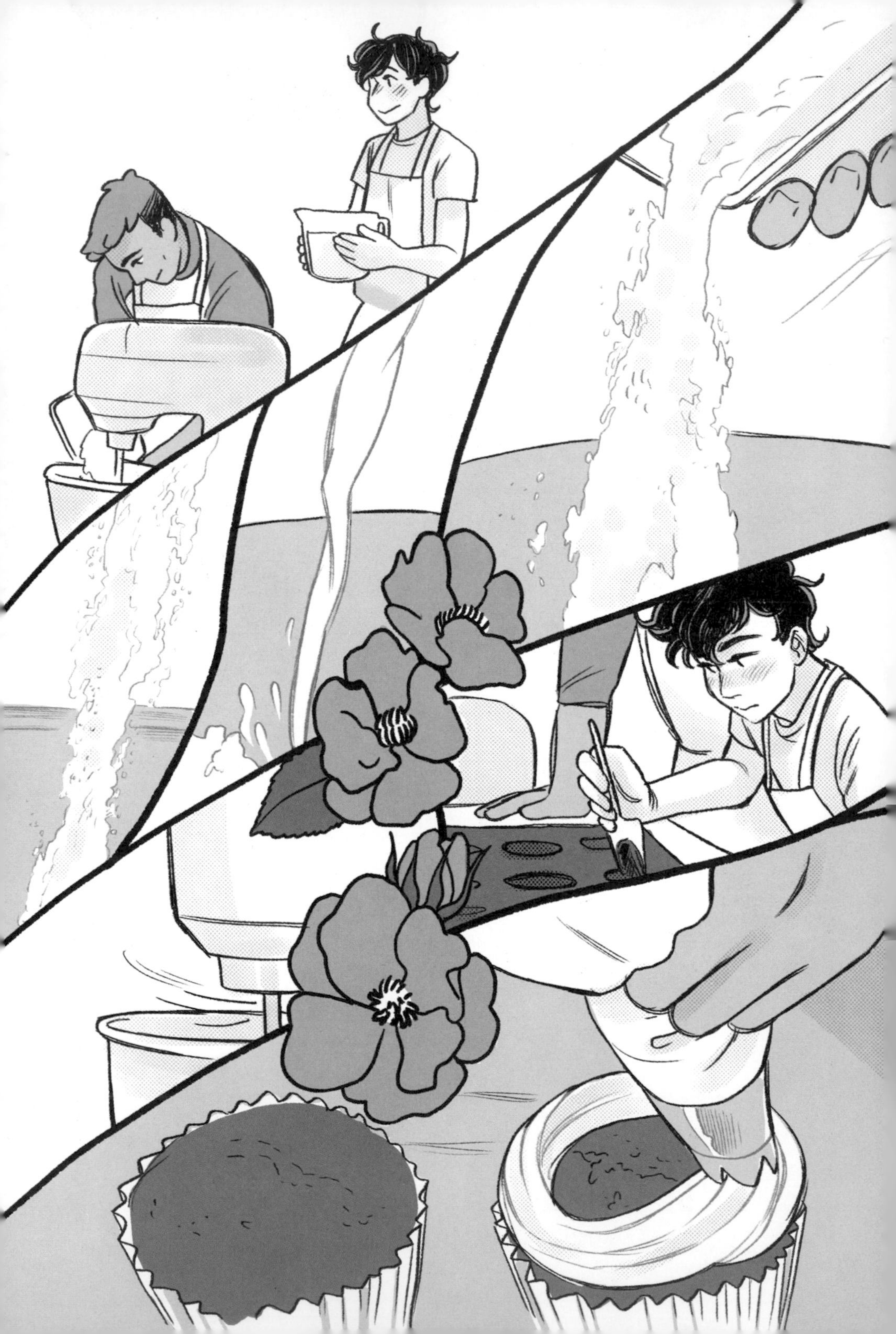

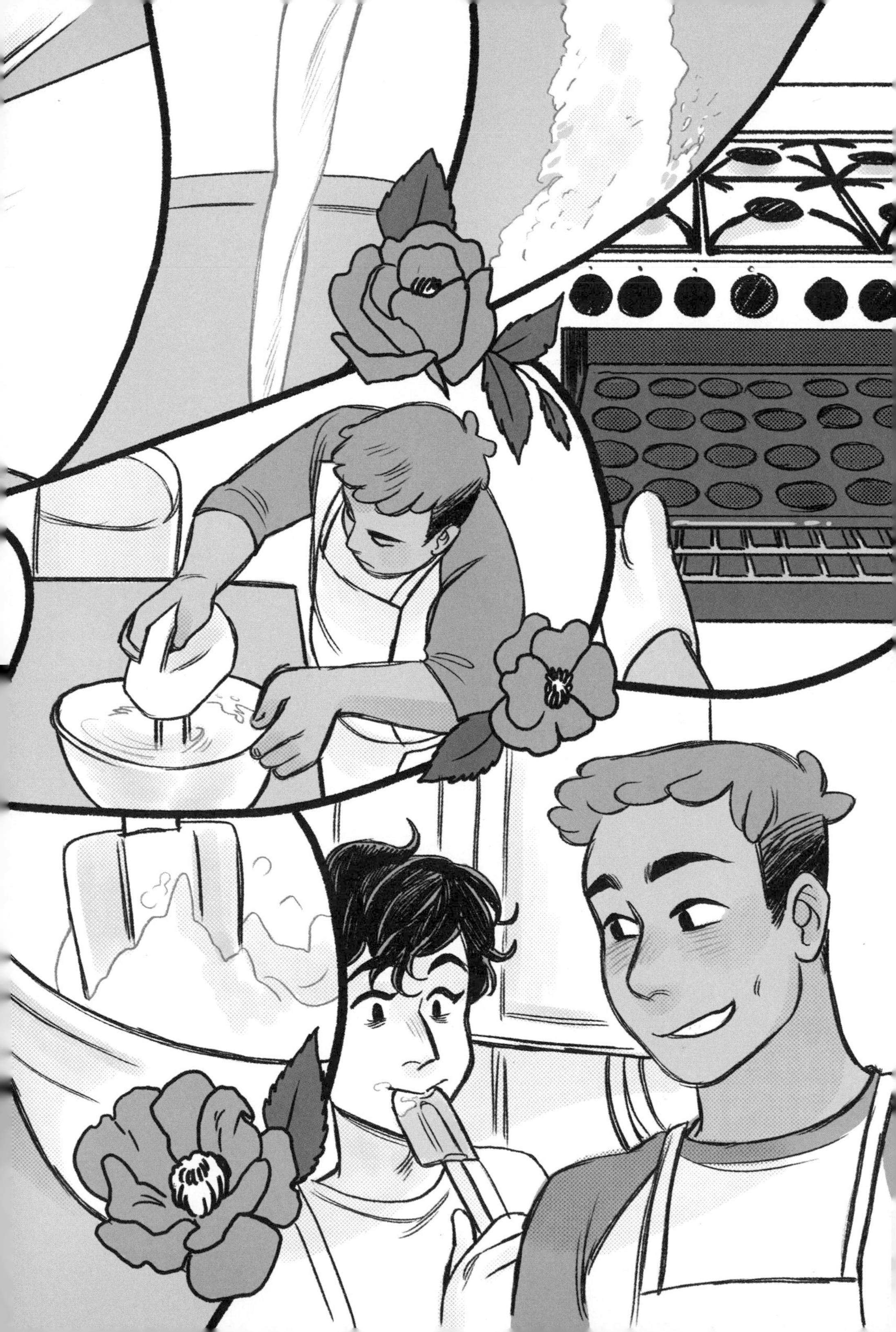

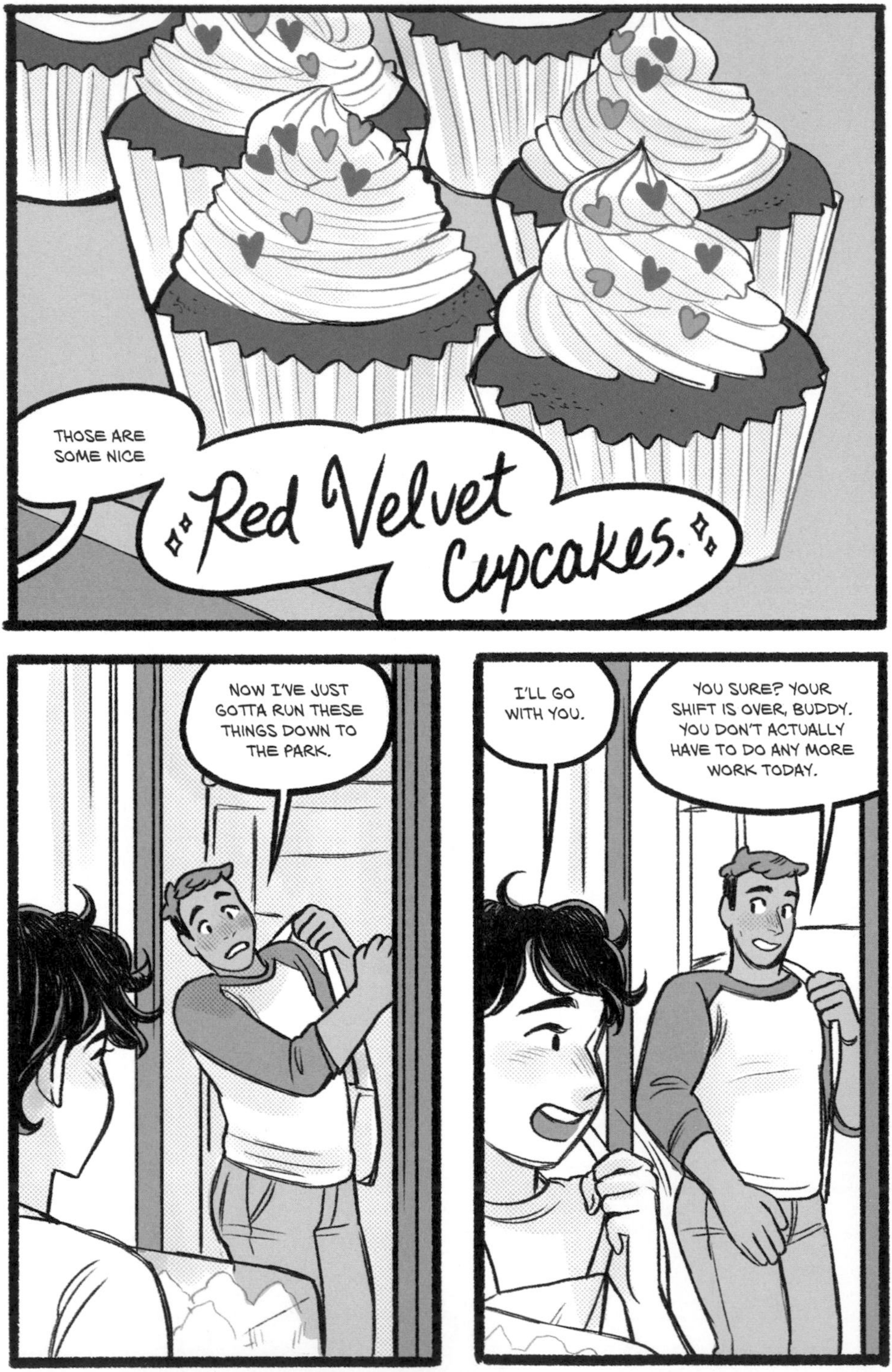
THOSE ARE SOME NICE
Red Velvet Cupcakes.
NOW I'VE JUST GOTTA RUN THESE THINGS DOWN TO THE PARK.
I'LL GO WITH YOU.
YOU SURE? YOUR SHIFT IS OVER, BUDDY. YOU DON'T ACTUALLY HAVE TO DO ANY MORE WORK TODAY.

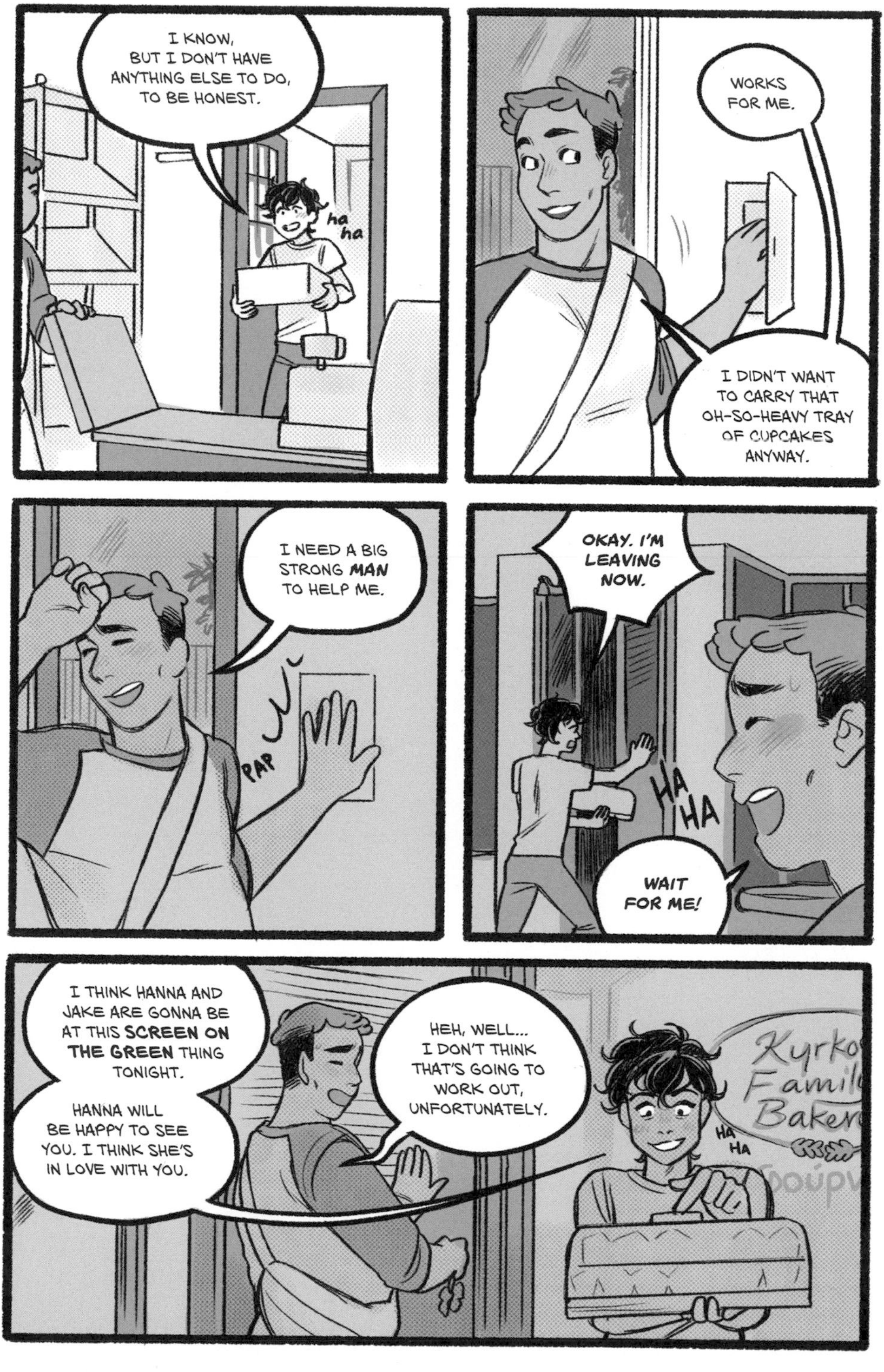

I KNOW, BUT I DON'T HAVE ANYTHING ELSE TO DO, TO BE HONEST.
ha ha
WORKS FOR ME.
I DIDN'T WANT TO CARRY THAT OH-SO-HEAVY TRAY OF CUPCAKES ANYWAY.
I NEED A BIG STRONG **MAN** TO HELP ME.
PAP
OKAY. I'M LEAVING NOW.
HA HA
WAIT FOR ME!
I THINK HANNA AND JAKE ARE GONNA BE AT THIS **SCREEN ON THE GREEN** THING TONIGHT.
HANNA WILL BE HAPPY TO SEE YOU. I THINK SHE'S IN LOVE WITH YOU.
HEH, WELL... I DON'T THINK THAT'S GOING TO WORK OUT, UNFORTUNATELY.
HA HA

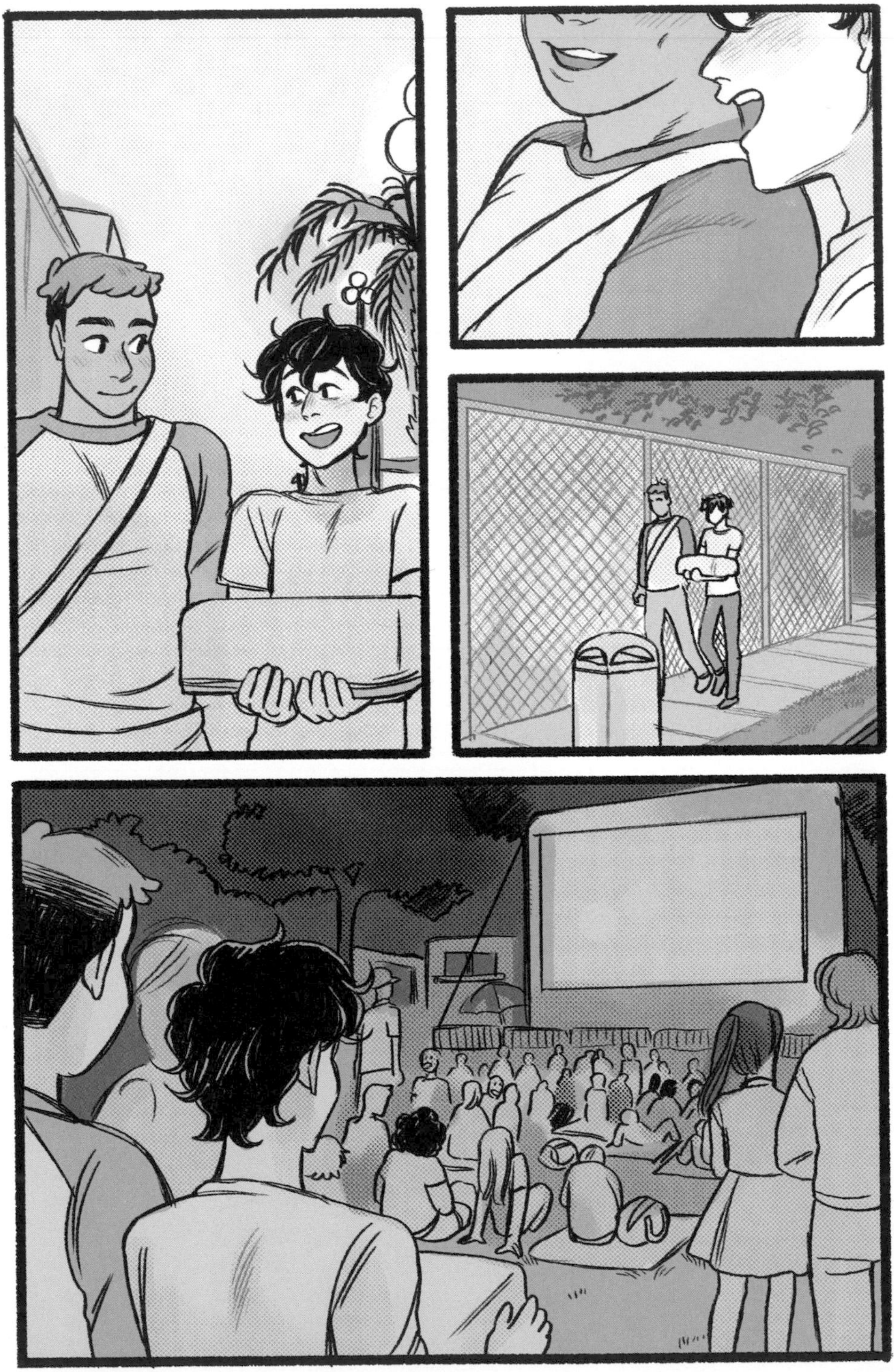

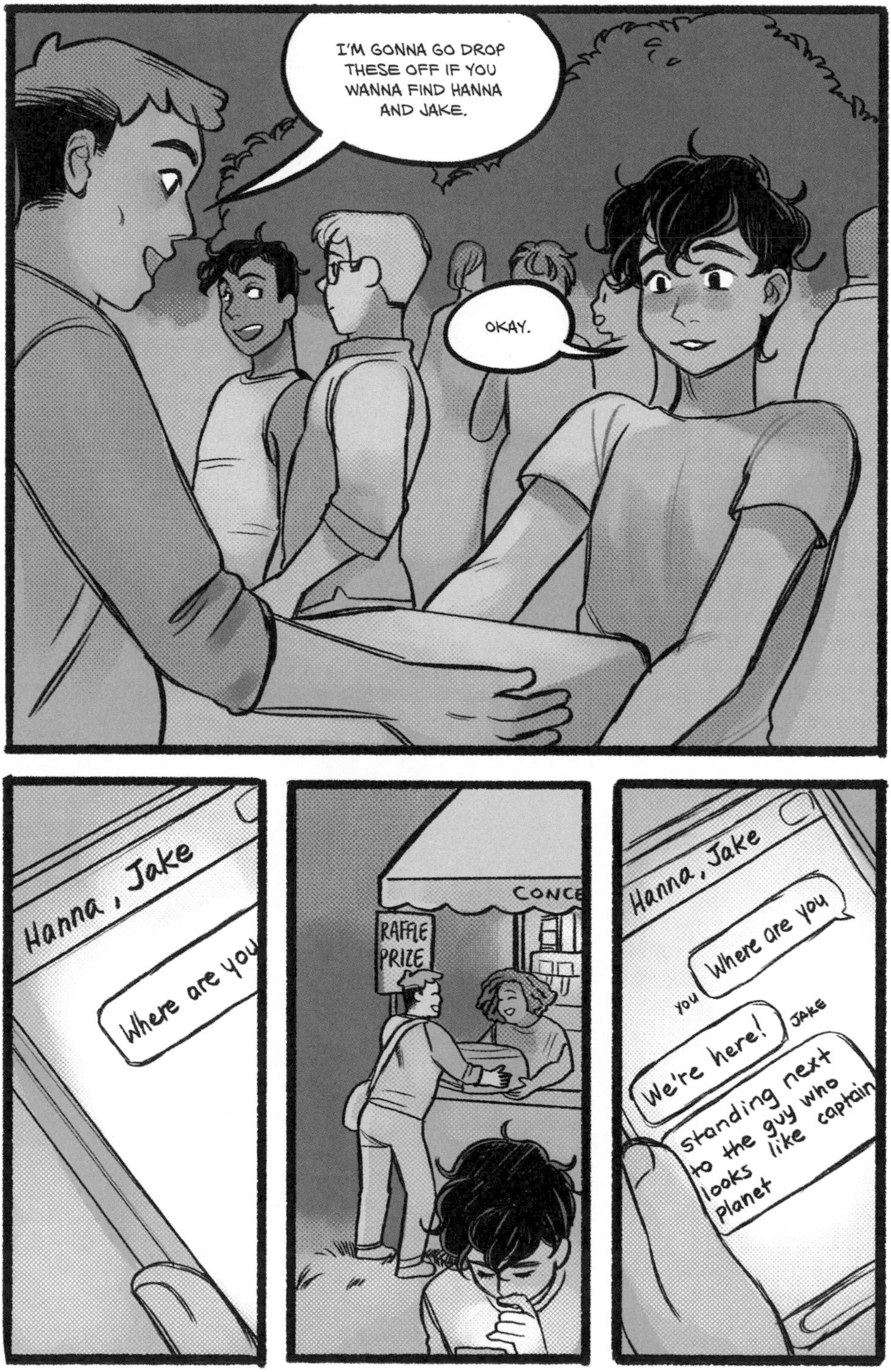
I'M GONNA GO DROP THESE OFF IF YOU WANNA FIND HANNA AND JAKE.
OKAY.
Hanna, Jake
Where are you
RAFFLE PRIZE
CONCE
Hanna, Jake
Where are you
YOU
We're here!
JAKE
standing next to the guy who looks like captain planet

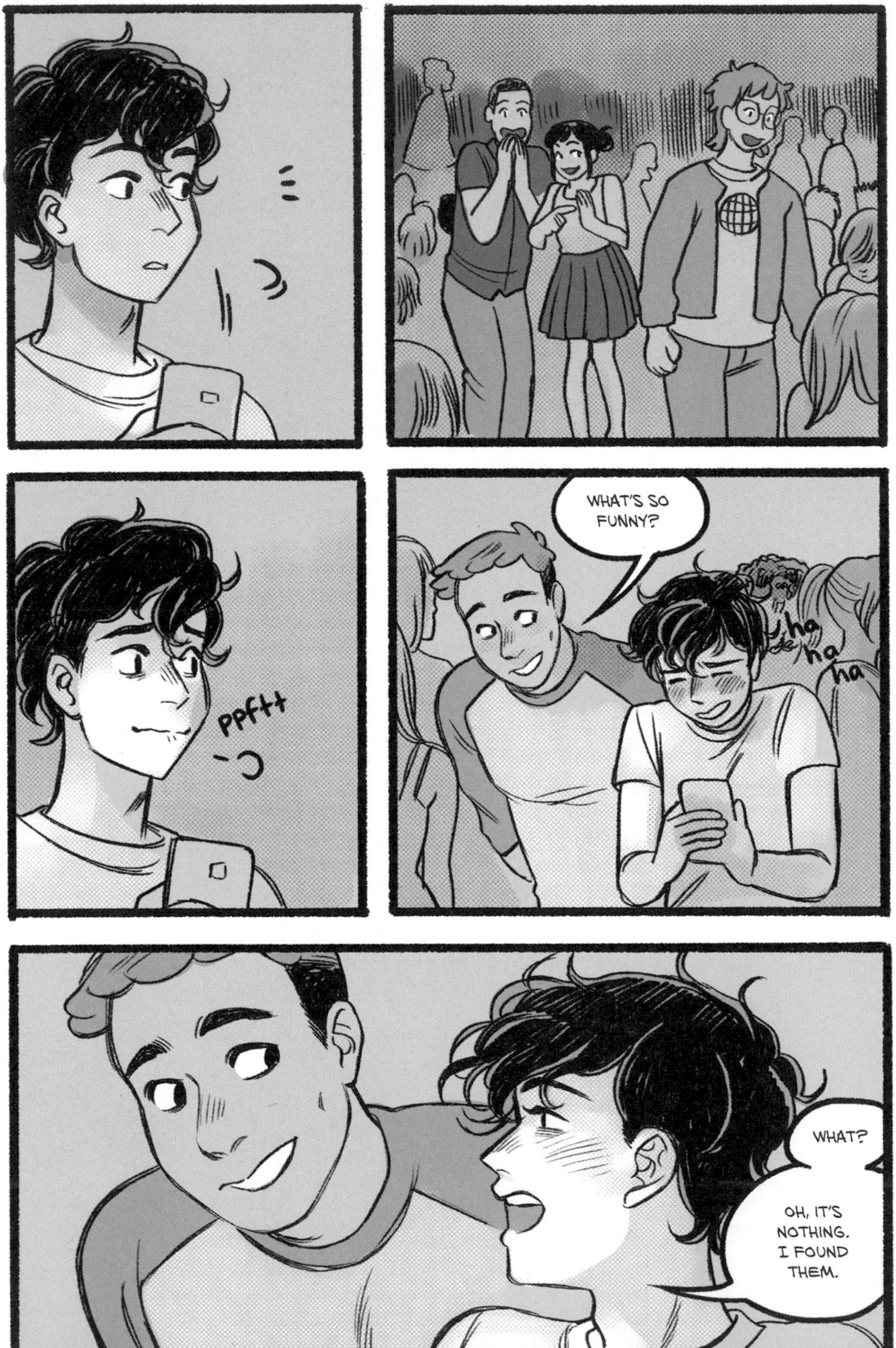
ppftt
WHAT'S SO FUNNY?
ha
ha
ha
WHAT?
OH, IT'S NOTHING. I FOUND THEM.

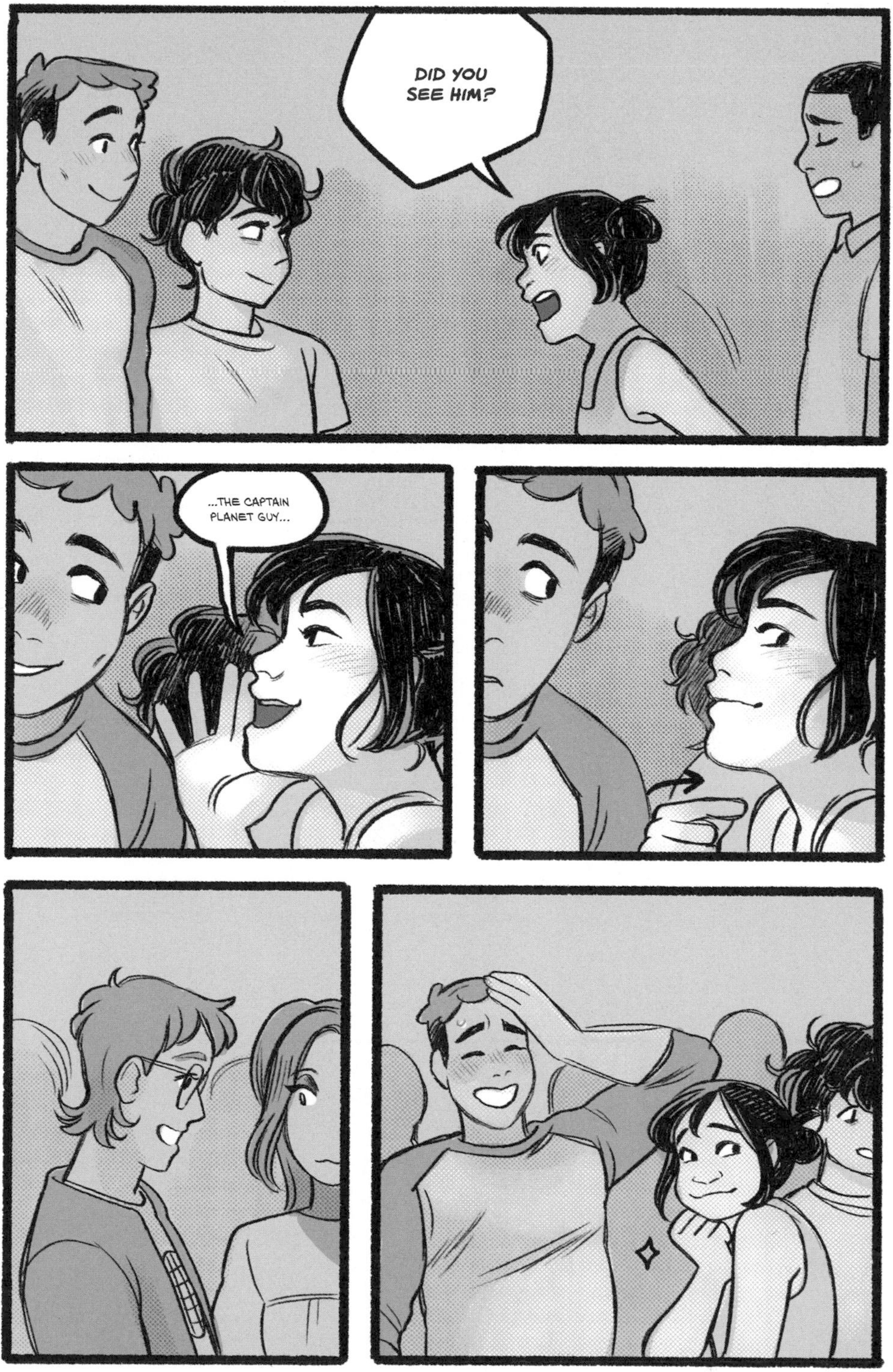
DID YOU SEE HIM?
...THE CAPTAIN PLANET GUY...

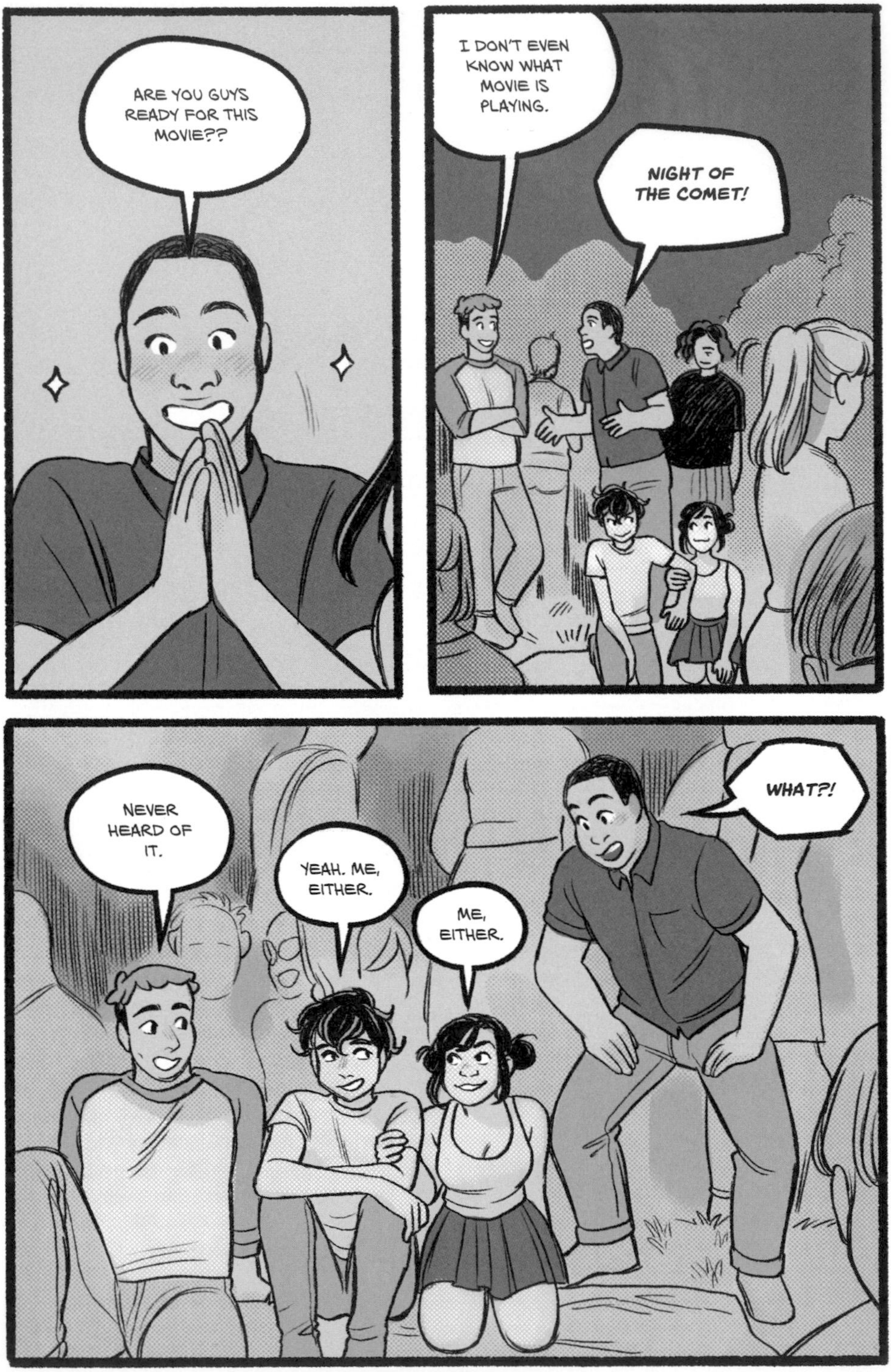
ARE YOU GUYS READY FOR THIS MOVIE??
I DON'T EVEN KNOW WHAT MOVIE IS PLAYING.
NIGHT OF THE COMET!
NEVER HEARD OF IT.
YEAH. ME, EITHER.
ME, EITHER.
WHAT?!

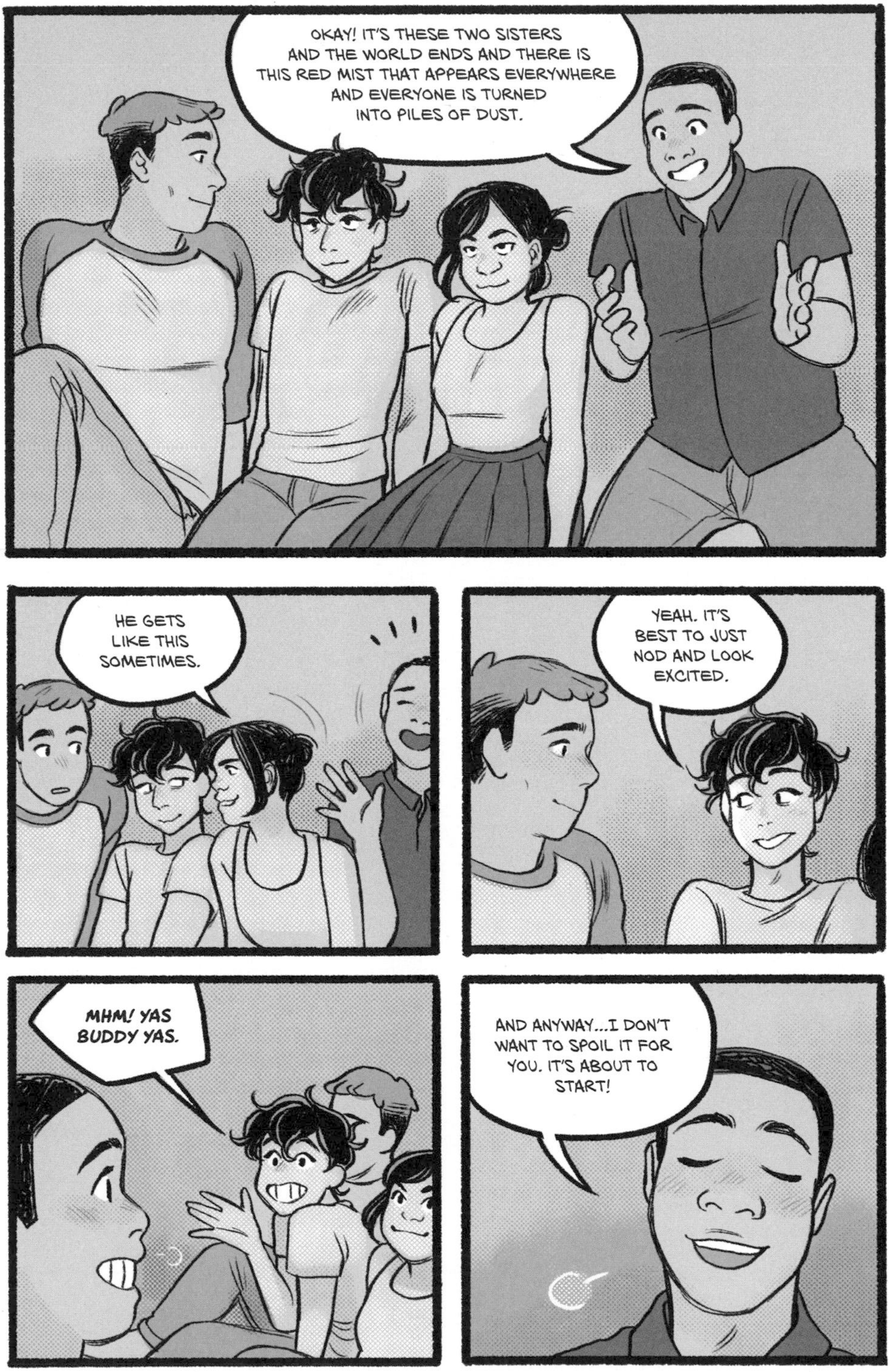
OKAY! IT'S THESE TWO SISTERS AND THE WORLD ENDS AND THERE IS THIS RED MIST THAT APPEARS EVERYWHERE AND EVERYONE IS TURNED INTO PILES OF DUST.
HE GETS LIKE THIS SOMETIMES.
YEAH. IT'S BEST TO JUST NOD AND LOOK EXCITED.
MHM! YAS BUDDY YAS.
AND ANYWAY...I DON'T WANT TO SPOIL IT FOR YOU. IT'S ABOUT TO START!

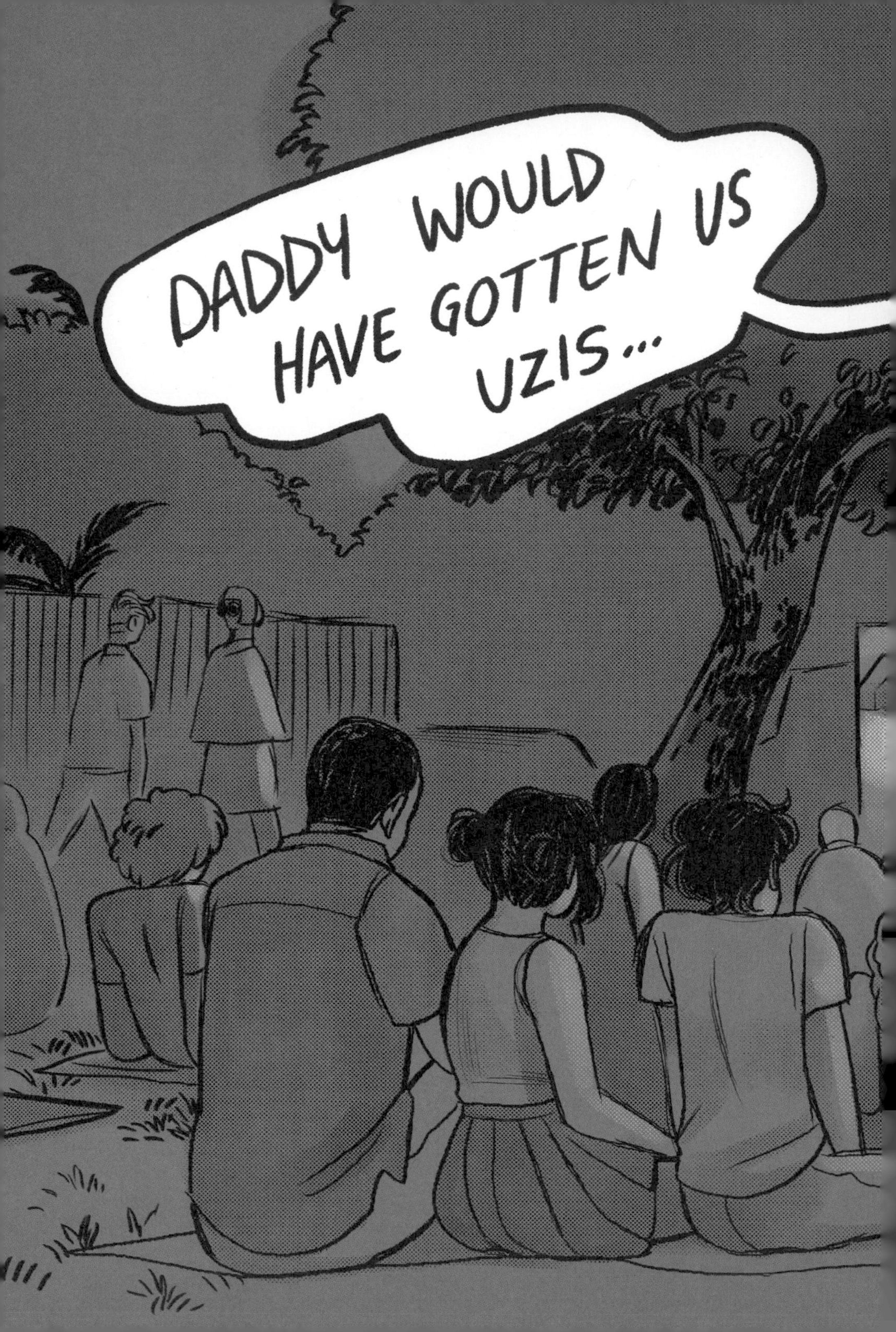
DADDY WOULD HAVE GOTTEN US UZIS...

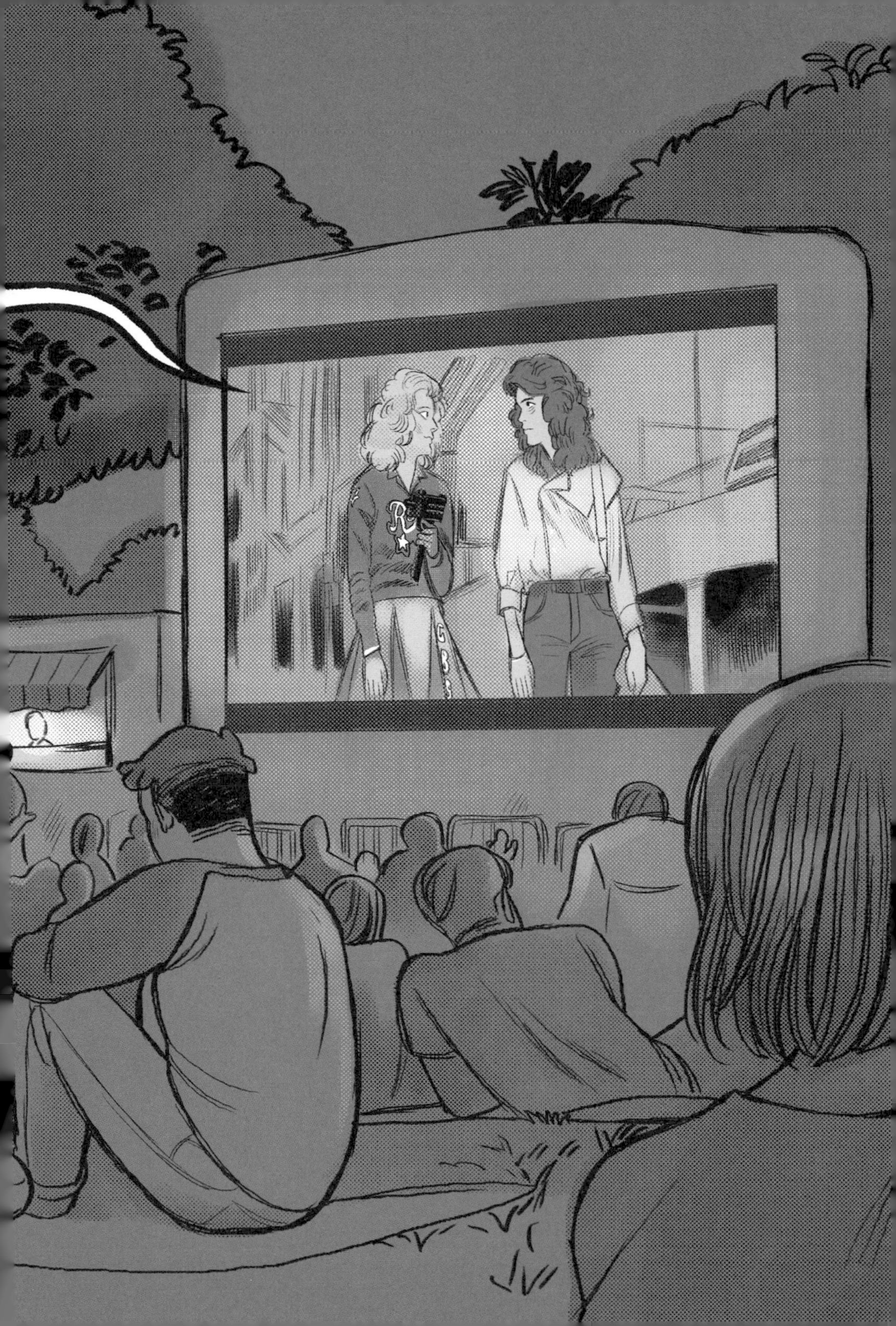

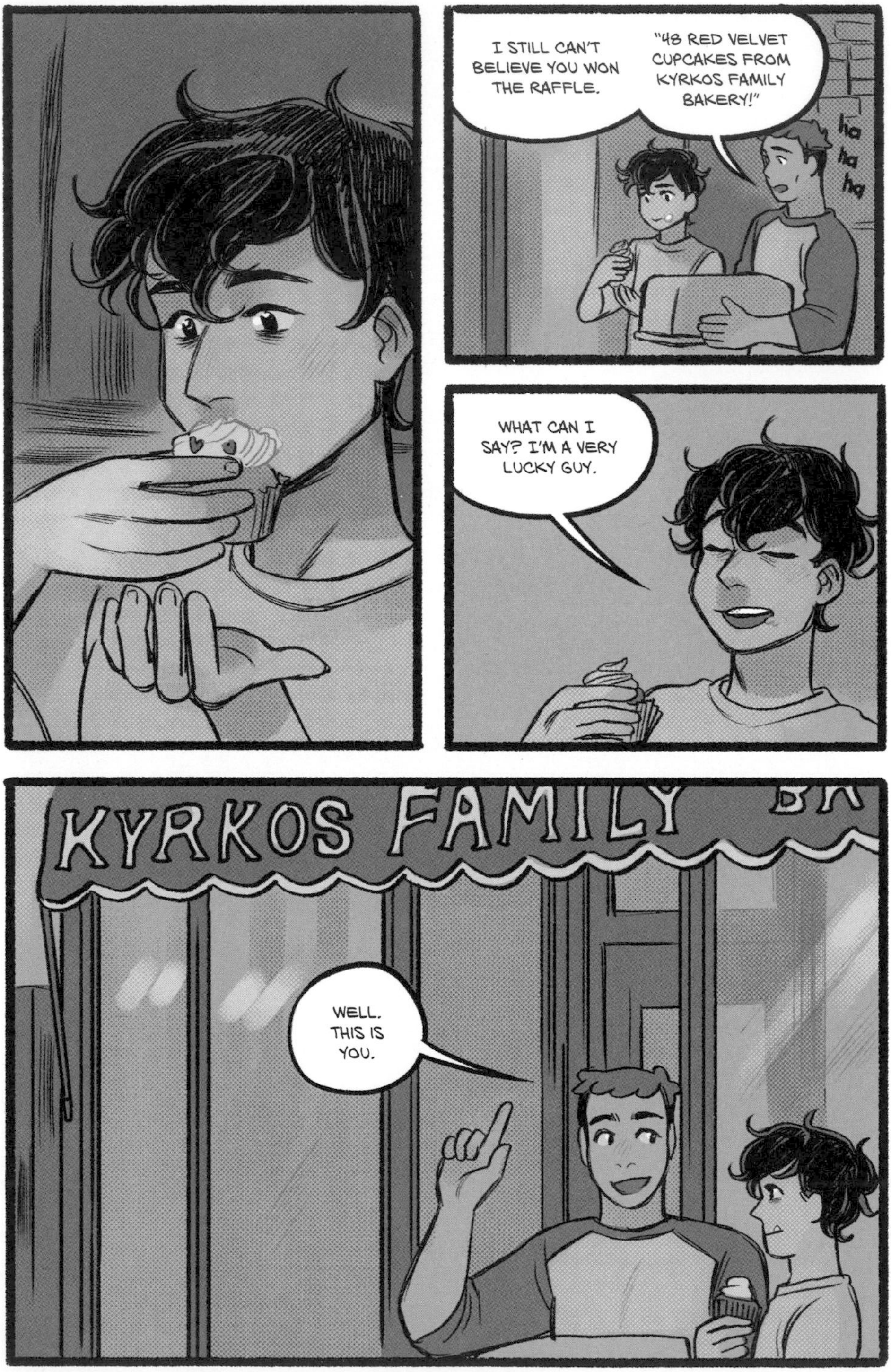
I STILL CAN'T BELIEVE YOU WON THE RAFFLE.
"48 RED VELVET CUPCAKES FROM KYRKOS FAMILY BAKERY!"
ha ha ha
WHAT CAN I SAY? I'M A VERY LUCKY GUY.
KYRKOS FAMILY BA
WELL. THIS IS YOU.

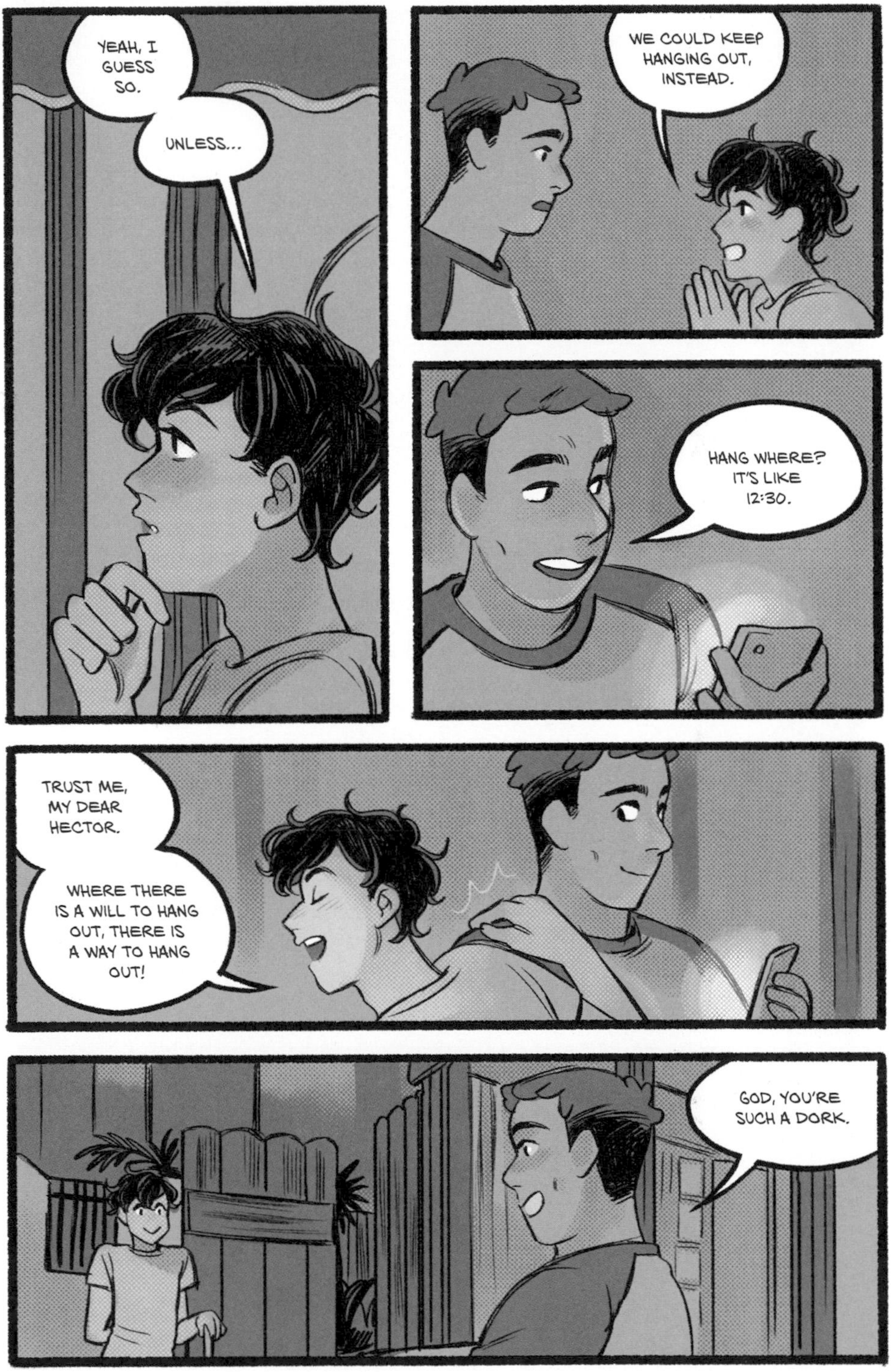
YEAH, I GUESS SO.
UNLESS...
WE COULD KEEP HANGING OUT, INSTEAD.
HANG WHERE? IT'S LIKE 12:30.
TRUST ME, MY DEAR HECTOR.
WHERE THERE IS A WILL TO HANG OUT, THERE IS A WAY TO HANG OUT!
GOD, YOU'RE SUCH A DORK.

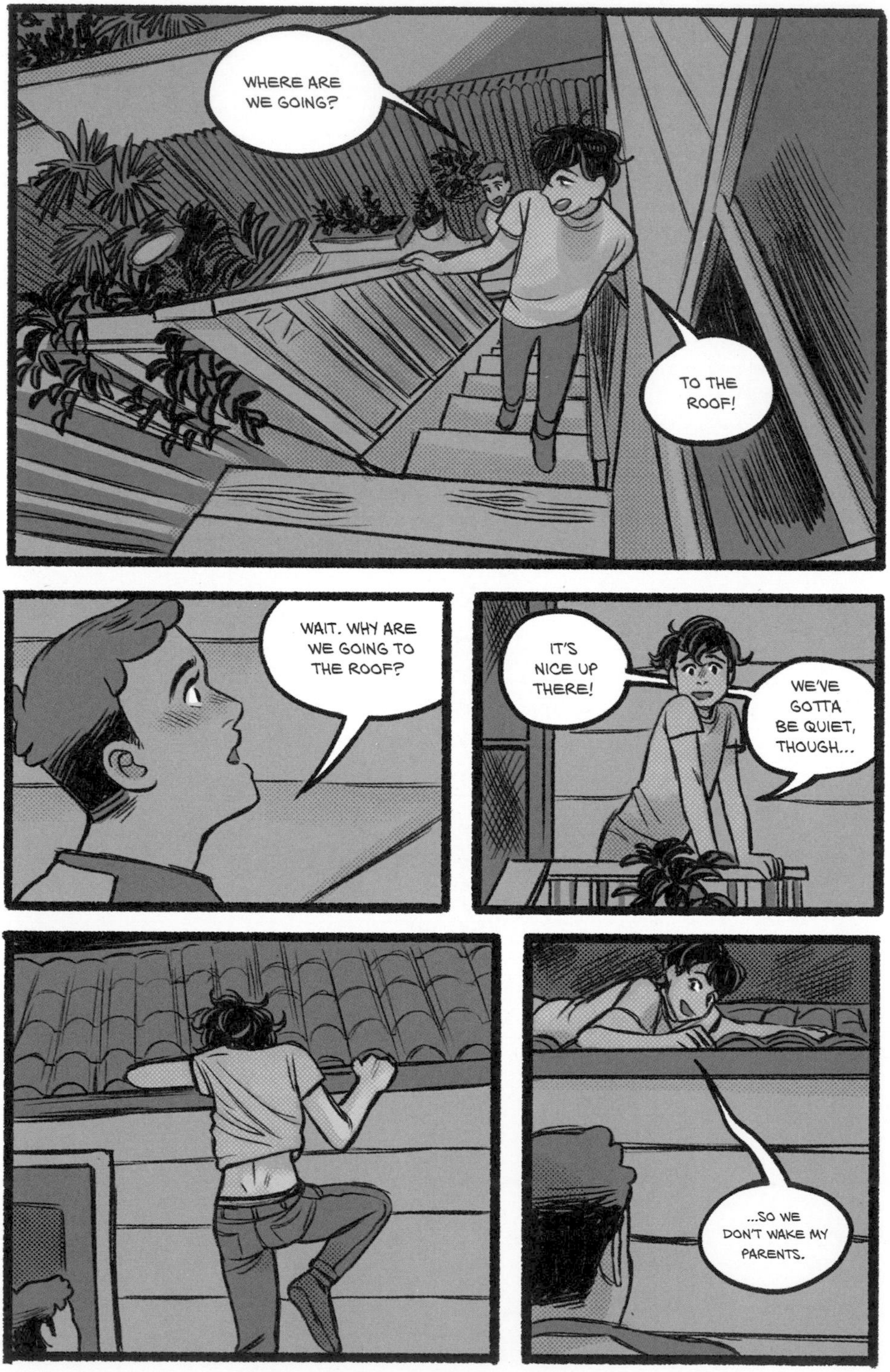
WHERE ARE WE GOING?
TO THE ROOF!
WAIT. WHY ARE WE GOING TO THE ROOF?
IT'S NICE UP THERE!
WE'VE GOTTA BE QUIET, THOUGH...
...SO WE DON'T WAKE MY PARENTS.

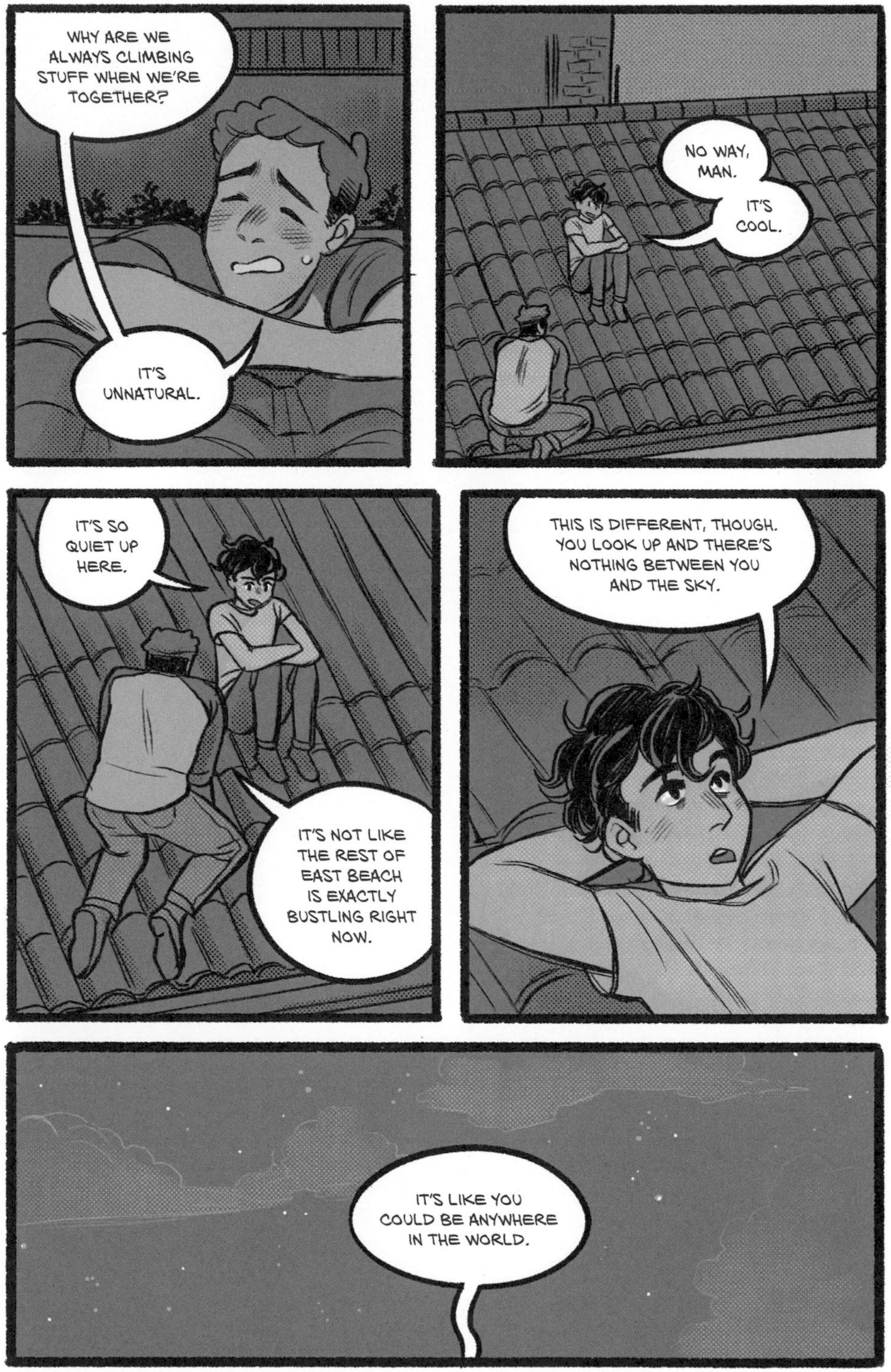
WHY ARE WE ALWAYS CLIMBING STUFF WHEN WE'RE TOGETHER?
IT'S UNNATURAL.
NO WAY, MAN.
IT'S COOL.
IT'S SO QUIET UP HERE.
IT'S NOT LIKE THE REST OF EAST BEACH IS EXACTLY BUSTLING RIGHT NOW.
THIS IS DIFFERENT, THOUGH. YOU LOOK UP AND THERE'S NOTHING BETWEEN YOU AND THE SKY.
IT'S LIKE YOU COULD BE ANYWHERE IN THE WORLD.

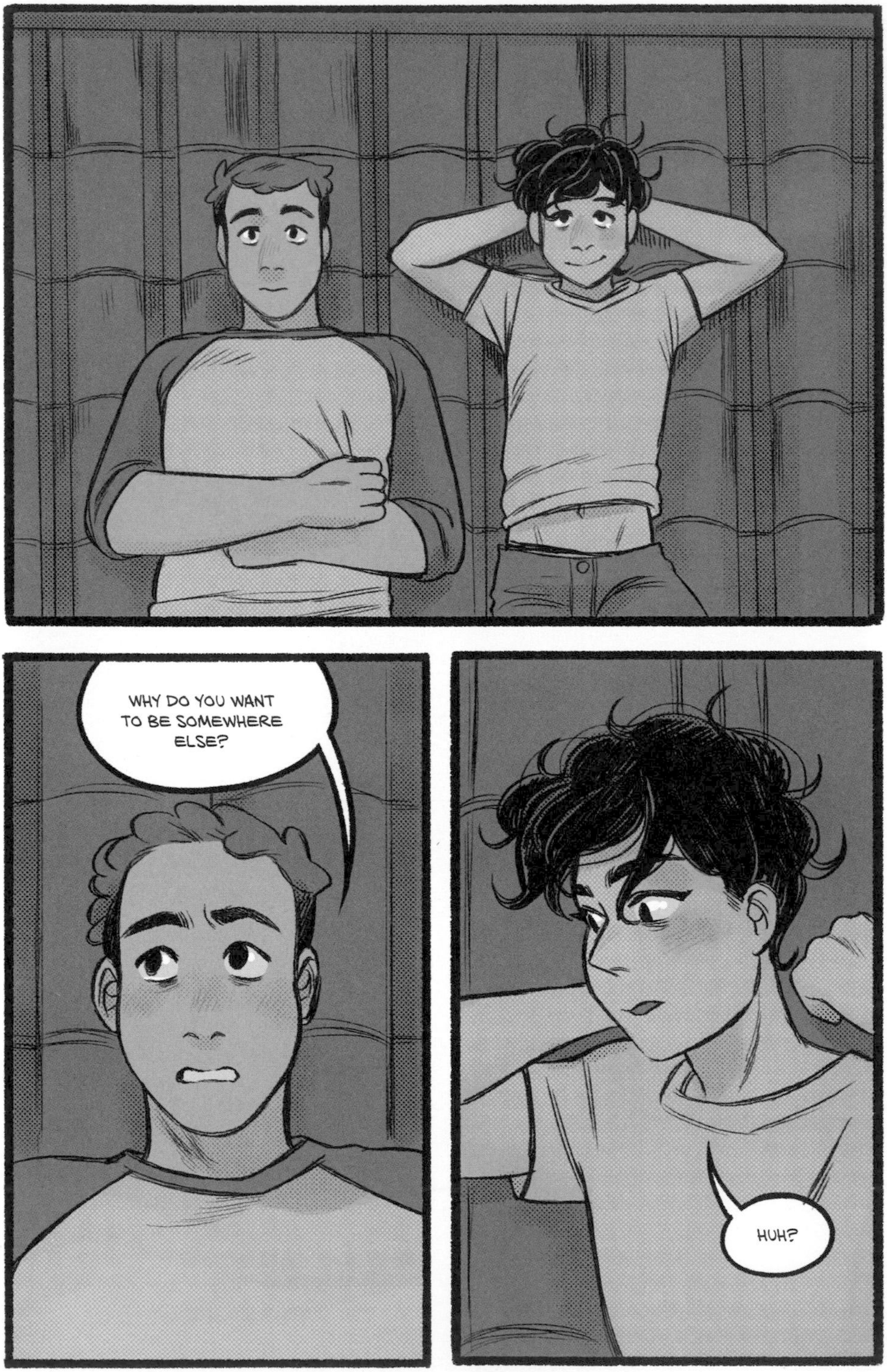
WHY DO YOU WANT TO BE SOMEWHERE ELSE?
HUH?

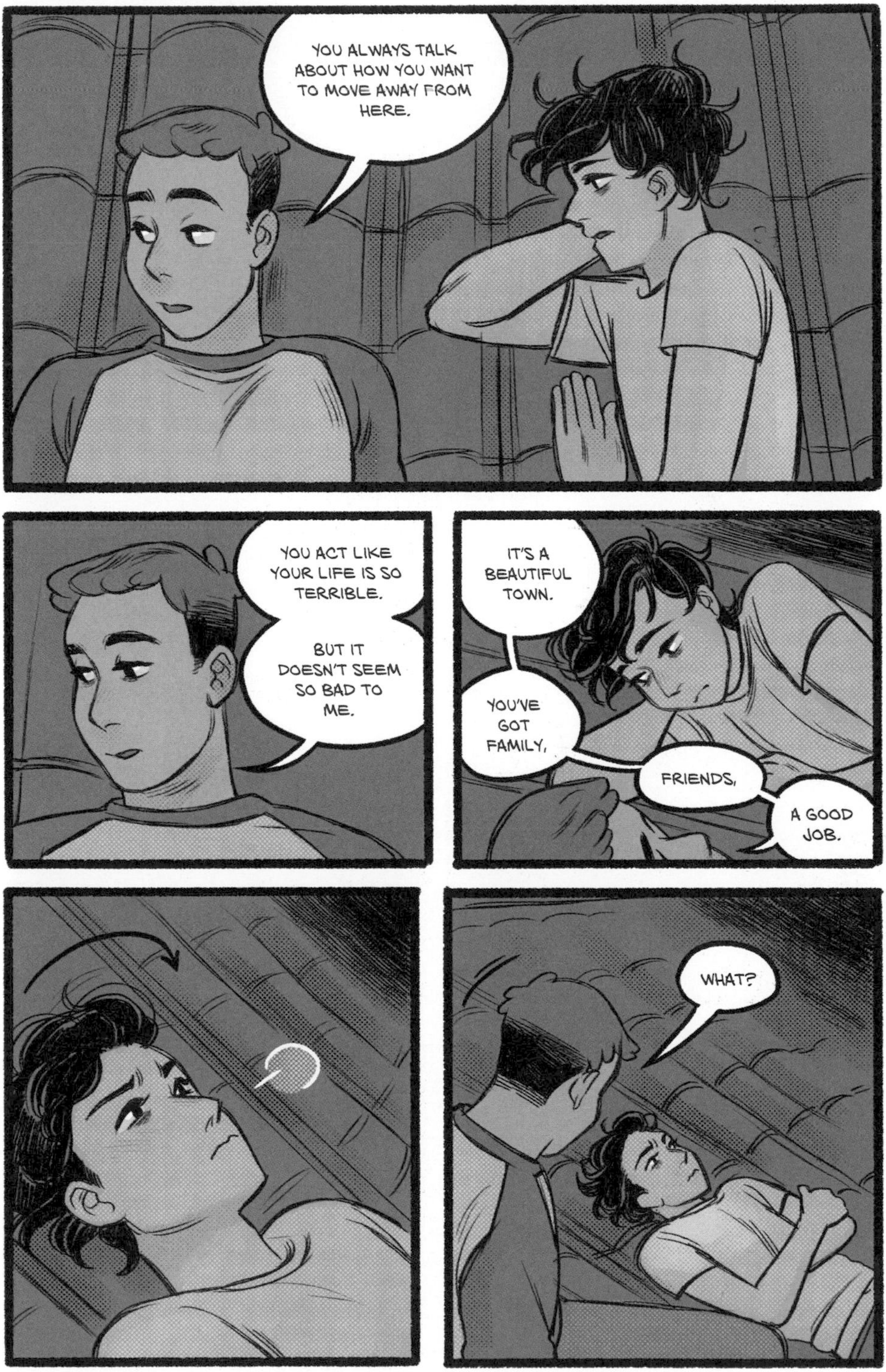
YOU ALWAYS TALK ABOUT HOW YOU WANT TO MOVE AWAY FROM HERE.
YOU ACT LIKE YOUR LIFE IS SO TERRIBLE.
BUT IT DOESN'T SEEM SO BAD TO ME.
IT'S A BEAUTIFUL TOWN.
YOU'VE GOT FAMILY,
FRIENDS,
A GOOD JOB.
WHAT?

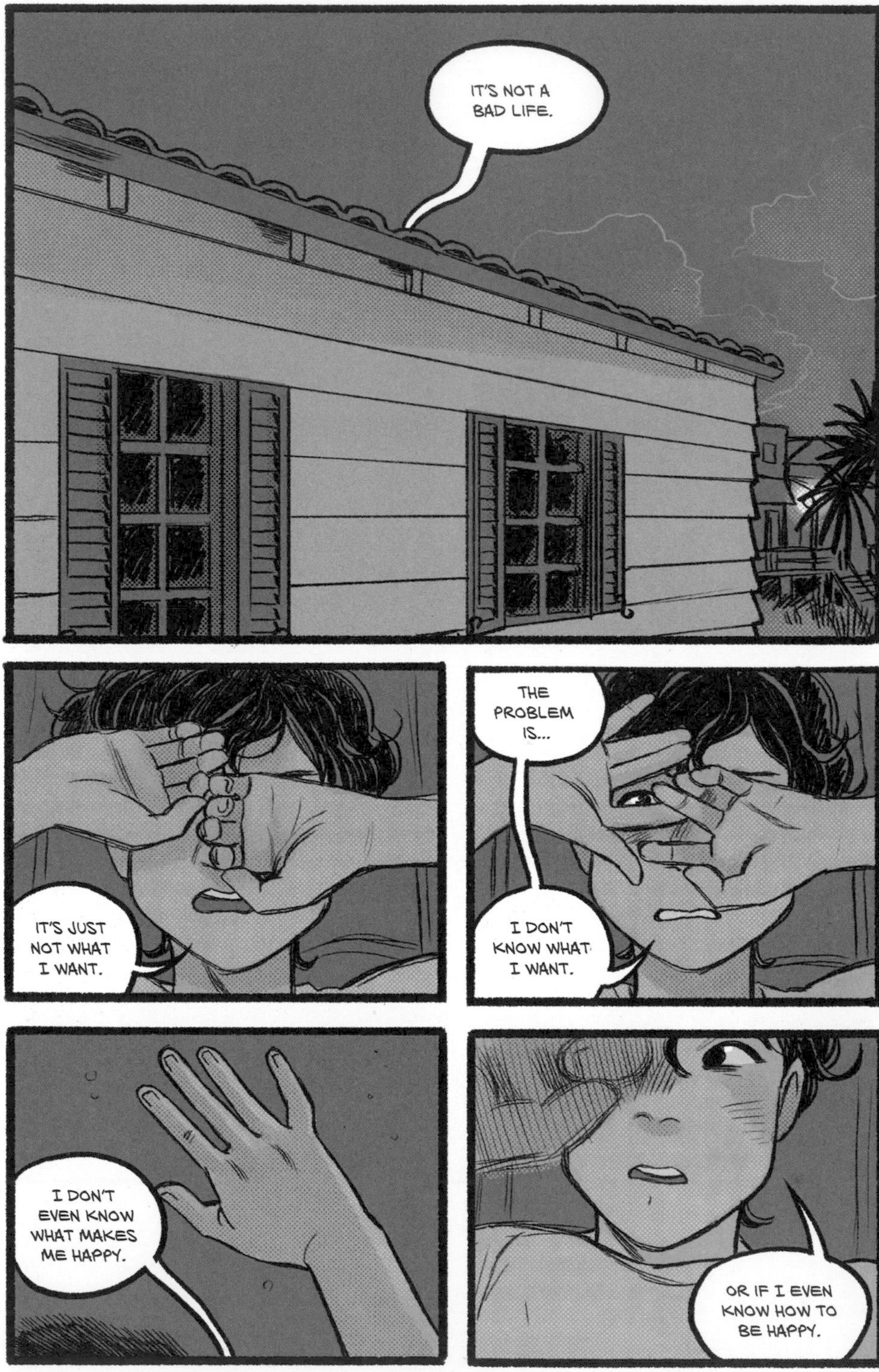
IT'S NOT A BAD LIFE.
IT'S JUST NOT WHAT I WANT.
THE PROBLEM IS...
I DON'T KNOW WHAT I WANT.
I DON'T EVEN KNOW WHAT MAKES ME HAPPY.
OR IF I EVEN KNOW HOW TO BE HAPPY.

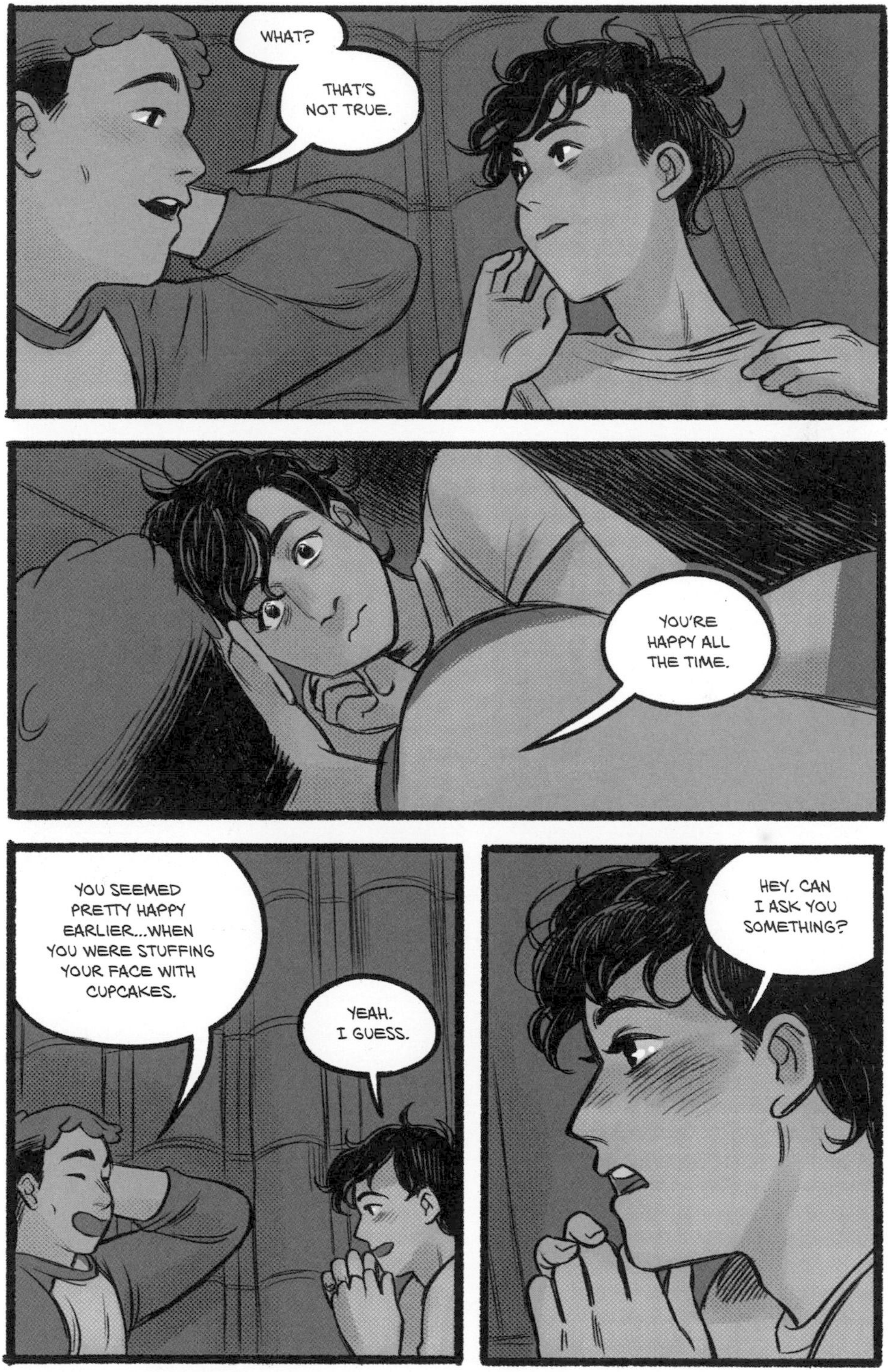
WHAT?
THAT'S NOT TRUE.
YOU'RE HAPPY ALL THE TIME.
YOU SEEMED PRETTY HAPPY EARLIER...WHEN YOU WERE STUFFING YOUR FACE WITH CUPCAKES.
YEAH. I GUESS.
HEY. CAN I ASK YOU SOMETHING?

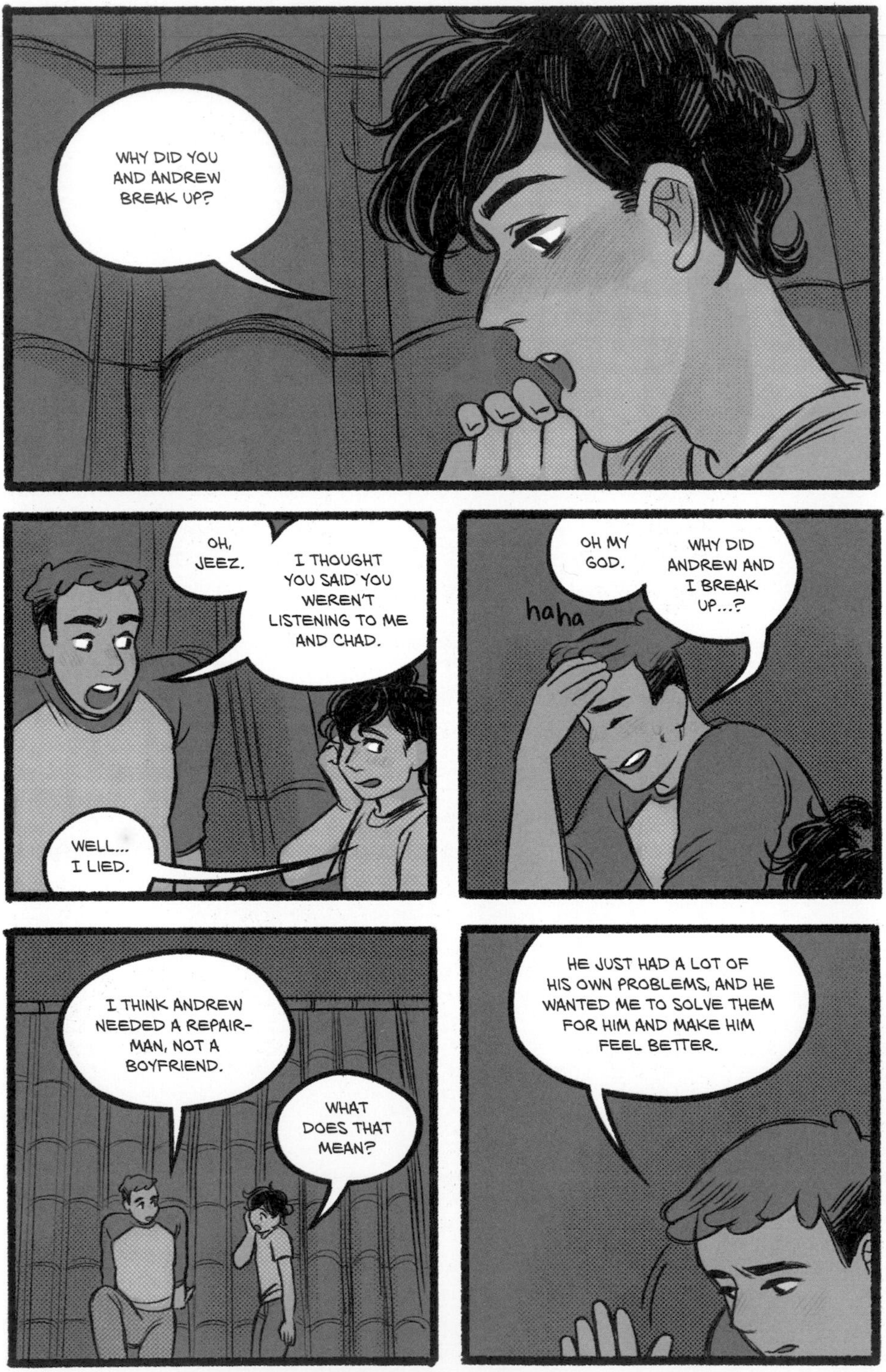
WHY DID YOU AND ANDREW BREAK UP?
OH, JEEZ.
I THOUGHT YOU SAID YOU WEREN'T LISTENING TO ME AND CHAD.
WELL... I LIED.
OH MY GOD.
WHY DID ANDREW AND I BREAK UP...?
haha
I THINK ANDREW NEEDED A REPAIR-MAN, NOT A BOYFRIEND.
WHAT DOES THAT MEAN?
HE JUST HAD A LOT OF HIS OWN PROBLEMS, AND HE WANTED ME TO SOLVE THEM FOR HIM AND MAKE HIM FEEL BETTER.

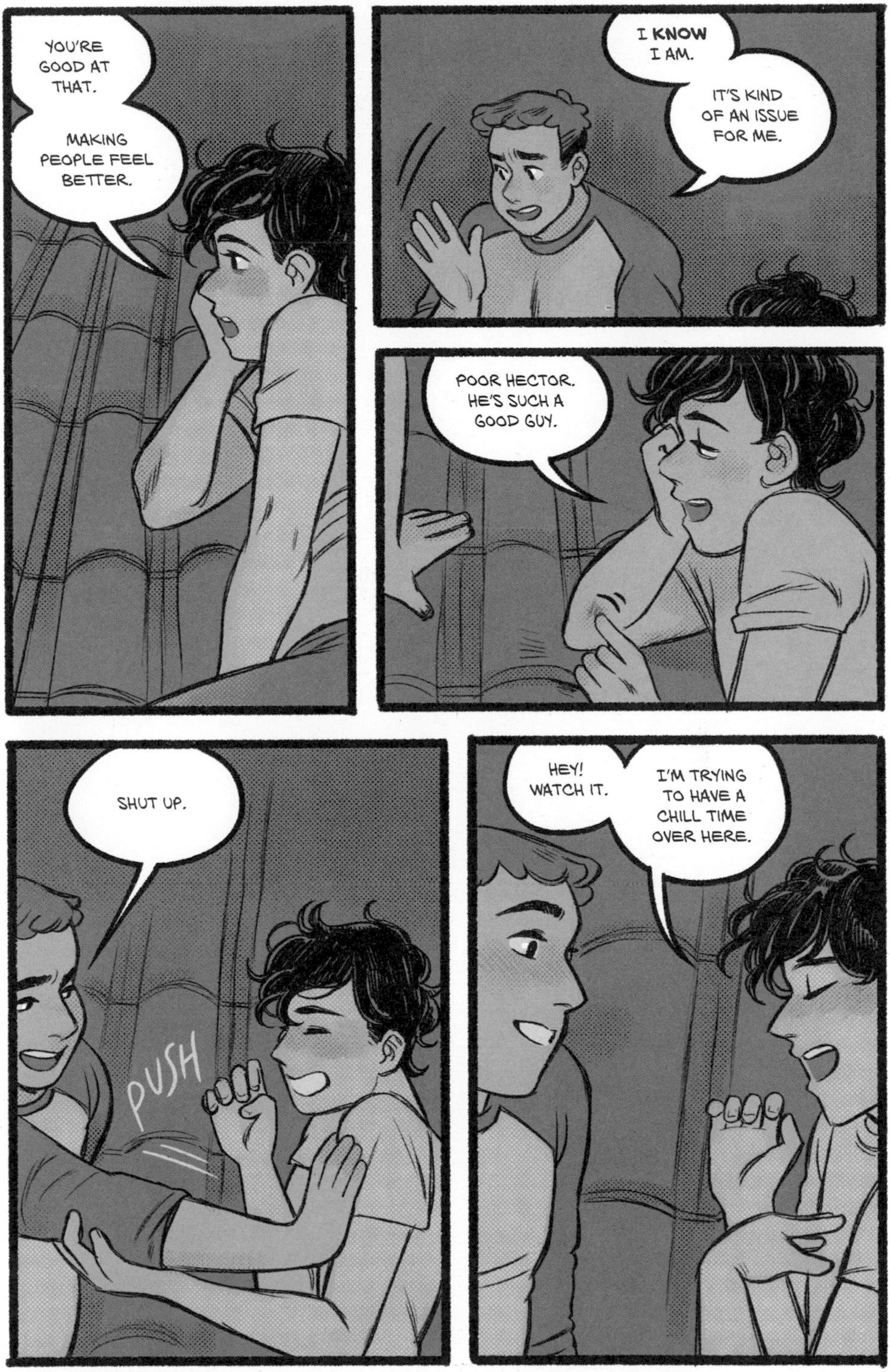
YOU'RE GOOD AT THAT.
MAKING PEOPLE FEEL BETTER.
I **KNOW** I AM.
IT'S KIND OF AN ISSUE FOR ME.
POOR HECTOR. HE'S SUCH A GOOD GUY.
SHUT UP.
PUSH
HEY! WATCH IT.
I'M TRYING TO HAVE A CHILL TIME OVER HERE.

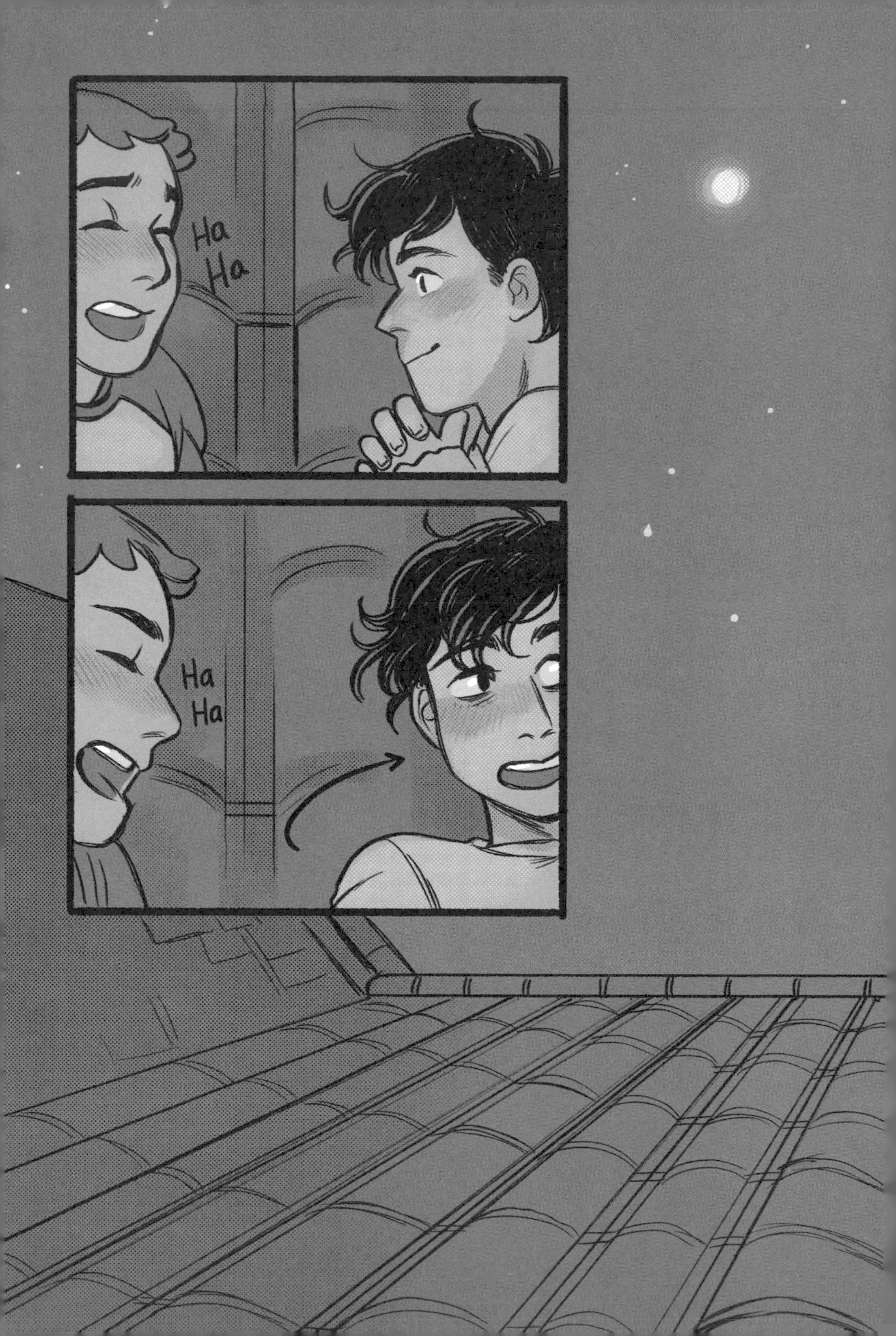
Ha
Ha
Ha
Ha

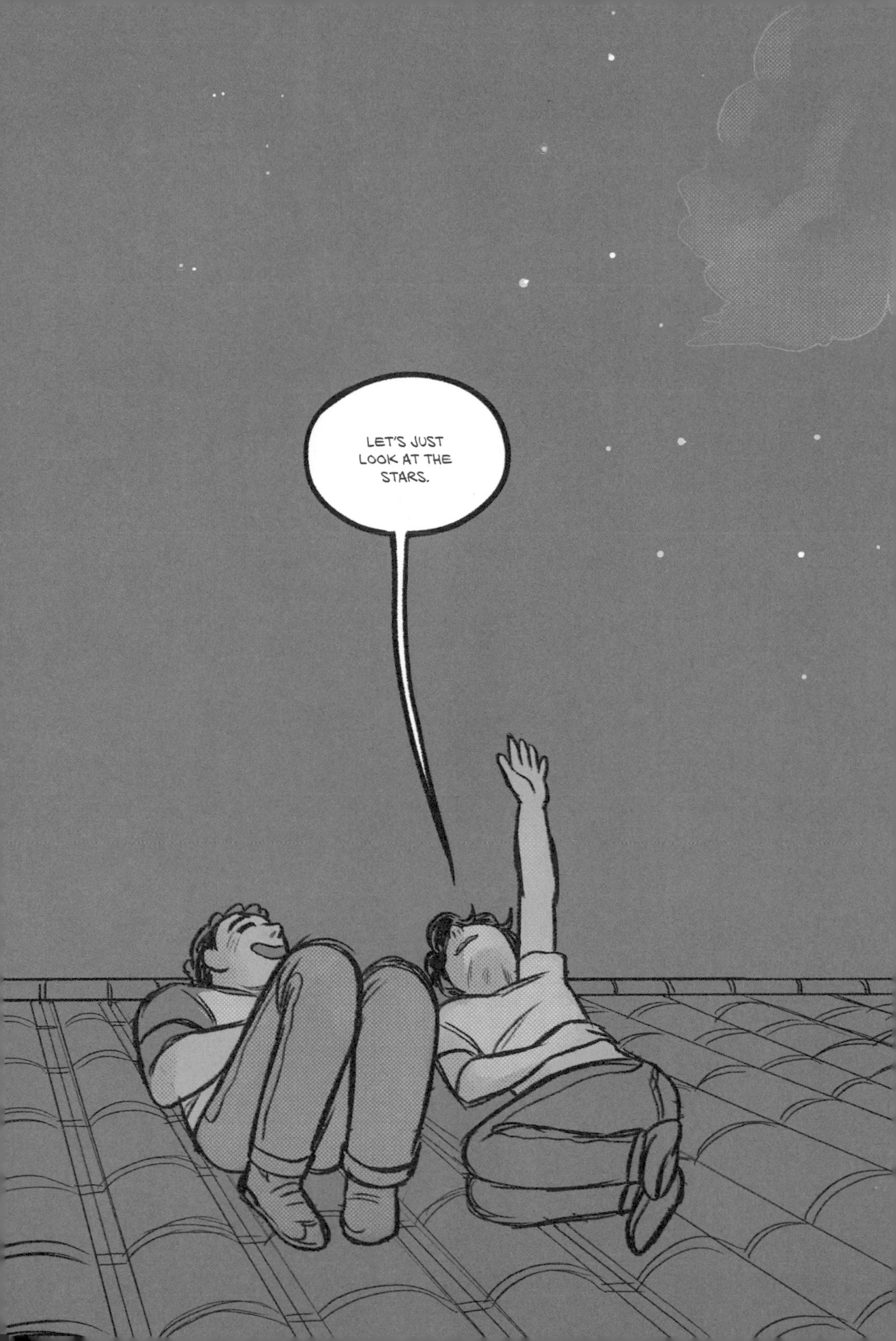
LET'S JUST LOOK AT THE STARS.

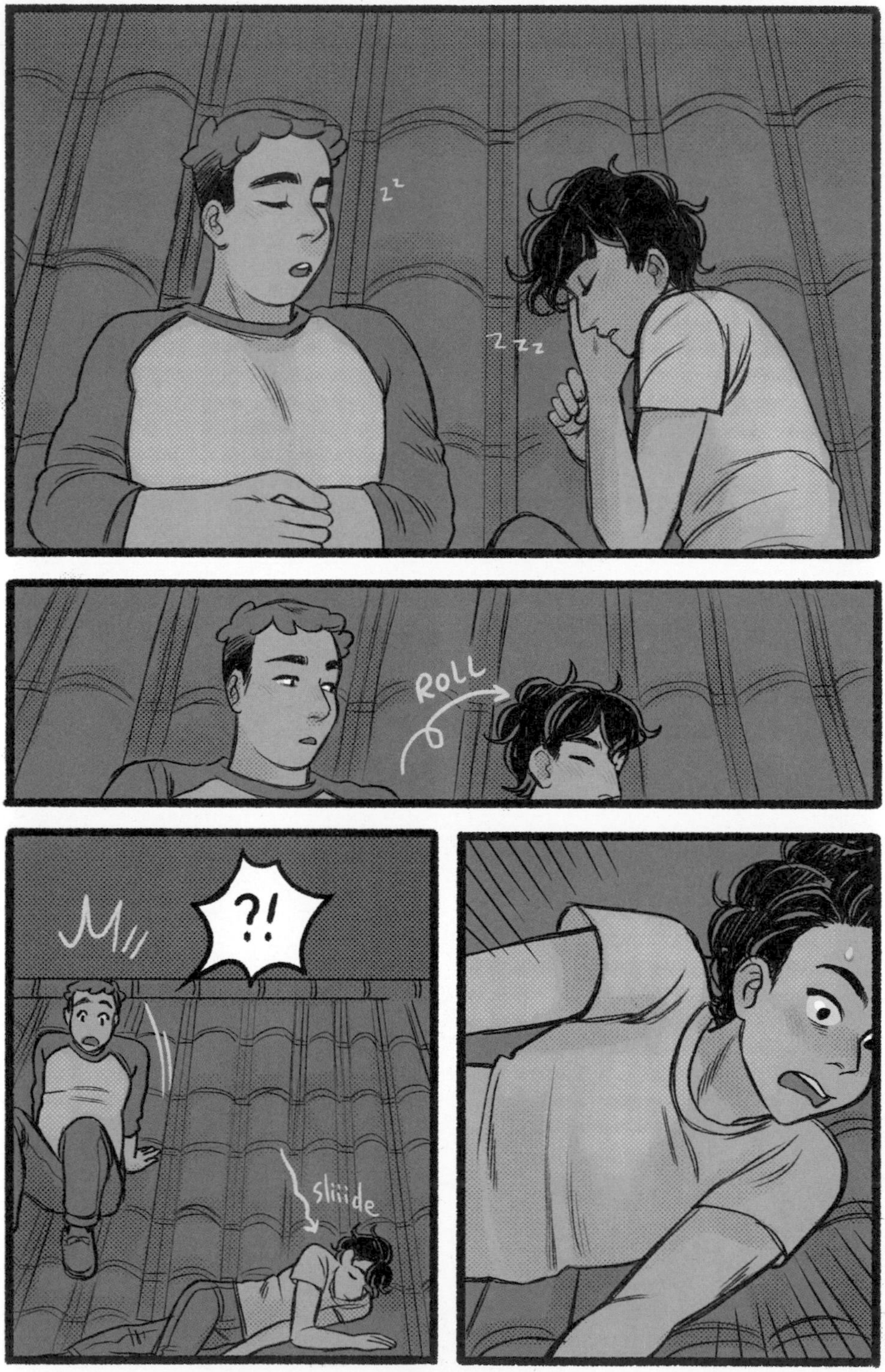

z z
z z z
ROLL
?!
sliiide

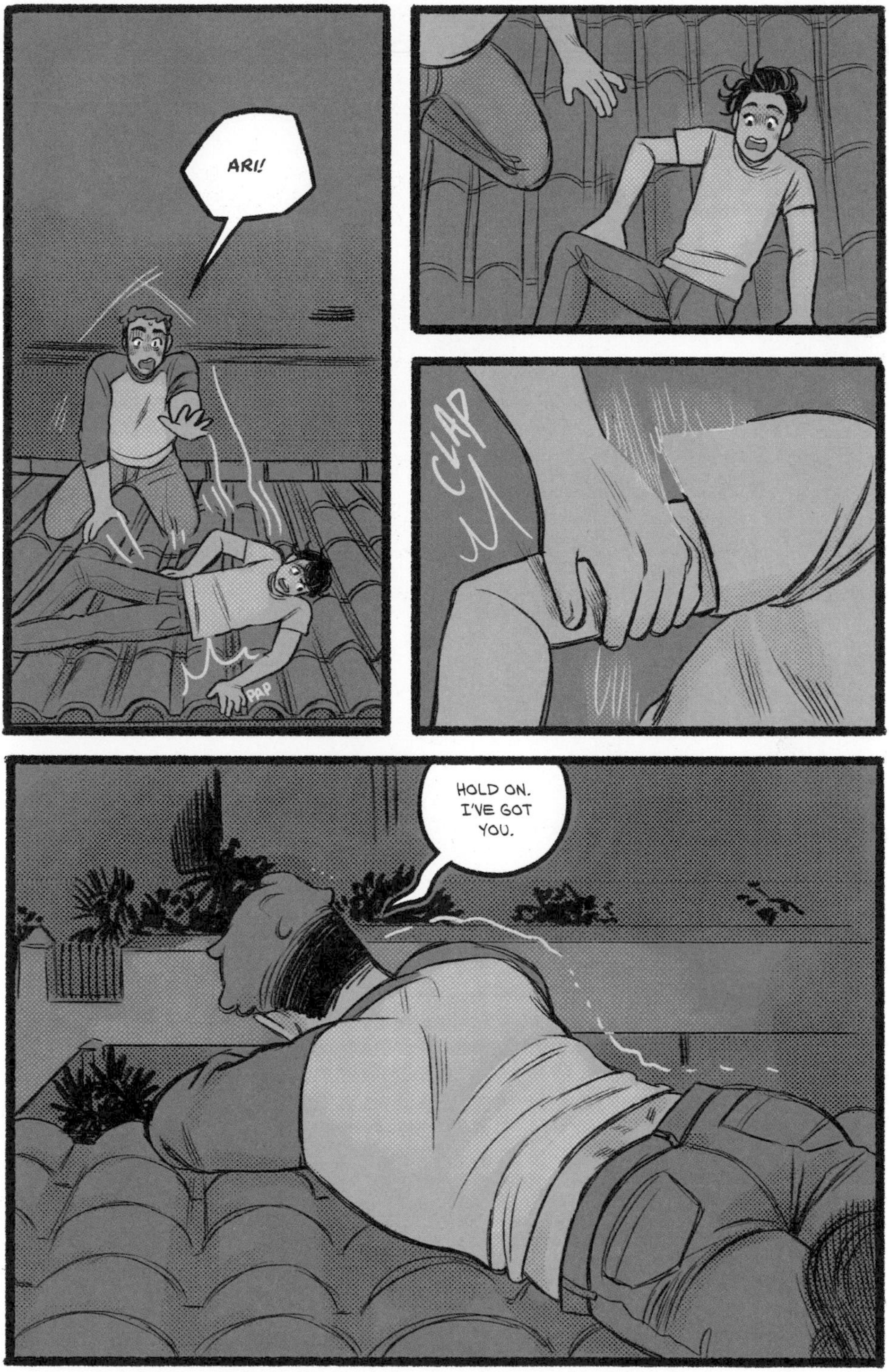
ARI!
PAP
CLAP
HOLD ON. I'VE GOT YOU.

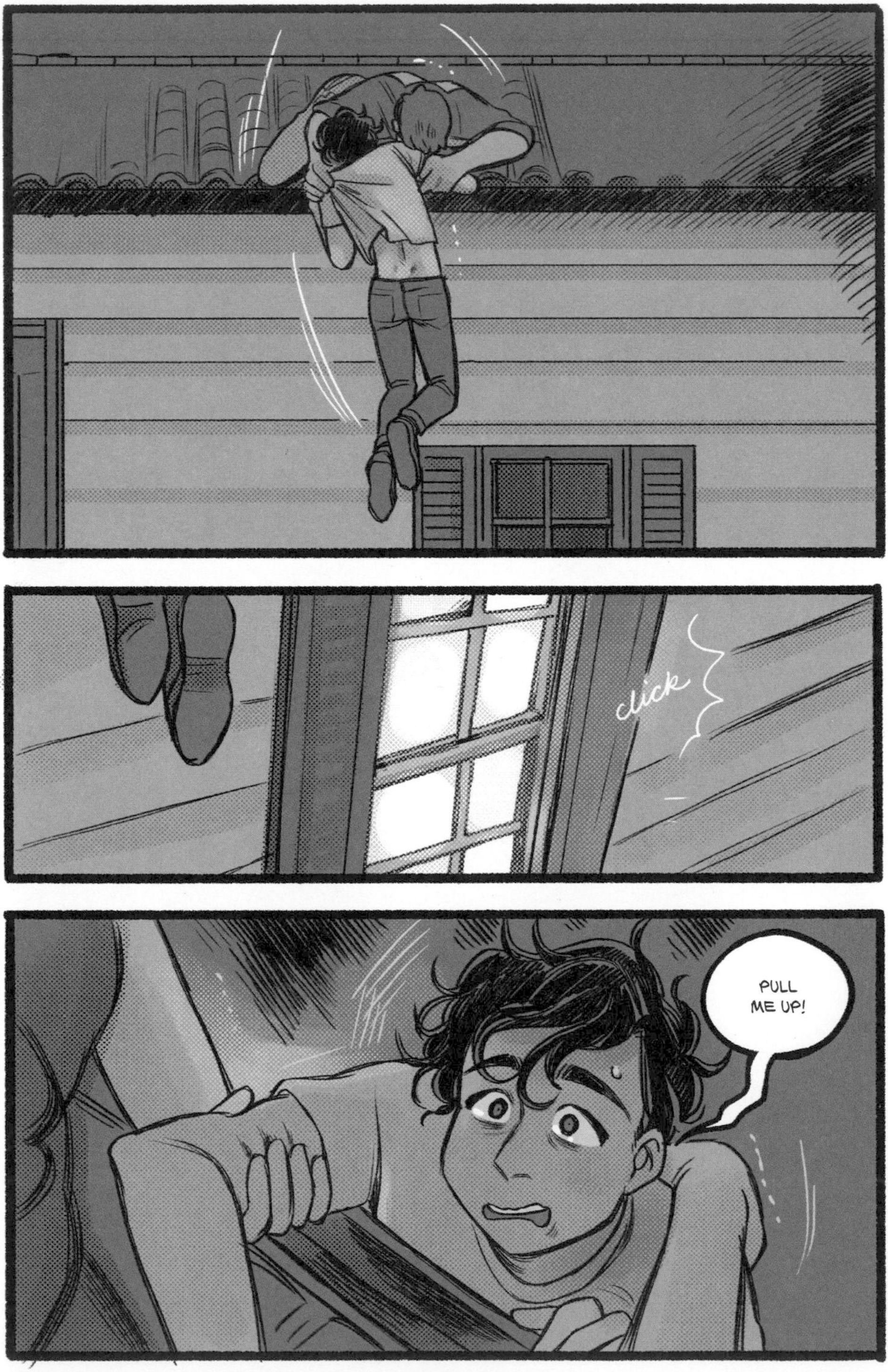
click
PULL ME UP!

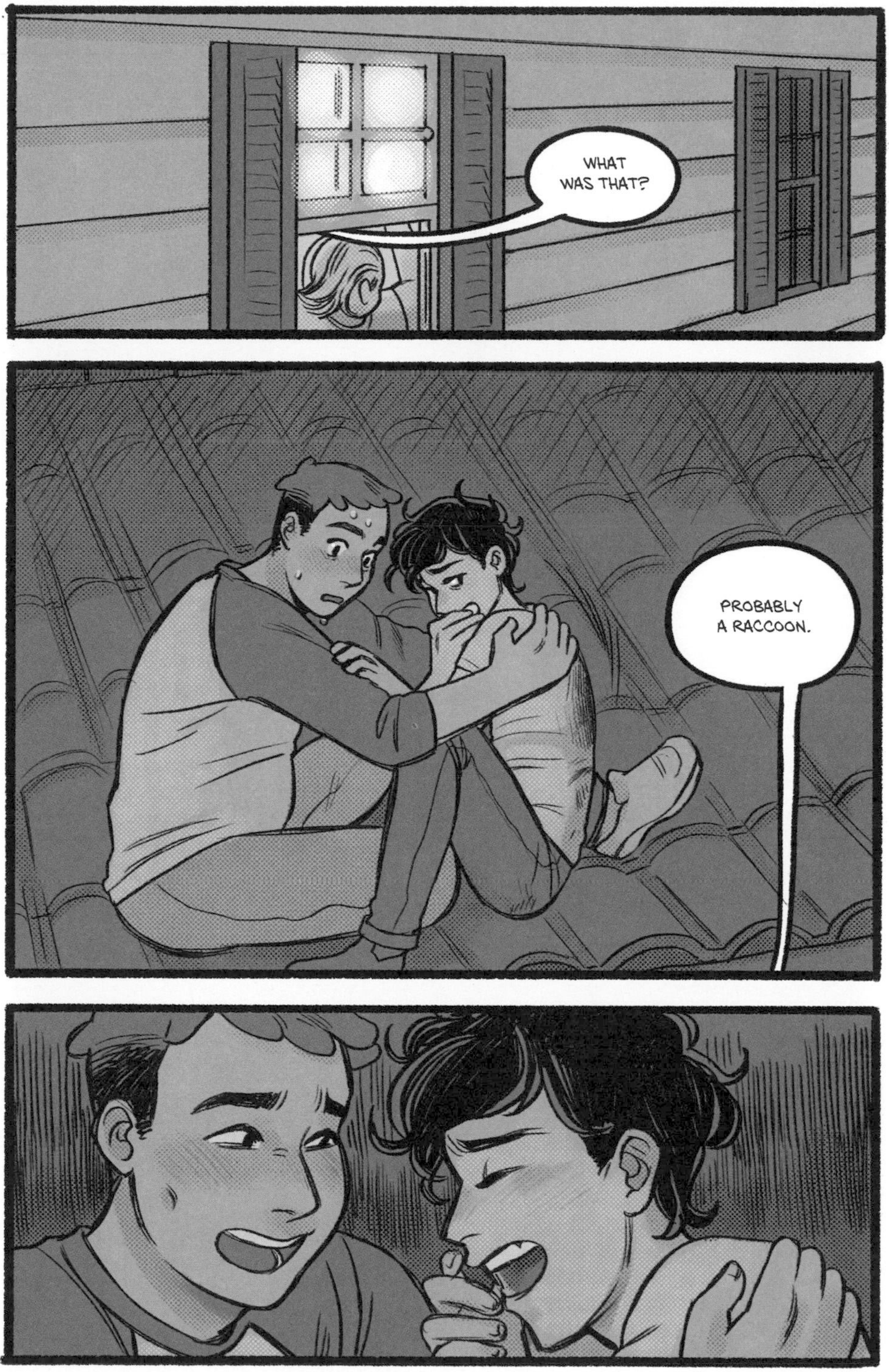
WHAT WAS THAT?
PROBABLY A RACCOON.

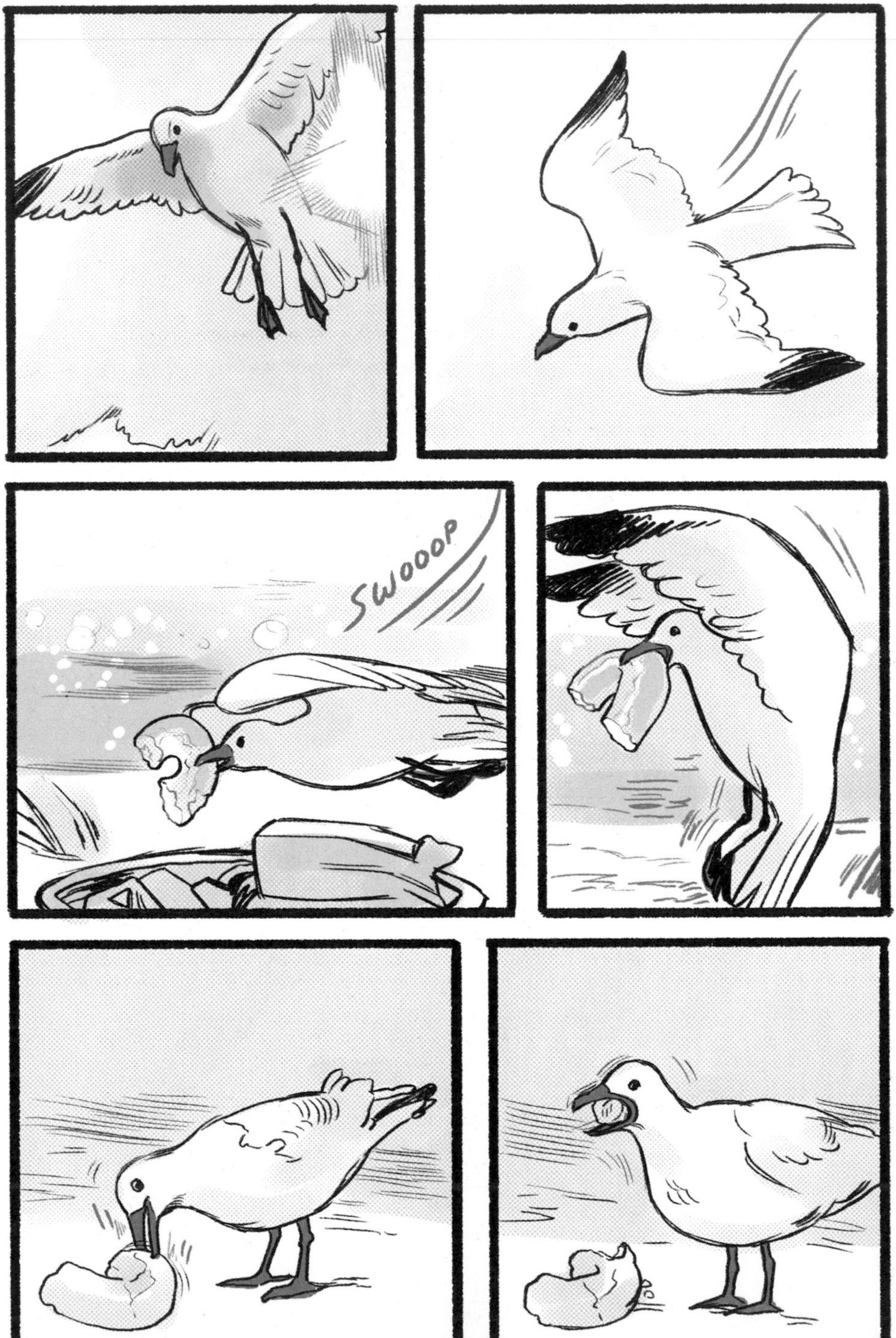
SWOOOP

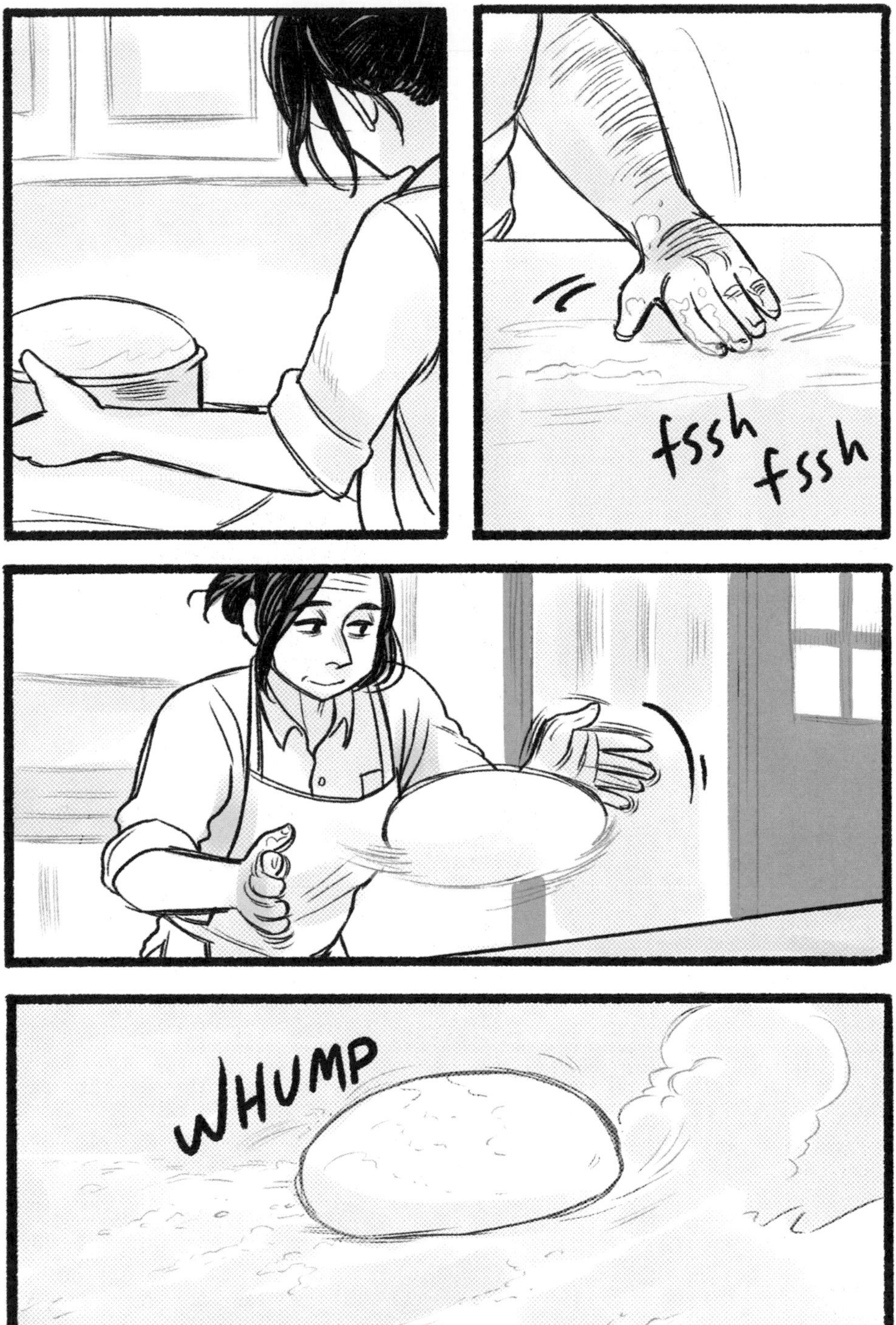
fssh
fssh
WHUMP

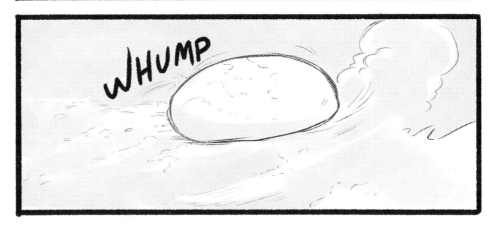

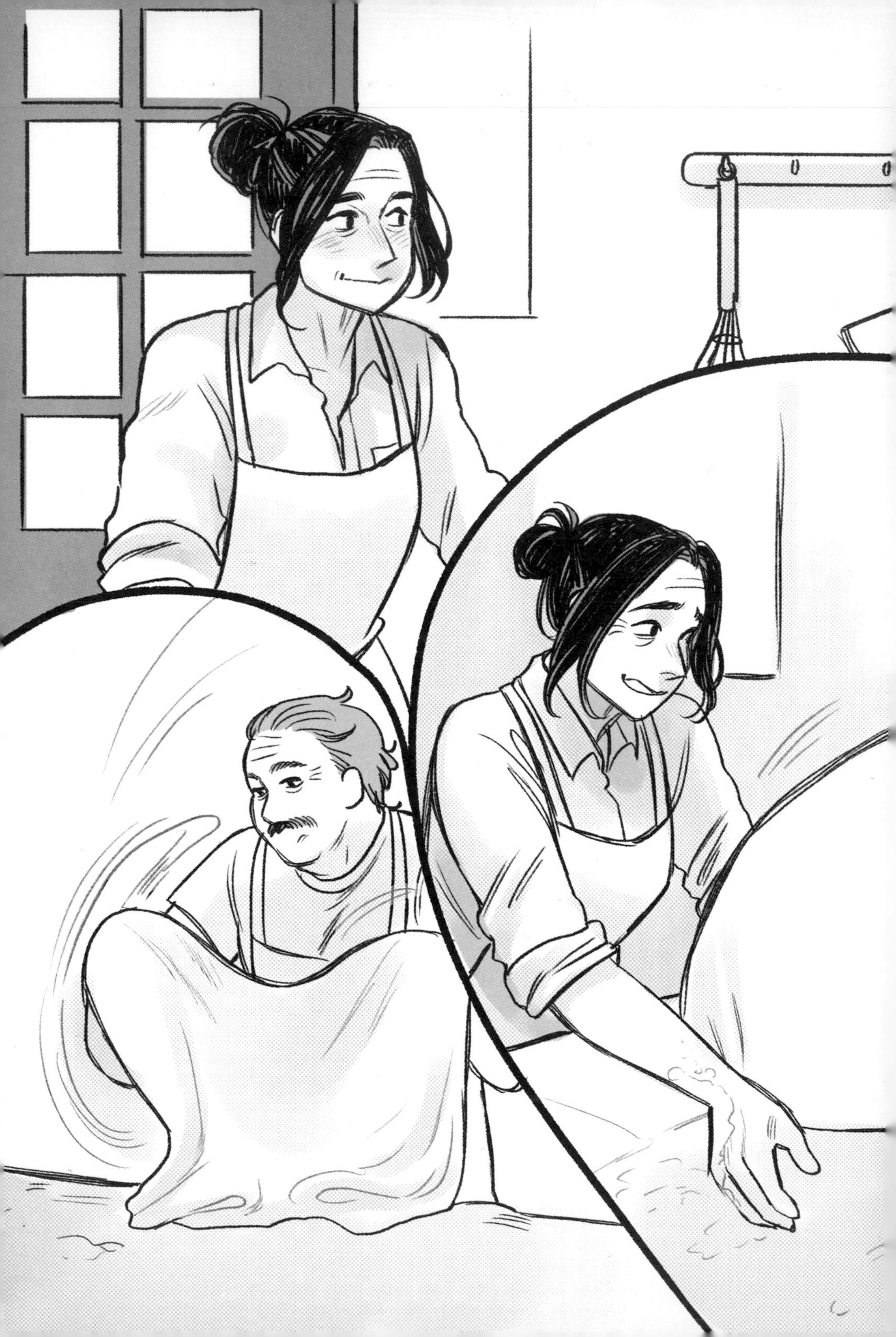

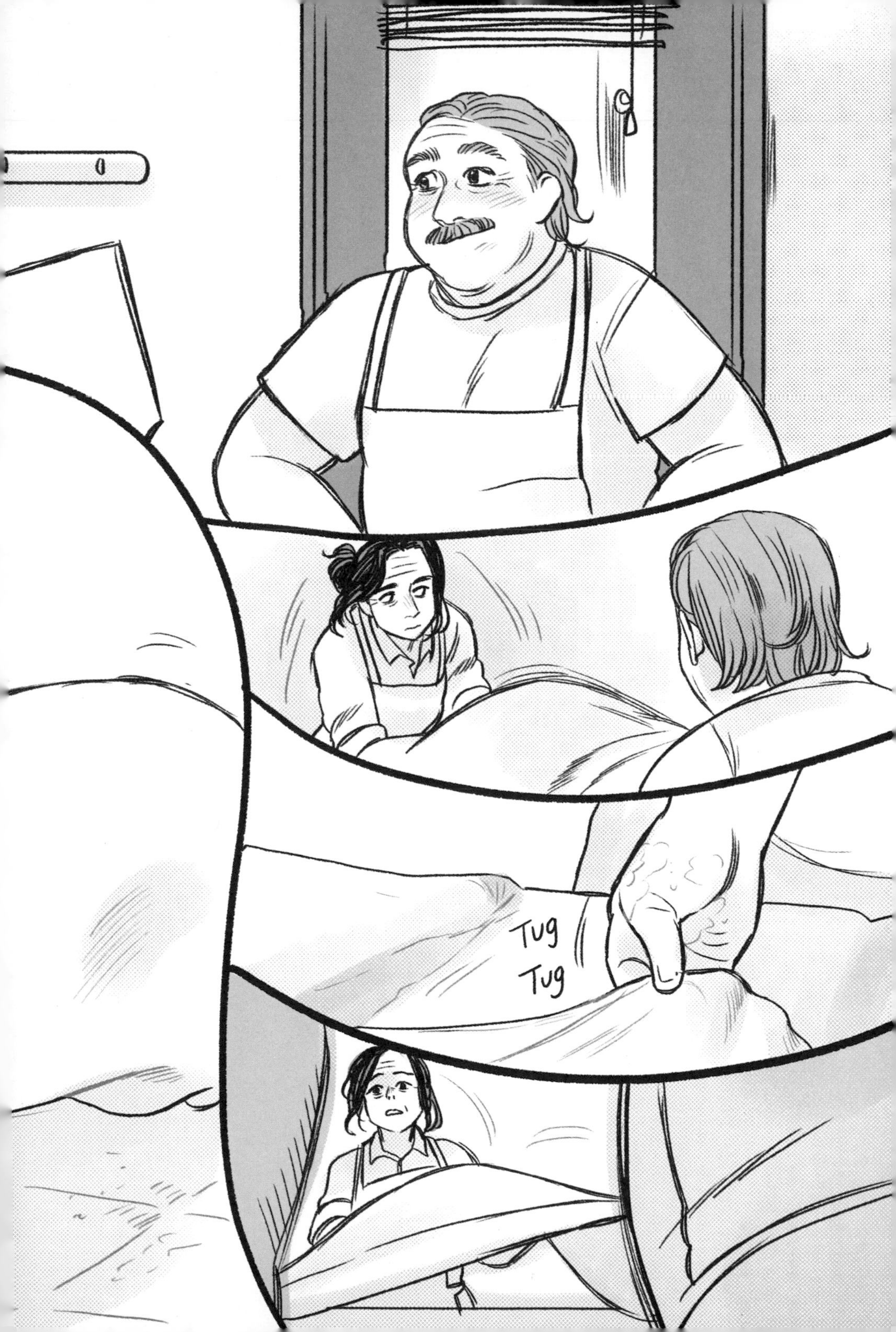
Tug
Tug

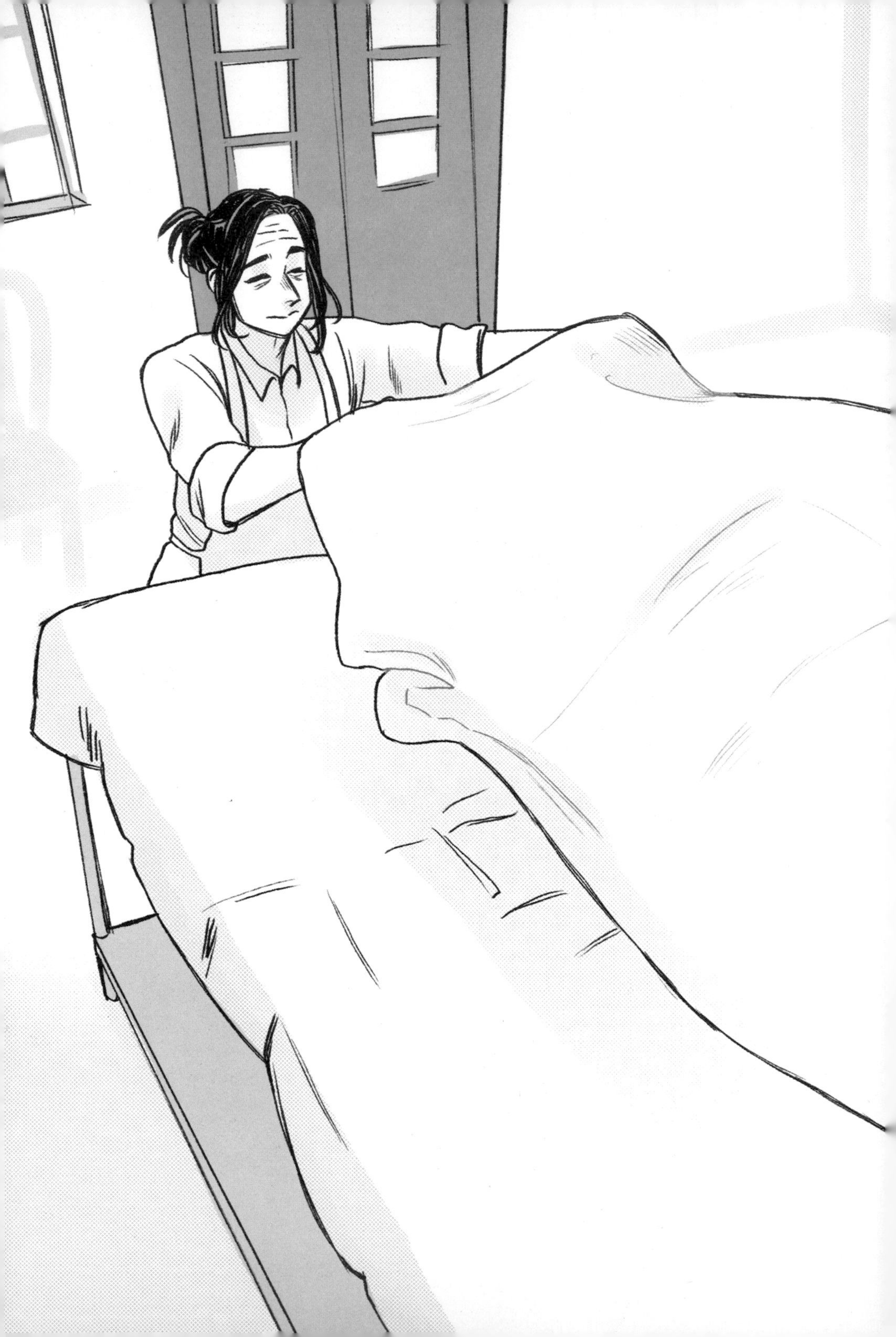

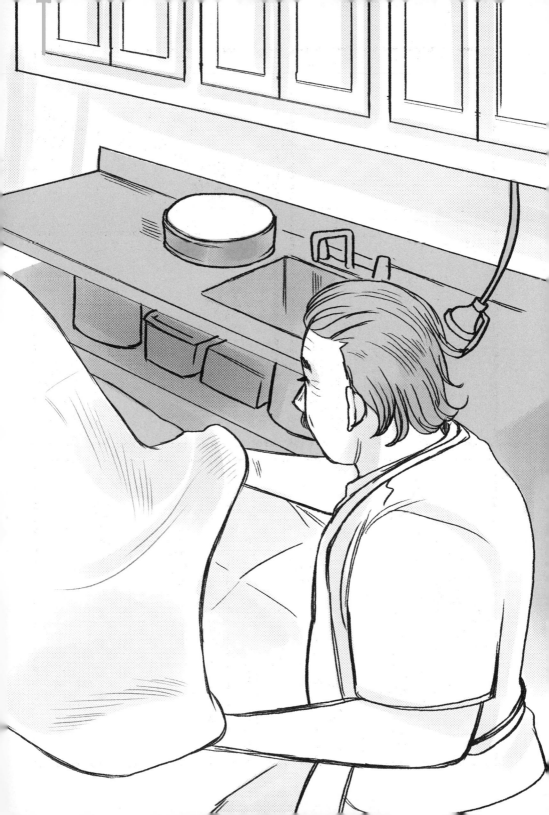

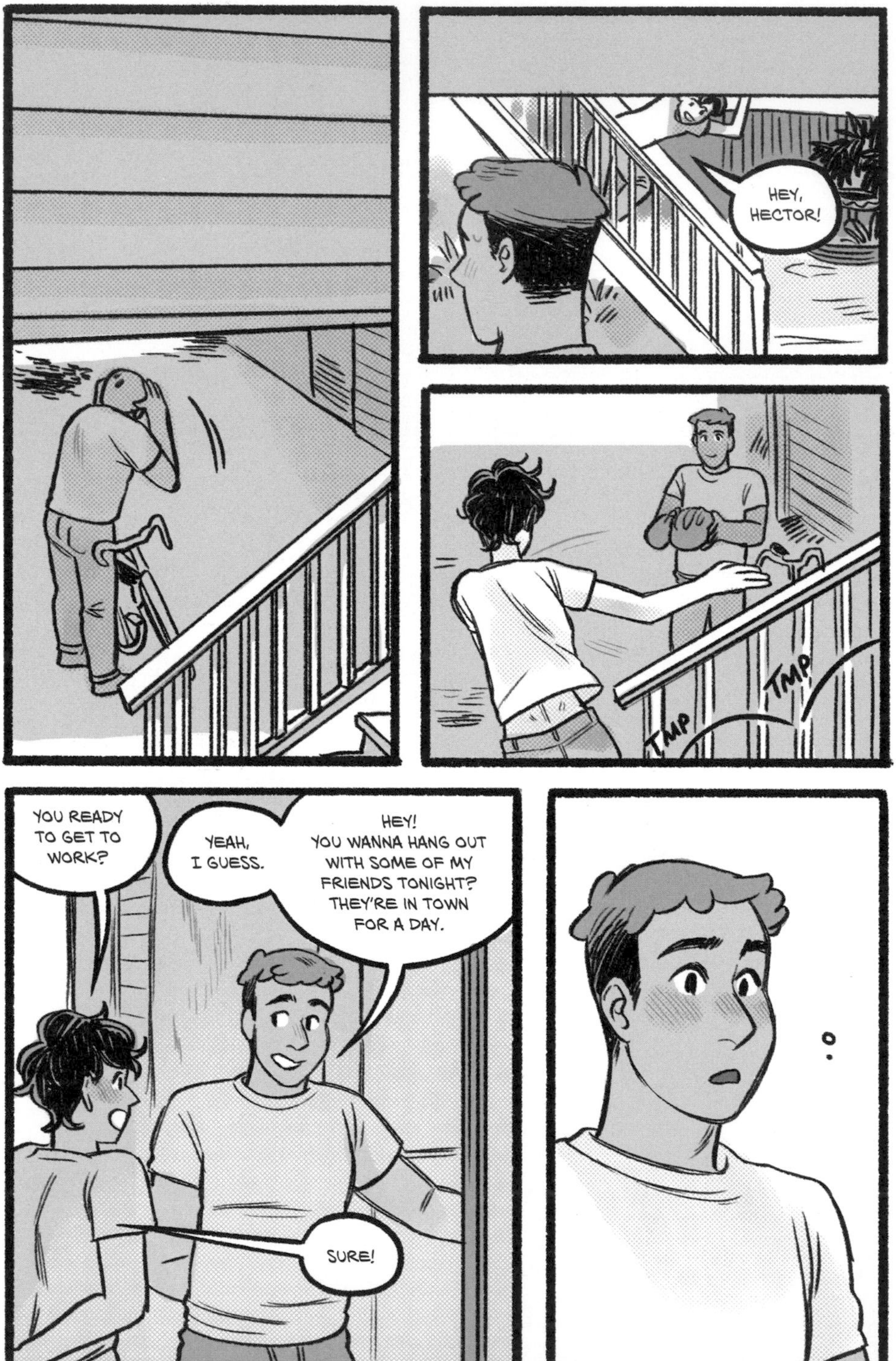
HEY, HECTOR!
TMP
TMP
YOU READY TO GET TO WORK?
YEAH, I GUESS.
HEY! YOU WANNA HANG OUT WITH SOME OF MY FRIENDS TONIGHT? THEY'RE IN TOWN FOR A DAY.
SURE!
o.

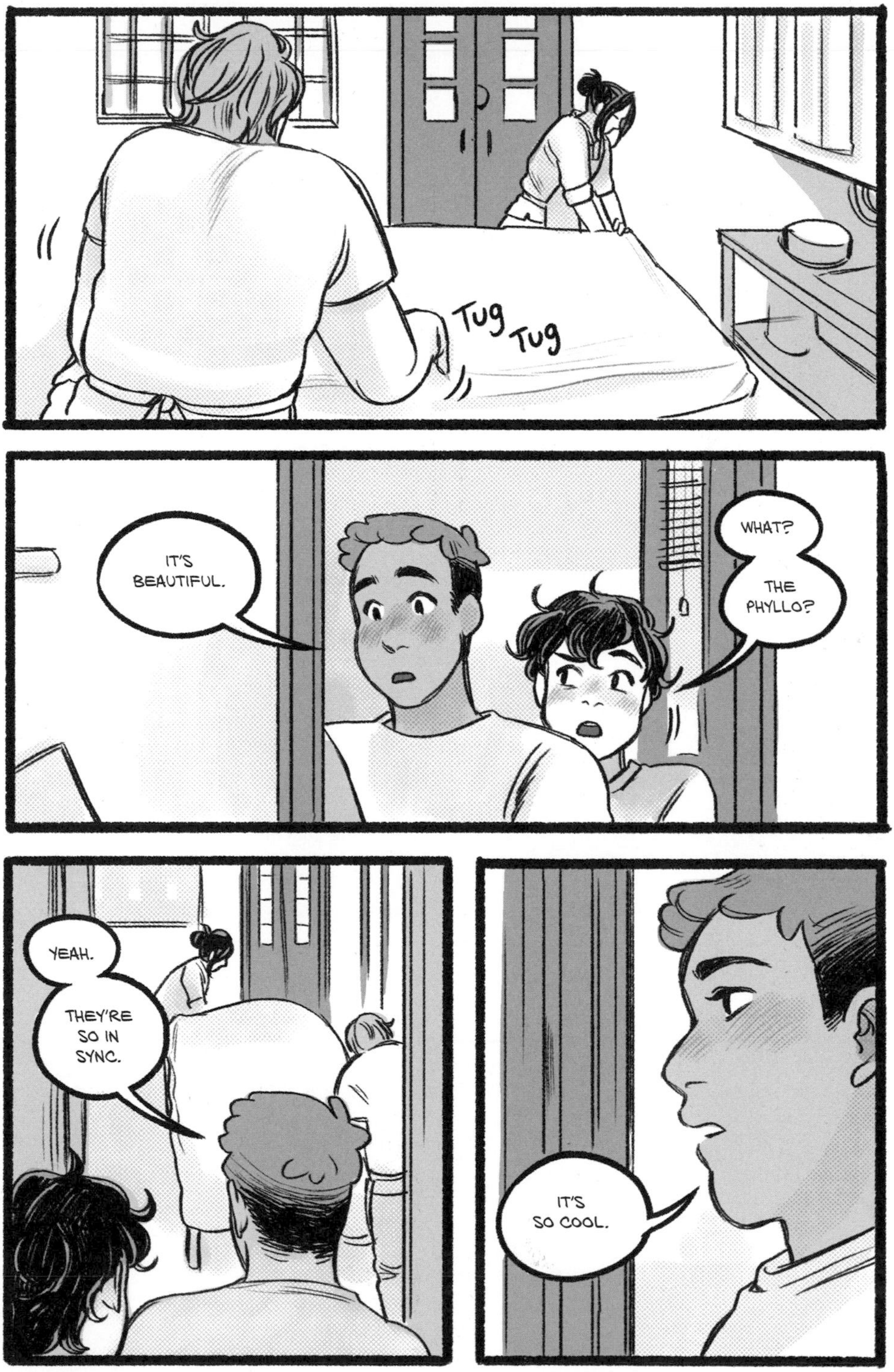
Tug
Tug
IT'S BEAUTIFUL.
WHAT?
THE PHYLLO?
YEAH.
THEY'RE SO IN SYNC.
IT'S SO COOL.

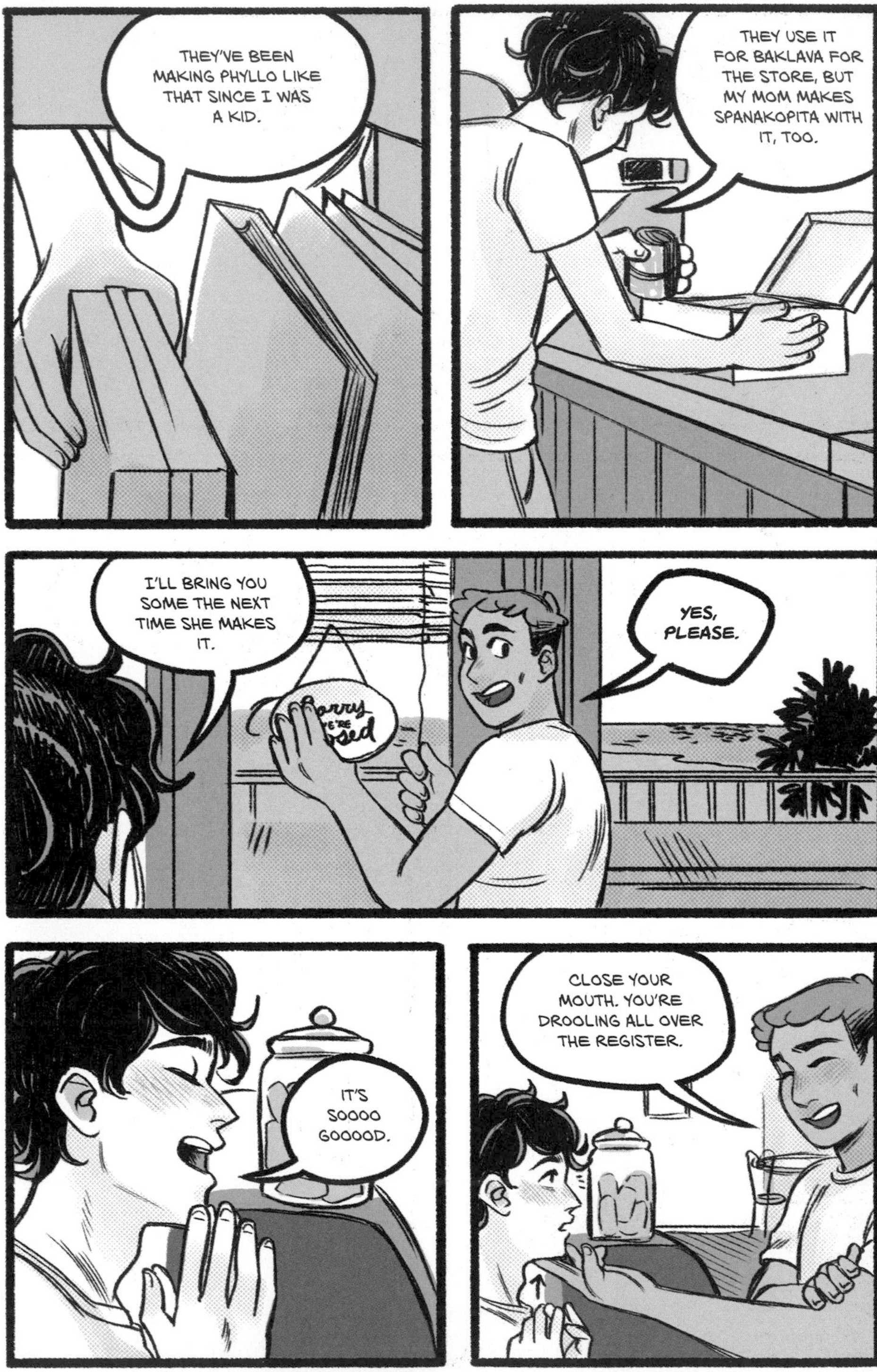
THEY'VE BEEN MAKING PHYLLO LIKE THAT SINCE I WAS A KID.
THEY USE IT FOR BAKLAVA FOR THE STORE, BUT MY MOM MAKES SPANAKOPITA WITH IT, TOO.
I'LL BRING YOU SOME THE NEXT TIME SHE MAKES IT.
YES, PLEASE.
IT'S SOOOO GOOOOD.
CLOSE YOUR MOUTH. YOU'RE DROOLING ALL OVER THE REGISTER.

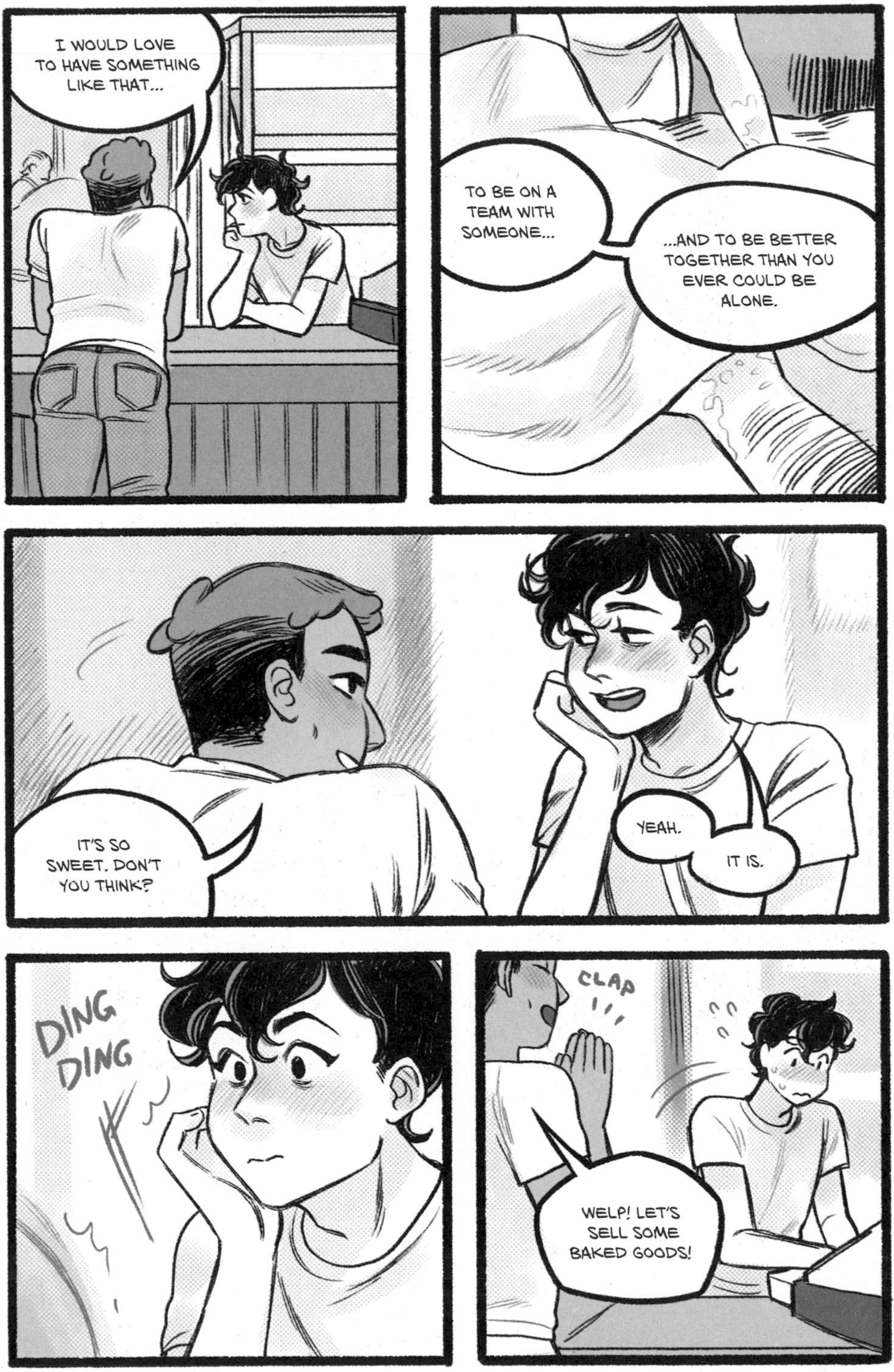
I WOULD LOVE TO HAVE SOMETHING LIKE THAT...
TO BE ON A TEAM WITH SOMEONE...
...AND TO BE BETTER TOGETHER THAN YOU EVER COULD BE ALONE.
IT'S SO SWEET. DON'T YOU THINK?
YEAH.
IT IS.
DING DING
CLAP
WELP! LET'S SELL SOME BAKED GOODS!

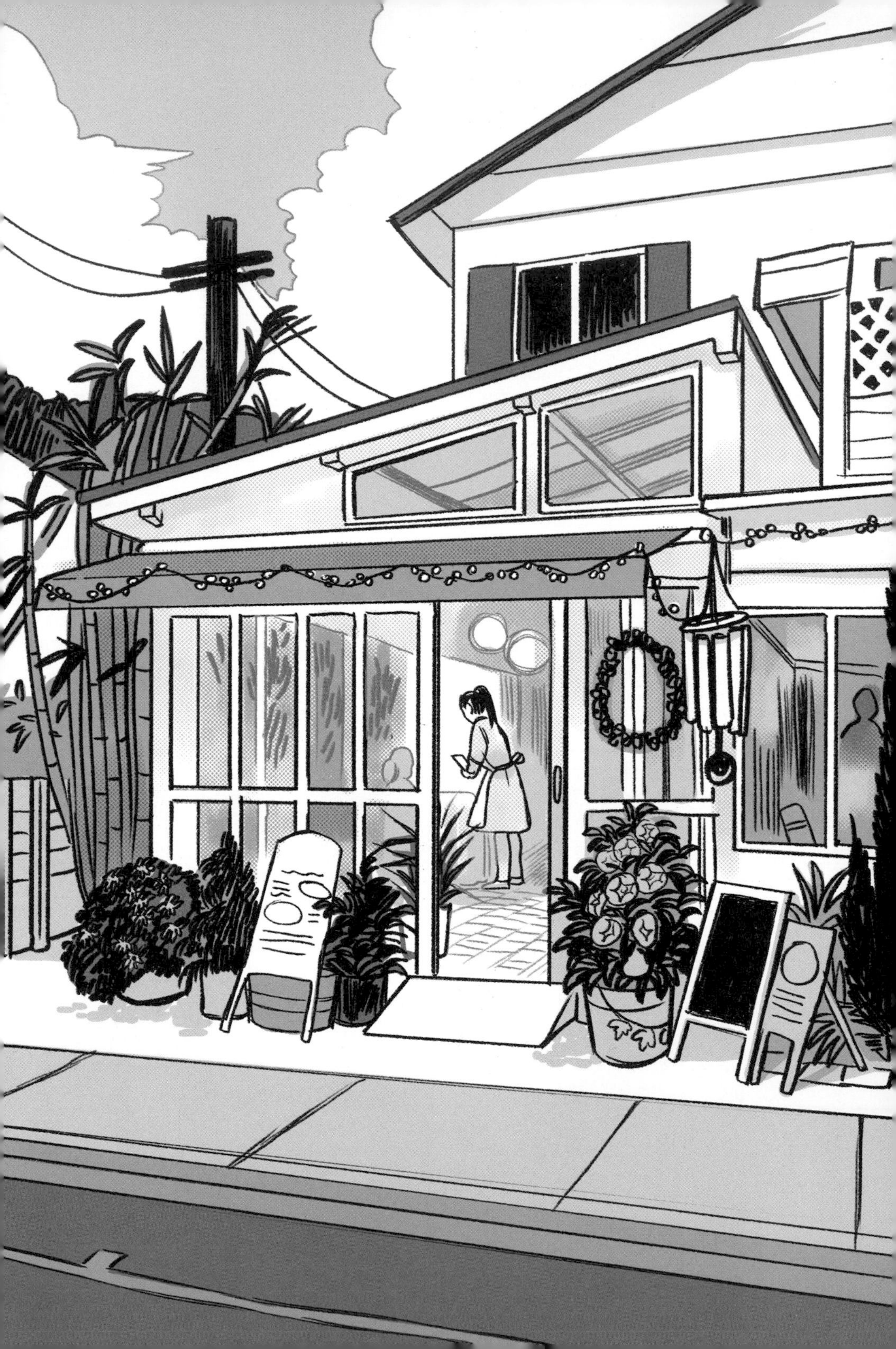

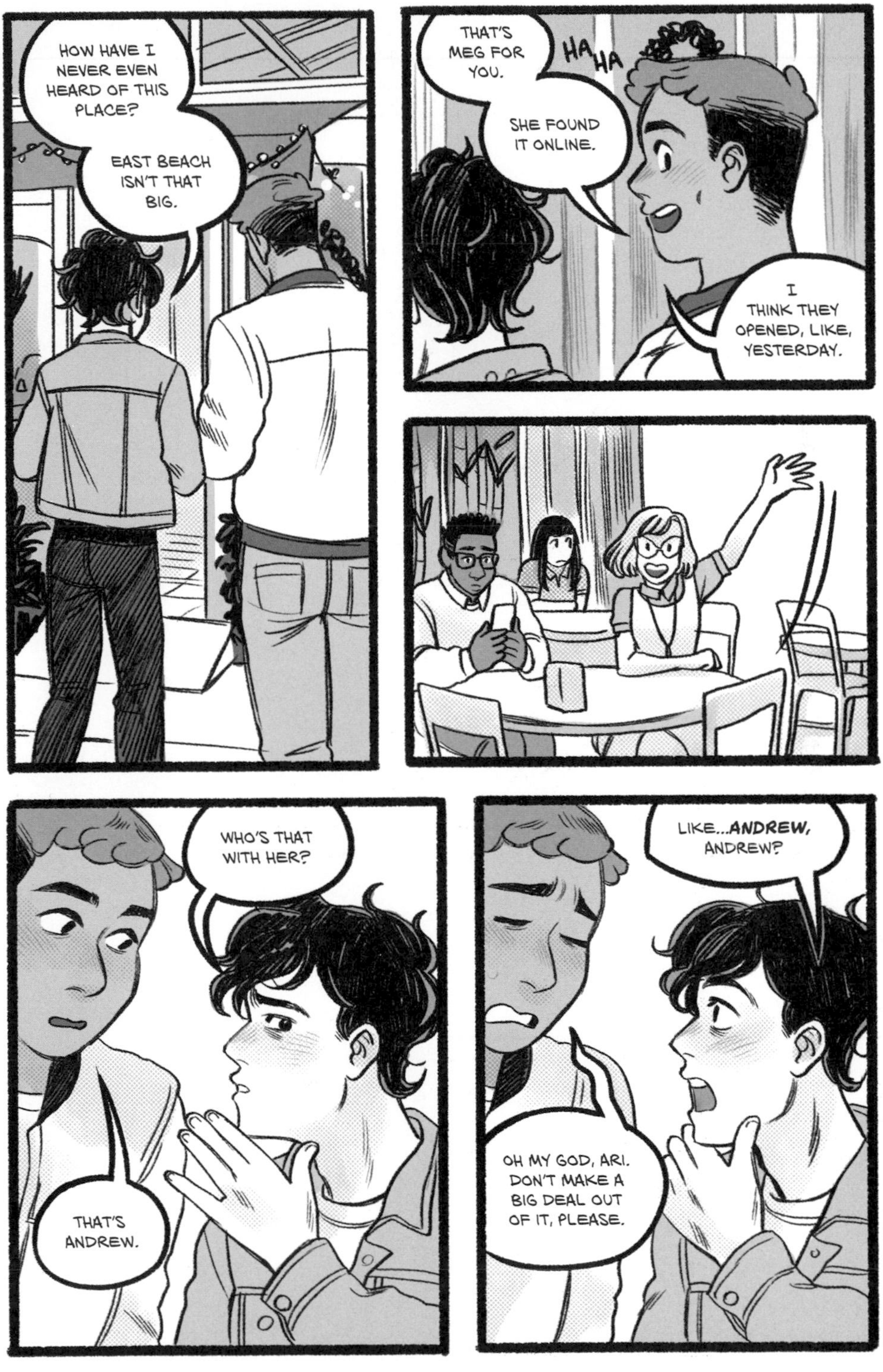
HOW HAVE I NEVER EVEN HEARD OF THIS PLACE?
EAST BEACH ISN'T THAT BIG.
THAT'S MEG FOR YOU.
HA HA
SHE FOUND IT ONLINE.
I THINK THEY OPENED, LIKE, YESTERDAY.
WHO'S THAT WITH HER?
THAT'S ANDREW.
LIKE...**ANDREW,** ANDREW?
OH MY GOD, ARI. DON'T MAKE A BIG DEAL OUT OF IT, PLEASE.

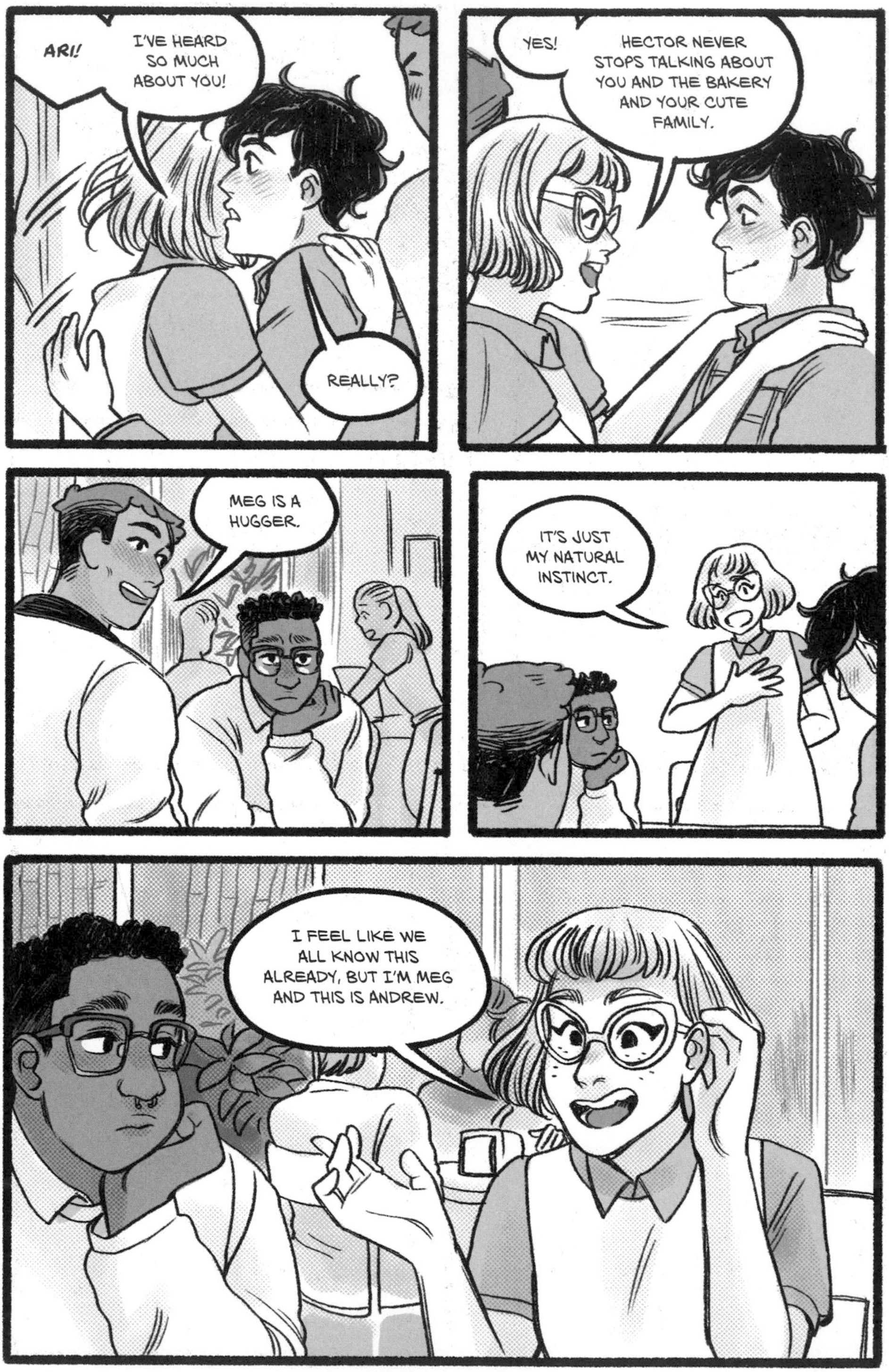
ARI!
I'VE HEARD SO MUCH ABOUT YOU!
REALLY?
YES!
HECTOR NEVER STOPS TALKING ABOUT YOU AND THE BAKERY AND YOUR CUTE FAMILY.
MEG IS A HUGGER.
IT'S JUST MY NATURAL INSTINCT.
I FEEL LIKE WE ALL KNOW THIS ALREADY, BUT I'M MEG AND THIS IS ANDREW.

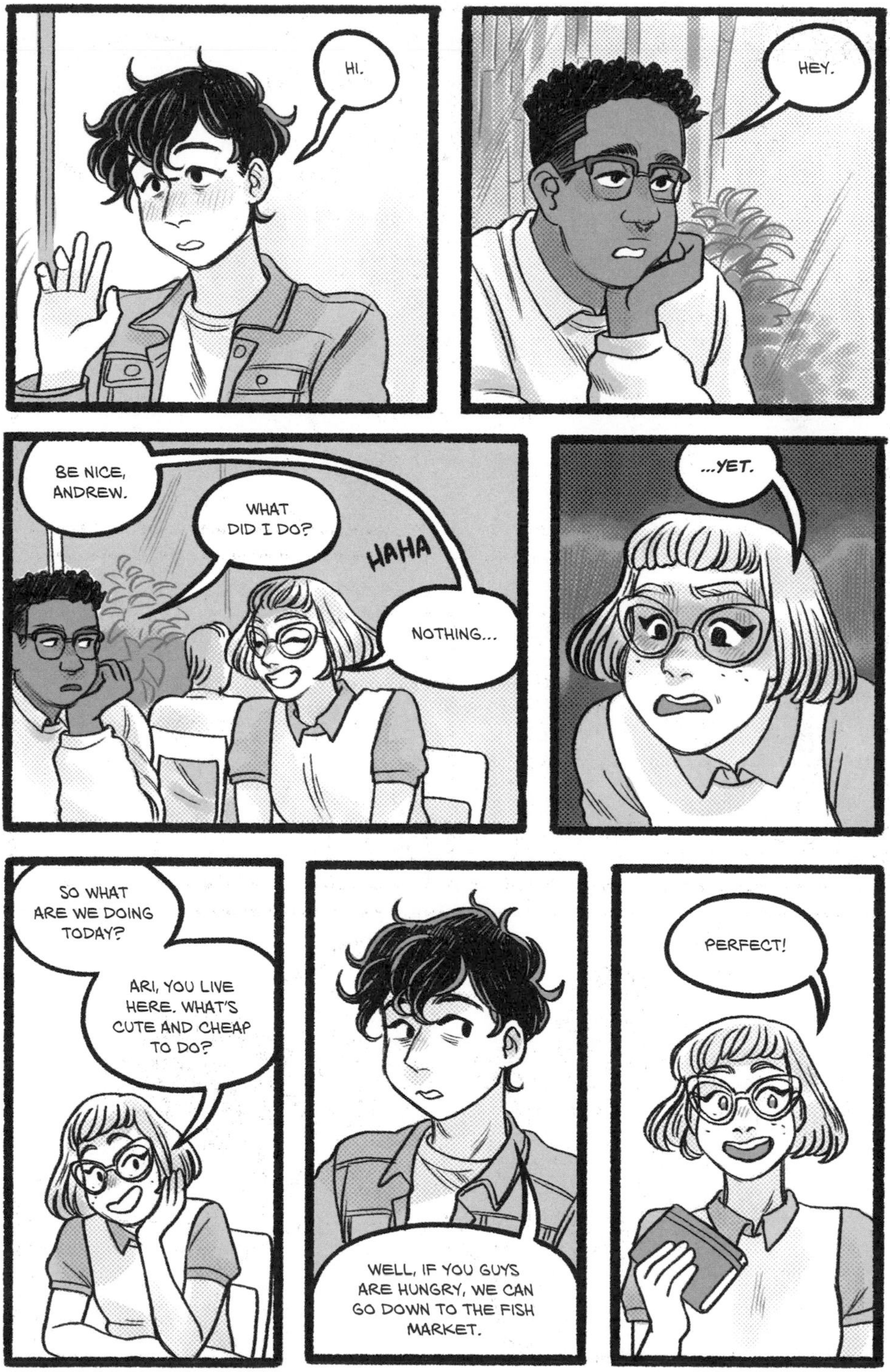
HI.
HEY.
BE NICE, ANDREW.
WHAT DID I DO?
HAHA
NOTHING...
...YET.
SO WHAT ARE WE DOING TODAY?
ARI, YOU LIVE HERE. WHAT'S CUTE AND CHEAP TO DO?
WELL, IF YOU GUYS ARE HUNGRY, WE CAN GO DOWN TO THE FISH MARKET.
PERFECT!

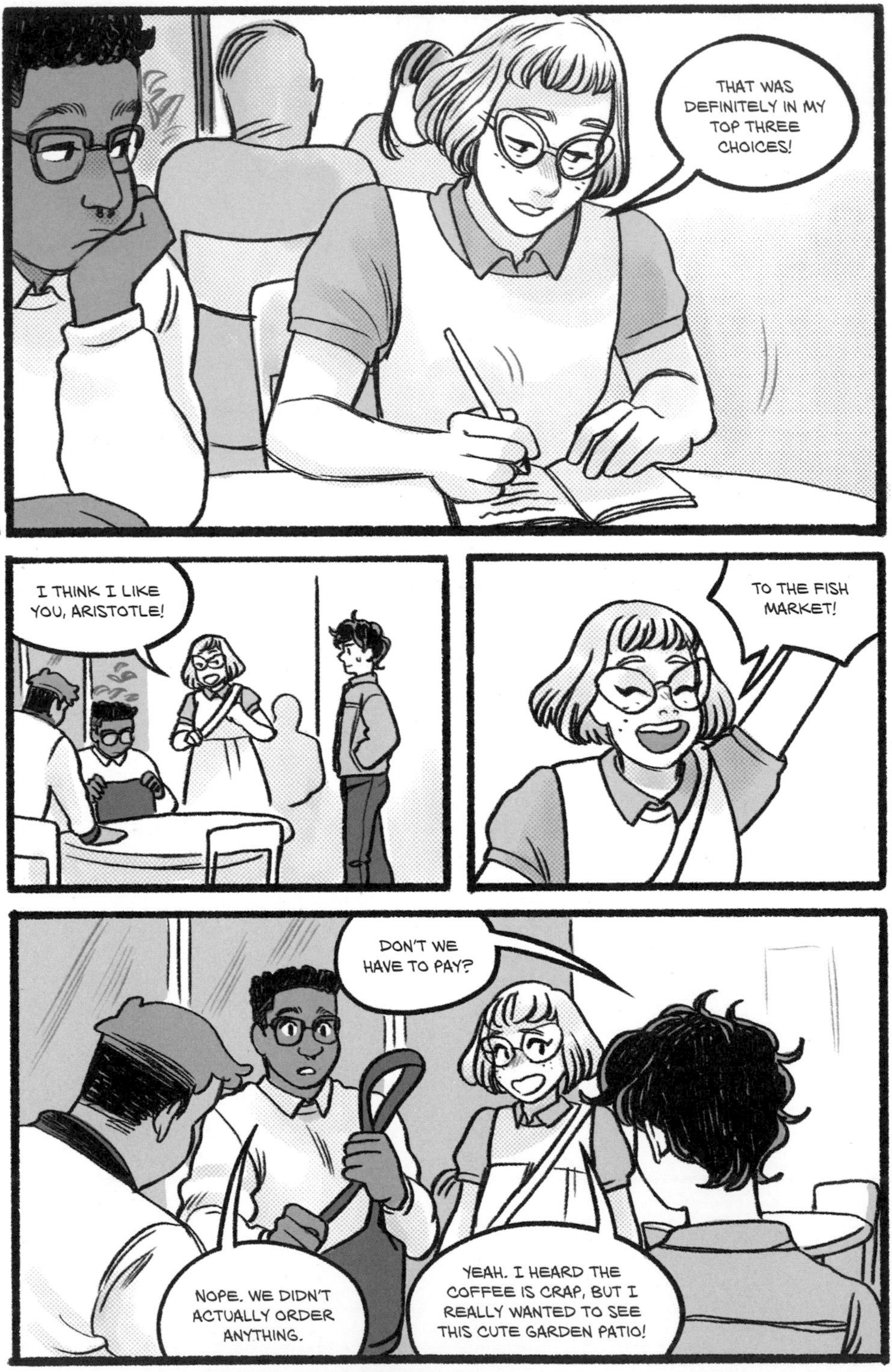
THAT WAS DEFINITELY IN MY TOP THREE CHOICES!
I THINK I LIKE YOU, ARISTOTLE!
TO THE FISH MARKET!
DON'T WE HAVE TO PAY?
NOPE. WE DIDN'T ACTUALLY ORDER ANYTHING.
YEAH. I HEARD THE COFFEE IS CRAP, BUT I REALLY WANTED TO SEE THIS CUTE GARDEN PATIO!

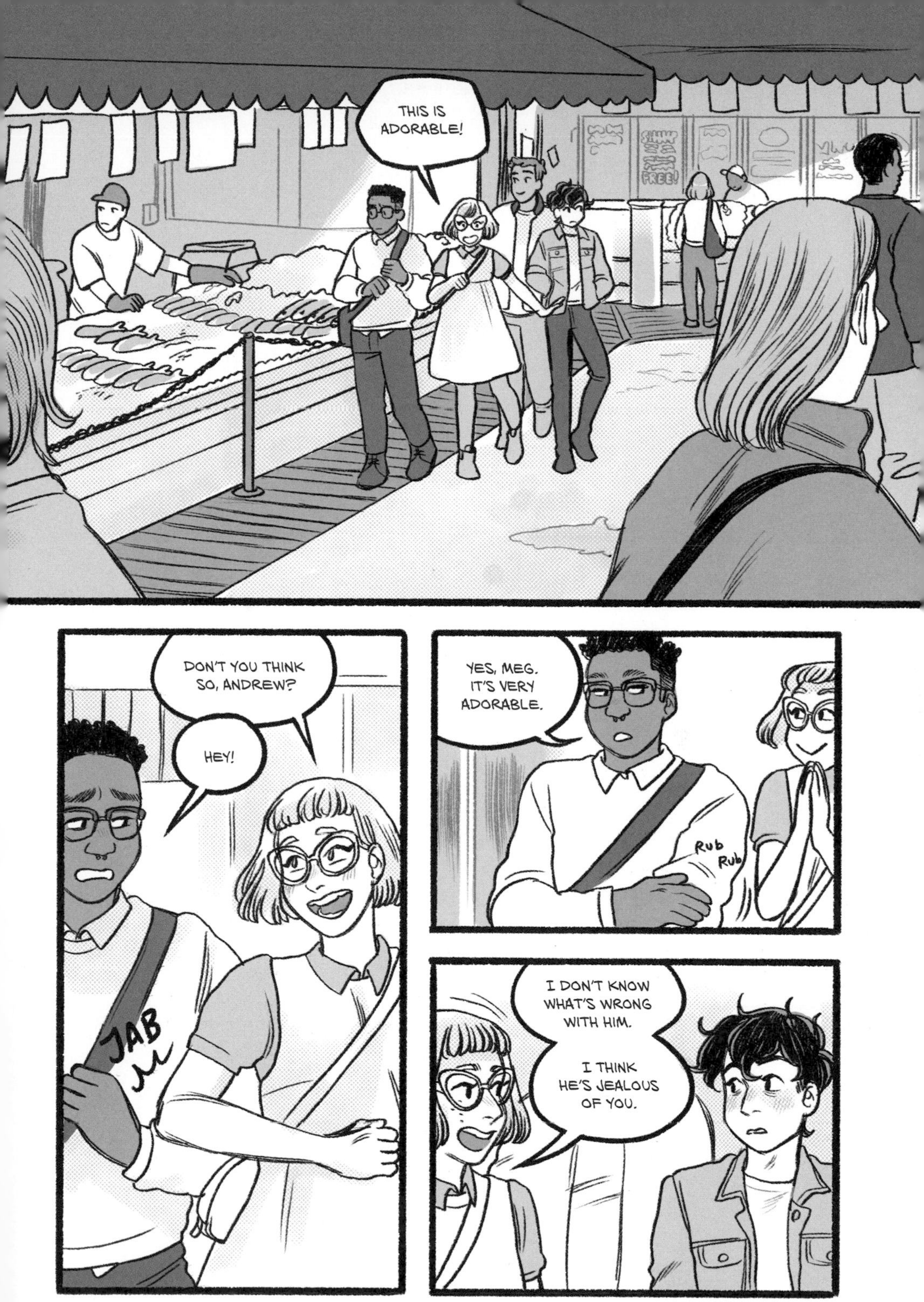
THIS IS ADORABLE!
SHUT FREE!
DON'T YOU THINK SO, ANDREW?
HEY!
JAB
YES, MEG. IT'S VERY ADORABLE.
Rub Rub
I DON'T KNOW WHAT'S WRONG WITH HIM.
I THINK HE'S JEALOUS OF YOU.

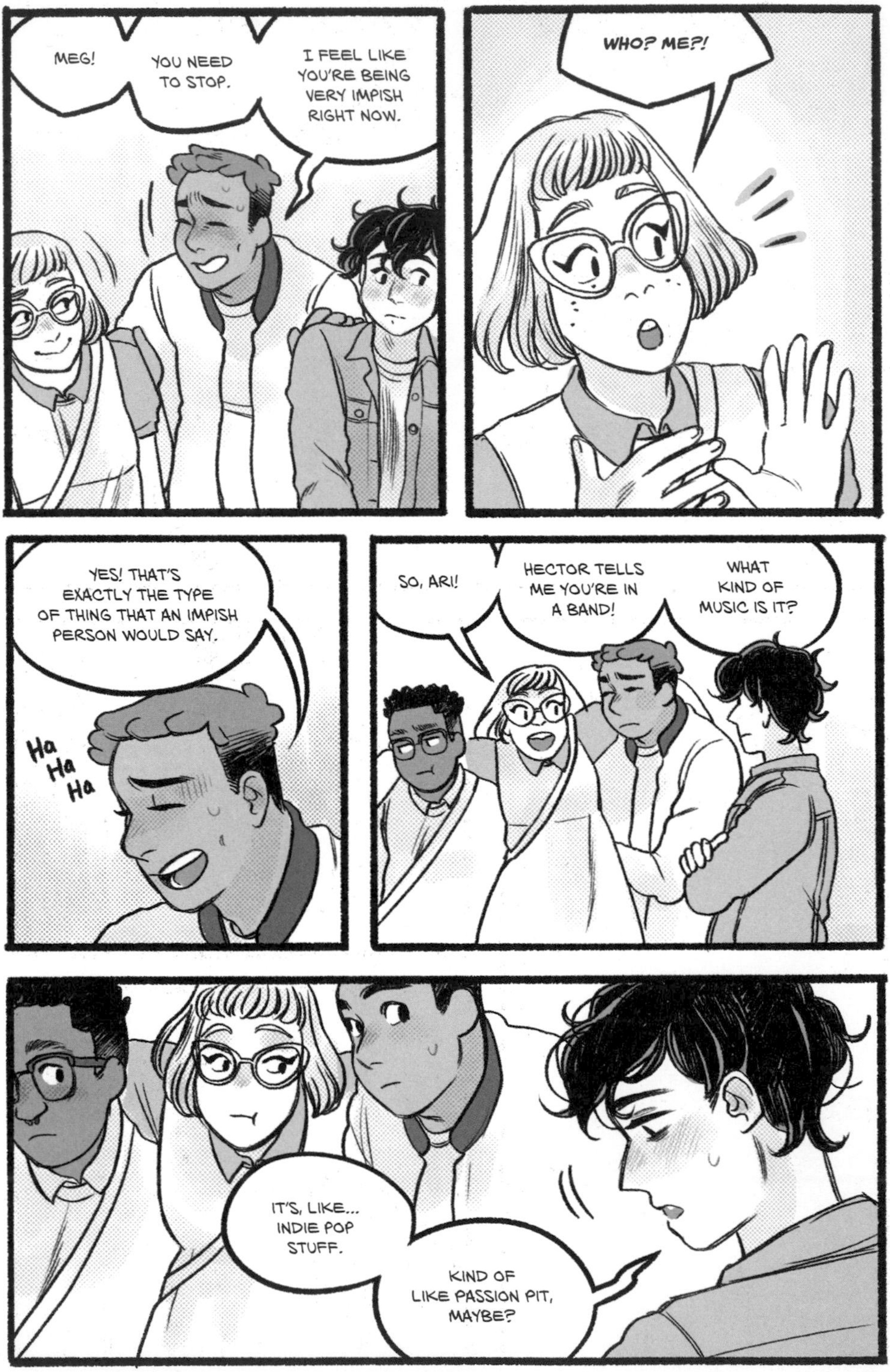
MEG!
YOU NEED TO STOP.
I FEEL LIKE YOU'RE BEING VERY IMPISH RIGHT NOW.
WHO? ME?!
YES! THAT'S EXACTLY THE TYPE OF THING THAT AN IMPISH PERSON WOULD SAY.
Ha Ha Ha
SO, ARI!
HECTOR TELLS ME YOU'RE IN A BAND!
WHAT KIND OF MUSIC IS IT?
IT'S, LIKE... INDIE POP STUFF.
KIND OF LIKE PASSION PIT, MAYBE?

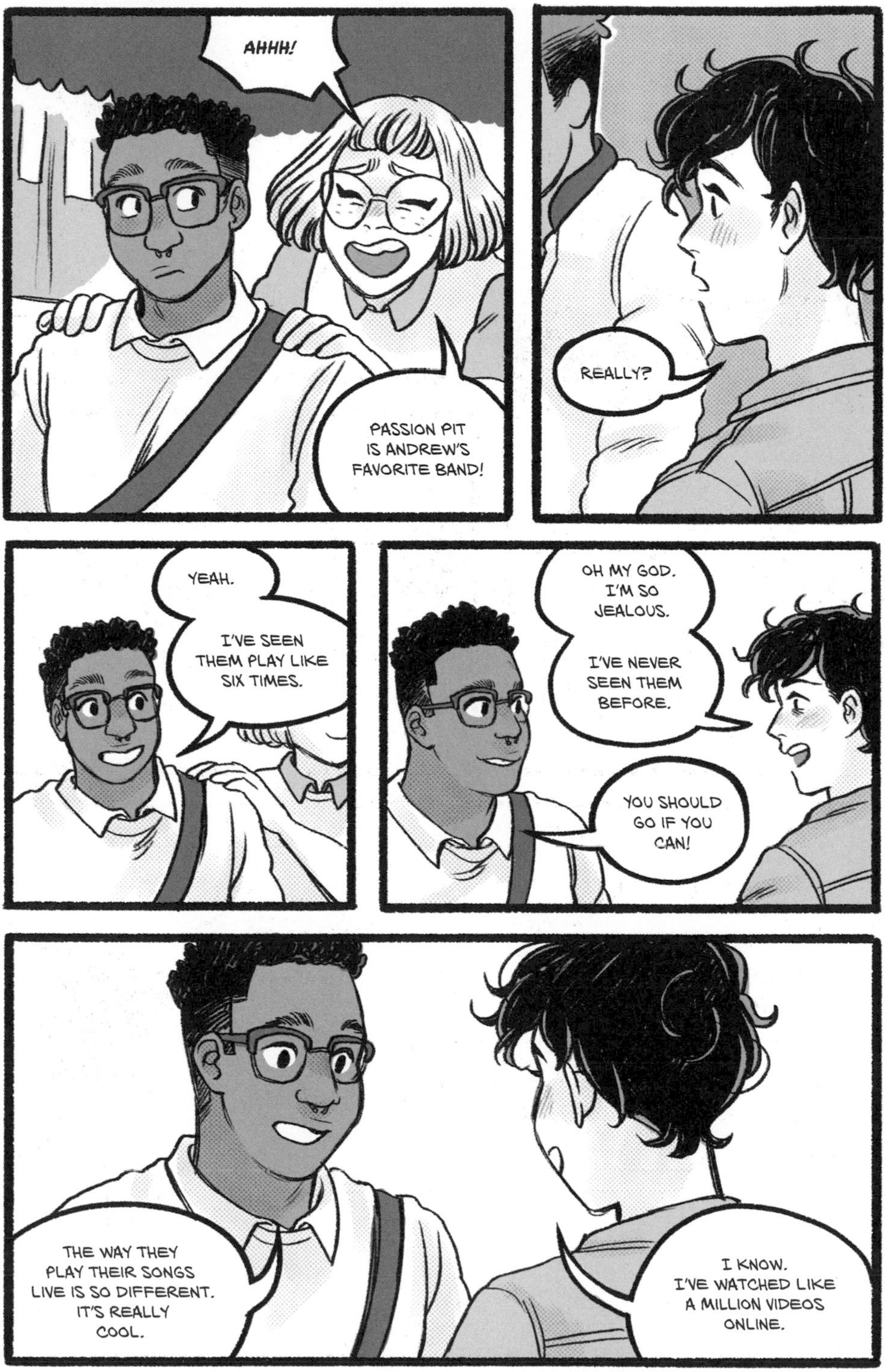
AHHH!
PASSION PIT IS ANDREW'S FAVORITE BAND!
REALLY?
YEAH.
I'VE SEEN THEM PLAY LIKE SIX TIMES.
OH MY GOD. I'M SO JEALOUS.
I'VE NEVER SEEN THEM BEFORE.
YOU SHOULD GO IF YOU CAN!
THE WAY THEY PLAY THEIR SONGS LIVE IS SO DIFFERENT. IT'S REALLY COOL.
I KNOW. I'VE WATCHED LIKE A MILLION VIDEOS ONLINE.

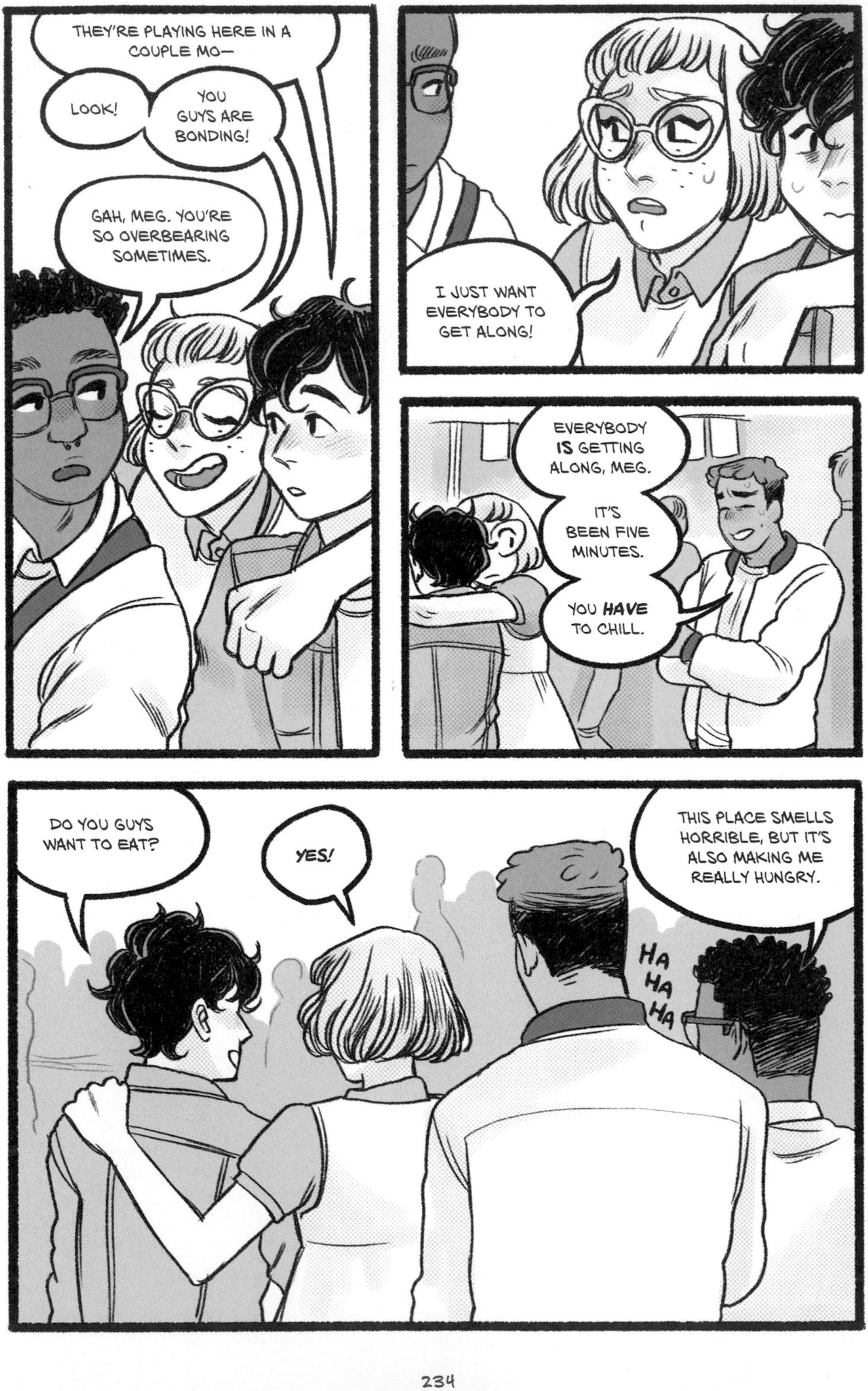
THEY'RE PLAYING HERE IN A COUPLE MO—
LOOK!
YOU GUYS ARE BONDING!
GAH, MEG. YOU'RE SO OVERBEARING SOMETIMES.
I JUST WANT EVERYBODY TO GET ALONG!
EVERYBODY IS GETTING ALONG, MEG.
IT'S BEEN FIVE MINUTES.
YOU HAVE TO CHILL.
DO YOU GUYS WANT TO EAT?
YES!
THIS PLACE SMELLS HORRIBLE, BUT IT'S ALSO MAKING ME REALLY HUNGRY.
HA HA HA

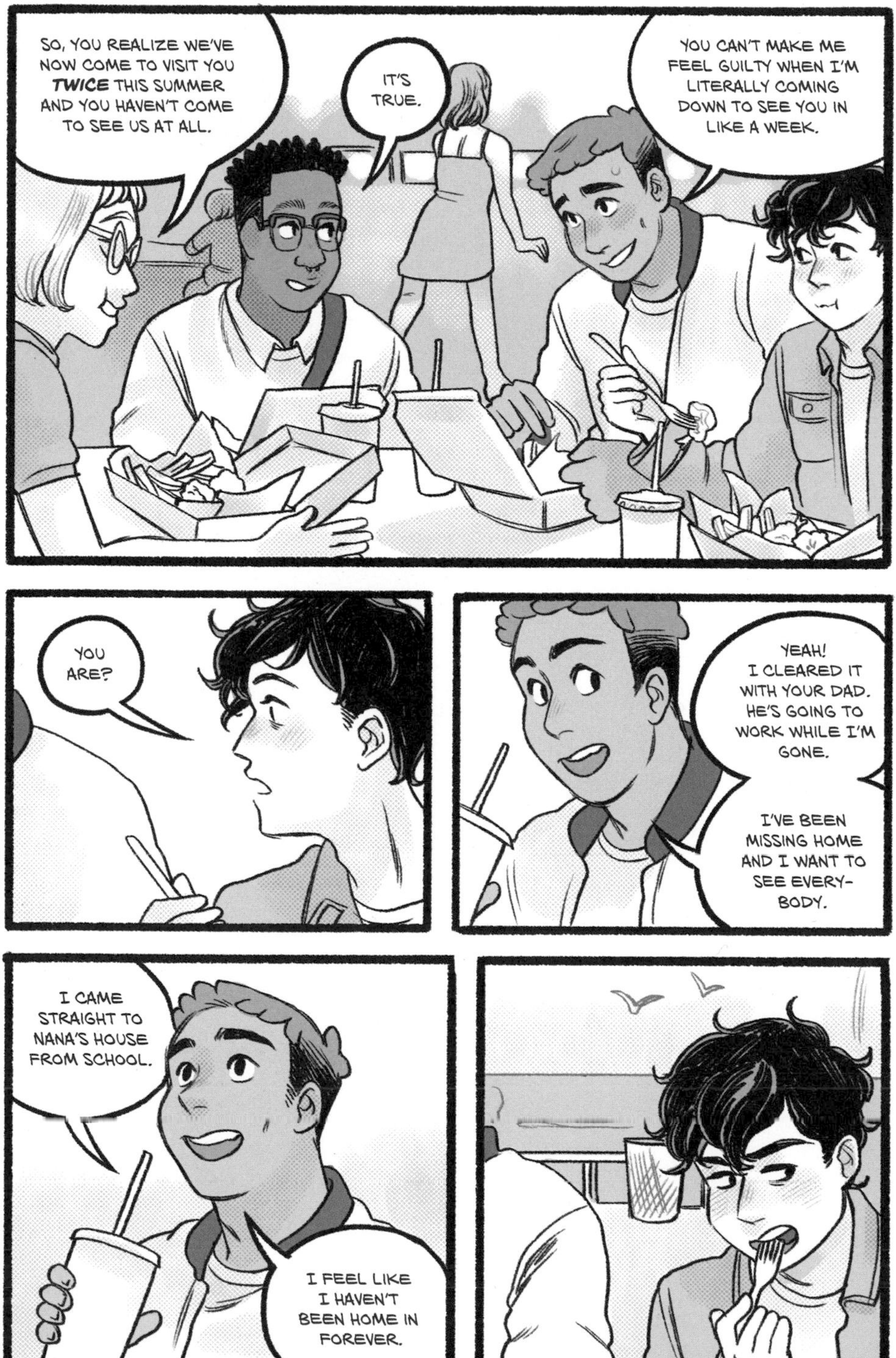
SO, YOU REALIZE WE'VE NOW COME TO VISIT YOU *TWICE* THIS SUMMER AND YOU HAVEN'T COME TO SEE US AT ALL.
IT'S TRUE.
YOU CAN'T MAKE ME FEEL GUILTY WHEN I'M LITERALLY COMING DOWN TO SEE YOU IN LIKE A WEEK.
YOU ARE?
YEAH! I CLEARED IT WITH YOUR DAD. HE'S GOING TO WORK WHILE I'M GONE.
I'VE BEEN MISSING HOME AND I WANT TO SEE EVERY-BODY.
I CAME STRAIGHT TO NANA'S HOUSE FROM SCHOOL.
I FEEL LIKE I HAVEN'T BEEN HOME IN FOREVER.

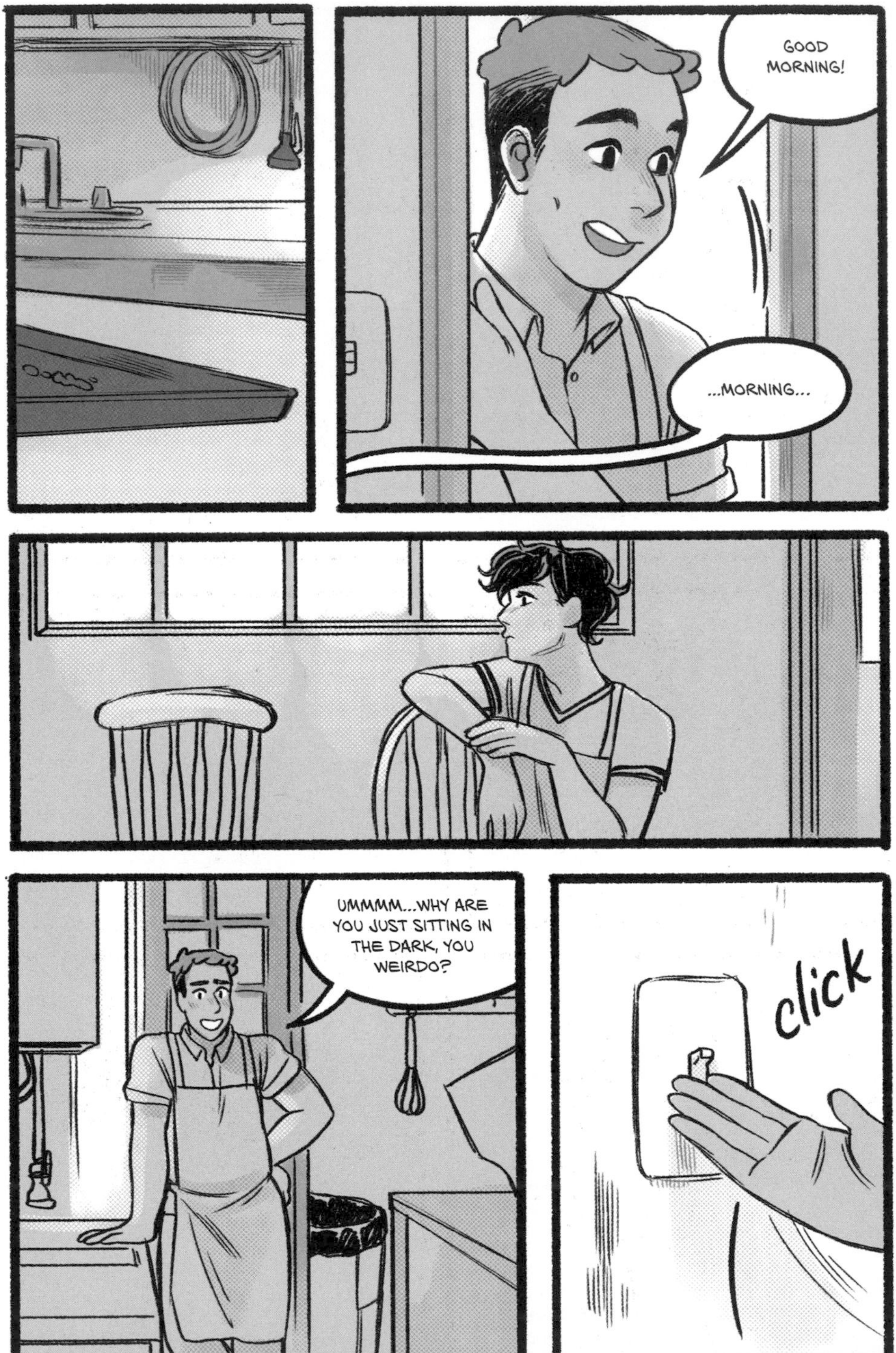
GOOD MORNING!
...MORNING...
UMMMM...WHY ARE YOU JUST SITTING IN THE DARK, YOU WEIRDO?
click

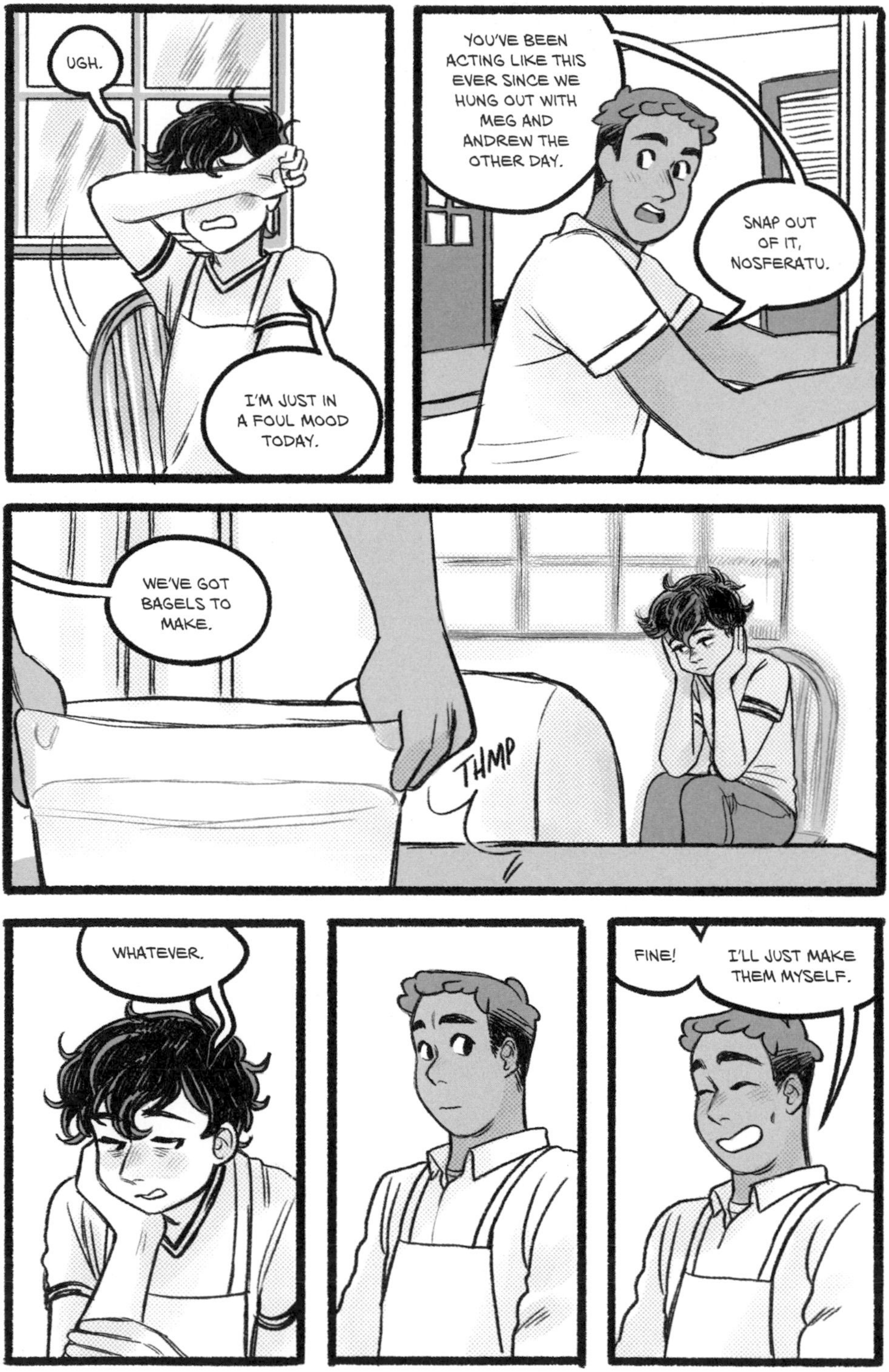
UGH.
I'M JUST IN A FOUL MOOD TODAY.
YOU'VE BEEN ACTING LIKE THIS EVER SINCE WE HUNG OUT WITH MEG AND ANDREW THE OTHER DAY.
SNAP OUT OF IT, NOSFERATU.
WE'VE GOT BAGELS TO MAKE.
THMP
WHATEVER.
FINE!
I'LL JUST MAKE THEM MYSELF.

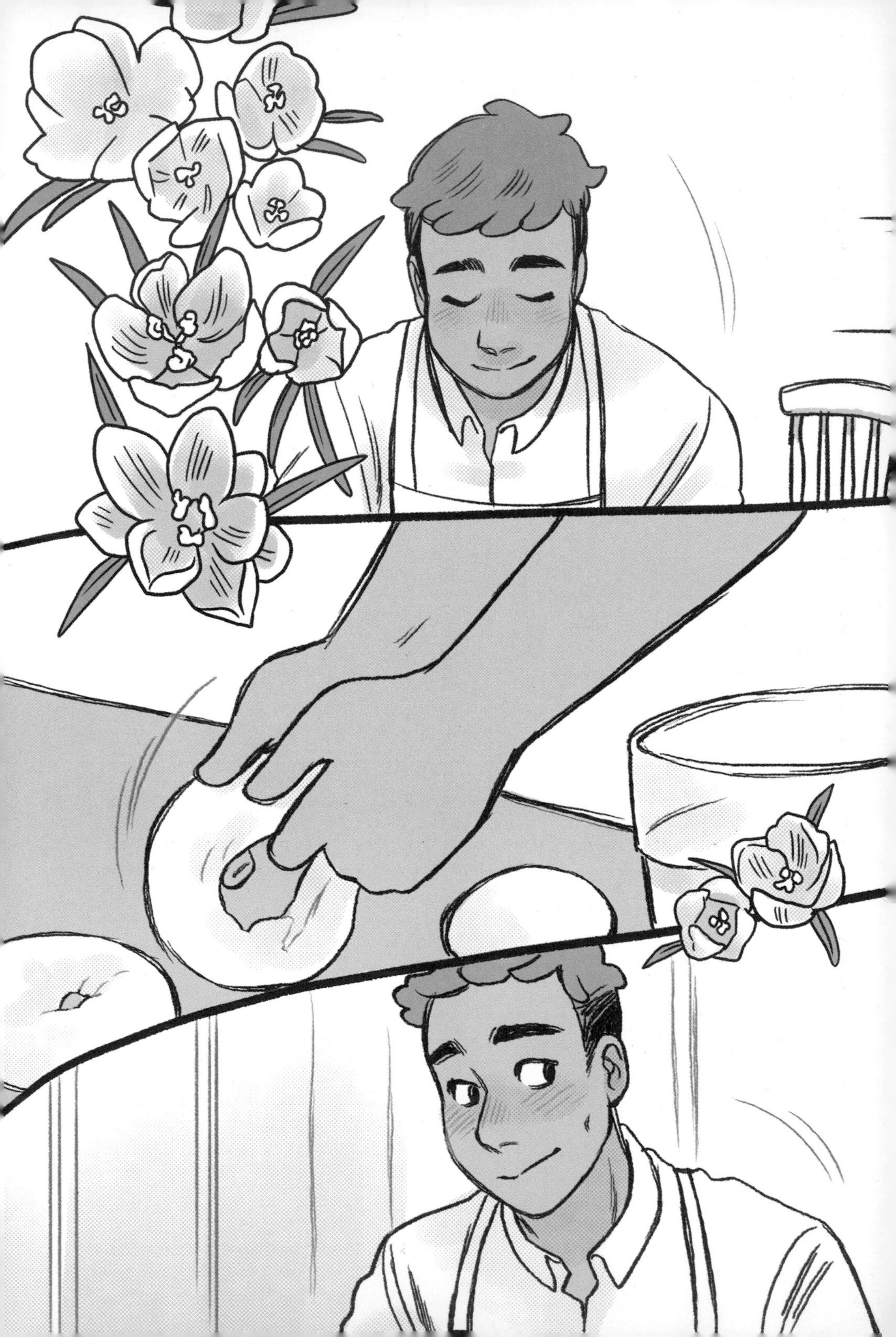

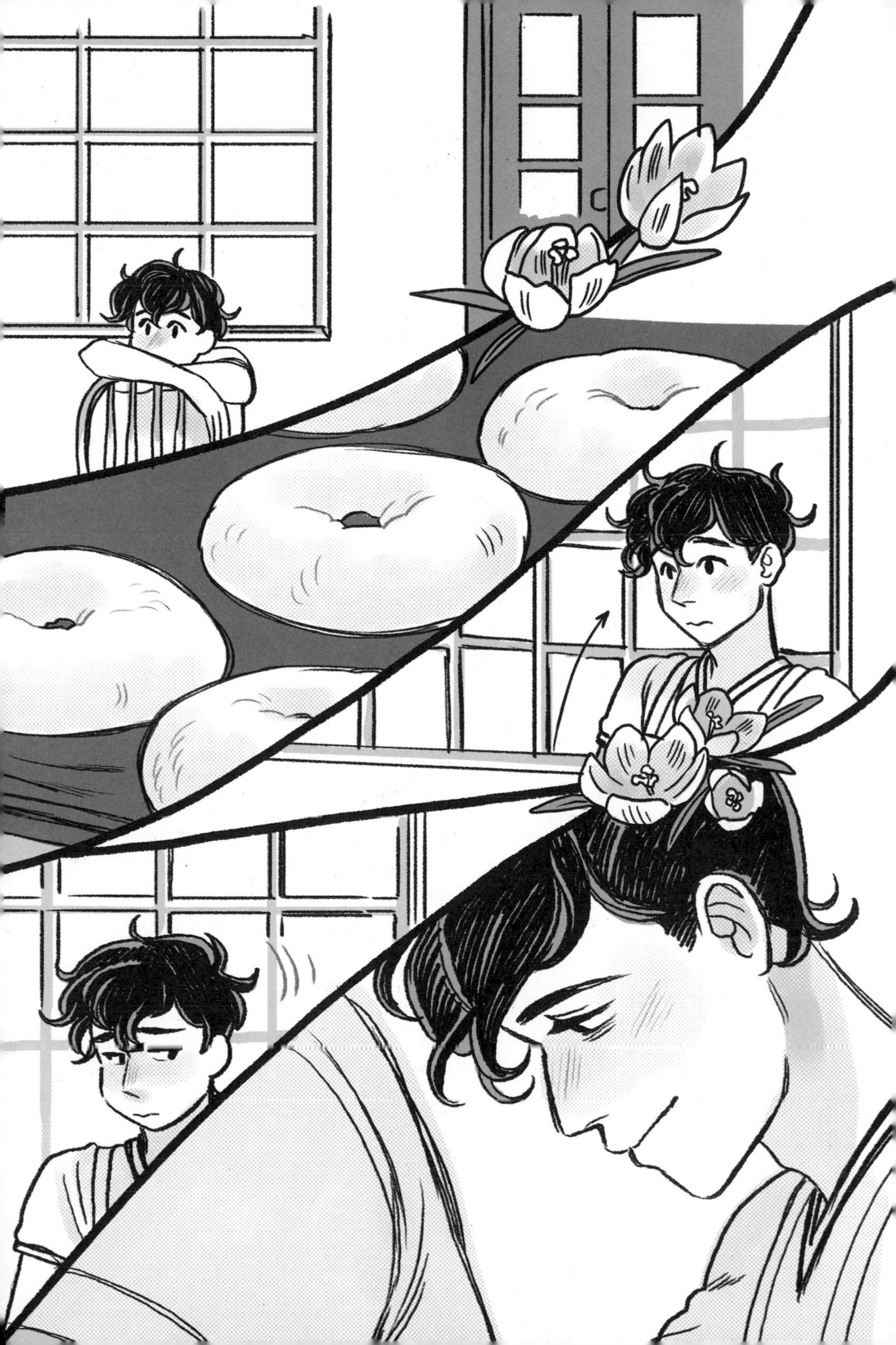

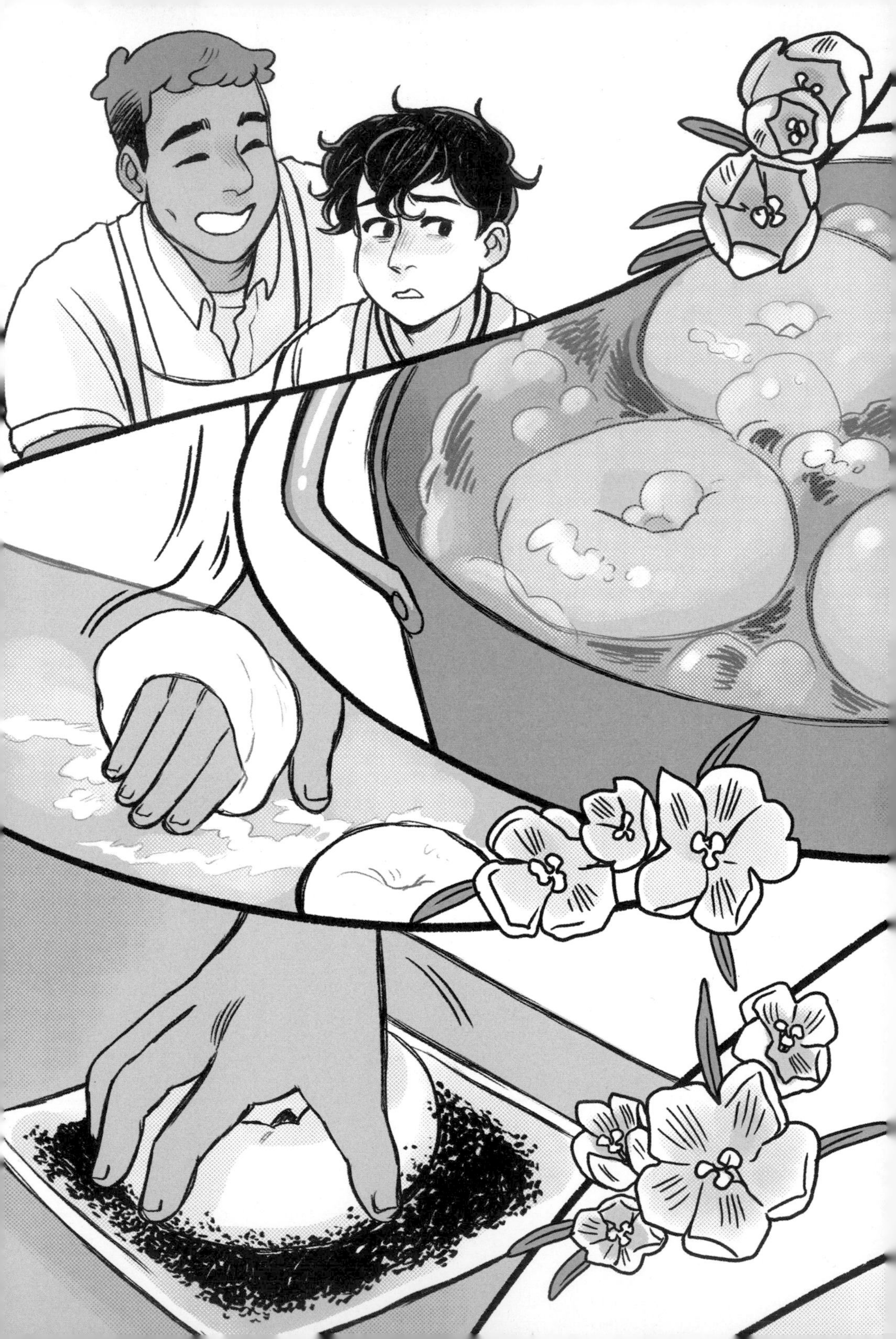

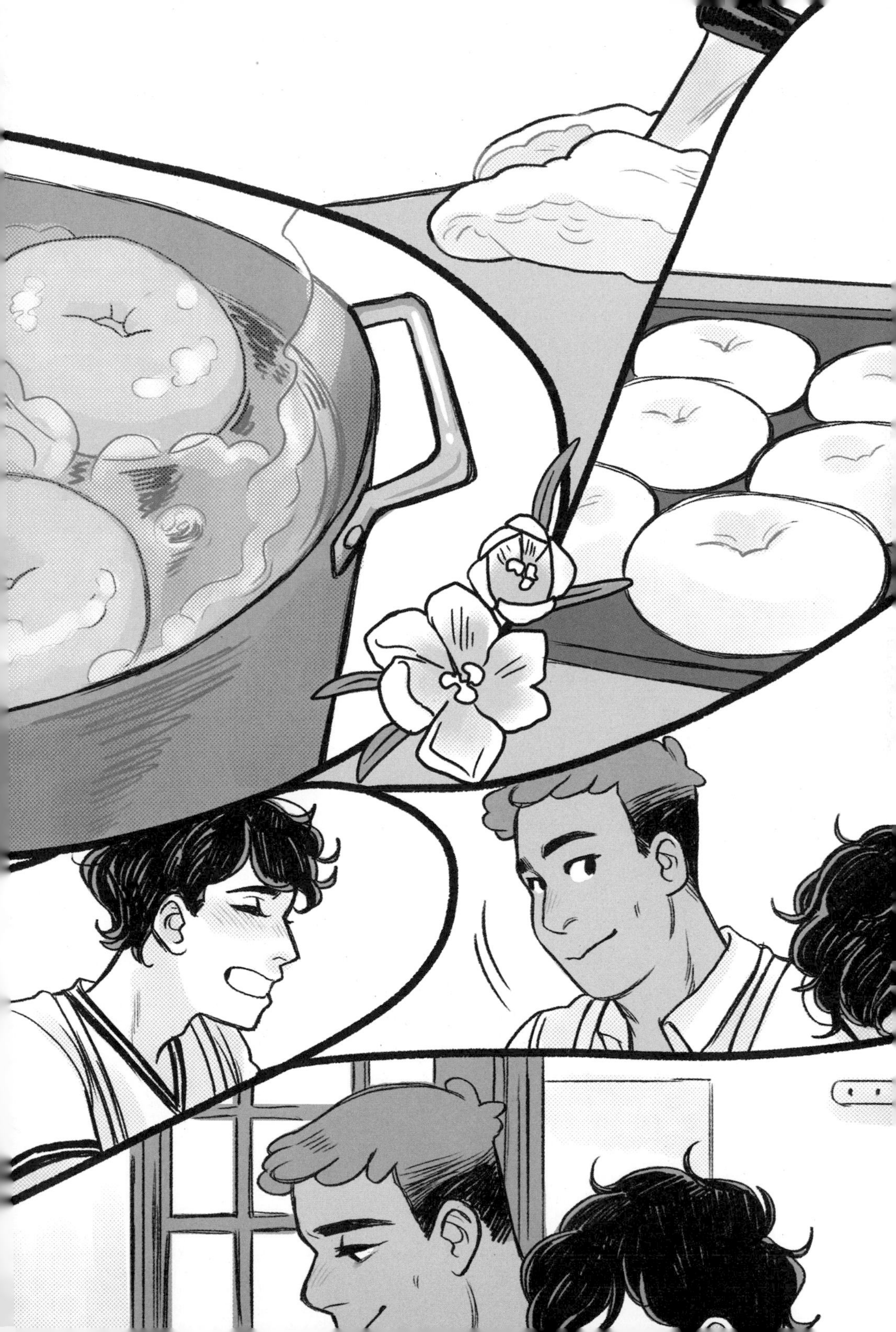

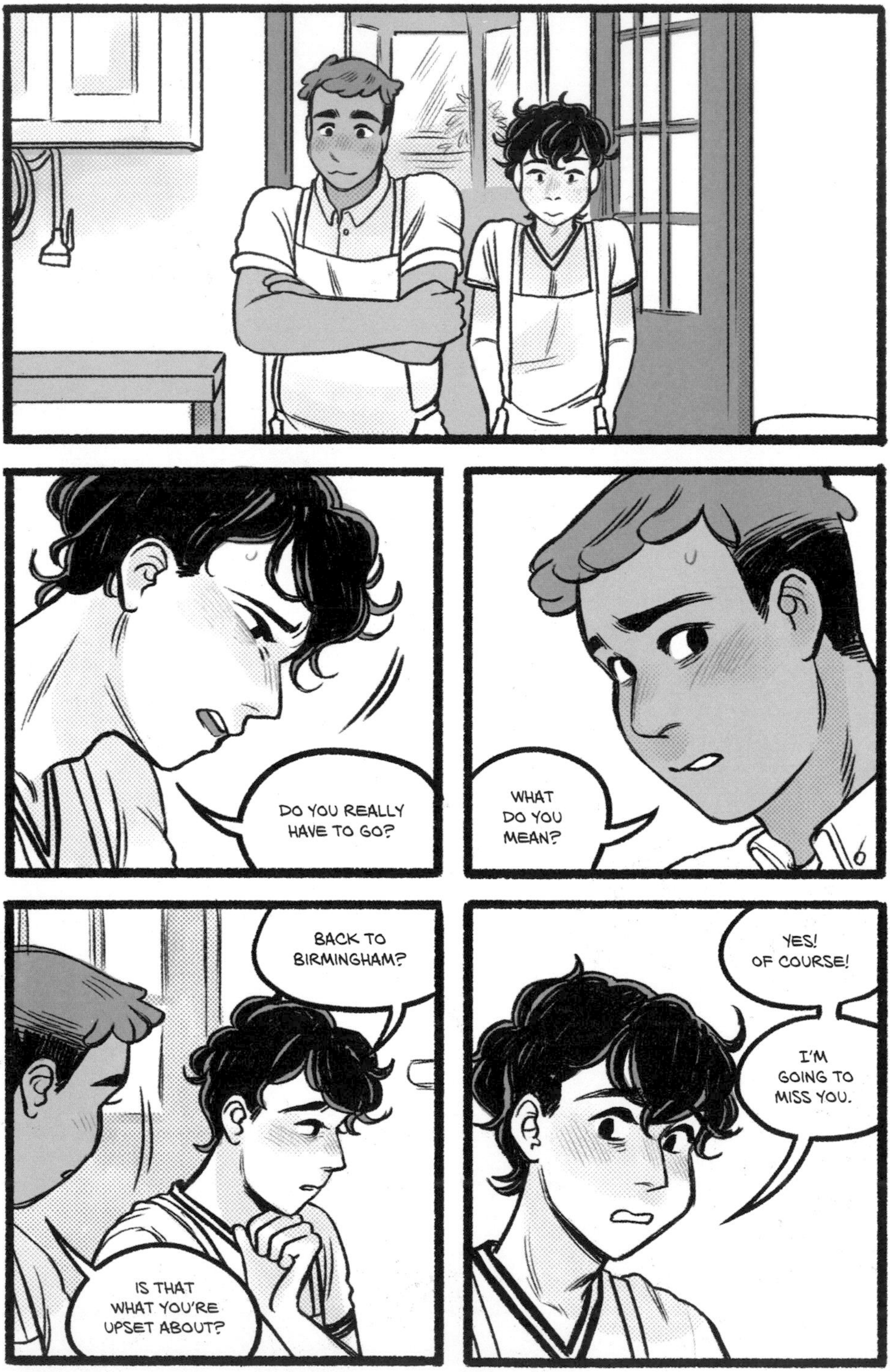
DO YOU REALLY HAVE TO GO?
WHAT DO YOU MEAN?
BACK TO BIRMINGHAM?
IS THAT WHAT YOU'RE UPSET ABOUT?
YES! OF COURSE!
I'M GOING TO MISS YOU.

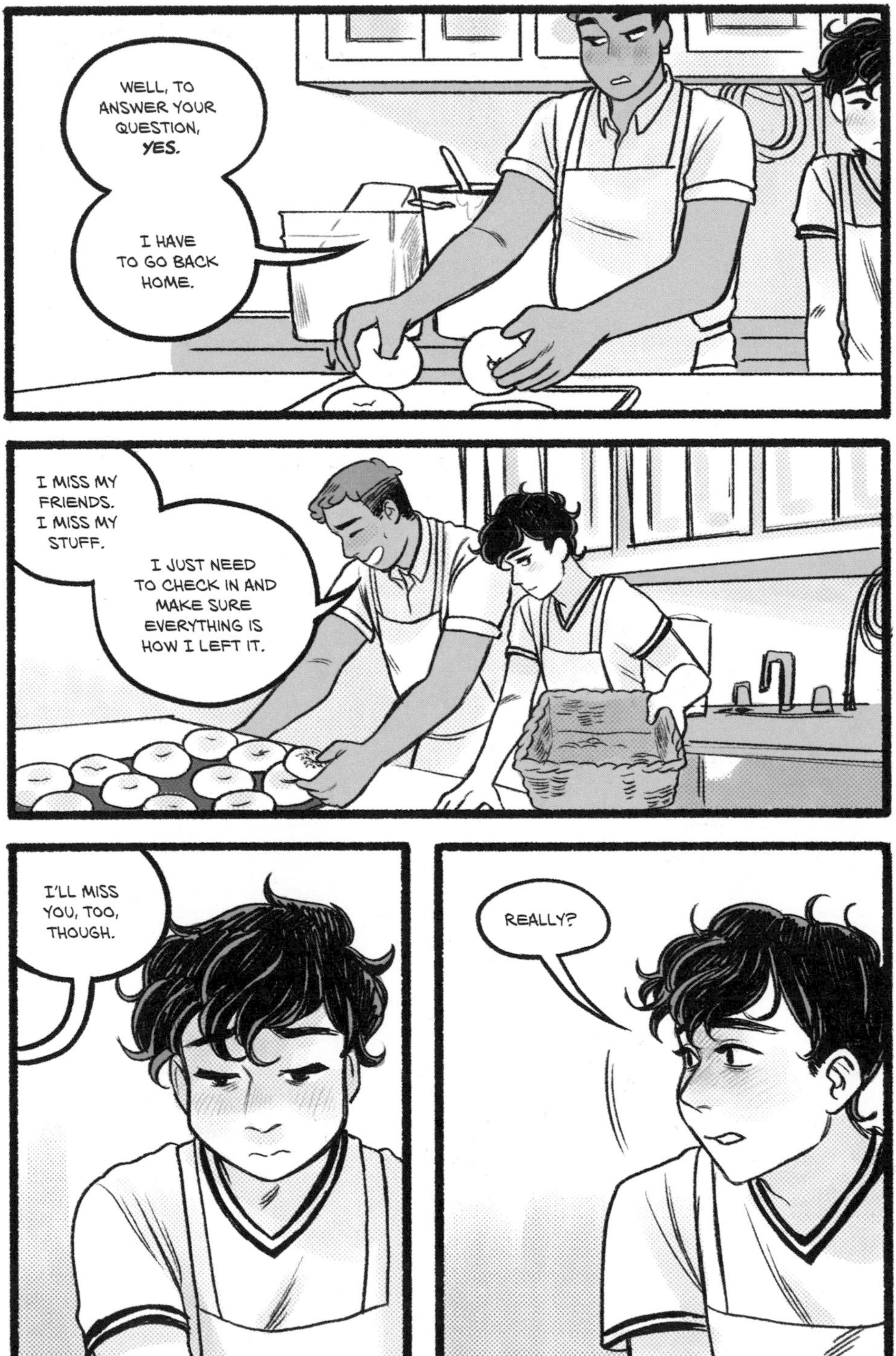
WELL, TO ANSWER YOUR QUESTION, **YES.**
I HAVE TO GO BACK HOME.
I MISS MY FRIENDS. I MISS MY STUFF.
I JUST NEED TO CHECK IN AND MAKE SURE EVERYTHING IS HOW I LEFT IT.
I'LL MISS YOU, TOO, THOUGH.
REALLY?

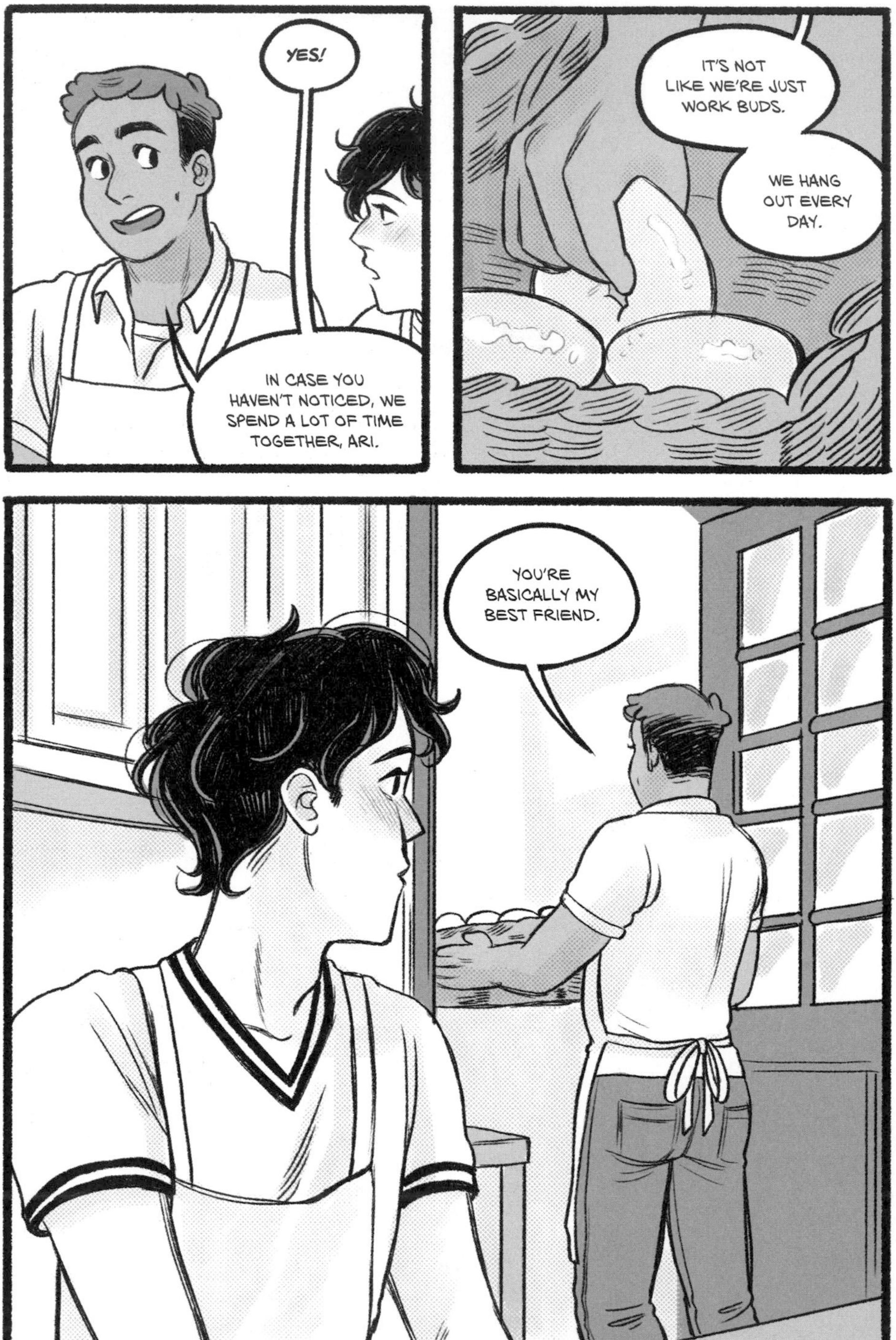
YES!
IN CASE YOU HAVEN'T NOTICED, WE SPEND A LOT OF TIME TOGETHER, ARI.
IT'S NOT LIKE WE'RE JUST WORK BUDS.
WE HANG OUT EVERY DAY.
YOU'RE BASICALLY MY BEST FRIEND.

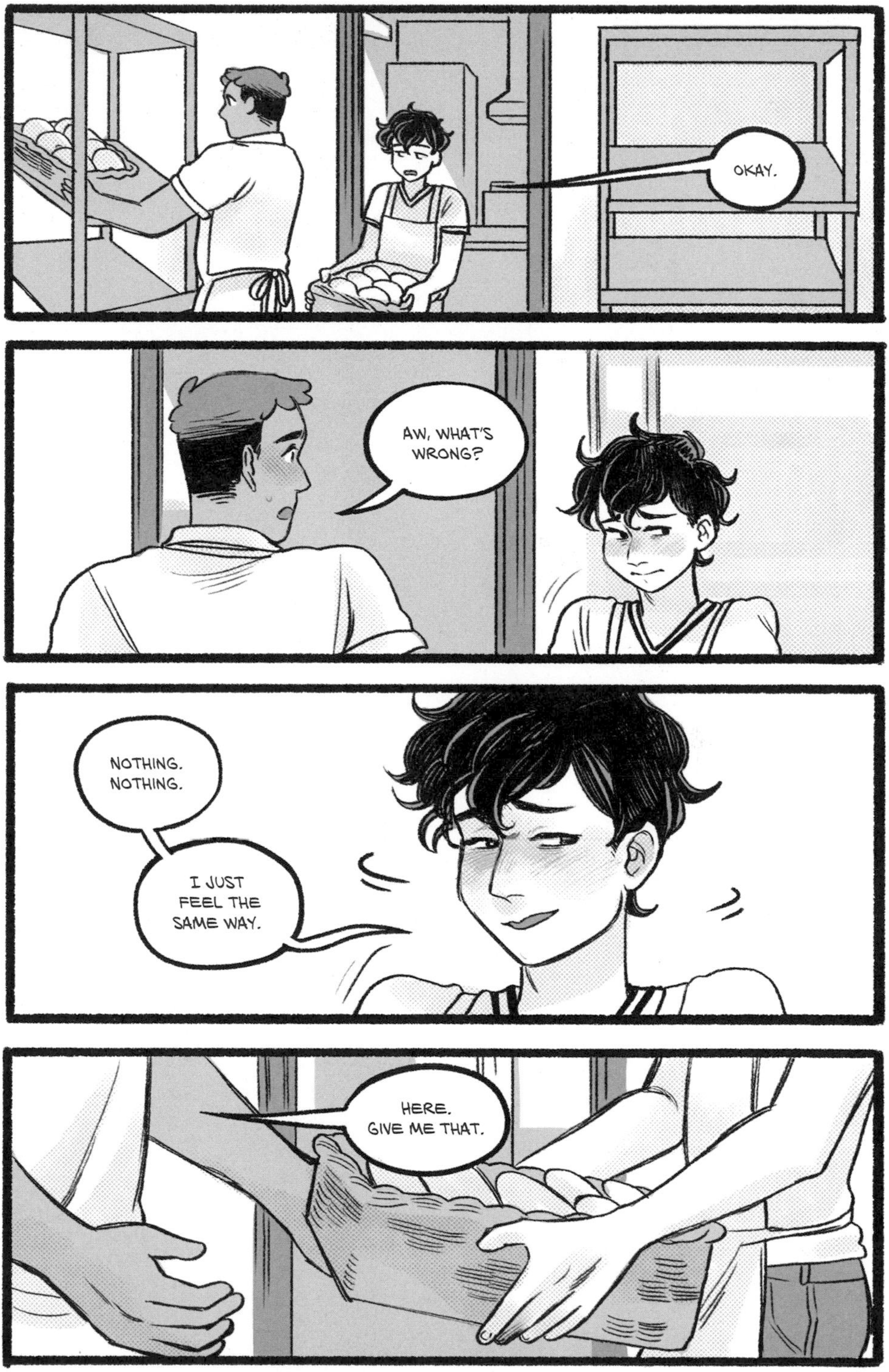
OKAY.
AW, WHAT'S WRONG?
NOTHING. NOTHING.
I JUST FEEL THE SAME WAY.
HERE. GIVE ME THAT.

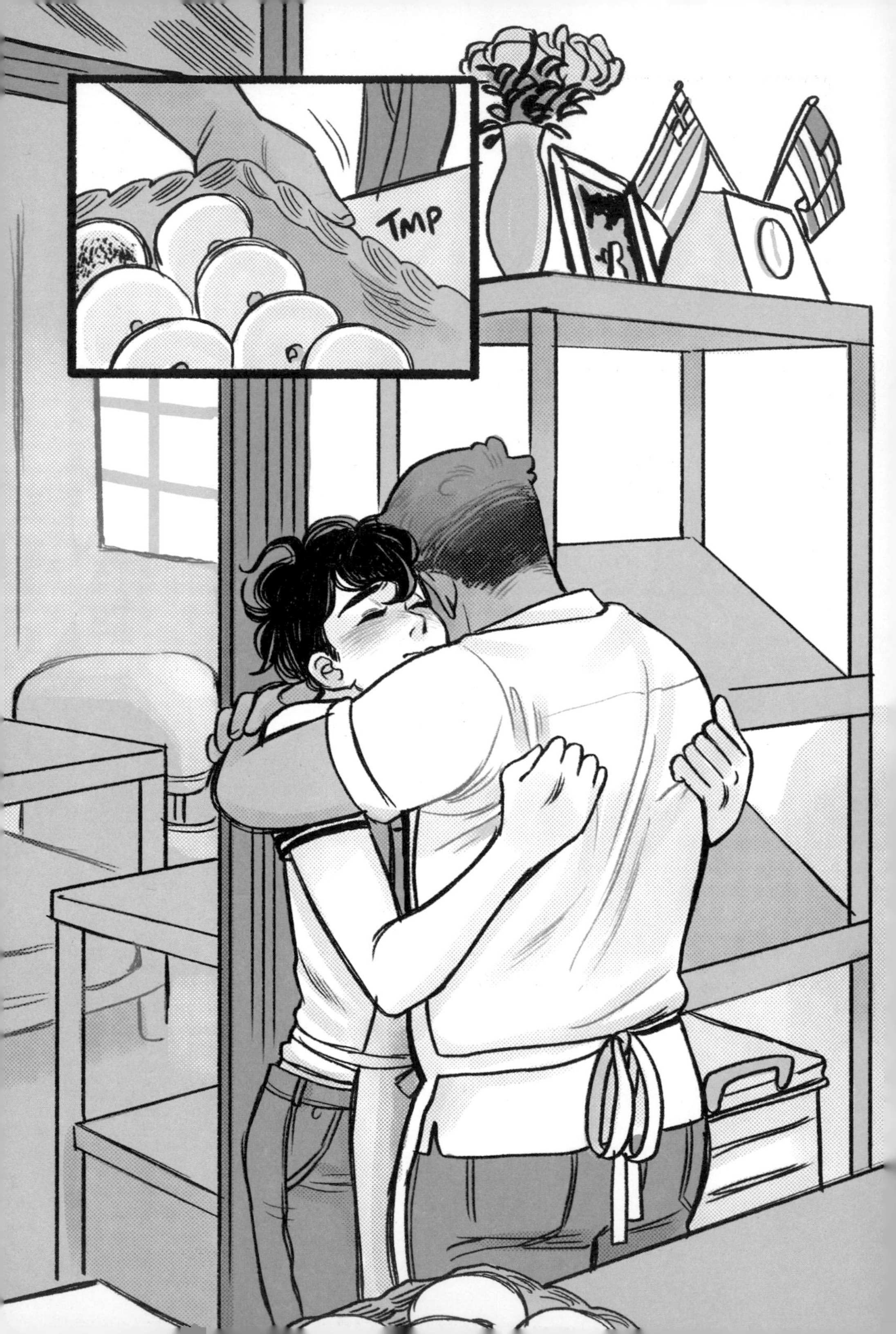
TMP

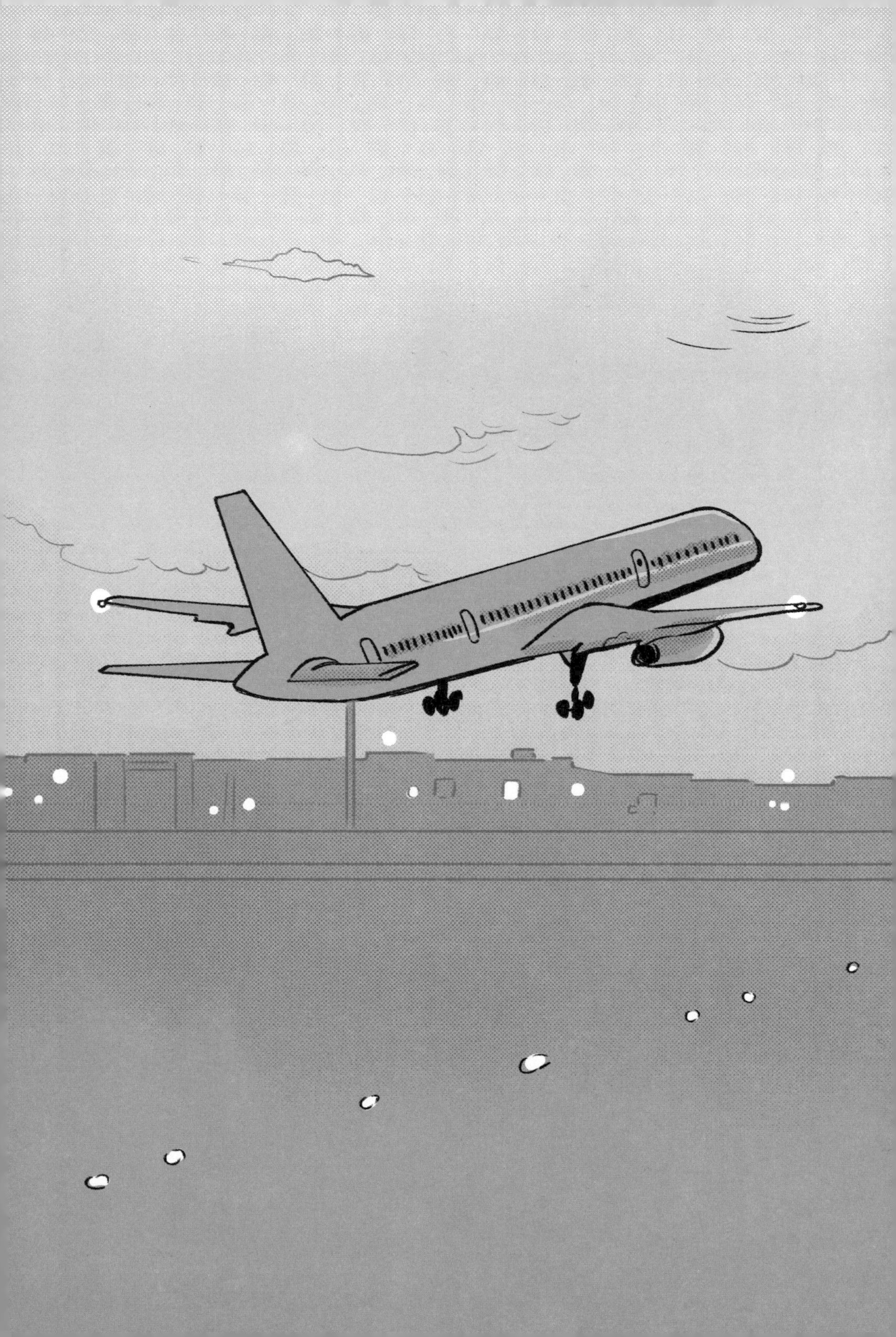

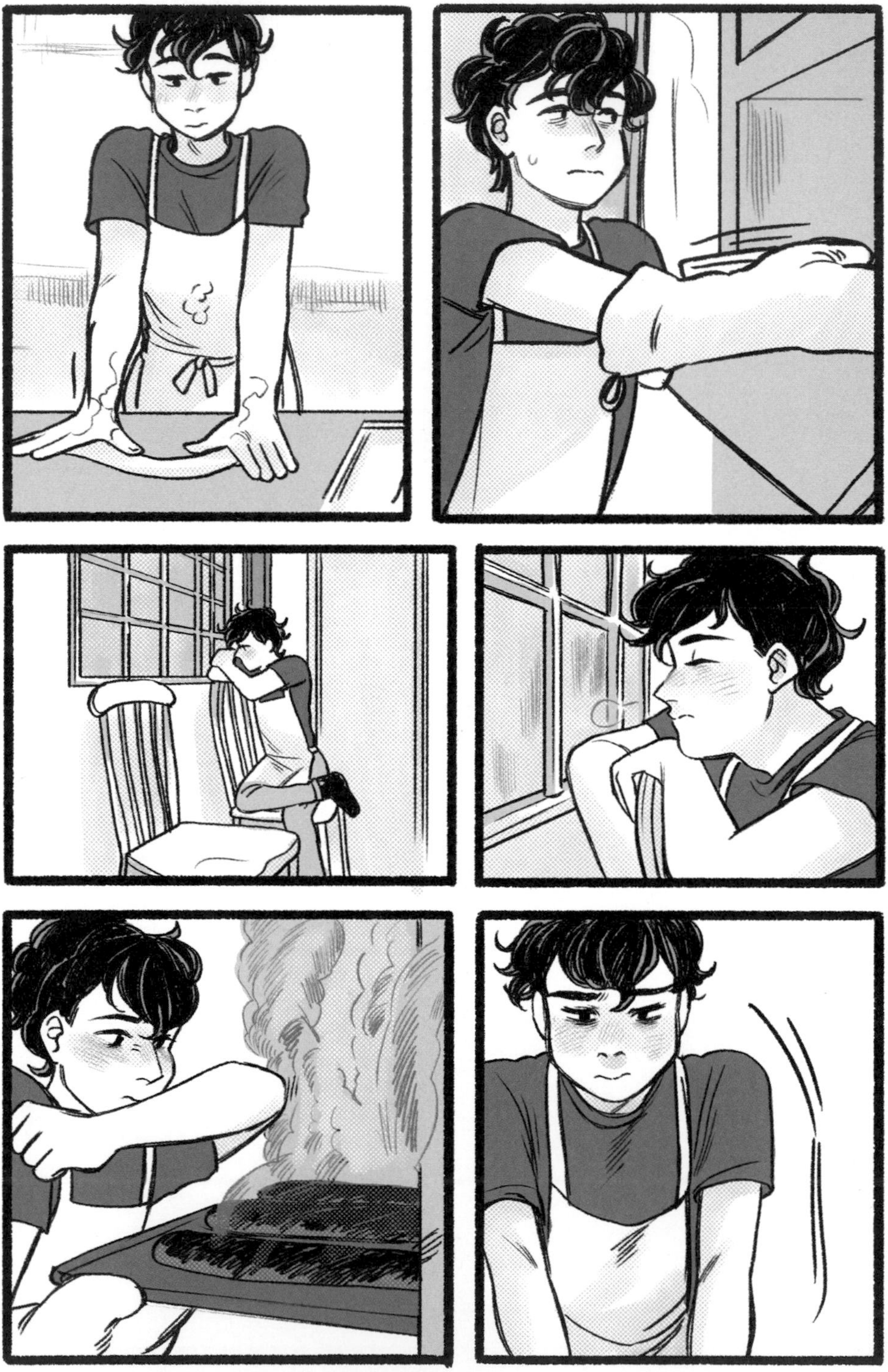

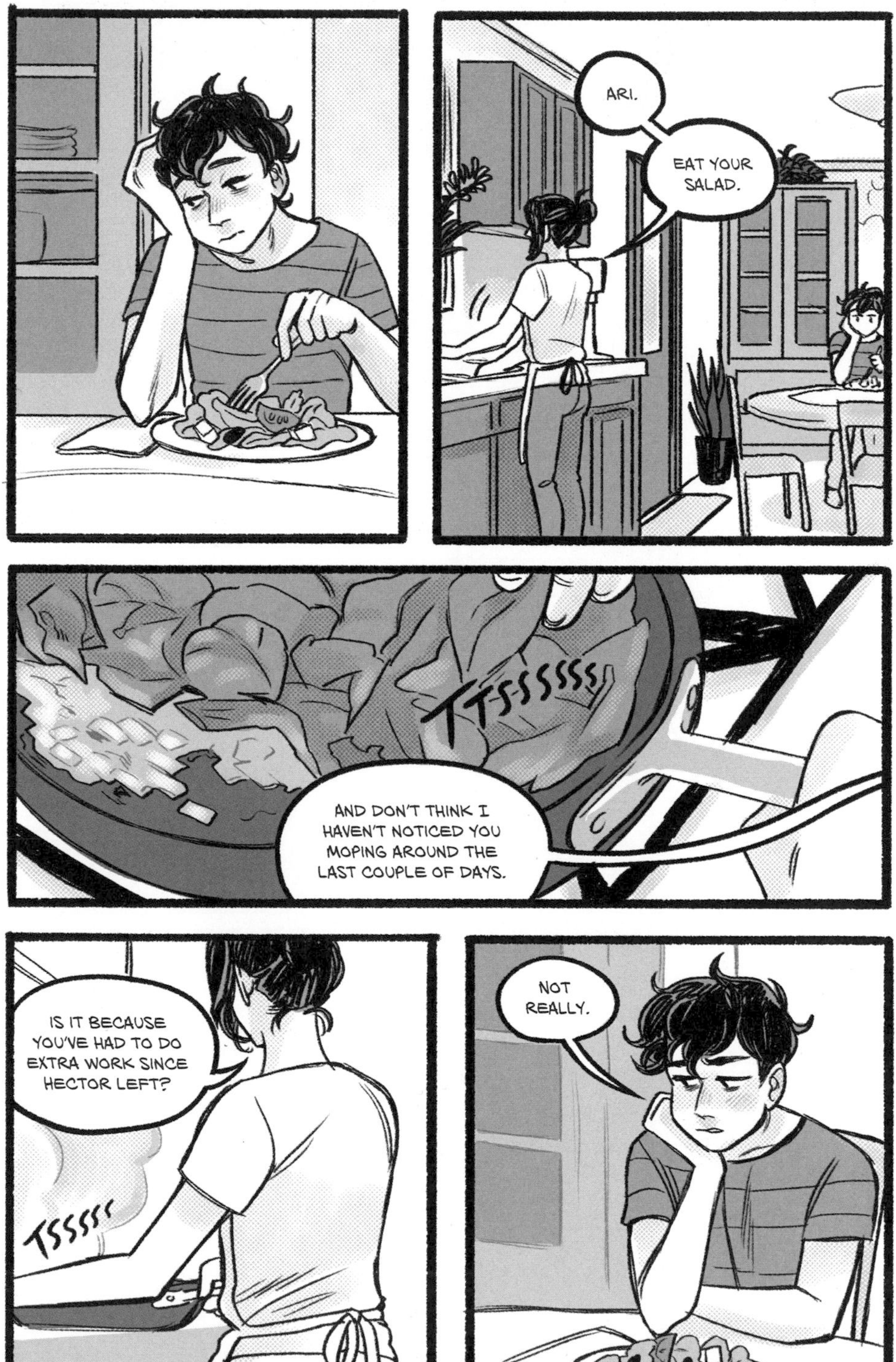
ARI.
EAT YOUR SALAD.
TT-S-S-S-S-S
AND DON'T THINK I HAVEN'T NOTICED YOU MOPING AROUND THE LAST COUPLE OF DAYS.
IS IT BECAUSE YOU'VE HAD TO DO EXTRA WORK SINCE HECTOR LEFT?
TSSSSS
NOT REALLY.

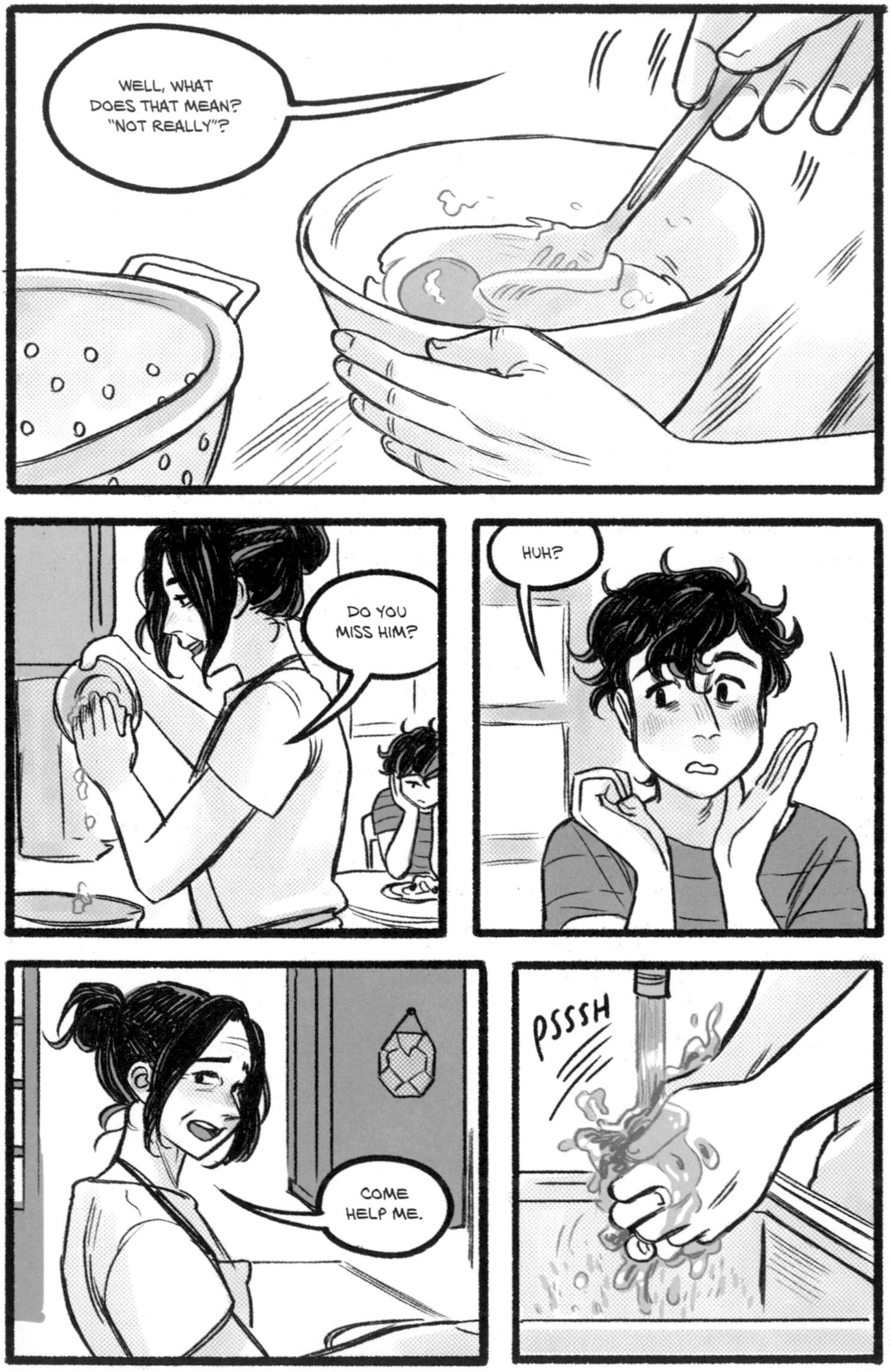
WELL, WHAT DOES THAT MEAN? "NOT REALLY"?
DO YOU MISS HIM?
HUH?
COME HELP ME.
PSSSH

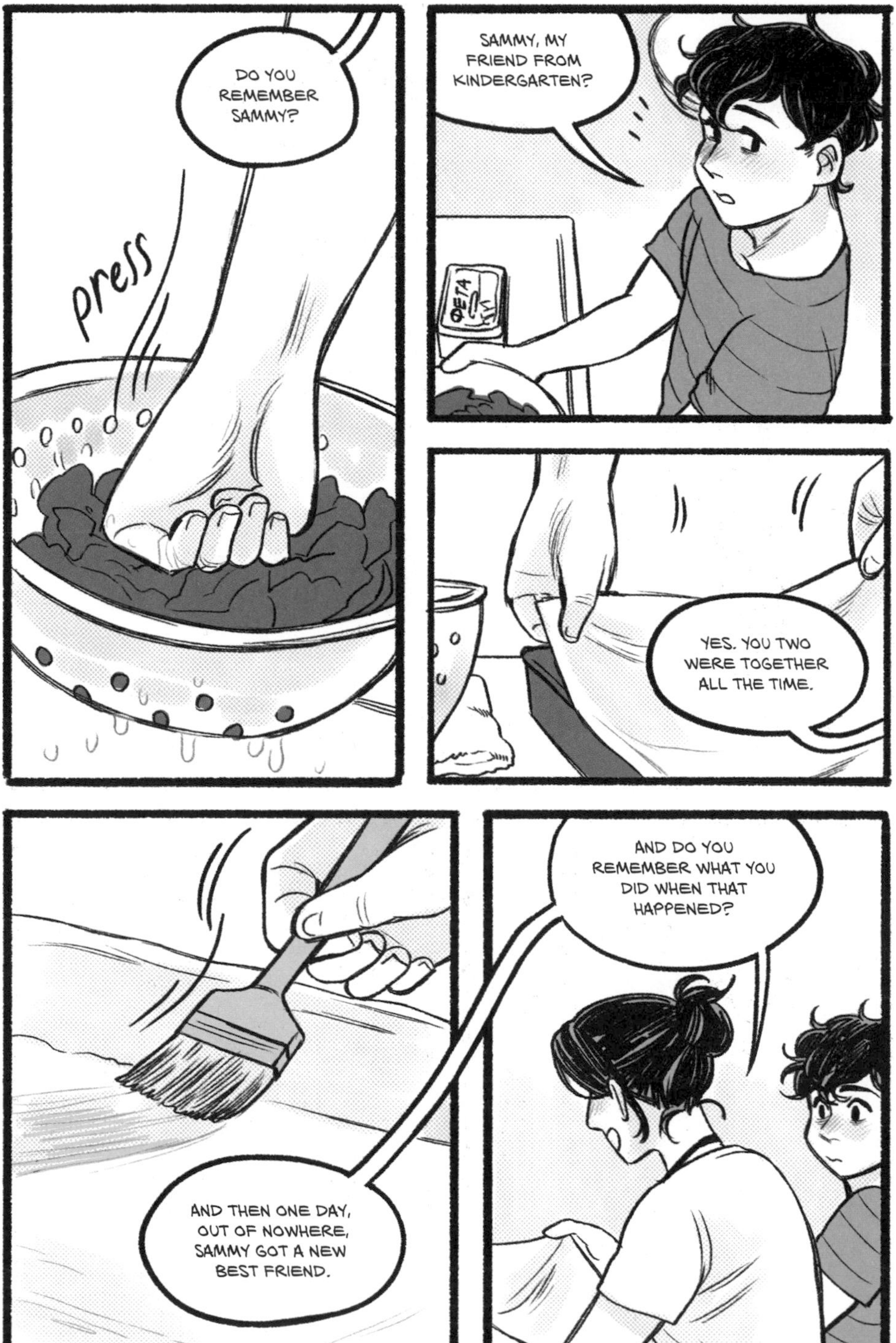
DO YOU REMEMBER SAMMY?
press
SAMMY, MY FRIEND FROM KINDERGARTEN?
ΦETA
YES. YOU TWO WERE TOGETHER ALL THE TIME.
AND THEN ONE DAY, OUT OF NOWHERE, SAMMY GOT A NEW BEST FRIEND.
AND DO YOU REMEMBER WHAT YOU DID WHEN THAT HAPPENED?

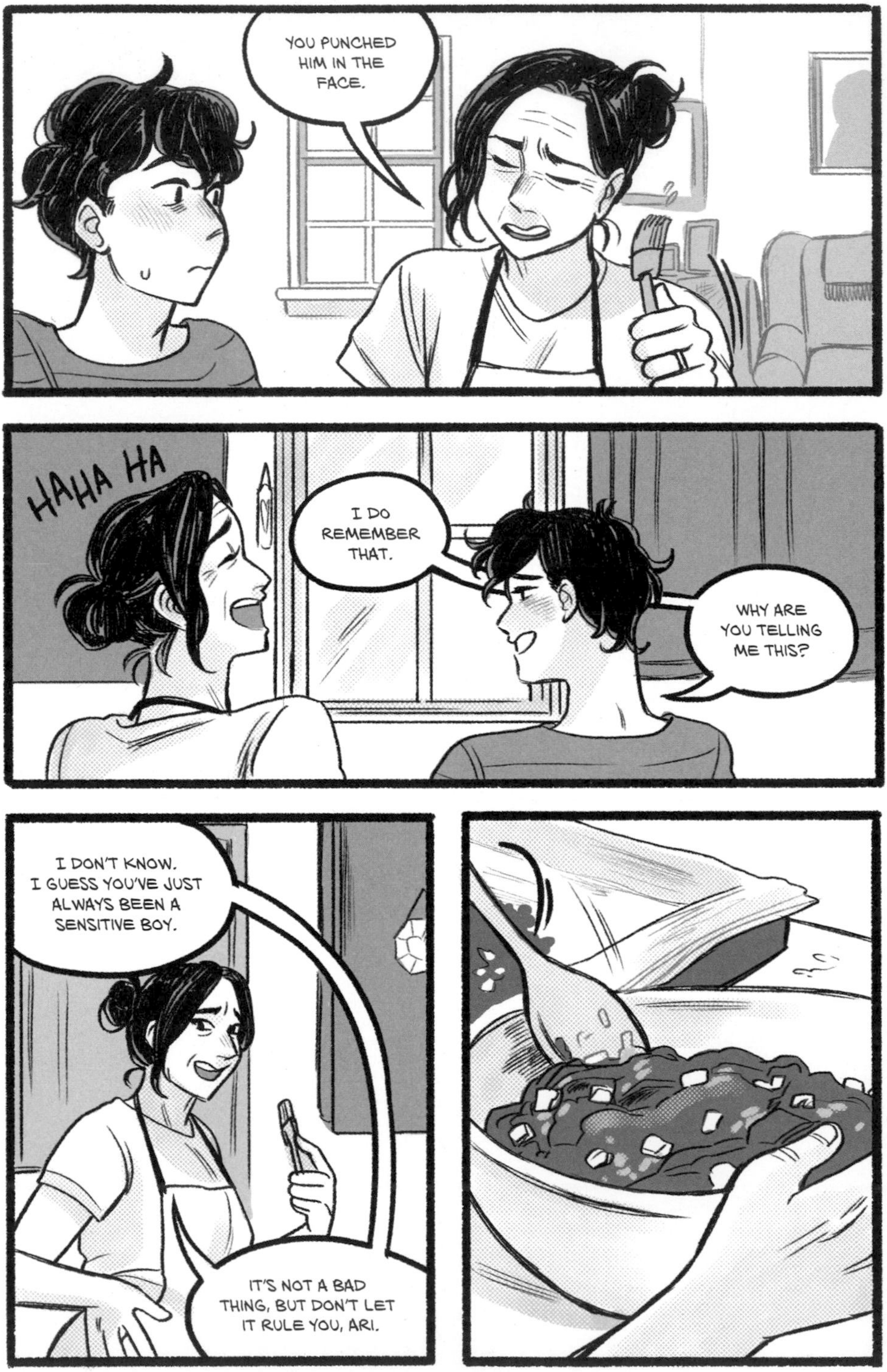
YOU PUNCHED HIM IN THE FACE.
HAHA HA
I DO REMEMBER THAT.
WHY ARE YOU TELLING ME THIS?
I DON'T KNOW. I GUESS YOU'VE JUST ALWAYS BEEN A SENSITIVE BOY.
IT'S NOT A BAD THING, BUT DON'T LET IT RULE YOU, ARI.

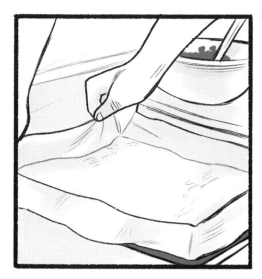

THANKS, MOM.

IT'S NO PROBLEM.

I LOVE YOU, MY SWEET BOY.

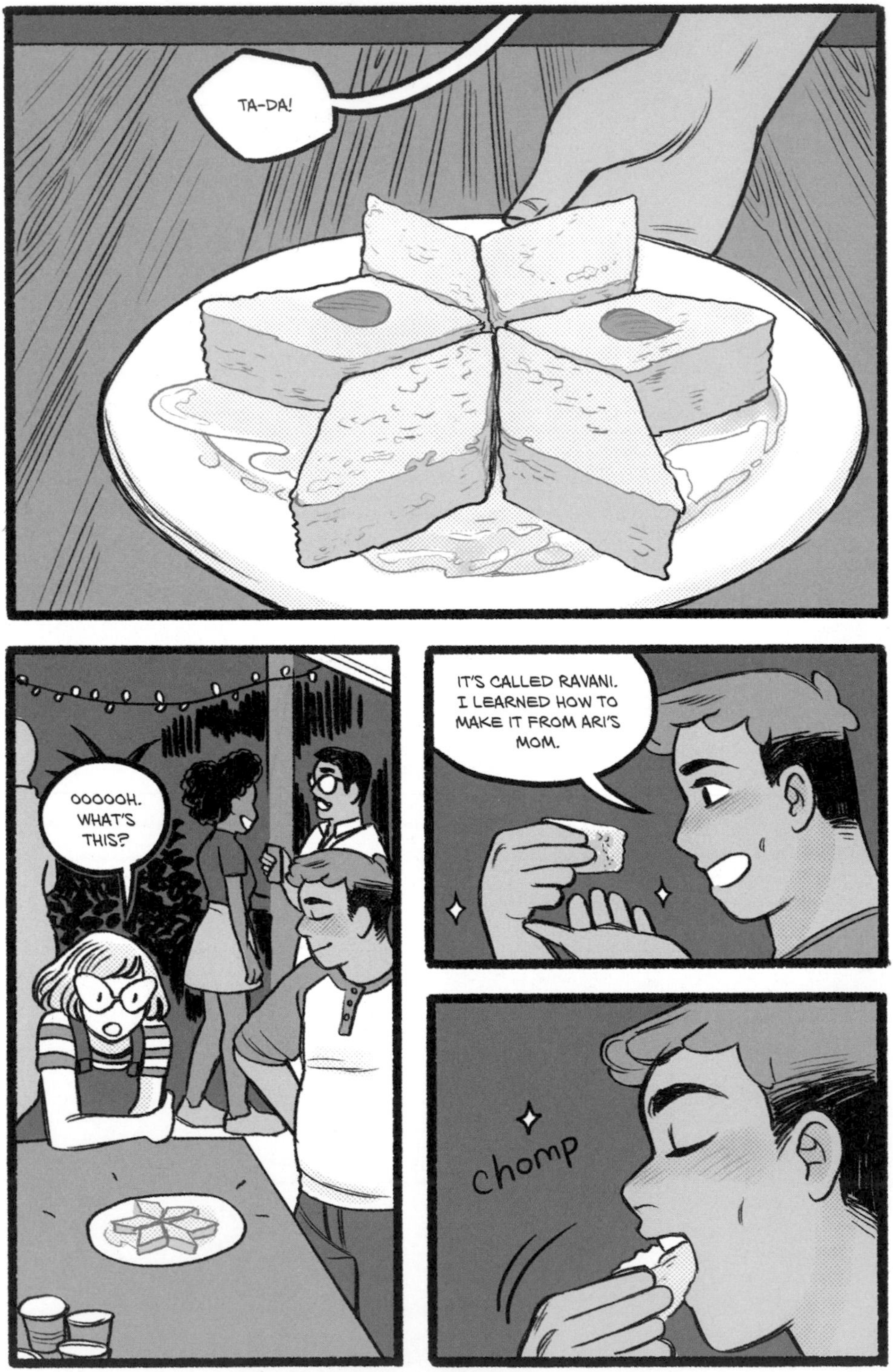
TA-DA!
OOOOOH. WHAT'S THIS?
IT'S CALLED RAVANI. I LEARNED HOW TO MAKE IT FROM ARI'S MOM.
chomp

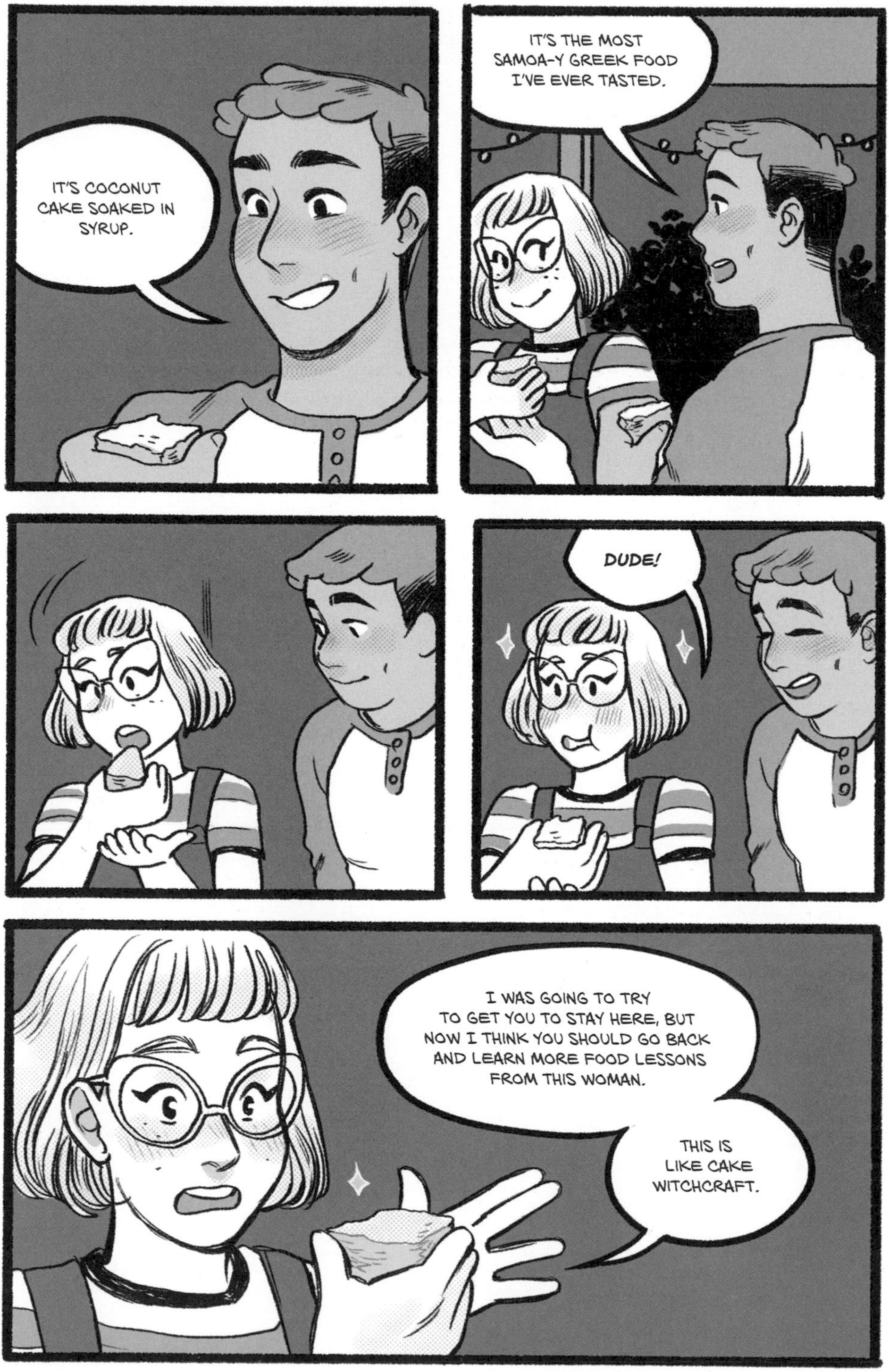
IT'S COCONUT CAKE SOAKED IN SYRUP.
IT'S THE MOST SAMOA-Y GREEK FOOD I'VE EVER TASTED.
DUDE!
I WAS GOING TO TRY TO GET YOU TO STAY HERE, BUT NOW I THINK YOU SHOULD GO BACK AND LEARN MORE FOOD LESSONS FROM THIS WOMAN.
THIS IS LIKE CAKE WITCHCRAFT.

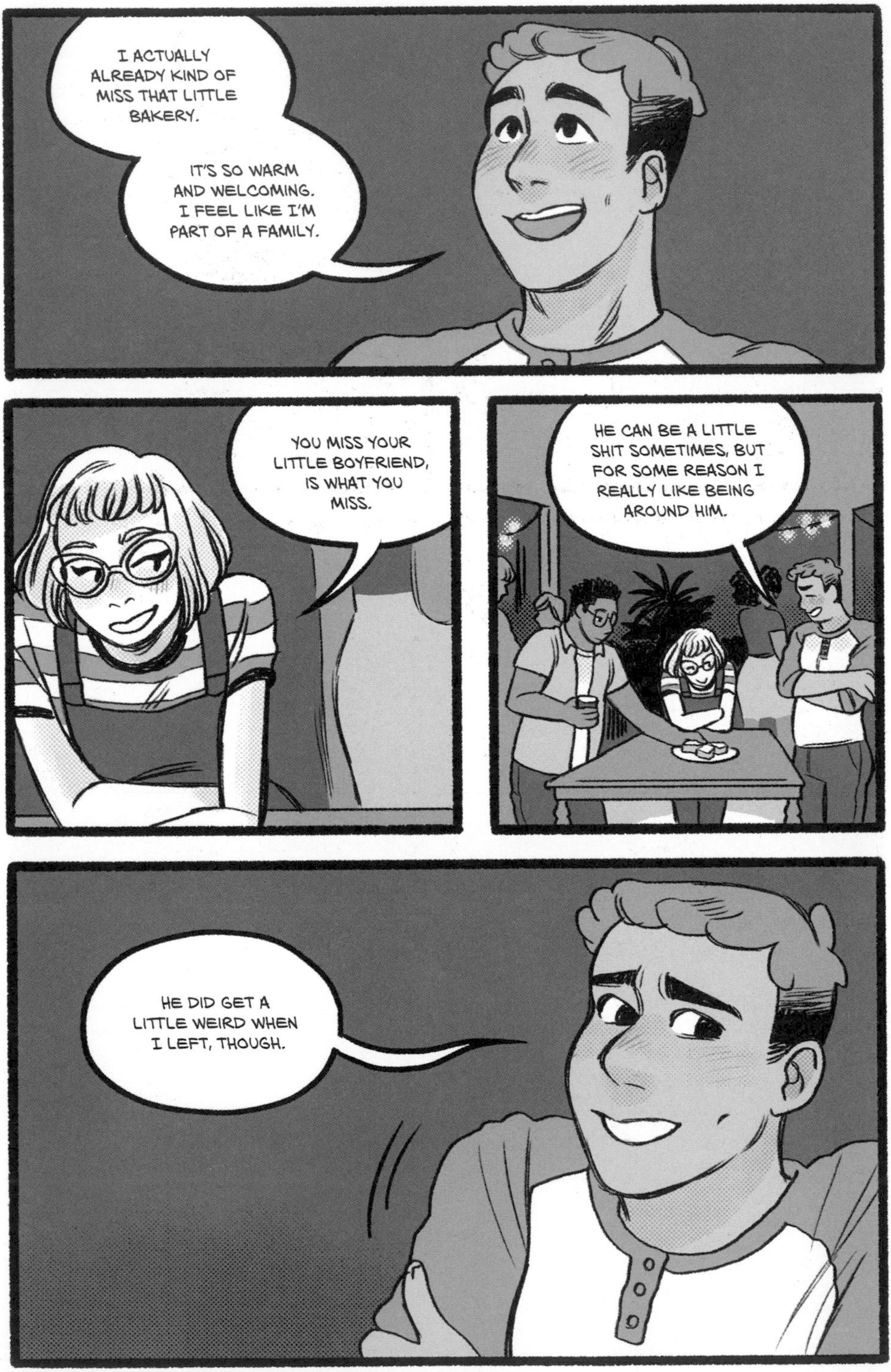
I ACTUALLY ALREADY KIND OF MISS THAT LITTLE BAKERY.
IT'S SO WARM AND WELCOMING. I FEEL LIKE I'M PART OF A FAMILY.
YOU MISS YOUR LITTLE BOYFRIEND, IS WHAT YOU MISS.
HE CAN BE A LITTLE SHIT SOMETIMES, BUT FOR SOME REASON I REALLY LIKE BEING AROUND HIM.
HE DID GET A LITTLE WEIRD WHEN I LEFT, THOUGH.

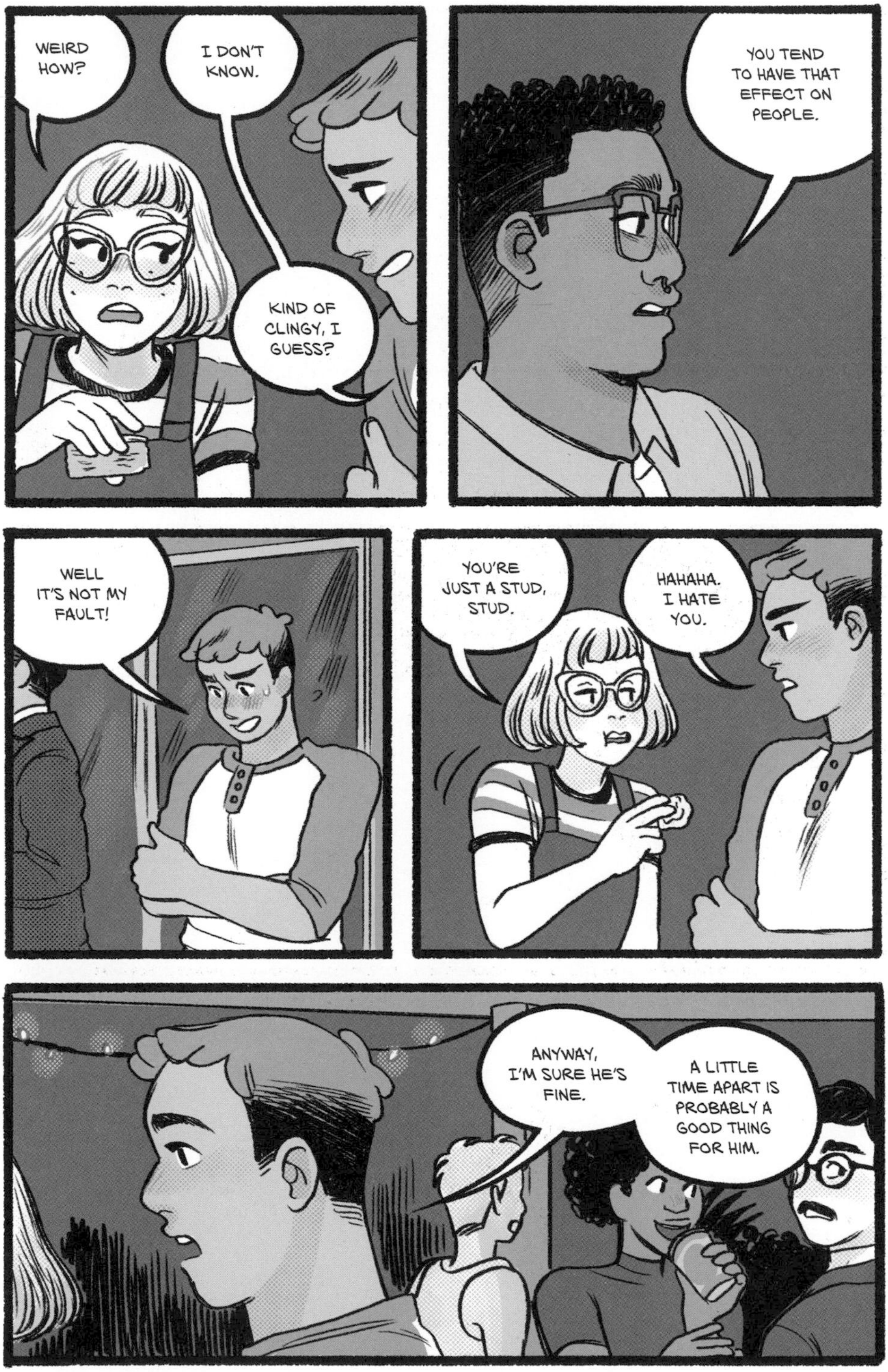
WEIRD HOW?
I DON'T KNOW.
KIND OF CLINGY, I GUESS?
YOU TEND TO HAVE THAT EFFECT ON PEOPLE.
WELL IT'S NOT MY FAULT!
YOU'RE JUST A STUD, STUD.
HAHAHA. I HATE YOU.
ANYWAY, I'M SURE HE'S FINE.
A LITTLE TIME APART IS PROBABLY A GOOD THING FOR HIM.

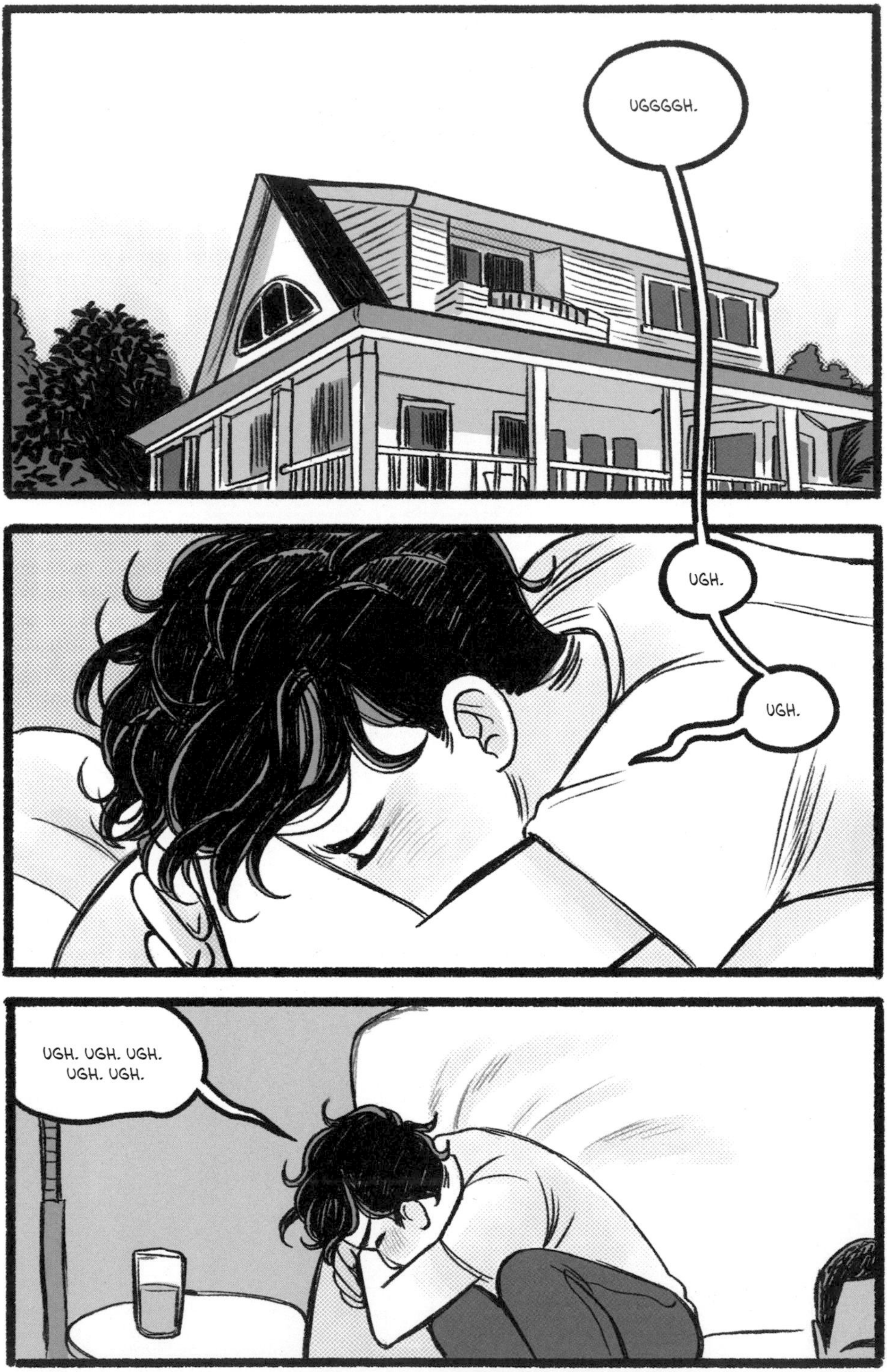
UGGGGH.
UGH.
UGH.
UGH. UGH. UGH.
UGH. UGH.

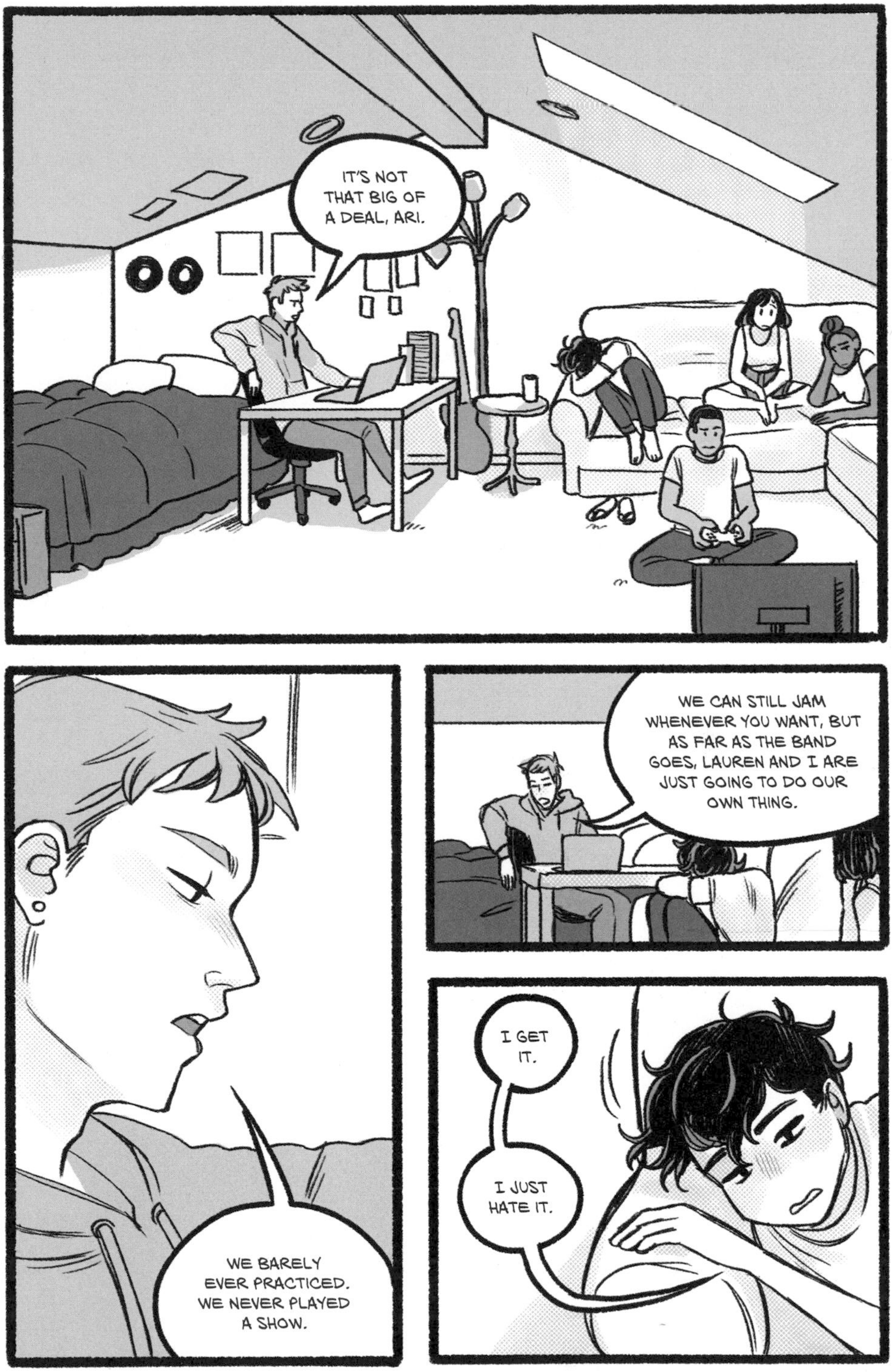
IT'S NOT THAT BIG OF A DEAL, ARI.
WE BARELY EVER PRACTICED. WE NEVER PLAYED A SHOW.
WE CAN STILL JAM WHENEVER YOU WANT, BUT AS FAR AS THE BAND GOES, LAUREN AND I ARE JUST GOING TO DO OUR OWN THING.
I GET IT.
I JUST HATE IT.

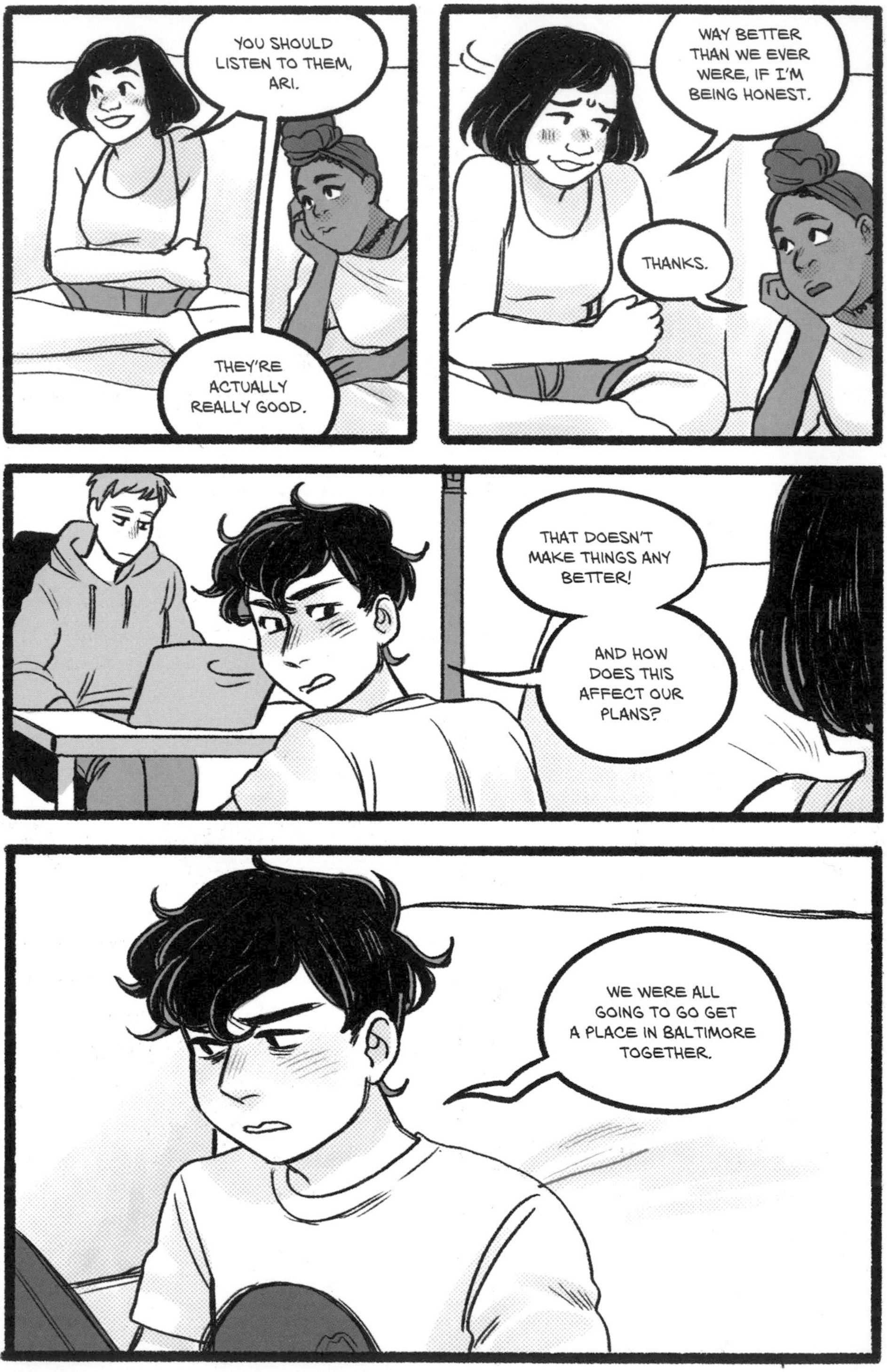
YOU SHOULD LISTEN TO THEM, ARI.
THEY'RE ACTUALLY REALLY GOOD.
WAY BETTER THAN WE EVER WERE, IF I'M BEING HONEST.
THANKS.
THAT DOESN'T MAKE THINGS ANY BETTER!
AND HOW DOES THIS AFFECT OUR PLANS?
WE WERE ALL GOING TO GO GET A PLACE IN BALTIMORE TOGETHER.

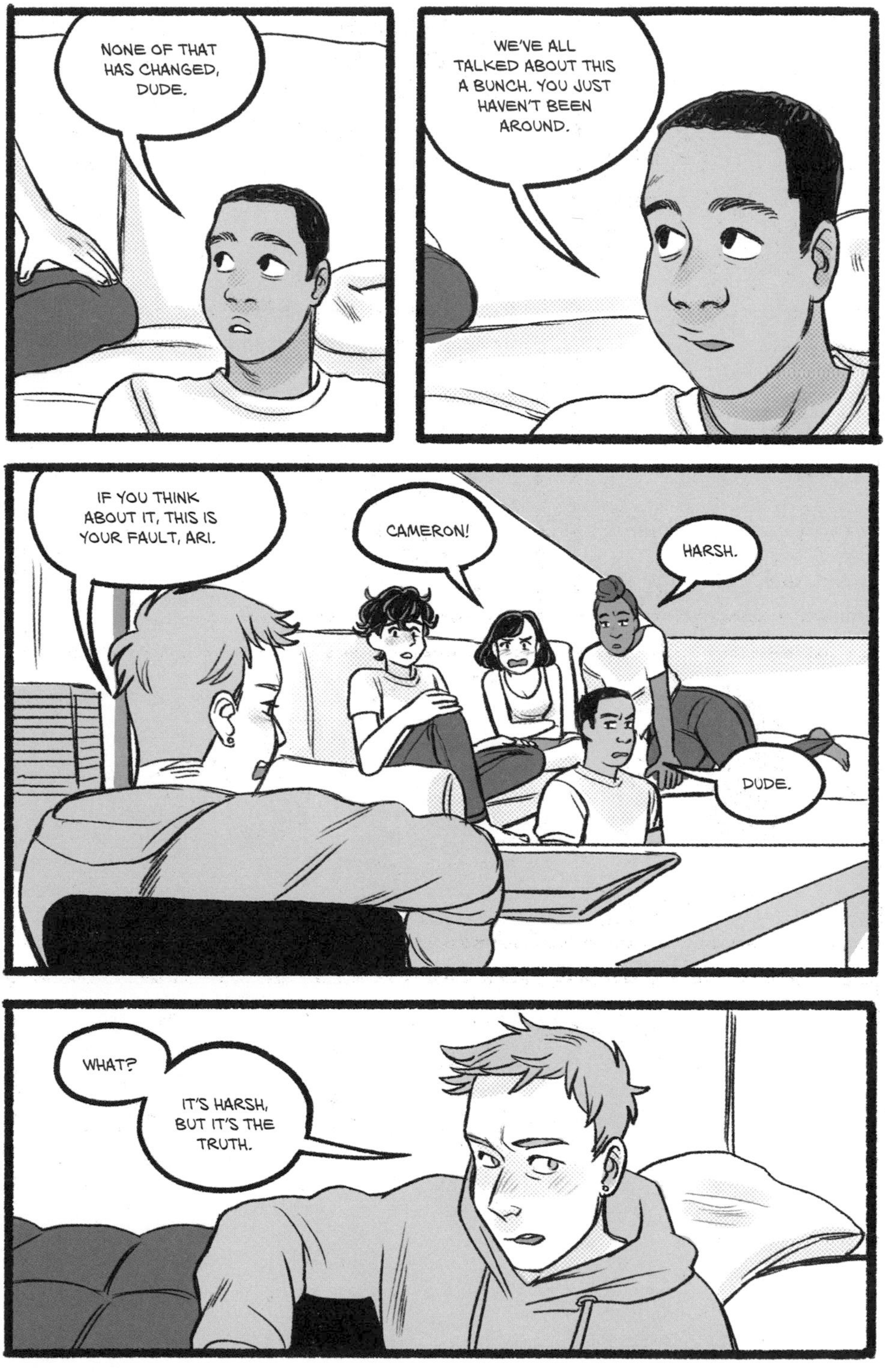
NONE OF THAT HAS CHANGED, DUDE.
WE'VE ALL TALKED ABOUT THIS A BUNCH. YOU JUST HAVEN'T BEEN AROUND.
IF YOU THINK ABOUT IT, THIS IS YOUR FAULT, ARI.
CAMERON!
HARSH.
DUDE.
WHAT?
IT'S HARSH, BUT IT'S THE TRUTH.

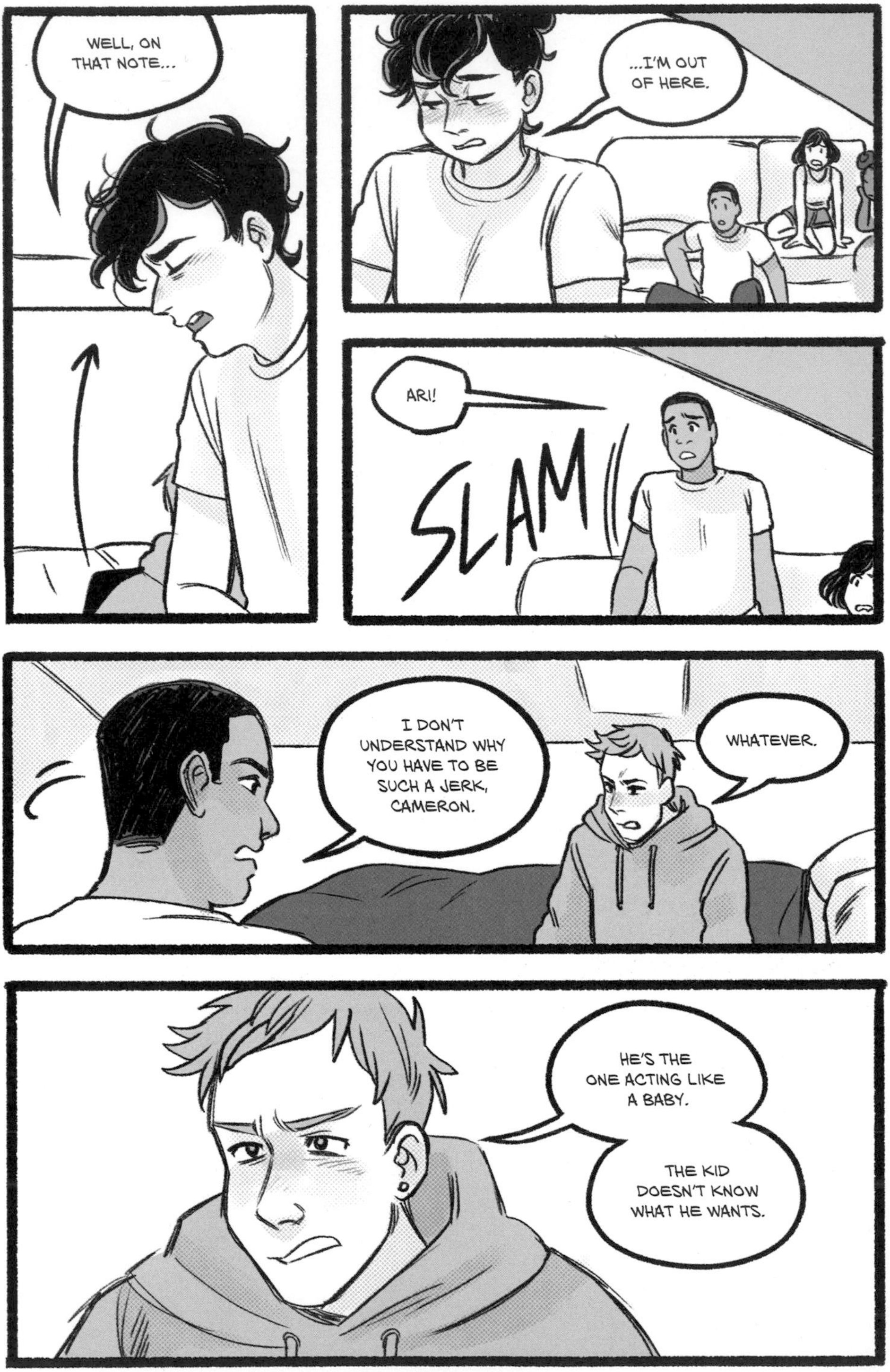
WELL, ON THAT NOTE...
...I'M OUT OF HERE.
ARI!
SLAM
I DON'T UNDERSTAND WHY YOU HAVE TO BE SUCH A JERK, CAMERON.
WHATEVER.
HE'S THE ONE ACTING LIKE A BABY.
THE KID DOESN'T KNOW WHAT HE WANTS.

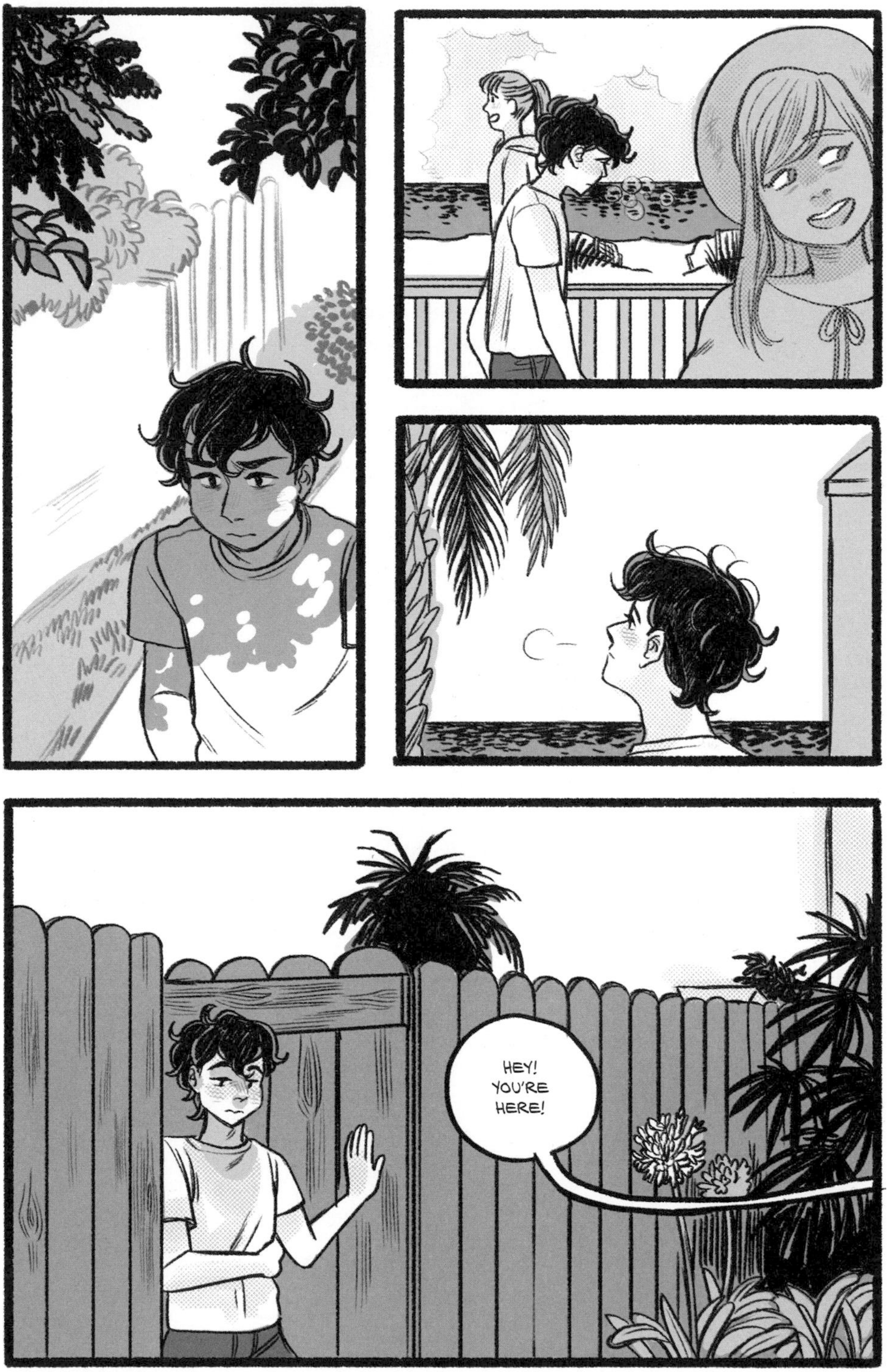
HEY! YOU'RE HERE!

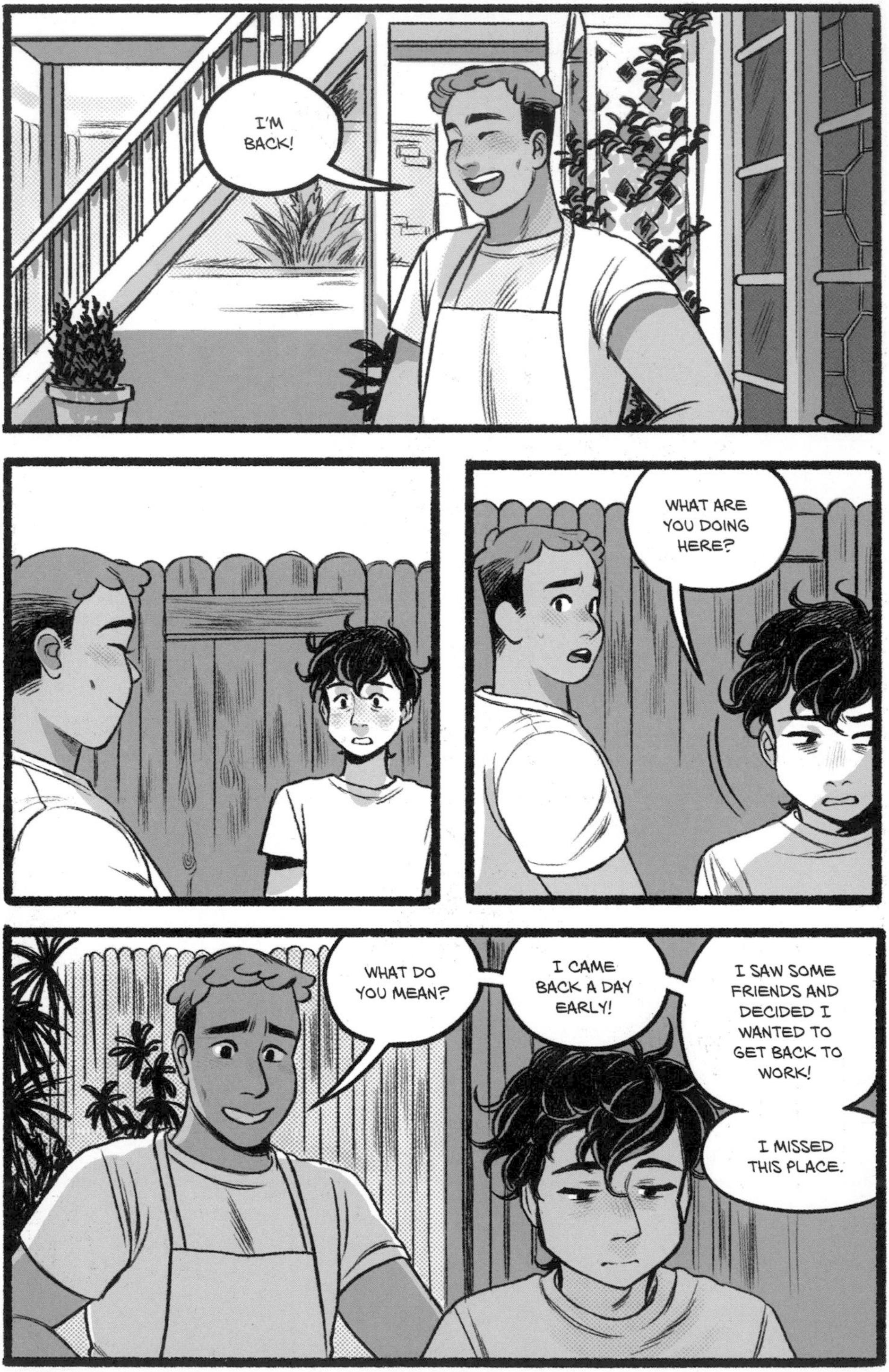
I'M BACK!
WHAT ARE YOU DOING HERE?
WHAT DO YOU MEAN?
I CAME BACK A DAY EARLY!
I SAW SOME FRIENDS AND DECIDED I WANTED TO GET BACK TO WORK!
I MISSED THIS PLACE.

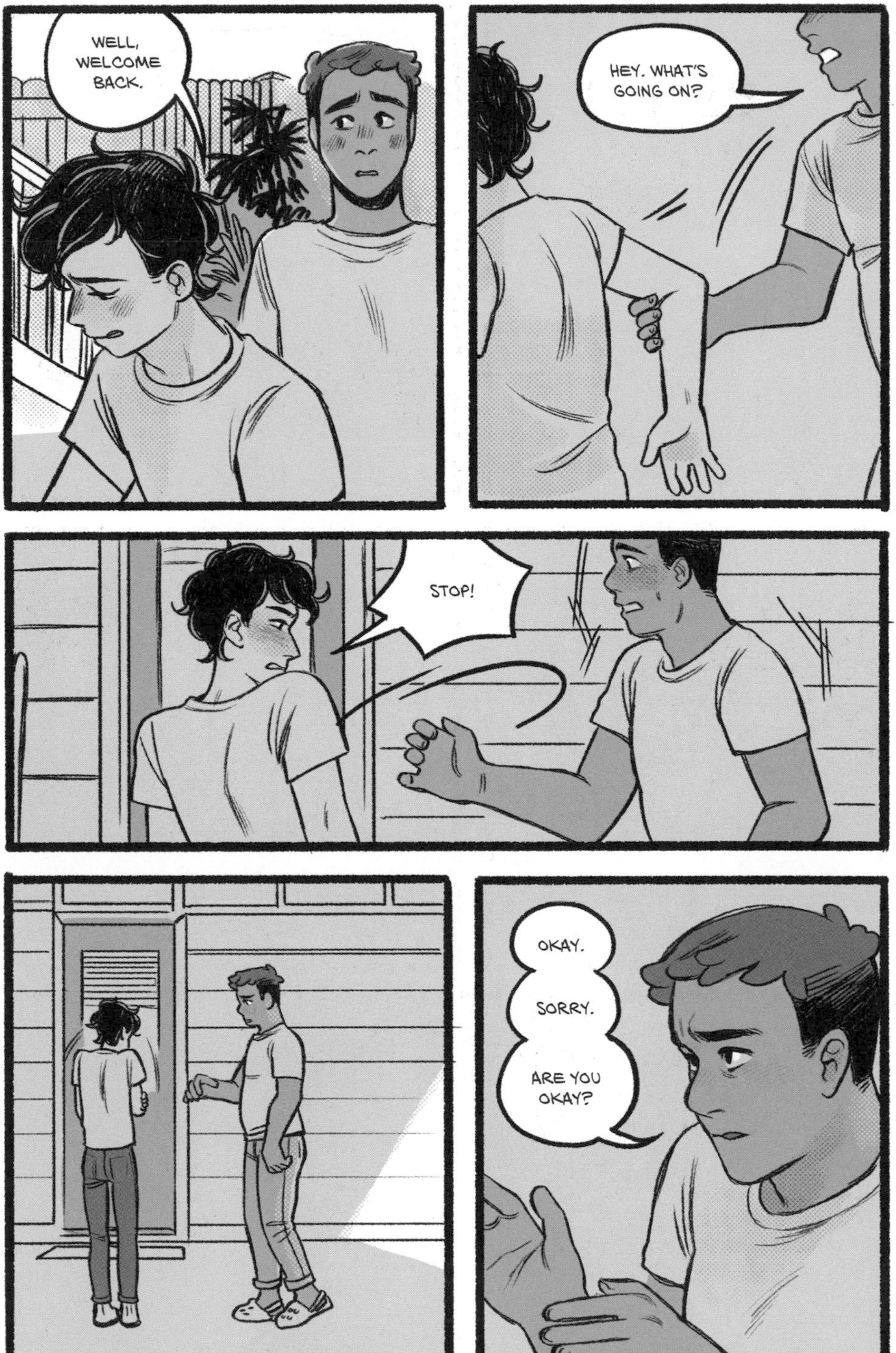
WELL, WELCOME BACK.
HEY. WHAT'S GOING ON?
STOP!
OKAY.
SORRY.
ARE YOU OKAY?

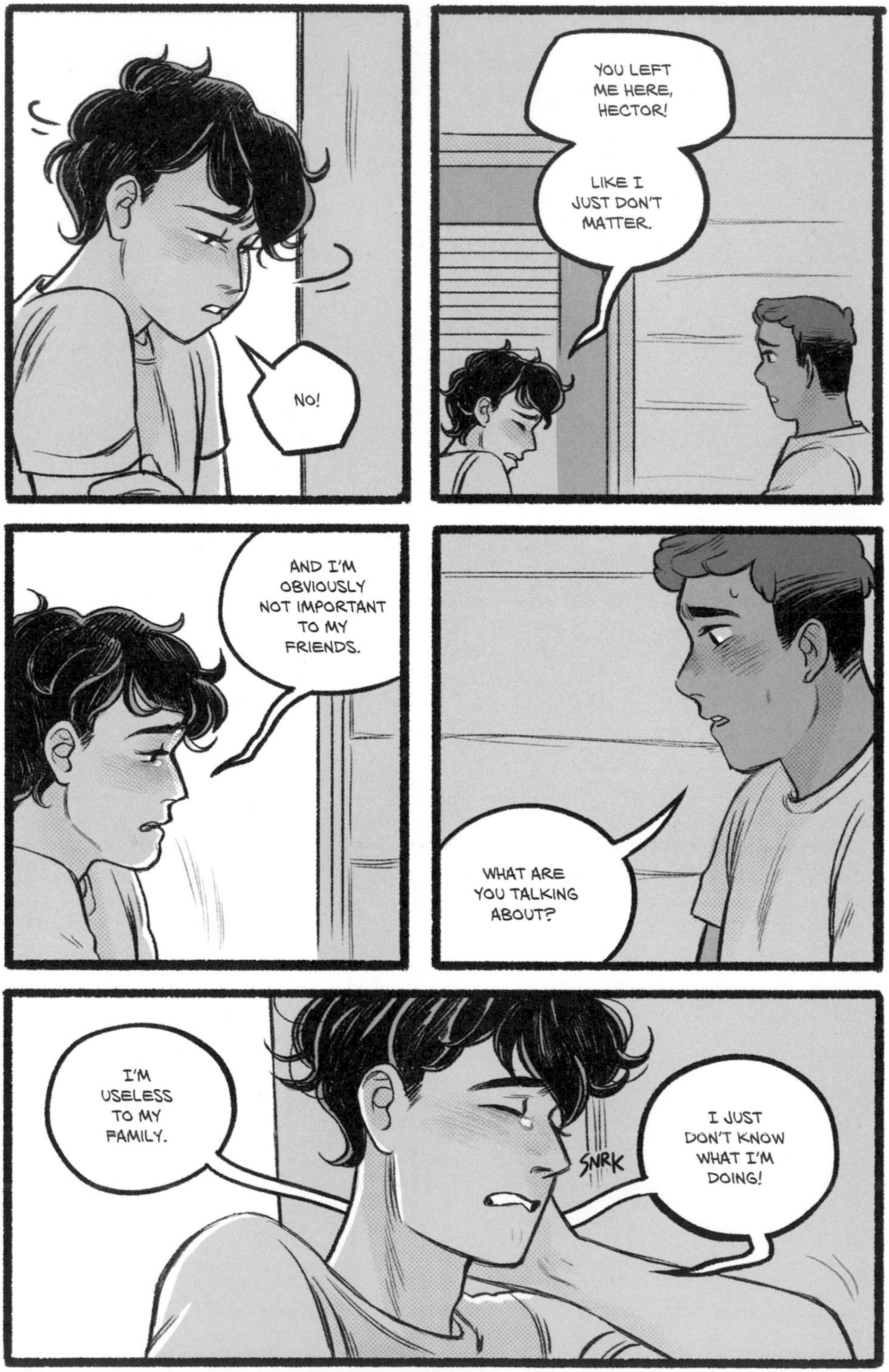
NO!
YOU LEFT ME HERE, HECTOR!
LIKE I JUST DON'T MATTER.
AND I'M OBVIOUSLY NOT IMPORTANT TO MY FRIENDS.
WHAT ARE YOU TALKING ABOUT?
I'M USELESS TO MY FAMILY.
SNRK
I JUST DON'T KNOW WHAT I'M DOING!

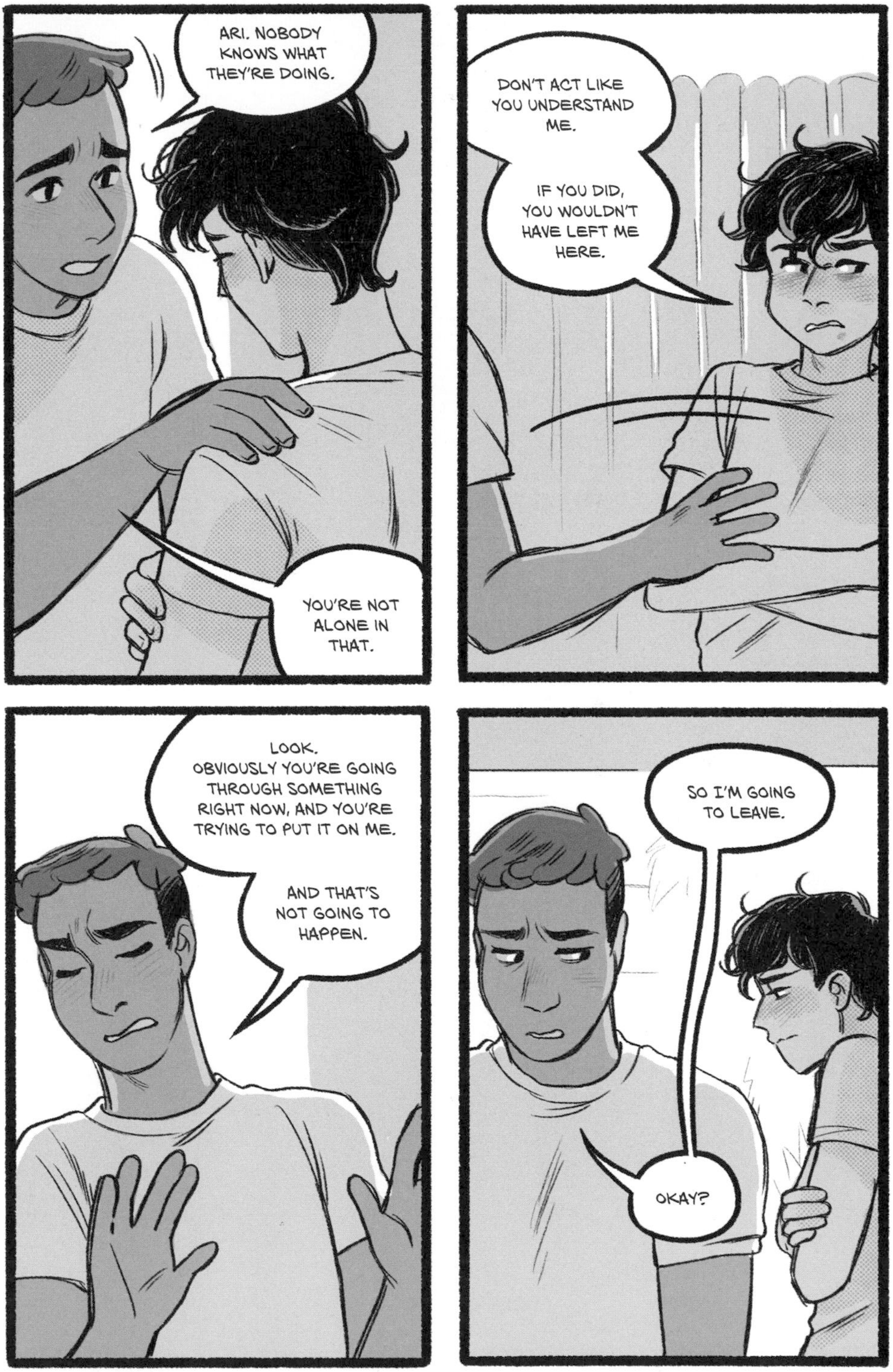
ARI. NOBODY KNOWS WHAT THEY'RE DOING.
YOU'RE NOT ALONE IN THAT.
DON'T ACT LIKE YOU UNDERSTAND ME.
IF YOU DID, YOU WOULDN'T HAVE LEFT ME HERE.
LOOK. OBVIOUSLY YOU'RE GOING THROUGH SOMETHING RIGHT NOW, AND YOU'RE TRYING TO PUT IT ON ME.
AND THAT'S NOT GOING TO HAPPEN.
SO I'M GOING TO LEAVE.
OKAY?

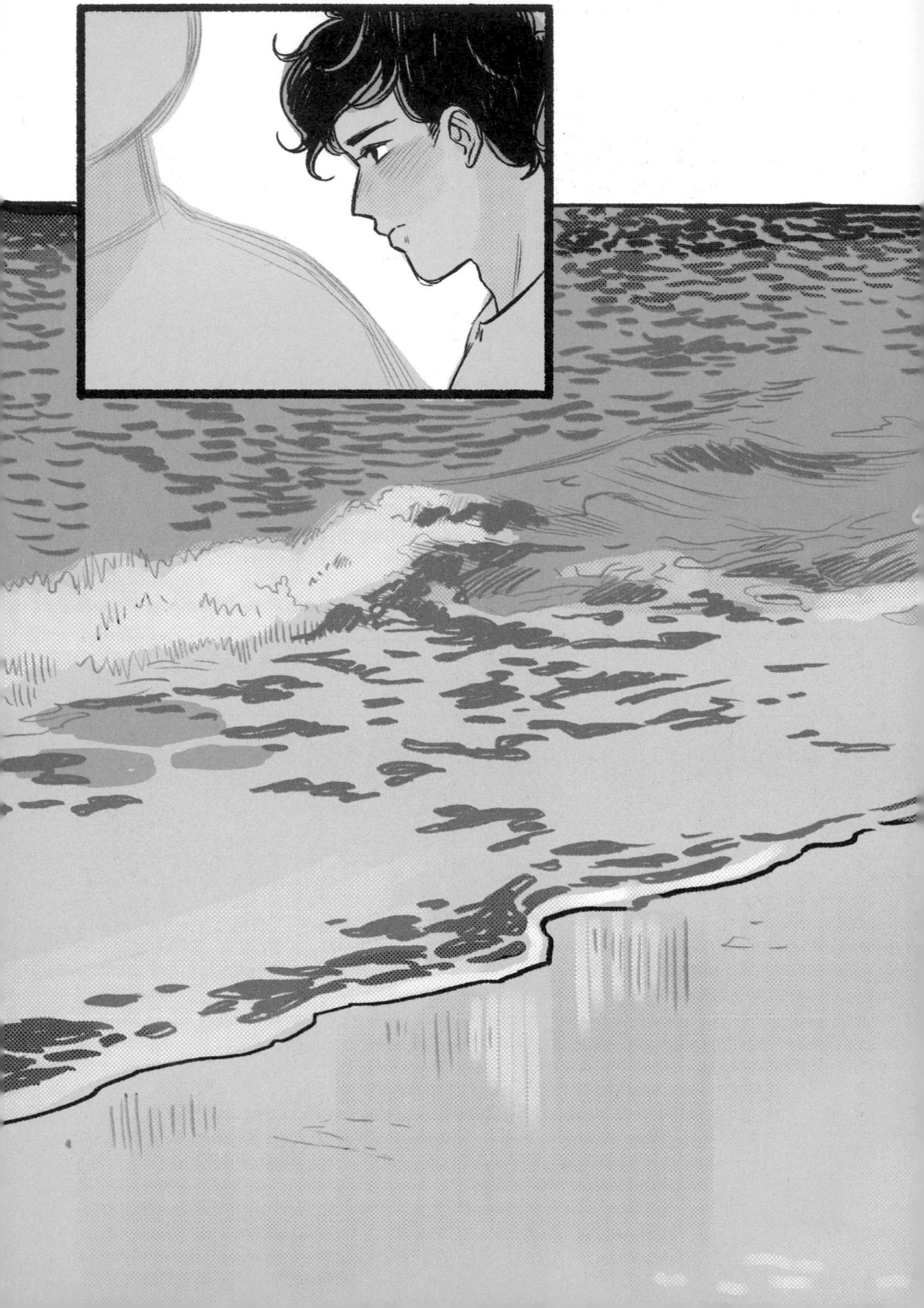

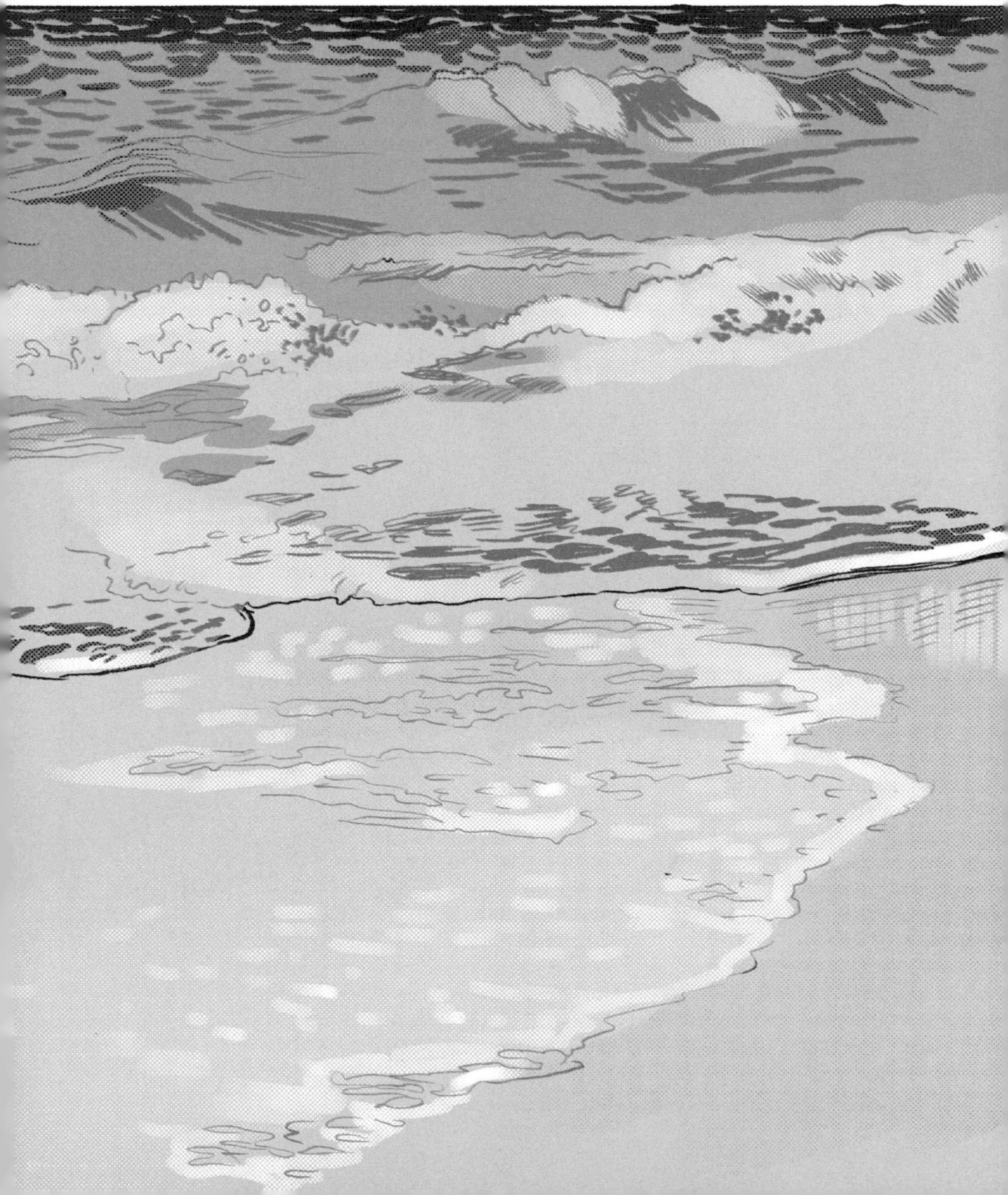

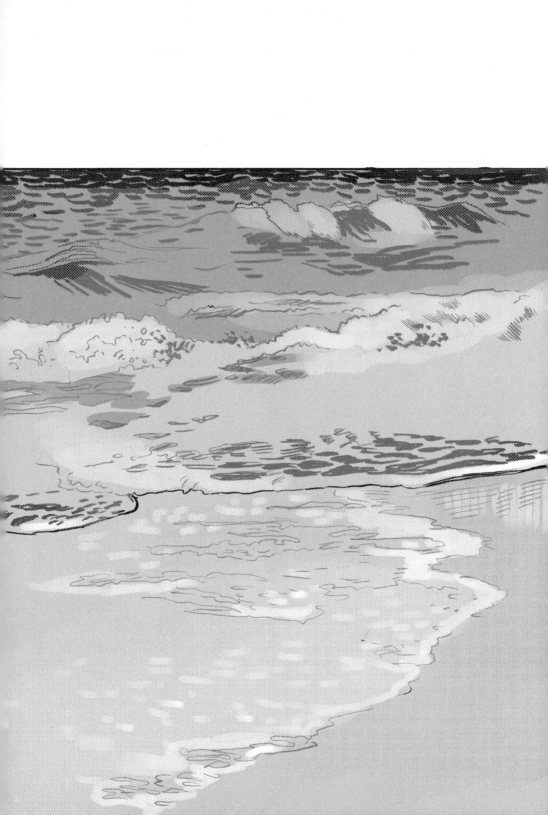

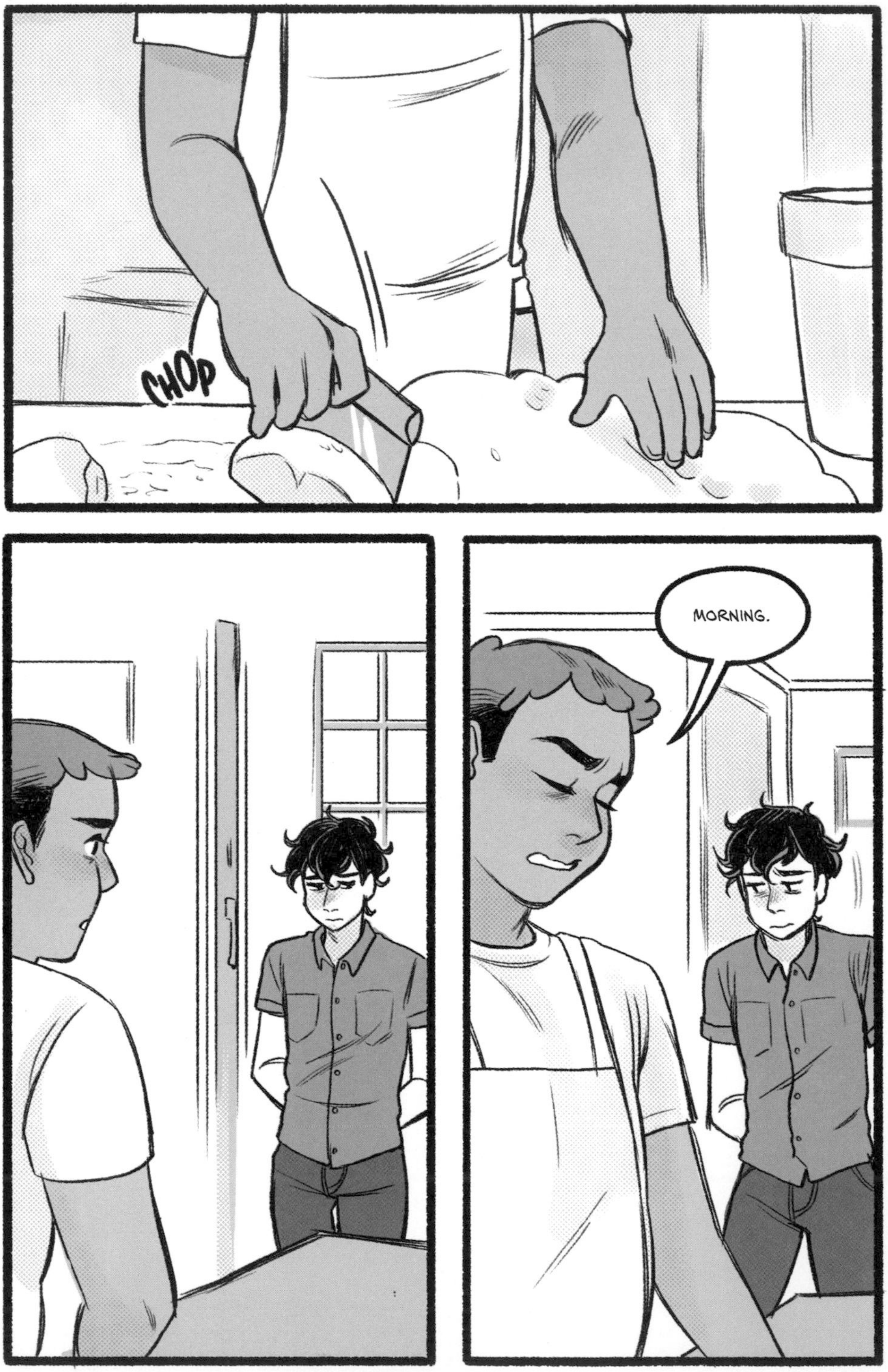
CHOP
MORNING.

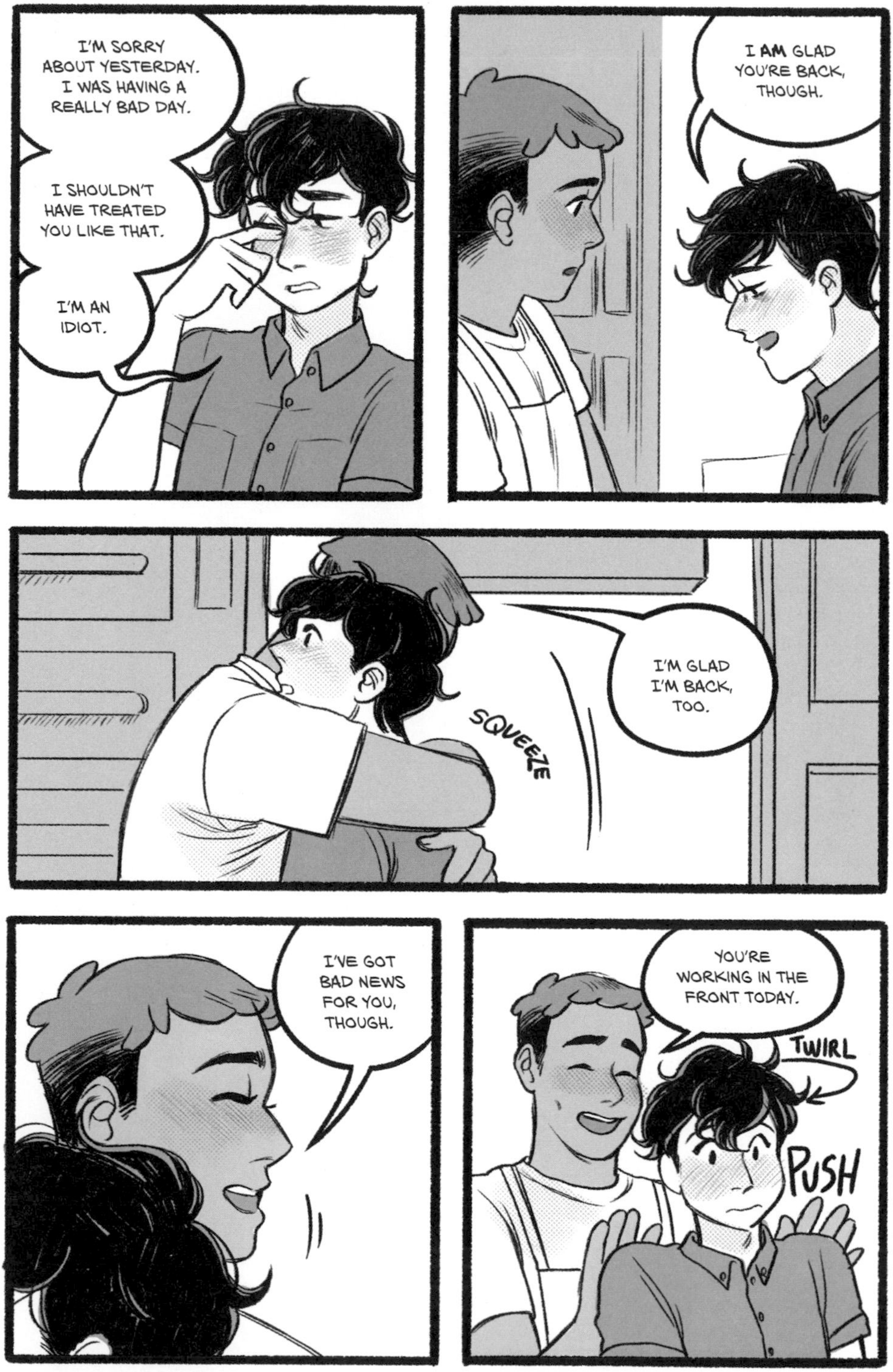
I'M SORRY ABOUT YESTERDAY. I WAS HAVING A REALLY BAD DAY.
I SHOULDN'T HAVE TREATED YOU LIKE THAT.
I'M AN IDIOT.
I AM GLAD YOU'RE BACK, THOUGH.
SQUEEZE
I'M GLAD I'M BACK, TOO.
I'VE GOT BAD NEWS FOR YOU, THOUGH.
YOU'RE WORKING IN THE FRONT TODAY.
TWIRL
PUSH

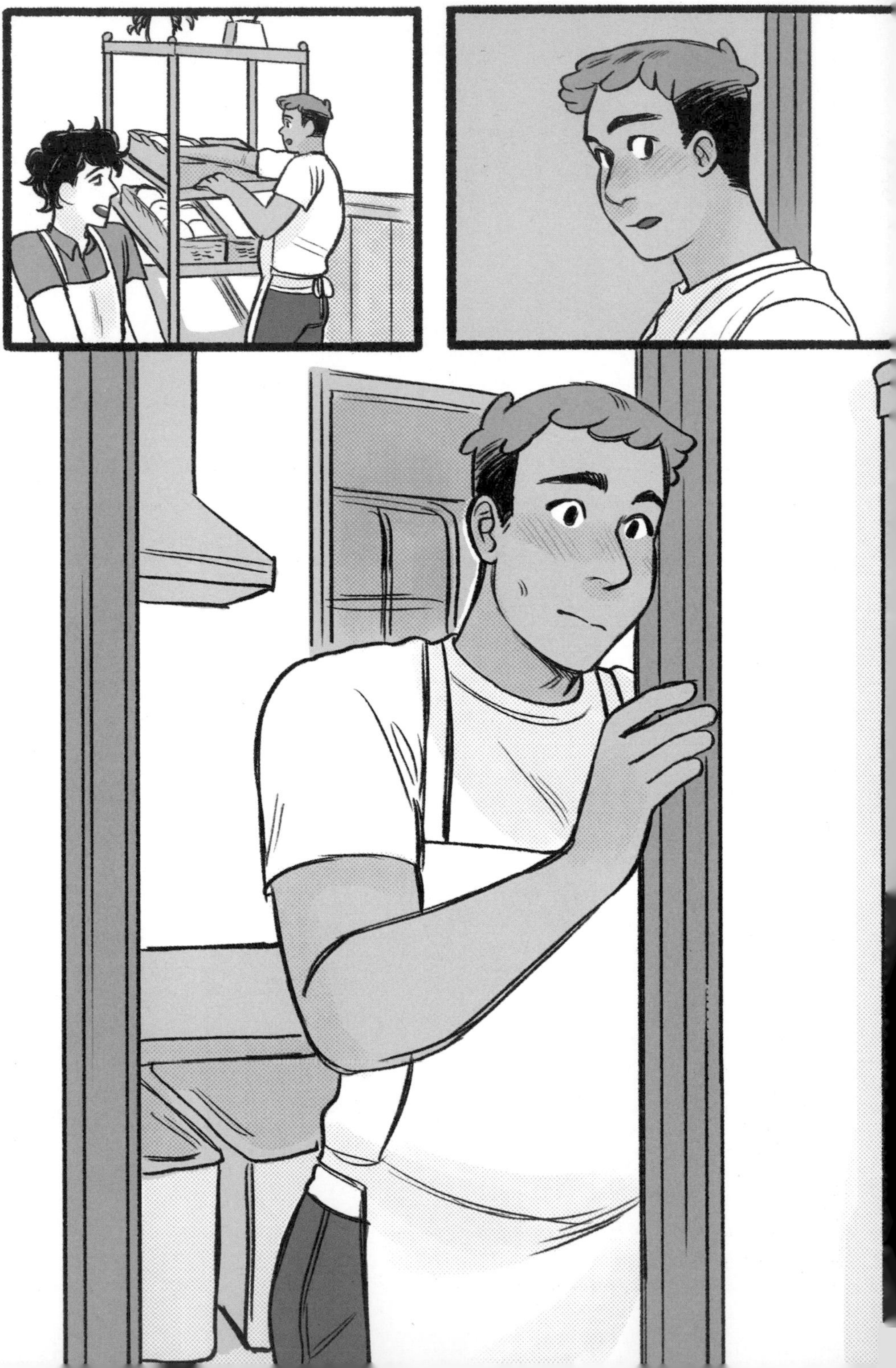

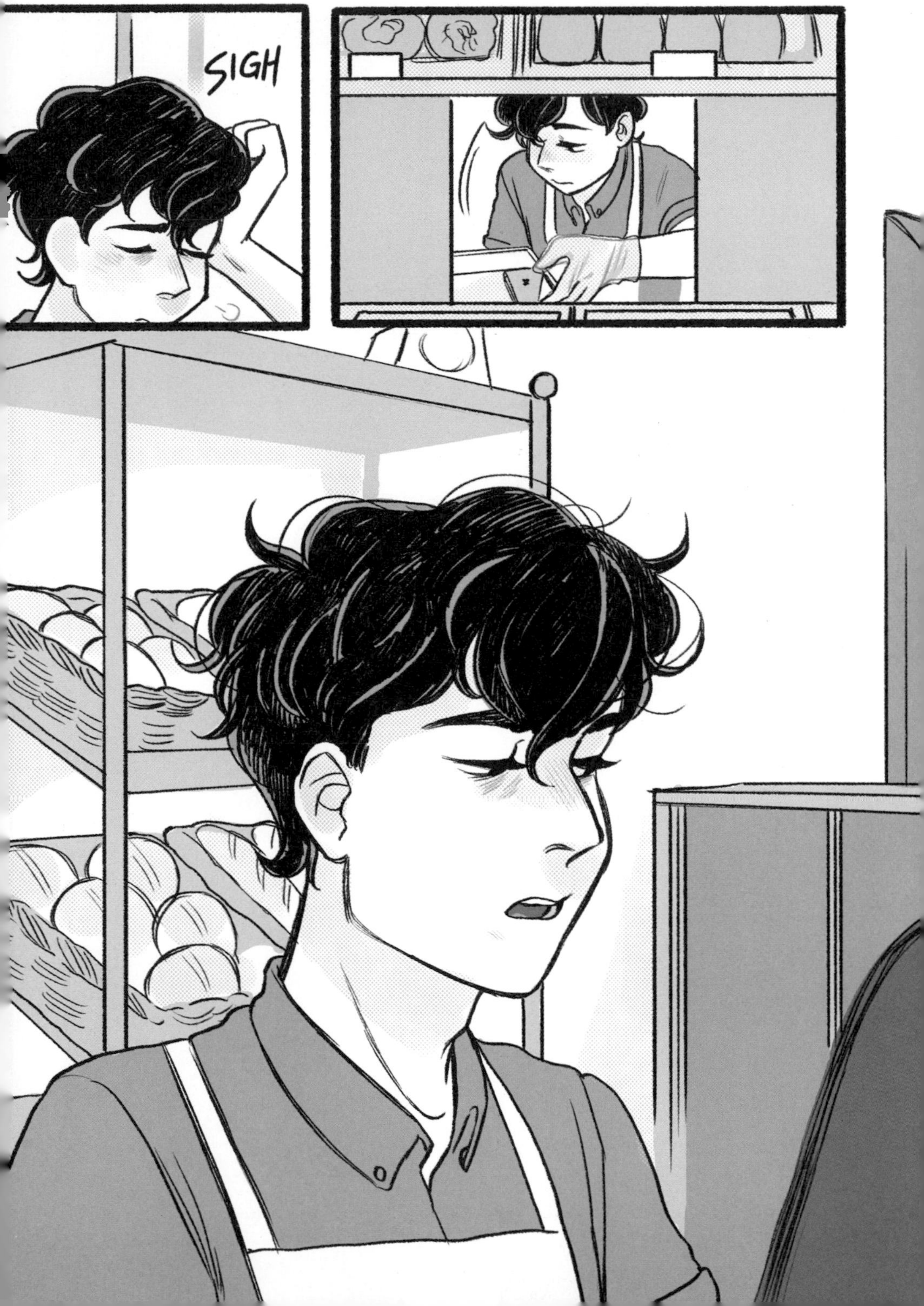
SIGH

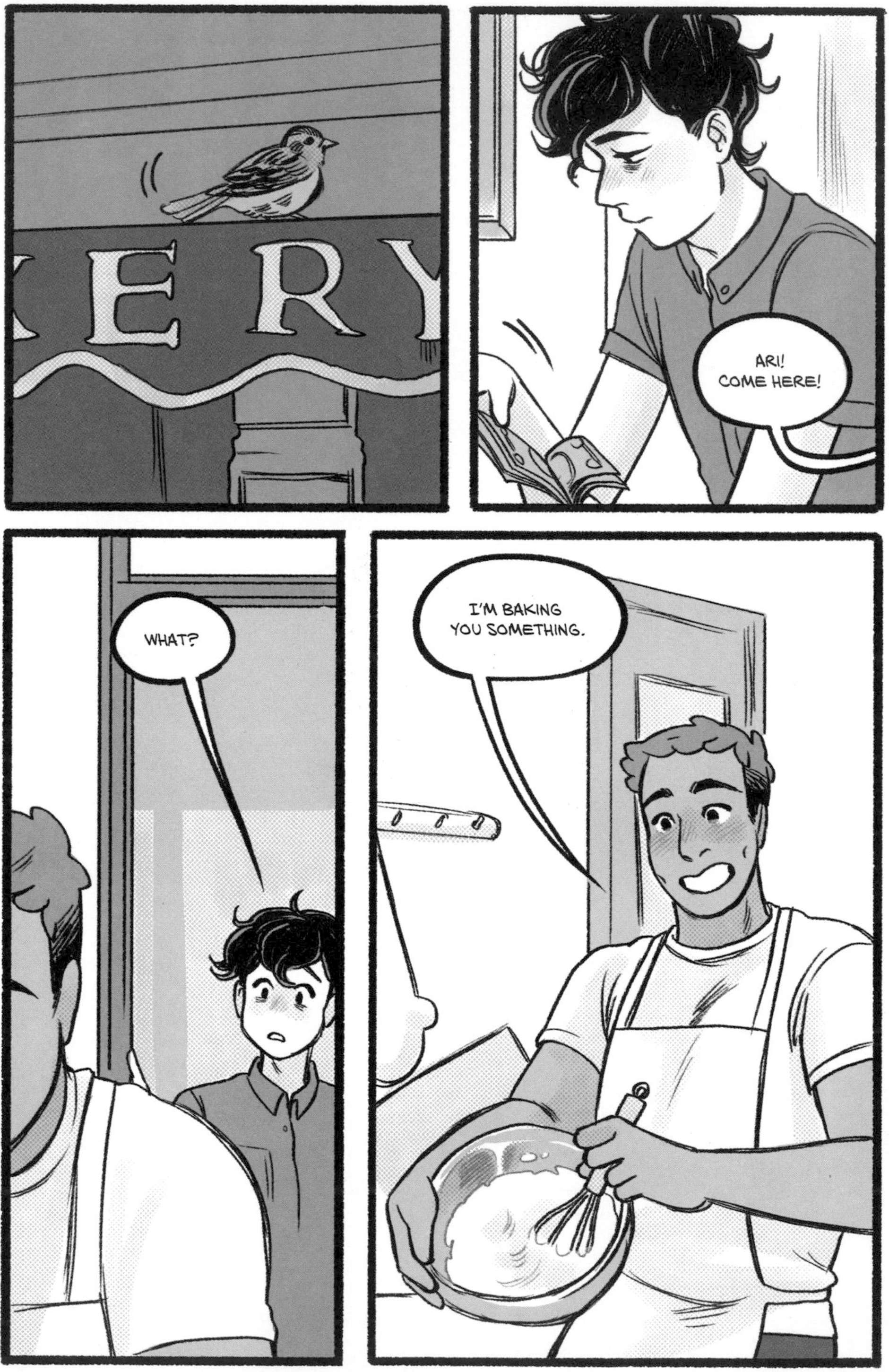
KERY
ARI!
COME HERE!
WHAT?
I'M BAKING
YOU SOMETHING.

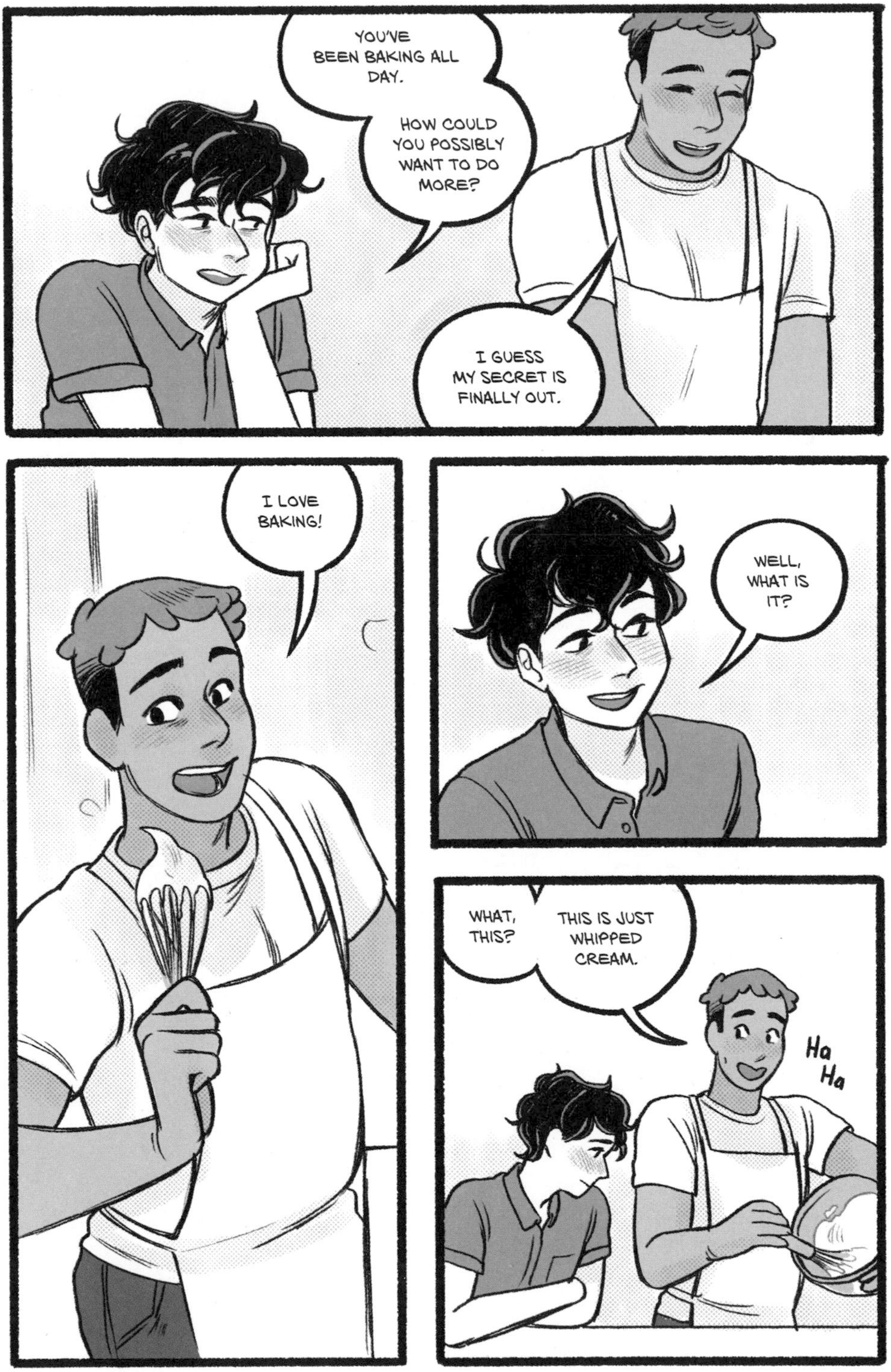
YOU'VE BEEN BAKING ALL DAY.
HOW COULD YOU POSSIBLY WANT TO DO MORE?
I GUESS MY SECRET IS FINALLY OUT.
I LOVE BAKING!
WELL, WHAT IS IT?
WHAT, THIS?
THIS IS JUST WHIPPED CREAM.
Ha Ha

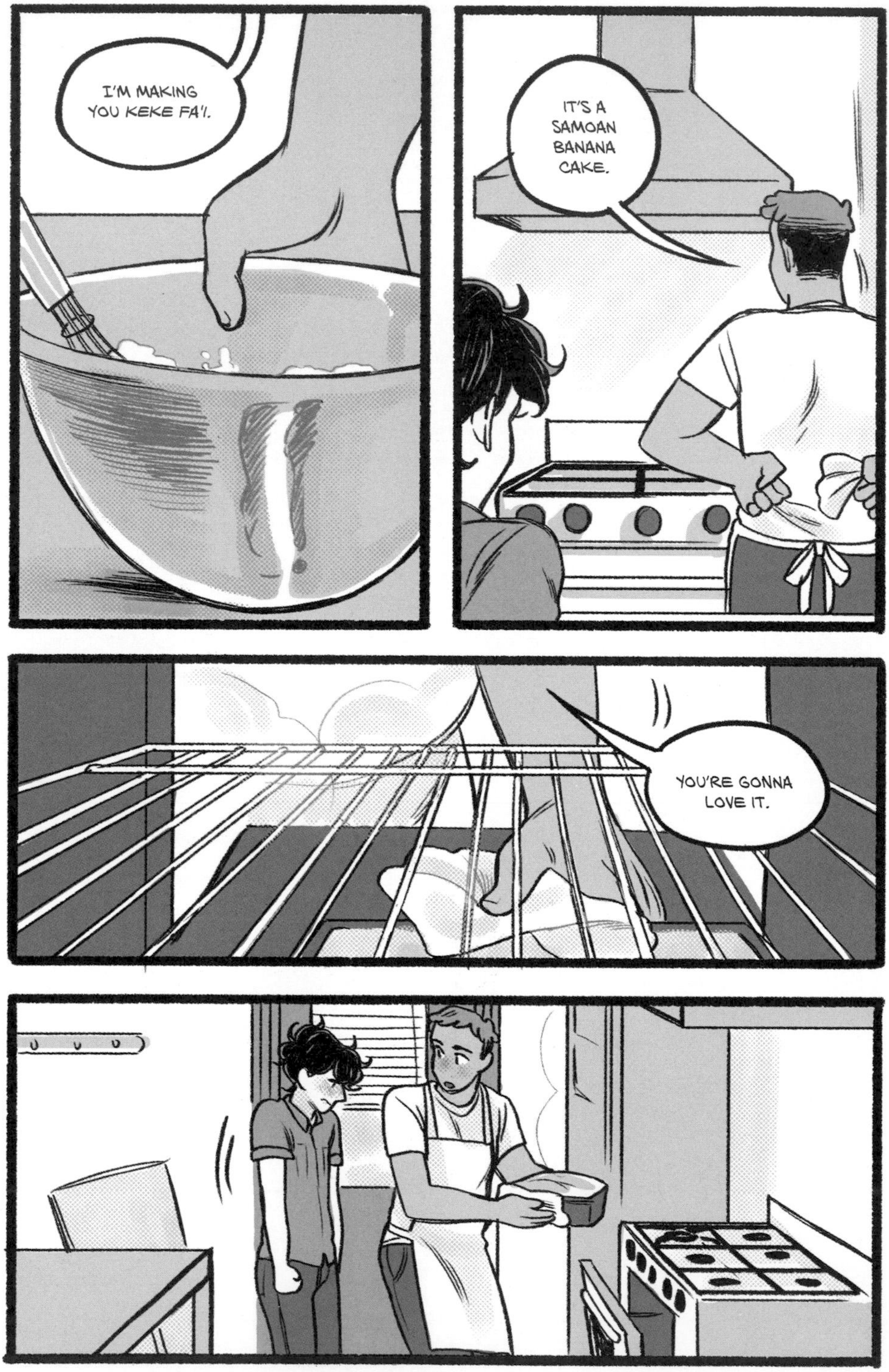
I'M MAKING YOU KEKE FA'I.
IT'S A SAMOAN BANANA CAKE.
YOU'RE GONNA LOVE IT.

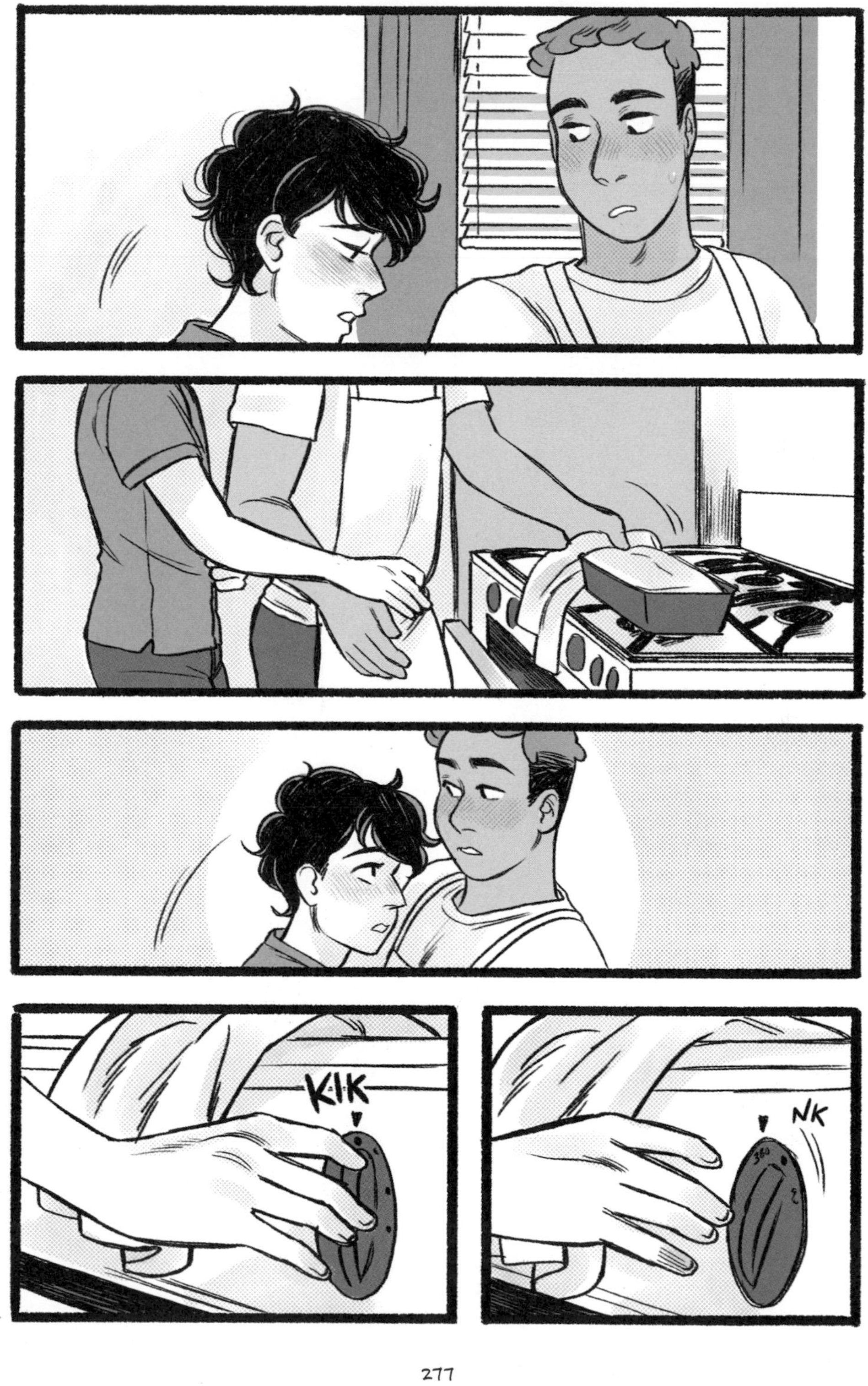
KIK
NK

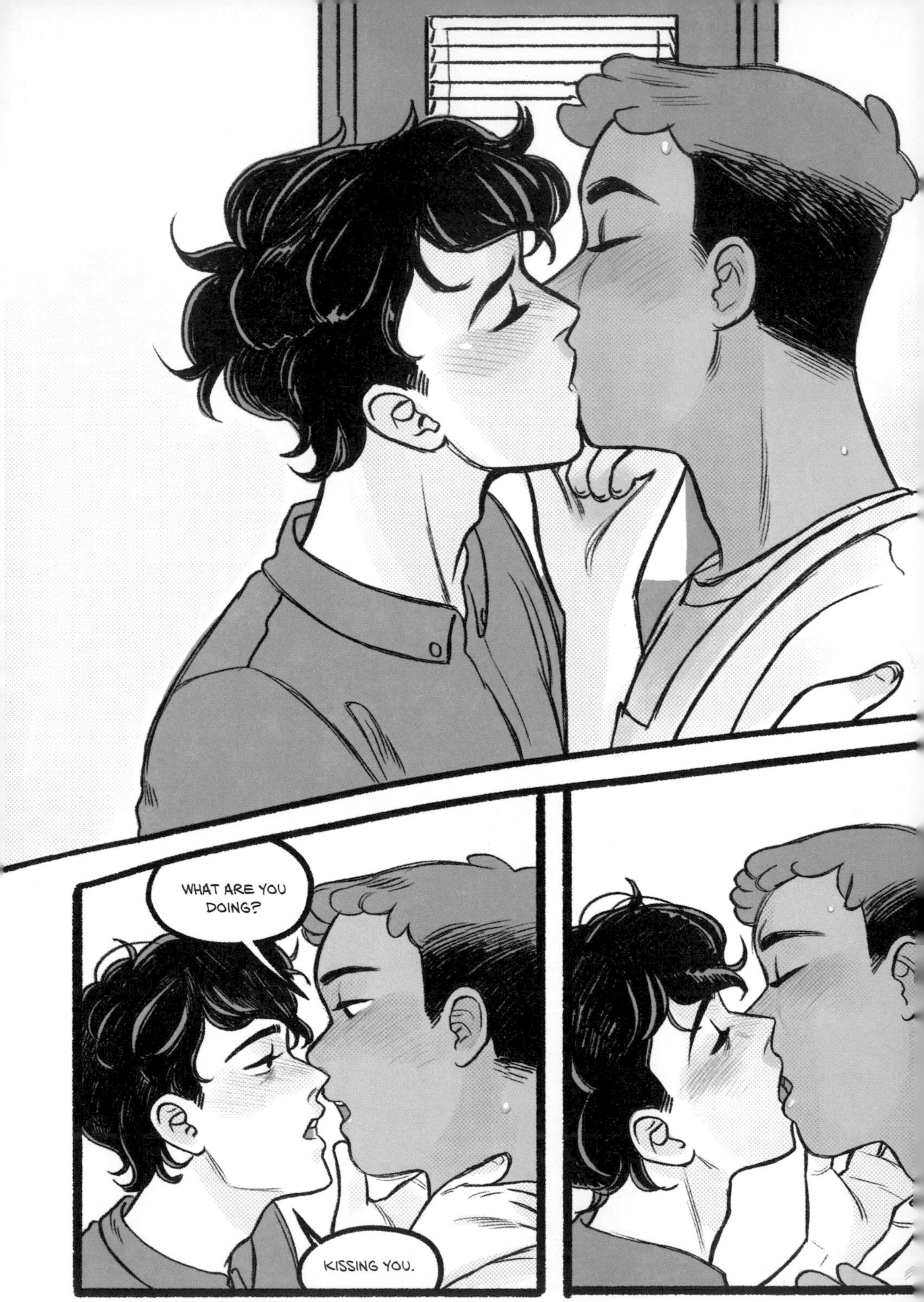
WHAT ARE YOU DOING?
KISSING YOU.

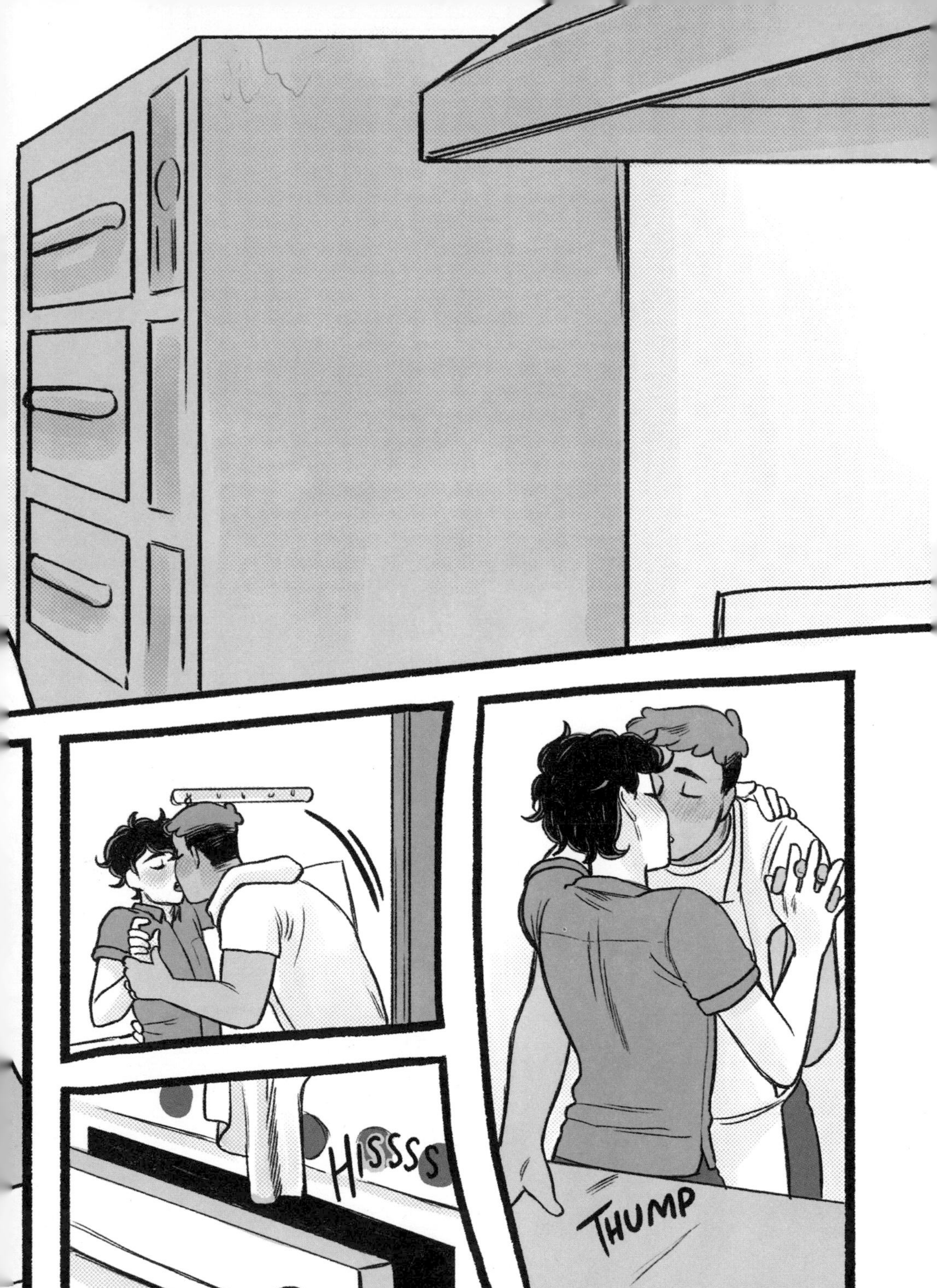
HISSSS
THUMP

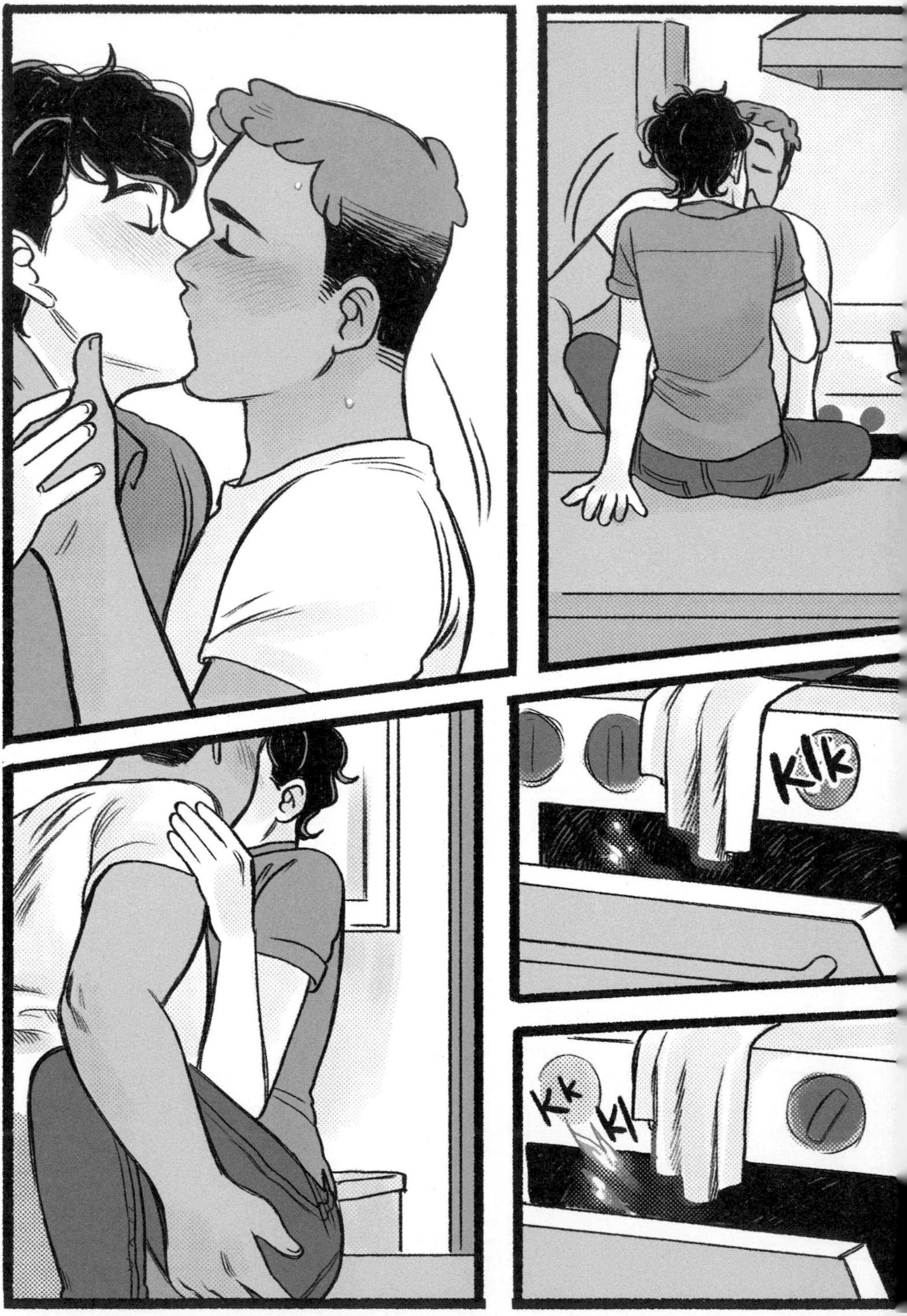
KIK
KK
KI

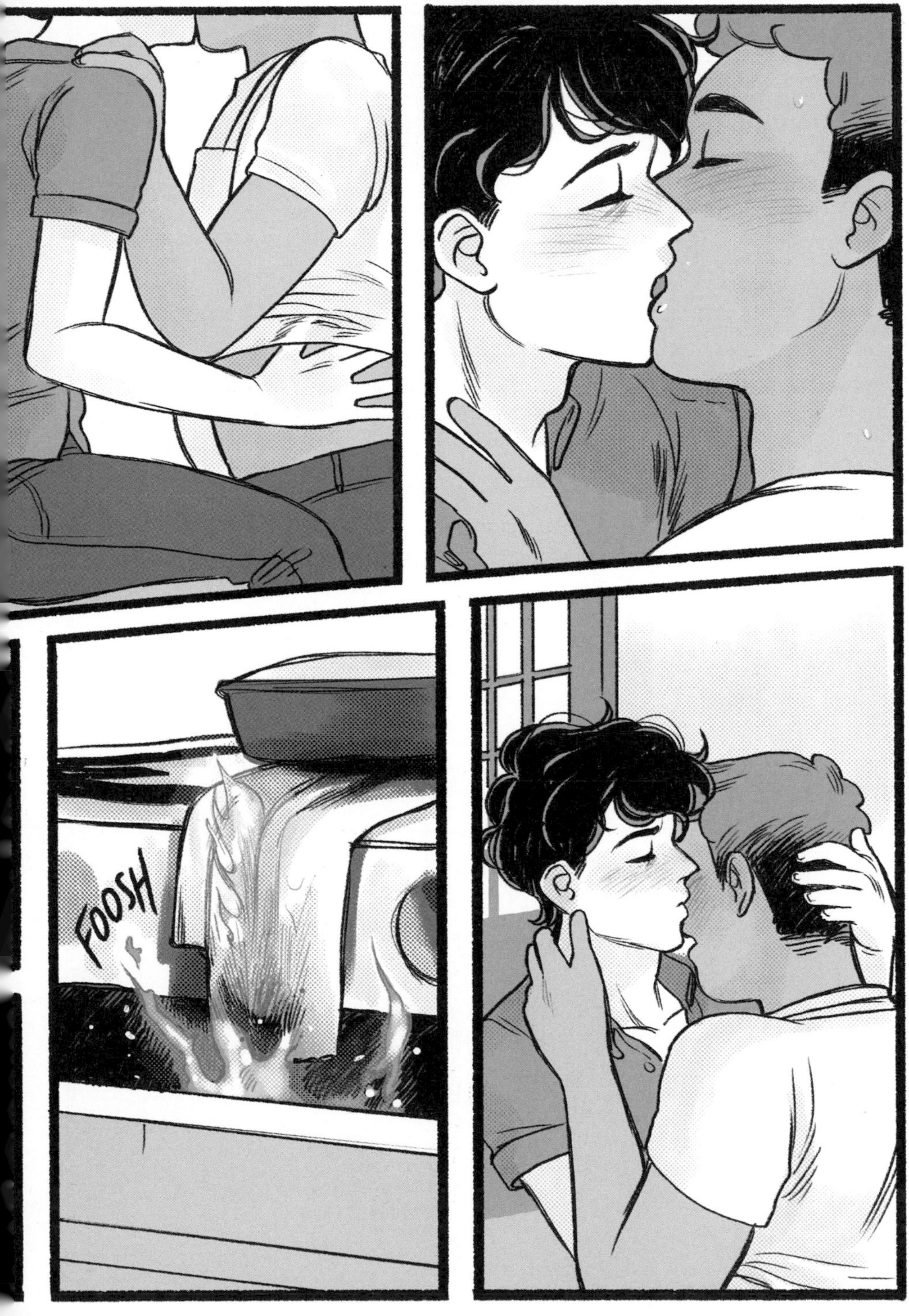
FOOSH

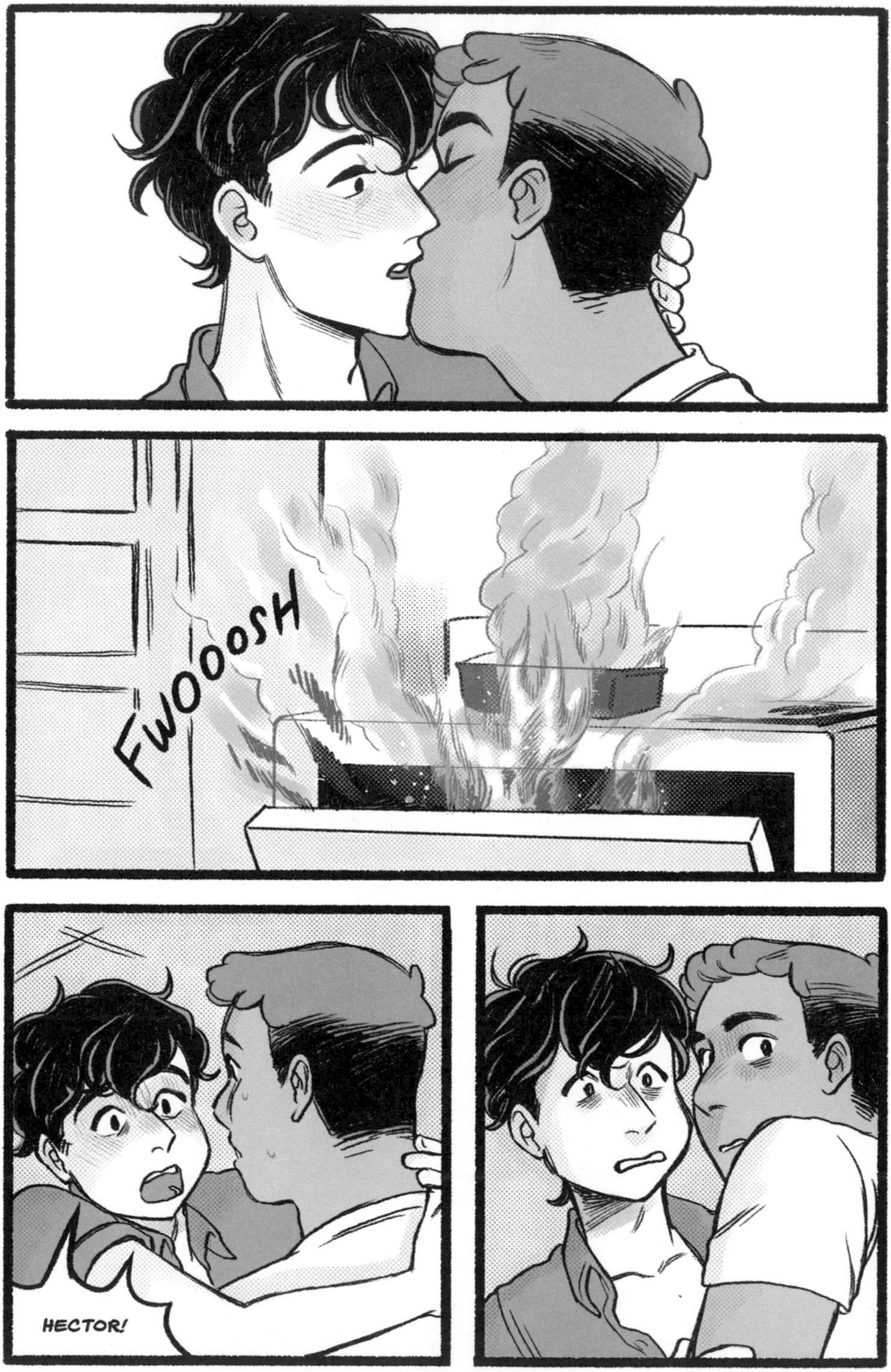
FWOOOSH
HECTOR!

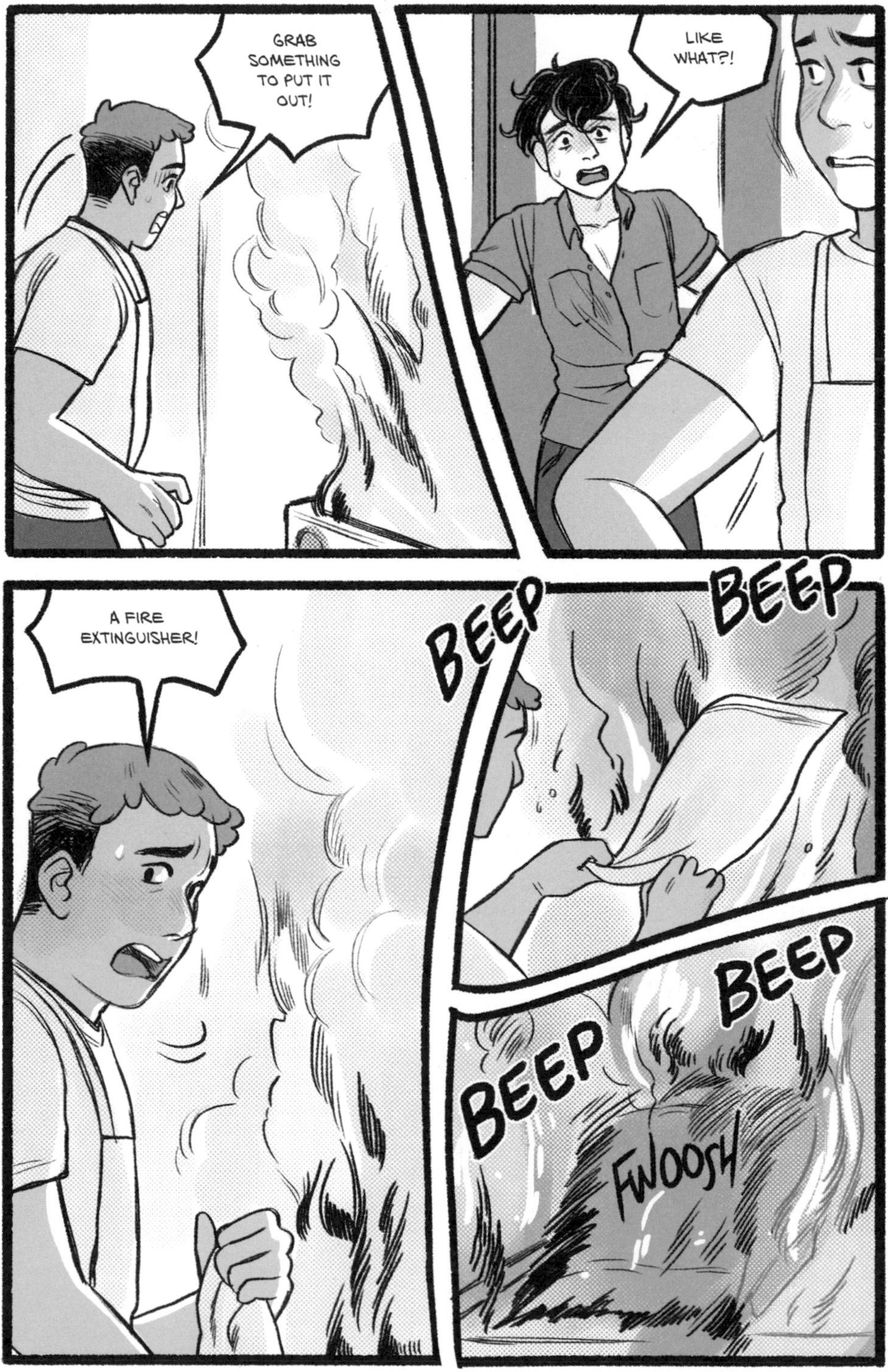
GRAB SOMETHING TO PUT IT OUT!
LIKE WHAT?!
A FIRE EXTINGUISHER!
BEEP
BEEP
BEEP
BEEP
FWOOSH

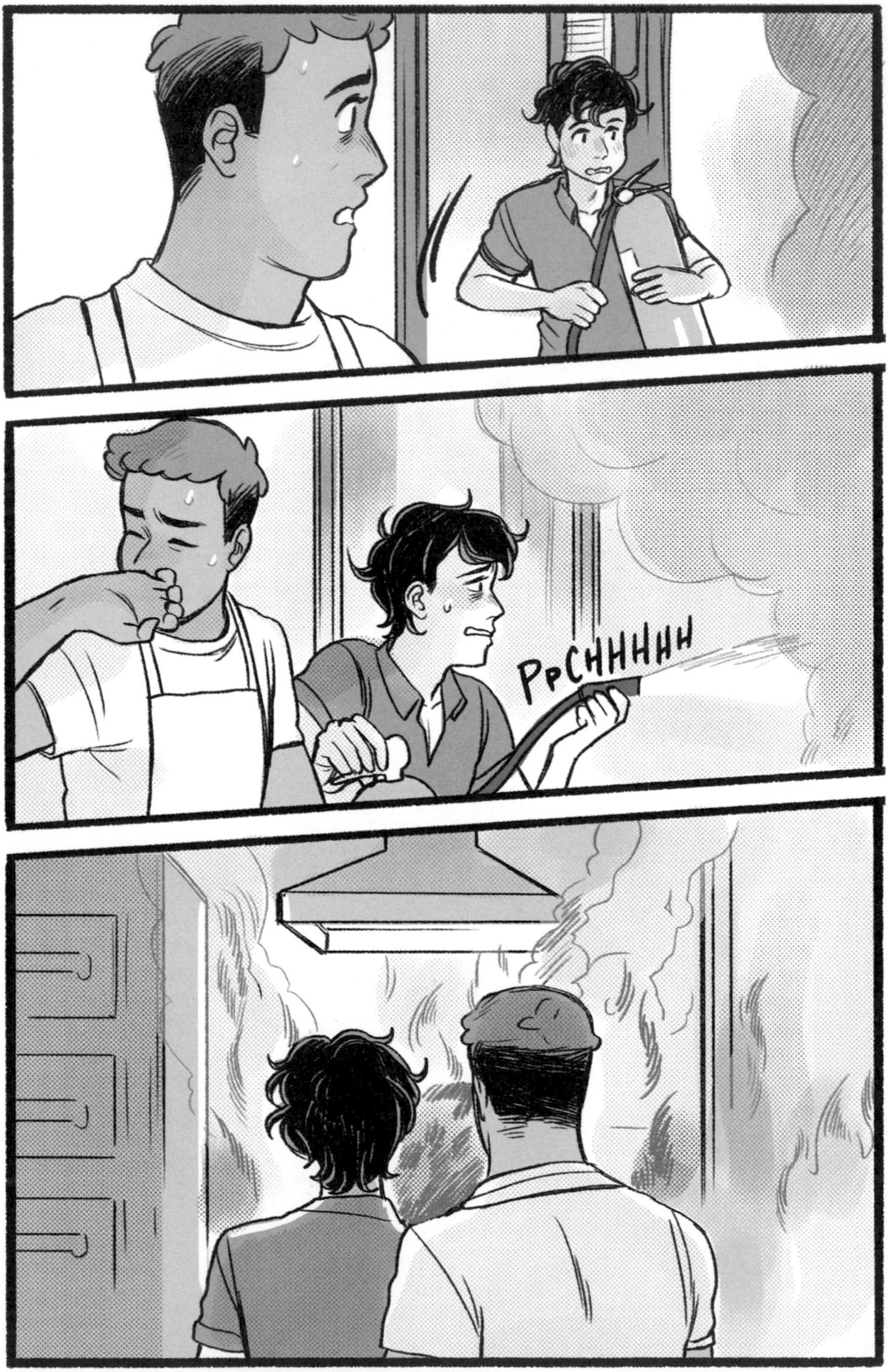
PPCHHHHHH

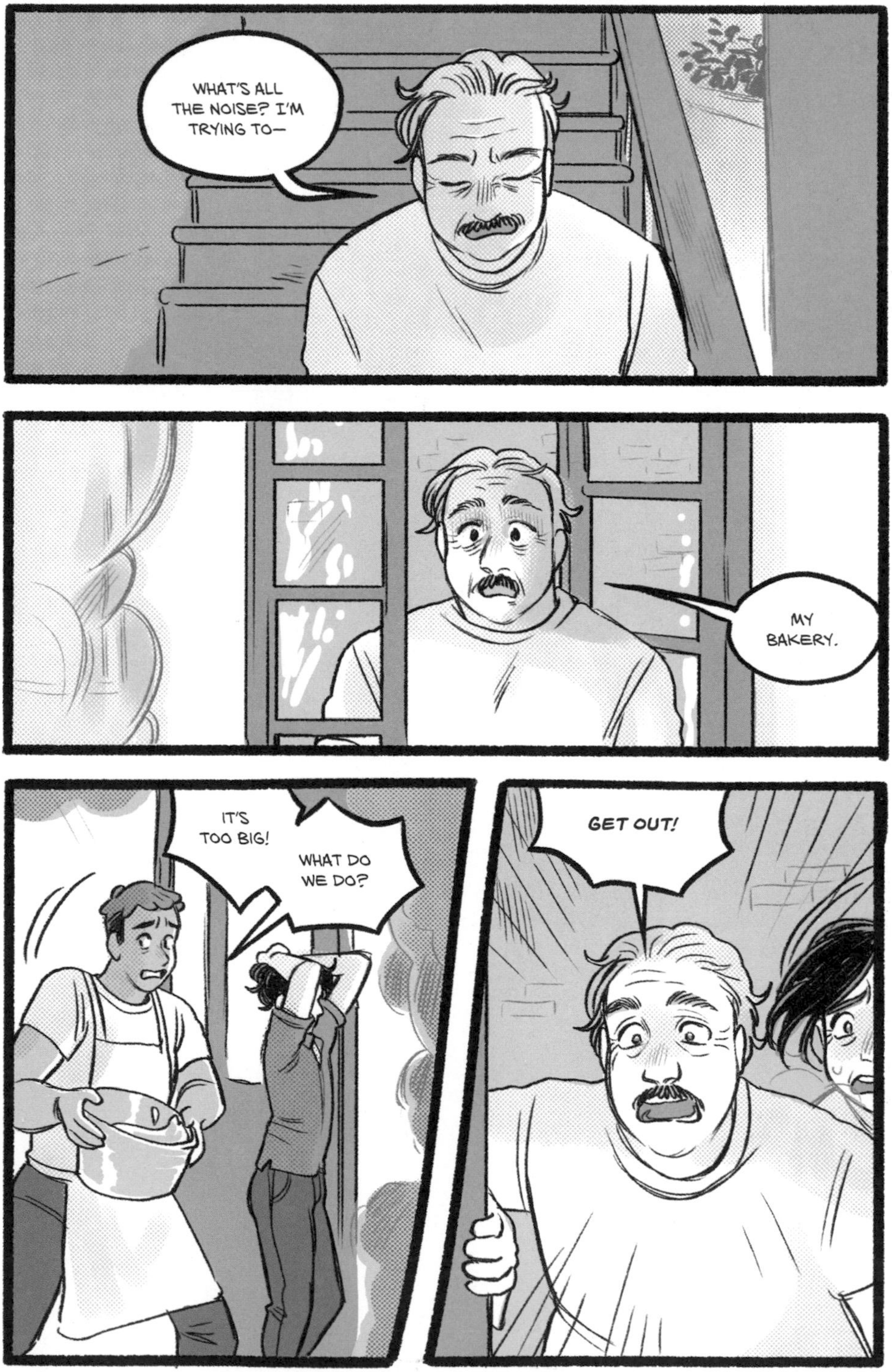
WHAT'S ALL THE NOISE? I'M TRYING TO—
MY BAKERY.
IT'S TOO BIG!
WHAT DO WE DO?
GET OUT!

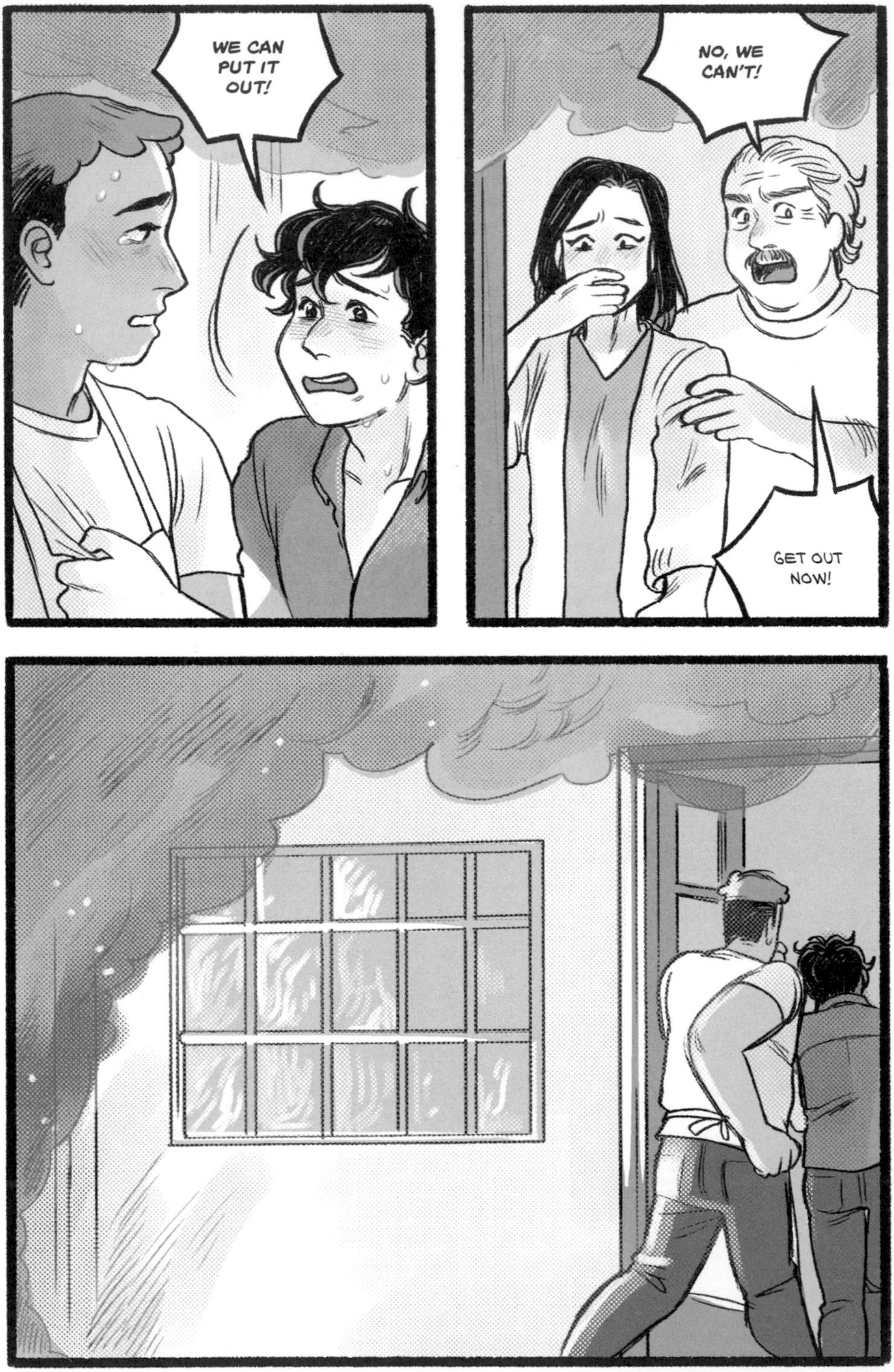
WE CAN PUT IT OUT!
NO, WE CAN'T!
GET OUT NOW!

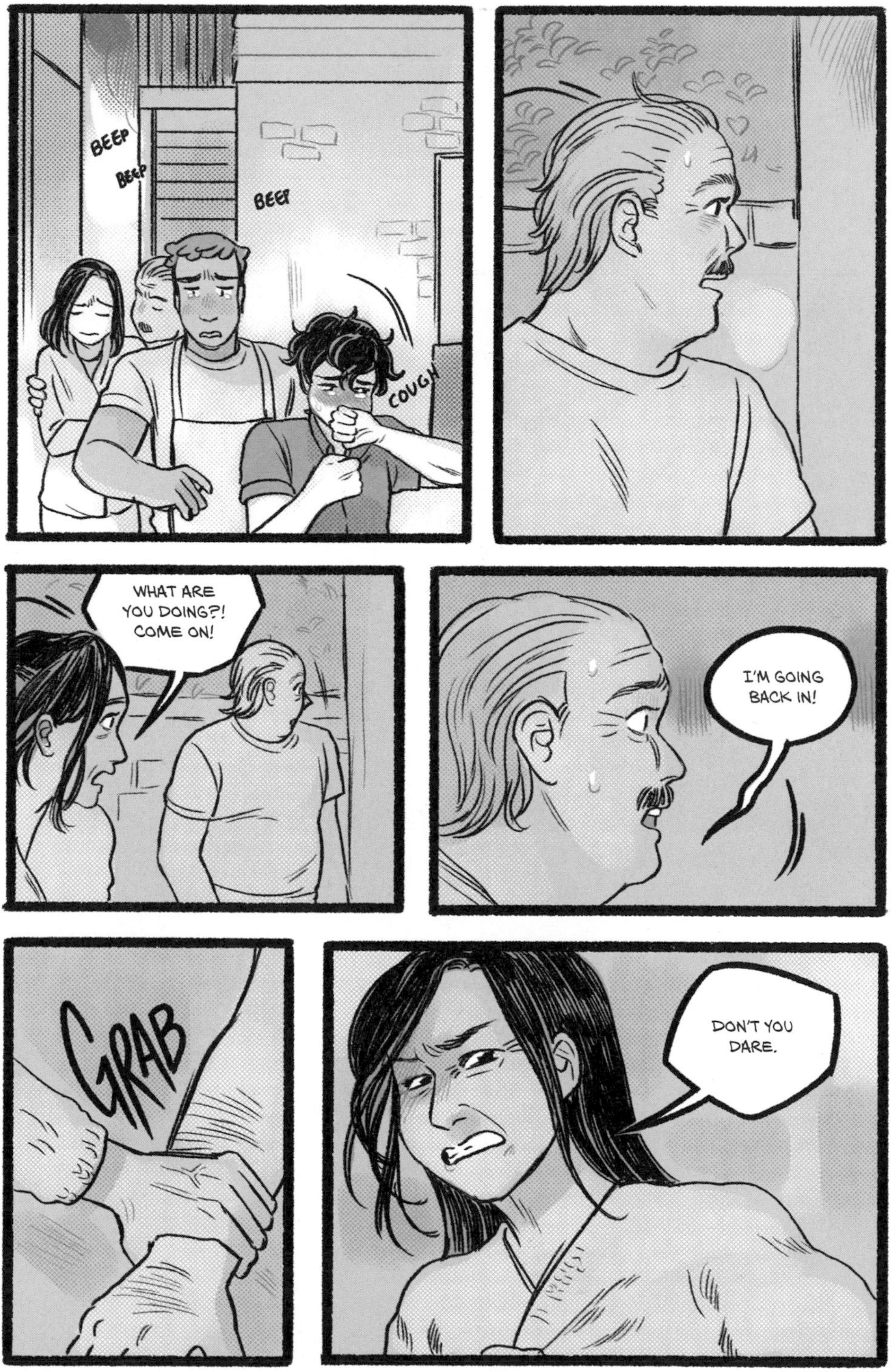
BEEP
BEEP
BEEP
COUGH
WHAT ARE YOU DOING?! COME ON!
I'M GOING BACK IN!
GRAB
DON'T YOU DARE.

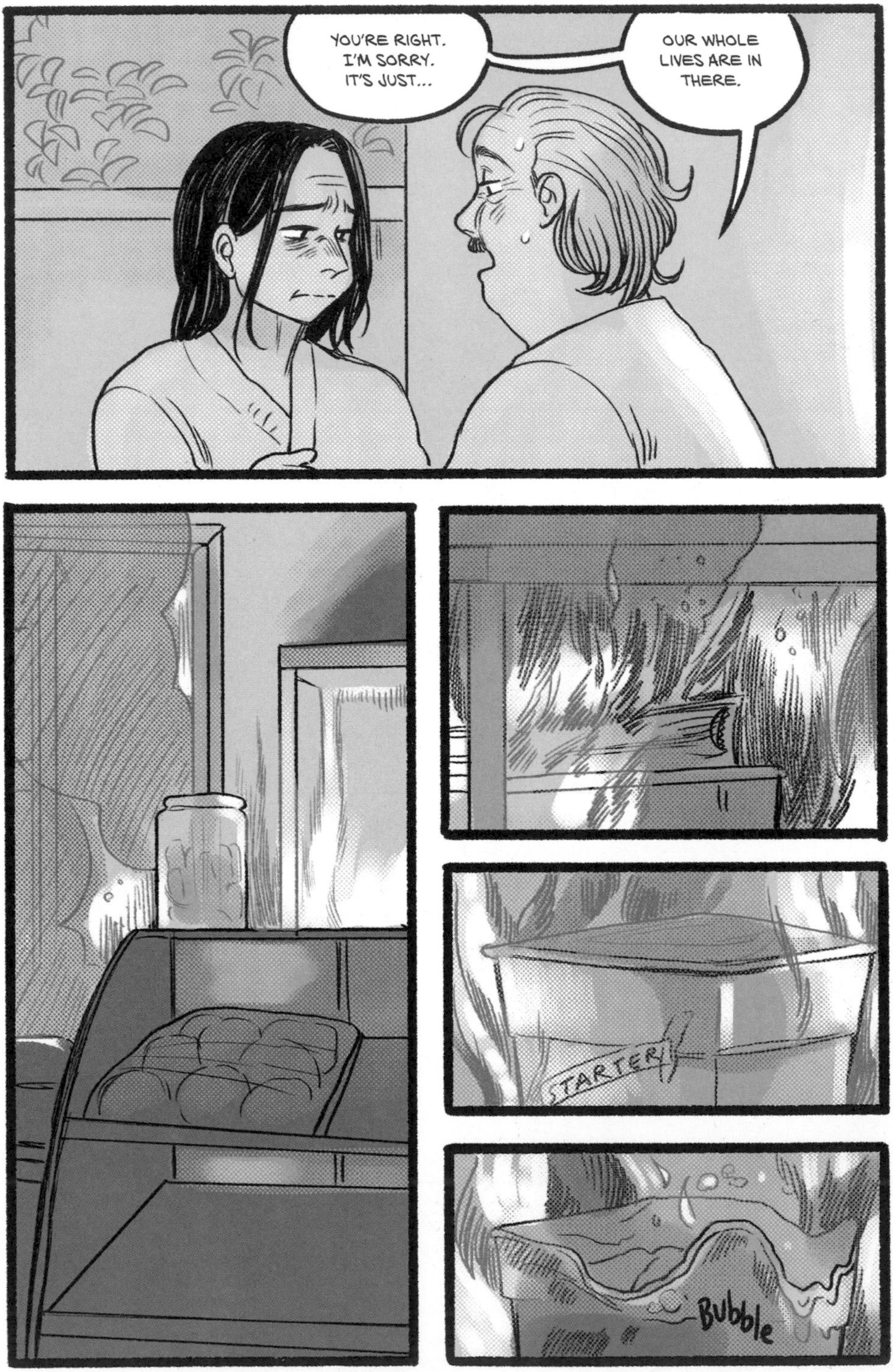
YOU'RE RIGHT. I'M SORRY. IT'S JUST...
OUR WHOLE LIVES ARE IN THERE.
STARTER
Bubble

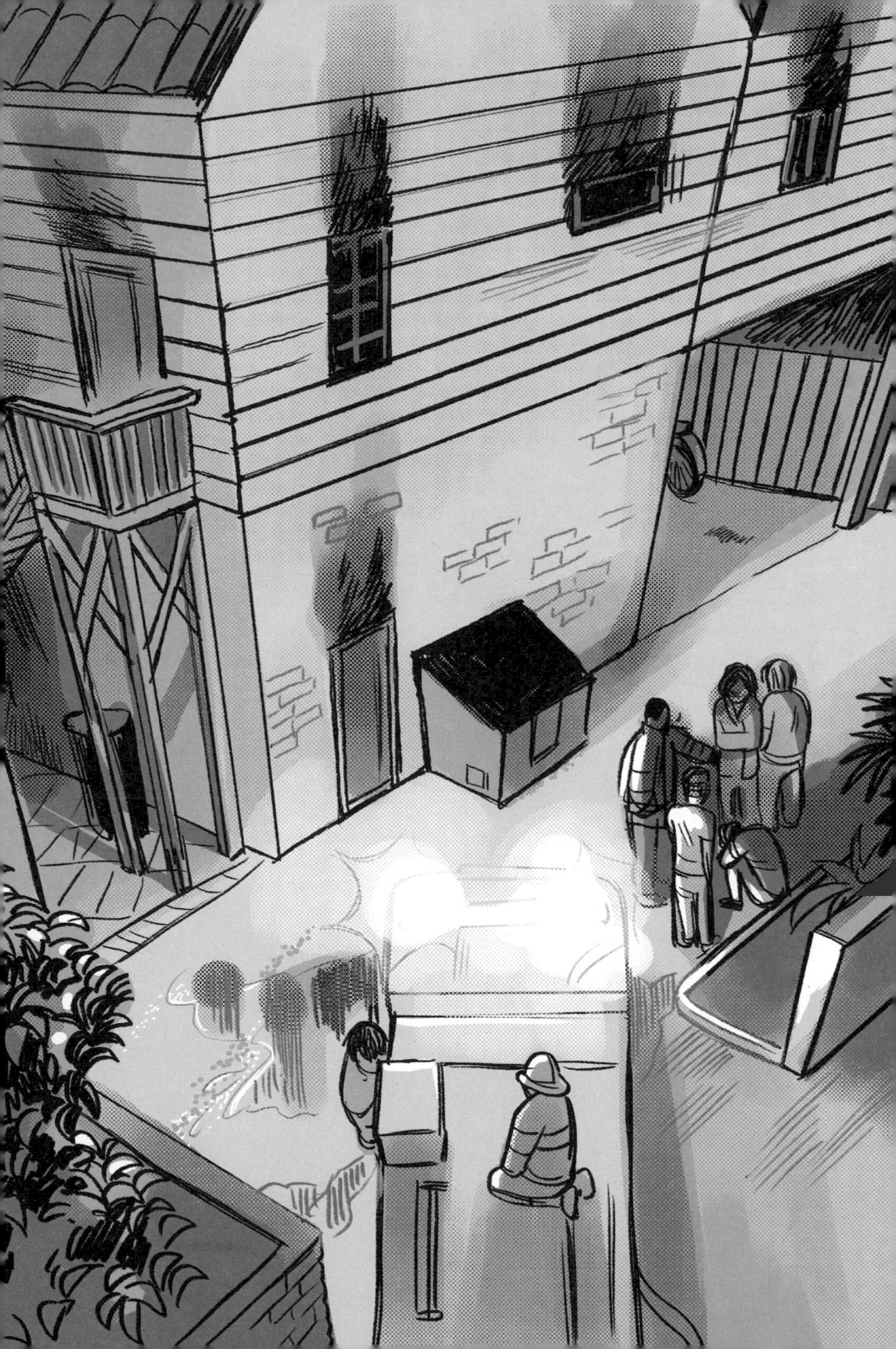

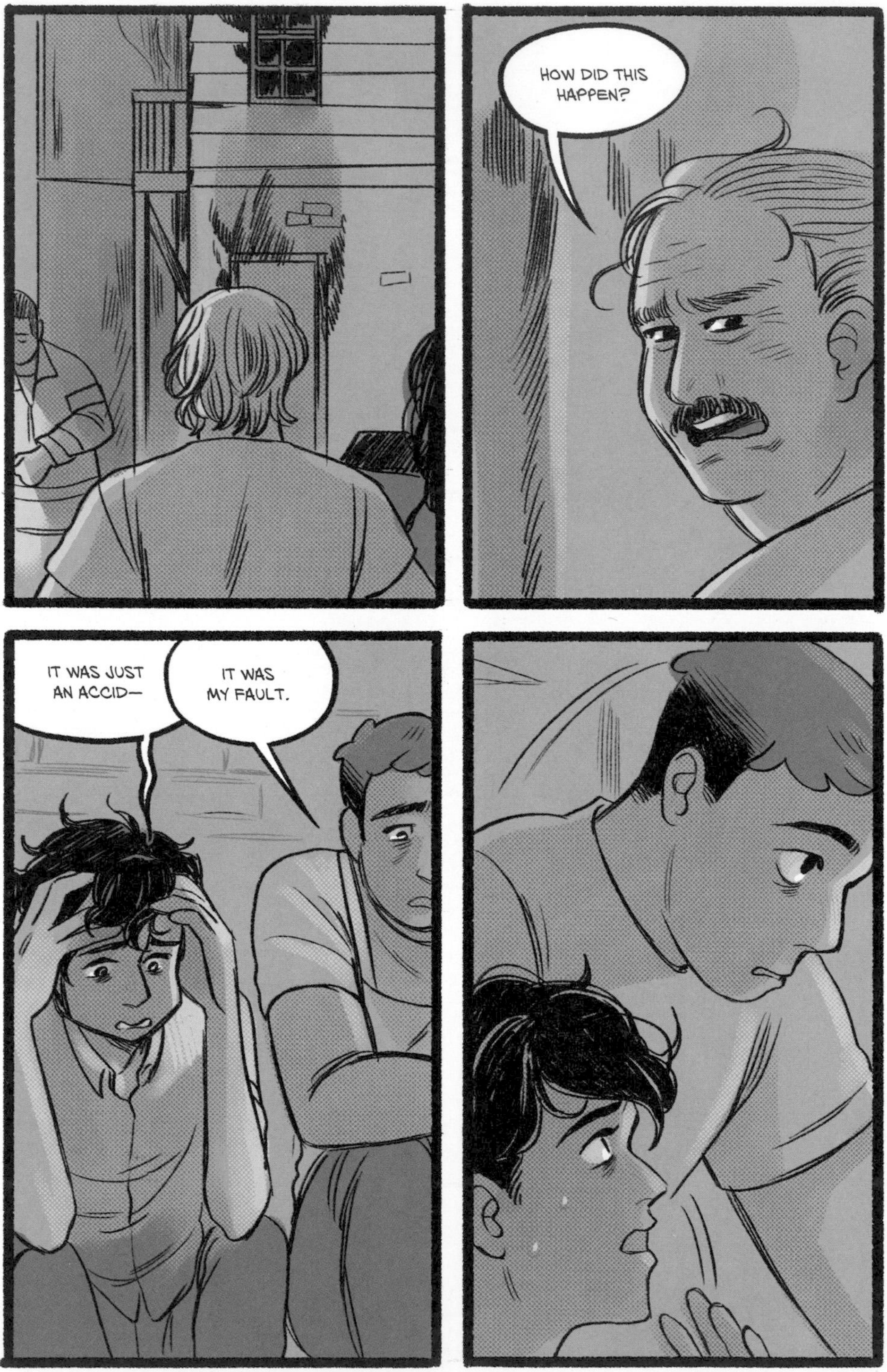
HOW DID THIS HAPPEN?
IT WAS JUST AN ACCID—
IT WAS MY FAULT.

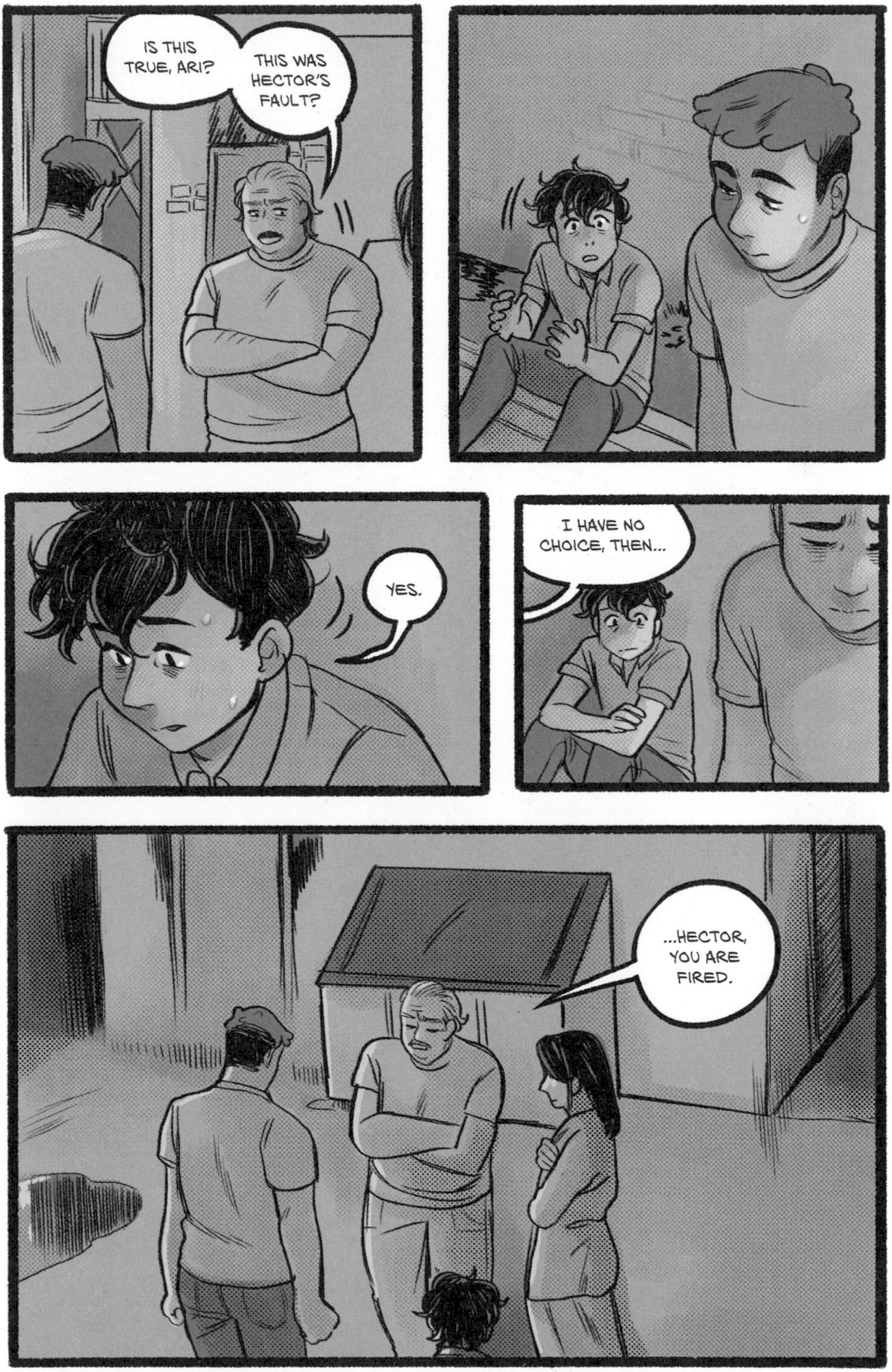
IS THIS TRUE, ARI?
THIS WAS HECTOR'S FAULT?
YES.
I HAVE NO CHOICE, THEN...
...HECTOR, YOU ARE FIRED.

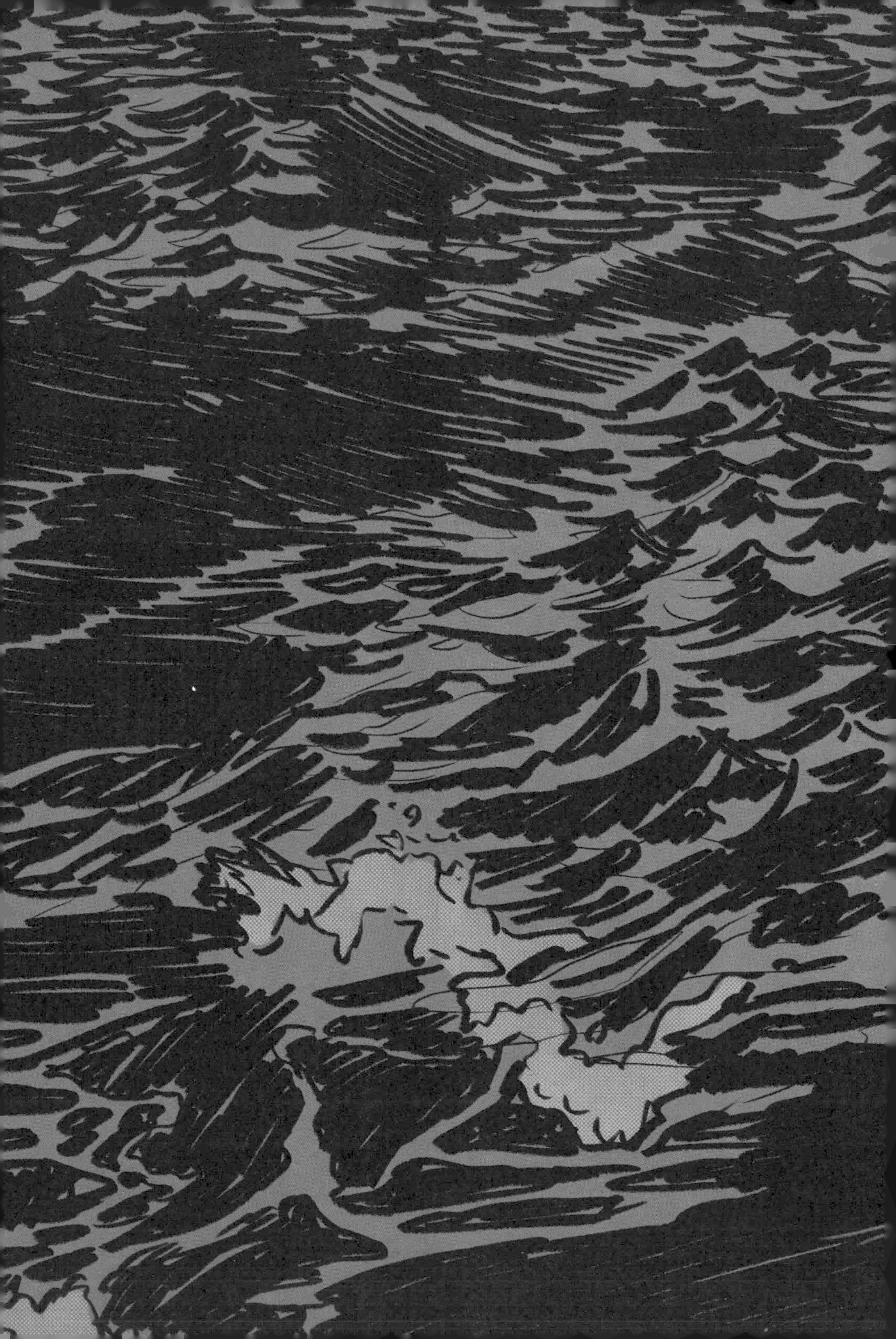

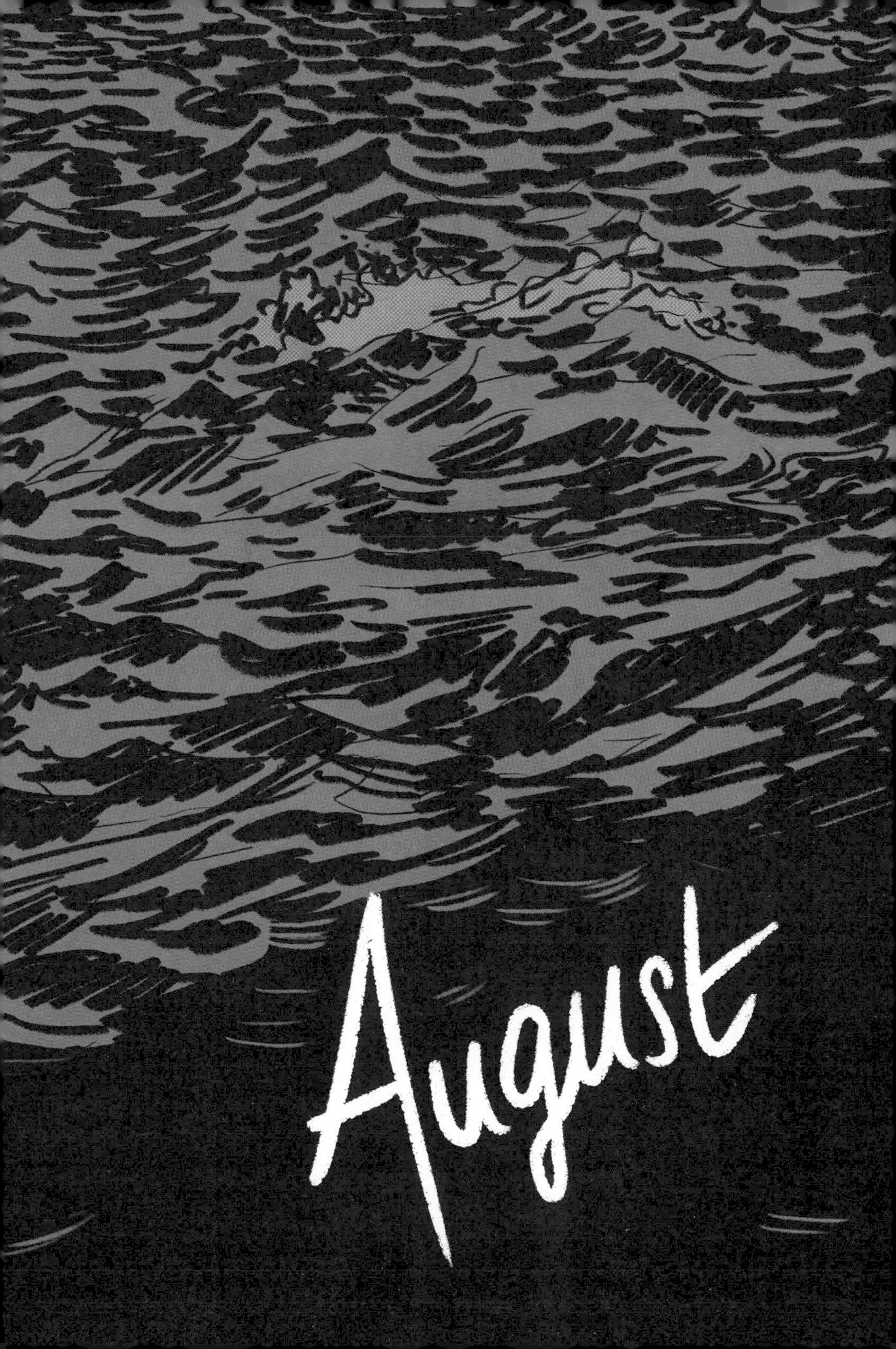
August

BARK
BARK

Weeeooo

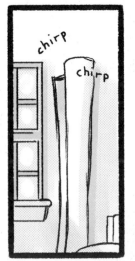

chirp

chirp

SMAK

WAKE UP,
DUDE.

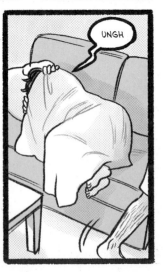

UNGH

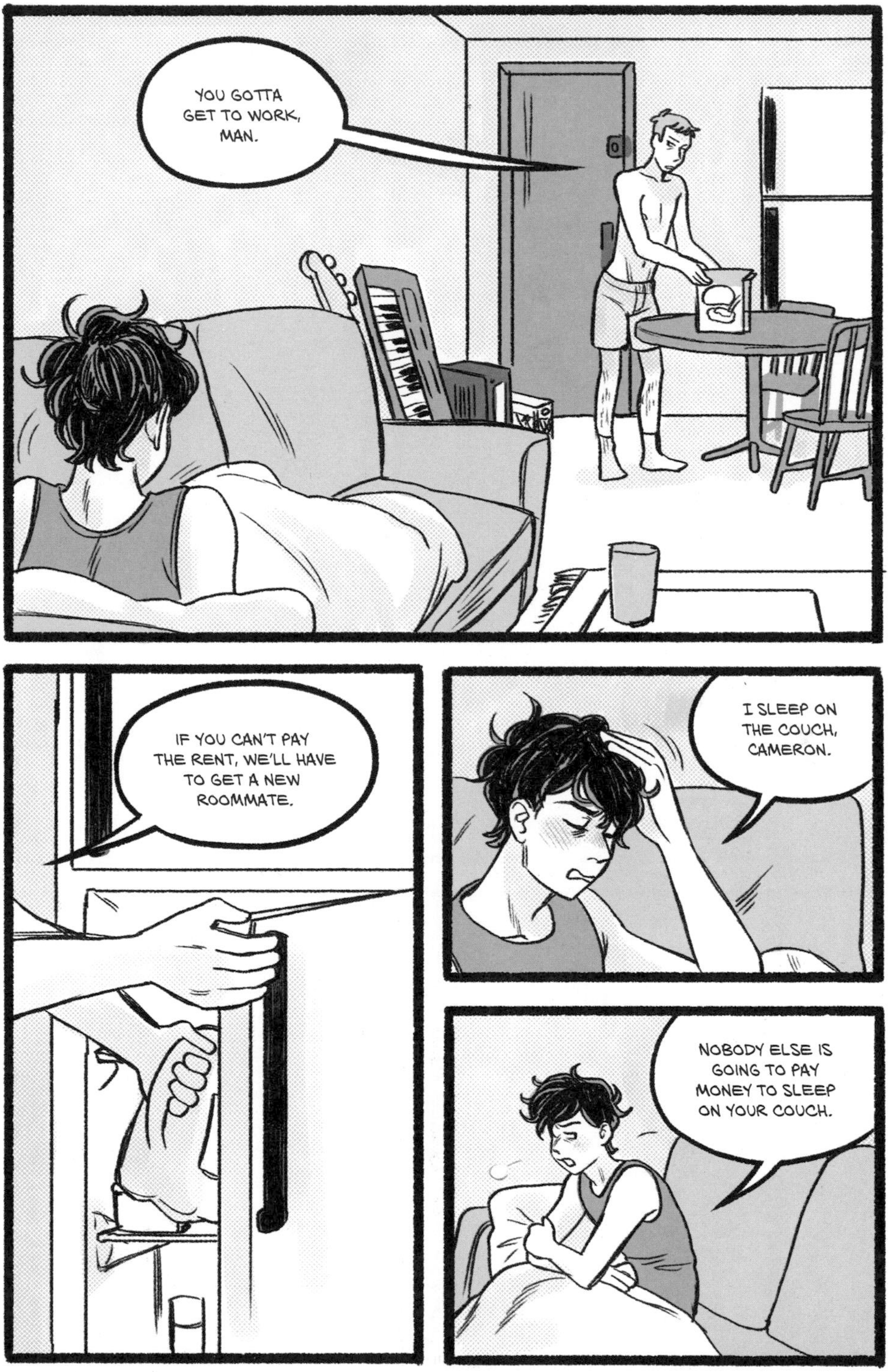
YOU GOTTA GET TO WORK, MAN.
IF YOU CAN'T PAY THE RENT, WE'LL HAVE TO GET A NEW ROOMMATE.
I SLEEP ON THE COUCH, CAMERON.
NOBODY ELSE IS GOING TO PAY MONEY TO SLEEP ON YOUR COUCH.

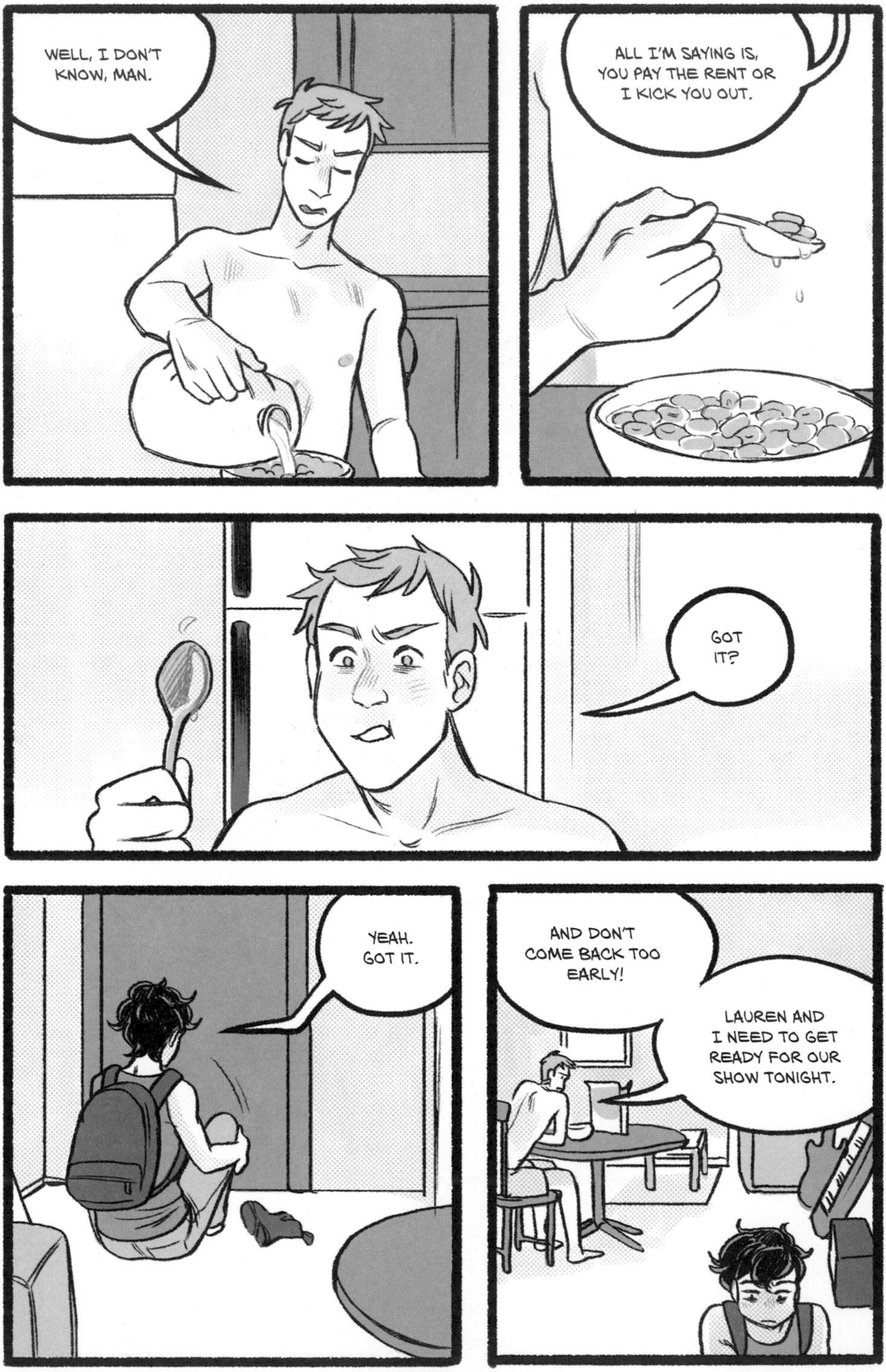
WELL, I DON'T KNOW, MAN.
ALL I'M SAYING IS, YOU PAY THE RENT OR I KICK YOU OUT.
GOT IT?
YEAH. GOT IT.
AND DON'T COME BACK TOO EARLY!
LAUREN AND I NEED TO GET READY FOR OUR SHOW TONIGHT.

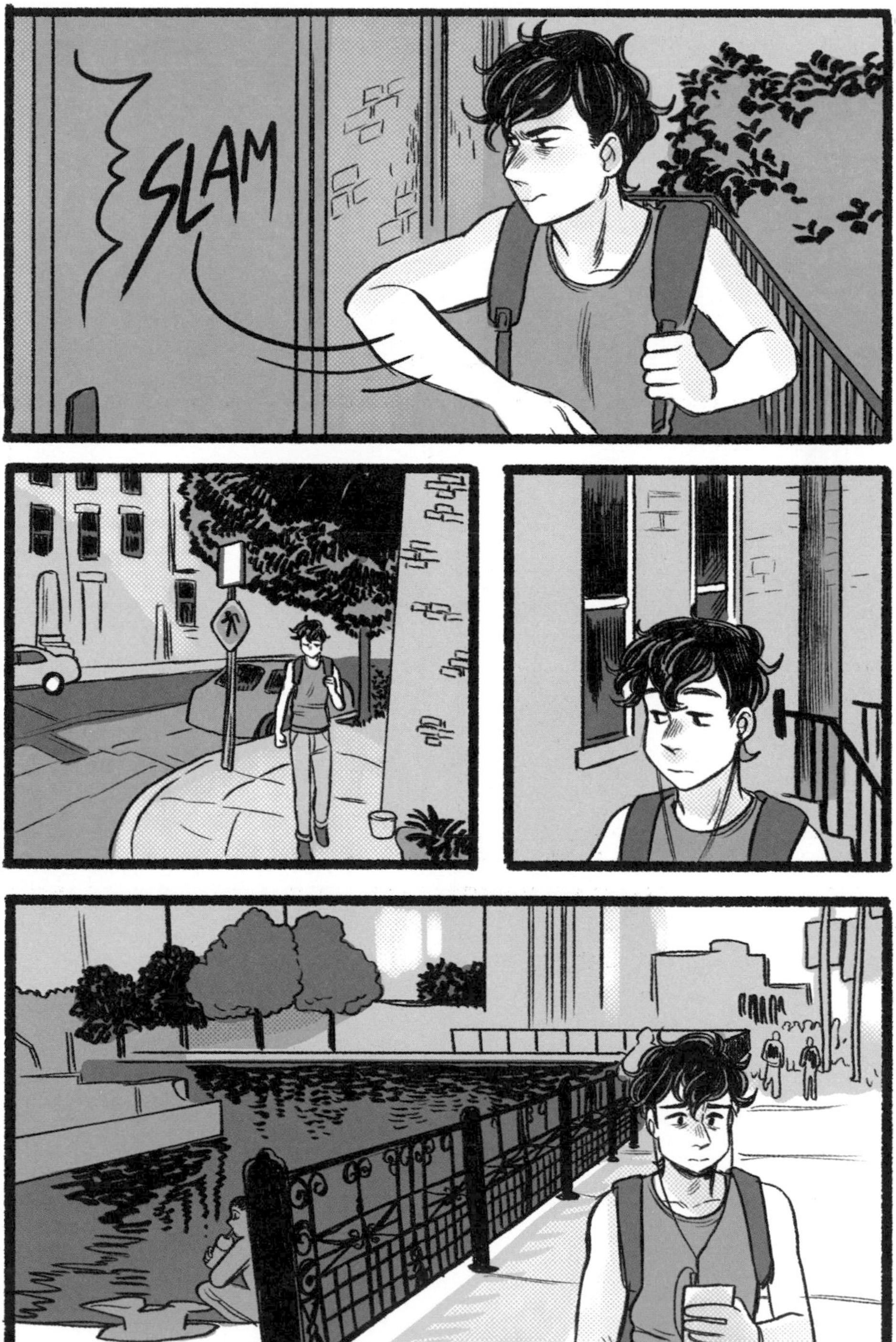
SLAM

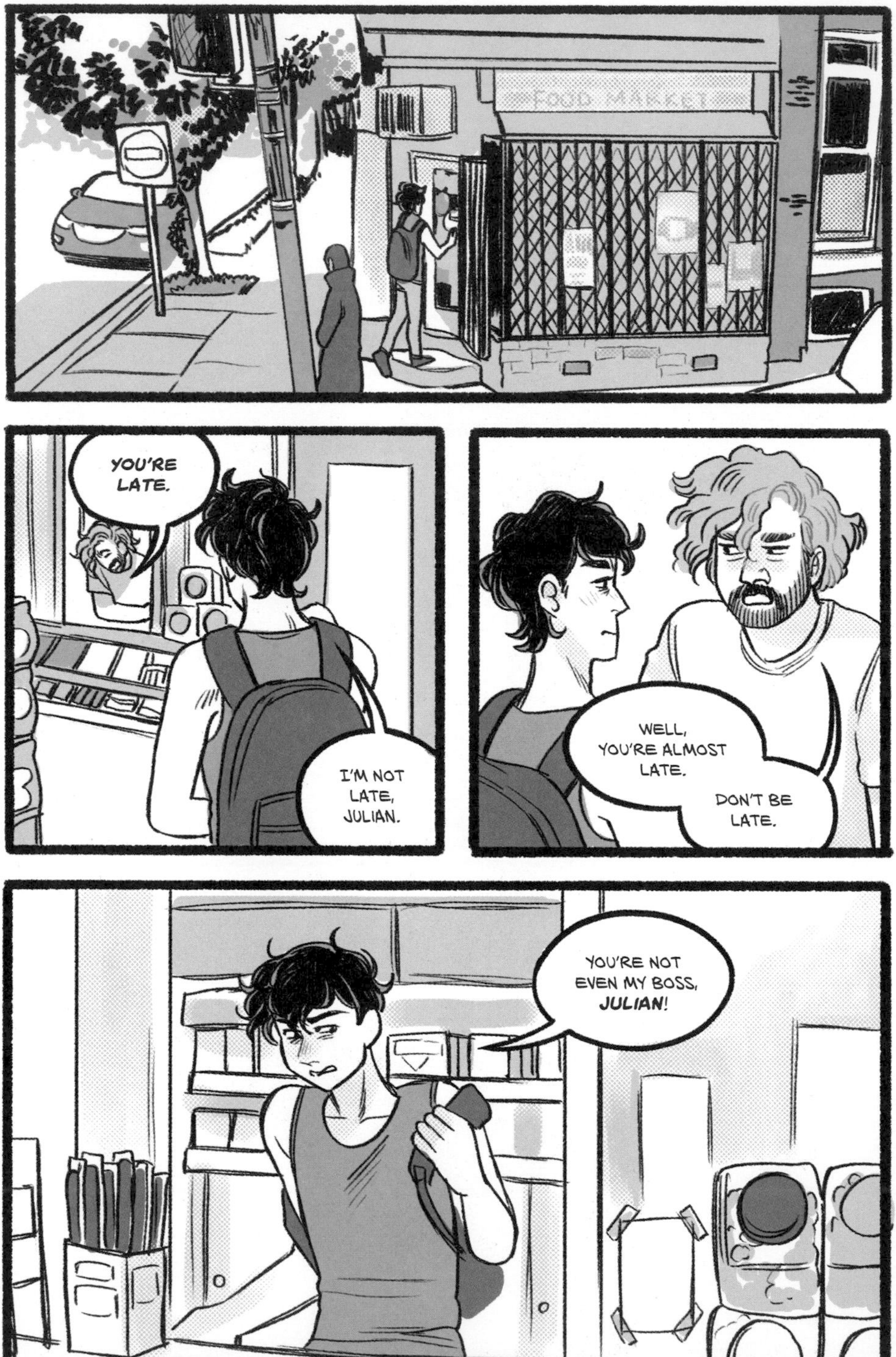
FOOD MARKET
YOU'RE LATE.
I'M NOT LATE, JULIAN.
WELL, YOU'RE ALMOST LATE.
DON'T BE LATE.
YOU'RE NOT EVEN MY BOSS, **JULIAN**!

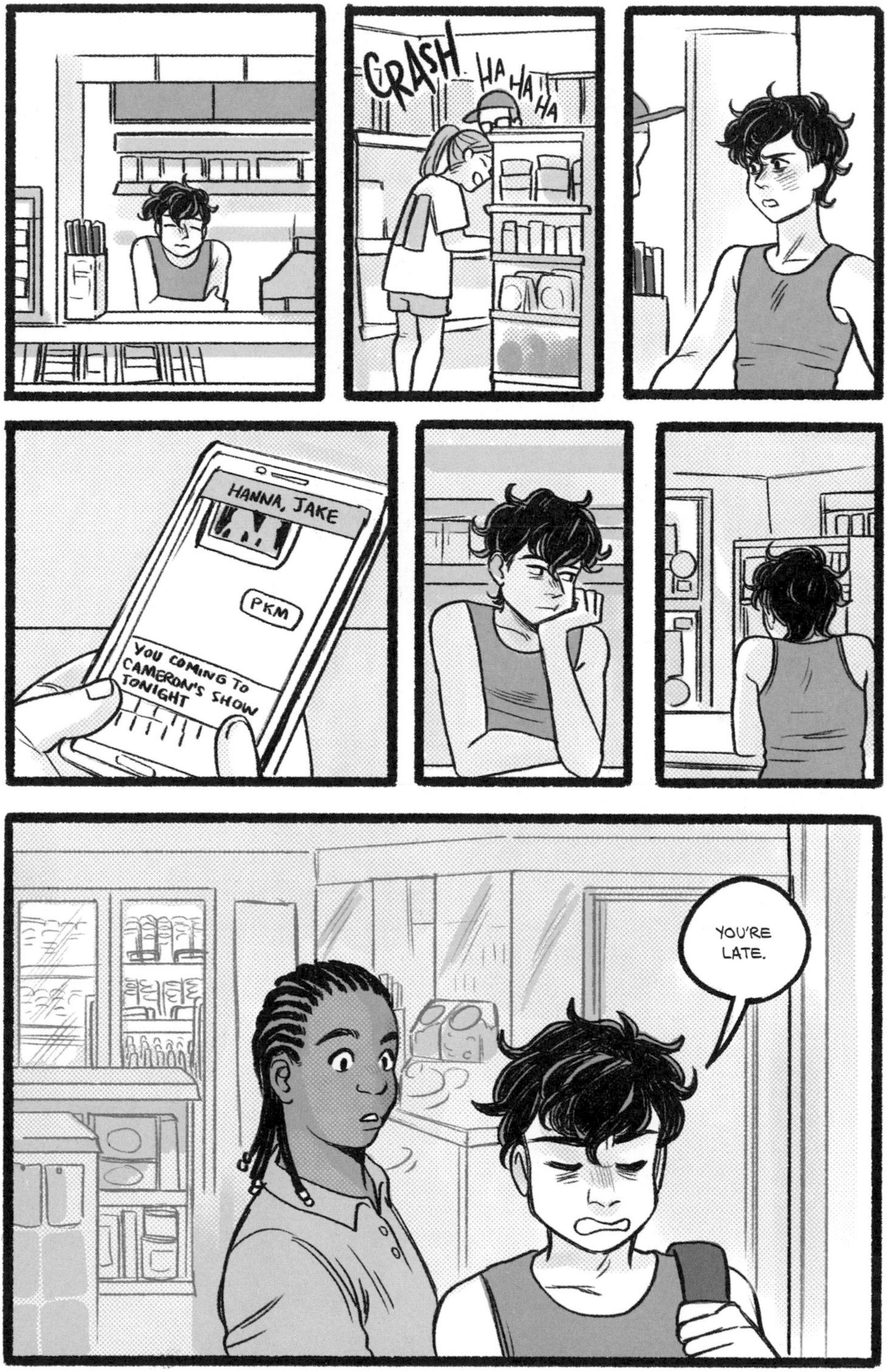
CRASH
HA HA HA
HANNA, JAKE
PKM
YOU COMING TO CAMERON'S SHOW TONIGHT
YOU'RE LATE.

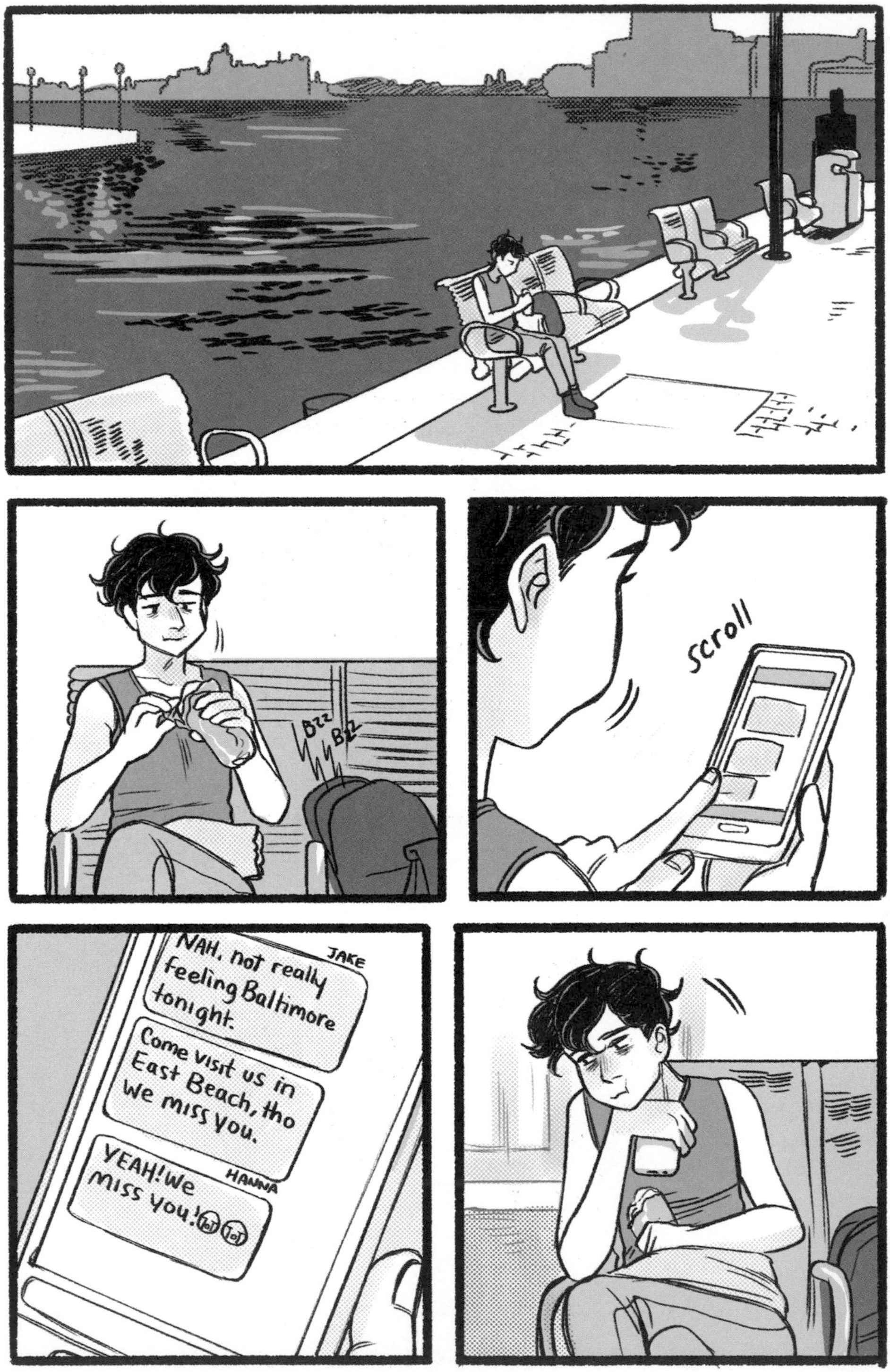
Bzz
Bzz
Scroll
JAKE
NAH, not really feeling Baltimore tonight.
Come visit us in East Beach, tho we miss you.
HANNA
YEAH! We miss you!

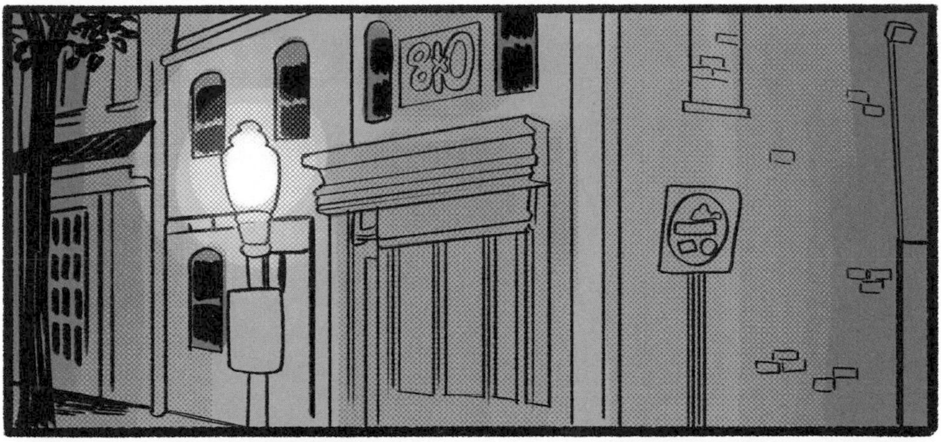

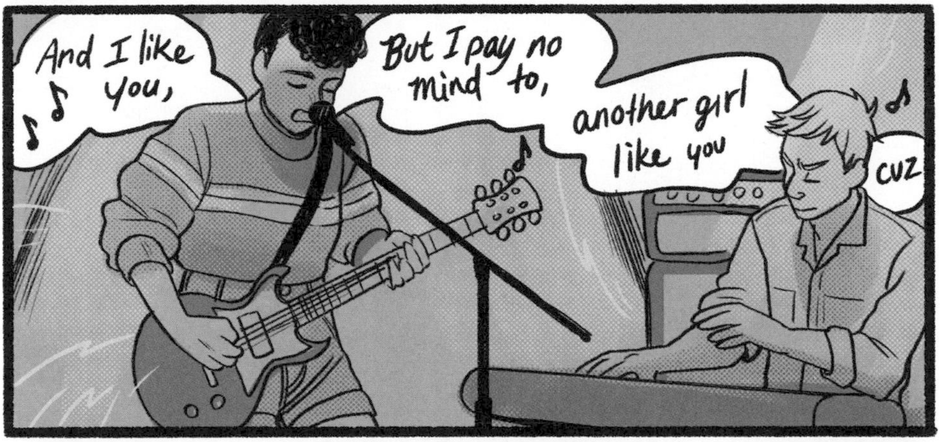
And I like you,
But I pay no mind to,
another girl like you
CUZ

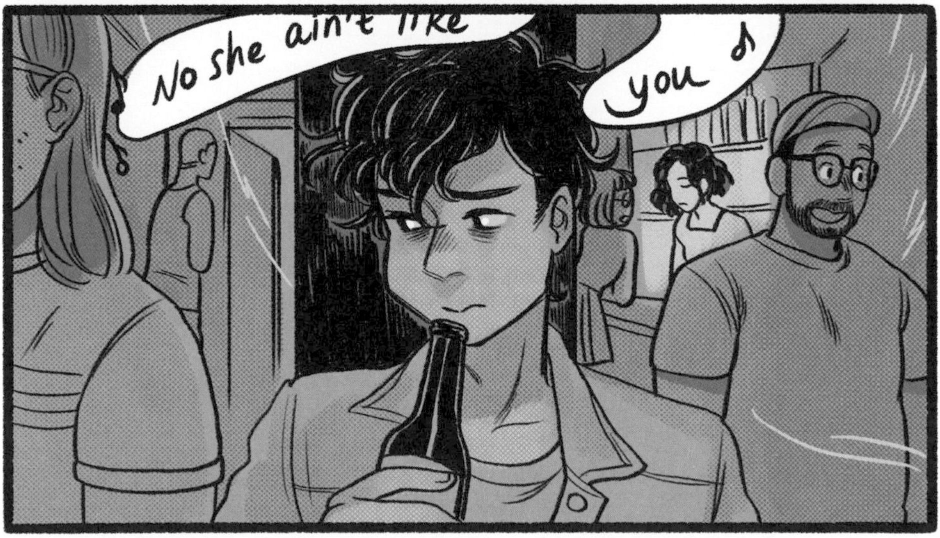
No she ain't like
you

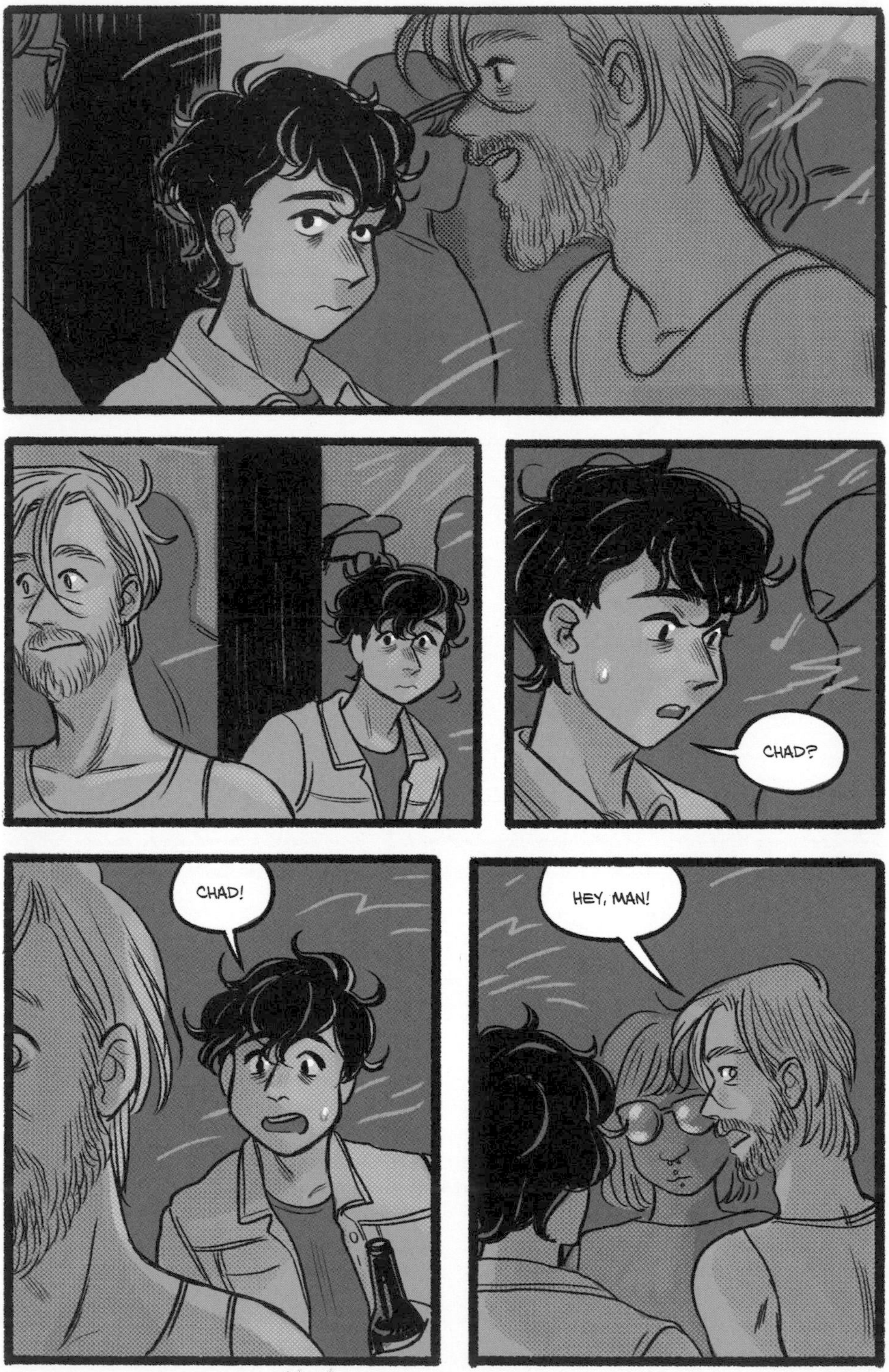
CHAD?
CHAD!
HEY, MAN!

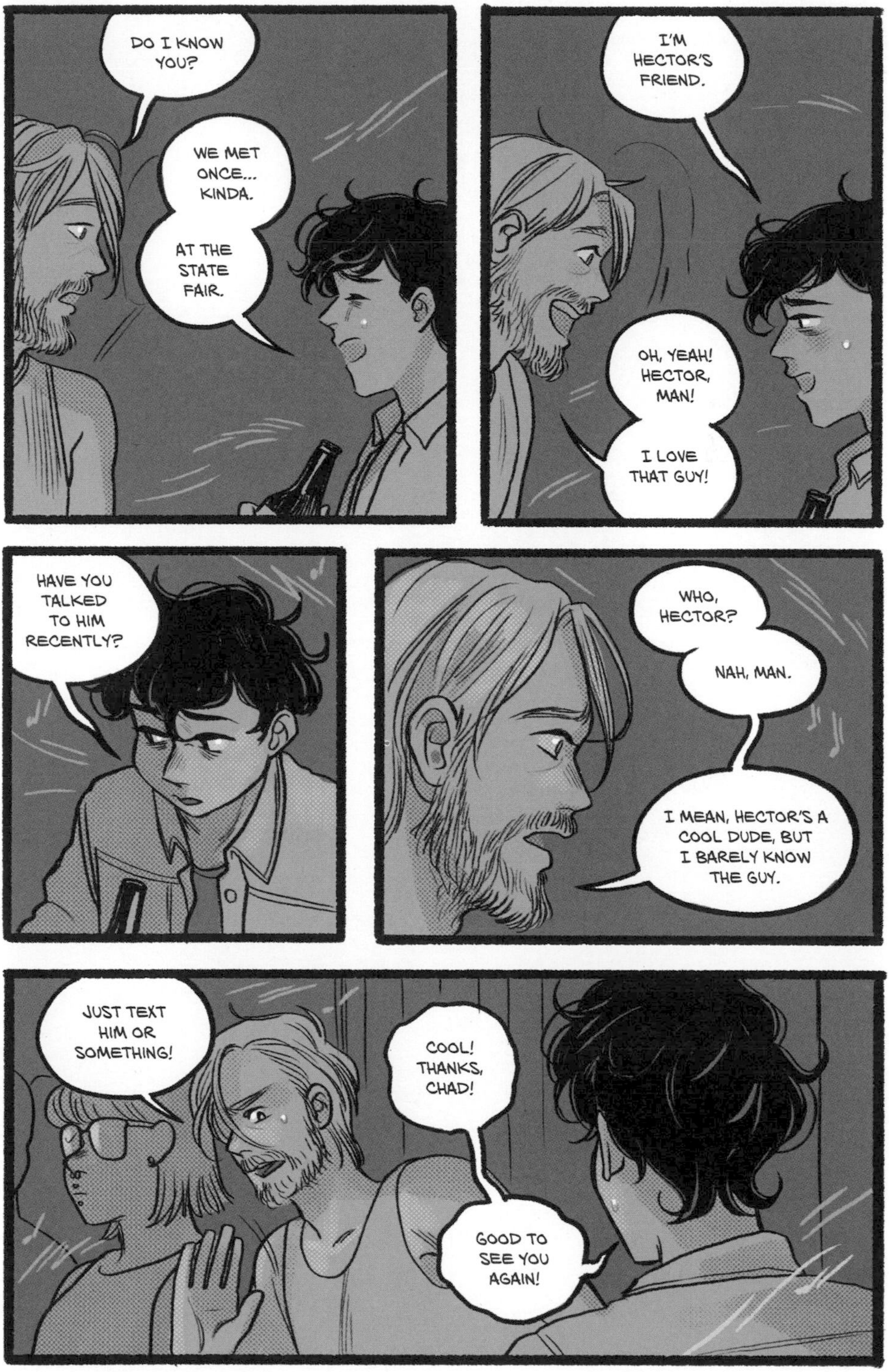
DO I KNOW YOU?
WE MET ONCE... KINDA.
AT THE STATE FAIR.
I'M HECTOR'S FRIEND.
OH, YEAH! HECTOR, MAN!
I LOVE THAT GUY!
HAVE YOU TALKED TO HIM RECENTLY?
WHO, HECTOR?
NAH, MAN.
I MEAN, HECTOR'S A COOL DUDE, BUT I BARELY KNOW THE GUY.
JUST TEXT HIM OR SOMETHING!
COOL! THANKS, CHAD!
GOOD TO SEE YOU AGAIN!

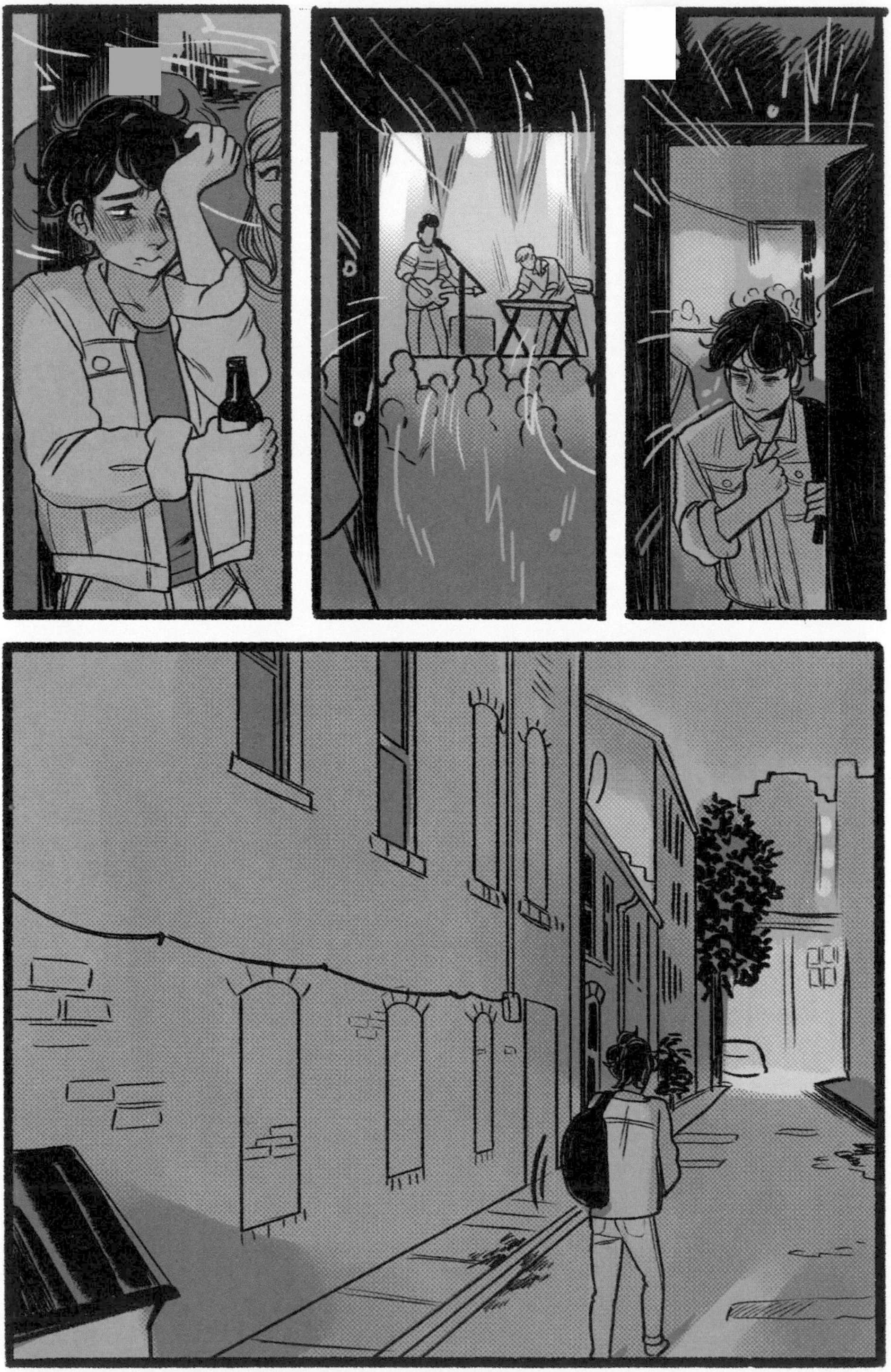

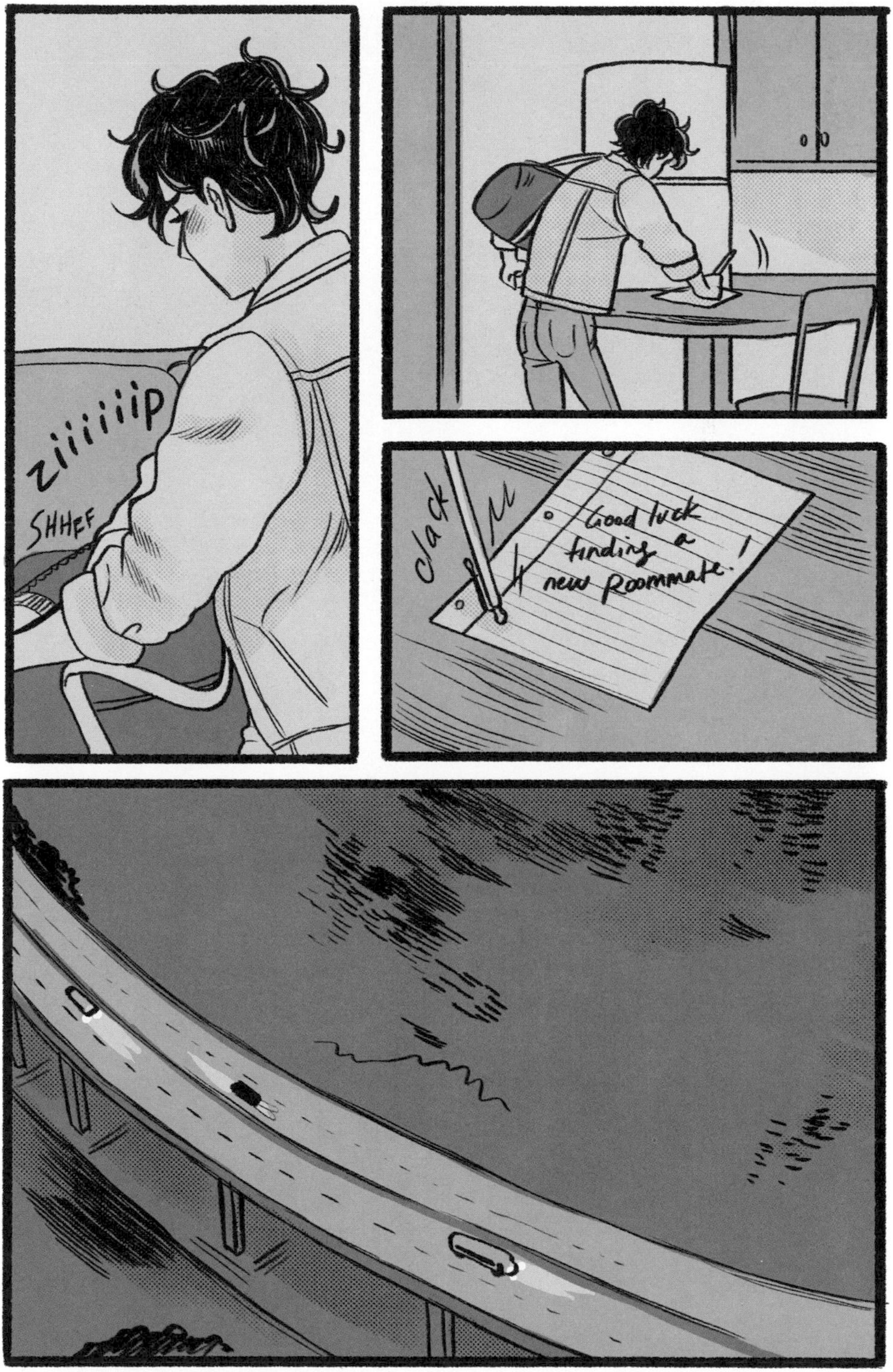
ziiiiiip
SHHEF
clack
Good luck finding a new Roommate!

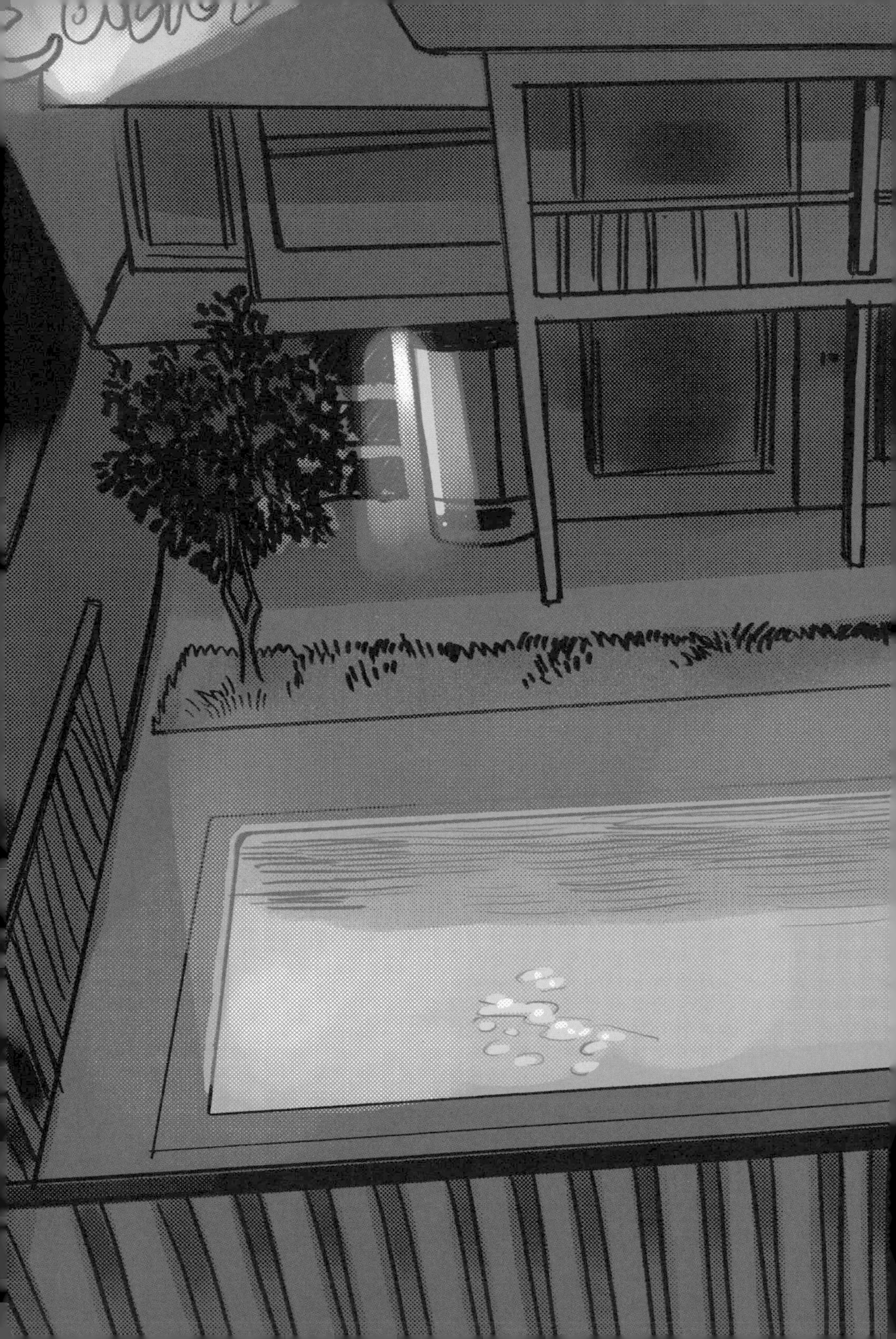

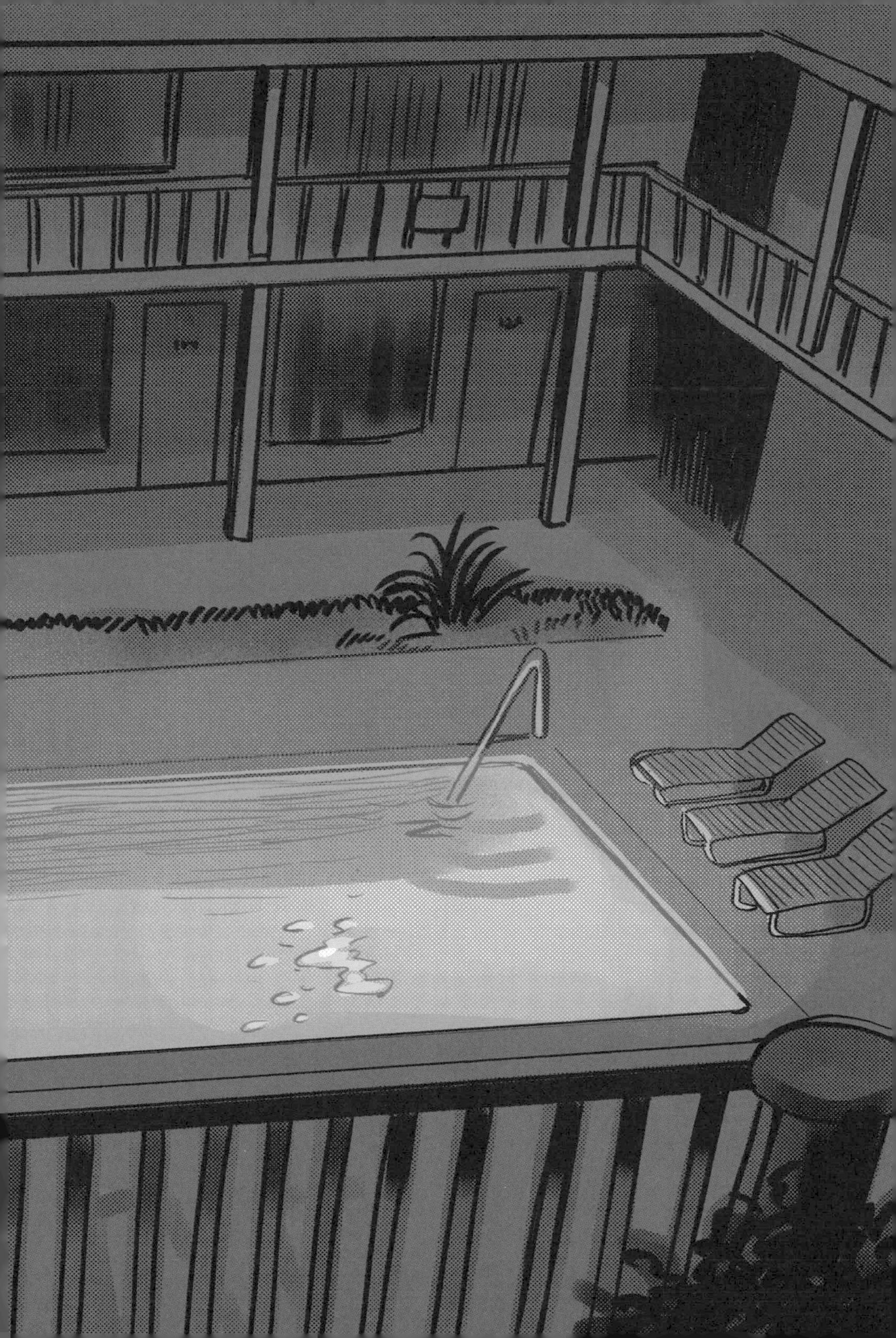

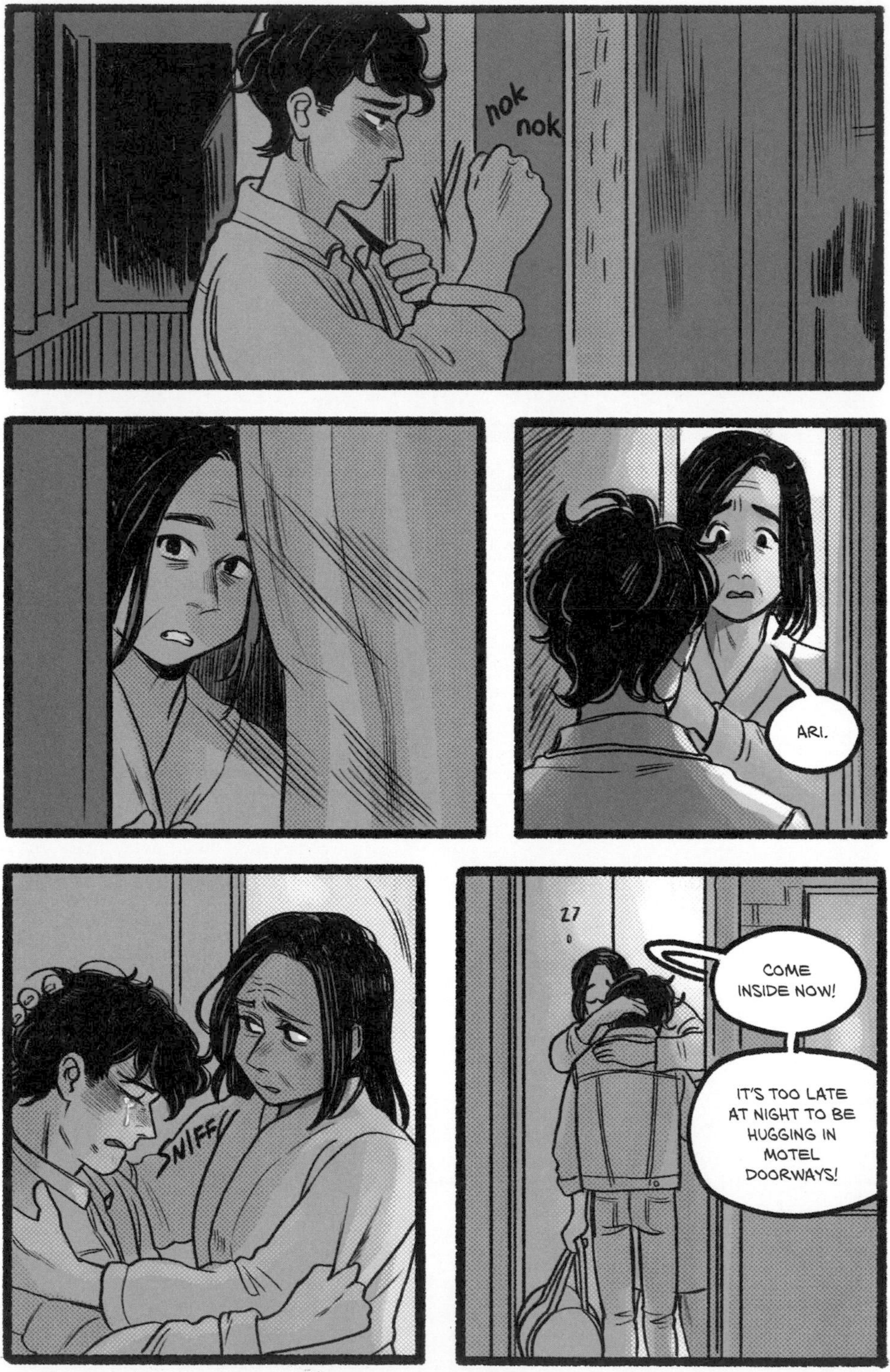
nok nok
ARI.
SNIFF
COME INSIDE NOW!
IT'S TOO LATE AT NIGHT TO BE HUGGING IN MOTEL DOORWAYS!

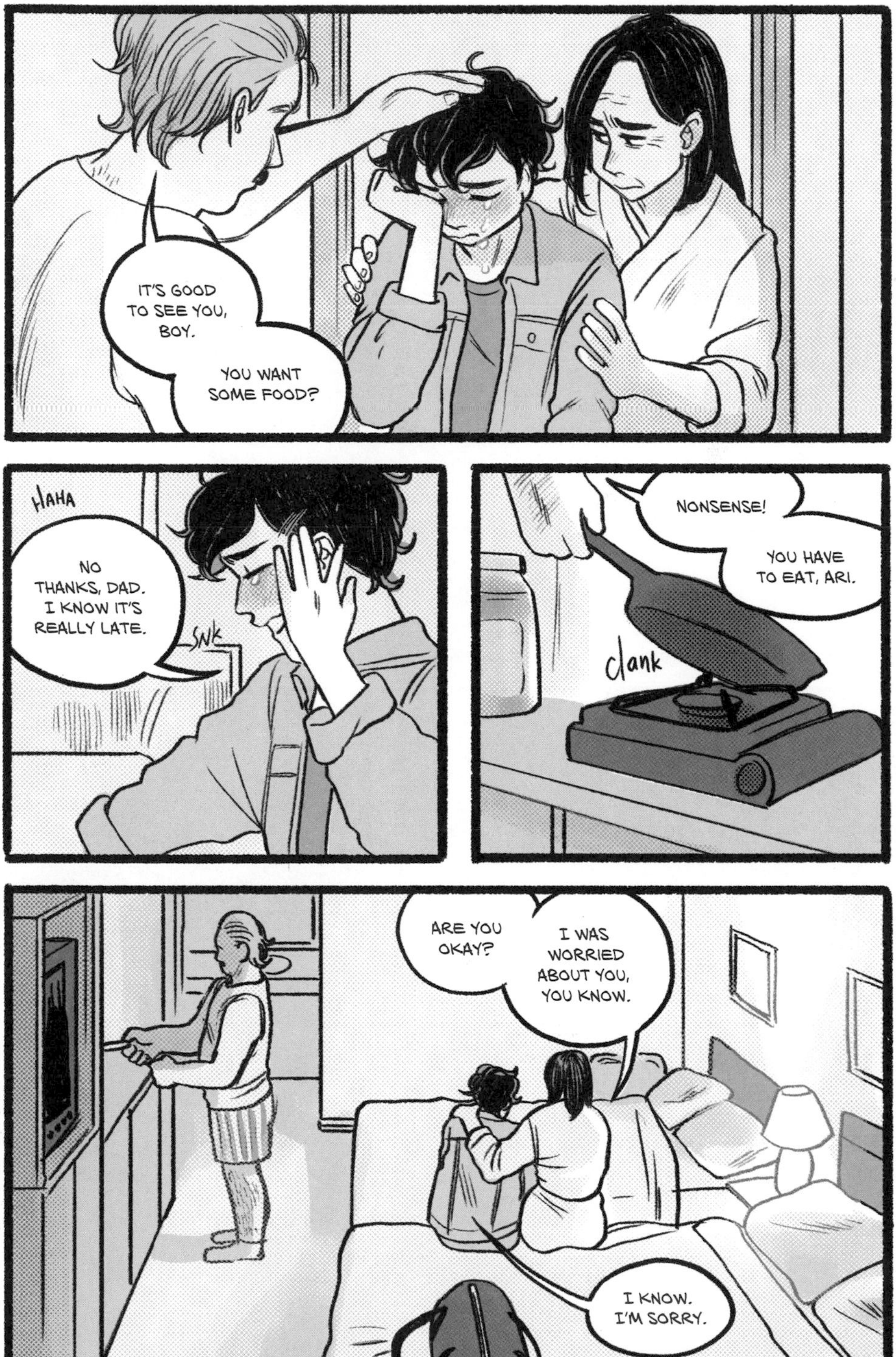
IT'S GOOD TO SEE YOU, BOY.
YOU WANT SOME FOOD?
HAHA
NO THANKS, DAD. I KNOW IT'S REALLY LATE.
SNK
NONSENSE!
YOU HAVE TO EAT, ARI.
clank
ARE YOU OKAY?
I WAS WORRIED ABOUT YOU, YOU KNOW.
I KNOW. I'M SORRY.

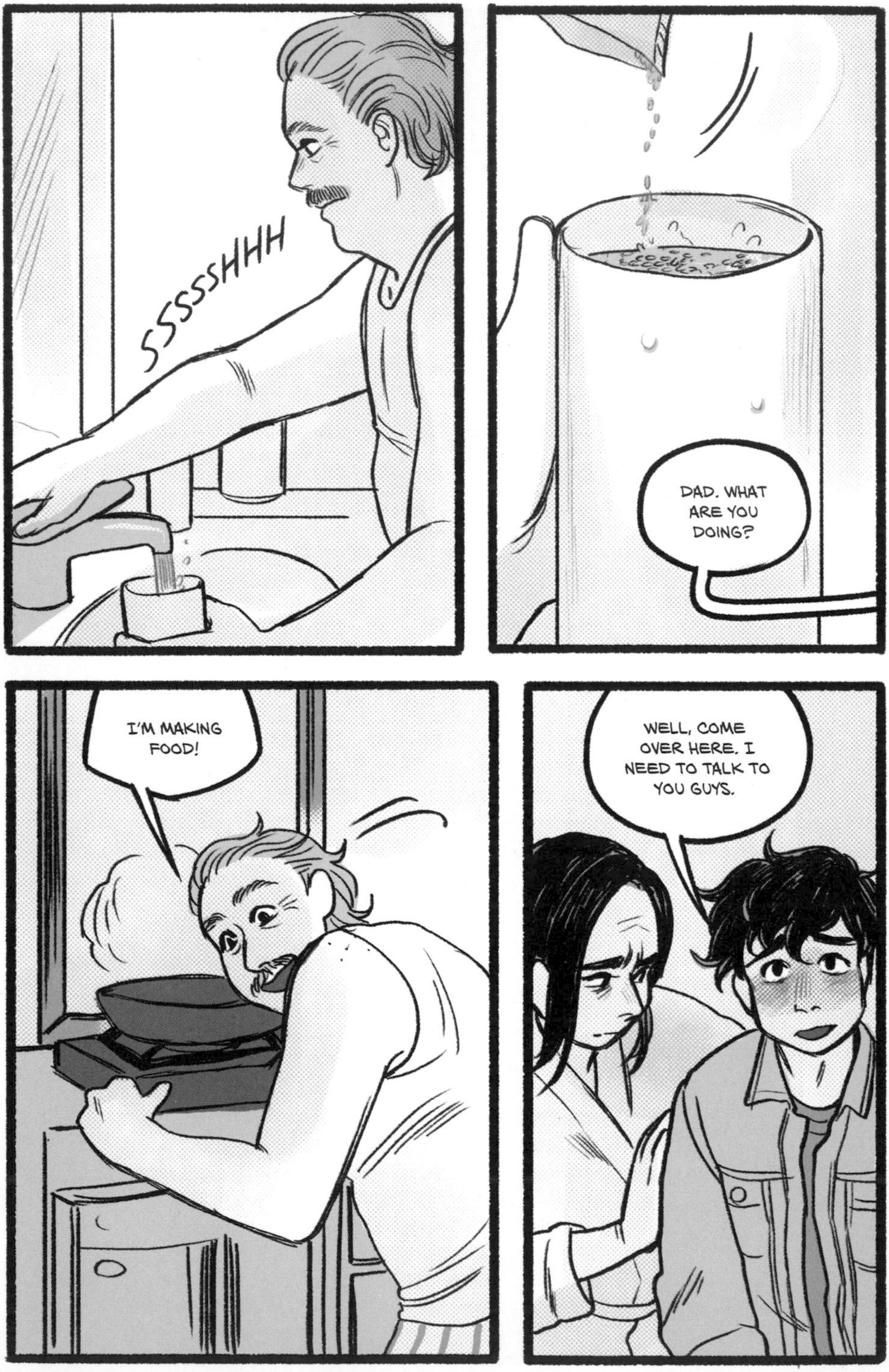
SSSSHHH
DAD. WHAT ARE YOU DOING?
I'M MAKING FOOD!
WELL, COME OVER HERE. I NEED TO TALK TO YOU GUYS.

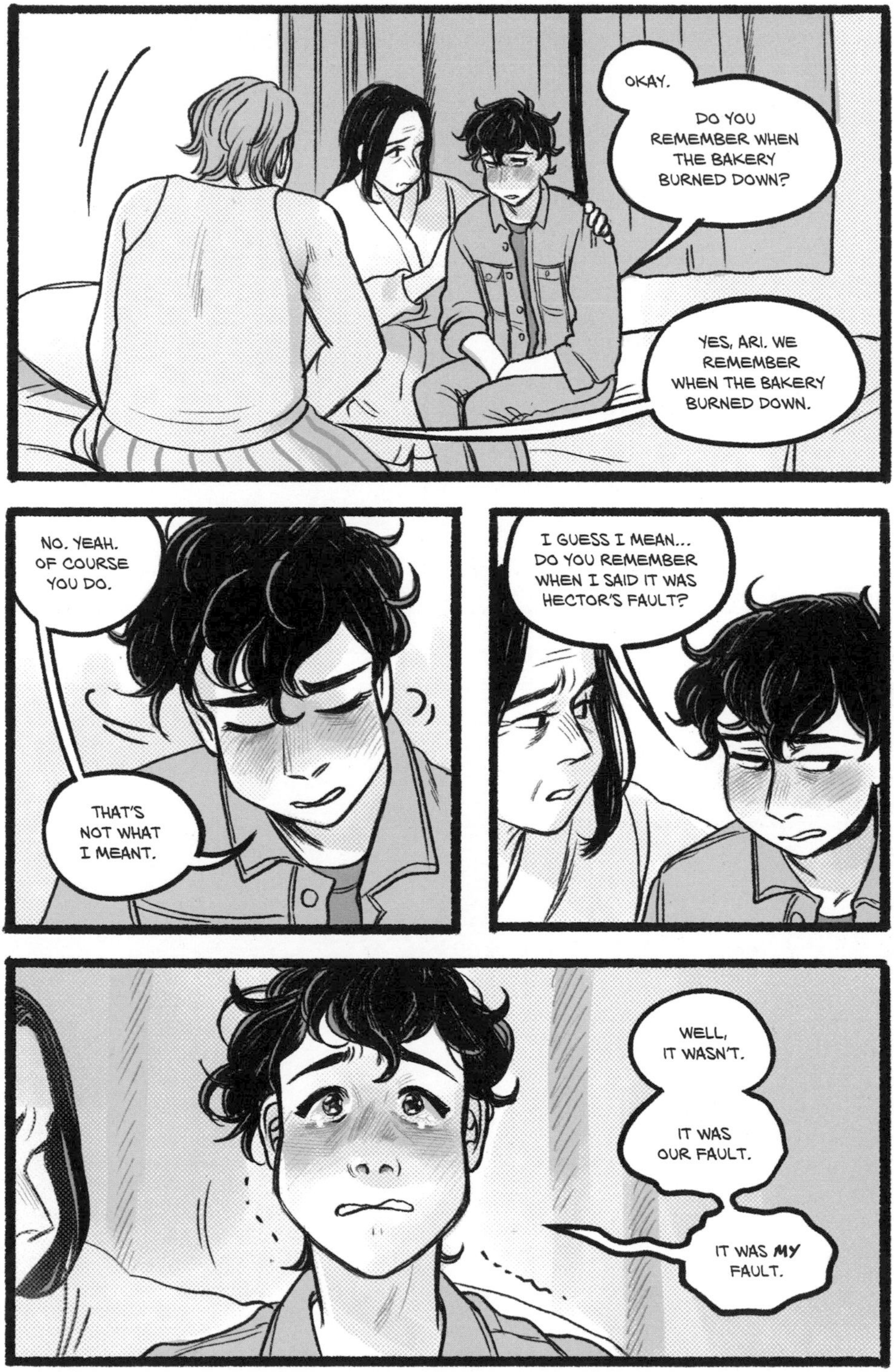
OKAY.
DO YOU REMEMBER WHEN THE BAKERY BURNED DOWN?
YES, ARI. WE REMEMBER WHEN THE BAKERY BURNED DOWN.
NO. YEAH. OF COURSE YOU DO.
THAT'S NOT WHAT I MEANT.
I GUESS I MEAN... DO YOU REMEMBER WHEN I SAID IT WAS HECTOR'S FAULT?
WELL, IT WASN'T.
IT WAS OUR FAULT.
IT WAS **MY** FAULT.

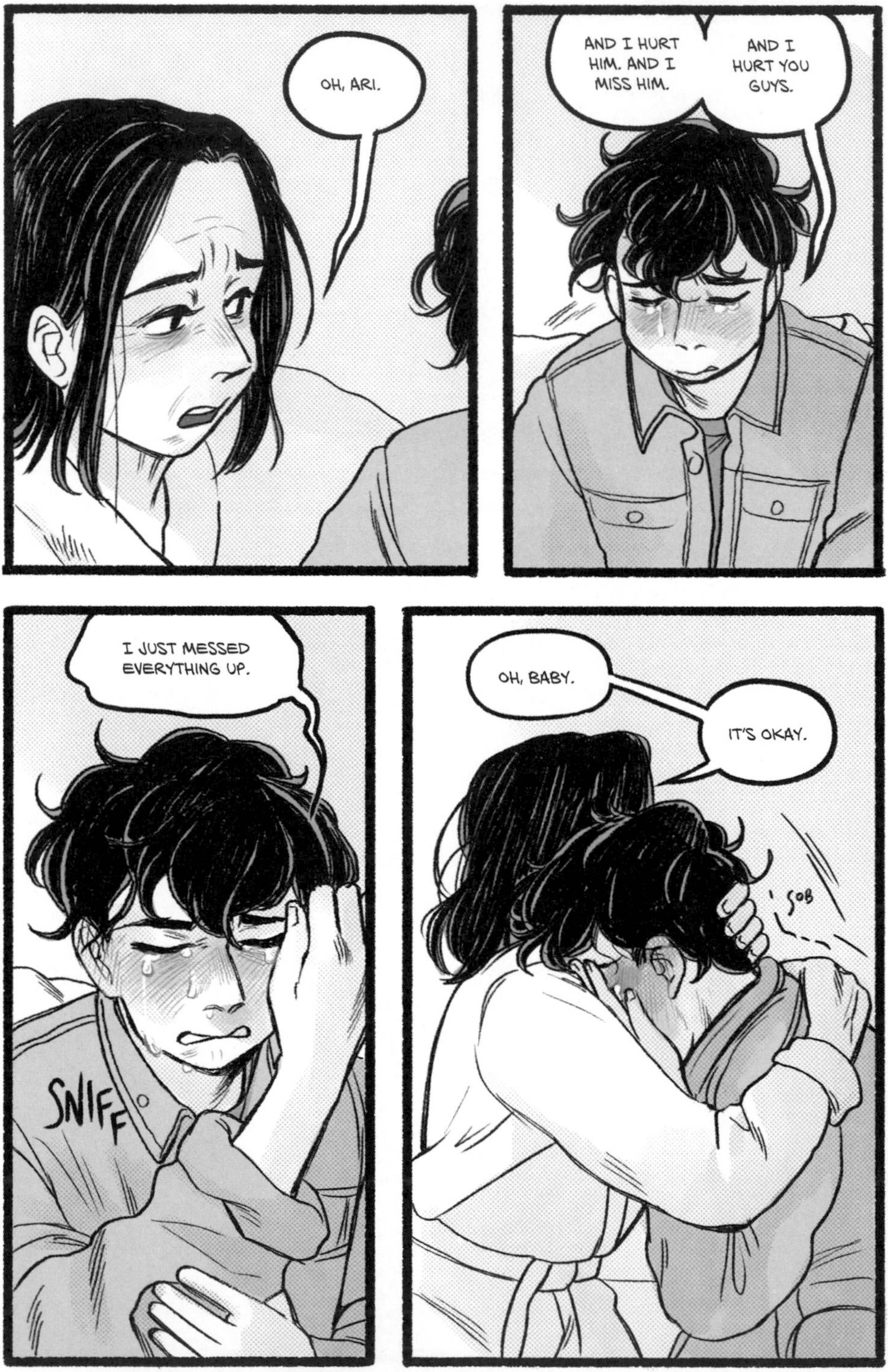
OH, ARI.
AND I HURT HIM. AND I MISS HIM.
AND I HURT YOU GUYS.
I JUST MESSED EVERYTHING UP.
SNIFF
OH, BABY.
IT'S OKAY.
SOB

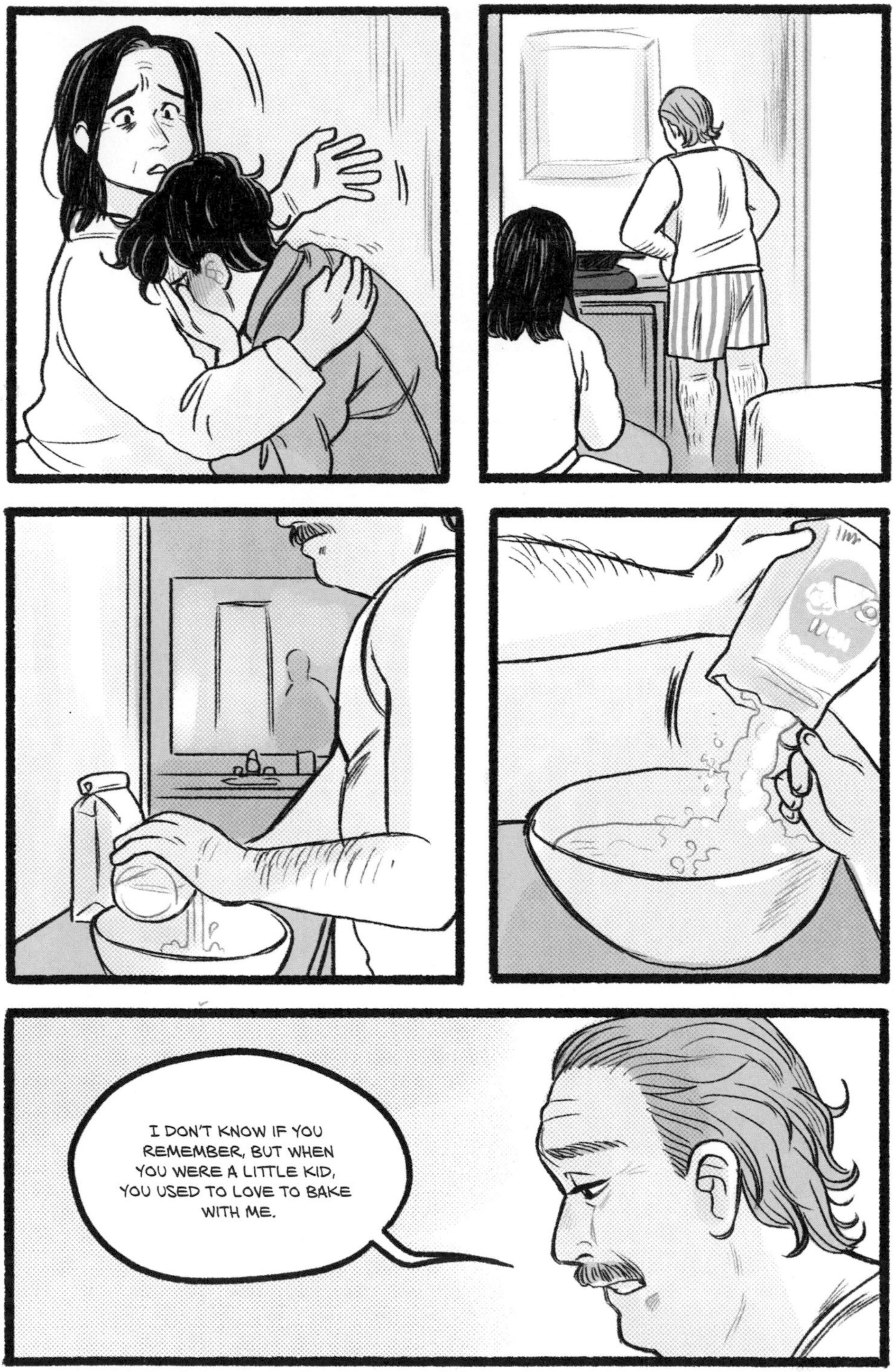
I DON'T KNOW IF YOU REMEMBER, BUT WHEN YOU WERE A LITTLE KID, YOU USED TO LOVE TO BAKE WITH ME.

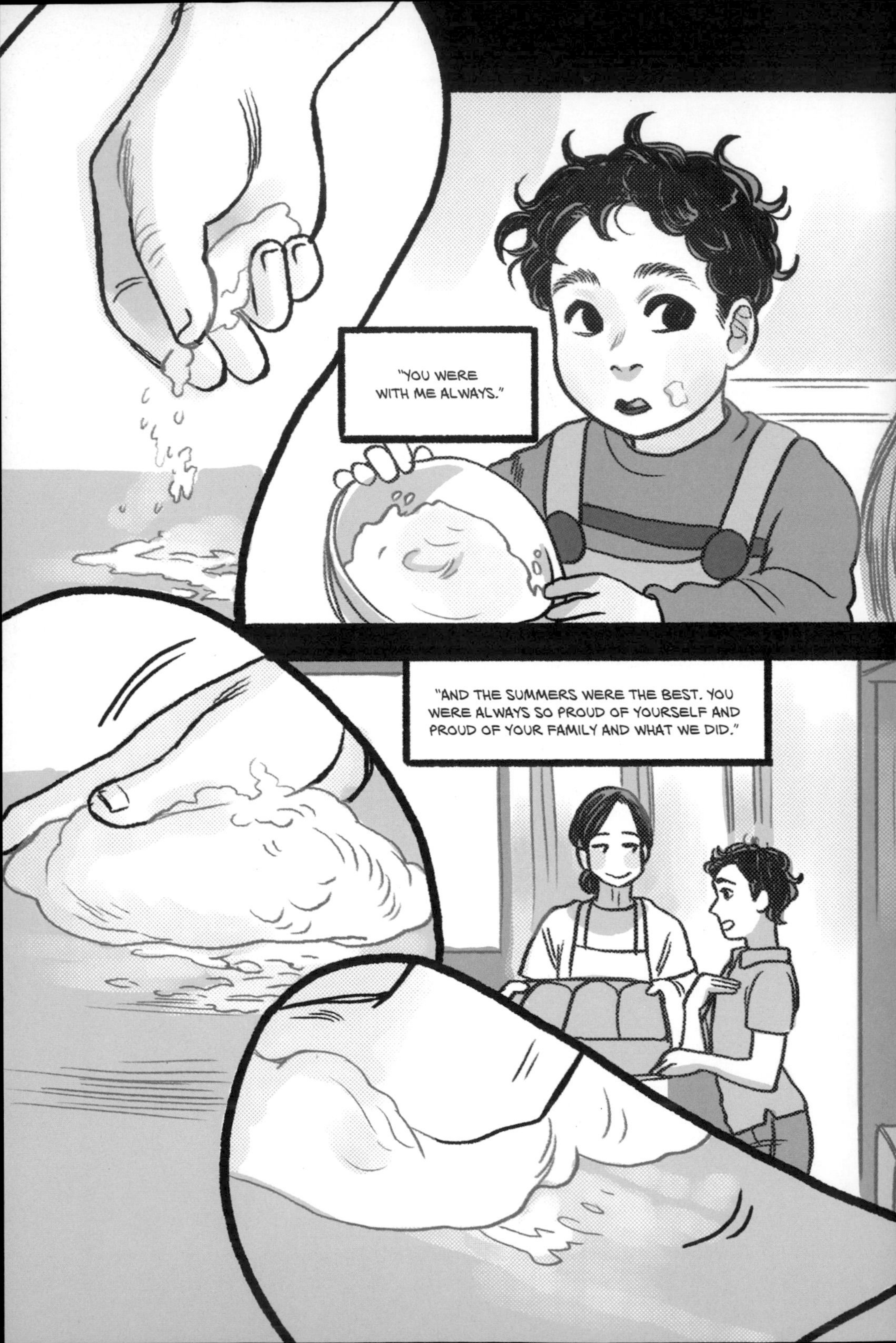
"YOU WERE WITH ME ALWAYS."
"AND THE SUMMERS WERE THE BEST. YOU WERE ALWAYS SO PROUD OF YOURSELF AND PROUD OF YOUR FAMILY AND WHAT WE DID."

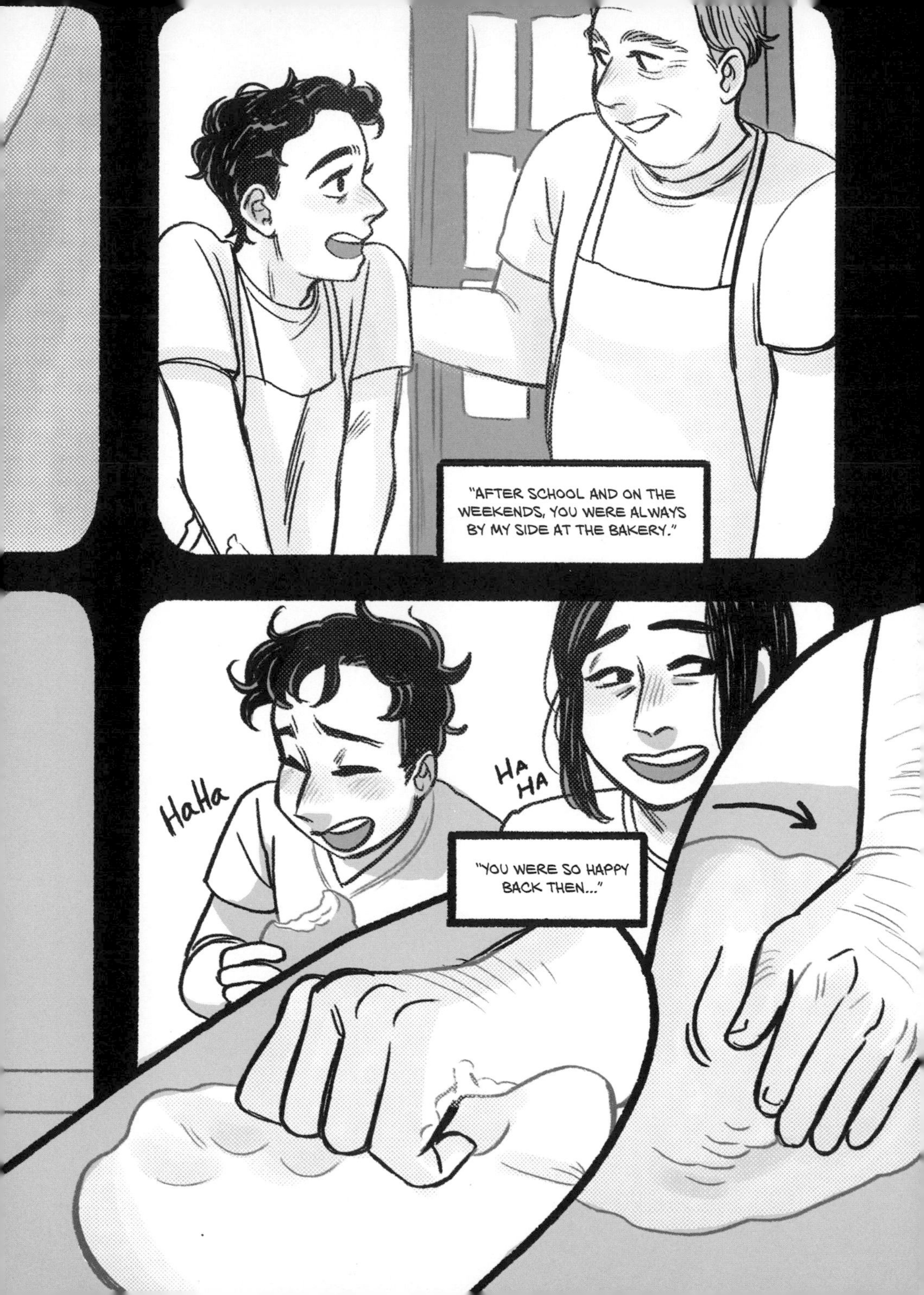
"AFTER SCHOOL AND ON THE WEEKENDS, YOU WERE ALWAYS BY MY SIDE AT THE BAKERY."
HaHa
HA HA
"YOU WERE SO HAPPY BACK THEN..."

...BUT I FEEL LIKE YOU LOST THAT SOMEWHERE ALONG THE WAY.

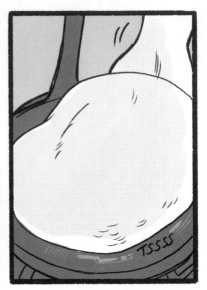

TSSSS

AND I FELT LIKE I LOST YOU.

LOST MY BOY.

BUT THEN SOMETHING HAPPENED THIS SUMMER.

YOU WERE LIKE YOUR OLD SELF FOR A LITTLE WHILE.

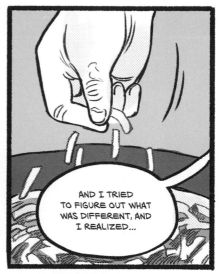

AND I TRIED TO FIGURE OUT WHAT WAS DIFFERENT, AND I REALIZED...

...IT WAS THE BOY. HECTOR.

SHAKE

HE HELPED YOU FIND THAT HAPPINESS YOU USED TO HAVE.

SHAKE

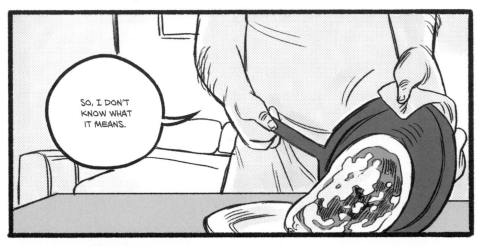

SO, I DON'T KNOW WHAT IT MEANS.

MAYBE JUST...DON'T TRY TO BE WHAT YOU THINK YOU SHOULD BE.

BE WHAT YOU LOVE.

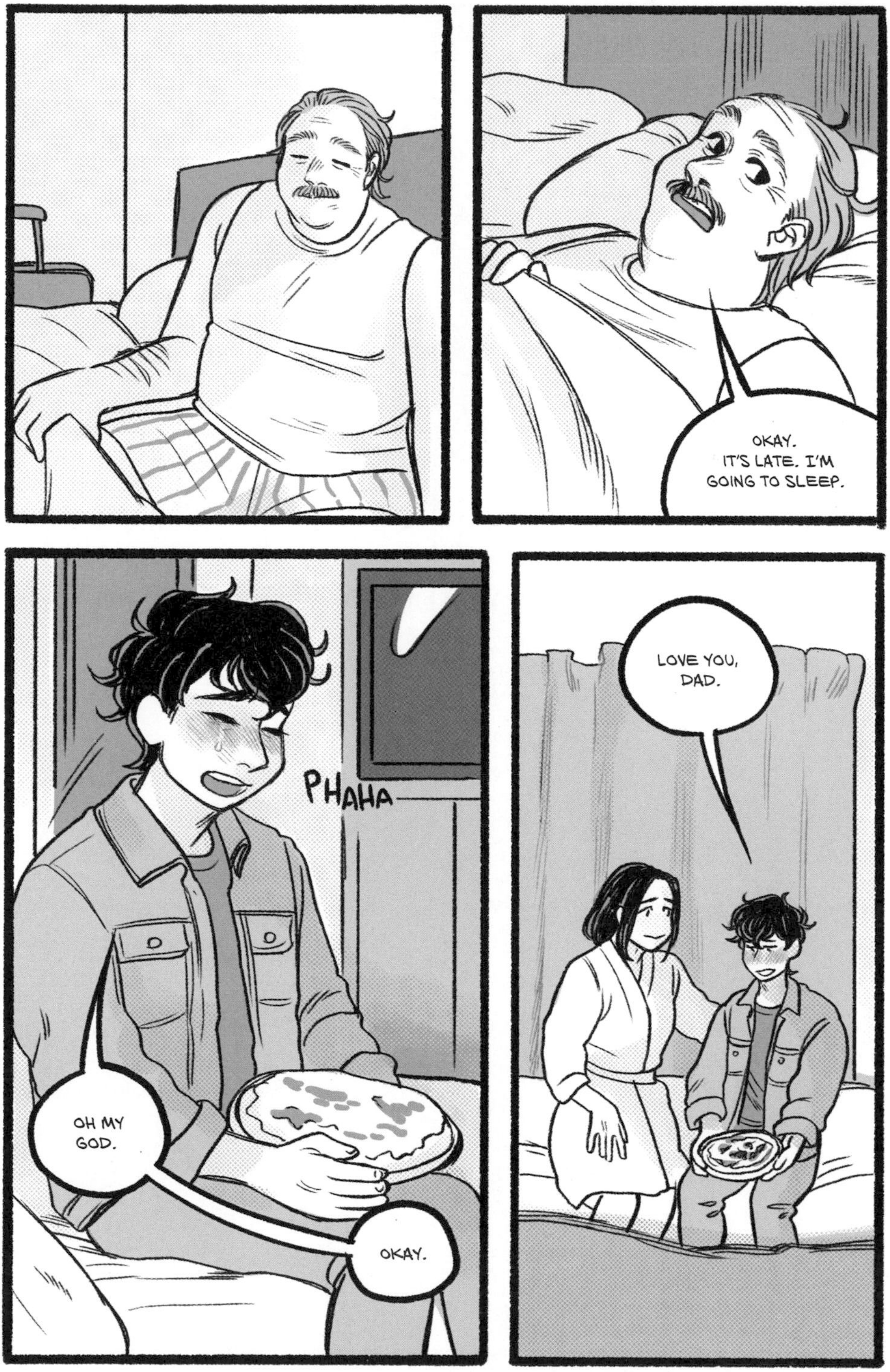
OKAY. IT'S LATE. I'M GOING TO SLEEP.
PHAHA
OH MY GOD.
OKAY.
LOVE YOU, DAD.

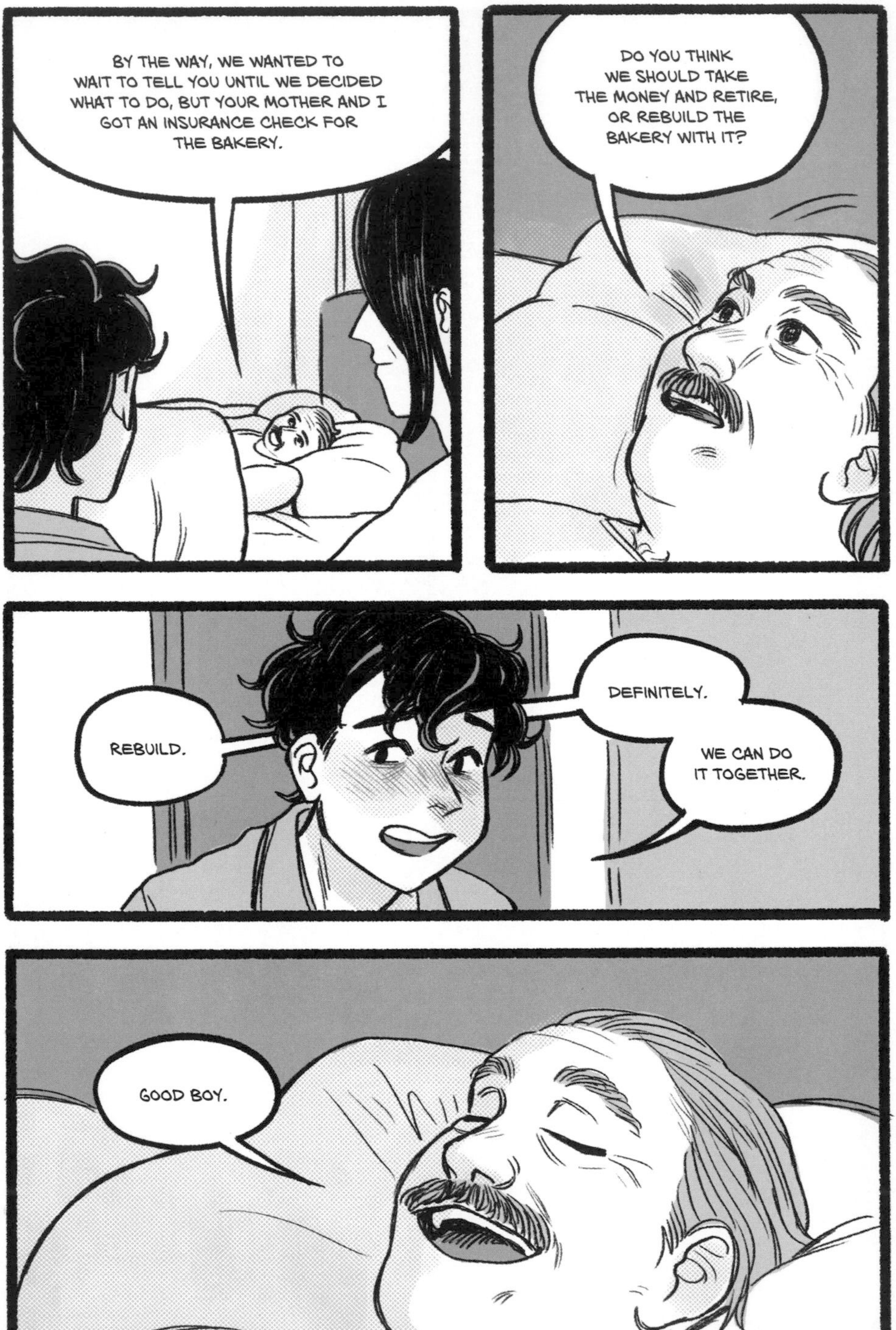
BY THE WAY, WE WANTED TO WAIT TO TELL YOU UNTIL WE DECIDED WHAT TO DO, BUT YOUR MOTHER AND I GOT AN INSURANCE CHECK FOR THE BAKERY.
DO YOU THINK WE SHOULD TAKE THE MONEY AND RETIRE, OR REBUILD THE BAKERY WITH IT?
REBUILD.
DEFINITELY.
WE CAN DO IT TOGETHER.
GOOD BOY.

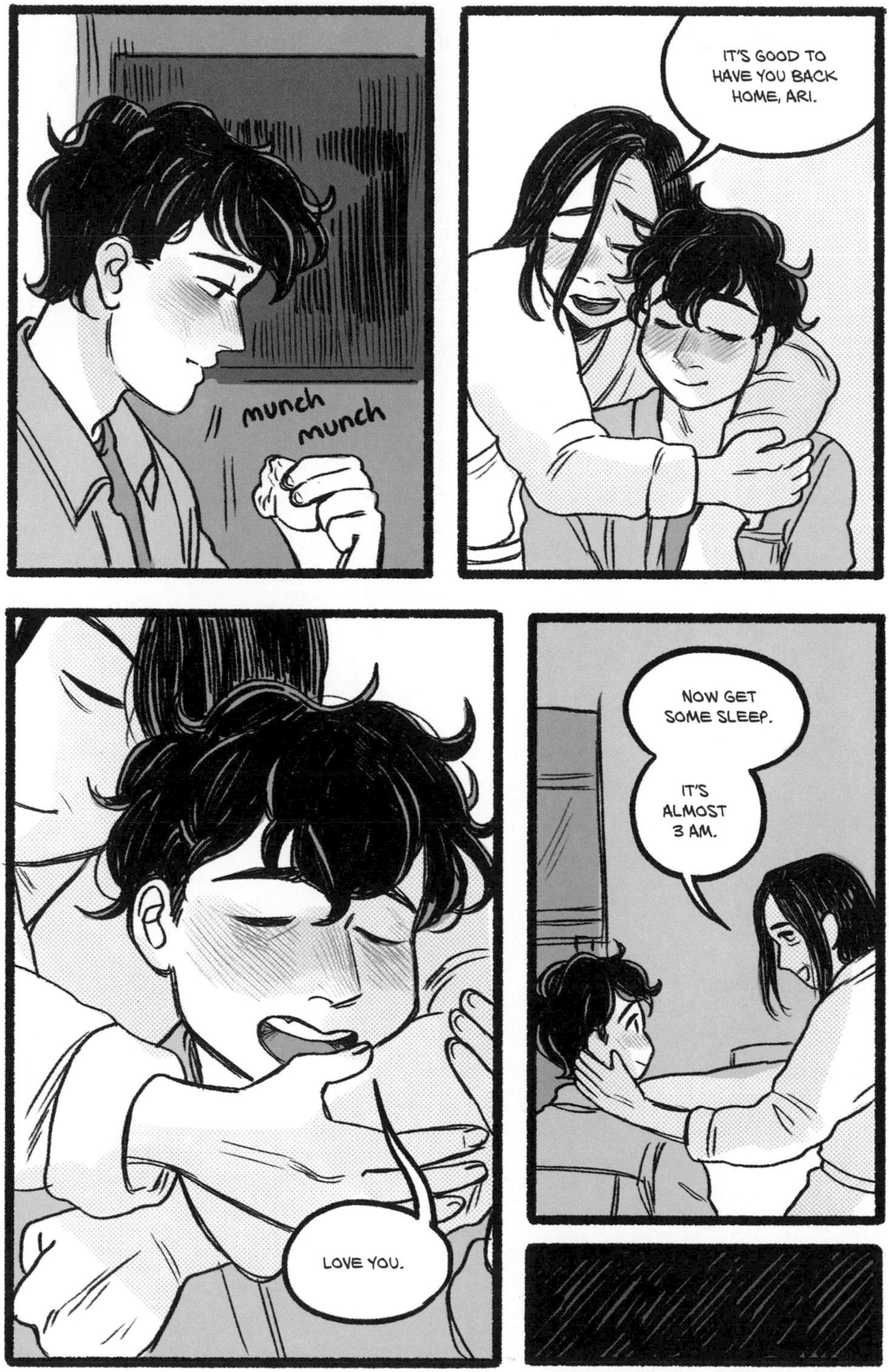
munch
munch
IT'S GOOD TO HAVE YOU BACK HOME, ARI.
LOVE YOU.
NOW GET SOME SLEEP.
IT'S ALMOST 3 AM.

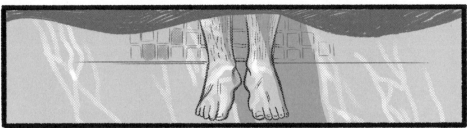

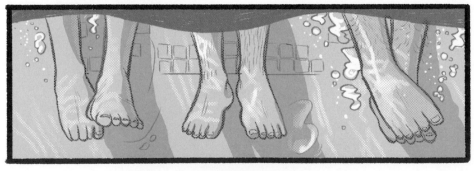

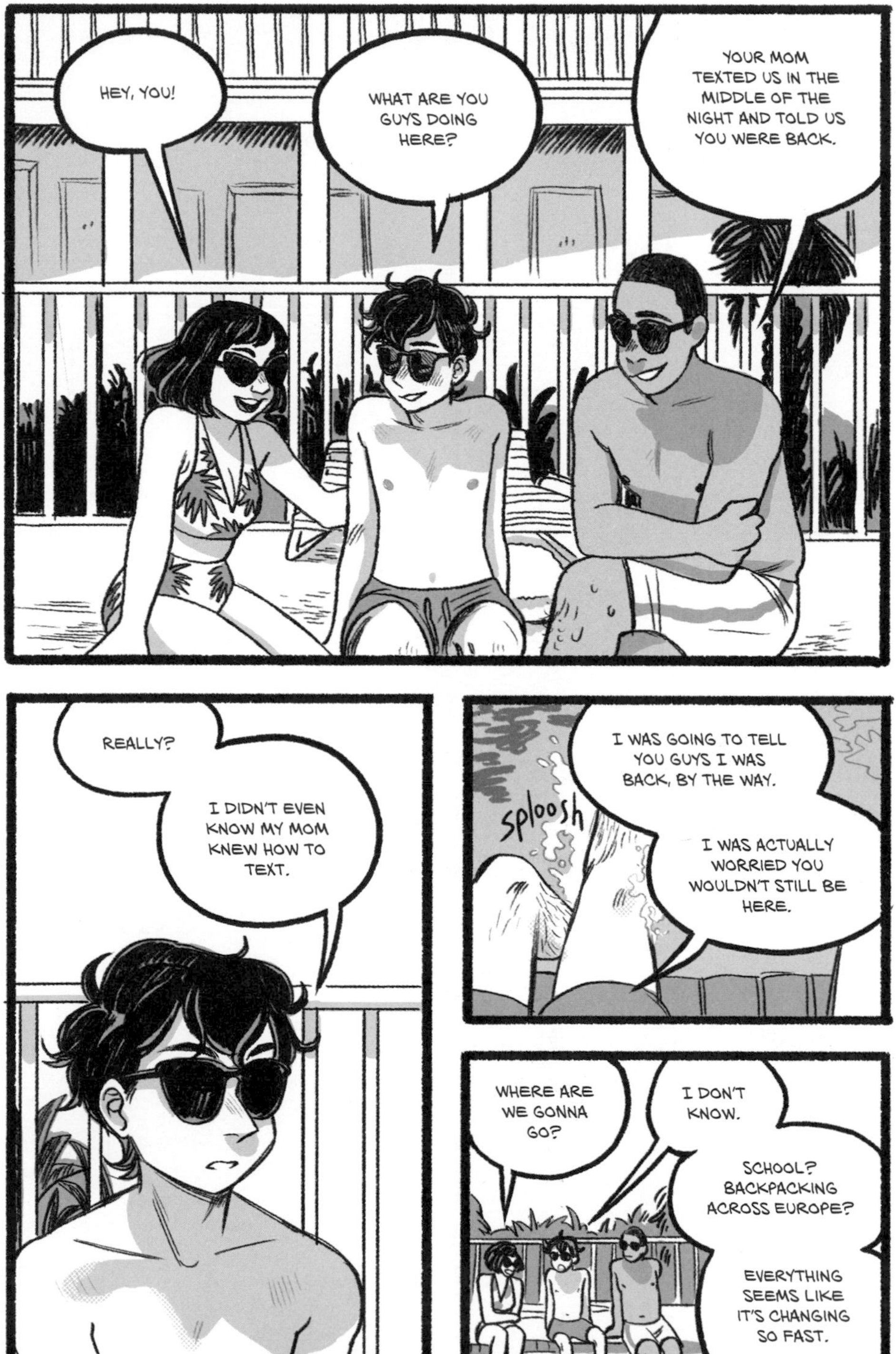
HEY, YOU!
WHAT ARE YOU GUYS DOING HERE?
YOUR MOM TEXTED US IN THE MIDDLE OF THE NIGHT AND TOLD US YOU WERE BACK.
REALLY?
I DIDN'T EVEN KNOW MY MOM KNEW HOW TO TEXT.
sploosh
I WAS GOING TO TELL YOU GUYS I WAS BACK, BY THE WAY.
I WAS ACTUALLY WORRIED YOU WOULDN'T STILL BE HERE.
WHERE ARE WE GONNA GO?
I DON'T KNOW.
SCHOOL? BACKPACKING ACROSS EUROPE?
EVERYTHING SEEMS LIKE IT'S CHANGING SO FAST.

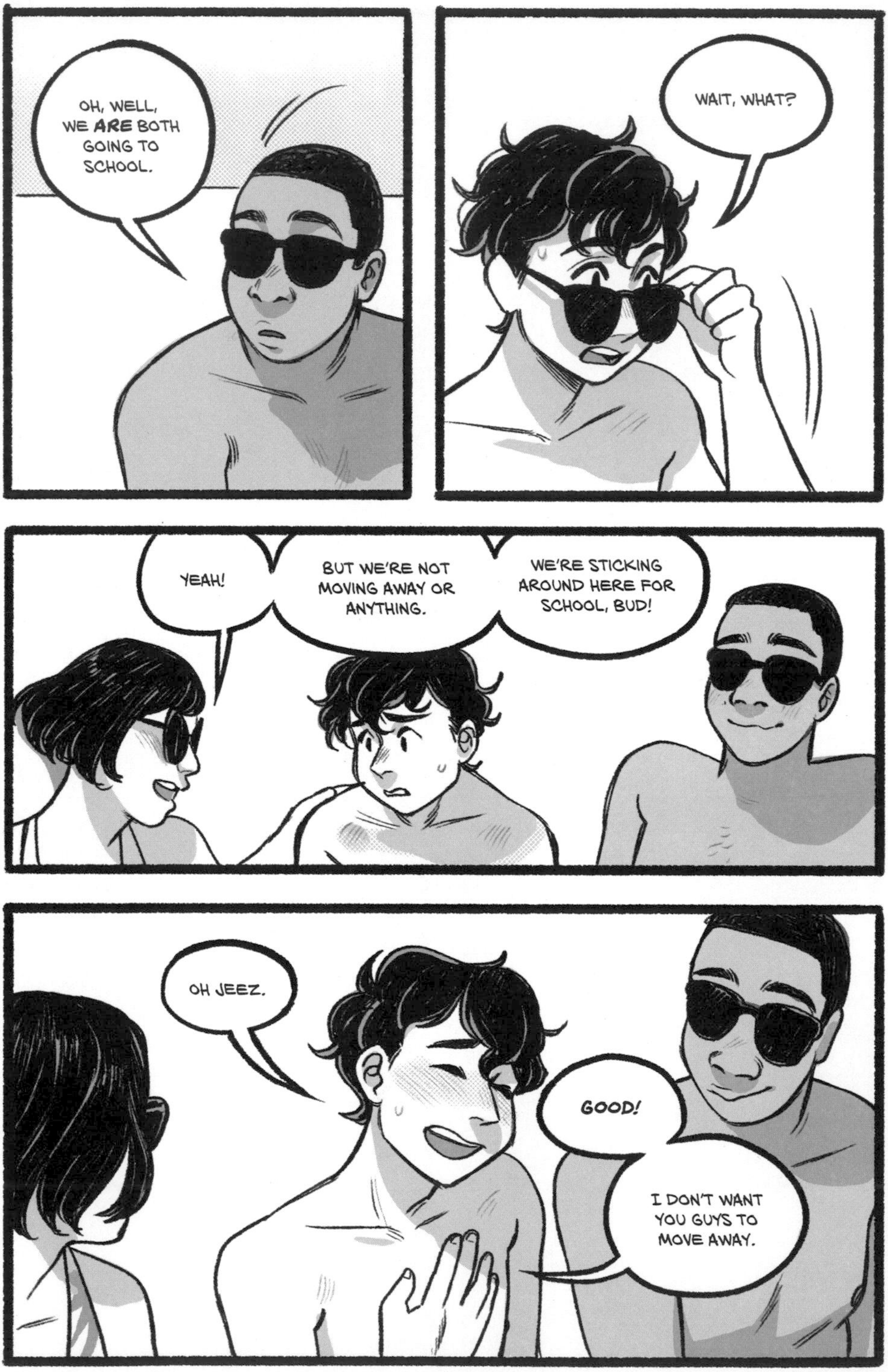
OH, WELL, WE ARE BOTH GOING TO SCHOOL.
WAIT, WHAT?
YEAH!
BUT WE'RE NOT MOVING AWAY OR ANYTHING.
WE'RE STICKING AROUND HERE FOR SCHOOL, BUD!
OH JEEZ.
GOOD!
I DON'T WANT YOU GUYS TO MOVE AWAY.

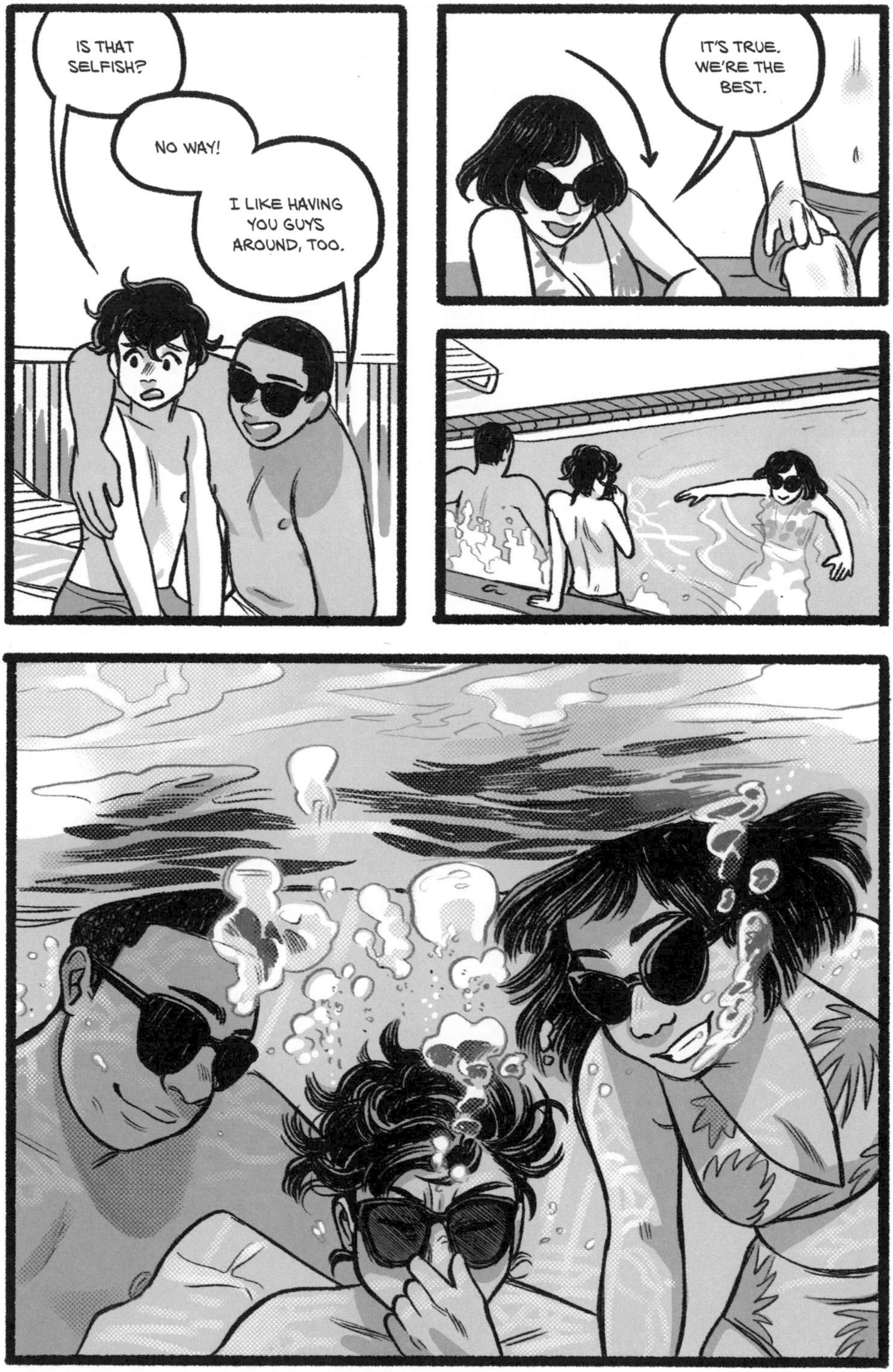
IS THAT SELFISH?
NO WAY!
I LIKE HAVING YOU GUYS AROUND, TOO.
IT'S TRUE. WE'RE THE BEST.

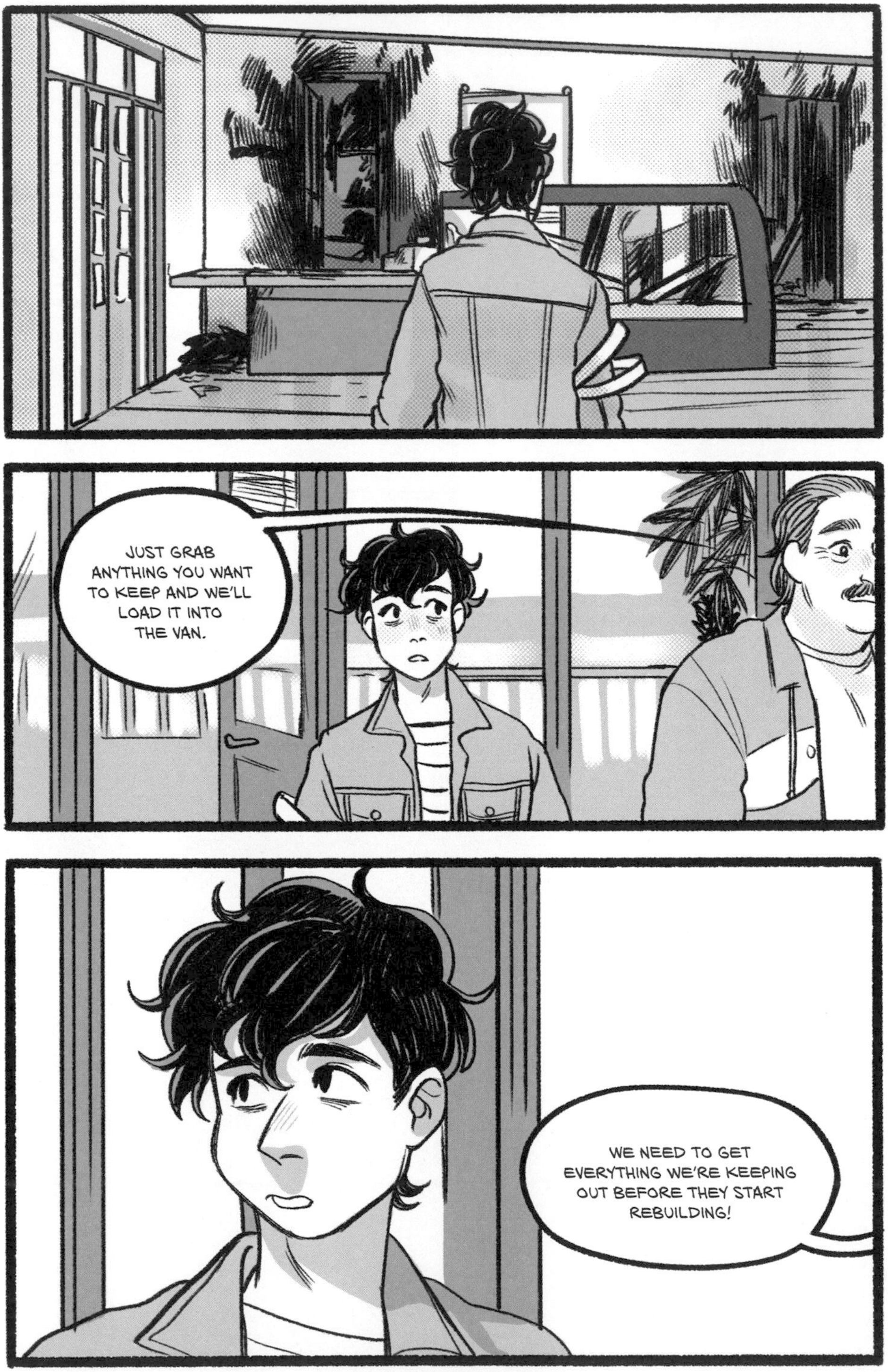
JUST GRAB ANYTHING YOU WANT TO KEEP AND WE'LL LOAD IT INTO THE VAN.
WE NEED TO GET EVERYTHING WE'RE KEEPING OUT BEFORE THEY START REBUILDING!

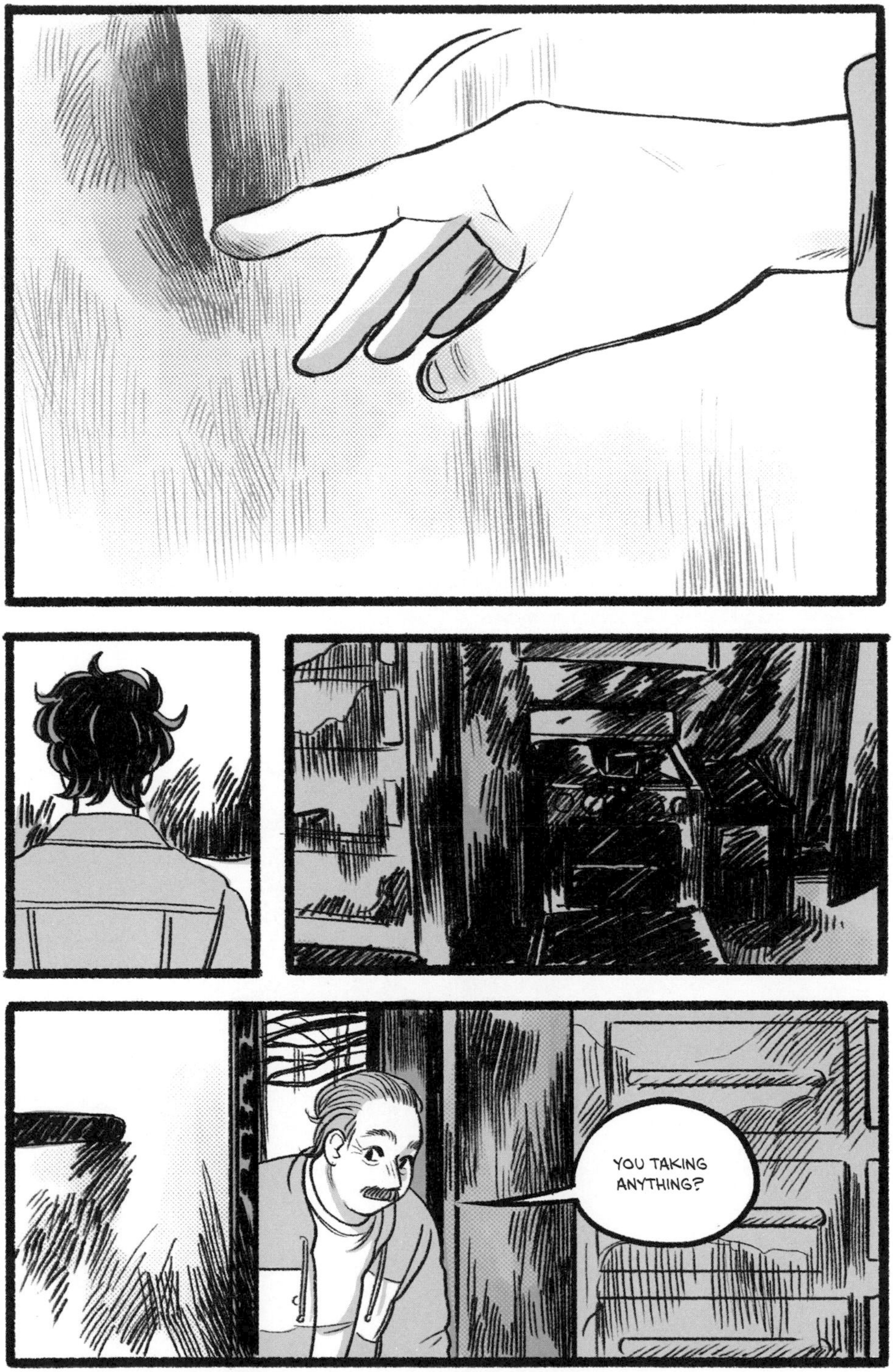
YOU TAKING ANYTHING?

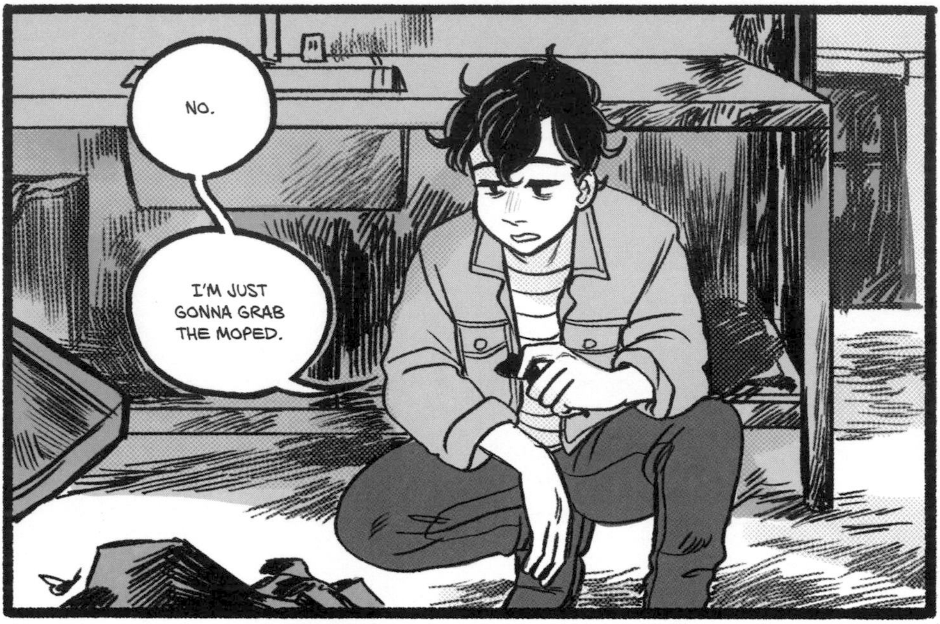
NO.
I'M JUST GONNA GRAB THE MOPED.

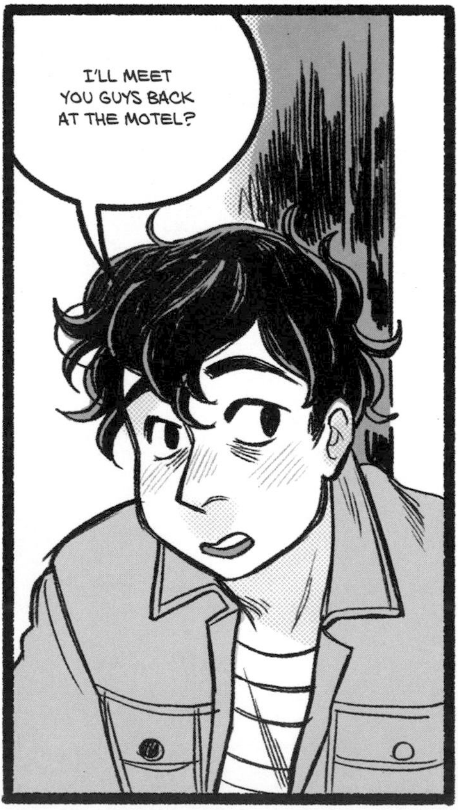
I'LL MEET YOU GUYS BACK AT THE MOTEL?

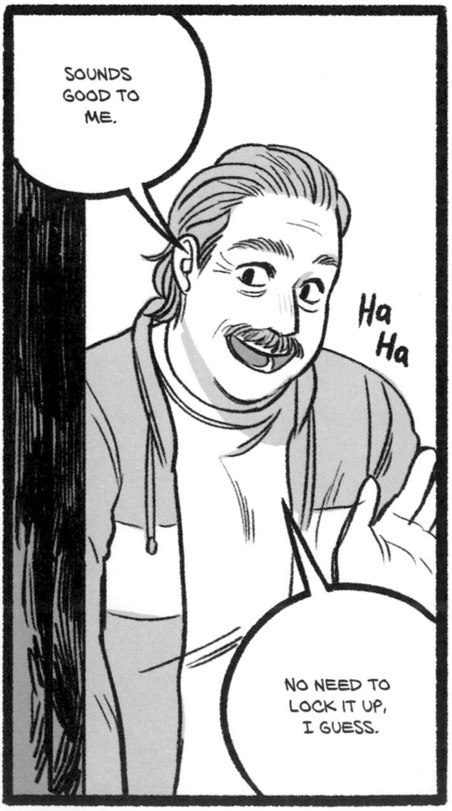
SOUNDS GOOD TO ME.
Ha Ha
NO NEED TO LOCK IT UP, I GUESS.

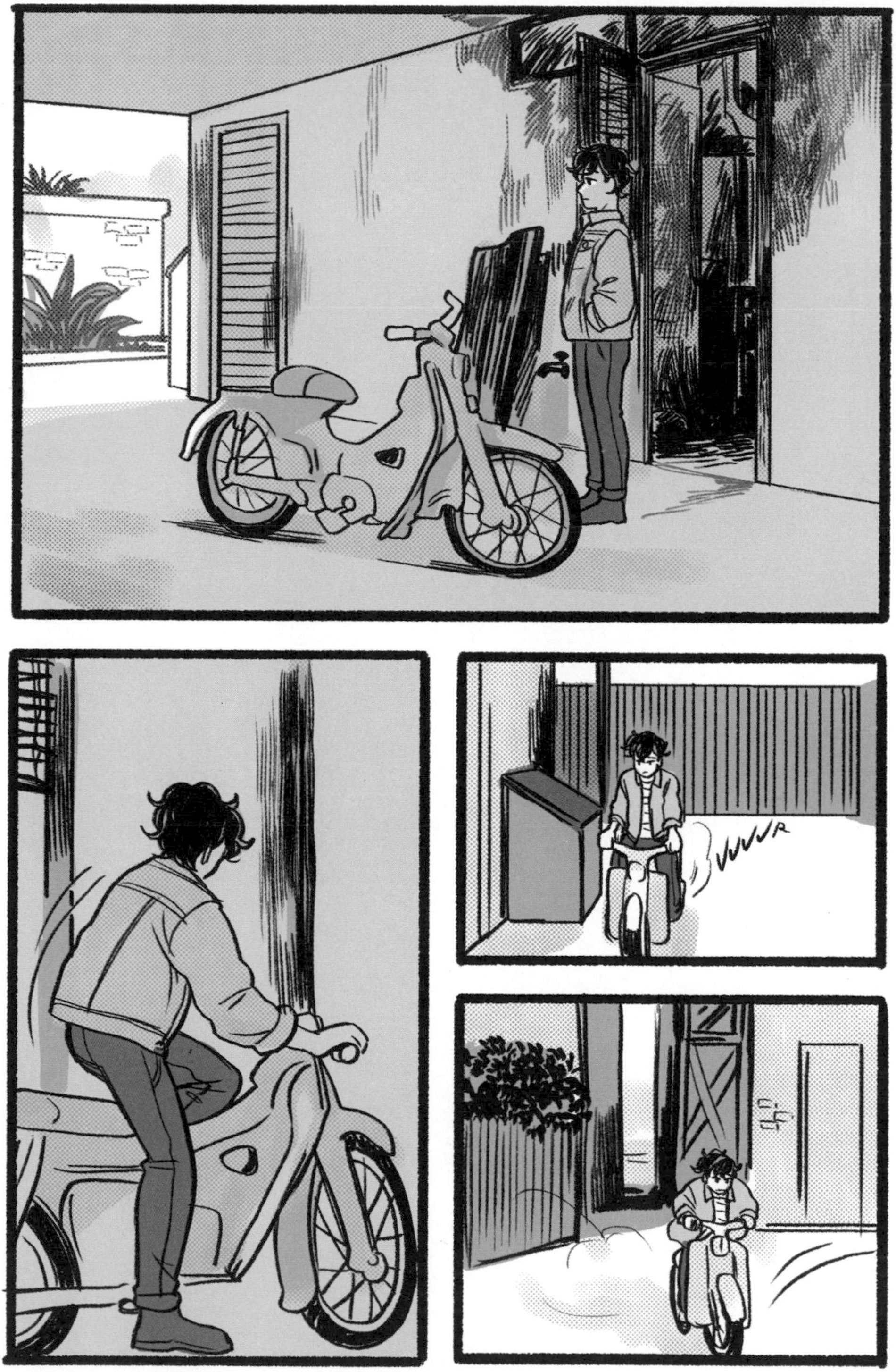
BVVVVR

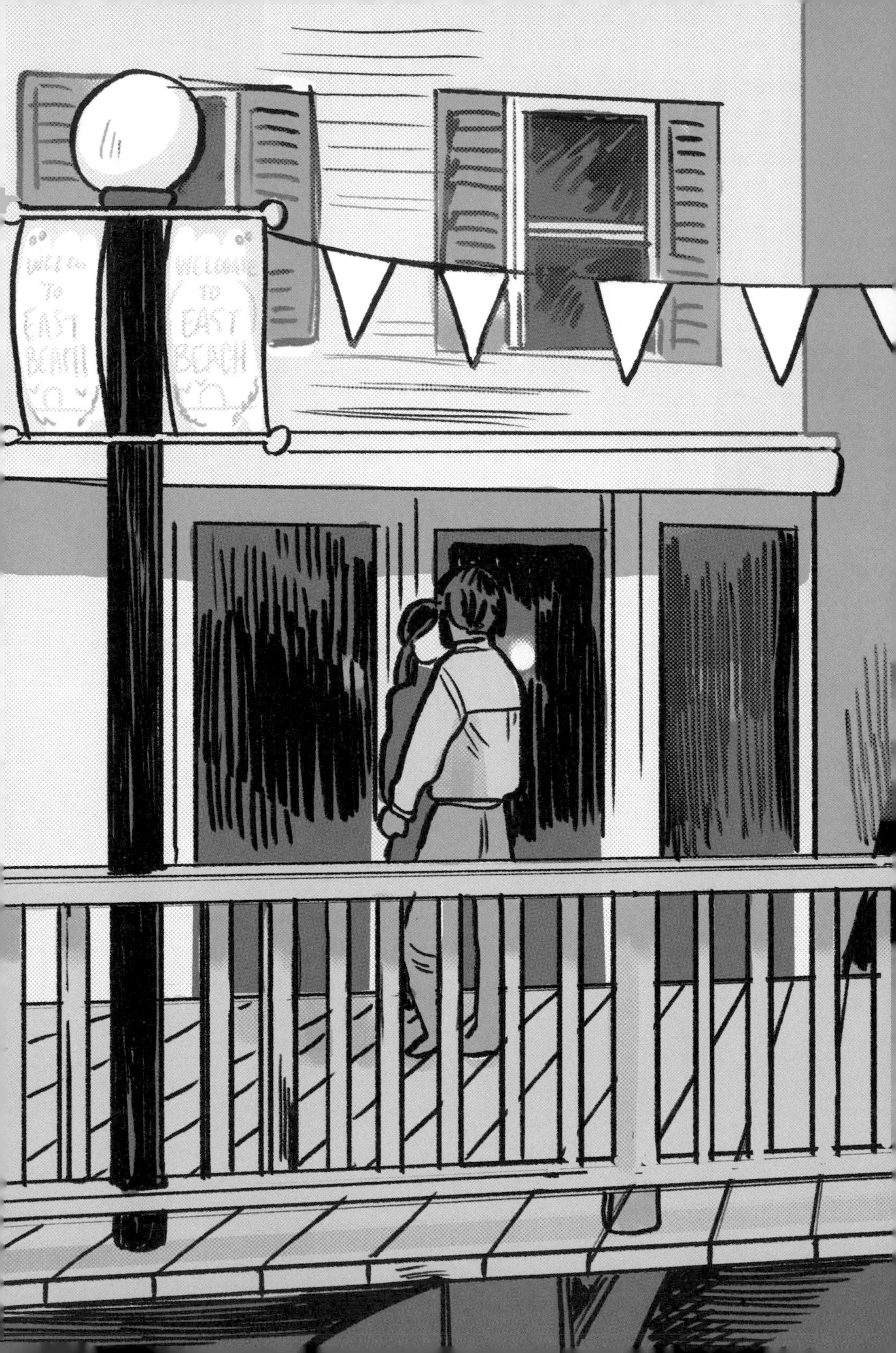
WELCOME TO EAST BEACH

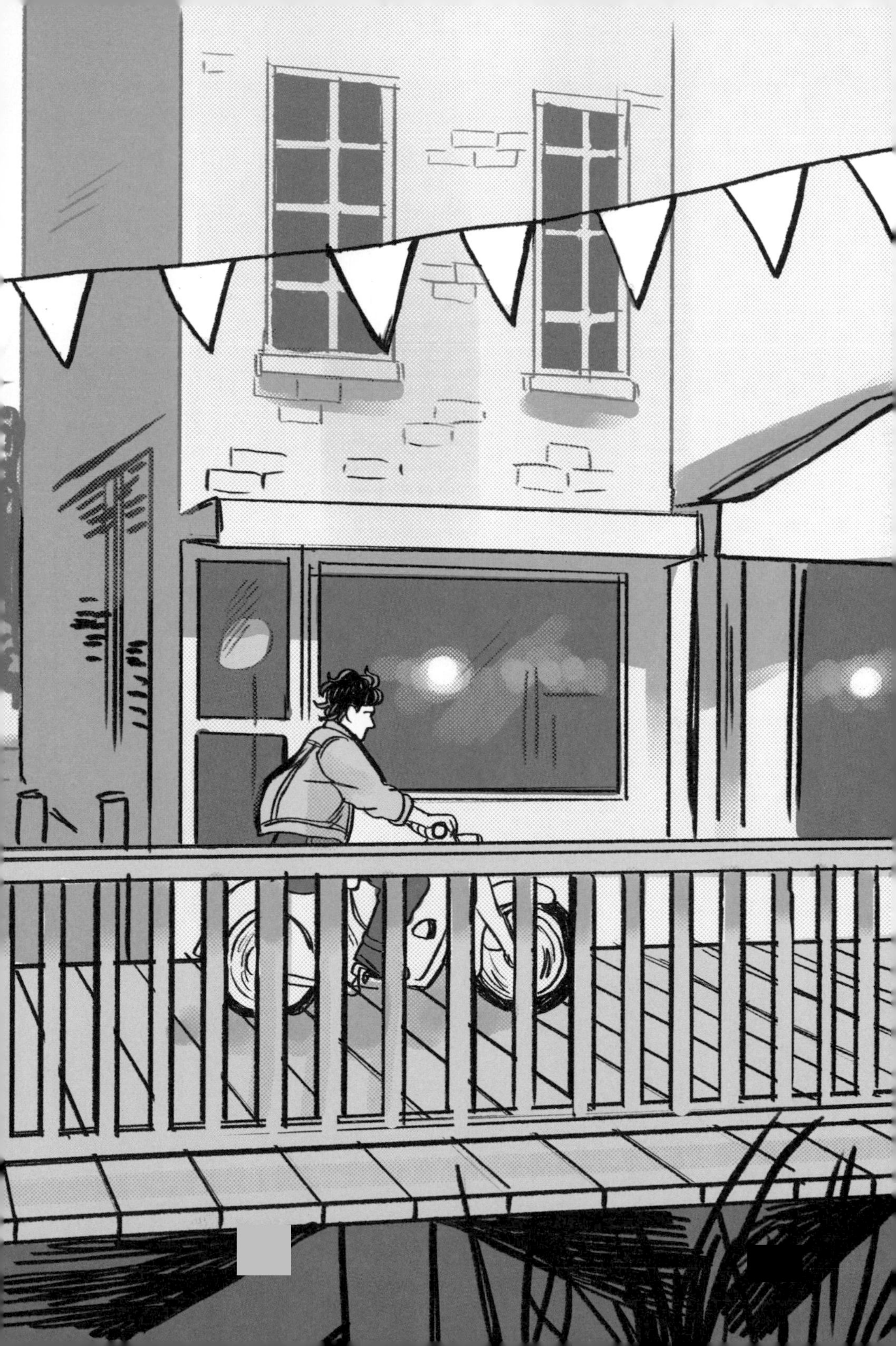

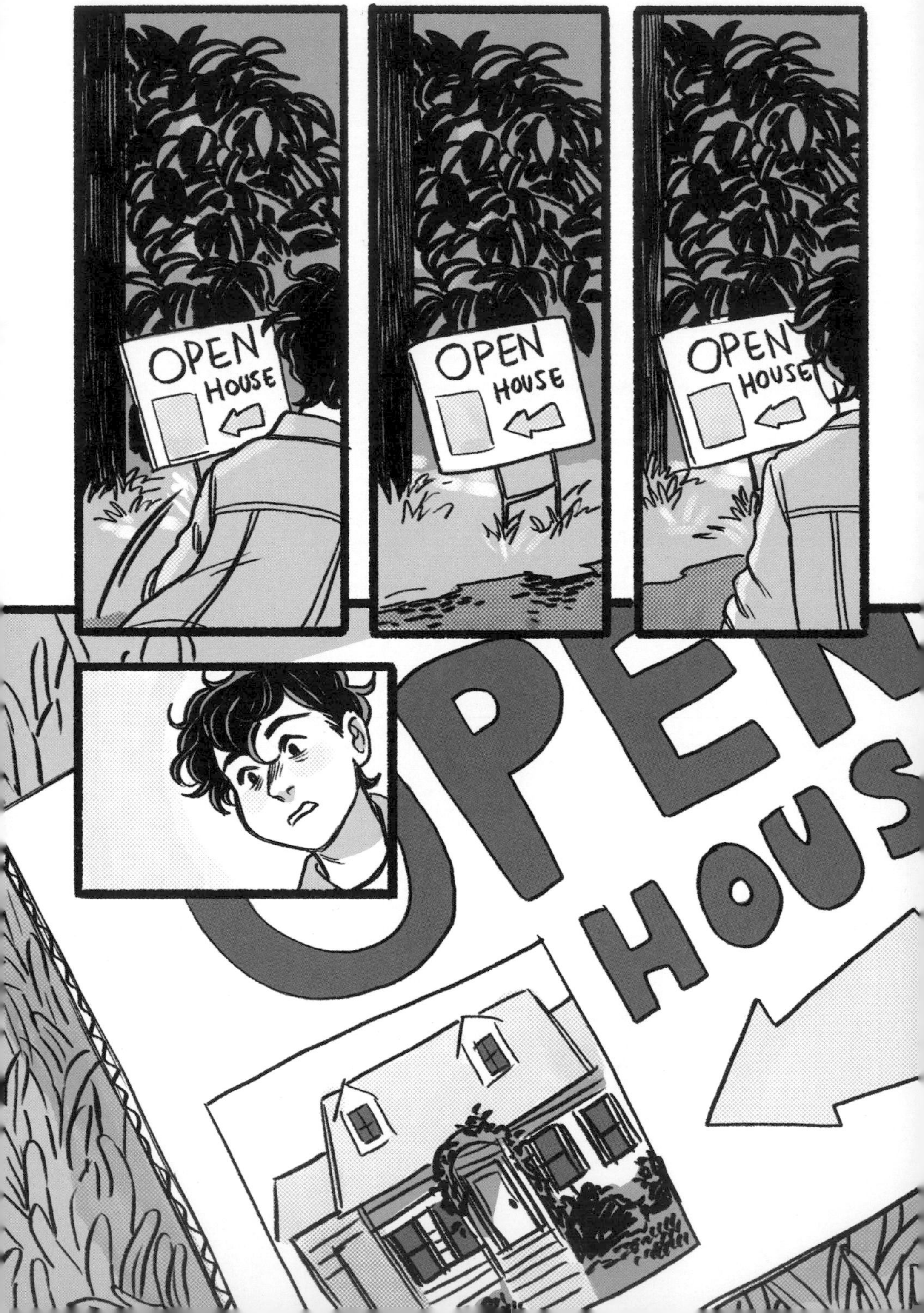
OPEN HOUSE
OPEN HOUSE
OPEN HOUSE
OPEN HOUSE

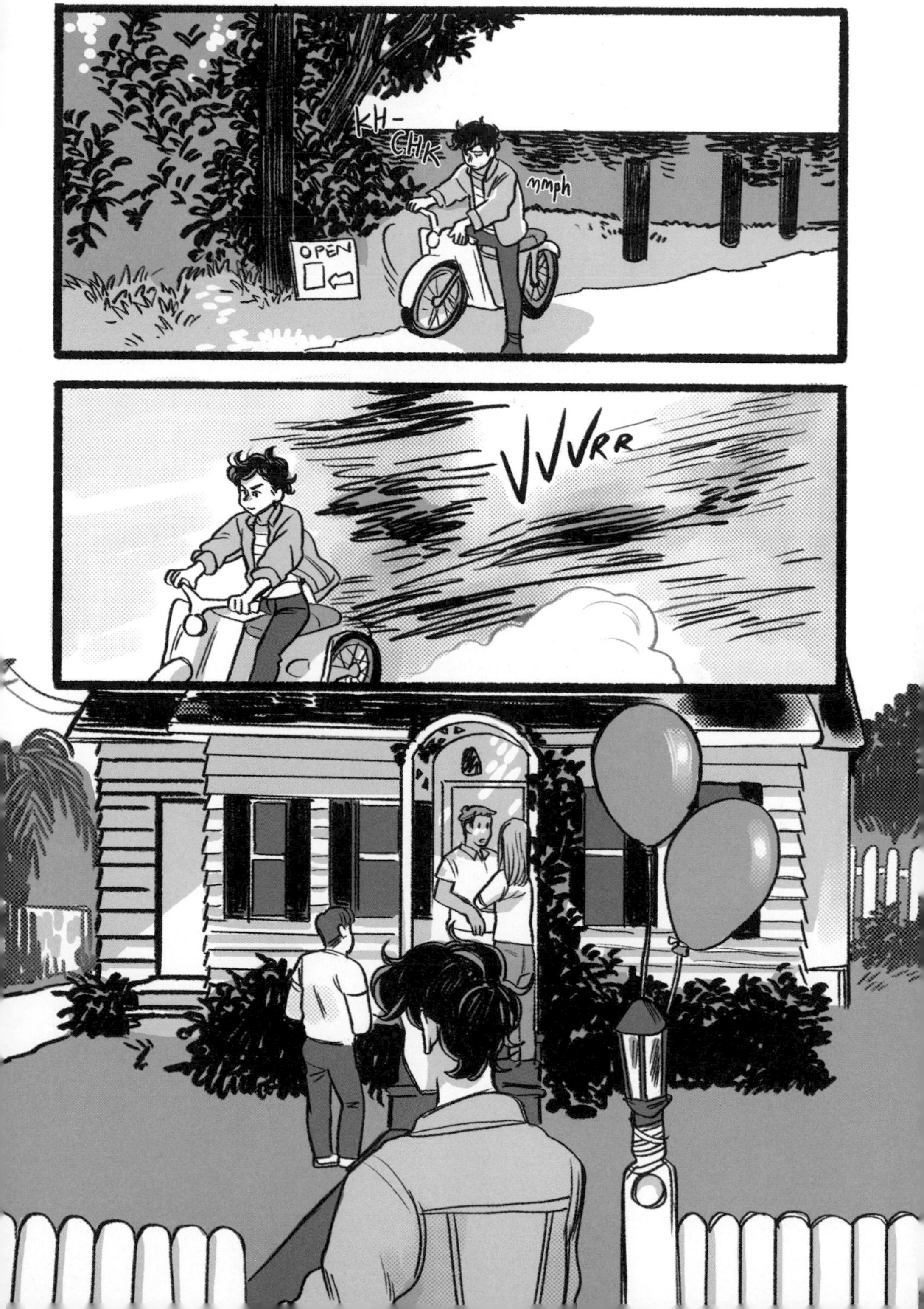
OPEN
KH-
CHK
mmph
VVVRR

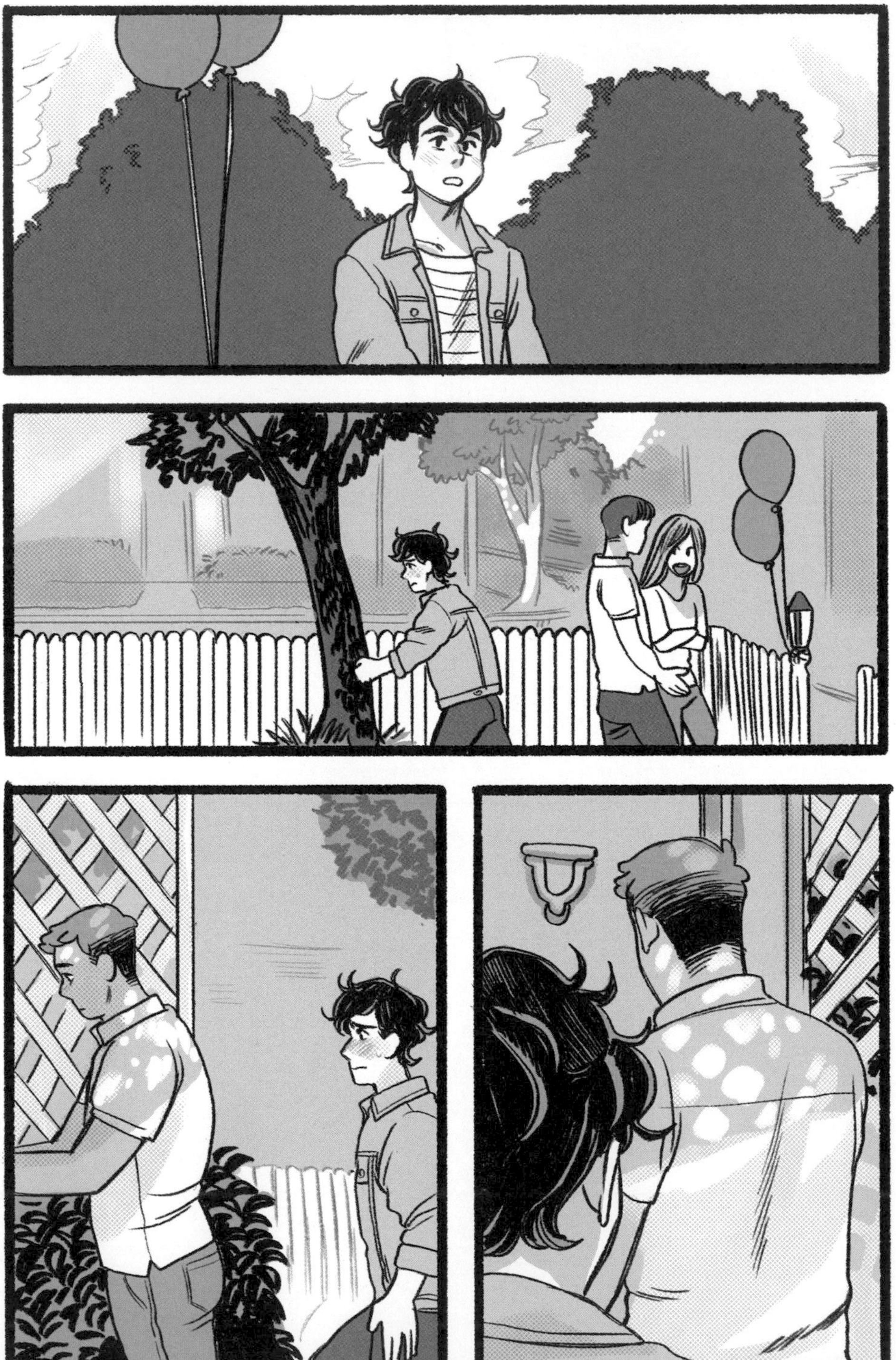

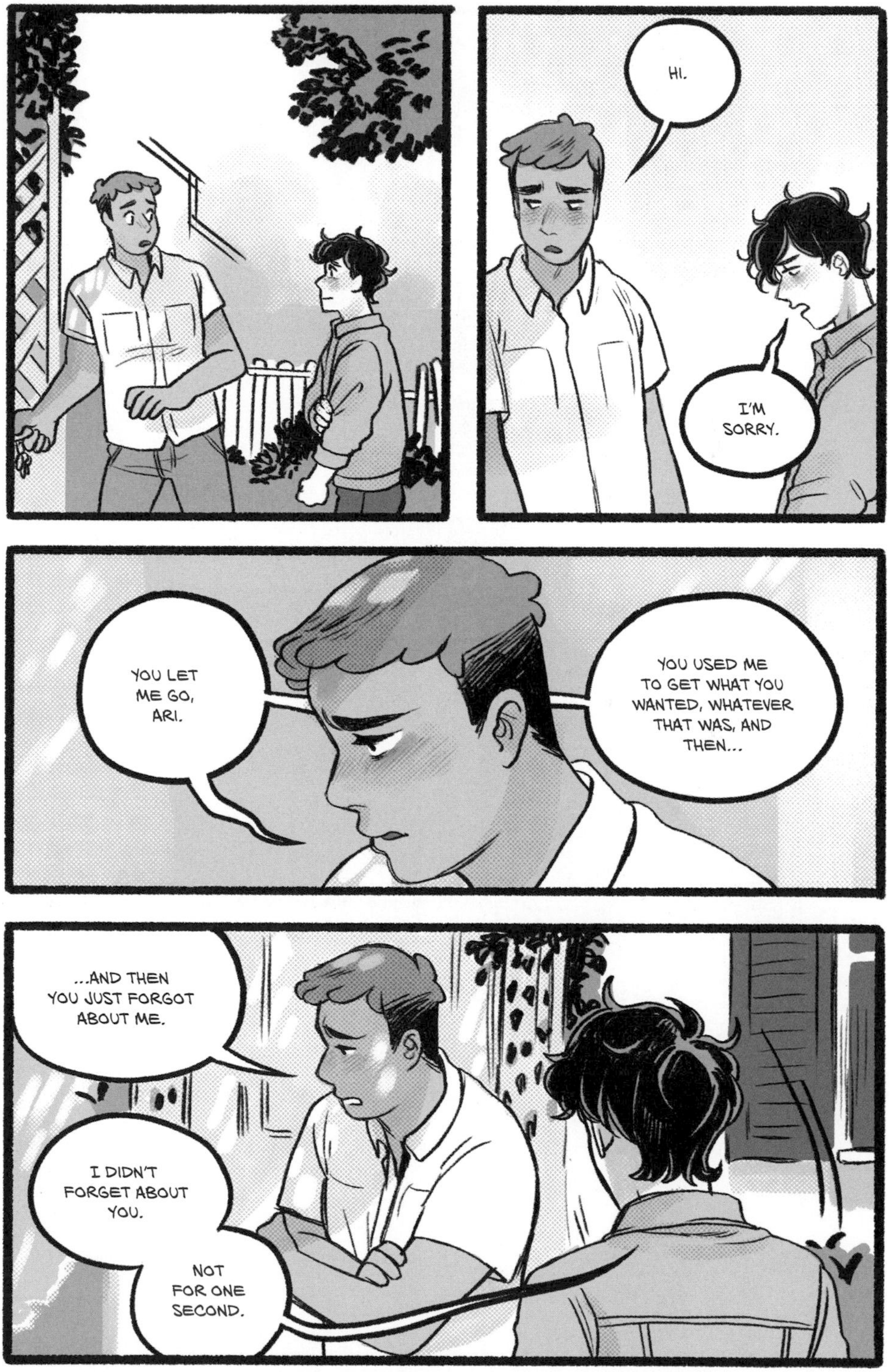
HI.
I'M SORRY.
YOU LET ME GO, ARI.
YOU USED ME TO GET WHAT YOU WANTED, WHATEVER THAT WAS, AND THEN...
...AND THEN YOU JUST FORGOT ABOUT ME.
I DIDN'T FORGET ABOUT YOU.
NOT FOR ONE SECOND.

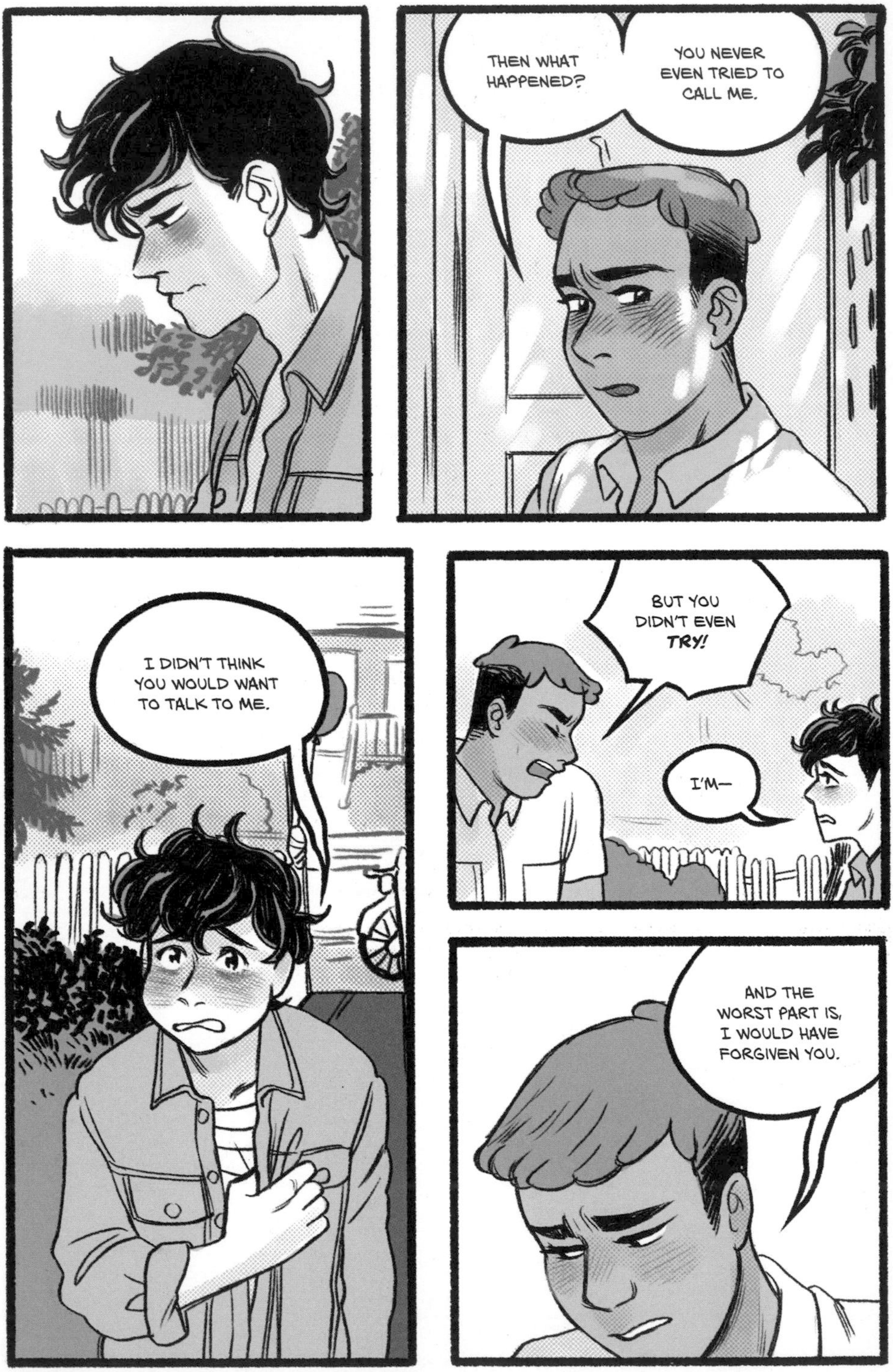
THEN WHAT HAPPENED?
YOU NEVER EVEN TRIED TO CALL ME.
I DIDN'T THINK YOU WOULD WANT TO TALK TO ME.
BUT YOU DIDN'T EVEN ***TRY!***
I'M—
AND THE WORST PART IS, I WOULD HAVE FORGIVEN YOU.

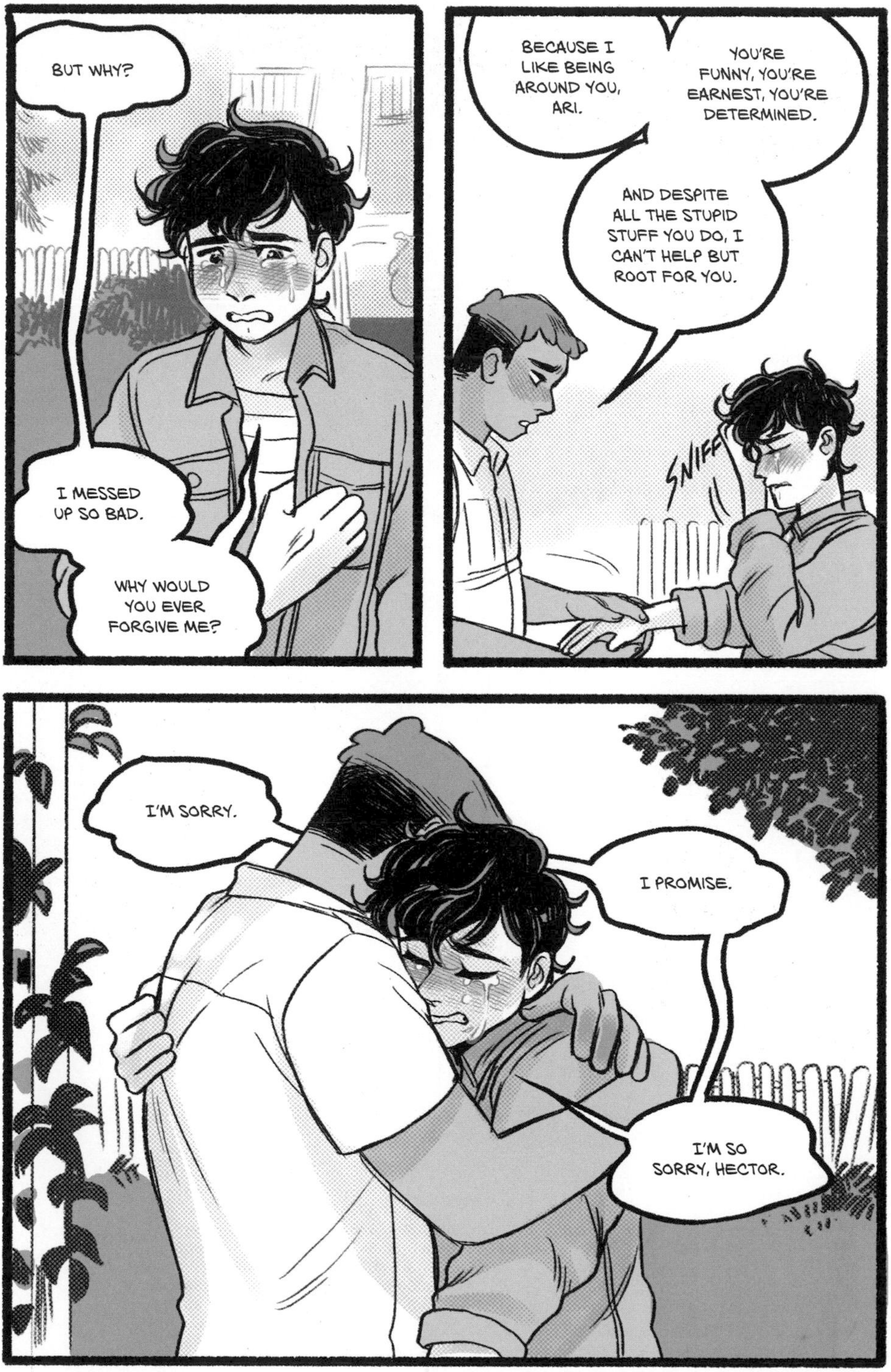
BUT WHY?
I MESSED UP SO BAD.
WHY WOULD YOU EVER FORGIVE ME?
BECAUSE I LIKE BEING AROUND YOU, ARI.
YOU'RE FUNNY, YOU'RE EARNEST, YOU'RE DETERMINED.
AND DESPITE ALL THE STUPID STUFF YOU DO, I CAN'T HELP BUT ROOT FOR YOU.
SNIFF
I'M SORRY.
I PROMISE.
I'M SO SORRY, HECTOR.

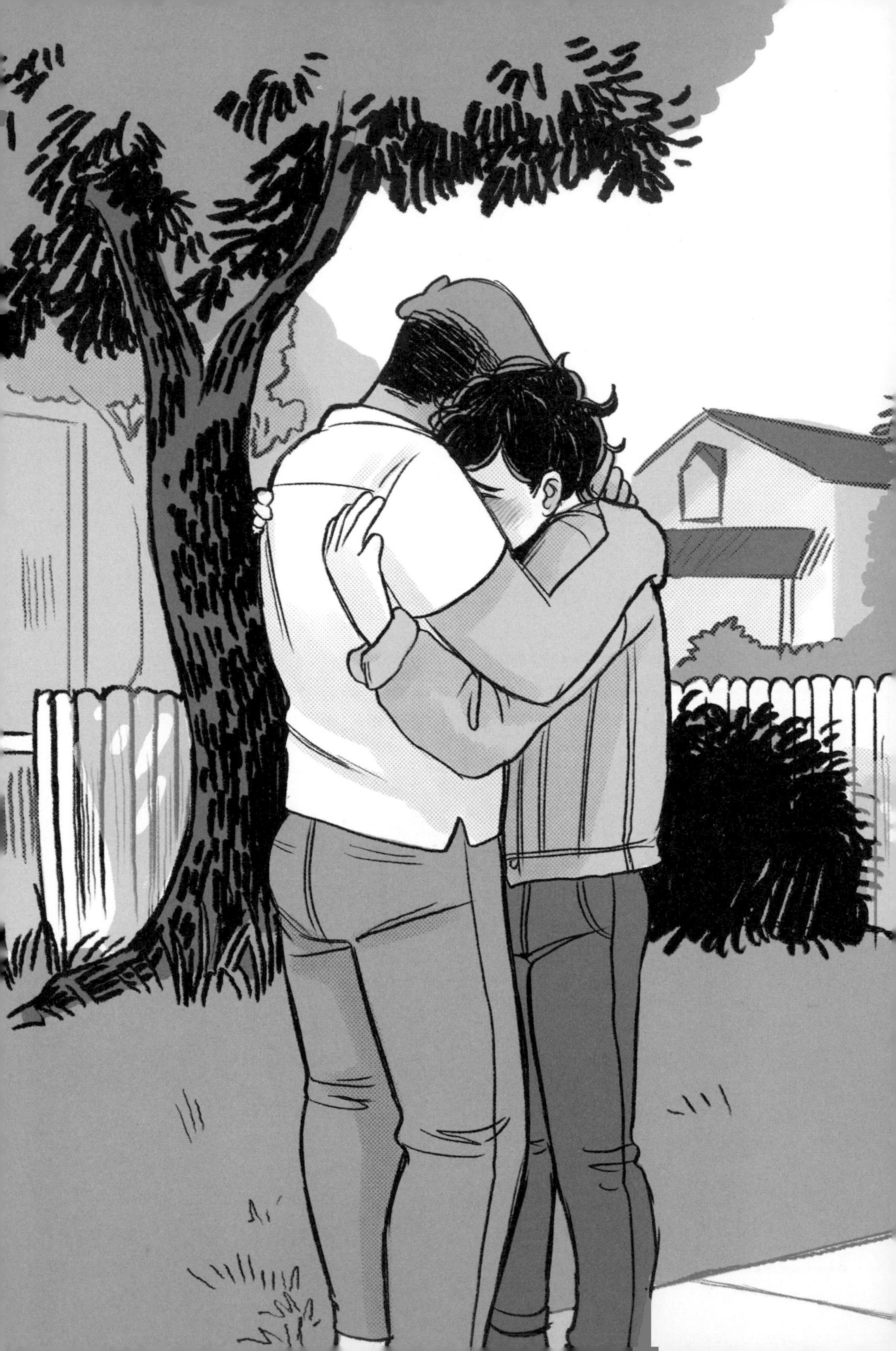

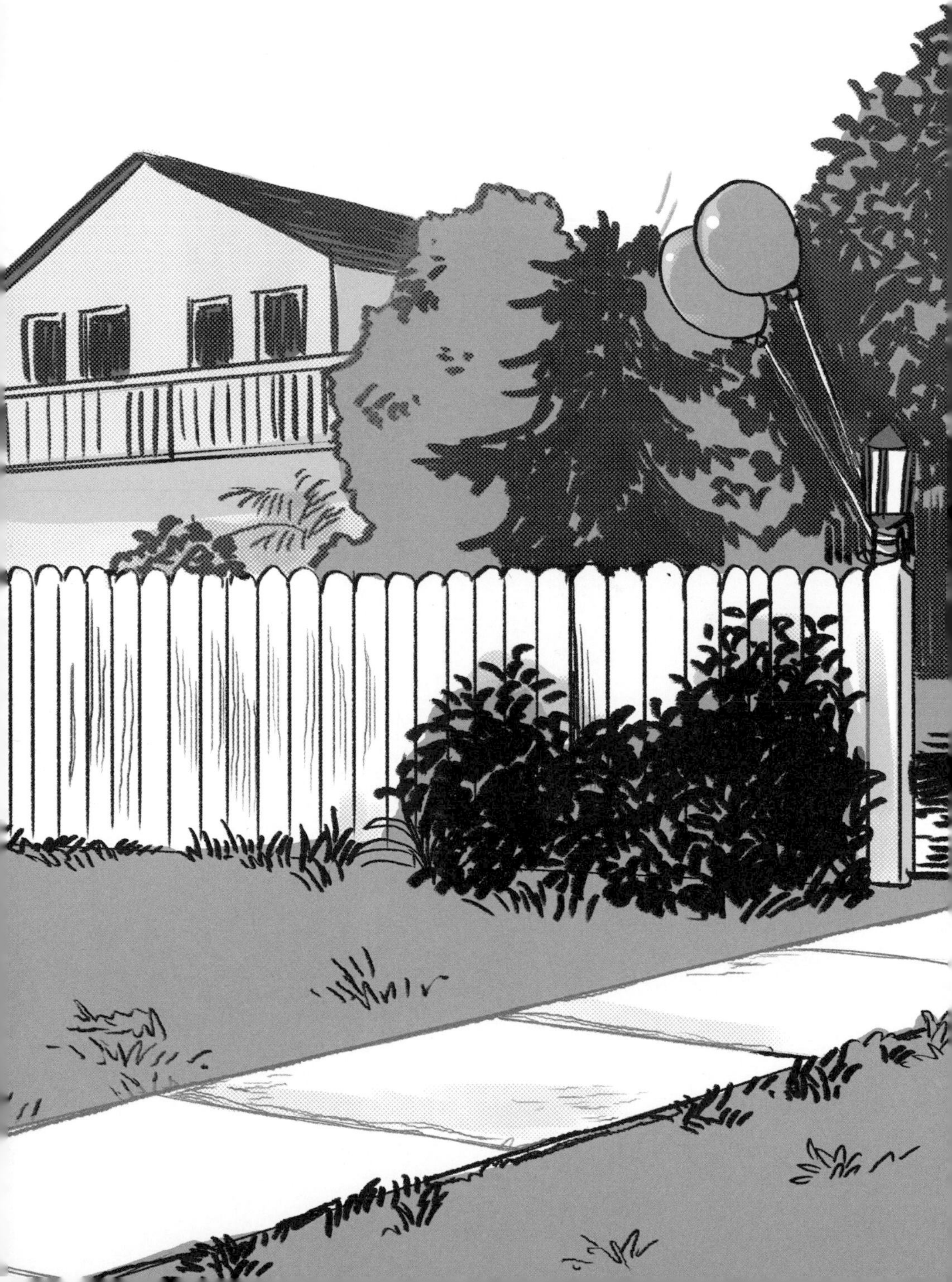

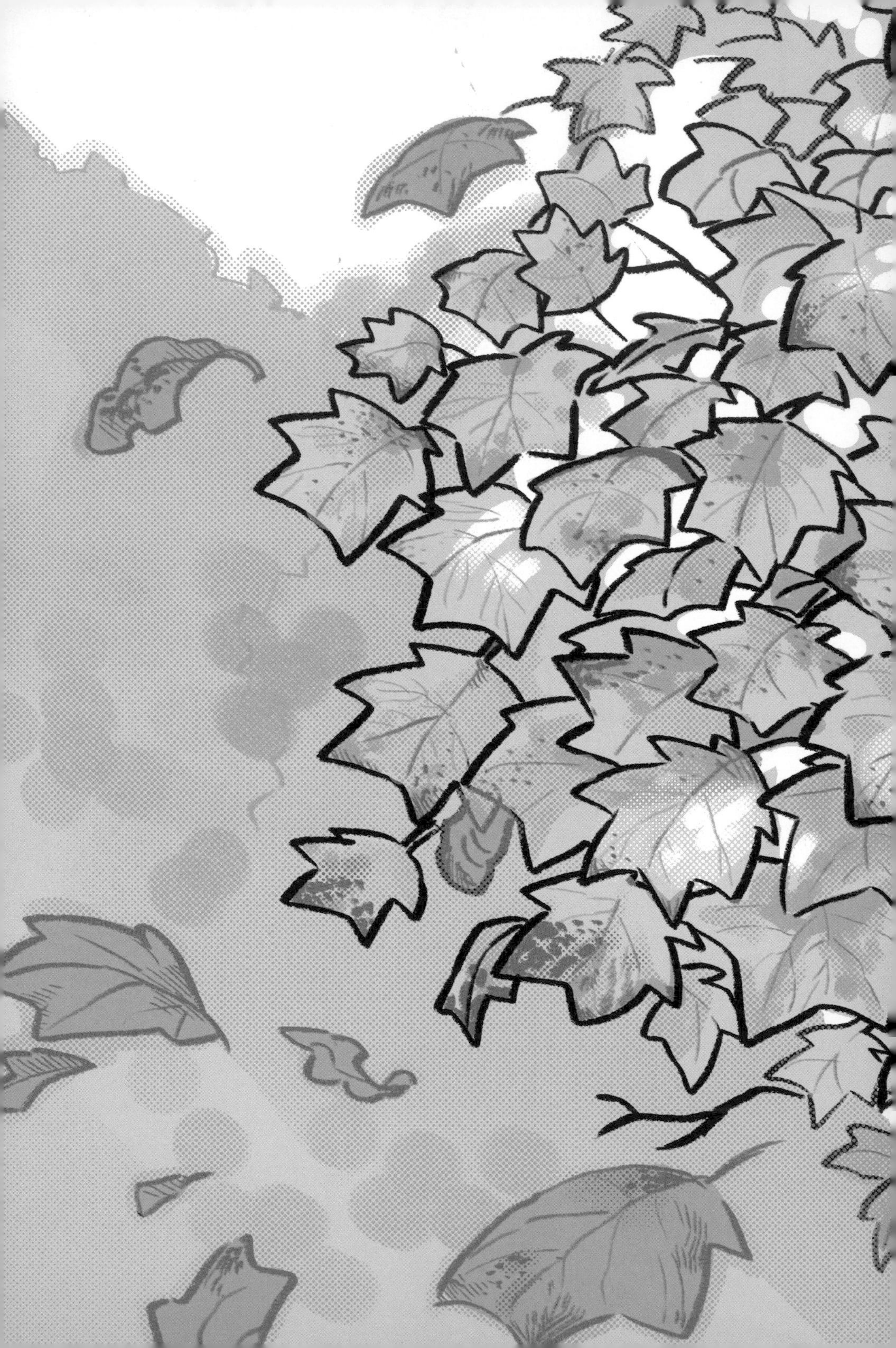

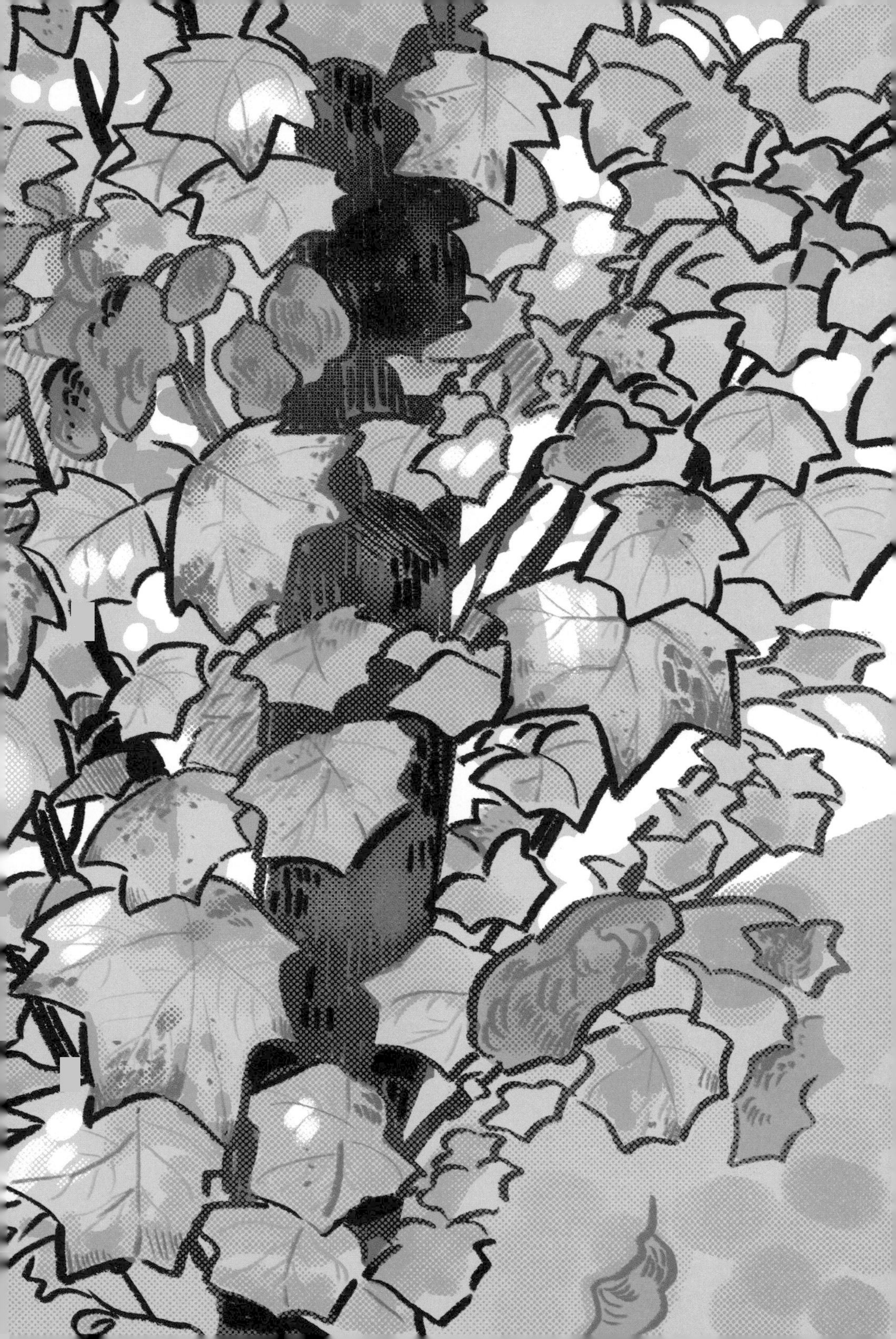

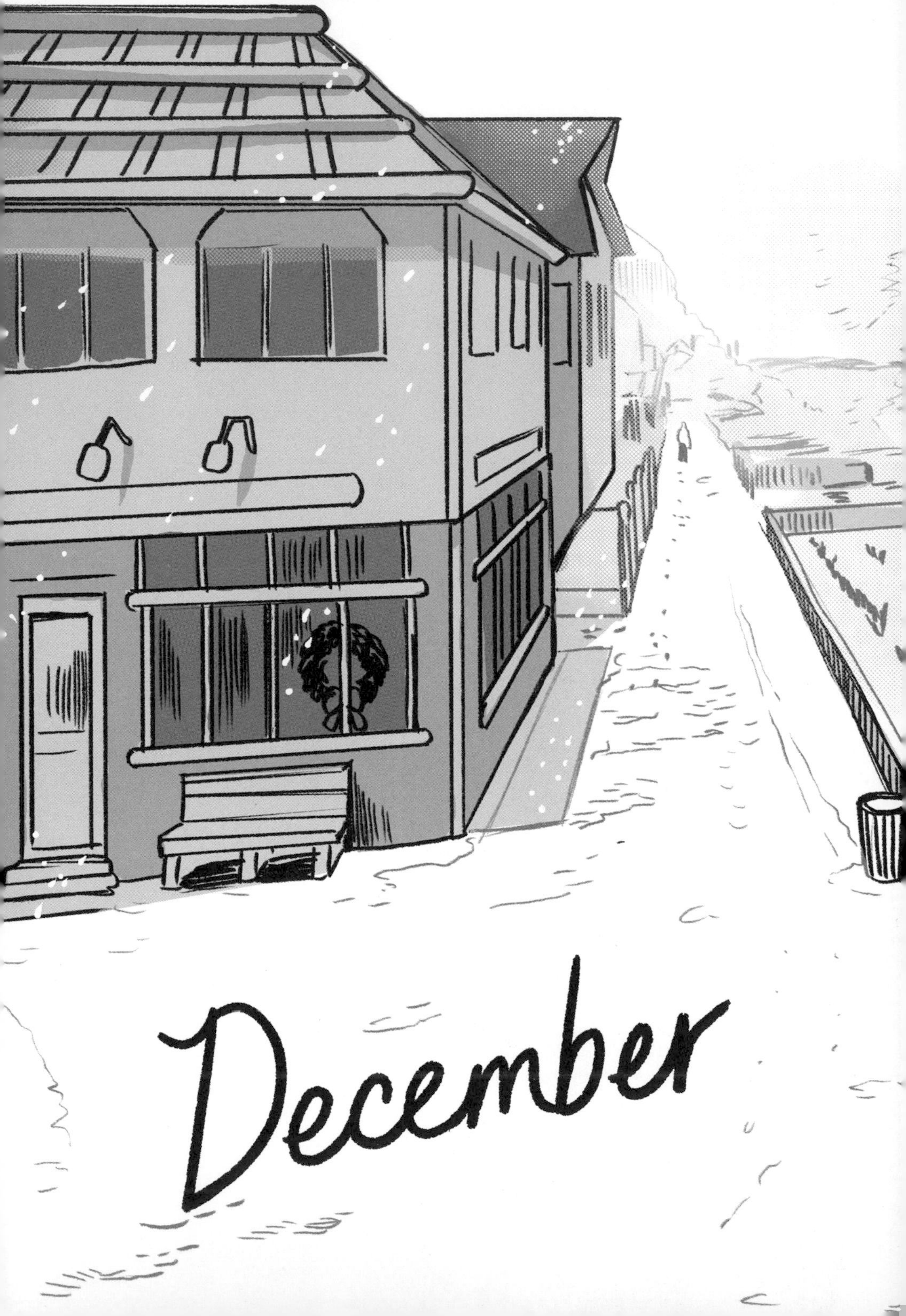
December

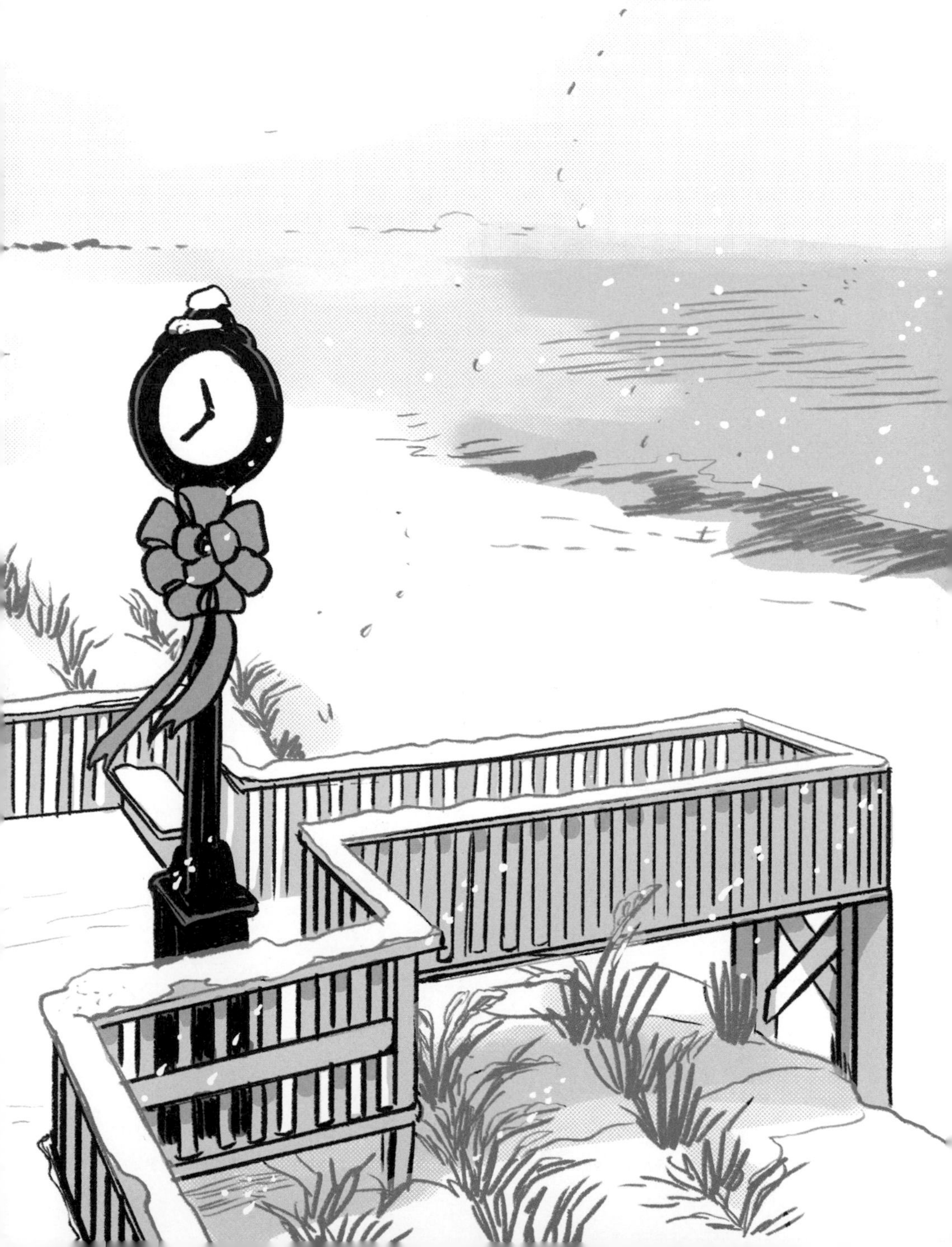

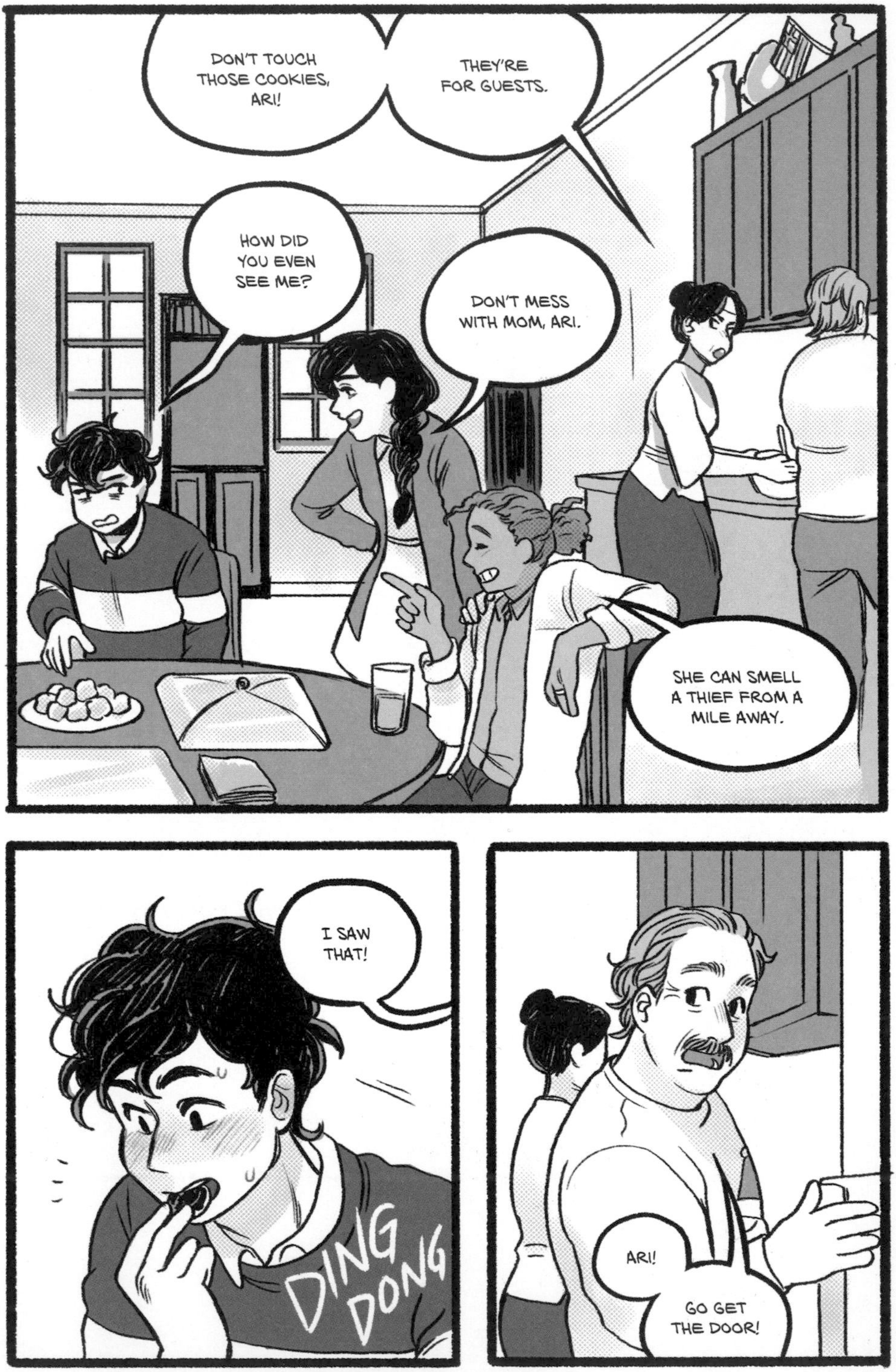
DON'T TOUCH THOSE COOKIES, ARI!
THEY'RE FOR GUESTS.
HOW DID YOU EVEN SEE ME?
DON'T MESS WITH MOM, ARI.
SHE CAN SMELL A THIEF FROM A MILE AWAY.
I SAW THAT!
DING DONG
ARI!
GO GET THE DOOR!

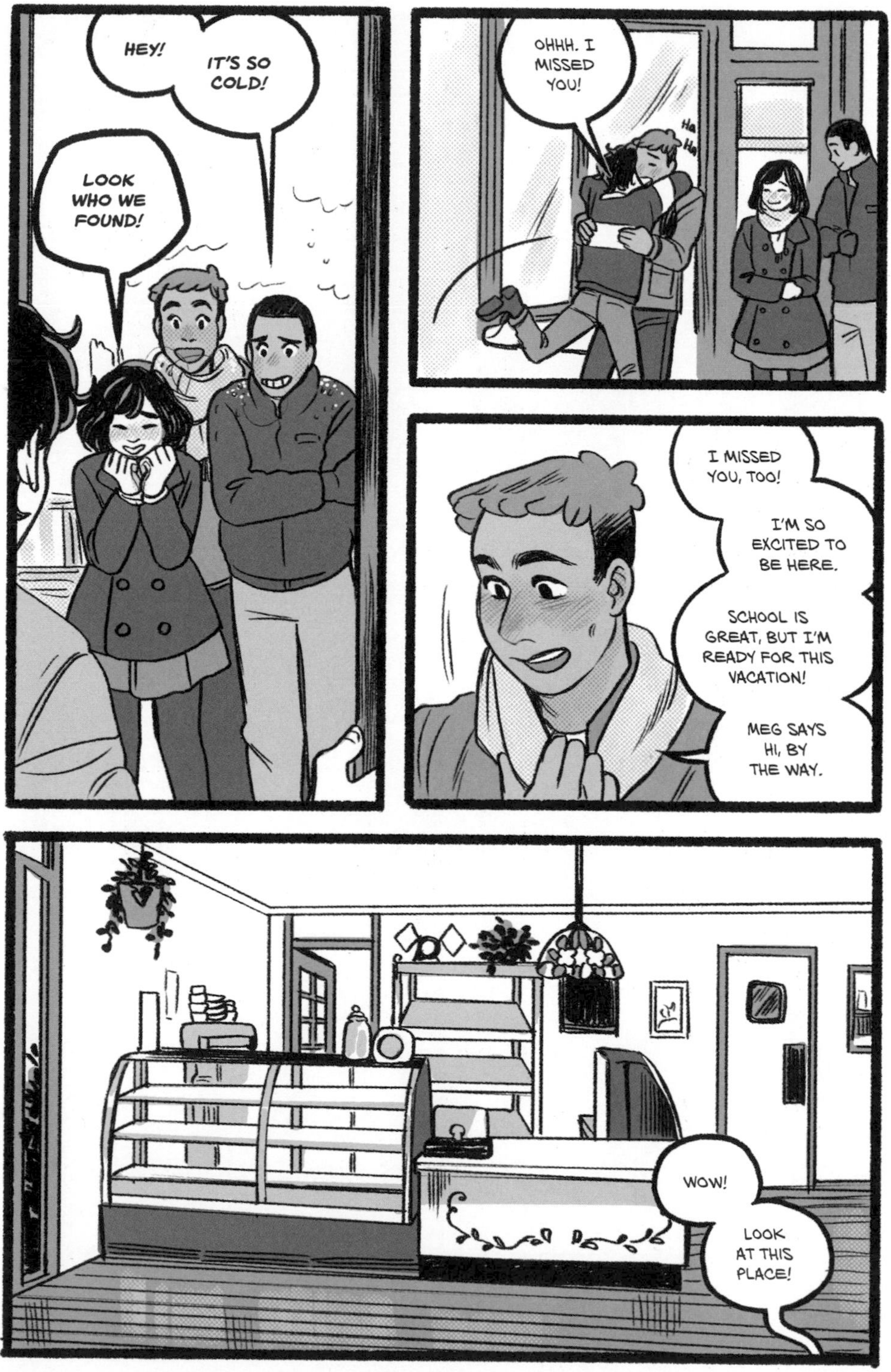

HEY!
IT'S SO COLD!
LOOK WHO WE FOUND!
OHHH. I MISSED YOU!
Ha Ha
I MISSED YOU, TOO!
I'M SO EXCITED TO BE HERE.
SCHOOL IS GREAT, BUT I'M READY FOR THIS VACATION!
MEG SAYS HI, BY THE WAY.
WOW!
LOOK AT THIS PLACE!

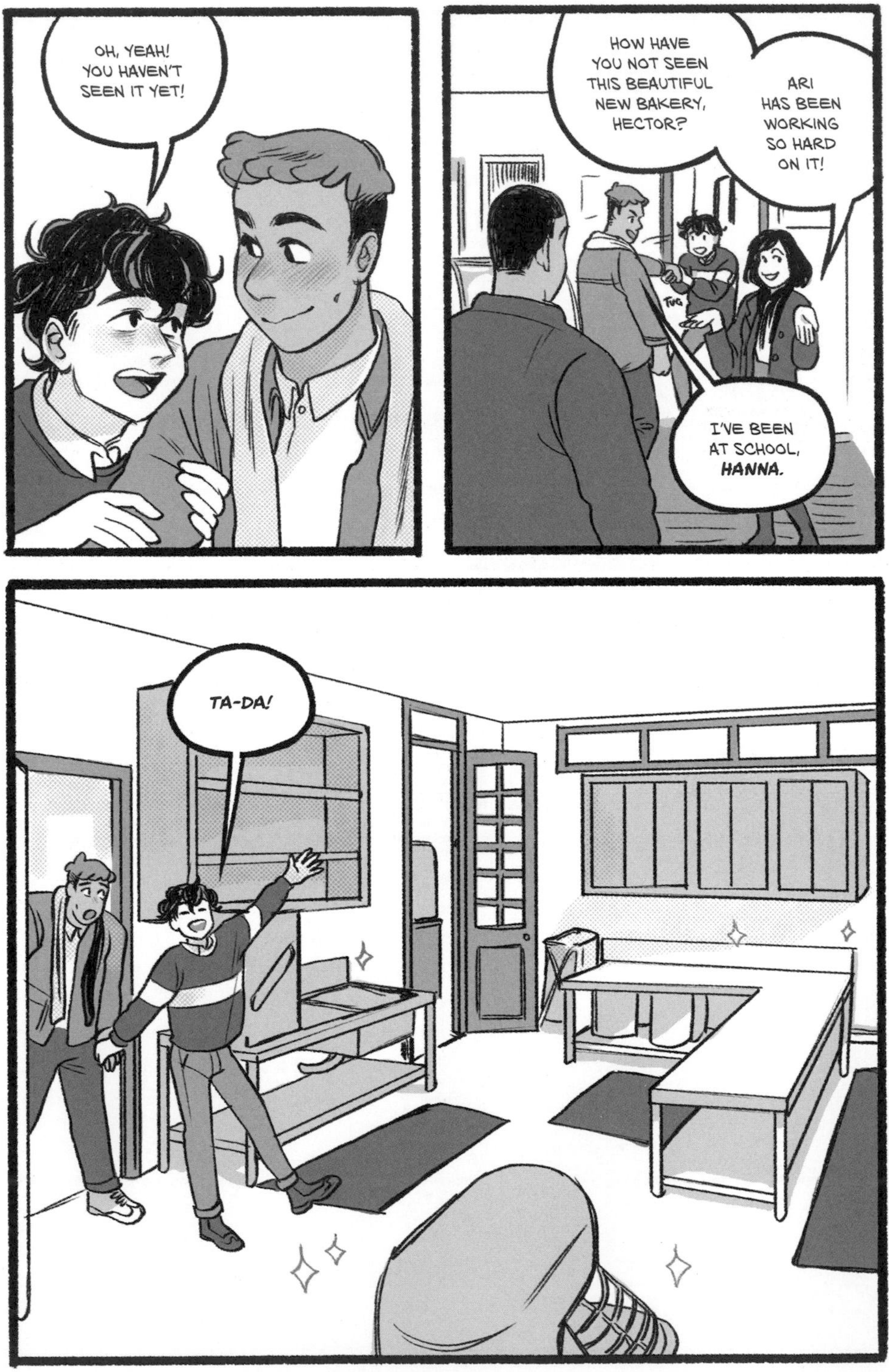
OH, YEAH! YOU HAVEN'T SEEN IT YET!
HOW HAVE YOU NOT SEEN THIS BEAUTIFUL NEW BAKERY, HECTOR?
ARI HAS BEEN WORKING SO HARD ON IT!
TUG
I'VE BEEN AT SCHOOL, **HANNA.**
TA-DA!

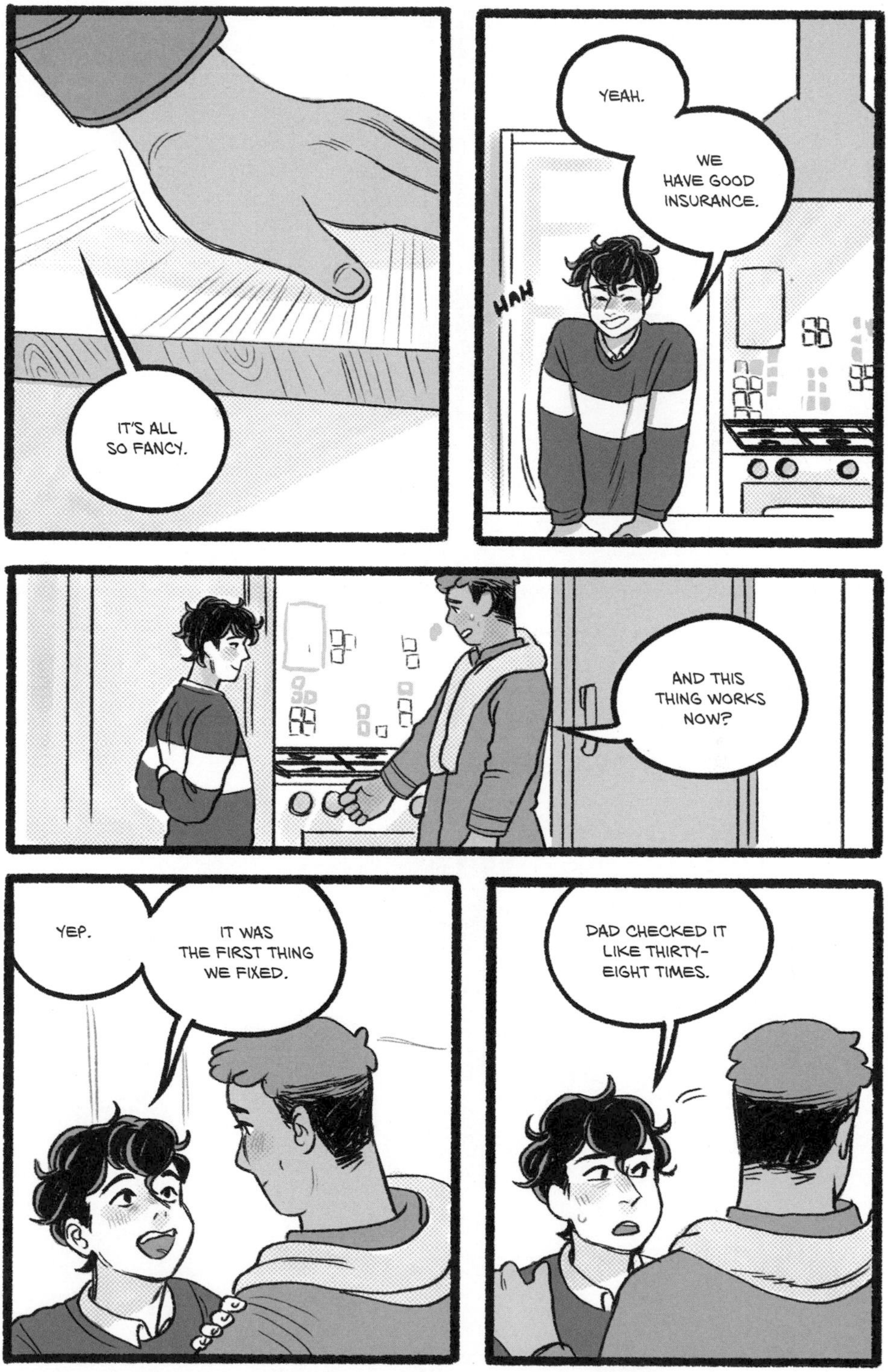
IT'S ALL SO FANCY.
YEAH.
WE HAVE GOOD INSURANCE.
HAH
AND THIS THING WORKS NOW?
YEP.
IT WAS THE FIRST THING WE FIXED.
DAD CHECKED IT LIKE THIRTY-EIGHT TIMES.

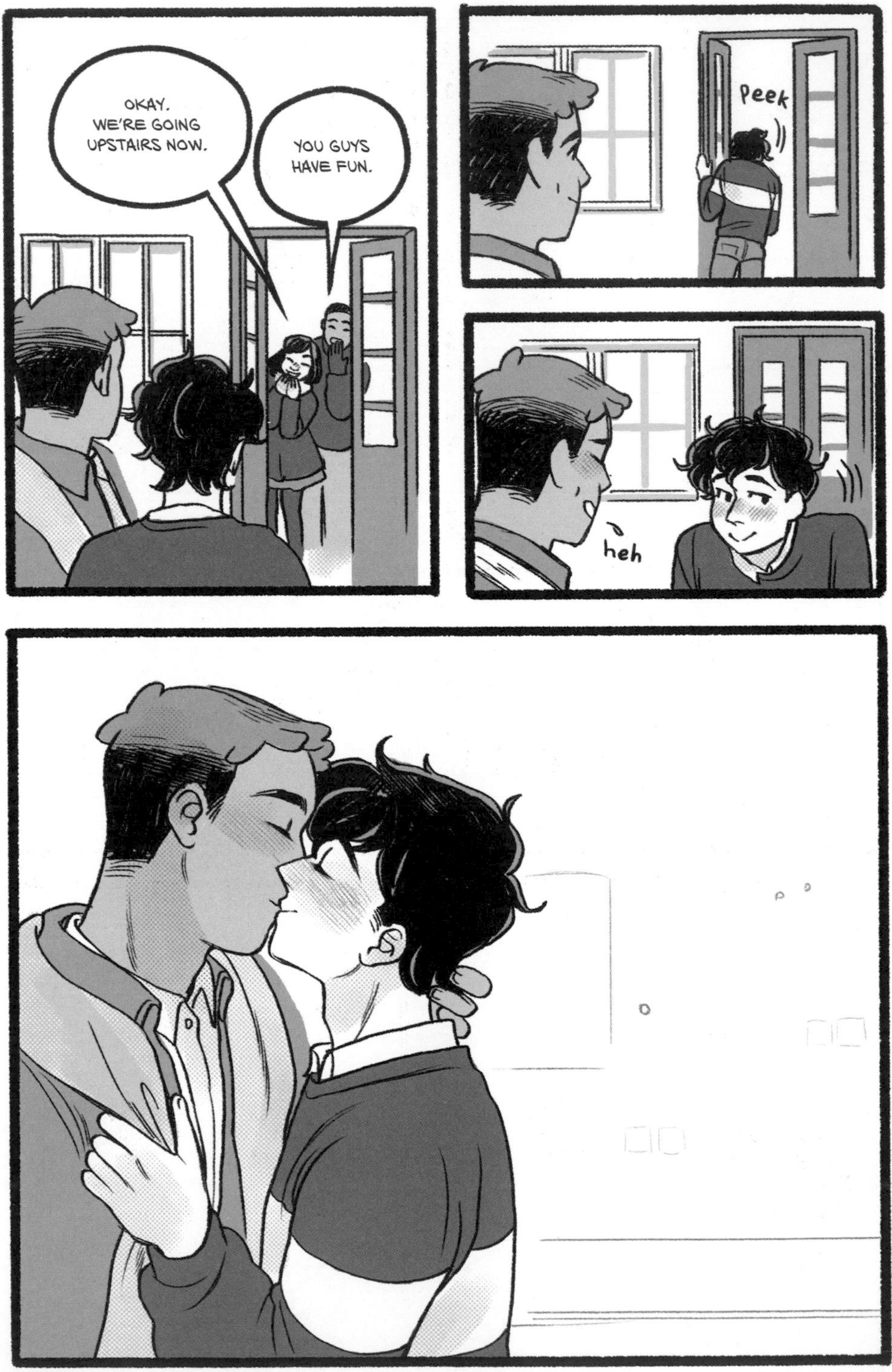
OKAY. WE'RE GOING UPSTAIRS NOW.
YOU GUYS HAVE FUN.
Peek
heh

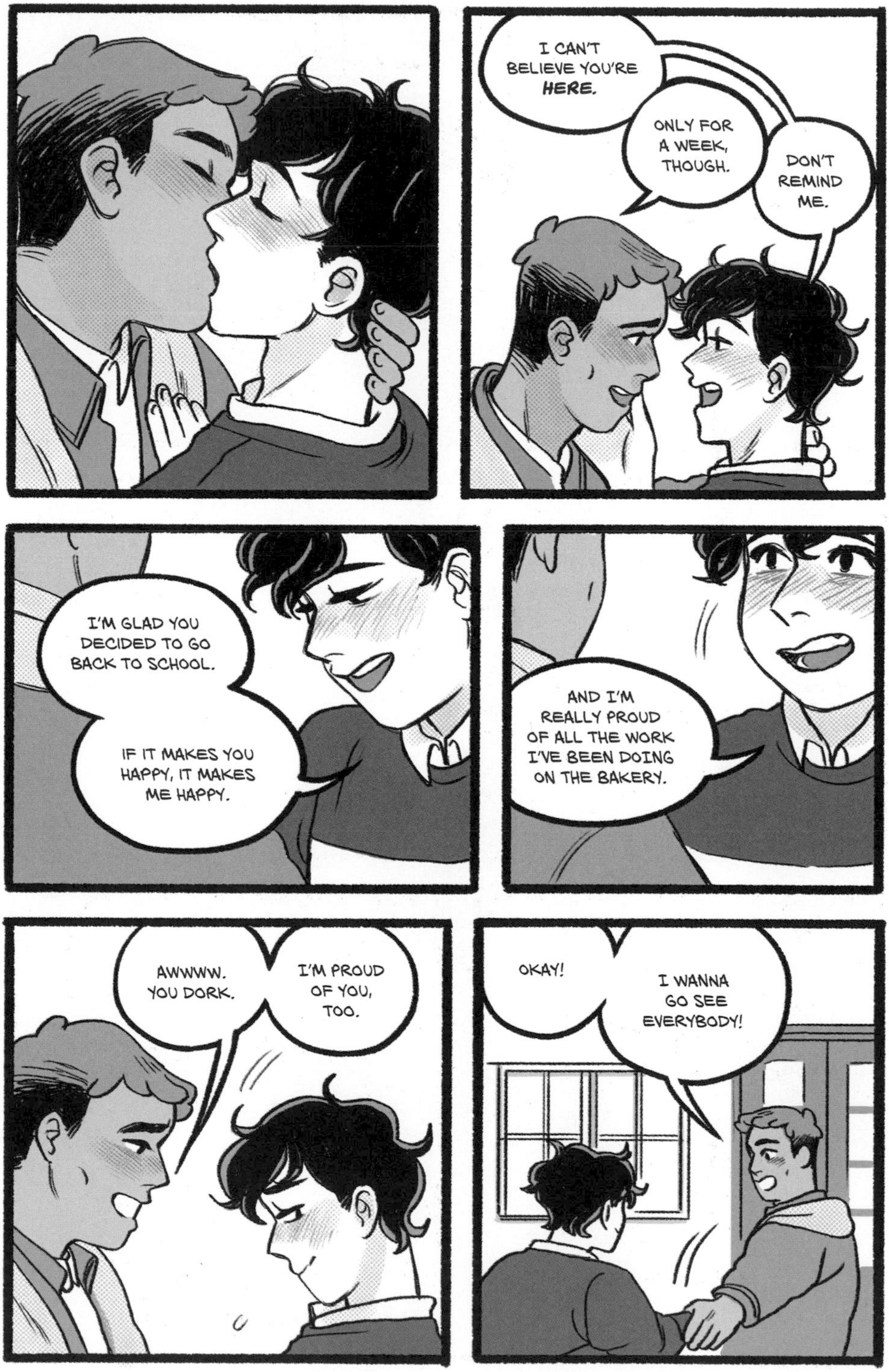

I CAN'T BELIEVE YOU'RE **HERE.**
ONLY FOR A WEEK, THOUGH.
DON'T REMIND ME.
I'M GLAD YOU DECIDED TO GO BACK TO SCHOOL.
IF IT MAKES YOU HAPPY, IT MAKES ME HAPPY.
AND I'M REALLY PROUD OF ALL THE WORK I'VE BEEN DOING ON THE BAKERY.
AWWWW. YOU DORK.
I'M PROUD OF YOU, TOO.
OKAY!
I WANNA GO SEE EVERYBODY!

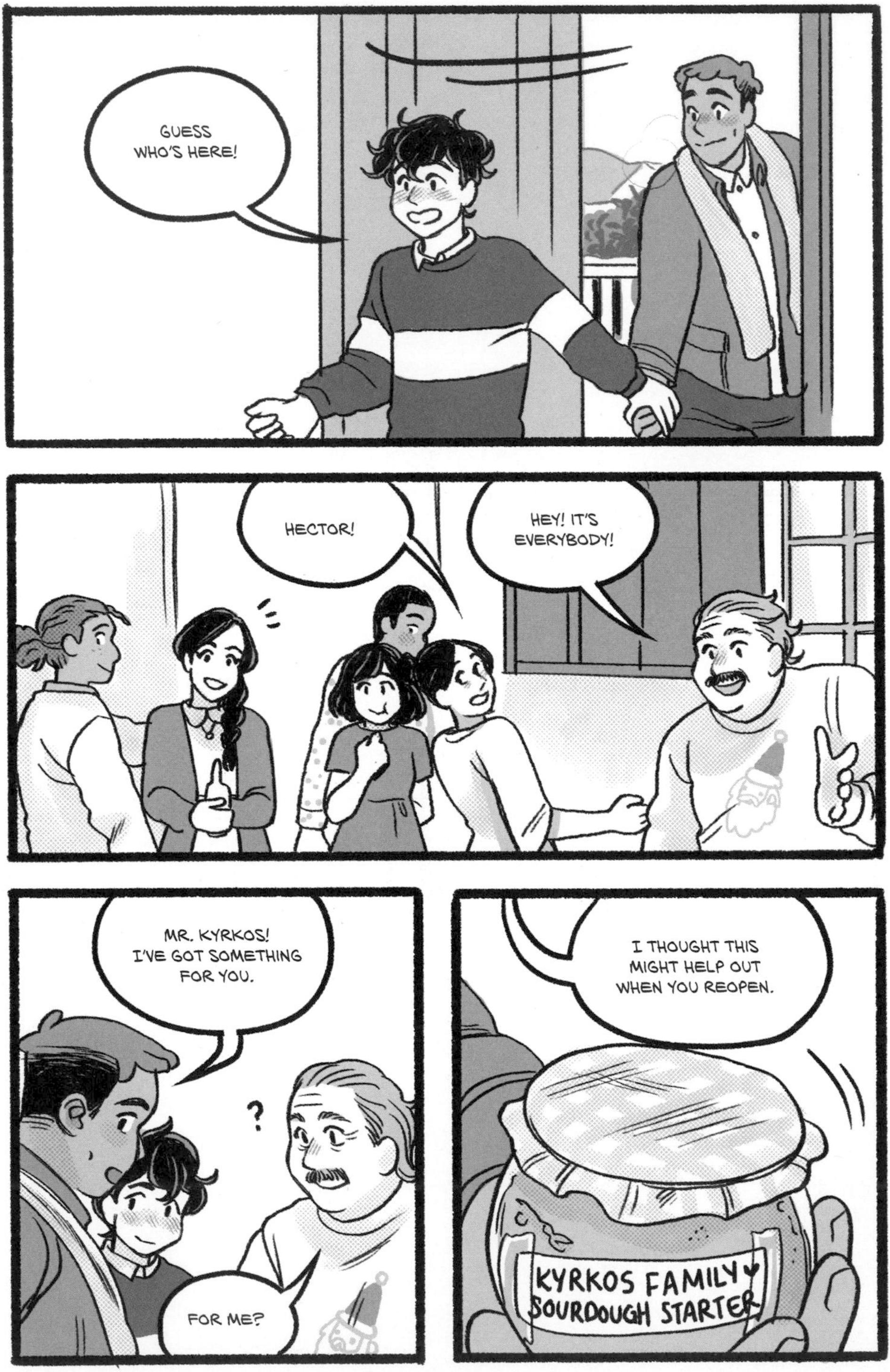
GUESS WHO'S HERE!
HECTOR!
HEY! IT'S EVERYBODY!
MR. KYRKOS! I'VE GOT SOMETHING FOR YOU.
?
FOR ME?
I THOUGHT THIS MIGHT HELP OUT WHEN YOU REOPEN.
KYRKOS FAMILY SOURDOUGH STARTER

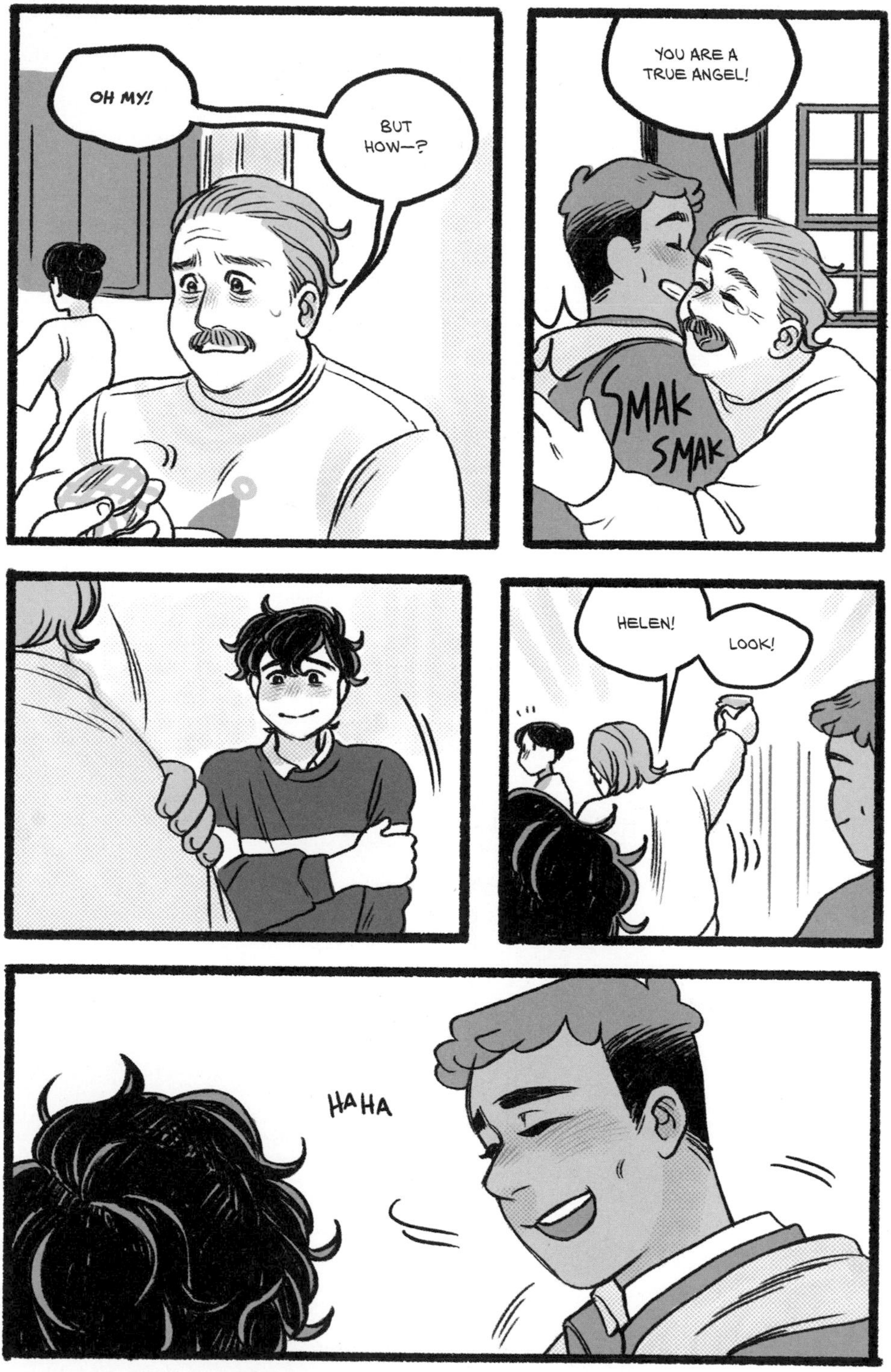
OH MY!
BUT HOW—?
YOU ARE A TRUE ANGEL!
SMAK SMAK
HELEN!
LOOK!
HAHA

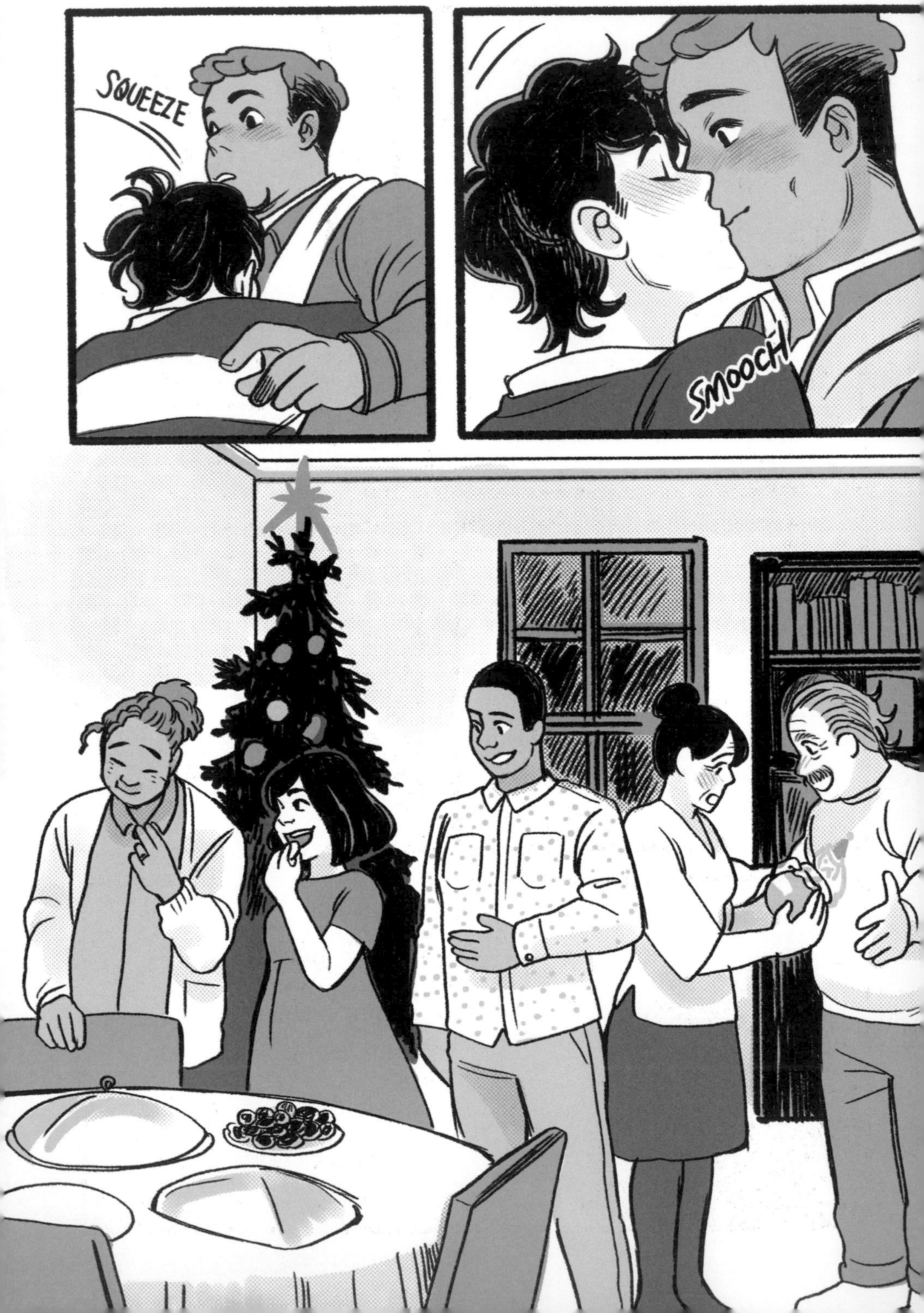
SQUEEZE
SMOOCH

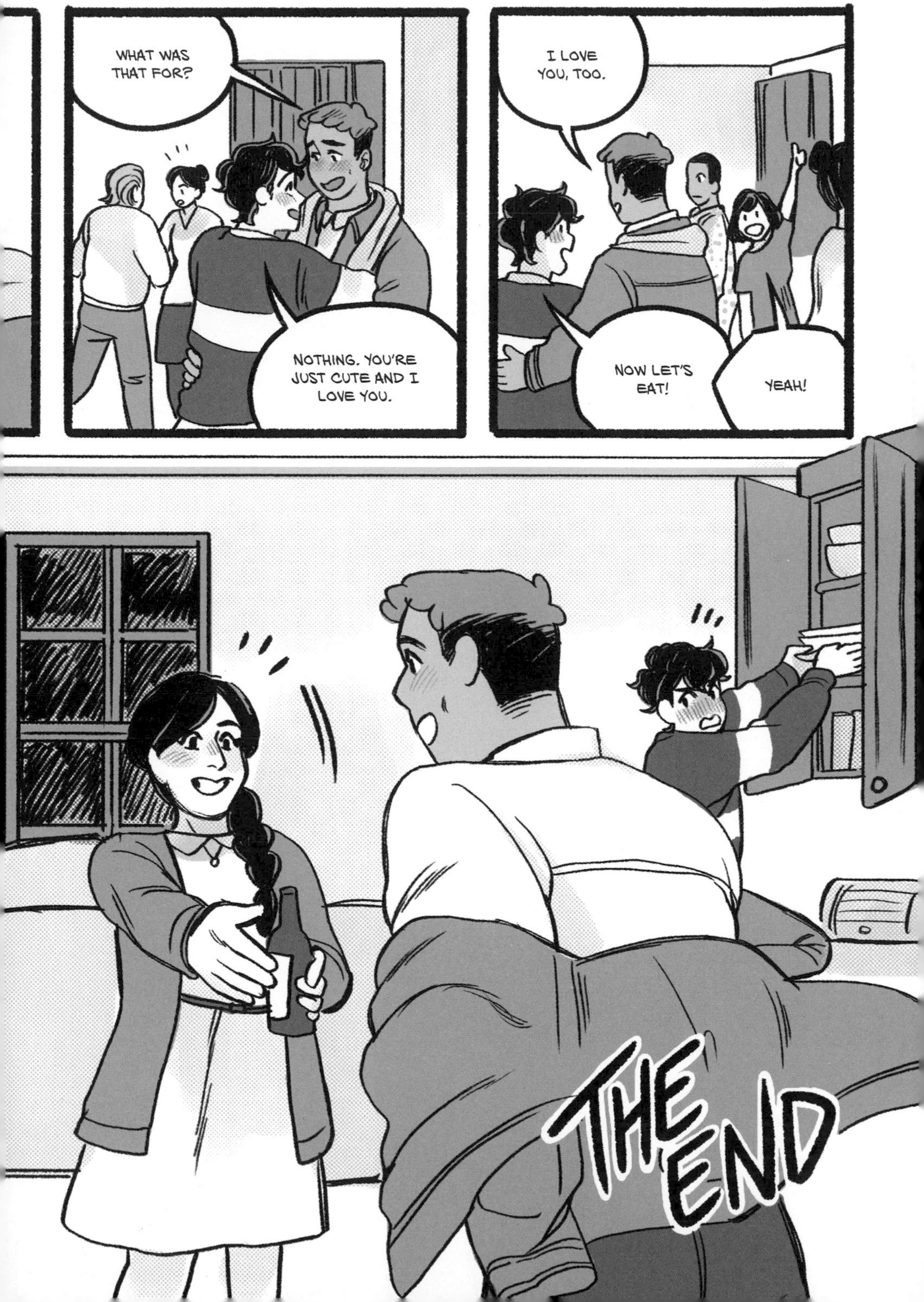
WHAT WAS THAT FOR?
NOTHING. YOU'RE JUST CUTE AND I LOVE YOU.
I LOVE YOU, TOO.
NOW LET'S EAT!
YEAH!
THE END

Thanks for reading ***Bloom***!

Baking and music are such a big part of this book. While working on *Bloom*, we would make the food baked by the characters and send each other music in order to help find the right tone for every scene. So when First Second asked us about what extras we wanted to put in the back of the book, it made perfect sense to include a recipe and a playlist, along with some production art!

Thanks again for reading, and we hope you enjoy baking the Kyrkos Family Bakery's Famous Sourdough Rolls as much as Ari and Hector did! Why not put on some tunes while you cook?

Savanna & Kevin

Special thanks to Nick, Brook, Stephen, Charlie, James, Paulina, and all our friends and family who made *Bloom* possible!

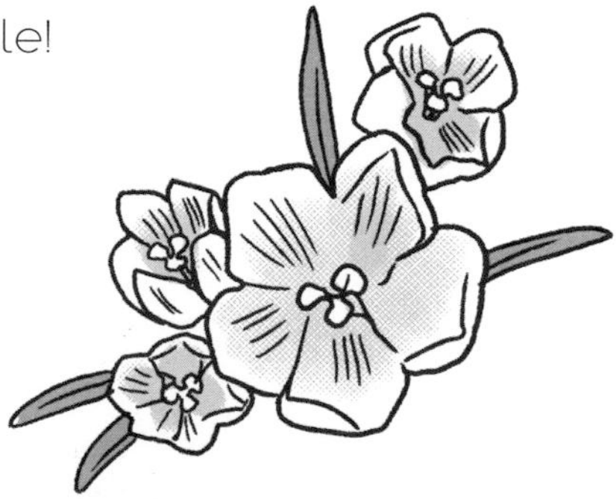

KYRKOS FAMILY BAKERY'S
Famous Sourdough Rolls

Ingredients:

1 cup sourdough starter (fresh)

1 cup whole wheat flour

2 ¼ teaspoons (one package) active dry yeast

2 teaspoons salt

3 tablespoons brown sugar

1 cup warm (110°F / 43°C) water

¼ cup melted butter

2 cups bread flour

1 tablespoon olive oil

1 egg

1 tablespoon water

Steps:

1. In a large bowl, mix starter, whole wheat flour, yeast, salt, and brown sugar until combined.
2. Stir in warm water and melted butter.
3. Stir in bread flour ½ cup at a time until a dough is formed.
4. Knead dough on a floured surface for 10 minutes until it becomes shiny and springy to the touch.
5. Oil the sides of a large bowl with the olive oil. Place the dough in the large oiled bowl and cover. Keep in a warm spot until the dough doubles in size (approximately 2 hours).
6. On a floured surface, punch dough down lightly to flatten. Cut dough into 10 equal-sized pieces and roll into balls.
7. Cut a simple leaf design (just barely) into the tops of the rolls.
8. Place dough balls on parchment-lined pan at least 2 inches apart.
9. Keep in a warm spot until the dough doubles in size again (approximately 1 hour).
10. Preheat oven to 400°F / 204°C.
11. Brush the top of the buns with egg wash (a mixture of 1 beaten egg and 1 tablespoon of water).
12. Bake rolls in oven for 25 minutes.
13. Remove the rolls and check the bottoms. They should be a rich brown color and sound hollow when you tap on them. If they're not ready, just pop the rolls back in and check them again at 3-minute intervals until they're done.

Production Art

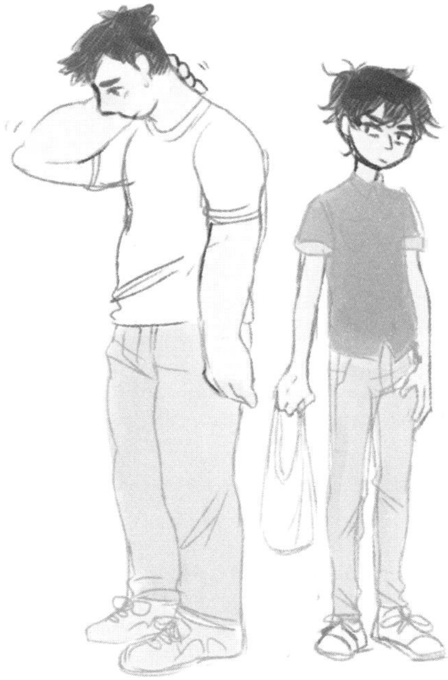

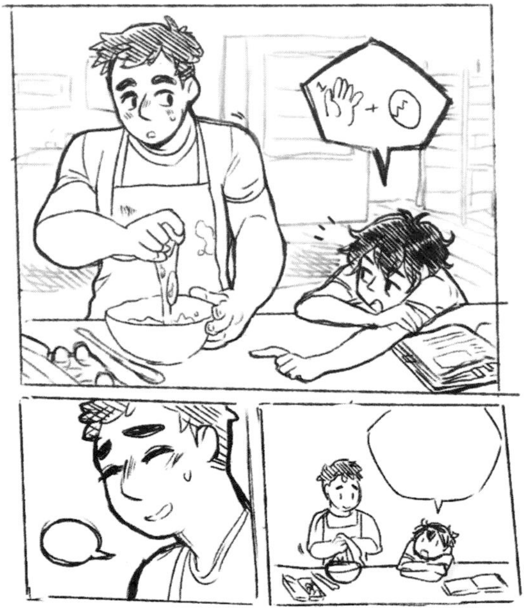

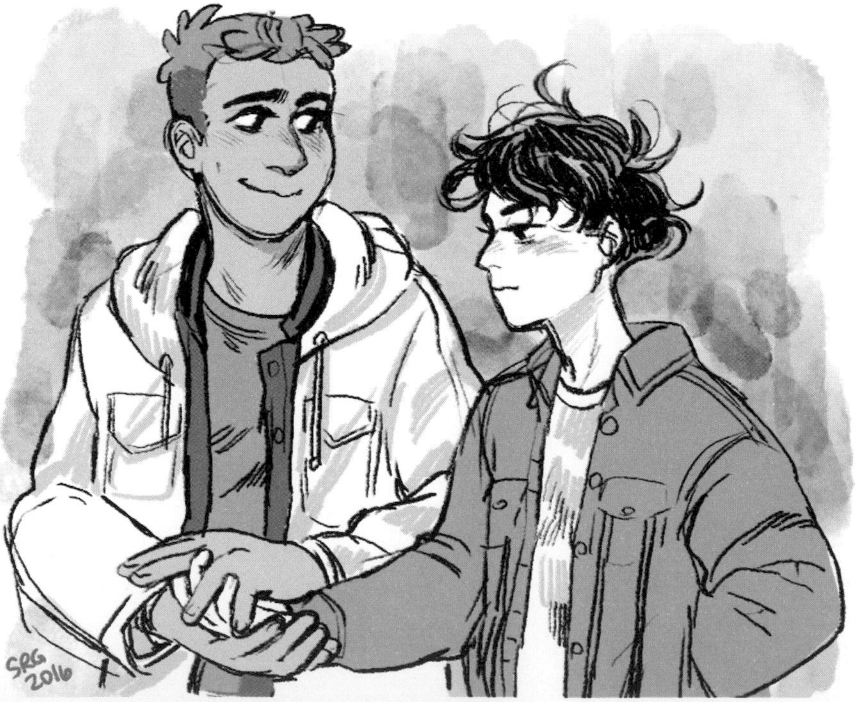
SRG
2016

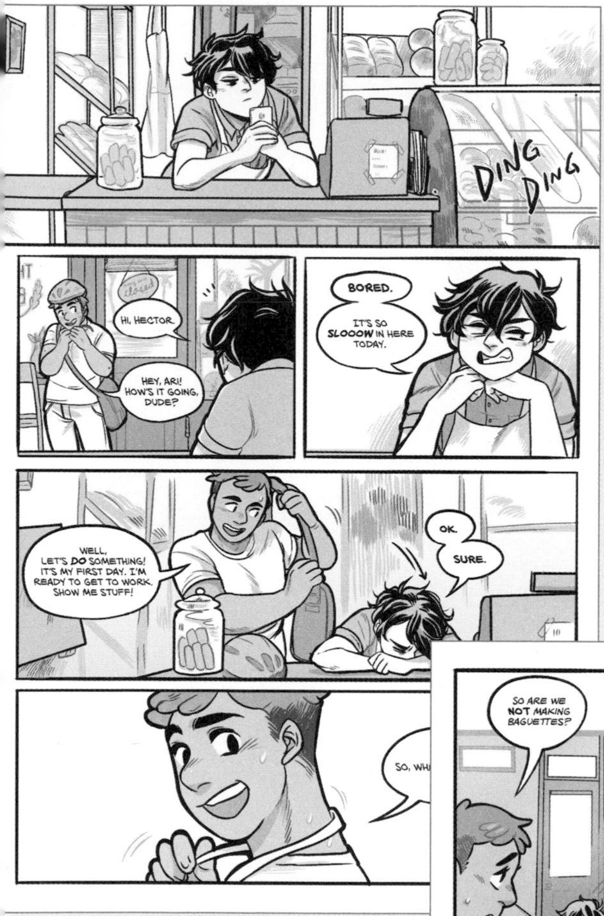
DING DING
HI, HECTOR.
HEY, ARI! HOW'S IT GOING, DUDE?
BORED.
IT'S SO SLOOOW IN HERE TODAY.
WELL, LET'S DO SOMETHING! IT'S MY FIRST DAY. I'M READY TO GET TO WORK. SHOW ME STUFF!
OK.
SURE.

Bloom pitch pages

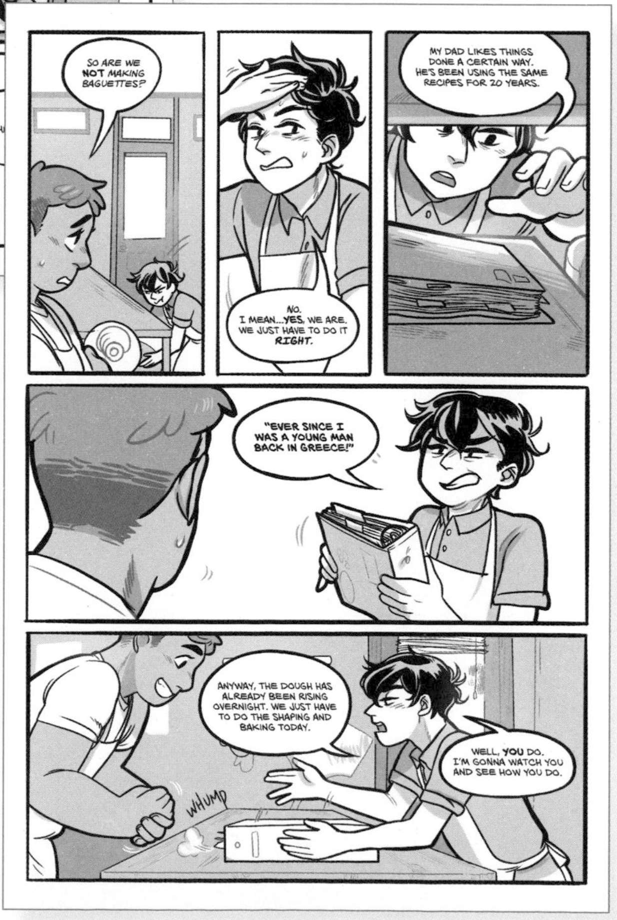
SO ARE WE NOT MAKING BAGUETTES?
NO. I MEAN...YES, WE ARE. WE JUST HAVE TO DO IT RIGHT.
MY DAD LIKES THINGS DONE A CERTAIN WAY. HE'S BEEN USING THE SAME RECIPES FOR 20 YEARS.
"EVER SINCE I WAS A YOUNG MAN BACK IN GREECE!"
ANYWAY, THE DOUGH HAS ALREADY BEEN RISING OVERNIGHT. WE JUST HAVE TO DO THE SHAPING AND BAKING TODAY.
WHUMP
WELL, YOU DO. I'M GONNA WATCH YOU AND SEE HOW YOU DO.

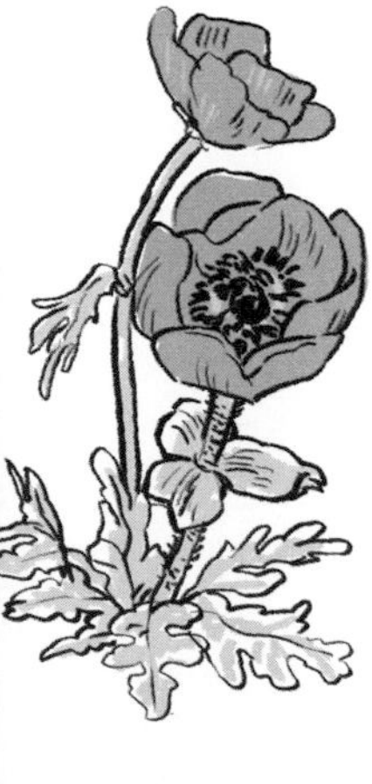

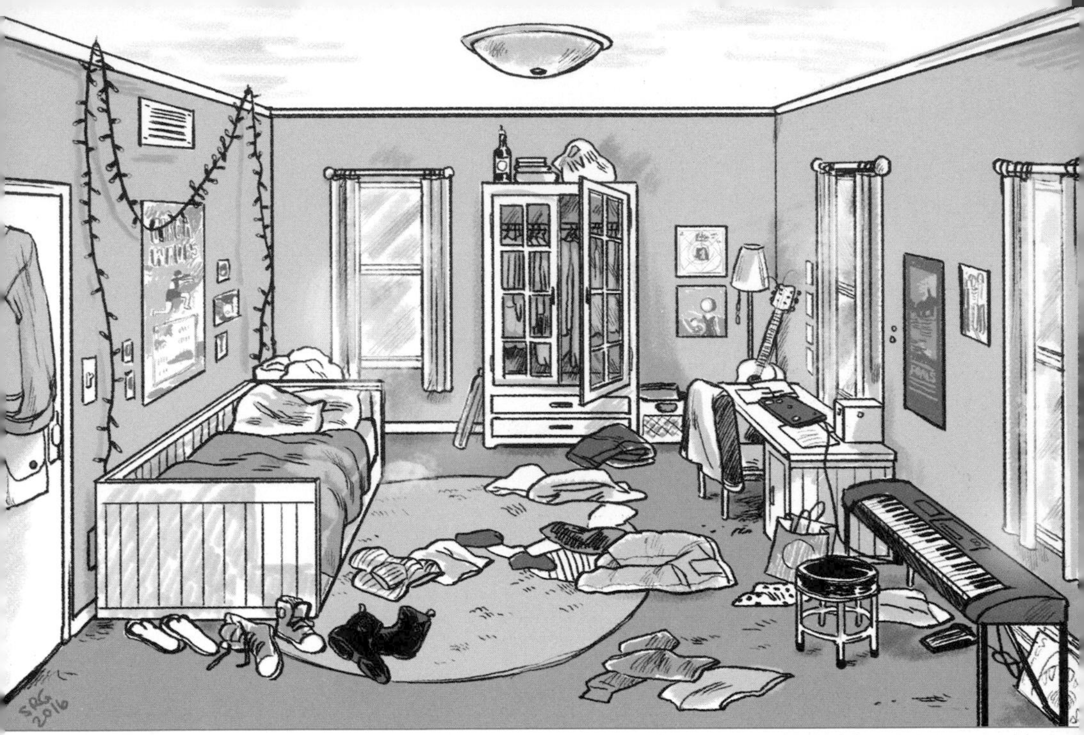

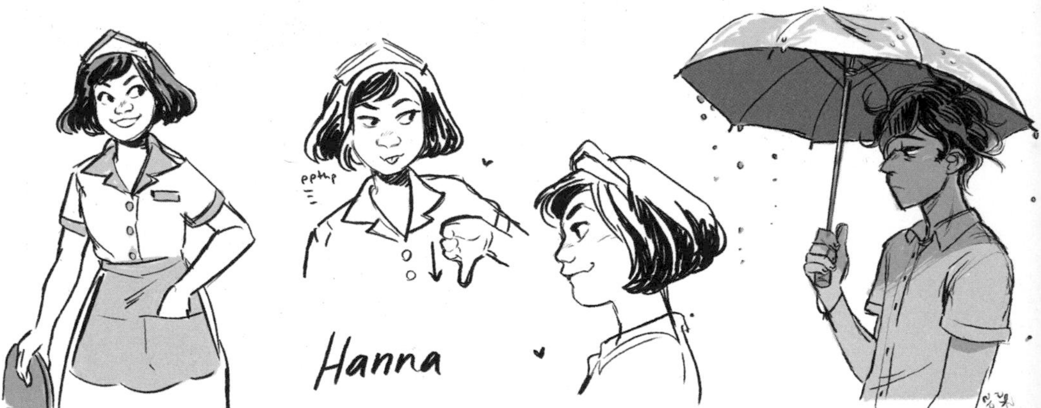

pp thp
Hanna

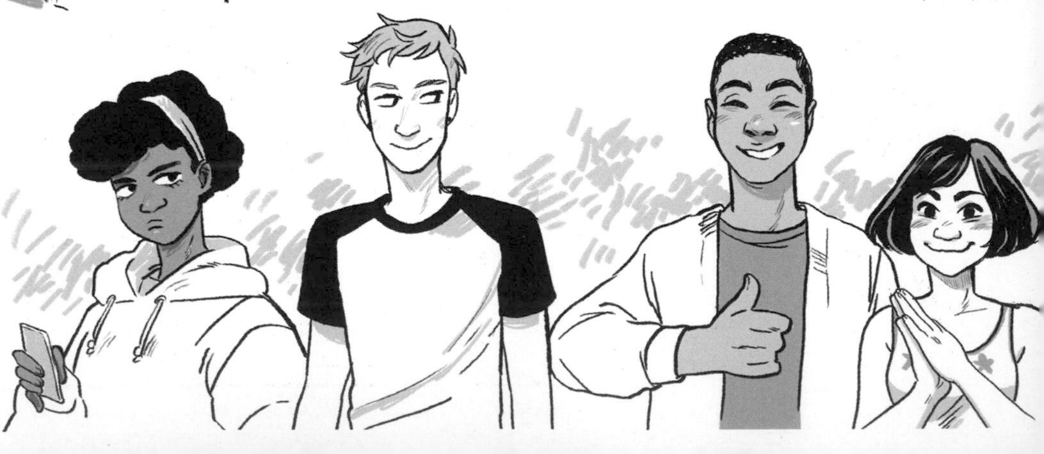

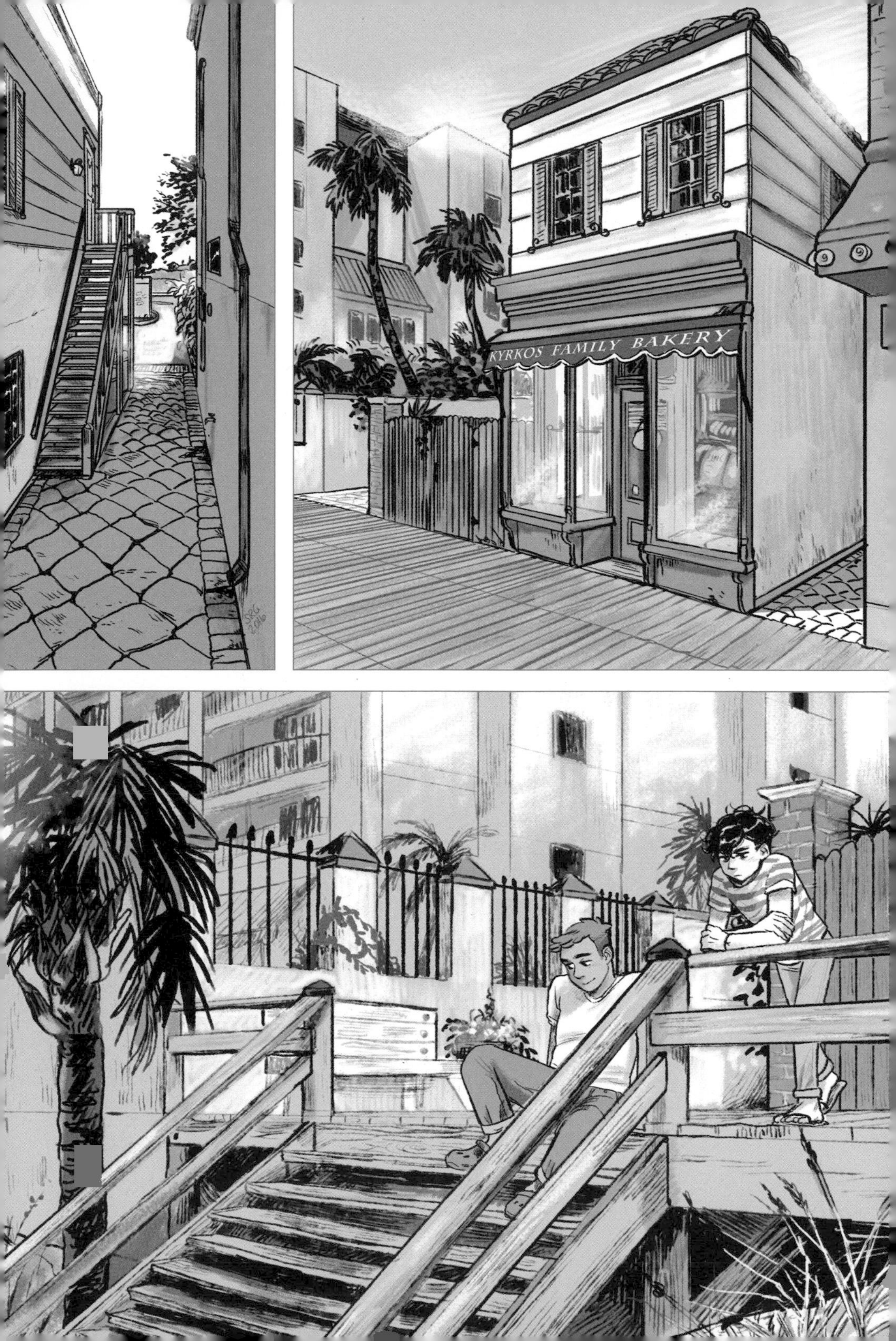
KYRKOS FAMILY BAKERY

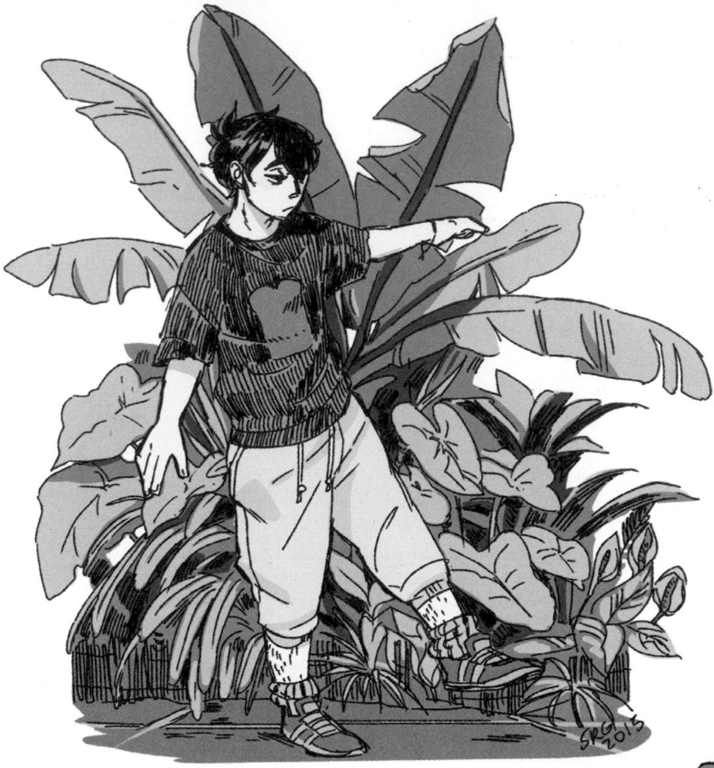
SRG
2015

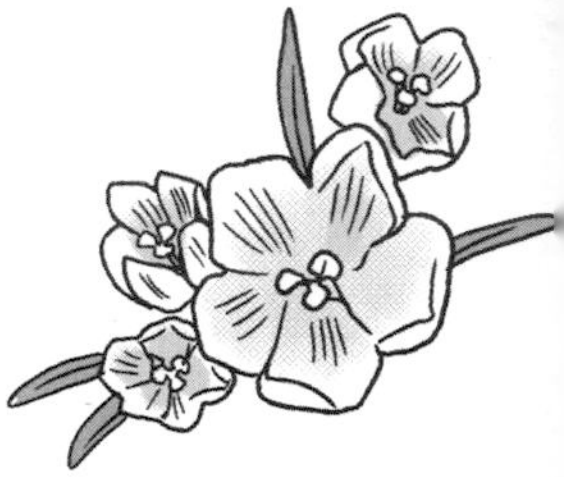

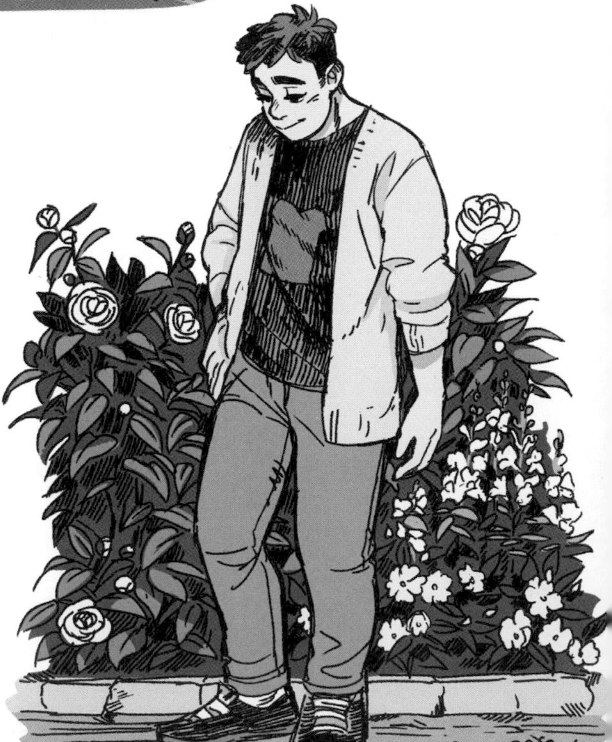
SRG
2015

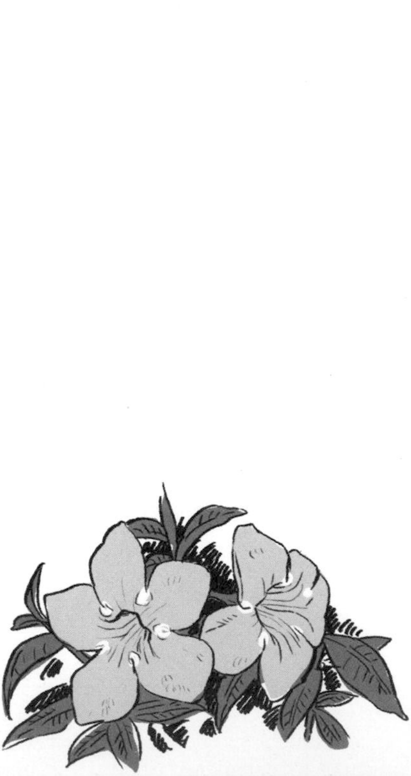

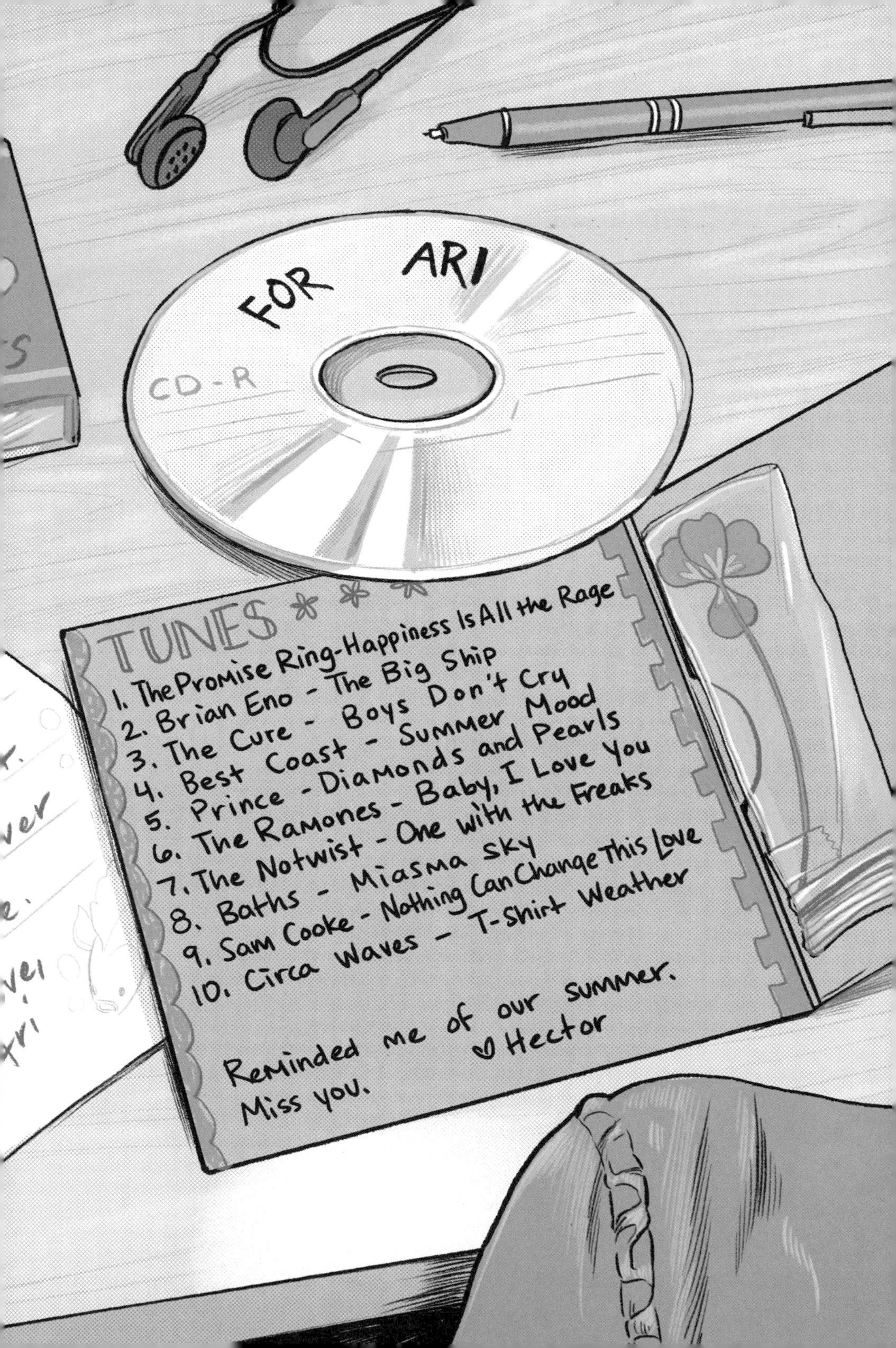
FOR ARI
CD-R
TUNES
1. The Promise Ring - Happiness Is All the Rage
2. Brian Eno - The Big Ship
3. The Cure - Boys Don't Cry
4. Best Coast - Summer Mood
5. Prince - Diamonds and Pearls
6. The Ramones - Baby, I Love You
7. The Notwist - One with the Freaks
8. Baths - Miasma Sky
9. Sam Cooke - Nothing Can Change This Love
10. Circa Waves - T-Shirt Weather
Reminded me of our summer.
Miss you.
♥ Hector

I LOVE GRAPHIC NOVELS!

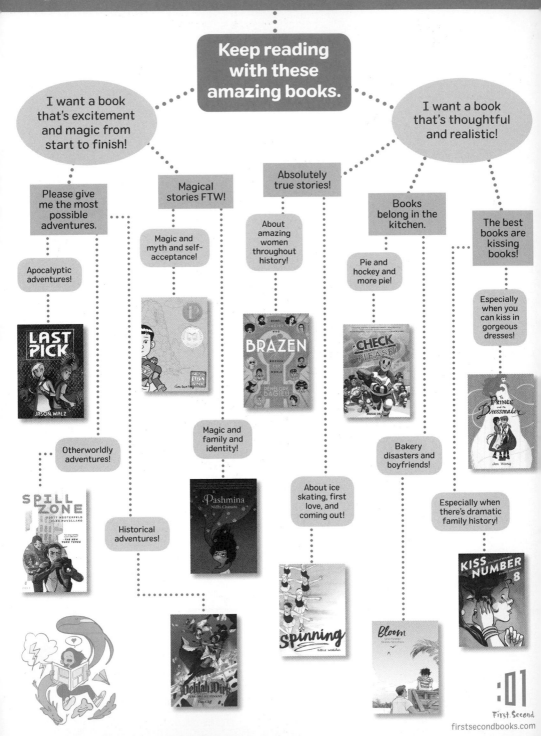

Keep reading with these amazing books.

I want a book that's excitement and magic from start to finish!

Please give me the most possible adventures.

Apocalyptic adventures!

LAST PICK
JASON WALZ

Otherworldly adventures!

SPILL ZONE
SCOTT WESTERFELD
ALEX PUVILLAND
—THE NEW YORK TIMES

Historical adventures!

Delilah Dirk
TURKISH LIEUTENANT
Tony Cliff

Magical stories FTW!

Magic and myth and self-acceptance!

AMERICAN BORN CHINESE

Magic and family and identity!

Pashmina
Nidhi Chanani

I want a book that's thoughtful and realistic!

Absolutely true stories!

About amazing women throughout history!

BRAZEN
PENELOPE BAGIEU

About ice skating, first love, and coming out!

Spinning
tillie walden

Books belong in the kitchen.

Pie and hockey and more pie!

CHECK, PLEASE!
NGOZI UKAZU

Bakery disasters and boyfriends!

Bloom

The best books are kissing books!

Especially when you can kiss in gorgeous dresses!

The Prince and the Dressmaker
Jen Wang

Especially when there's dramatic family history!

KISS NUMBER 8